CONDENSED BOOKS

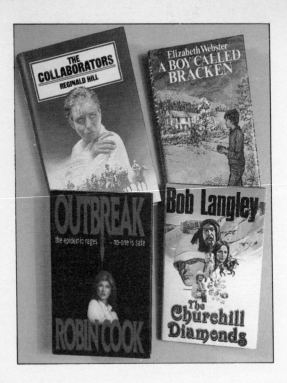

THE READER'S DIGEST ASSOCIATION LIMITED
25 Berkeley Square, London W1X 6AB
THE READER'S DIGEST ASSOCIATION
SOUTH AFRICA (PTY) LTD
Reader's Digest House, 130 Strand Street, Cape Town
Printed by Petty & Sons Ltd, Leeds
Bound by Hazell, Watson & Viney Ltd, Aylesbury
Original cover design by Jeffery Matthews FSIAD
For information as to ownership
of copyright in the material in this book see last page

CONDENSED BOOKS

OUTBREAK
by Robin Cook

Dr. Marissa Blumenthal is delighted with her new post as a medical officer investigating epidemic outbreaks at the Centers for Disease Control, in Atlanta. Her first task, however, is a daunting and terrifying one: to find the source of a deadly, highly contagious virus which is striking hospitals all over the country.

As Marissa sets out to track the virus down, she finds her work being mysteriously hampered from the start, and soon her investigations are taking increasingly bizarre turns. Slowly she realizes that behind the killer disease is an even more frightening force, which intends to keep her silent.

Tense medical drama from one of the acclaimed masters of the genre.

THE COLLABORATORS
by Reginald Hill

Abwehr officer Günter Mai has arrived in Paris with the German army of occupation. His job: to find informers, French citizens willing to collaborate. Like amiable Miche Boucher, eager to make a living; Maurice Melchior, a flamboyant homosexual and Jew who needs protection at any price; or the Croziers, simple folk who just want to keep their *boulangerie* in business. Then Mai meets Janine Simonian, desperate for news of her missing husband, and sees in her a potential agent. But as trust grows between them, the German finds his duty and his feelings in conflict.

A powerful novel about divided loyalties, and the courage and love which outlive them.

A BOY CALLED BRACKEN
by Elizabeth Webster

Jake Farrant is a high-powered Fleet Street journalist. When he learns that he has only months to live, he retreats to the Gloucestershire countryside, determined to spend the rest of his time in solitude. Instead he meets Bracken, a beguiling gipsy boy whose affinity with nature has made him wise beyond his years.

With Bracken as his guide, Jake learns to appreciate and help the creatures around him: an injured kestrel; an orphaned badger cub. Before long, Bracken's infectious and simple joy rubs off on the tired news-paperman, and he finds a contentment he's never known before.

This radiant novel celebrates life—and nature—in all its seasons.

THE CHURCHILL DIAMONDS
by Bob Langley

When the legendary Churchill Diamonds are stolen from the Coffey Foundation's vaults, Thomas Kengle, president of the multimillion pound business empire, is mystified. Who would want to steal a collection of diamonds so famous that it is unsaleable? Kengle turns to the one woman who may know the answer. She has a fascinating story to tell. It began back in 1898, when a handsome cavalry lieutenant rode out across the sun-baked Sudanese desert to rescue her mother from the hands of barbarous savages—and stumbled across a bag of shiny, rough-hewn stones . . .

A lively tale of hair-raising adventure and stirring romance.

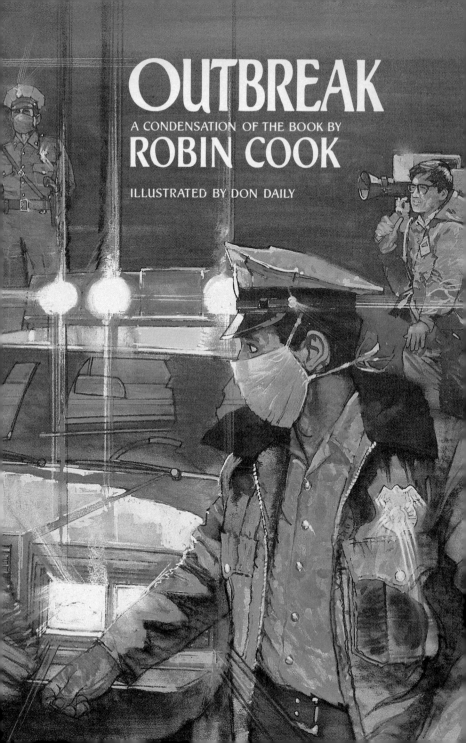

OUTBREAK

A CONDENSATION OF THE BOOK BY

ROBIN COOK

ILLUSTRATED BY DON DAILY

Panic grips a Californian clinic.
Already seven patients are dying—victims
of a mysterious disease. Swift to strike,
highly contagious and untreatable,
it claims new victims daily. No one
knows what to do.

Dr. Marissa Blumenthal of the
Centers for Disease Control is called in to
investigate. At first she too is baffled.
Is this outbreak the forerunner of a new
killer epidemic? Where did the virus come
from? Where will it strike next?

As Marissa's medical sleuthing
starts paying off, she begins to feel
uneasy. Her colleagues seem
uncooperative, hostile. Chillingly,
she senses that there's something very
wrong—something highly sinister
behind this outbreak.

PROLOGUE

Zaire, Africa
September 7, 1976

A twenty-one-year-old Yale biology student by the name of John Nordyke woke up at dawn at the edge of a village north of Bumba, Zaire. Rolling over in his sweat-drenched sleeping bag, he stared out through the mesh flap of his nylon mountain tent, hearing the sounds of the tropical rain forest mixed with the noises of the awakening village. High above him he caught glimpses of monkeys skittering through the lush vegetation that shielded the sky from his view.

He had slept fitfully, and as he pulled himself upright he was unsteady and weak. He felt distinctly worse than he had the night before, when he'd been hit by chills and fever. He guessed he had malaria, even though he'd been careful about taking his chloroquine-phosphate pills. The problem was that it had been impossible to avoid the clouds of mosquitoes that emanated each evening from the hidden pools in the swampy jungle.

John quickly broke camp, stuffed his tent and sleeping bag into his backpack and made his way into the village, where he inquired about the nearest clinic. An itinerant priest told him that there was a Belgian mission hospital in Yambuku, a small town located a few kilometres to the east. Sick and frightened, he set out for Yambuku.

John was on a six-month leave from college and had come to Africa to photograph animals, such as the highland gorilla, that were threatened by extinction. It was the fulfilment of a boyhood dream.

Yambuku was scarcely larger than the village he'd just left, and the mission hospital did not inspire confidence. It was no more than a meagre collection of broken-down breeze-block buildings.

9

After checking in with a nun, who spoke only French, John was sent to wait among a throng of natives in such states of debility and disease that he wondered if he wasn't likely to catch something worse than what he already had.

Finally he was examined by a harassed doctor and, as John had already surmised, the diagnosis was a "touch" of malaria. The doctor ordered an injection of chloroquine and advised John to return if he didn't feel better.

The examination over, John was sent into the treatment room to wait in line for his injection. The nurse did not have disposable needles but merely rotated three syringes. John was certain that their short stay in the sterilizing solution was not nearly long enough to render them germ-free. When it was his turn, he was tempted to say something, but his French was not fluent enough, and he knew he needed the medicine.

During the next few days, John began to feel better. By the third day he was preparing to journey up the Zaire River when his health took a rapid turn for the worse. The first thing he noticed was a violent headache, followed in rapid succession by chills, fever, nausea and diarrhoea. He took to his tent and shivered through the night. Next morning, feeling weak and dehydrated, he made his way slowly to the mission hospital. When he arrived in the clinic, he vomited blood and collapsed on the floor.

An hour later he woke in a room occupied by two other patients, both suffering from drug-resistant malaria. The doctor who'd examined John on his previous visit was alarmed by the severity of John's condition and noted some curious additional symptoms: a strange rash over his chest and small surface haemorrhages in his eyes. Although the doctor's diagnosis was still malaria, he was troubled. It was not a typical case.

DR. LUGASA, District Health Commissioner for the Bumba region, reread the letter he'd just received from the Yambuku Mission Hospital concerning the deaths on September 14 of an American male, one John Nordyke, and a farmer from a plantation near the Ebola River. The mission doctor claimed that their deaths had been caused by an unknown infection that spread rapidly; four members of the farmer's family and ten of the clinic's outpatients had since come down with severe cases of the same illness.

Dr. Lugasa knew that he had two choices. He could do nothing, which was undoubtedly the wisest choice—who knew what kind of rampant endemic diseases there were out there in the bush? His second option was to fill out a bewildering array of official forms reporting the incident to Kinshasa, where someone higher on the bureaucratic ladder would decide to do nothing. With a twinge of guilt he let the letter slip into the wastepaper basket.

A week later Dr. Lugasa watched the aged DC-3 aircraft land at Bumba airport. First out was Dr. Bouchard, Dr. Lugasa's superior from Kinshasa. The day before, Dr. Lugasa had telephoned Dr. Bouchard to inform him that a serious outbreak of an unknown disease was in progress in the area around the Yambuku Mission Hospital. He had not mentioned the letter he'd received some seven days before.

The two doctors greeted each other on the tarmac and then climbed into Dr. Lugasa's Toyota. Dr. Bouchard asked if there was any more news from Yambuku. Dr. Lugasa cleared his throat, still upset about what he'd learned that morning from the wireless. Apparently eleven of the medical staff of seventeen were already dead, along with one hundred and fourteen villagers. The hospital was closed, since there was no one well enough to run it.

Dr. Bouchard decided that the entire Bumba region had to be quarantined to contain the highly contagious and very deadly disease. He quickly made the necessary calls to Kinshasa and then asked Dr. Lugasa to arrange transport for the following day so that they could visit Yambuku and assess the situation at firsthand.

The next morning, when the two doctors pulled into the deserted courtyard of the Yambuku Mission Hospital, they were greeted by an eerie stillness and a putrid odour. Holding handkerchiefs over their noses, they reluctantly got out of the car and looked into the nearest building. It contained two corpses, both beginning to decay in the heat. It wasn't until they'd peered into the third building that they found someone still alive, a nurse delirious with fever. Though fearful for their own health, they tended to the sick nurse and then searched for more of the staff. There were no other survivors.

THE NURSE, who had been airlifted to Kinshasa, died six days later. No diagnosis was made, but after the autopsy samples of her blood, liver, spleen and brain were sent to the Institut de Médecine Tropicale Prince Léopold in Antwerp, Belgium; to the Microbiological Research Establishment in Porton Down, England; and to the Centers for Disease Control in Atlanta, USA. In the Yambuku area there were now two hundred and ninety-four known cases of the illness, with a fatality rate of ninety per cent.

In mid-October the Yambuku virus was isolated almost simultaneously at the three international laboratories. It was noted to be structurally similar to the Marburg virus, first seen in 1967 in a fatal outbreak among German laboratory workers handling green monkeys from Uganda. The new virus, considerably more virulent than Marburg, was named Ebola, after the Ebola River, which is north of Bumba. It was immediately thought to be the most deadly micro-organism seen since the bubonic-plague bacillus.

11

NEARLY THREE MONTHS after the initial outbreak, the unknown disease in Yambuku was considered successfully contained, since no new cases had been reported in the area for several weeks. The Ebola virus was evidently once again residing only in its original source, but what that source was remained a complete mystery. An international team of professionals, including Dr. Cyrill Dubchek, an American virologist with the Centers for Disease Control, had scoured the area, searching for a reservoir for the Ebola virus within mammals, birds and insects. They had no success whatsoever. Not even a clue.

Los Angeles, California
January 14, Present Day

Dr. Rudolph Richter, a tall, dignified ophthalmologist originally from West Germany, cofounder of the Richter Clinic in Los Angeles, looked over the advertising proofs laid out on the circular table in the clinic's conference room. His brother and partner, William, a business-school graduate, was examining the proofs with equal attention. The advertisement was for the next quarter's drive for new prepaid subscribers to their health-care plan. It was aimed at young people, who as a group were relatively healthy. That was where the real money was in the prepaid health-care business, William had been quick to point out.

Rudolph picked up an ad scheduled for the *Los Angeles Times* Sunday magazine. It portrayed carefree bikini-clad girls on a Malibu beach playing volleyball with some handsome young men. It reminded Rudolph of a Pepsi ad, though it extolled the concept of prepaid health maintenance as delivered by an organization like the Richter Clinic in contrast to conventional fee-for-service medicine. The ad was perfect, the first good thing that had happened to him all day. It was a day that had begun badly when an AIDS patient with some weird complication had coughed in his face while he tried to examine the man's retinas. And if that wasn't enough, he'd been bitten by one of the monkeys used in his ocular herpes project. What a day!

After a brief discussion with his brother about the ad, Dr. Richter returned to his office. He caught up on his correspondence, then did his evening rounds: two retinal detachments with difficult medical histories. Both were doing well. Walking back to his office, he thought about how little surgery he was doing lately. It was disturbing, but with all the ophthalmologists in town, he was lucky to have what he did. He was thankful that his brother had talked him into the clinic idea eight years ago.

Dr. Richter changed his white coat for a blue blazer, picked up his briefcase and left the clinic. It was after 9 o'clock, and the garage was almost empty. Musing about the economics of the clinic, he was unaware of two men who had been waiting in the shadows of the garage, even after they fell in step behind him. The taller of the two had an arm that seemed permanently frozen into a flexed position. In his hand was a briefcase, which he held high due to the immobility of the elbow joint.

Nearing his car, Dr. Richter suddenly sensed footsteps behind him. He cast a nervous glance over his shoulder and caught sight of the two men, who seemed to be coming directly towards him. As they passed beneath an overhead light Dr. Richter saw that they were dressed in dark business suits and felt a little better. Even so, he quickened his pace, rounding the back end of his car. Fumbling for the keys, he unlocked the driver's door, tossed in his briefcase and slid into the welcome smell of coach leather. He started to close the door when a hand stopped him.

"Could you tell me the time, Doctor?" asked the man politely.

"Certainly," said Richter, glad to have a safe explanation for the man's presence. But before he had a chance to look at his watch, he was pulled from the car and knocked to the ground by a blow to the side of his face. Hands roughly searched for his wallet, and he heard fabric tear. One of the men said, "Open the briefcase."

It was over as quickly as it had begun. Dr. Richter heard footsteps recede and a car door slam, then the screech of tyres. For a few minutes he lay without moving, glad to be alive. As a surgeon, his primary concern was for his hands; he checked them even before he picked himself up off the ground. Getting to his feet, he began to examine the rest of himself. His shirt and tie were smeared with oil, his trousers torn from the right front pocket all the way down to the knee.

He returned to his office and reported the incident to security, but the idea of bad publicity for the clinic made him decide not to call the Los Angeles police. And really, what could they do now? He went into the lavatory to examine his face in the mirror. There was an abrasion over the right cheekbone. As he blotted it with antiseptic he tried to estimate how much he had contributed to the muggers' welfare. He guessed he'd had about a hundred dollars in his wallet, as well as all his credit cards and identification.

THE FOLLOWING DAY Dr. Richter did not feel well, but he attributed his symptoms to shock. By 5:30, though, he felt ill enough to consider cancelling a rendezvous he had with his mistress, a secretary in the medical records department. In the end he went to her apartment but left early to get some sleep, only to spend the night tossing restlessly in his bed.

The next day Dr. Richter was really ill. When he stood up from his desk, he was light-headed and dizzy. He tried not to think about the monkey bite or being coughed on by the AIDS patient. He was well aware that AIDS was not transmitted by such casual contact; it was the patient's undiagnosed complications that worried him. By 3:30 Richter had a chill and the beginnings of a headache of migraine intensity. Thinking he had developed a fever, he cancelled the rest of the afternoon's appointments and headed home. His wife took one look at his pale face and red-rimmed eyes and sent him to bed. By 8 o'clock his headache was so bad that he took a Percodan. By nine he had violent stomach cramps and diarrhoea. He took some Dalmane and fell asleep. At four he woke up and dragged himself into the bathroom, where he vomited blood. His terrified wife called an ambulance to take him to the clinic. He knew that he was sicker than he'd ever been in his life.

CHAPTER 1

Something disturbed Marissa Blumenthal. Whether the stimulus came from within her own mind or from some minor external change, she did not know. Nonetheless, her concentration was broken. As she raised her eyes from the book in her lap she realized that the light outside the window had changed from its pale wintry white to inky blackness. She glanced at her watch. No wonder. It was nearly 7 o'clock.

"Holy Toledo," muttered Marissa, using one of her expressions left over from childhood. She stood up quickly. She had been sprawled out on two chairs in a corner of the library of the Centers for Disease Control (CDC) in Atlanta for hours, but had planned on being home by 6:30.

Carrying the ponderous virology textbook she'd been reading, she made her way over to the reserve desk.

"Need help getting that monster back on the shelf?" teased Mrs. Campbell, the motherly librarian.

As in all good humour, there was some basis in truth for Mrs. Campbell's comment. The textbook weighed ten pounds—one tenth as much as Marissa's hundred-pound frame. She was only five feet tall, and to return the book she had to swing it back and then almost toss it into place.

"The kind of help I need with this book," answered Marissa, "is to get the contents into my brain."

Mrs. Campbell laughed in her subdued fashion. She was a warm, friendly person, like most people at the CDC. Marissa said goodnight and went upstairs to her office. It was a windowless cubbyhole with just enough room for a metal desk, filing cabinet, lamp and swivel chair, but she was lucky to have it. Competition for space at the CDC was intense.

Yet despite being hopelessly inadequate in terms of space, the CDC worked. Marissa was well aware of the phenomenal medical service the agency had delivered over the years. She remembered how the Center had solved the Legionnaires' Disease mystery a number of years back.

There had been hundreds of such cases since the organization had been started in 1942 as the Office of Malaria Control. In 1946 it had been renamed the Communicable Disease Center, with separate labs set up for bacteria, fungi, parasites, viruses and Rickettsia. The following year a lab was added for zoonoses, diseases that can be transmitted from animals to man, like plague, rabies and anthrax. In 1970 the organization was renamed again, this time the Centers for Disease Control. Three years later it had officially become an agency of the federal government. In 1980, after being reorganized with separate centres for various concerns such as environmental health, education and prevention services, as well as infectious diseases, the organization took the plural name Centers for Disease Control.

Marissa's awareness of the past successes of the CDC had been one of the prime reasons for her coming to the Center. After completing a pediatric residence in Boston, she had applied to and had been accepted by the Epidemic Intelligence Service (EIS) of the CDC as an Epidemic Intelligence Service officer. It was like being a medical detective. Only three and a half weeks previously, just before Christmas, she'd completed her introductory course in public health administration, biostatistics and epidemiology—the study and control of health and disease in a given population.

A wry smile appeared on Marissa's face as she pulled on her dark blue overcoat. She'd taken the introductory course, all right, but she felt totally ill-equipped to handle a real emergency. It was going to be an enormous leap from the classroom to the field if and when she was sent out on an assignment. Analysing textbook cases of a specific disease in a way that would reveal cause, transmission and host factors was a far cry from deciding how to control a real outbreak involving real people and a real disease.

At the completion of the training she'd been assigned to the Department of Virology, Special Pathogens Branch—her first choice—but she had little background in virology, which was the reason she'd been spending so much time in the library. However, she'd asked to be assigned to the department because the current epidemic of AIDS had catapulted virology into the forefront of research. It was where the action was, and Marissa wanted to be a part of it.

Picking up her briefcase, she turned off the light and headed down the hall. She took the lift to the main floor, where she stood in line to sign out, a requirement after 5:00.

It was a short drive from the CDC to her rented house in Peachtree Place, a small two-storey wood-frame building that Marissa described as cute. Since she was going out that evening, she did not put her car in the garage but parked it outside her back door. As she ran up the steps she heard Taffy barking a welcome.

Marissa had never planned on having a dog, but six months previously a long-term relationship that she had assumed was leading to marriage had suddenly ended. Roger, a neurosurgical resident at Massachusetts General Hospital, had shocked her with the news that he had accepted a fellowship at University College Los Angeles and that he wanted to go by himself.

As the baby in the family, with three older brothers and a dominating neurosurgeon for a father, Marissa had never had much confidence. She took the breakup very badly and had been barely able to drag herself out of bed each morning to get to the hospital. In the midst of her depression a friend had presented her with the cocker spaniel puppy. At first Marissa had been irritated, but Taffy—the name the puppy had worn on a large bow tied round her neck—soon won Marissa's heart and helped her to focus on something besides her hurt. When she had come to the CDC, Marissa's only worry had been what to do with Taffy when she was sent out in the field. The issue weighed heavily on her until her neighbours, the Judsons, fell in love with the puppy and offered to take her any time Marissa had to go out of town.

Opening the door, Marissa had to fend off Taffy's excited jumps until she could turn off the burglar alarm. When the owners of the house had first explained the system to Marissa, she'd listened with only half an ear. But she was glad she had it. She felt much more isolated at night here in the suburbs than she had in Boston. She even appreciated the "panic button" she carried in her coat pocket, which she could use to set off the alarm from the driveway if she saw unexpected lights or movements inside the house.

While Marissa looked over her mail, she let Taffy expend some of her pent-up energy racing about in the front garden. Unfortunately, Marissa had to cut the puppy's exuberant exercise short since it was already after seven and she was expected at a dinner party at eight. The host, Ralph Hempston, was a successful ophthalmologist at University Hospital. He had taken her out several times, and though she was still not over Roger, she enjoyed Ralph's sophisticated company. He seemed content to let the relationship grow at its own pace, and Marissa was grateful, even though she suspected the reason might be the difference in their ages; she was thirty-one and he was fifty-three.

Oddly enough, the only other man Marissa was dating was four years younger than she. Tad Schockley, a microbiologist PhD who also worked in the Virology Department, was boyishly shy—the exact opposite of Ralph Hempston. Fortunately, Tad, like Ralph, was not pushy in a physical sense.

Marissa showered quickly and put on a silk skirt-and-blouse set she'd been given for Christmas. Slipping on a pair of black shoes, she eyed herself in the mirror. Except for her height, Marissa was happy with her looks. Her eyes were dark brown and thickly lashed, her features small but delicate, and her thick, shoulder-length, wavy hair was the colour of expensive sherry.

It was only a five-minute drive to Ralph's house, a three-storey Victorian affair situated on a large piece of property. An octagonal tower dominated the right front corner, and a large porch, defined by a complicated gingerbread trim, started at the tower, extended along the front of the house and swept round the left side. Above the double-doored front entrance was a circular balcony roofed with a cone that was complemented by one on top of the tower.

Marissa drove round to the left. As she passed the house she glanced up at the fire escape coming down from the second floor. Ralph had explained that when the previous owners had built servants' quarters, the city building department had insisted the fire escape be added. The black iron stood out grotesquely against the white wood.

Marissa parked in front of the garage, whose trim matched that of the house. She knocked on the back door. No one seemed to hear her. Looking through the window, she could see the caterer's people bustling about in the kitchen.

She walked round to the front of the house and rang the bell. Ralph opened the door immediately and greeted her with a hug. "Thanks for coming early," he said, helping her off with her coat.

"Early? I thought I was late."

"No, not at all," said Ralph. "The guests aren't supposed to be here until eight thirty." He hung her coat in the hall cupboard.

Marissa couldn't help thinking that Ralph looked the quintessential physician: strong, sympathetic features and hair greying in just the right places.

"You look stunning, as always," he continued as he led Marissa into the living room and explained that he'd asked her to come early in the hope that she'd act as hostess. A little surprised—after all, she'd only been out with Ralph five or six times—Marissa agreed.

Fifteen minutes later the first guests arrived. Marissa had never been good at keeping track of people's names, but she remembered a Dr. and Mrs. Hayward because of his silver hair. Then there was a Dr. and Mrs. Jackson, she sporting a diamond the size of a golf ball.

When almost everyone was standing in the living room with drinks in hand, the doorbell sounded again. Ralph was not in sight, so Marissa opened the door. To her utter surprise she recognized Dr. Cyrill Dubchek, her boss at the Department of Virology.

"Hello, Dr. Blumenthal," said Dubchek, taking Marissa's presence in his stride.

Marissa was visibly flustered. She'd not expected anyone from the CDC. Dubchek took off his coat and handed it to a maid. He was wearing a dark blue Italian-tailored suit. A striking man with coal-black intelligent eyes and an olive complexion, his features were sharp and aristocratic.

Dubchek smiled at Marissa and moved towards the crowded living room as the doorbell rang again. This time Marissa was even more flabbergasted. Standing before her was Tad Schockley.

"Marissa!" said Tad, genuinely surprised.

Marissa recovered and greeted Tad. While she took his coat, she asked, "How do you know Dr. Hempston?"

"Just from meetings. I was surprised when I got an invitation in the mail." Tad smiled. "But who am I to turn down a free meal, on my salary?"

Marissa grinned in spite of herself. Tad, with his short sandy hair and fresh complexion, looked too young to be a PhD. He was dressed in a corduroy jacket, a knitted tie and grey flannels.

"Hey," he said. "How do *you* know Dr. Hempston?"

"He's just a friend," said Marissa evasively, gesturing for Tad to head into the living room for a drink.

Once all the guests had arrived, Marissa felt free to move away from the front door. At the bar she got herself a glass of white wine and began to mingle. She found herself in conversation with Dr. and Mrs. Jackson.

"How did you happen to come to the CDC?" asked Dr. Jackson. His voice was deep and resonant. He not only looked like Charlton Heston, he actually sounded as if he could play Ben Hur.

Trying not to stare at Mrs. Jackson's ring, Marissa wondered how to answer his question. She certainly wasn't going to mention anything about her former lover's flight to Los Angeles and her need for a change. That wasn't the kind of commitment people expected at the CDC. "I've always been fascinated by stories of medical detective work." She smiled. At least that was the truth.

"Dinner is served," called Ralph over the din of conversation. Marissa and the Jacksons moved into the dining room. Looking at the place cards, Marissa discovered that Ralph had seated himself at one end of the table and had placed her at the other. To her immediate right was Dr. Jackson, and to her left was the silver-haired Dr. Hayward.

As the meal progressed, the conversation turned to the sorry state of American medicine and how prepaid health-care groups were eroding the foundations of private practice. Glancing at their clothes and jewels, Marissa didn't feel that anyone present was suffering too much.

"How about the CDC?" asked Dr. Hayward, looking across at Dubchek. "Have you been experiencing budgetary constraints?"

Dubchek laughed ruefully, his smile forming deep creases in his cheeks. "Every year we have to do battle with the Office of Management and Budget as well as the House Appropriations Committee. We've lost five hundred jobs due to budgetary cuts."

Dr. Jackson cleared his throat. "What if there were a serious outbreak of influenza, like the pandemic of nineteen eighteen? Do you have the manpower for such an eventuality?"

Cyrill Dubchek shrugged. "It depends on a lot of variables. If the strain doesn't mutate its surface antigens and we can grow it readily in tissue culture, we could develop a vaccine quite quickly. How quickly, I'm not sure. Tad?"

"A month or so," said Tad. "If we were lucky. Longer to produce enough to make a significant difference."

Marissa felt a hand on her shoulder. Turning, she found herself looking at one of the waitresses.

"There is a phone call for you, Dr. Blumenthal," said the girl.

Marissa excused herself and followed the waitress to the kitchen. Then it dawned on her, and she felt a stirring of fear. It had to be the CDC. After all, she was on call and she'd left Ralph's number.

"Congratulations on your first assignment, Dr. Blumenthal," said the CDC duty officer when Marissa picked up the phone. "There has been an epidemic-aid request from the California State Epidemiologist. He'd like CDC help on a problem in Los Angeles—an outbreak of an unknown but apparently serious illness in a hospital called the Richter Clinic. We've made a reservation for you on a Delta flight that leaves at one ten am, and we've arranged hotel accommodation at the Beverly Hilton. Good luck!"

Replacing the receiver, Marissa left her hand on the phone for a moment while she caught her breath. She didn't feel prepared at all. Those poor unsuspecting people in California had called the CDC expecting to get an epidemiological expert, and instead they were going to get her, Marissa Blumenthal. All five feet of her. She made her way back to the dining room to say goodbye.

CHAPTER 2

By the time Marissa had collected her suitcase from the baggage carousel, hired a car and had somehow managed to find the Beverly Hilton, the sky had begun to lighten.

She washed her hands and face, combed her hair and freshened her lipstick. With no other plausible reason for delay, she drove to the Richter Clinic. The palms of her hands were damp against the steering wheel.

The building was situated on a wide thoroughfare. The entire structure was modern, including the garage, where she parked her hired car, the outpatient clinic and what Marissa guessed was the hospital, which appeared to be seven storeys tall.

Inside, Marissa noted the familiar hospital odour of disinfectant and felt instantly at home. She asked a maintenance man who was mopping the floor how to get to the hospital wing, and he pointed to a red stripe on the floor. Marissa followed it to the emergency room. There were a few patients in the waiting room, and a nurse was behind the main desk. Marissa sought out the on-call doctor and explained who she was.

"Oh, great!" he said enthusiastically. "Dr. Navarre, our chief of medicine, has been waiting all night for you. Let me get him."

Soon the door to the on-call room opened, and a handsome black-haired man appeared. Blinking in the bright emergency room light, he came directly towards Marissa. "Dr. Blumenthal, we are so glad to see you. You have no idea."

They shook hands, then Dr. Navarre inquired about her flight and asked if she was hungry.

Marissa said that she was fine, adding, "I think it would be best to get right down to business."

Dr. Navarre readily agreed. He led Marissa to the hospital conference room, where he motioned her to sit at the circular table. Once he himself was seated, Dr. Navarre pulled some patient-record cards from his pocket and said, "Now, let me bring you up to date. We have seven cases of an undiagnosed, but obviously severe, febrile illness. The first patient who was hospitalized is one of the founders of the clinic, Dr. Richter. The next, a woman from the medical records department." Dr. Navarre began placing his record cards on the table.

Opening her briefcase, Marissa extracted her notebook and a pencil. She knew that she needed to break the information down into understandable categories. First the disease: was it really something new? She had to characterize it even if she couldn't make a specific diagnosis. The next step would be to determine host factors in the victims, such as age, sex, health, eating habits, hobbies, then to determine time, place and circumstances in which each patient displayed initial symptoms, in order to learn what elements of commonality existed. Then there would be the question of transmission of the illness, which might lead to the infectious agent. Finally, the host or reservoir would have to be eradicated. It sounded so easy, but Marissa knew it would be difficult.

"So," she said, staring at the blank page. "Since no diagnosis has been made, what's being considered?"

"Everything," said Dr. Navarre.

"Influenza?" asked Marissa, hoping she wasn't sounding overly simplistic.

"No," said Dr. Navarre. "Serological testing has been negative for influenza virus in all seven patients."

"Any other ideas?" asked Marissa.

"All the cultures we've tested have been negative," said Dr. Navarre. "Blood, urine, sputum, stools, even cerebrospinal fluid. We thought about malaria, but the blood smears were negative for the parasites. We even treated for typhoid with chloramphenicol, despite negative cultures. There was no effect whatsoever. The patients are all going downhill, no matter what we do."

"How long has Dr. Richter been hospitalized?" asked Marissa.

"This is his fifth day. I think you should see the patients to have an idea of what we are dealing with." Dr. Navarre stood up without waiting for a response, and Marissa followed him through swing doors into the hospital proper. Nervous as she was, she could not help being impressed by the luxurious surroundings.

They took the lift up to the fourth floor and walked to the nurses' station. "All seven patients are on this floor," explained Dr. Navarre. "It has some of our most experienced personnel. The two patients in a critical condition are in separate cubicles in the Intensive Care Unit just across the hall. The rest are in private rooms. Here are the charts." He thumped a pile of folders stacked on the countertop. "I assume you'd like to see Dr. Richter first." Dr. Navarre handed Richter's chart to Marissa.

The first thing she looked at was the vital-sign sheet. The doctor's blood pressure was falling and his temperature was rising; not a good omen. Then she read the section entitled "History of the Present Illness". Something jumped out at her right away. Six weeks previous to the onset of symptoms Dr. Richter had attended an ophthalmological convention in Nairobi, Kenya. She read on, her interest aroused. One week prior to his illness Dr. Richter had attended an eyelid-surgery conference in San Diego. Two days prior to admission he'd been bitten by a *Cercopithecus aethiops*, whatever that was. She showed it to Dr. Navarre.

"It's a type of monkey," he said. "Dr. Richter always has a few of them on hand for his ocular herpes research."

Marissa nodded. She glanced at the laboratory values and noted that the patient had a low white count, a low ESR and low thrombocytes. Other lab values indicated liver and kidney malfunction. Even the ECG showed mild abnormalities. Dr. Richter was virulently sick.

Marissa laid the chart down on the counter.

"Ready?" questioned Dr. Navarre.

Marissa nodded that she was. However, she had no delusions of grandeur that she would uncover some heretofore missed but significant physical sign and thereby solve the mystery.

She followed Dr. Navarre into the Intensive Care Unit, with its familiar backdrop of complicated electronic machinery. There was the smell of alcohol, the sound of respirators and cardiac monitors. There was also the usual high level of nursing activity.

21

"We've isolated Dr. Richter in this side room," said Dr. Navarre, stopping at a closed doorway. "I think you'd better put on a mask and gown. We're observing isolation precautions on all the patients for obvious reasons."

"By all means," said Marissa, trying not to sound too eager. She slipped on the gown and helped herself to a hat, mask, bootees and rubber gloves. Dr. Navarre did likewise.

They entered the room to find the patient stretched out beneath a canopy of intravenous bottles. His colour was ashen, his eyes sunken, his skin slack. There was a bruise over his right cheekbone; his lips were dry, and dried blood was caked on his front teeth. Behind him was a cathode ray tube with a continuous ECG tracing flashing across its screen.

As Marissa stared down at the stricken man his eyes fluttered open. She noticed some haemorrhages in the whites.

"Is it true you were in Africa a month ago?" she asked.

"Six weeks ago," said Dr. Richter.

"Did you come in contact with any animals?" She had to lean over to hear the man, and her heart went out to him.

"No," managed Dr. Richter after a pause.

"Did you attend anyone who was ill?"

He shook his head. Speaking was obviously difficult for him.

Marissa pointed to the abrasion under the patient's right eye. "Any idea what this is?" she asked Dr. Navarre.

Dr. Navarre nodded. "He was mugged two days before he was hospitalized. He hit his cheek on the pavement."

"Poor guy," said Marissa, wincing at Dr. Richter's misfortune. Then she added, "I think I've seen enough for now."

Just inside the door leading back to the ICU proper there was a large frame holding a plastic bag. Both Dr. Navarre and Marissa peeled off their isolation apparel and dumped it before returning to the nurses' station.

"What about the monkey that bit Dr. Richter?" she asked.

"We have him quarantined," said Dr. Navarre. "We've also cultured him in every way possible. He appears to be healthy."

Marissa took a deep breath. They seemed to have thought of everything. Suddenly she remembered reading about a category of diseases called "viral haemorrhagic fevers". They were extremely rare, but deadly, and a number of them came from Africa. She mentioned the possibility.

"VHF was already brought up," said Dr. Navarre. "That was one of the reasons we called the CDC so quickly."

Just then Dr. Navarre was paged for an emergency. "I'm terribly sorry," he said, "but I'm needed in the ER. Is there anything I can do before I go?"

"Well, I think it would be better to improve the isolation of the patients. I think you should place them in a completely isolated wing and begin total barrier nursing, at least until we have some idea as to the communicability of the disease."

Dr. Navarre stared at Marissa. For a moment she wondered what he was thinking. Then he said, "You're absolutely right."

Marissa took the seven charts into a small room behind the nurses' station. Studying them, she learned that besides Dr. Richter there were four women and two men who presumably had the same illness. Somehow they all had to have had direct contact with each other or to have been exposed to the same source of contamination. Going back to Dr. Richter's chart, Marissa read everything. In her notebook she listed every bit of information that could possibly have significance, including the fact that the man had presented with an episode of haematemesis—vomiting blood. The whole time she was working, her mind kept returning to the fact that Dr. Richter had been in Africa six weeks previously. That had to be significant, even though a month's incubation was unlikely, given the symptomology. Of course, there were viral diseases like AIDS with longer incubation periods, but AIDS was not an acute viral infectious disease. The incubation period for such a disease was usually about a week.

Marissa painstakingly went through all seven charts, amassing diverse data on age, sex, lifestyle, occupation and living environment, and recording her findings on a separate page in her notebook for each of the patients. In addition to Dr. Richter there was a secretary who worked in medical records at the clinic, two housewives, a plumber, an insurance salesman and a real estate agent. Opportunity for commonality seemed remote with a group this diverse, yet all of them must have been exposed to the same source.

Reading the charts also gave Marissa a better clinical picture of the illness. Apparently it began rather suddenly, with severe headaches, muscle pain and high fever. Then the patients experienced some combination of abdominal pain, diarrhoea, vomiting, sore throat, cough and chest pain. A shiver went down Marissa's spine as she thought about having been exposed to the disease. She rubbed her eyes. They felt gritty from lack of sleep, but it was time to visit the other patients, whether she wanted to or not.

She started with the medical secretary and worked her way through to the last patient to be admitted. Before seeing each case, she dressed in full protective clothing. None of the patients felt like talking. Still, with each one Marissa went through her list of questions, concentrating on whether the patient was acquainted with any of the other people who were ill. The answer was always no, except that each one knew Dr. Richter and all were members of the Richter Clinic prepaid health plan.

24

One possible answer seemed so obvious that she was surprised no one had spotted it. Dr. Richter might have spread the disease himself! She asked the ward clerk to call for all the patients' outpatient records.

While she was waiting, Dr. Navarre telephoned. "I'm afraid we have another case," he said. "He's one of the lab techs here at the clinic. He's in the emergency room."

"Is he isolated?" asked Marissa.

"As well as we can do it down here," said Dr. Navarre. "We're preparing an isolation wing on the fourth floor."

"The sooner the better," said Marissa. "For the time being I recommend that all nonessential lab work be postponed."

"That's OK by me," said Dr. Navarre. "What about this boy down here? Do you want to see him?"

"I'm on my way," said Marissa, unable to shake off the fear that they were on the brink of a major epidemic. Concerning the lab technician, there were two equally disturbing possibilities: either he had contracted the illness in the same fashion as the others—from some active source of deadly virus in the clinic—or, more probably, he had been exposed to the agent by handling infected material from the existing cases.

The ER personnel had placed the new patient in one of the psychiatric cubicles. Marissa read the technician's chart. He was a twenty-four-year-old male by the name of Alan Moyers. His temperature was 103.4. After donning protective clothing, Marissa entered the tiny room.

"I understand you're not feeling too well," she said. "What was the first thing you noticed?"

"The headache," said Alan. "Then I started to get chills."

"Has anything abnormal happened to you in the lab recently?"

"Like what?" asked Alan, closing his eyes.

"Were you bitten by any animals?"

"Nope. I never handle any animals. What's wrong with me?"

"How about Dr. Richter? Do you know him?"

"Sure. Everybody knows Dr. Richter. Oh, I remember something. I stuck myself with a Vacutainer needle."

"Do you remember the patient's name on the Vacutainer?"

"No. All I remember is that the guy didn't have AIDS. I was worried about that, so I looked up his diagnosis."

"What was it?"

"It didn't say. I don't have AIDS, do I?"

"No, Alan, you don't have AIDS," said Marissa.

"Thank goodness," said Alan. "For a moment there, I was scared."

Leaving the lab technician, Marissa headed for the lifts. While she was waiting, she felt a tap on her arm. She turned to face a stocky man with a beard and wire-rimmed glasses. "Are you Dr. Blumenthal from the CDC?" he asked.

Surprised at being recognized, Marissa nodded.

"I'm Clarence Herns, with the *Los Angeles Times*. My wife works up in the medical ICU. What is it that Dr. Richter has?"

"At this point no one knows," said Marissa.

"My wife says he is dying and that there are six other similar cases. Sounds to me like the beginnings of an epidemic."

"I'm not sure that epidemic is the right word. There does seem to be one more case today, but that's the only one for two days. I hope it will be the last, but no one knows."

"Sounds scary," said the reporter.

"I agree," said Marissa. "But I can't talk any longer. I'm in a hurry."

Dodging the insistent Mr. Herns, Marissa boarded the next lift. She returned to the chart room behind the fourth floor nurses' station and put through a call to Dr. Dubchek at the CDC.

"So, how's your first field assignment?" he asked.

"It's a bit overwhelming," said Marissa. She described the eight cases she'd seen, admitting that she had not learned anything that the Richter Clinic doctors didn't already know.

"That shouldn't bother you," said Dubchek. "You have to keep in mind that a clinician looks at each case in particular, whereas you, as an epidemiologist, are looking at the whole picture; so the same data can mean different things. Tell me about the illness."

Marissa described the clinical syndrome. Dubchek was particularly interested in the fact that two of the patients had vomited blood and that three had conjunctival haemorrhages in their eyes. When Marissa said that Dr. Richter had been to an ophthalmology meeting in Africa, Dubchek exclaimed, "My heavens, do you know what you are describing?"

"Not exactly," said Marissa.

"Viral haemorrhagic fever," said Dubchek. "And if it came from Africa, it could be Marburg or Ebola . . . perhaps Lassa fever."

"But Richter's visit was over six weeks ago."

"Darn," said Dubchek almost angrily. "The longest incubation period is about two weeks."

"The doctor was also bitten by a monkey two days before he became ill," offered Marissa.

"And that's too short an incubation period. It should be five or six days. Where's the monkey now?"

"Quarantined," said Marissa.

"Good. If the animal is involved, we have to consider the Marburg virus. In any case, the illness certainly sounds like a viral haemorrhagic fever, and until proven otherwise, we'd better consider it as such."

"What about the mortality rate?" asked Marissa.

"High. Tell me, does Dr. Richter have a skin rash?"

26

Marissa couldn't remember. "I'll check."

"The first thing I want you to do is draw blood, obtain urine samples and do throat swabs for viral culture on all the cases, and have them rushed to the CDC. From the monkey, too, if you can. Pack the samples in dry ice and send them by air. Also make sure that all the patients are totally isolated, with complete barrier nursing. And tell whoever is in charge not to do any lab work until I get there."

"I have," said Marissa. "You're coming yourself?"

"You bet I am," said Dubchek. "This could be a national emergency. But it is going to take some time to prepare the mobile isolation lab. Meanwhile, start setting up a quarantine for contacts, and try to get in touch with the people who sponsored that eye meeting in Africa and see if any of the other doctors who went are ill. And one other thing: don't say anything to the press. There could be widespread panic. And Marissa, I want you to wear full protective clothing, including goggles, when you see the patients. I'll be there as soon as possible."

Hanging up, Marissa experienced a rush of anxiety. She wondered if she'd already exposed herself to the virus. Then she worried about having talked to Clarence Herns from the *Los Angeles Times*. Well, what was done was done. She was glad that Dubchek was coming. She knew she'd been in over her head from the moment she arrived in LA.

MARISSA GOT GOGGLES from pathology. She'd never thought about catching an illness through her eyes, but she was aware that the surface of the eye was a mucous membrane and was therefore vulnerable to viral assault. When she was fully attired in hood, goggles, mask, gown, gloves and bootees, she went to Dr. Richter's room to begin obtaining her samples.

Before she started, she examined him for a skin rash. His arms were clear, but he did have a curious red area about the size of a coin on his right thigh. Lifting up his hospital gown, Marissa noted a fine definite rash covering most of his body. She was impressed that Dubchek had anticipated it.

She drew blood first, then filled a urine container from the catheter bag. After each sample was sealed, she washed its exterior with sodium hypochlorite, then put it in a second bag. After the exterior of the second bag was washed in the disinfectant, she allowed it to be removed from the room.

Disposing of her protective clothes and then donning fresh ones, Marissa went on to the next patient, the medical secretary, whose name was Helen Townsend. Marissa noted that Helen also had a faint rash on her body, but no red circle on her thigh. None of the patients were well enough to question Marissa much as she went about her sampling.

As for the monkey, Marissa didn't even attempt to get a blood sample.

The animal keeper was out for the day, and she had no intention of trying to handle the job alone.

Once Marissa completed the packing of the samples, she personally drove to the airport and saw the boxes safely on their way to Atlanta.

Back at the Richter Clinic, Marissa called Dr. Navarre and said that they should get together to talk about systematically quarantining all contacts. Dr. Navarre agreed, shocked to hear that Dubchek thought they might actually be dealing with viral haemorrhagic fever.

Marissa then went to the library. There she found a few standard texts that included sections on viral diseases. She scanned the entries for Lassa fever, Marburg and Ebola viruses, and understood Dubchek's reaction on the telephone. These were the most deadly viruses known to man.

Returning to the fourth floor, Marissa found that the clinic records she'd ordered had arrived. She sat down to study them.

The first belonged to Harold Stevens, the insurance salesman. Stevens had chronic open-angle glaucoma and saw Dr. Richter on a regular basis. His last checkup had been on January 15, four days before he was admitted to the hospital.

With a sense of growing certainty Marissa looked at the last entry on each chart. There it was. Each patient had seen Dr. Richter on either January 15 or 16. All except Helen Townsend, the secretary from the medical records, and Alan, the lab tech. Still, it was a strong suggestion that Dr. Richter was the source of the illness. The fact that he'd seen five of the patients just as he was developing symptoms had to be significant.

Marissa could explain the lab tech's getting the illness by his injecting himself with a contaminated needle, but she couldn't explain Helen Townsend. Marissa had to assume that Helen had seen Dr. Richter some time earlier in the week. She had come down with the illness just forty-eight hours after the doctor.

Marissa's musings were interrupted by a call from Dr. Navarre asking if she would come down to the hospital conference room.

Returning to the room where she'd started the day reminded Marissa of how long she'd been working. She felt bone weary as Dr. Navarre closed the door and introduced her to Dr. Richter's brother, William.

"Thank you for being here," said William. "Dr. Navarre has told me your tentative diagnosis, and I want to assure you that we will support your effort to contain the illness. But we are also concerned about the negative impact a quarantine could have on our clinic. I hope you agree that no publicity would be the best publicity."

Marissa felt outraged, when so many lives were at stake, but Dubchek himself had said essentially the same thing about publicity.

"I understand your concern," she said. "But we must initiate further quarantine measures." Marissa went on to explain that they would have to separate the possible contacts into primary and secondary groups. Primary contacts were people who had spoken with or touched one of the current eight patients. Secondary were those who had had contact with the primary contacts.

"Dr. Blumenthal," said Navarre. "You're talking about thousands of people."

"Besides, shouldn't we wait until we have a firm diagnosis before we initiate further quarantine measures?" said Richter.

"If we wait, it may be too late," said Marissa.

"There is no way we'll keep this from the press," moaned Richter.

"I think the press can help us," said Marissa, "in reaching all the contacts. Primary contacts must be instructed to stay as isolated as possible for a week and to take their temperatures twice a day. If they run a fever of a hundred and one or over, they'll have to come to the clinic. Secondary contacts can go about their business but should take their temperatures once a day."

Marissa stood up and stretched. "What I've outlined is standard CDC procedure. I'll leave its implementation to the Richter Clinic. My job is to try to find out where the virus originated."

Leaving two stunned men in her wake, Marissa walked out of the conference room. After getting directions at the inquiry desk, she made her way up to Dr. Richter's office.

His secretary was dutifully behind her desk. "Can I help you?" she asked. She was fiftyish, with silver-grey, tightly permed hair. Her name tag said Miss Cavanagh.

Marissa explained who she was, adding, "I need to reconstruct Dr. Richter's schedule for a week or two prior to his getting sick. Could you help me do that? I'm going to ask his wife to do the same."

"I suppose I could," said Miss Cavanagh.

"Good. I would also like to have the phone numbers of the sponsoring organizations for the medical meetings Dr. Richter attended in Africa and San Diego. Then I'd like to have a list of all the patients Dr. Richter saw during the two weeks before his illness. And finally, do you know Helen Townsend?"

Miss Cavanagh sighed disapprovingly. "Does Helen Townsend have the same illness as Dr. Richter?"

"We believe she does," said Marissa, watching Miss Cavanagh's face as she toyed with the keys of her typewriter. "Was Helen Townsend a patient of Dr. Richter's?" she prodded.

Miss Cavanagh looked up. "No. She was his mistress."

Marissa stared at the woman. It all fitted into place. She could now relate all the known cases to Dr. Richter. Epidemiologically, that was extremely important. It meant that Dr. Richter was an index case and that he, and only he, had been exposed to the unknown reservoir of the virus. Now it was even more important to reconstruct Dr. Richter's schedule in minute detail.

"Is there a chance I might get ill?" asked the secretary.

Marissa didn't want to frighten the woman, but she could not lie. After all, the secretary was a primary contact.

"It's possible," said Marissa. "We'd like you to restrict some of your activities during the next week or so and to check your temperature twice a day. Personally, however, I think you will be fine, since you haven't experienced any symptoms so far."

Back on the fourth floor, Marissa ran into Dr. Navarre. He looked as tired as Marissa felt. "Dr Richter's condition is deteriorating," he said. "He's bleeding from everywhere: injection sites, gums. He's on the brink of kidney failure, and his blood pressure is way down. The Interferon we gave him had no effect whatever, and none of us knows what else to try."

"What about Helen Townsend?" asked Marissa.

"She's worse, too," said Dr. Navarre. "She's also starting to bleed." He sat down heavily.

Marissa hesitated for a minute and then reached for the phone. She placed another call to Atlanta, hoping Dubchek was already on his way. Unfortunately, he wasn't. He came on the line.

"Things are pretty bad here," reported Marissa. "Two patients are experiencing significant haemorrhagic symptoms. Clinically, it is looking more and more like viral haemorrhagic fever, and no one knows what to do for these people."

"There's little that can be done," said Dubchek. "They can try heparinization. Otherwise, supportive therapy—that's about it. When we make a specific diagnosis we may be able to use hyperimmune serum, if it is available. On that track, we've already got your samples, and Tad has begun processing them."

"When will you be coming?" asked Marissa.

"Shortly," said Dubchek. "The mobile isolation lab is all packed."

MARISSA WOKE UP with a start. Thank goodness no one had come into the little chart room behind the nurses' station. She looked at her watch. It was 10:15 at night. She'd only been asleep for five or ten minutes.

Her head ached and she had the beginnings of a sore throat. She prayed that her symptoms were a product of exhaustion and not the onset of viral haemorrhagic fever.

It had been a busy evening. Four more cases had presented themselves in the ER. The new patients were all family members of the previous victims, underlining the need for strict quarantine. The virus was already into the third generation. Recognizing that she was at the limit of her strength, Marissa decided to go back to her hotel. She walked out to her car and drove to the Beverly Hilton, where she fell directly into bed.

CHAPTER 3

Arriving at the clinic the next morning, Marissa was surprised to see a number of TV trucks pulled up at the hospital entrance. When she entered through the car park, she was stopped by a policeman and had to show her CDC identification.

"Quarantine," the policeman explained, and told her to enter the clinic through the main hospital entrance, where the TV trucks were located.

Marissa obeyed, wondering what had been happening during the hours she'd been away. TV cables snaked their way along the floor to the conference room, and she was amazed at the level of activity in the main corridor. Spotting Dr. Navarre, she asked him what was going on.

"Your people have scheduled a news conference," he explained. His face was haggard and unshaven, and it seemed obvious he had not been to bed. He took a newspaper from under his arm and showed it to Marissa. "A New AIDS Epidemic" shouted the headline. The article carried the by-line of Clarence Herns. "Dr. Dubchek felt that such a misconception could not be allowed to continue," said Dr. Navarre.

Marissa groaned. "I didn't tell the reporter anything."

"It doesn't matter," said Dr. Navarre, patting her on the shoulder. "Dr. Richter died during the night, and with the four new cases there was no way we could have kept this from the press."

"When did Dr. Dubchek arrive?" asked Marissa.

"A little after midnight," said Dr. Navarre.

"Why the police?" she said.

"After Dr. Richter died, patients started signing themselves out of the hospital, until the State Commissioner of Health issued an order placing the whole building under quarantine."

Marissa excused herself and made her way into the conference room. She was glad Dubchek had arrived but wondered why he hadn't been in touch with her. When she entered the room, Dubchek was just starting to speak.

He began by introducing himself and the other doctors from the CDC. There was Dr. Mark Vreeland, Chief of Medical Epidemiology, and Dr. Clark Layne, Director of the Hospital Infectious Disease Program. Dubchek then went on to say that the problem was not "a new AIDS epidemic" by any stretch of the imagination. He said that the California State Epidemiologist had requested aid from the CDC to look into a few cases of unexplained illness thought to be of viral origin.

Looking at the reporters, Marissa could tell they were not buying Dubchek's calm assessment. The idea of a new, unknown and frightening viral illness made for exciting news.

Dubchek continued by saying that there had only been a total of twelve cases and that he thought the problem was under control. He added that experience proved this kind of illness could be controlled by strict hospital isolation.

At this Clarence Herns got to his feet, asking, "Did Dr. Richter bring this virus back from his African conference?"

"We don't know," said Dubchek. "It is a possibility, but doubtful. The incubation period would be too long, since Dr. Richter returned from Africa over a month ago. The incubation period for this kind of illness is usually about a week."

Another reporter jumped in. "If the incubation period for AIDS can be five years, how can you limit this to a week?"

"That's exactly the point," said Dubchek. "The AIDS virus is totally different from our current problem. It is essential that the media understand this and communicate it to the public."

"Have you isolated the new virus?" asked another reporter.

"Not yet," admitted Dubchek.

"If the virus hasn't been isolated," continued the same reporter, "how can you say it's different from the AIDS virus?"

Dubchek stared at the man. Calmly he said, "Over the years we've come to realize that totally different clinical syndromes are caused by totally different micro-organisms. Now, that is all for today, but we will keep you informed."

The conference room erupted as each reporter tried to get one more question answered. Dubchek ignored them as he and the other doctors made their exit. Outside the conference room the uniformed policeman kept the reporters from entering the hospital proper. After showing her CDC identity card, Marissa was allowed to pass. She caught up with Dubchek at the lifts.

"There you are!" he said, his dark eyes lighting up. His voice was friendly as he introduced Marissa to the other doctors.

"I didn't know you were all coming," Marissa said.

"We didn't have much choice," said Dr. Layne.

Dr. Vreeland nodded. "Despite Cyrill's comments at the news conference, this outbreak is extraordinarily serious. An appearance of African viral haemorrhagic fever in the developed world has been a nightmare we've dreaded since the illness first surfaced."

"If it really is African viral haemorrhagic fever," added Dr. Layne.

"I'm convinced the monkey will turn out to be the culprit," said Dr. Vreeland as they boarded the lift.

"I didn't get samples from the monkey," admitted Marissa.

"That's OK," said Dubchek. "Last night we put the animal to sleep and sent liver and spleen sections back to the Center."

They arrived on the fourth floor, where two technicians from the CDC were running samples in the mobile isolation lab.

"I'm sorry about that *Los Angeles Times* article," said Marissa, when she could speak to Dubchek alone.

"No matter," he said. "Just don't let it happen again." He smiled and winked.

Marissa had no idea what the wink meant, nor the smile, for that matter. "Why didn't you call me when you arrived?" she asked.

"I knew you'd be exhausted," explained Dubchek. "We spent most of the night getting the lab set up and autopsying the monkey. You are to be congratulated. You've done a fine job so far. For the moment I'm buried in administrative detail," continued Dubchek, "but I do want to hear what you've learned. Could you and I have dinner tonight at the hotel? I'll have something sent up to my room, and we'll go over your notes while we eat."

"Fine," said Marissa.

She returned to her room behind the nurses' station and phoned the sponsoring organizations for the two medical meetings Dr. Richter had attended. She told them she needed to know if any of the other attendees had become ill with a viral disease. Then, gritting her teeth, she left the clinic and drove to Dr. Richter's home, where she had an appointment to interview his widow.

Anna Richter, a well-dressed, attractive woman in her late thirties, did her best to be helpful, but she was desperately upset. She kept folding and unfolding some papers in her hands. Finally she handed them to Marissa, saying, "This is a list of Rudolph's activities over the last weeks. Maybe it will help some other poor family." Her eyes filled with tears. "He was such a good man . . . a good father . . . My poor children."

Despite knowing of his affair with Helen Townsend, Marissa decided that Dr. Richter must have been a pretty good husband. Anna's grief seemed real, and Marissa left as soon as she politely could.

The notes, which she read before starting the car, were surprisingly detailed. After a further interview with Miss Cavanagh and a close look at the doctor's appointment book, Marissa felt she'd have a good picture of Richter's last few weeks.

Back at the fourth-floor chart room that had become her office, Marissa was surprised to receive a call from Tad Schockley. "I need to speak to Dubchek," he said. "The hospital operator seemed to think that you might know where he was."

"If he's not in the CDC room, then I guess he's gone to the hotel."

"Well, I'll try the hotel, but in case I don't get him, could you give him a message?"

"Of course," said Marissa.

"It's not good news."

Straightening up, Marissa pressed the phone to her ear.

"It's about the virus you people are dealing with," said Tad. "The samples you sent were great, especially Dr. Richter's. His blood was loaded with virus—more than a billion per millilitre."

"Could you tell what it was?" asked Marissa.

"Absolutely," said Tad excitedly. "Dr. Richter has Ebola haemorrhagic fever."

"Had," said Marissa, mildly offended by Tad's callous enthusiasm. "He died last night."

"It's not surprising. The illness has a ninety-per-cent-plus fatality rate."

"My heavens! That must make it the deadliest virus known."

"Just about," said Tad. "And except for a couple of outbreaks in Africa, it's an unknown entity. You're going to have your work cut out trying to explain how it popped up in Los Angeles."

"Maybe not," said Marissa. "Dr. Richter had been bitten just prior to his illness by a monkey that had come from Africa. Dr. Vreeland is pretty sure the monkey was the source."

"He's probably right," agreed Tad. "Monkeys were responsible for an outbreak of haemorrhagic fever in sixty-seven. The virus was named Marburg, after the town in Germany where it occurred. The Marburg virus looks a lot like Ebola."

"We'll soon know," said Marissa. "Liver and spleen sections from the monkey are on the way."

"I'll check them as soon as they arrive," said Tad. "Let Dubchek and the others know they're dealing with Ebola. I'll talk with you soon. Take care of yourself."

DUBCHEK OPENED his hotel room door with a smile and motioned for Marissa to come in. He was on the phone, talking to Tad. She sat down and tried to follow the conversation. It seemed that the samples from the monkey had arrived and they had tested clear.

As Marissa watched Dubchek she realized the man had a disturbing effect on her. She recalled how unnerved she'd been when he'd turned up at Ralph's dinner party, and was upset to find herself inexplicably attracted to him now. From time to time he looked up, and her glance was trapped by an unexpected glint in his dark eyes.

Finally he hung up and walked over to her, grinning. "You're the best-looking thing I've seen today. And I gather your friend Tad would agree. He seemed very concerned that you don't put yourself at risk."

"I'm in no more danger than anyone else involved in this," she said, vaguely annoyed. Then, changing the subject, she asked about the monkey's liver and spleen sections.

"Clean so far," said Dubchek. "But that was only by electron microscopy. Tad has also planted the usual viral cultures. We'll know more in a week."

Marissa handed her notes to Dubchek and in a chronological fashion

34

began to describe what she'd been doing since her arrival in Los Angeles. She made a convincing argument that Dr. Richter was the index case, spreading the disease to some of his patients. She explained his relationship with Helen Townsend and described the two medical conventions that Dr. Richter had attended. The sponsoring organizations were sending complete lists of the attendees, with their addresses and phone numbers.

Throughout her monologue Dubchek nodded to indicate that he was listening, but somehow he seemed distracted, concentrating more on her face than on what she was saying. With so little feedback Marissa trailed off. Dubchek smiled. "Good job," he said simply. He stood up at the sound of a knock on the door. "That must be dinner. I'm starved."

The food was mediocre and lukewarm. As for the conversation, Marissa had thought that Dubchek intended to talk business, but the topics ranged from Ralph's dinner party to the CDC and whether she was enjoying her assignment. Towards the end of the meal he suddenly said, "I wanted to tell you that I am a widower."

"I'm sorry to hear that," said Marissa sincerely, wondering why he was bothering to inform her about his personal life.

"I just thought you should know," he added. "My wife died two years ago in a car accident."

Marissa nodded, uncertain how to reply.

"What about you?" asked Dubchek. "Are you seeing anyone?"

Marissa paused, toying with the handle of her coffee cup. "No, not at the moment." She wondered if Dubchek knew that she was dating Tad. It had not been a secret, but it wasn't public knowledge either. Looking at Dubchek, she couldn't help but acknowledge that she found him attractive. Perhaps that was why he made her feel so uncomfortable. She wasn't sure she was interested in a personal relationship with him, however.

Dubchek stood up. "If we're going back to the clinic, maybe we should be on our way."

Marissa went over to the coffee table to pick up her papers. As she straightened up, Dubchek came up behind her, putting his hands on her shoulders and turning her round. The action so surprised her that she stood frozen. For a brief moment their lips met. Then she pulled away, her papers dropping to the floor.

"I'm sorry," he said. "I wasn't planning that at all, but ever since you arrived at the CDC I've been tempted to do that. Lord knows I don't believe in dating anyone I work with, but it's the first time since my wife died that I've been interested in a woman. My wife was a musician, and when she played she had the same excited expression I've seen you get from your work."

Marissa was silent. She knew that Dubchek certainly had not been harassing her, but she felt embarrassed and awkward and was unable to say anything to ease the situation.

"Marissa," he said gently, "I'm telling you that I'd like to take you out when we get back to Atlanta, but if you're involved with Ralph or just don't want to . . ." His voice tailed off.

Marissa bent down and gathered up her notes. "We'd better go now," she said curtly.

He stiffly followed her out of the door, to the lift. Later, sitting silently in her car, Marissa berated herself. Dubchek was the most attractive man she'd met since Roger. Why had she behaved so unreasonably?

CHAPTER 4

Almost five weeks later, as she entered her house in Peachtree Place, Marissa was wondering if she would be able to reestablish a pleasant, professional relationship with Dubchek now that they were both back in Atlanta. He had left a few days after their exchange at the Beverly Hilton, and the few meetings they'd had at the Richter Clinic had been awkward.

After paying the driver and turning off the alarm, Marissa hurried over to the Judsons' and retrieved Taffy. The dog was ecstatic to see her, and the Judsons couldn't have been nicer. Rather than making Marissa feel guilty about being gone for so long, they seemed truly sad to see Taffy leave.

Back in her own house, Marissa turned up the heat to a comfortable level. Having a puppy there made all the difference in the world. The dog wouldn't leave her side and demanded almost constant attention.

She had just begun to leaf through five weeks' worth of mail when the phone rang. She picked up the receiver and was pleased to hear Tad's voice welcoming her home. "How about going out for a drink?" he asked. "I can pop over and pick you up."

Marissa thanked him for the offer but said she was exhausted after her trip. Then, remembering that on her last call from Los Angeles he'd told her he was hard at work on what he called "her" Ebola virus, she asked how those tests were going.

"Fine!" said Tad. "The stuff grows like wildfire."

"I can't wait to see what you're doing," said Marissa.

"I'll be happy to show you what I can," said Tad. "Unfortunately, the majority of the work is done inside the maximum containment lab, and you don't have clearance yet."

Marissa knew that the only way deadly viruses such as Marburg, AIDS and Ebola could be handled was in a facility that did just what its name suggested—contained the micro-organisms. For safety reasons, entry was restricted to authorized individuals, and having witnessed Ebola's devastating potential, Marissa was determined to get clearance as soon as she could.

"Can I take a rain check on that drink?" Marissa asked.

"Sure," said Tad.

OVER THE NEXT FEW DAYS Marissa readjusted to life in Atlanta, enjoying her home and her dog. At work, she threw herself into the study of Ebola. Making use of the CDC library, she obtained detailed material about the previous outbreaks of Ebola: Zaire '76, Sudan '76, Zaire '77 and Sudan '79. During each outbreak the virus had appeared out of nowhere and then disappeared. A great deal of effort had been expended trying to determine what organism served as the reservoir for the virus, all to no avail.

Marissa found the description of the first Zairean outbreak particularly interesting. Transmission of the illness had been linked to a health-care facility called the Yambuku Mission Hospital. She wondered what possible points of similarity existed between the Yambuku hospital and the Richter Clinic. There couldn't be very many.

She was sitting at a back table in the library, reading virology texts. She was boning up on tissue cultures, as an aid to practical work in the main virology lab. Tad had been helpful in setting her up with some relatively harmless viruses so that she could familiarize herself with the latest virology equipment.

Marissa checked her watch. It was a little after 2:30. At 3:15 she had an appointment with Dr. Dubchek. The day before, she'd given his secretary a letter formally requesting permission to use the maximum containment lab and outlining the experimental work she wanted to do on the communicability of the Ebola virus. Marissa was not particularly sanguine about Dubchek's response. He'd all but ignored her since her return from Los Angeles.

A shadow fell across her page, and Marissa glanced up. "Well! She is still alive," said a familiar voice.

"Ralph," whispered Marissa, shocked by his unexpected presence in the CDC library. She took his hand and led him into the hallway, where they could talk. She felt a surge of affection as she looked up at his welcoming smile. "It's good to see you," she said, giving him a hug. She felt a twinge of guilt at not having contacted him since returning to Atlanta. They'd talked on the phone about once a week during her stay in Los Angeles.

They went down to the CDC cafeteria for coffee and sat by a window overlooking the courtyard. "How about dinner?" Ralph asked, leaning forward and putting a hand on Marissa's. "I'm dying to hear the details of your triumph over Ebola in Los Angeles."

"I'm not sure that twenty-one deaths can be considered a triumph," said Marissa. "Worse still, from an epidemiological point of view we failed. We never found out where the virus came from, and we have no idea if and when Ebola will appear again. It's so unbelievably deadly."

Ralph squeezed her hand. "They couldn't figure out where Ebola came from in Africa either," he said. "I think you should consider your time in Los Angeles successful because you were able to contain what could have been an epidemic."

Marissa smiled. She realized that Ralph was trying to make her feel good, and she appreciated the effort. "Thank you," she said. "You're right. The outbreak could have have been much worse. Thank goodness it responded to the quarantine, because it carried better than a ninety-per-cent fatality rate, with only two survivors. Even the Richter Clinic has become a victim. Its reputation is ruined."

Marissa glanced at her watch. It was after 3 o'clock. "I have a meeting in a few minutes," she apologized. "See you tonight."

"Until dinner, then," said Ralph.

Marissa hurried up three flights of stairs and crossed to the virology building. It was 3:17 when she stood in front of Dubchek's secretary. It was silly of her to have rushed. She had to wait more than half an hour before the door to Dubchek's office opened and he motioned her to come in.

His office was small and cluttered, with reprinted articles stacked on the desk, on the filing cabinet and on the floor. Dubchek was in his shirt sleeves, his tie tucked between the second and third buttons of his shirt. There was no apology as to why she'd been kept waiting. In fact, there was a suggestion of a grin on his face that particularly galled Marissa.

"I trust that you received my letter," she said, keeping her voice businesslike.

"I did indeed," said Dubchek. "But a few days' lab experience is not enough to work in the maximum containment lab."

"What do you suggest?" asked Marissa.

"Exactly what you are doing. Continue working with less pathogenic viruses until you gain sufficient experience."

"How will I know when I've had enough experience?" Marissa realized that Dubchek had a point, but she wondered if his answer would have been different had they been dating. It bothered her even more that she didn't have the nerve to withdraw her earlier rebuff. He was a handsome man, one who attracted her far more than Ralph, whom she was happy enough to see for dinner.

"I believe *I* will know when you have had adequate experience," said Dubchek. "Meanwhile, I've got something more important to talk with you about. I've just been on the phone with the Missouri State

Epidemiologist. They have a case of a severe viral illness in St. Louis that might be Ebola. I want you to leave immediately, assess the situation, send Tad samples and report back. Here's your flight reservation." He handed Marissa a piece of paper that said, "Delta, Flight 1083, departure 5:34 pm".

Marissa was stunned. With rush-hour traffic it was going to be a near thing. She knew that she should always have a bag packed, but she didn't, and there was Taffy to think of, too.

Dubchek extended his hand to wish her good luck, but Marissa was so preoccupied with the thought of possibly facing the deadly Ebola virus again that she walked out without noticing. Glancing at her watch, she broke into a run. It was going to be close.

THE GREATER ST. LOUIS Community Health Plan Hospital was an impressive modern structure, with travertine-marble facing. The interior was mostly fumed oak and bright red carpeting. A receptionist directed Marissa to the administration offices.

"Dr. Blumenthal!" cried a diminutive Oriental man, jumping up from his desk and relieving her of her suitcase, which she was carrying as well as her briefcase, since she'd not taken the time to stop at her hotel. "I'm Dr. Harold Taboso," he said. "I'm the Medical Director here. And this is Dr. Peter Austin, the Missouri State Epidemiologist. We've been waiting for you." Marissa shook hands with Dr. Taboso and with Dr. Austin, a tall, thin man with a ruddy complexion.

"We are thankful that you could come so quickly," said Dr. Taboso. "We're aware of what happened in Los Angeles, and we're concerned that we might be dealing with the same problem here. We admitted one suspicious case this morning, and two more have arrived while you were en route."

Marissa bit her lip. She was troubled by the idea of another probable Ebola outbreak appearing so quickly. How had the virus come to St. Louis? Was this a separate outbreak from Los Angeles or merely an extension? Could there be an Ebola Mary, like the infamous Typhoid Mary? There were many questions, none of which made Marissa cheerful. She sank into the chair that Dr. Taboso proffered and said, "What have you learned so far?"

"Not much, I'm afraid," replied Dr. Austin. "The first case was admitted about four am. The patient was immediately isolated, hopefully minimizing contacts here at the hospital."

"Was any lab work done?" said Marissa.

"Yes," said Dr. Taboso. "It was ordered immediately on admittance, before we had any suspicion of the diagnosis."

"Have you been able to make any association with the Los Angeles outbreak? Did any of the patients come from Los Angeles?"

"No," said Dr. Austin. "We have inquired about such a possibility, but there has been no connection that we could find."

"Well," said Marissa, standing up, "let's see the patients."

They crossed the lobby to the lifts. Riding up in the lift, Marissa asked, "Have any of the patients been to Africa recently?"

"I don't believe so," said Dr. Taboso.

Marissa had not expected a positive answer. That would have been too easy. The lift stopped on the seventh floor.

As they walked down the corridor Marissa realized that none of the rooms they were passing were occupied. When she looked closer, she realized that most weren't even fully furnished.

Dr. Taboso noticed Marissa's expression. "I should have explained," he said. "When the hospital was built, too many beds were planned, and the seventh floor was never completed. It's ideal for isolation, so we decided to use it for this emergency."

When they arrived at the nurses' station, Marissa picked up the first patient's chart. She opened the metal cover and read the man's name: Dr. Carl M. Zabriski. Raising her eyes to Dr. Taboso, she asked incredulously, "Is the patient a physician?"

"I'm afraid so," answered Taboso. "He's an ophthalmologist here at the hospital."

Turning to Dr. Austin, she asked, "Did you know the index case in Los Angeles was also an ophthalmologist?"

"I was aware of the coincidence," said Dr. Austin.

Marissa directed her attention back to the chart. There were no references to recent travel or animal contact, but the vital-sign page showed high fever and low blood pressure. And although not all the lab tests were back, those that were suggested severe liver and kidney involvement. So far everything was consistent with Ebola haemorrhagic fever.

After Marissa had finished with the chart, she got together the materials necessary for drawing and packing viral samples. When all was ready, she was taken to the isolation area, where she donned hood, mask, gloves, goggles and bootees.

Inside Zabriski's room, the first thing Marissa noticed was the rash over the man's body. The second thing was signs of haemorrhage. Dr. Zabriski was conscious, but just barely. He certainly couldn't answer any questions. Clinically, the patient resembled Dr. Richter to a horrifying degree. Until proved otherwise, it had to be assumed that Dr. Zabriski and the other two admissions had Ebola haemorrhagic fever.

A nurse helped Marissa obtain a nasal swab as well as blood and urine samples. Marissa handled them as she'd done in Los Angeles, double bagging the material and disinfecting the outsides of the bags with sodium hypochlorite. Then, after removing her protective clothing and washing her hands, she returned to the nurses' station to call Dubchek.

The phone conversation was short and to the point. Marissa said that it was her clinical impression that they were dealing with another Ebola outbreak.

"We'll be there as soon as possible," said Dubchek. "Probably tonight. Meanwhile, I want you to stop all further lab work and supervise a thorough disinfection. Also, have them set up the same kind of quarantine that we used in Los Angeles."

Marissa was about to reply when she realized that Dubchek had hung up. She sighed as she replaced the receiver; such a wonderful working relationship!

Marissa turned to the nurse on duty and asked for the charts on the other two patients. As the nurse handed them to her she said, "I don't know if Dr. Taboso mentioned it, but Mrs. Zabriski is waiting in the ground-floor lounge."

Marissa put down the two new charts. She wanted to see Mrs. Zabriski, since she had very few details regarding the doctor's recent schedule. As she made her way downstairs to the lounge Marissa was unsure how she would recognize Mrs. Zabriski, but it turned out she was the only person in the room.

"Mrs. Zabriski," said Marissa softly. The woman raised her head. Her eyes were red-rimmed from crying.

"I'm Dr. Blumenthal. I'm sorry to bother you, but I need to ask you some questions."

Panic clouded the woman's eyes. "Is Carl dead?"

"No," said Marissa, sitting down next to the woman.

"He's going to die, isn't he?"

"Mrs. Zabriski," said Marissa, wanting to avoid such a sensitive issue, "I'm not one of your husband's doctors. I'm here to help find out what kind of illness he has and how he got it. Has he done any travelling over the last two months?"

"Yes," Mrs. Zabriski said wearily. "He went to a medical meeting in San Diego last month."

"Was that an eyelid-surgery conference?" asked Marissa.

"I believe so," said Mrs. Zabriski.

Marissa's mind whirled. Dr. Zabriski had attended the same meeting as Dr. Richter! "Do you know whether your husband was bitten by or was around any monkeys recently?" she asked.

"No," said Mrs. Zabriski. At least none that she knew of.

Finally, Marissa inquired if Dr. Zabriski knew Dr. Richter. The answer was negative, so she thanked the woman and apologized for bothering her.

As she left the lounge Marissa suddenly remembered that she hadn't called Ralph to cancel their dinner date. She found a pay phone and made the call. After she had explained what had happened, Ralph said that he would forgive her only if she promised to call him every couple of days to let him know if she was all right. Marissa agreed.

Returning to the isolation ward, she went back to the charts. The two other admissions with Ebola-like symptoms were a Carol Montgomery and a Dr. Brian Cester.

After gathering the material necessary for taking viral samples, Marissa dressed in protective clothing and visited Carol Montgomery. The patient was one year older than Marissa, who found it hard not to identify with her. Marissa asked her if she had done any recent travelling. The answer was no. Marissa asked if she knew Dr. Zabriski. Carol said that she did. Dr. Zabriski was her ophthalmologist. She had seen him four days ago.

Marissa obtained the samples and left the room with a heavy heart. She hated making a diagnosis of a disease with no available treatment. The fact that she'd been able to uncover information that mirrored the earlier outbreak was small compensation.

After changing into fresh protective clothing, she visited Dr. Cester. She asked the same questions and got the same replies, except when she asked if he was one of Dr. Zabriski's patients.

"No," said Dr. Cester after a spasm of abdominal pain had subsided. "I occasionally give anaesthesia for him, and I often play tennis with him. In fact, I played with him just four days ago."

Having obtained samples from Dr. Cester, Marissa left, feeling more confused than ever. She had begun to think that close contact—particularly one involving a mucous membrane, such as the surface of the eye—was needed to communicate the disease. Playing tennis with someone did not fit.

After sending off the second set of viral samples to Atlanta, Marissa reread Dr. Zabriski's chart. She then began the same type of diary she'd drawn up for Dr. Richter. Although this procedure had not resulted in determining the reservoir of the virus in the Los Angeles outbreak, Marissa hoped that by repeating it with Dr. Zabriski she might find some common element in addition to both doctors having been to the same eye conference in San Diego.

IT WAS PAST MIDNIGHT when Drs. Dubchek, Vreeland and Layne arrived from Atlanta. After a cursory greeting they all but ignored Marissa as they struggled to get the mobile isolation laboratory functioning and to improve the isolation of the patients. Marissa went back to her charts, but soon exhausted the information they could supply. Getting up, she wandered to the isolation lab, where Dubchek was working with two CDC technicians.

"I would like a minute to go over my findings with you," said Marissa, eager to discuss the fact that Dr. Zabriski had attended the same San Diego medical meeting as Dr. Richter had.

"It will have to wait," said Dubchek coolly. "Getting this lab functioning takes precedence over epidemiological theories."

Marissa seethed. She did not expect or deserve Dubchek's sarcasm. She considered her options. She could stay, hoping he might allow her ten minutes at his convenience, or she could go and get some sleep. Sleep won out.

THE OPERATOR WOKE Marissa at 7 o'clock. As she showered and dressed, she realized that her anger towards Dubchek had dissipated. After all, he was under a lot of stress. If Ebola raged out of control, it was his neck on the line, not hers.

At the nurses' station in the isolation ward, things were chaotic. Dr. Zabriski had died during the night, and five more patients had been admitted with a presumptive diagnosis of Ebola haemorrhagic fever. Marissa collected their charts.

Although she'd expected Dr. Zabriski's death, she was still upset. Unconsciously, she had been hoping for a miracle. She sat down and put her face in her hands. After a moment she forced herself to go over the new charts. It was easier to keep busy. Without meaning to, she caught herself touching her neck for swelling. There was an area of tenderness. Could it be a swollen lymph node?

Marissa was pleased to be interrupted by Dr. Layne, the director of the CDC's hospital infectious disease programme.

"Looks like this is going to be just as bad as Los Angeles," he said, sitting down wearily. "We have two more patients in the ER."

"I've just started looking at the new charts," said Marissa.

"Well, I can tell you one thing," said Dr. Layne. "All the new patients seem to have got their disease from the hospital."

"Are they all patients of Dr. Zabriski's?" asked Marissa.

"Those are," said Dr. Layne, pointing at the charts in front of Marissa. "They all saw Zabriski recently. The new cases are both Dr. Cester's patients. He was the anaesthetist when they had surgery during the last ten days."

"Do you think that Dr. Cester contracted the disease the same way that Dr. Zabriski did?" asked Marissa.

Dr. Layne shook his head. "Nope. I talked at length with Dr. Cester, and I found out that he and Dr. Zabriski were tennis partners. Four days before Zabriski became ill, Cester borrowed his towel between sets. I think that's what did it. Transmission seems to depend on actual contact with body fluids. I think Zabriski is another index case, just like Dr. Richter."

Marissa felt stupid. She had stopped questioning Dr. Cester just one question short of learning a crucial fact. She hoped that she wouldn't make the same mistake again.

"If we only knew how the Ebola got into the hospital in the first place," said Dr. Layne rhetorically.

Dubchek, looking tired but as carefully dressed as always, arrived at the nurses' station. Marissa quickly told both doctors that Zabriski had attended the same San Diego medical conference as Richter had.

"It's too long ago to be significant," Dubchek said dogmatically. "That conference was over six weeks ago."

"But it appears to be the only association between the two doctors," protested Marissa. "I think I should follow up on it."

"Suit yourself," said Dubchek. "But now I'd like you to go down to pathology and make sure they take every precaution when they do the Zabriski autopsy. Tell them that we want samples of liver, kidney, heart, brain and spleen for viral isolation."

Marissa went off feeling like an errand girl.

In pathology, she was directed to the autopsy rooms, which were gleaming with white tiles and stainless steel. There was a pervading aroma of formaldehyde, which made her eyes water. One of the technicians told her that Zabriski's autopsy was scheduled for room 3. "If you intend to go, you have to suit up."

With the fear of catching Ebola, Marissa was more than happy to comply. When she entered the room, Dr. Zabriski's body was still enclosed in a large, clear plastic bag. The pathologist, who was just about to begin, looked up from the table of horrific tools.

Marissa conveyed the CDC's request to him, and he agreed to supply the samples. He then cut into the plastic bag and exposed Zabriski's body to the air. Marissa debated whether she should go or stay. Indecision resulted in inaction; she stayed.

Speaking into an overhead microphone activated by a foot pedal, the pathologist began his description of the external markings of the body. Suddenly Marissa was startled to hear him describe a sutured scalp laceration. That hadn't been in Zabriski's chart, nor had the cut on the right elbow nor the circular bruise, about the size of a coin, on the right thigh.

"Did these abrasions happen before or after death?" she asked.

"Before," answered the pathologist.

"How old do you think they are?" said Marissa.

"About a week old, give or take a couple of days."

Marissa thought about this evidence of trauma. There was probably some simple explanation; perhaps Dr. Zabriski had fallen playing tennis. As soon as the autopsy was finished and she had seen that the tissue samples were correctly done, she decided to try to track down the cause of the bruises.

Since Zabriski's office was in the clinic, she decided to see if any of his staff were in. She found his secretary at her desk. Her name was Judith, and she was a frail young woman in her twenties. Marissa could tell that she'd been crying. But she was more than sad, she was terrified.

"Mrs. Zabriski is sick," she blurted out as soon as Marissa introduced herself. "She's downstairs in the emergency room. They think she has the same thing that her husband had. My God, am I going to get it too?"

With some difficulty Marissa calmed the woman enough to explain that in the Los Angeles outbreak the doctor's secretary had not come down with the illness.

"I'm getting out of here," said Judith. "And I'm not the only one who wants to go," she added.

"I understand how you feel," said Marissa. "But I need to ask you a question. Dr. Zabriski had some abrasions and a cut on his head. Do you know anything about that?"

"That was nothing," said Judith. "He was mugged about a week ago while he was shopping for a birthday gift for his wife."

So much for the mysterious question of trauma, thought Marissa. For a few minutes she stood watching Judith as she emptied her desk drawers. Marissa couldn't think of any further questions, so she said goodbye and headed for the isolation ward.

The ward was more chaotic than ever. "Welcome to bedlam," said Dr. Layne. "We've got five more admissions, including Mrs. Zabriski."

"So I've heard," said Marissa, sitting down. If only Dubchek would treat her as he did—as a colleague.

"Tad Schockley called earlier. It *is* Ebola."

The sound of the patient-lift doors opening caught Marissa's attention. She watched as a trolley emerged, covered by a clear plastic isolation tent. As it went by, she recognized Mrs. Zabriski. A shiver ran down Marissa's spine.

CHAPTER 5

Marissa took another forkful of the kind of dessert that she allowed herself only on rare occasions. It was her second night back in Atlanta, and Ralph had taken her to an intimate French restaurant. After five weeks of gulping down meals in a hospital cafeteria, the gourmet meal had been a delight.

While she'd been in St. Louis, Marissa had got into the habit of calling Ralph every few days. Talking with him had provided a sounding board for her theories as well as a way to relieve her frustration at Dubchek's continued insistence on ignoring her. In both cases Ralph had been understanding and supportive.

There had been thirty-seven deaths, and just before Marissa left St. Louis, Dr. Taboso had sadly told her he expected the hospital to close when the quarantine was lifted.

"You know, I'm still worried about getting sick myself," she admitted now with a self-conscious laugh. "Every time I get a headache I think, This is it. And though we still have no idea where the virus came from, Dubchek's position is that the virus reservoir is somehow associated with medical personnel, which doesn't make me any more comfortable."

"Do you believe that?" asked Ralph.

"I'm supposed to," said Marissa. "And if it is true, then you should consider yourself particularly at risk. Both index cases were ophthalmologists."

"Don't say that," Ralph laughed, "I'm superstitious."

Marissa leaned back as the waiter served coffee.

After he left, she continued, "If Dubchek's position is correct, then somehow both eye doctors came into contact with the reservoir of the virus. I've puzzled over this for weeks without coming up with a single explanation. Dr. Richter had contact with monkeys, and monkeys have been associated with a related virus called Marburg. But Dr. Zabriski had no contact with any animals at all."

"I thought you told me that Dr. Richter had been to Africa," said Ralph. "It seems to me that is the crucial fact. After all, Africa is where this virus is endemic."

"True," said Marissa. "But the time frame is all wrong. His incubation period would have been six weeks, when all the other cases averaged only two to five days. Then consider the problem of relating the two outbreaks. Dr. Zabriski hadn't been to Africa. The only point of connection was that the two doctors attended the same medical conference in San Diego. It's crazy." Marissa waved her hands as if she were giving up. Then she added, "There is one thing about the two index cases that I find curious. Both men were mugged just a few days before they got sick."

"Very suspicious," said Ralph with a wink. "Are you suggesting that there is an 'Ebola Mary' who spreads the disease?"

Marissa laughed. "I know it sounds stupid. That's why I haven't said anything to Dubchek." Thinking of him reminded her to ask, "By the way, how do you know Dr. Dubchek?"

"I met him when he addressed the ophthalmology residents at University Hospital," said Ralph. "Some rare viruses like Ebola and even AIDS have been localized in tears and the aqueous humour, some of them even causing anterior uveitis."

"Oh," said Marissa, nodding as if she understood. Actually, she had no idea what anterior uveitis was, but she had decided this was as good a point as any to ask Ralph to drive her home.

EVERY TIME THE PHONE rang over the next few days, Marissa expected to be called out for another Ebola outbreak. She packed a suitcase and kept it ready in her cupboard. She could be out of her house in a matter of minutes if the need arose.

At work Tad helped her to write up a research proposal on Ebola. Unable to come up with a working hypothesis for a possible reservoir for Ebola, Marissa concentrated instead on the issue of transmission. From the data she'd amassed in Los Angeles and St. Louis, she constructed case maps to show the spread of the illness from one person to another. She also compiled detailed profiles on the people who had been primary contacts but had not come down with the disease. As Dr. Layne had suggested, close personal contact was needed, presumably viral contact with a mucous membrane.

Marissa wanted to validate her hypothesis by using guinea pigs. Of course, such work required the use of the maximum containment lab, and she still had not obtained permission.

One afternoon, as Marissa and Tad relaxed over coffee in his office, she said, "Tad, you told me that there were all sorts of viruses stored in the maximum containment lab, including Ebola."

"Yes. We have samples from every outbreak. There are even samples frozen and stored from your two outbreaks."

Marissa wasn't at all sure how she felt about people referring to the recent epidemics as hers. "Is there any place else that the Ebola virus is stored, other than here at the CDC?" she asked.

Tad thought for a moment. "The army probably has some in Fort Detrick, at the Center for Biological Warfare. The fellow that runs the place used to be here at the CDC, and he had an interest in viral haemorrhagic fevers. He was one of the team sent out to cover the initial Ebola outbreak in Zaire."

"Does the army have a maximum containment lab?"

Tad whistled. "They've got everything."

Marissa sipped her coffee. She was beginning to get an idea, one so unpleasant that she could barely consider it as a hypothesis.

"ONE MOMENT, MA'AM," said the uniformed sentry with a southern accent.

Marissa had stopped at the main gate to Fort Detrick. Despite several days of trying to argue herself out of the suspicion that the army might have somehow been responsible for Ebola being loosed on an unsuspecting public, she had finally decided to use her day off to investigate. Those two muggings continued to nag her.

It had been an hour-and-a-half flight to Maryland from Atlanta, and a short drive in a hired car. Marissa had used her field experience with Ebola as an excuse to talk to anyone else familiar with the rare virus and

Colonel Woolbert had responded to her request with enthusiasm.

The sentry returned to Marissa's car. "You are expected at building eighteen." He handed her a pass to wear on her lapel. Ahead of her the black and white gate tipped up and she drove onto the base.

Building 18 was a windowless concrete structure with a flat roof. A middle-aged man in civilian clothes waved as Marissa got out of her car. It was Colonel Kenneth Woolbert. He was friendly, and unabashedly pleased about Marissa's visit. He told her straight away that she was the prettiest and the smallest EIS officer he'd ever met. Marissa smiled.

The building felt like a bunker. Entry was obtained through a series of sliding steel doors activated by remote control. Small TV cameras were mounted above each door. The laboratory was like any other modern hospital facility, complete with the omnipresent coffeepot over the Bunsen burner. The only difference was the lack of windows.

After a quick tour during which the presence of a maximum containment lab was not mentioned, Colonel Woolbert took Marissa to their snack shop. He got her a coffee and they sat down at a small table.

Without any prompting, Colonel Woolbert explained that he'd started at the CDC as an EIS officer in the late fifties and had become increasingly interested in microbiology, and ultimately virology. He told Marissa that there had been a history of movement between Detrick and the CDC and that the army had come to him with an offer he couldn't refuse.

"Doesn't the ultimate goal of the organization bother you?" asked Marissa.

"No," said Colonel Woolbert. "Three quarters of the work here involves defending the US against biological attack, so most of my efforts are directed towards neutralizing viruses like Ebola."

Marissa nodded. She'd not thought of that.

"Besides," continued Colonel Woolbert, "I can work on whatever I want to."

"And what is that just now?" asked Marissa innocently. There was a pause. The colonel's light blue eyes twinkled.

"I suppose I'm not violating the confidentiality of the military, since I've been publishing a string of articles on my results. For the last three years my interest has been the influenza virus."

"Not Ebola?" asked Marissa.

Colonel Woolbert shook his head. "No, my last research on Ebola was years ago."

"Is anyone here at the centre working on Ebola?" asked Marissa.

"No. No one is working on Ebola, including the Soviets, mainly because there is no vaccine or treatment for it. It was generally felt that once started Ebola haemorrhagic fever would spread like wildfire to both friendly and hostile forces."

48

"But it hasn't," said Marissa.

"I know," said Colonel Woolbert with a sigh. "I've read with great interest about the last two outbreaks. We'll have to review our assessment of the organism."

"Please, not on my account," said Marissa. The last thing she wanted to do was to encourage the army to work with Ebola. "I understand you were part of the international team that was sent to Yambuku in nineteen seventy-six," she said.

"Which makes me appreciate what you're doing. I can tell you, when I was in Africa I was scared stiff."

Marissa grinned. "You are the first person to admit to being afraid," she said. "I've been struggling with my fear from the first day I was sent to LA."

"And with good reason," said Colonel Woolbert. "Ebola's a strange bug. Even though it seems it can be inactivated quite easily, it is extraordinarily infective, meaning that only a couple of organisms have to make entry to produce the disease."

"What about the reservoir?" asked Marissa. "I know that no reservoir was discovered in Africa. But did you have an opinion?"

"I think it is an animal disease," said Colonel Woolbert. "I think it will eventually be isolated to some equatorial African monkey and is therefore a zoonosis, or a disease of vertebrate animals that occasionally gets transmitted to man."

"So you agree with the current CDC official position about these recent US outbreaks?" asked Marissa.

"Of course," said Colonel Woolbert. "What other position is there?"

Marissa shrugged. "Do you have any Ebola here?"

"No," said Colonel Woolbert. "But I know where we can get it."

"I know, too," said Marissa. Well, that wasn't quite true, she thought. It was in the maximum containment lab at the CDC, but exactly where she did not know, yet.

MARISSA WAS IN a troubled sleep, tortured by nightmares of being chased through alien landscapes, when she realized that her phone was ringing. She shook herself awake and picked up the receiver. "Dr. Blumenthal," she said.

The voice on the other end of the wire was anything but calm. The caller introduced himself as Dr. Guy Weaver, the Arizona State Epidemiologist. "I've been called in on a severe problem at Medica Hospital in Phoenix," he explained. "Are you familiar with Medica Hospital?"

"Can't say that I am," said Marissa, glancing at the time. It was 4 am, which meant it was 2 am in Phoenix.

"It's part of a chain of for-profit hospitals that provide prepaid comprehensive care in this part of Arizona. We're terrified that the hospital's been hit with Ebola."

"Have you isolated the patient?" asked Marissa.

"Dr. Blumenthal," said Dr. Weaver, "it's not one case. It's eighty-four."

"Eighty-four!" she exclaimed in disbelief.

"We have forty-two doctors, eighteen registered nurses, eleven LPNs, four lab techs, six of the administrative staff, one food-service employee and two maintenance men."

"All at once?" asked Marissa.

"All this evening," said the epidemiologist.

"I'll be there as soon as possible," said Marissa.

MEDICA HOSPITAL was another elaborate modern structure, and as Marissa's taxi pulled up at the entrance it occurred to her that Ebola favoured such contemporary edifices.

Despite the early hour, the street in front of the hospital was crowded with TV trucks, reporters and uniformed police, some of whom were actually wearing surgical masks. In the early light the whole scene had a surreal look.

Marissa showed her identification card to one of the policemen, but he had to ask his sergeant if it was OK to let her pass. The hospital had already been quarantined. A group of reporters, hearing that she was from the CDC, crowded round and asked for a statement.

"I have no direct knowledge of the situation," protested Marissa. She was grateful for a policeman who shoved the press aside and allowed her through.

Unfortunately, things inside the hospital were even more chaotic. The lobby was jammed with people, and as Marissa entered, she was again mobbed. Apparently she was the first person to pass either in or out of the building for several hours.

"Please! Let me through." A heavy-set man with bushy eyebrows made his way to Marissa's side. "Dr. Blumenthal?"

"Yes," said Marissa with relief.

"I'm Lloyd Davis, director of the hospital," he said, taking her suitcase and briefcase. "I'm sorry about all this turmoil. We have a panic on our hands." Pushing his way through the crowd, he led Marissa to his office. "The staff is waiting to talk with you," he added as he deposited Marissa's belongings next to his desk.

"What about the patients with suspected Ebola?" asked Marissa. "Our first priority has to be to isolate them properly."

"They are well isolated," Davis assured her. "Right now I'd like you to talk with the staff before I'm faced with mutiny."

"I hope it's not that bad," said Marissa. It was one thing if the patients were upset, quite another if the staff was hysterical.

Mr. Davis ushered her out of the office. "A lot of people are terrified at being forced to stay in the hospital."

"How many more presumed cases have been diagnosed since you called the CDC?"

"Sixteen. No more staff; all the new cases are Medica Plan subscribers."

That suggested that the virus was already into its second generation, having been spread by the initially infected physicians. At least that was what had happened in the two previous outbreaks. With so many people infected, Marissa wondered if they would be able to contain the problem as they had in Los Angeles and St. Louis. The horror of the thought of Ebola passing into the general community was beyond comprehension.

"Do you know if any of the initial cases had been mugged recently?" asked Marissa. Davis raised his eyebrows as if she were crazy. So much for that, thought Marissa, remembering Ralph's response.

Davis led Marissa into the hospital auditorium and onto the stage. It was not a big room; there was seating for approximately one hundred and fifty people. Every seat was occupied, and all eyes were upon Marissa as she nervously walked towards the podium. A tall, exceptionally thin man stood up from a chair behind the podium and shook her hand. Davis introduced him as Dr. Guy Weaver, the man she'd spoken to on the phone.

"Dr. Blumenthal," said Dr. Weaver, "you have no idea how happy I am to see you." He stepped to the microphone and began describing Marissa in glowing terms, as if she were synonymous with all the triumphs of the CDC. Then, with a sweep of his long arm, he turned the microphone over to her.

Marissa was totally nonplussed. She had no idea what to say. Glancing at the audience, she noted that about half were wearing surgical masks. Everyone was watching her expectantly.

"The first thing we will do is ascertain the diagnosis," began Marissa in a hesitant voice at least an octave above her normal pitch. She tried to assure the audience, even though she wasn't sure herself, that the outbreak would be controlled by strict isolation of the patients and complete barrier nursing.

"Will we all get sick?" shouted a woman from the back of the room. A murmur rippled through the audience. This was their major concern.

"I have been involved in two recent outbreaks and haven't been infected," said Marissa. "Close personal contact is necessary to spread Ebola. Airborne spread is not a factor." Marissa noticed that a few of the people in the audience removed their masks.

"Is it really necessary for us to remain within the hospital?" demanded a man wearing a physician's long white coat.

"For the time being," said Marissa. She described what they had done in Los Angeles and St. Louis, explaining that none of the people who'd been quarantined had come down with the illness unless they had had direct contact with someone already ill.

When Marissa had finished, Dr. Weaver led her out of the auditorium. She told him that she wanted to see one of the initial cases before she called the CDC, and he offered to take her himself. En route he explained that they had placed all the cases on two floors of the hospital and that laboratory work had been restricted to what could be done on the isolated floors.

As for the quarantine situation, he told Marissa that mattresses had been brought in and the outpatient department had been turned into a huge dormitory, separating primary and secondary contacts. All food and water were also being brought in.

Before entering the isolation floor, Marissa and Dr. Weaver gowned. Then, before entering one of the rooms, they double-gowned, adding hoods, goggles, masks, gloves and bootees.

The patient, one of the clinic's general surgeons, was an Indian, originally from Bombay. Marissa glanced at the man's chart and saw no mention of foreign travel, monkeys, or contact with the Los Angeles or St. Louis outbreaks. The clinical picture mirrored the terminal phase of Ebola: high fever, low blood pressure, the typical skin rash, with signs of haemorrhage from mucous membranes. Marissa knew the man would not last another twenty-four hours.

She drew her viral samples immediately, and Dr. Weaver arranged to have them packed and shipped off to Tad Schockley.

Leaving the floor, Marissa first requested access to a telephone, then said she wanted physician volunteers to help her interview the patients. If many were as sick as the Indian doctor, they would have to work quickly to get any information at all.

Marissa was given the phone in Mr. Davis's office. It was already after 11 o'clock in Atlanta, and she reached Dubchek immediately.

"Does it look like Ebola?" he asked.

"It does," said Marissa. "The chief difference is, this outbreak involves one hundred cases at this point."

"I hope that you have instituted the proper isolation," was Dubchek's only reply.

Marissa had expected Dubchek to be overwhelmed. "Aren't you surprised by the number of cases?" she asked.

"Ebola is a relatively unknown entity," said Dubchek. "Nothing surprises me. I'm more concerned about containment."

"The isolation arrangements are fine," said Marissa.

"Good," said Dubchek. "We will be leaving within the hour."

Marissa found herself holding a dead phone. He'd hung up. She hadn't even had a chance to warn him that the entire hospital was under quarantine—that if he entered, he'd not be allowed to leave. "It'll serve him right," she said aloud.

When she left the office, she discovered that Dr. Weaver had assembled eleven doctors to help interview patients. Marissa explained what she needed: complete histories on as many of the first eighty-four cases as possible. She explained that in both the Los Angeles and the St. Louis incidents there had been an index case to which all other patients could be traced. Obviously, here in Phoenix it was different. With so many simultaneous cases there was the suggestion of a food- or water-borne disease.

"If it were water-borne, wouldn't more people have been infected?" asked one of the doctors.

"If the entire hospital supply was involved," said Marissa. "But perhaps a certain water fountain . . . ." Her voice trailed off. "Ebola has never been a water- or food-borne infection," she admitted. "It is all very mysterious, and it just underlines the need for complete histories to find some area of commonality. Were all the patients on the same shift? Were they all in the same areas of the hospital? Did they all drink coffee from the same pot, eat the same food, come in contact with the same animal?"

Before the group disbanded, Marissa reminded everyone to adhere to the isolation procedures. Then she thanked them and went to review the material that was already available.

As she had done in Los Angeles, Marissa took over the chart room behind the nurses' station on one of the isolation floors as her command post. As the doctors finished their history-taking they brought their notes to Marissa, who had begun the burdensome task of collating them.

By midday fourteen more cases had been admitted. All the new patients were prepaid health-care subscribers who had been treated by one of the original forty-two sick physicians before the physicians developed symptoms.

During the evening Marissa learned that the CDC team had arrived. Relieved, she went to find Dubchek, who was helping to set up the mobile isolation lab.

"You might have told me the hospital was quarantined," he snapped, when he saw her.

"You didn't give me a chance," she said, wishing there was something she could do to improve their relationship, which seemed to be getting worse. She gave Dubchek her notes.

"I'm not sure it was a good idea to use the regular hospital staff to take these histories," he said, as he began to leaf through them.

"There were so many cases," Marissa said defensively. "I couldn't possibly interview all of them quickly enough."

"That's still not reason enough to expose doctors who aren't trained

53

epidemiologists. If any of these doctors become ill, the CDC might be held responsible."

"But they—" protested Marissa.

"Enough!" interrupted Dubchek. "I'm not here to argue. What have you learned?"

Marissa tried to organize her thoughts and control her emotions. It was true that she'd not considered the legal implications, but the quarantined doctors were already considered contacts.

"One of the initial patients, an ophthalmologist," she began, "attended the same San Diego conference as Drs. Richter and Zabriski. Another, an orthopaedic surgeon, went on safari to East Africa two months ago. Two of the initial cases have used monkeys in their research. As a group, all eighty-four cases developed symptoms within a six-hour period, suggesting that all were exposed at the same time. The severity of the initial symptoms suggests that they all received an overwhelming dose of the infective agent. It seems to me we are dealing with a food- or water-borne infection, and in that regard the only commonality is that all eighty-four had lunch in the hospital cafeteria three days ago."

"What about contact with any of the patients in the Los Angeles or St. Louis episodes?" asked Dubchek.

"None that we can discover," said Marissa.

Dubchek headed for the door. "I think you should redouble your efforts to associate this outbreak with one of the other two. There has to be a connection."

"What about the cafeteria?" asked Marissa.

"Ebola has never been spread by food, so I can't see how the cafeteria could be associated . . ." He pulled open the door. "Still, the coincidence is curious, and I suppose you'll follow your own instincts no matter what I recommend."

Almost as if Dubchek's last words had been a challenge, Marissa decided to visit the cafeteria, which was in a separate wing.

When she entered, a stout but attractive middle-aged woman appeared and told her that the cafeteria was closed. Marissa introduced herself and asked if she could ask a few questions.

"Certainly," replied the woman, who said that her name was Jana Beronson and that she was the cafeteria manager.

Marissa asked to see the lunch menu for three days ago. Miss Beronson got it out of the file, and Marissa scanned the page. It was a typical cafeteria menu, with three entrees, two soups and a selection of desserts.

"Was this all the food offered?"

"Those are all the specials," answered Miss Beronson. "We also offer a selection of sandwiches and salads and beverages."

Marissa asked if she could keep the menu. She decided that she would go back to each of the initial cases and find out what they had eaten for lunch three days ago. She would also question a control group made up of people who ate from the same menu but who did not become ill.

As she put the menu in her bag Marissa asked Miss Beronson, "Wasn't one of your employees stricken?"

"Yes. Maria Gonzales. She was in charge of desserts and salads."

Marissa thanked Miss Beronson for her help and left the cafeteria.

MARISSA ROCKED BACK in the swivel chair and rubbed her eyes. It was 11:00 of her second day in Phoenix, and she'd only managed four hours' sleep the previous night.

Behind her, she heard the door open. She turned and saw Dubchek holding the front page of a local newspaper. The headline read "CDC believes hidden source of Ebola in USA". Looking at his expression, Marissa saw that he was, as usual, angry.

Dubchek smacked the newspaper. "It says here that Dr. Blumenthal of the CDC said that there is a reservoir of Ebola in the USA, and that the outbreak in Phoenix was spread by either contaminated food or water. Marissa, I don't mind telling you that you are in a lot of trouble!"

Marissa took the paper and read the article quickly. It was true that her name was mentioned, but only at second hand. The source of the information was one of the doctors who'd helped take patients' histories. She pointed this fact out to Dubchek.

"Whether you talk directly to the press or to an intermediary who talks to the press is immaterial. The effect is the same. It suggests that the CDC supports your opinion, which is not the case. We have no evidence of a food-related problem, and the last thing we want to do is cause mass hysteria."

Marissa bit her lower lip. It seemed that every time Dubchek spoke to her, it was to find fault. Controlling her temper, she handed him a paper. "I think you should take a look at this."

"What is it?" he asked irritably.

"It's the result of a second survey of the initially infected patients. Except for two people who couldn't remember, all the patients had eaten custard in the hospital cafeteria four days ago. In my first survey, lunch in the cafeteria on that day was the only point of commonality. You'll also see that a group of twenty-one people who ate in the cafeteria on the same day but did not eat the custard remained healthy."

Dubchek put the paper down on the countertop. "You are forgetting one important fact: Ebola is not a food-borne disease."

"I know that," said Marissa. "But you cannot ignore the fact that this outbreak started with an avalanche of cases, then slowed to a trickle after isolation."

Dubchek took a deep breath. "Listen," he said condescendingly, "Dr. Layne has confirmed your finding that one of the initial patients had been to the San Diego conference with Richter and Zabriski. That fact forms the basis of the official position: Richter brought the virus back from its endemic habitat in Africa and spread it to other doctors in San Diego, including the ophthalmologist here at Medica Hospital."

"But that position ignores the known incubation period for haemorrhagic fever."

"I know there are problems," admitted Dubchek tiredly, "but at the moment that's our official position. I don't mind you following up the food-borne possibility, but remember that you are here in an official capacity. I don't want you conveying your personal opinions to anyone, particularly the press. Understood?"

Marissa nodded. Dubchek started through the door, then hesitated. Looking back, he said more kindly, "You might be interested to know that Tad has started to compare the Ebola from the Los Angeles and St. Louis outbreaks with this one. His preliminary work suggests that they're all the same strain. That does support the opinion that it is really one related outbreak." He gave Marissa a brief, self-satisfied smile, then left the room.

56

Marissa closed her eyes and thought about what she could do. Unfortunately, no custard had been left over from the fatal lunch. That would have made things too easy. She decided to send samples of the custard ingredients to Tad to check for viral contamination. Yet she doubted she would learn anything from the ingredients. The virus was known to be extremely sensitive to heat, so it could only have been introduced into the custard after it had cooled. But how could that be? Marissa stared at her stacks of papers. The missing clue had to be there. If she'd only had a bit more experience, perhaps she'd be able to see it.

CHAPTER 6

It was nearly a month later, and Marissa was back in Atlanta in her little office at the CDC. The epidemic in Phoenix had finally been contained, without any answers as to what caused the outbreak or whether it could be prevented from recurring.

With a mixture of disappointment and anger she was staring at a memo that began, "I regret to inform you . . ." Once again Dubchek had turned down her proposal to work with Ebola in the maximum containment lab. This time she felt truly discouraged. She still believed that the outbreak in Phoenix had been connected with the custard, and she desperately wanted to vindicate her position by experimenting on animal systems with the virus itself. If she could understand the transmission of the virus, she might understand where it came from.

Marissa glanced at the large sheets of paper that traced the transmission of the Ebola virus from one generation to another in all three US outbreaks. She had also constructed similar diagrams concerning the transmission of Ebola in the first two outbreaks, in 1976. They had occurred almost simultaneously, one in Yambuku, Zaire, and the other in Nzara, Sudan.

One thing that continued to interest her about the African experience was that a reservoir had never been found. Mosquitoes, bedbugs, monkeys, mice, rats—all sorts of creatures were suspected and ultimately ruled out. It was a mystery in Africa just as it was in the United States.

Marissa tossed her pencil onto her desk with a sense of frustration. She had not been surprised by Dubchek's memo. He seemed determined to maintain the position that the Ebola virus had been brought back from Africa by Dr. Richter, who had then passed it on to his fellow ophthalmologists at the eyelid-surgery conference in San Diego. Dubchek was convinced that the long incubation period was an aberration.

Impulsively she got to her feet and went to find Tad. After some protest she managed to drag him away from the virology lab to get an early lunch.

"You'll just have to try again in a few weeks," Tad said, when she told him the bad news.

After they were seated at a table in the cafeteria, Marissa asked if he had had a chance to check the custard ingredients that she'd sent back from Phoenix.

"No Ebola," he said laconically, then added, "I should warn you. Dubchek came across the work and he was annoyed. Marissa, what's going on between you two? Did something happen in Phoenix?"

Marissa was tempted to tell Tad the whole story but decided it would only make a bad situation worse. To answer his question, she explained that she'd been the inadvertent source of a news story that differed from the official CDC position.

Tad took a bite of his sandwich. "Was that the story that said there was a hidden reservoir of Ebola in the US?"

Marissa nodded. "I'm certain the Ebola was in the custard. And I'm convinced that we're going to face further outbreaks."

Tad shrugged. "My work seems to back up Dubchek's position. I've been analysing viruses from all three outbreaks, and astonishingly enough, they are identical. It means that the exact same strain of virus is involved. It's strange, because normally Ebola mutates to some degree. Even the two original African outbreaks, in Yambuku and Nzara, involved slightly different strains."

"But what about the incubation period?" protested Marissa. "During each outbreak, the incubation period of new cases was always two to four days. There were three months between the conference in San Diego and the problem in Phoenix."

"OK," said Tad. "But that is a no bigger stumbling block than figuring out how the virus was introduced into the custard."

"The lady serving the dessert got sick herself. Perhaps she contaminated the custard," said Marissa.

"Fine," said Tad. "But how did she get a virus that lives only in darkest Africa?"

They ate in exasperated silence for a few minutes.

"There is only one place I know of that the dessert server could have got the virus," said Marissa at last.

"And where's that?"

"Here at the CDC."

Tad put down the remains of his sandwich and looked at her with wide eyes. "Marissa, do you know what you're suggesting?"

"I'm not suggesting anything," she said. "I'm merely stating a fact. The only known reservoir for Ebola is in our own maximum containment lab."

Tad shook his head in disbelief.

"Tad," said Marissa, "I'd like to ask you a favour. Would you get a printout from the Office of Biosafety of all the people who've been in and out of the lab for the last year?"

"I don't like this," said Tad, leaning back in his seat.

"Oh, come on," said Marissa. "I'm sure you can think up a reason to justify such a request."

"The printout is no problem," he said. "What I don't like is encouraging your paranoid theory, much less getting between you and Dubchek."

"Fiddlesticks," said Marissa. "How will he know?"

"He won't," said Tad reluctantly.

"Good," said Marissa, as if the matter had been decided. "I'll stop over at your apartment this evening to pick it up."

She smiled at Tad. He was a wonderful friend. She had the feeling that he'd do almost anything for her, which was reassuring, because she had another favour to ask him. She wanted to go into the maximum containment lab.

THE MOMENT MARISSA saw Tad that evening, she knew that he had got what she wanted. It was the way he smiled when he opened the door of his apartment.

Marissa plopped herself onto an overstuffed sofa, and sure enough, Tad produced the computer printout. "I told them that we were doing an internal audit of frequency of entry," he explained.

Turning back the first page, Marissa traced down the list with her index finger, recognizing few names. The one that appeared most often was Tad's.

"Everybody knows I'm the only one at the CDC who works," he said with a laugh.

Marissa noticed Colonel Woolbert's name listed a number of times, as well as that of a man named Arnold Heberling, who had visited fairly regularly until September. Then his name disappeared. Marissa asked about him.

"Heberling took another job six months ago," explained Tad. "There's been a bit of mobility in academic virology of late because of the huge grants generated by the AIDS scare."

"Where'd he go?" asked Marissa.

Tad shrugged. "Don't know. At one point he wanted to go to the Center for Biological Warfare, but he didn't get the job. Heberling's smart, but not the easiest guy in the world to get along with."

Marissa rolled up the list. "It's a little longer than I expected," she admitted. "But I appreciate your effort. There is another thing, though. You told me that the Ebola in Los Angeles, St. Louis and Phoenix were all the identical strain. I'd sure like to see exactly how you determined that."

"All that data is in the maximum-containment lab," said Tad.

"So?"

"You don't have clearance," Tad reminded her.

"I don't have clearance to do a study," said Marissa. "That means I can't go in by myself. But it's different if I'm with you. What could be so terrible about showing me what you're doing with the Ebola in the lab right now and then going out for a drink? It's nine pm. No one will be there."

Tad thought for a moment. He'd never been specifically told that he could not take other staff members into the lab, so he could always plead ignorance. Although he knew he was being manipulated, it was hard to withstand Marissa's charm. Besides, he was proud of his work and wanted to show it off.

"All right," he said. Marissa retrieved her bag, noting that Tad's access card was on the shelf by the door.

"I'm still not sure about this," admitted Tad as he pulled into the CDC car park a few minutes later.

"Relax," said Marissa. "I'm an EIS officer, for goodness' sakes."

They walked in silence to the main entrance, where they displayed their CDC identity cards and signed in under the watchful eyes of the security guard. Under the heading "Destination" Marissa wrote "office". They took the lift up to the second floor. After walking the length of the main building, they went through an outside door to a wire-enclosed catwalk that connected the main building to the virology labs.

"Security is tight for the maximum containment lab," said Tad as he opened the door to the virology building. "We store every pathological virus known to man."

"How are the viruses preserved?" Marissa asked.

"Frozen with liquid nitrogen," explained Tad.

"Are they infective?"

"Just have to thaw them out."

They were walking down an ordinary hall past a myriad of small, dark offices. When the hall turned sharply to the right, they were confronted by a massive steel door. Just above the doorknob was a grid of push buttons similar to Marissa's alarm system. Below that was a slot, like the opening for a credit card at an automatic cash dispenser.

Tad inserted his card. "The computer is recording the entry," he said. Then he tapped out his code number on the push-button plate: 43 23 39.

There was a mechanical click as the bolt released, then the door swung open. Marissa felt as if she had entered another world. Instead of the drab hallway, she found herself in a room almost two storeys high. She was surrounded by colour-coded pipes, gauges and other futuristic paraphernalia.

The lighting was dim until Tad opened a cabinet door, exposing a row of circuit breakers, which he threw in order. The first turned on the lights in the room in which they were standing. The next circuit breaker lit up a row of porthole-like windows that lined the sides of a ten-foot-high cylinder that protruded into the room. At the end of the cylinder was an oval door like the watertight hatch on a submarine.

The final circuit breaker caused a whirring noise. "Compressors," said Tad in response to Marissa's questioning look. He turned a large wheel to open the airtight door and motioned Marissa to go inside. He followed her, then closed and bolted the door. A feeling of claustrophobia almost overwhelmed her, especially when she had to swallow to clear her ears due to the pressure change.

Along both sides of the cylinder, beneath the porthole-like windows, were benches and upright lockers. At the far end was another oval airtight door.

"Surprise!" said Tad as he tossed Marissa a set of scrub clothes. "No street clothes allowed."

Marissa vainly glanced around for some privacy. Embarrassed as she was to be stripping down to her underwear in front of Tad, he seemed more self-conscious than she. He made a big production of facing away from her while she changed.

They then went through a second door. "Each room that we enter as we go into the lab is more negative in terms of pressure than the last. That ensures that the only movement of air will be into the lab, not out."

The second room was about the size of the first but with no windows. A number of large blue plastic suits hung on pegs. Tad searched until he found one he thought would fit Marissa. It looked like a spacesuit and covered her entire body, complete with hood, gloves and bootees. Issuing from the back, like a long tail, was an air hose.

Tad pointed out green piping that ran along the sides of the room at chest height, saying that the entire lab was laced with such pipes. At frequent intervals were rectangular lime-green air manifolds with adapters to take the air hoses from the suits. Tad explained that the suits were filled with clean, positive-pressure air so that the air in the lab itself was never breathed. He rehearsed with Marissa the process of attaching and detaching the air hose until he was convinced she felt secure.

"OK, time to suit up," said Tad as he showed Marissa how to start working her way into the bulky garment. The process was complicated, particularly getting her head inside the hood. As she looked out through the clear plastic face mask it fogged.

Tad told her to attach her air hose, and instantly Marissa's mask cleared and the fresh air cooled her body. Tad zipped up the front of her suit and with practised movements climbed into his own. He inflated his suit, then detached his air hose and, carrying it in his hand, moved down to the far door. Marissa did the same. She had to waddle to walk.

To the right of the door was a panel. "Interior lights for the lab," explained Tad in a muffled voice as he threw the switches. They went through another airtight door, and the next room was smaller than the first two, with walls and piping all covered with a white chalky substance. The floor was a plastic grate.

They attached their air hoses for a moment. Then they moved through a final door into the lab itself. This was a large rectangular chamber with a central island of lab benches surmounted by protective exhaust hoods. The walls were lined with all sorts of equipment: centrifuges, incubators, microscopes, computer terminals and a host of things Marissa did not recognize. To the left there was a bolted, insulated door.

"Over here," called Tad after they'd both hooked up to a manifold. He took her to one of the lab benches, where there was a complicated set-up of glassware, and began explaining how he was analysing the Ebola virus.

What Marissa really wanted to see was where they stored the Ebola. She eyed the bolted, insulated door. If she had to guess, she'd guess somewhere in there. As soon as Tad paused, she asked him where they kept the virus.

"Over there," he said, pointing in the direction of the insulated door.

"Can I see?" asked Marissa.

Motioning her to follow him, Tad waddled over to the side of the room and indicated an appliance next to one of the tissue-culture incubators. He wasn't pointing at the door.

"In there?" questioned Marissa with surprise. "It looks just like my parents' freezer."

"It is. We simply modified it to take liquid-nitrogen coolant."

Around the freezer and through the handle was a chain secured by a combination lock. Tad lifted the lock and twirled the dial. "Whoever set this had a sense of humour. The magic sequence is six six six."

"It doesn't seem very secure," said Marissa.

"No one can get in the lab without an access card," said Tad, opening the lock and pulling off the chain.

Big deal, thought Marissa as Tad lifted the top of the freezer. She peered within, half expecting something to jump out at her. What she saw through a frozen mist were thousands of tiny plastic-capped phials in metal trays.

With his plastic-covered hand Tad wiped the frost off the inside of the freezer's lid, revealing a chart locating the various viruses. He found the tray number for Ebola, then rummaged in the freezer like a shopper looking for frozen fish.

"Here's your Ebola," he said, selecting a phial and pretending to toss it at Marissa.

In a panic, she threw her hands out to catch the phial. She heard Tad's laughter, which sounded hollow and distant coming from within his suit.

Marissa felt a stab of irritation. This was hardly the place for such antics.

"Doesn't look like much, but there's about a billion viruses in there," he said.

"Well, now that I've seen it, I guess you may as well put it away." She didn't talk as he replaced the phial in the metal tray, closed the freezer and redid the lock. Marissa then glanced round the lab. It was an alien environment, but the individual pieces of equipment seemed relatively commonplace.

"Is there anything here that's not in any regular lab?" she asked.

Tad looked round the room. His eyes rested on the protective exhaust hoods over the workbenches. "Those are unique," he said, pointing. "They're called type-three HEPA filter systems—High Efficiency Particulate Air."

"Are they only used for maximum containment labs?"

"Absolutely. They have to be custom constructed."

Marissa walked over to the hood in place over Tad's set-up. It was like a giant extractor fan over a stove. A metal label affixed to the side said "Lab Engineering, South Bend, Indiana". Marissa wondered if anyone had ordered similar hoods lately. She knew the idea in the back of her mind was crazy, but ever since she'd decided that the Phoenix episode had been related to the custard, she hadn't been able to stop wondering if the outbreaks had been deliberately caused. Or, if not, whether a physician had been doing some research that had got out of control.

"Hey, I thought you were interested in my work," said Tad.

"I am," insisted Marissa. "I'm just overwhelmed by this place."

Tad began a complicated description of his latest work, which included development of a convalescent serum from the Los Angeles outbreak. Marissa listened, but just barely. She made a mental note to write to Lab Engineering.

"So what do you think?" asked Tad when he had finally finished.

"I'm impressed," said Marissa.

Before they left, Tad led Marissa down a passageway to a maze of animal cages. There were monkeys, rabbits, guinea pigs, rats and mice.

There was one last surprise. When they returned to the room with chalky walls, they were drenched by a shower of phenolic disinfectant. Looking at Marissa's shocked face, Tad grinned. "Now you know what a toilet bowl feels like."

While they were changing into their street clothes, Marissa asked Tad what was behind the bolted insulated door.

"Just a large freezer," he said, waving off the question.

When they left the lab, Tad took Marissa into his office and showed her how closely all his final results matched one another, suggesting that all the recent outbreaks were really one and the same.

"Have you compared the American strain with the African ones?" she asked him.

"Not yet," admitted Tad. He stepped over to his filing cabinet and extracted two manila folders. "Here's the one for the Sudan and here's Zaire."

Marissa opened both folders. The strains looked similar to her, but Tad pointed out significant differences in almost all the six Ebola proteins.

Then, while Marissa continued to study the Sudan strain, Tad leaned forward and picked up the Zaire folder and placed it next to the notes he'd just completed on the three American outbreaks.

"I don't believe this."

"What?" asked Marissa.

"I'm going to have to run all these through a spectrophotometer tomorrow just to be sure."

"Sure of what?"

"There's almost complete structural homology here," said Tad.

"Speak English!" said Marissa. "What are you saying?"

"The Zaire seventy-six strain is exactly the same as the strain from your three outbreaks."

Marissa and Tad stared at one another for a few moments. Finally Marissa spoke. "That means there's been just one outbreak, from the one in Zaire nineteen seventy-six to the one in Phoenix this year."

"That's impossible," said Tad.

"But that's what you're saying," said Marissa.

"I know," said Tad. "I guess it's just a statistical freak." He shook his head. "It's amazing, that's all I can say."

They left Tad's office. After crossing the catwalk to the main building, Marissa made Tad wait in her office while she typed a short letter to Lab Engineering in South Bend, Indiana.

"Why on earth are you writing to them?" Tad asked.

"I want some information about a type-three HEPA filter system."

"Why?" Tad asked with a glimmer of concern.

"Come on!" Marissa laughed. "If Dubchek continues to refuse me authorization to use the maximum containment lab, I'll just have to build my own."

Tad started to say something, but Marissa grabbed his arm and pulled him towards the lifts.

"I'm thirsty," she said. "Let's get that drink."

MARISSA WAS BACK in her office by 8:30 the next morning. She was eager to calculate the statistical probability of all the US strains of Ebola being the same as the 1976 Zairean strain. If the chances were as infinitesimally small as she thought, then she'd have a scientific basis for her suspicions.

64

But Marissa did not get far. On her desk was a terse message telling her to come to Dr. Dubchek's office immediately.

She crossed the catwalk to the virology building. Dubchek's secretary had not come in yet, so Marissa knocked on the open door.

Dubchek was at his desk, hunched over correspondence. When he looked up, he told her to close the door and sit down. Marissa did as she was told, conscious the whole time of Dubchek's onyx eyes following her every move.

"Dr. Blumenthal," he began, "I understand that you were in the maximum containment lab last night."

Marissa said nothing.

"I thought I made it clear that you were not allowed in there until you'd been given clearance. I find your disregard for my orders upsetting, to say the least, especially after getting Tad to do unauthorized studies on food samples from Medica Hospital."

"I'm trying to do my job as best I can," said Marissa.

"Then your best is clearly not good enough," snapped Dubchek. "I don't think you recognize the extent of the responsibility that the CDC has to the public."

"You are wrong," said Marissa, returning Dubchek's glare. "I take our responsibility to the public very seriously, and I believe that minimizing the threat of Ebola is a disservice. I'm doing my best to trace the source before we face another outbreak."

"Dr. Blumenthal, you are not in charge here!"

"I'm well aware of that fact, Dr. Dubchek. If I were, I wouldn't subscribe to the official position that Dr. Richter brought Ebola back from Africa and then experienced an unheard-of six-week incubation period. And if Dr. Richter didn't bring back the virus, the only known source of it is here at the CDC!"

"It is just this sort of irresponsible conjecture that I will not tolerate."

"You can call it conjecture," said Marissa, rising to her feet. "I call it fact. Even the army doesn't have the virus at its Center for Biological Warfare. Only the CDC has it, and it is stored in a freezer closed with a bicycle lock. Some security for the deadliest virus known to man! And if you think the maximum containment lab is secure, just remember that I was able to get into it."

As MARISSA ENTERED University Hospital and asked directions to the cafeteria she felt terrible, still remembering Dubchek's face as he'd ordered her out of his office. Uncertain what to do and sure that her EIS career had come to an end, Marissa had decided to call Ralph and seek his advice. She'd caught him between surgical cases, and he'd agreed to meet her for lunch.

The cafeteria at University Hospital was a pleasant affair, with yellow-topped tables and white-tiled floor. Marissa saw Ralph waving from a corner table. He was wearing his scrub clothes.

"Thanks for finding time to see me," she said as she sat down.

"I always have time for you," said Ralph. "What's wrong? You sounded really upset on the phone."

"Let's get our food first," said Marissa.

The interruption helped; Marissa was in better control of her emotions when they returned with their trays. "I'm having some trouble at the CDC," she confessed. She told Ralph about Dubchek's behaviour in Los Angeles and the incident in the hotel room. "From then on things have been difficult."

"That doesn't sound like Dubchek," said Ralph. "Can I speak frankly?"

Marissa nodded, wondering what was coming.

"I have heard through the grapevine that certain people at the CDC are not happy with you because you've not been toeing the official line. In a bureaucratic system you have to keep your own opinions to yourself until the right time."

"Obviously, you are referring to my stand on Ebola," said Marissa defensively. "But I can't remain silent. I cannot accept the CDC's position on Ebola. There are too many inconsistencies."

"Such as?"

"It's known that Ebola mutates constantly. Yet the three US strains are identical, and more astounding, they are the same as the strain in an outbreak in Zaire way back in nineteen seventy-six. To me it doesn't sound as if the disease is spreading naturally."

"You may be right," said Ralph. "But you are in a political situation, and you have to act accordingly. And even if there is another outbreak, which I hope there won't be, I have full confidence that the CDC will be capable of controlling it."

"That is a big question mark," said Marissa. "The statistics from Phoenix were not encouraging. Do you realize there were three hundred and forty-seven deaths and only thirteen survivors?"

"I know the statistics," said Ralph. "But with eighty-four initial cases, I think you people did a superb job."

"Oh, no!" said Marissa suddenly. "I've been so concerned about myself, I completely forgot about Tad. Dubchek must know it was Tad who took me into the maximum containment lab. I'd better get back and check on him."

"I'll let you go on one condition," said Ralph. "Tomorrow's Saturday. Let me take you to dinner."

"You are a dear. Dinner tomorrow night would be a treat."

Marissa gave Ralph a kiss on the forehead. He was so kind.

She drove back to the CDC and found Tad in the virology lab. When he caught sight of her, he shielded his face with his arms in mock defence.

"I'm sorry," said Marissa. "How did Dubchek find out?"

"He asked me," said Tad.

"And you told him?"

"Sure. I wasn't about to lie. He also asked if I was dating you."

"And you told him that, too?" asked Marissa, mortified.

"Why not?" said Tad.

Marissa took a deep breath. Maybe it was best to have everything out in the open. She put her hand on Tad's shoulder. "I'm really sorry I've caused you trouble. Can I try to make it up to you by fixing supper tonight?"

His face brightened. "Sounds good to me."

AT SIX O'CLOCK TAD came to Marissa's office and then followed her in his car to the supermarket, where they bought lamb chops, potatoes and salad. When the groceries were stashed in Marissa's boot, Tad insisted that he stop to buy some wine. He said he'd meet her at her house.

It had begun to rain when Marissa stopped at a bakery and picked up some bread. When she pulled up behind her house, she was pleased to see that she'd beaten Tad. The sun had not set yet, but it was as dark as if it had. Marissa had to fumble with her keys to put the proper one in the lock and then turn on the kitchen light with her elbow before dumping the two brown bags on the kitchen table. As she deactivated the alarm she called out to Taffy, wondering why the dog hadn't rushed to greet her. But the house remained unnaturally still.

She walked down the short hall to the living room and snapped on the light next to the couch. "Ta-a-a-affy," she called, drawing out the dog's name. She started for the stairs in case the dog had got shut into one of the bedrooms. Then she saw Taffy lying on the floor near the window, her head bent at an alarming angle.

"Taffy!" she cried as she ran to the dog and sank to her knees. But before she could touch the animal, she was grabbed from behind and her head jerked upright with such force that the room spun. Instinctively she reached up and gripped the arm, noticing that it felt like wood under the cloth of the suit. Even with all her strength she could not budge the man's grip on her neck. She tried to twist round to see her attacker, but she couldn't.

The panic button for the alarm system was in her jacket pocket. She reached in and juggled it in her fingers, desperately trying to turn it on. Just as she succeeded, a blow to her head sent her sprawling to the floor. Then, hearing Tad's voice shouting above the screech of the alarm, she turned groggily, to see him struggling with a tall, heavy-set man.

She managed to get up and rush to the front door. She threw it open, screaming for help from the Judsons. When she saw Mr. Judson opening his front door, she yelled to him to call the police, but didn't wait to explain. She turned on her heel and rushed back inside the house. The living room was empty. She raced down the hall to the kitchen. The back door was ajar. Reaching over to the panel, she turned the alarm off. There was no sign of Tad.

Mr. Judson came running up to the back door, brandishing a poker. "My wife is calling the police," he said.

"There was a friend with me," gasped Marissa, her anxiety increasing. "I don't know where he is."

"Here comes someone," said Mr. Judson, pointing.

A figure approached through the evergreen trees. It was Tad. Relieved, she ran out to him and threw her arms round his neck, asking him what had happened.

"I got knocked down," he told her, touching the side of his head. "When I got up, the guy was outside. He had a car waiting."

Marissa took Tad into the kitchen and cleaned his head with a wet towel. It was only a superficial abrasion.

"His arm felt like a club," said Tad.

"Could you identify him?" asked Mr. Judson.

Tad shrugged. "I doubt it. It all happened so quickly. All I noticed was that he had a briefcase."

"A briefcase? What kind of burglar carries a briefcase?"

In the distance they heard the sound of a police siren.

"Taffy!" cried Marissa suddenly. She ran back into the living room with Tad and Mr. Judson close behind.

The dog had not moved, and Marissa bent down and gingerly lifted the animal. Taffy's head dangled limply. Her neck had been broken.

Up until that moment Marissa had maintained control of her emotions, but now she began to weep hysterically. Mr. Judson took the dog. Tad put his arms around Marissa, trying to comfort her.

The police car pulled up with lights flashing. Two uniformed policemen came inside. They found the point of entry, a broken living-room window, and explained that the alarm hadn't sounded initially because the intruder had knocked out the glass and climbed through without lifting the sash.

Unfortunately, neither Marissa nor Tad could give much of a description of the man, save for his stiff arm. Asked if anything was missing, Marissa had to say that she had not yet checked. When she told them about Taffy, she began to cry again.

After saying they'd be in touch, the police left. Then Mr. Judson departed, and Marissa and Tad found themselves alone, sitting at the kitchen table, with the groceries still in their bags.

"Why don't we go out for dinner?" suggested Tad.

"I really am not up to a restaurant," said Marissa, rubbing her sore neck. "But I don't want to stay here. Would you mind if I fixed the meal at your place?"

"Absolutely not. Let's go!"

CHAPTER 7

It was Monday morning, and Marissa was filled with a sense of dread. It had not been a good weekend. Friday had been the worst day of her life, starting with the episode with Dubchek, then being attacked and losing Taffy. On Saturday night she'd seen Ralph as planned, and he'd suggested she ask for some time off. He felt that a short vacation might let things at the CDC cool down. When Marissa insisted that she must go back to work, he suggested she concentrate on something other than Ebola, but she shook her head to that, too. "Well, at least don't make more waves," Ralph counselled.

Dreading another confrontation with Dubchek but resolved to make amends, Marissa went to her office only to find another memorandum waiting on her desk. It was from Dr. Carbonara, the administrator of the EIS programme and hence Marissa's real boss. He wanted to see her immediately. That didn't sound good.

Dr. Carbonara's office was on the first floor. When Marissa entered, he motioned her to sit while he finished a phone call. When he hung up, he smiled warmly. The smile made Marissa relax a little. He didn't act as though he were about to fire her. Then he surprised her by commiserating with her about the assault and the death of her dog. Except for Tad, Ralph and the Judsons, she hadn't thought anyone knew about Taffy.

"I'm prepared to offer you some vacation time," continued Dr. Carbonara. "After such a harrowing experience a change of scene might do you good."

"I appreciate your consideration," said Marissa. "But to tell you the truth, I'd rather keep working. It will keep my mind occupied, and I'm convinced the outbreaks are not over."

Dr. Carbonara cleared his throat and said, "Unfortunately, there are some difficulties relating to the Ebola situation. As of today, we are transferring you from the Department of Virology to the Department of Bacteriology. I'm certain you will find this new position equally as challenging as your last."

Marissa was devastated. In her mind the transfer was tantamount to being fired.

"The truth of the matter is that the head of the CDC, Dr. Morrison, personally asked that you be moved out of virology and away from the Ebola problem," said Dr. Carbonara.

"I don't buy that," snapped Marissa. "It was Dr. Dubchek!"

"It wasn't Dr. Dubchek," said Dr. Carbonara with emphasis. Then he added, "Although he was not against the decision."

Marissa laughed sarcastically.

"Marissa, I am aware that there has been a clash of personalities between you and Dr. Dubchek. Perhaps it would be in everyone's best interests if I told you the whole story. Dr. Morrison received a call from Congressman Calvin Markham of Texas, who is a senior member of the House Appropriations Subcommittee for the Department of Health and Human Services. As you know, that subcommittee handles the CDC's annual appropriations. It was the Congressman who insisted that you be put off the Ebola team, not Dr. Dubchek."

Marissa was speechless. For a United States Congressman to call the head of the CDC to have her removed from the Ebola investigation seemed unbelievable. "Congressman Markham used my name specifically?" she asked when she found her voice.

"Yes," said Dr. Carbonara. "I questioned it, too."

"But why?" asked Marissa.

"There was no explanation," said Dr. Carbonara. "And it was an order, not a request. For political reasons, we have no choice."

Marissa shook her head. "I don't understand. But it does make me change my mind about that vacation offer. I think I need the time after all."

"Splendid," said Dr. Carbonara. "I'll arrange it—effective immediately. I want to reassure you that we have no quarrel with your work. Those Ebola outbreaks had us all terrified. You'll be a significant addition to the staff working on enteric bacteria."

Marissa left his office and headed home, her mind in turmoil. She hadn't accepted Dr. Carbonara's story that Dr. Dubchek had no role in shuffling her off the Ebola case. In fact, she was sure that if she checked, she would discover that Congressman Markham was a friend of Dubchek's. But instead of just giving in and accepting the situation, she resolved to do something. The question was what.

At home, she decided to do a therapeutic load of washing. Sorting her dirty clothes, she had an idea.

Impulsively she picked up the phone and called Delta Air Lines to make a reservation for the next flight to Washington DC.

"THERE'S AN INFORMATION desk just inside the door," said the knowledgeable cabdriver as he pointed up the stairs of the Cannon House Office Building.

Inside, Marissa went through a metal detector while a guard checked the contents of her bag. She asked for Congressman Markham's office and was told that it was on the fourth floor.

She found it easily. The outer door was ajar, so she walked in unannounced. Unfortunately, the Congressman was not in.

"He's not due back from Houston for three days," said a secretary. "Would you like to make an appointment? Or would you care to talk with Mr. Abrams, the Congressman's administrative assistant?"

While Marissa was deliberating, an earnest young man came up to her and introduced himself as Michael Abrams. "What can I do for you?" he said, extending a hand.

"Is there somewhere we can talk privately?" she asked him.

"By all means," said Abrams. He guided her into the Congressman's office, a large, high-ceilinged room with a huge mahogany desk flanked by an American flag on one side and a Texas state flag on the other.

"My name is Dr. Blumenthal," began Marissa as soon as she was seated. "I'm from the CDC in Atlanta." She watched to see if there was any unusual response. There wasn't.

"I'm interested in the Congressman's association with the Center," Marissa continued. "Is it one of his concerns?"

"He's concerned about all areas of health care," said Abrams. "In fact, Congressman Markham has recently sponsored bills limiting the immigration of foreign medical-school graduates, a bill for compulsory arbitration of malpractice cases and a bill limiting federal subsidies for the development of HMOs—health maintenance organizations."

"Impressive," said Marissa. "Obviously, he takes a real interest in American medicine. But as far as you know, he does not concern himself with any specific projects at the CDC?"

"Not that I know of," said Abrams.

"Well, thank you for your time," said Marissa, getting to her feet. Intuitively she knew she wasn't going to learn anything more from Michael Abrams.

Returning to the street, Marissa felt newly frustrated. She just couldn't understand why a man in Markham's position should bother with her, even if he were a friend of Dubchek's. Suddenly she got the glimmer of an idea. Hailing a cab, she hopped in and said, "Federal Election Commission."

Fifteen minutes later the cab pulled up in front of a drab building in downtown Washington. Uncertain which department she wanted, Marissa went into a ground-floor office. Four women were typing busily behind grey metal desks.

As Marissa approached, one looked up and asked if she could be of assistance.

"I'm interested in a Congressman's campaign finances," said Marissa. "I understand that's part of the public record."

"Certainly is," agreed the woman, getting to her feet. "Are you interested in contributions or disbursements?"

"Contributions, I guess," said Marissa with a shrug.

"What's the Congressman's name?"

"Markham," said Marissa. "Calvin Markham."

The woman padded over to a round table covered with loose-leaf books. She found the appropriate one and opened it at the Ms, explaining that the numbers following the Congressmen's names referred to microfilm cassettes. She then led Marissa to a cassette rack, picked out the relevant one and loaded it into the microfilm reader. "Which election?" she asked.

"The last one, I suppose," said Marissa. She wasn't sure what she was after—perhaps just some way to link Markham to Dubchek.

The machine whirred to life. "It's five cents a copy," said the woman, "if you want any. If you run into trouble, just yell."

Marissa reviewed the names and addresses of all contributors to Markham's considerable reelection coffers. She noted that he appeared to get support on a national scale, not just from Texas. She also noted that many of the donors were physicians, which made sense in the light of Markham's record on health legislation.

The names were in alphabetical order, and though she carefully scanned the Ds, she failed to find Dubchek's name. It had been a crazy idea anyway, she told herself.

At the end of the list of individual contributors was one of corporate supporters. The Physicians' Action Congress Political Action Committee had donated more money than any number of Texas oil companies. Going back to the previous election, Marissa found the same group. She made a copy of the lists, deciding to go over them at her leisure.

After thanking the woman for her help, Marissa went outside and hailed a cab. As it inched through rush-hour traffic to the airport Marissa looked again at the list of individual names. Suddenly she almost dropped the sheets. Dr. Ralph Hempston's name leaped out from the page. It was a coincidence, to be sure, but thinking it over, she was not surprised. Ralph was extremely conservative politically. It would be just like him to support a Congressman like Markham.

At the airport, waiting for her plane back to Atlanta, Marissa went to a pay phone to call Ralph. He asked her where she was.

"Washington," she explained, "but I'm on my way home."

"What's your flight number? I'll pick you up."

"Thanks, but it's not necessary," said Marissa. "I left my car at the airport."

"Then stop over on your way home."

"It might be late," said Marissa, thinking that it might be more pleasant at Ralph's than in her own empty house. "I'm planning on stopping by the CDC."

"That doesn't sound a good idea," said Ralph. "What are you up to?"

"Believe me, not much," said Marissa. "I just want one more quick visit to the maximum containment lab."

"I thought you didn't have authorization."

"I can manage it, I think. Ralph?" she said, screwing up her courage to ask the question. "Do you know Congressman Markham?"

There was a pause. "I know of him."

"Have you ever contributed to his campaign fund?"

"Yes," said Ralph. "Several times. I like the man's position on a lot of medical issues."

Marissa hung up feeling relieved. She was pleased she'd broached the subject of Markham and was even happier that Ralph had been so forthright about his contributions.

Once the plane took off, though, Marissa felt a sense of unease. A theory still undeveloped in the back of her mind was so terrifying she was afraid to try to flesh it out.

More horrifying yet, she was beginning to wonder if having her house broken into and her dog killed was something more than the random attack she'd taken it for.

MARISSA LEFT THE AIRPORT and headed for Tad's apartment. She'd not called, thinking it would be better just to drop in, even though it was almost 9 o'clock. She pulled up in front of his apartment, pleased to see lights blazing in the living room on the first floor.

"Marissa!" said Tad, opening his door. "What a surprise! Come on in."

Marissa entered ahead of Tad. Glancing at the shelf in the hall, she saw that his lab access card was there.

"I've been calling all day," he said. "Where have you been?"

"Out," said Marissa vaguely.

"I was told you'd been transferred from virology to bacteriology. Then I heard that you were on vacation. What's happening?"

"I wish I knew," said Marissa, dropping onto the sofa. "Do you have any idea why I've been transferred?"

"I'd guess that Dubchek requested it."

"Nope," said Marissa. "It was a US Congressman from Texas named Calvin Markham. He called Dr. Morrison directly. He sits on the Appropriations Subcommittee that decides on the CDC budget, so Morrison had to comply. But that's pretty weird, isn't it? I mean, I'm only an EIS officer."

"I suppose it is," agreed Tad. He was becoming very nervous.

Marissa reached out and put her hand on his shoulder. "What's the matter?"

"All this worries me," said Tad. "I like you; you know that. But trouble seems to follow you around, and I don't want to be drawn into it. I happen to like my job."

"I don't want to involve you, but I need your help just one last time. That's why I came here so late."

"Please don't ask me to break any more rules, Marissa."

"I have to get back into the maximum containment lab," she said. "Only for a few minutes."

"No!" said Tad decisively. "I can't take the risk. I'm sorry."

"There won't be anyone there at this hour," said Marissa.

"No," said Tad. "I won't do it."

Marissa could tell he was adamant. "I understand," she said.

"You do?" said Tad, surprised that she'd given in so easily.

"I really do. But if you can't take me into the lab, at least you could get me something to drink."

"Of course," he said, eager to please. "What's your pleasure?"

"A beer would be nice."

Tad disappeared into the kitchen. When Marissa heard the sound of the refrigerator opening, she tiptoed to the front door. Looking on the shelf, she was pleased to see Tad had two access cards. Maybe he wouldn't even notice that she'd borrowed one, she thought, as she slipped it into her jacket pocket. She was back on the sofa before Tad returned with the beer.

He handed her a bottle, keeping one for himself. Marissa asked about his latest research, but it was obvious she wasn't paying close attention to his answers.

"You don't like your beer?" asked Tad, noticing that she'd hardly touched hers.

"It's fine," she said, yawning. "I guess I'm more tired than thirsty. I suppose I ought to be going." She pushed herself to her feet.

"I'm sorry about the lab," said Tad, bending to kiss her.

"I understand," said Marissa. She headed out of the door before he could get his arms round her.

Tad waited until he heard the outer door close before going back inside his apartment. From where he was standing he was looking directly at the shelf where he kept his access cards. Suddenly he realized that one of the cards was gone. He carefully looked through all the junk he'd removed from his pockets, and then searched the shelves. His spare card was gone.

"Damn!" he said. He should have expected a trick when she'd given up so easily. He went to the phone and began dialling.

DRIVING TO THE CDC, Marissa worried that Dubchek might have warned the guards she was no longer working in virology. But when she flashed her identity card, the guard just smiled.

As a precaution, Marissa first went to her own office. There were a few letters on her desk: two advertisements from pharmaceutical houses and an envelope from Lab Engineering in South Bend. Marissa ripped this one open. A salesman thanked her for her inquiry concerning their type-3 HEPA filter systems and went on to say that such equipment was only built to custom specifications. If she was interested, she should retain an architectural firm specializing in health-care construction. He ended by answering the question that had prompted her letter: Lab Engineering had built only one system in the last year and that had been for Professional Labs in Grayson, Georgia.

Marissa searched through her drawers, knowing she had a Georgia road map somewhere. Finally she found it in the filing cabinet. Grayson was a small town a few hours' drive east of Atlanta. What on earth were they doing with a type-3 HEPA filter system?

After putting the letter in her pocket, Marissa checked the corrridor. It was quiet, and the lift was still at her floor; it had not been used. The time was right to make her move.

Marissa left the main building and crossed to the virology building via the catwalk. She was pleased that there were no lights on in any of the offices. When she passed Dubchek's door, she stuck out her tongue. It was childish but satisfying.

Turning the corner, she confronted the steel security door. She held her breath as she inserted Tad's card and tapped out his access number: 43 23 39. There was a resounding mechanical click, and the heavy door swung open.

Marissa felt her pulse begin to race. As she crossed the threshold she had the uncomfortable feeling she was entering a house of horrors. The dimly lit, cavernous two-storey space, filled with its confusion of pipes and their shadows, gave the impression of a gigantic spider's web.

As she'd seen Tad do on her previous visit, Marissa opened the small cabinet by the entrance and threw the circuit breakers, turning on the lights and activating the compressors and ventilation equipment. The sound of the machinery was much louder than she recalled, the lab even more intimidating. Every second she feared that someone would discover her.

With sweaty palms she grasped the releasing wheel on the airtight door and tried to turn it. The wheel would not move. Finally, using all her strength, she got it to turn. The seal broke with a hiss, and the door swung outwards. She climbed through, hearing the door close behind her with an ominous thud.

She felt her ears pop as she scrambled into a set of scrub clothes. The second airtight door opened more easily, but the fewer problems she encountered, the more she worried about the real risks she was taking.

Locating a small plastic isolation suit, she found it much harder to get into without Tad's help. She was sweaty by the time she zipped it closed.

At the switch panel, she only turned on the lights for the main lab; the rest were unnecessary. She had no intention of visiting the animal area. Then, carrying her air hose, she crossed the disinfecting chamber and climbed through the final airtight door into the main part of the lab.

She quickly hooked up to a manifold and let the fresh air clear her mask. She was already sorry that she'd not turned on all the lights. The shadows at the far end of the lab created a sinister backdrop for the deadly viruses, heightening her fear.

Swinging her legs widely to accommodate the bulky isolation suit, Marissa started for the freezer. Just short of it she paused, eyeing the insulated bolted door to the left. After having learned that the viruses were not stored behind it, she had wondered just what it did protect. Nervously she reached out and drew the bolt. A cloud of vapour rushed out as she opened the door and stepped inside. For a moment she felt as if she had stepped into a freezing cloud. Then the heavy door swung back against her air hose, plunging her into nearly total darkness.

When her eyes adjusted, she spotted a light switch and hit it. Overhead lights flickered on.

Marissa moved deeper into the room, fanning the air with her arms. Almost immediately a ghastly image caught her eye. She screamed, the sound echoing horribly within her suit. At first she thought she was seeing ghosts. Then she realized that she was facing a row of frozen nude corpses, only partially visible through the swirling mist. As she came closer Marissa recognized the first body. It was the Indian doctor whom she had seen in Phoenix, his face frozen in an agonized death mask. For a moment Marissa thought she was going to pass out.

There were at least half a dozen human bodies as well as the carcasses of monkeys and rats, frozen in grotesque positions. Although Marissa knew that such freezing was necessary for the viral study of gross specimens, she was totally unprepared for the sight. She backed out of the room, turning off the light and bolting the door. She shivered both from distaste and actual chill.

Chastised for her curiosity, Marissa turned her attention to the freezer Tad had shown her. In spite of the clumsiness caused by the plastic suit, she worked the combination lock and got the chain off. She lifted the lid of the freezer.

Rubbing the frost off the inner side of the lid, Marissa tried to decipher the index code. The viruses were in alphabetical order. "Ebola, Zaire '76" was followed by "97, E11-E48, F1-F12". Marissa guessed that the first number referred to the appropriate tray and that the letters and numbers that followed located the virus within the tray. There were, then, fifty phials of the Zaire '76 strain.

As carefully as possible, Marissa lifted tray 97 free and set it on a nearby countertop while she scanned the slots. Each was filled with a small black-topped phial. Marissa located the Zaire '76 strain and lifted out sample E11. The tiny frozen ball inside looked innocuous, but she knew that it contained millions of tiny viruses, any one or two of which, when thawed, would be capable of killing a human being.

Slipping the phial back into its slot, Marissa lifted the next, checking to see if the ice ball appeared intact. She continued this process without seeing anything suspicious until finally she reached phial E39. The phial was empty!

Quickly Marissa went through the rest of the samples. Only E39 was empty. All her unarticulated fears that the outbreaks had stemmed from accidental or even deliberate misuse of a CDC phial of the Ebola virus seemed to be confirmed.

Suddenly a movement caught Marissa's attention. The wheel on the door leading into the disinfecting chamber was turning. Someone was coming in!

Marissa was gripped with a paralysing panic. For a moment she just stared helplessly. When she'd recovered enough to move, she put the empty phial back in the tray, returned it to the freezer and closed the lid. She thought about running or hiding, but there was no place to go. She heard the seal break on the door and saw two people entering the lab, both dressed in plastic isolation suits. The smaller of the two seemed familiar with the lab, showing his larger companion where he should plug in his air hose.

Terrified, Marissa stayed where she was. There was always the faint chance that they were CDC scientists, checking on some ongoing experiment. That hope faded quickly when she realized they were coming directly towards her. It was at that point she noticed that the smaller person was holding a syringe. Her eyes flicked to the other one, who lumbered forward, his left elbow fixed at an odd angle, stirring an unpleasant memory. The glare off the masks made it impossible to make out any features.

"Blumenthal?" asked the smaller of the two in a harsh, masculine voice. He reached out and rudely angled Marissa's mask against the light. Apparently he recognized her, because he nodded to his companion, who reached for the zip on her suit.

"No!" screamed Marissa, realizing these men were about to attack her, just as she'd been attacked in her house. Desperately she snatched the lock from the freezer and threw it. The confusion gave Marissa just enough time to detach her air hose and run towards the darkened area by the animal cages.

The larger man came after her, but as he was about to grab her he was pulled up short by his air hose, like a dog on a leash.

Marissa moved as quickly as she could into the dark corridors between the stacked animal cages, hearing the frightened chatter of monkeys, rats, guinea pigs and who knew what else. Hoping to create a diversion, she began opening the cages. The animals who weren't too sick to move, immediately fled. Soon, her breathing became laboured.

Finding an air manifold, which was not easy in the darkness, Marissa plugged in. Welcoming the rush of cool, dry air, she moved down the line of cages to where she could see into the main area of the room. Silhouetted against the light, the man with the stiff arm was moving towards her. She had no idea if he could see her or not, but she stayed still, mentally urging him down a different aisle. But he was unswerving. He was walking right at her. The hairs on the back of her neck stood on end.

Reaching up, she detached her air hose and tried to move round the far end of the row of cages. Before she could do so, the man caught her left arm. The strength of his grip made resistance useless, but over his shoulder she glimpsed a red handle marked "Emergency Use Only".

In desperation Marissa reached up with her free hand and pulled the lever down. Instantly an alarm sounded, and a sudden shower of phenolic disinfectant drenched the whole lab, sending up clouds of mist and reducing the visibility to zero. Shocked, the man released Marissa's arm. She dropped to the floor. Discovering that she could slither beneath the row of cages, she crawled away, hoping she was heading back towards the main lab. Her breathing was becoming painfully laboured. She needed fresh air.

Something jumped in front of her, and she nearly screamed. But it was only one of the monkeys, tortured by the lethal atmosphere. Gasping, Marissa reached up and ran her hand along the pipes. Touching an air manifold, she connected her line.

Over the sound of the alarm Marissa heard a commotion in the next aisle, then muffled shouts. She guessed that her pursuer could not find a manifold.

Gambling that the second man would go to the aid of his accomplice, Marissa detached her own air hose and moved towards the main part of the lab, her arms stretched out in front of her like a blind man. Moving towards the wall, she banged into the freezer and remembered seeing a manifold just above it. She hooked up for several quick breaths. Then she felt her way to the door. The second she found it she released the seal and pulled it open, and was standing in the disinfecting room.

Having already been drenched with disinfectant, she didn't wait through the usual shower. In the next room, she struggled out of her plastic suit, then ran into the room beyond, where she tipped the lockers holding the scrub clothes over against the pressure door. She didn't think it would stop the door from being opened, but it might slow her pursuers down. She raced into her street clothes and left the cylinder. Then she flicked all the circuit breakers, throwing even the dressing rooms into darkness and turning off the ventilation system.

Once outside the maximum containment lab, Marissa ran the length of the virology building, across the catwalk and down the stairs to the main floor. Taking a deep breath, she tried to look relaxed as she went through the front lobby. The security guard was on the phone, explaining to someone that a biological alarm had gone off, not a security-door alarm.

Marissa trembled violently while signing out. The guard was explaining to the person he was talking to that the operators were busy searching for the head of the Virology Department.

"Hey!" yelled the guard as Marissa started for the door. Her heart leaped into her mouth. For a moment she thought of fleeing. Then she heard the guard say, "You forgot to put the time."

Marissa marched back and filled in the blank. A second later she was outside, running to her car.

She was halfway to Ralph's before she was able to stop shaking and think about her terrible discovery. The missing ball of frozen Ebola couldn't have been a coincidence. It was the same strain as each of the recent outbreaks. Someone was using the virus, and whether intentionally or by accident, the deadly disease was infecting doctors and hospitals in disparate areas at disparate times.

That the missing sample from phial E39 was the mysterious reservoir for the recent Ebola outbreaks was the only explanation that answered the questions posed by the apparently long incubation periods and the fact that all the outbreaks involved the same strain. Worse still, someone did not want that information released. That was why she'd been taken off the Ebola team and why she had just nearly been killed. The realization that frightened her most was that only someone with maximum containment lab access—presumably someone on the CDC staff—could have found her there. She cursed herself for not having looked in the logbook as she signed out, to see who'd signed in.

She had turned down Ralph's street, anxious to tell him her fears, when she realized that it wasn't fair to involve him. She'd already taken advantage of Tad's friendship, and by the next day, when he saw her name on the log, she would be a total pariah. Her one hope was that her two assailants would not report her presence in the lab, since they would then be implicated in the attempt on her life. It would be their word against hers, and by tomorrow her word wouldn't mean much at the CDC. For all she knew, the police might be looking for her by morning.

Stopping at her house to pick up her suitcase, Marissa headed for the nearest motel. As soon as she reached her room she called Ralph.

He answered sleepily on the fifth ring. "Why didn't you come by?" he asked.

"It's a long story," said Marissa. "I can't explain now, Ralph, but I'm in real trouble. Do you know a good lawyer?"

"*Lawyer?* Marissa, just what in the world is going on?"

"I don't want to drag you into it," said Marissa. "All I can say is that the whole situation has become serious, and for the moment I'm not ready to go to the authorities. I guess I'm a fugitive." Marissa laughed hollowly.

"Why don't you come over? You'd be safe here."

"Ralph, I'm serious about not wanting to involve you. But I do need a lawyer. Could you find me one?"

"Of course," said Ralph. "I'll help you in any way I can. Where are you?"

"I'll be in touch," said Marissa evasively. "And thanks."

CHAPTER 8

Marissa slept very badly. When the early light coming through the window woke her, it was a relief. She turned on the morning television news. Halfway through the programme the commentator said that there had been a problem at the CDC. There was no mention of the maximum containment lab, but it was reported that a technician had been treated at University Hospital after inhaling phenolic disinfectant. The item continued with a phone interview with Dr. Cyrill Dubchek.

"The injured technician was the only casualty," Dubchek said. "An emergency safety system was triggered by accident. Everything is under control, and we are searching for a Dr. Marissa Blumenthal in relation to the incident."

The commentators capped the item with the words that if anyone knew the whereabouts of Dr. Blumenthal, he should notify the Atlanta police. For about ten seconds they showed the photograph that had accompanied her CDC application.

Marissa turned off the TV. Although she had joked about being a fugitive, she'd meant it figuratively. Now she realized that the joke had become serious. She was a wanted person. Quickly getting her things together, she went to check out of the motel. The whole time she was in the office she felt nervous, since her name was there in black and white for the desk clerk to see. But all he said was, "Have a nice day."

She grabbed a quick coffee and a doughnut at a cafe and drove to her bank. She tried to conceal her face at the drive-in window in case the clerk had seen the morning news, but the man seemed uninterested. Marissa withdrew most of her savings, amounting to $4650. With the money in her bag, she relaxed a little. Grayson, Georgia, was going to be her next stop.

THE TOWN OF GRAYSON was exactly as Marissa had imagined. The main street was lined with a handful of brick and wood-frame buildings. There was a bankrupt cinema, and the largest commercial establishment was the hardware store. Professional Labs was probably a little way outside the town. She'd have to inquire, but of whom? She did not want to go to the local police. She passed a general store that also boasted a sign that read "US Post Office".

"Professional Labs? Yeah, they're out on Bridge Road," said the proprietor. "Take a right at the fire station, then take a left. You'll find it. It's the only thing out there 'cept for cows."

Following the man's directions, Marissa drove out of the town. He was right about there being nothing about but cows. After a while the road wasn't even surfaced, and Marissa began to wonder if she was on a wild-goose chase. But then the road entered a pine forest, and up ahead she could see a building.

With a thump Marissa's car hit a hard surface as the road widened into an asphalt parking area. There were two other vehicles: a white van with "Professional Labs, Inc." lettered on the side, and a cream-coloured Mercedes.

Marissa pulled up next to the van. The building had pointed roofs and lots of mirrored glass, which reflected the attractive tree-lined setting. The fragrant smell of pine surrounded her as she walked to the entrance. She searched for a bell, but there was none, so she knocked a couple of times. When there was no answer, she gave the door a pull, but it didn't move. Giving up on the front door, Marissa started to walk round the building.

"Do you know you are trespassing?" said an unfriendly voice. "This is private property." The speaker was a stocky middle-aged man with a bloated face and coarse features. He was dressed in blue overalls.

"Ummm . . ." voiced Marissa, desperately trying to think of an excuse for her presence.

"You did see the sign?" asked the man, gesturing to a no-trespassing notice by the car park.

"Well, yes," admitted Marissa. "But you see, I'm a doctor. I heard you have a viral lab here. I was interested to know if you do viral diagnostic work."

"Well, you heard wrong. We do molecular biology here. And you'd better leave unless you'd like me to call the police."

"That won't be necessary," said Marissa. Involving the police was the last thing she wanted. "I certainly apologize. I don't mean to be a bother. I would like to see your lab, though."

"Out of the question." The man led Marissa back to her car.

"Is there someone that I might contact to get a tour?" she asked as she slid behind the wheel.

"I'm the boss," the man said flatly. "I think you'd better go."

Having run out of bright ideas, Marissa started the engine and headed back to Grayson.

82

The man stood watching until her car was lost in the trees. Then he turned and walked back to the building.

The front door opened automatically, revealing an interior that was in the same contemporary style as the exterior. He went down a short tiled corridor and entered a small lab. At one end was a desk, at the other was an airtight steel door like the one leading into the CDC's maximum containment lab, behind which was a lab bench equipped with a type-3 HEPA filter system.

Another man was sitting at the desk. He looked up. "Why the hell didn't you let me handle her?" Speaking made him cough violently, bringing tears to his eyes.

"Because we don't know who knows she was coming here," said the man in the blue overalls. He picked up the phone and punched the number he wanted with unnecessary force.

"Dr. Jackson's office," answered a cheerful voice.

"This is Dr. Arnold Heberling. I want to talk to the doctor."

"I'm sorry, but he's with a patient."

"Honey, I don't care if he's with God. Put him on."

"One moment, please."

Turning to the desk, Heberling said, "Paul, would you get my coffee from the counter."

Paul heaved himself out of his chair. It took a bit of effort because he was a big man and his left arm was frozen at the elbow joint. He'd been shot by a policeman when he was a boy.

Paul gave Heberling his coffee, then returned to the desk.

"Heberling!" shouted Dr. Joshua Jackson at the other end of the line. "I told you never to call me at my office!"

"The Blumenthal girl was here," said Heberling.

"How the hell did she find out about the lab?"

"I don't know and I don't care. The fact of the matter is that she was here. Something has to be done about her."

"I'll be there around five," said Jackson, slamming down the receiver.

WHILE MARISSA DROVE back into town, she considered her options. She couldn't go back to the CDC. Her chances of working out what Professional Labs was doing with a sophisticated HEPA filter system seemed slim since the place was built like a fortress. Perhaps it was time to call Ralph and ask if he'd found a lawyer; except . . .

In her mind's eye Marissa pictured the white van in the lab's car park. It had "Professional Labs, Inc." printed on its side. It was the "Inc." that interested her.

Driving down the main street, Marissa parked in front of an office building she remembered passing. The door was frosted glass, with "Ronald Davis, Attorney and Estate Agent" stencilled on it in gold leaf.

A bell jangled as she entered. A man came out of an inside room. He was dressed in a white shirt, bow tie and red braces, and although he appeared to be no more than thirty, he was wearing grandfatherly wire-rimmed glasses. "Can I help you?" he asked, with a southern accent.

"Are you Mr. Davis?" asked Marissa.

"Yup." He hooked his thumbs through his braces.

"I have a couple of simple questions," said Marissa. "About corporate law. Do you think you could answer them?"

"Maybe," said Mr. Davis. He motioned Marissa into his office.

It looked like a set for a 1930s film, complete with a desk-top fan that slowly rotated back and forth, rustling the papers. Mr. Davis sat down and leaned back, putting his hands behind his head. Then he said, "What is it you want to know?"

"If a business is incorporated, can I find out the names of the owners?" asked Marissa.

"Maybe and maybe not," Mr. Davis said, smiling. "If the company is a public corporation, it would be hard to find out all the stockholders. But if the company is a partnership, then it would be easy."

"How would I go about finding out if a company is a partnership or a public corporation?"

"Easy," said Mr. Davis. "All you do is go to the Secretary of State's office at the State House in Atlanta and ask for the corporate division. Just tell the clerk the name of the company, and he can look it up. It's a matter of public record, and if the company is incorporated in Georgia, it will be listed there."

"Thank you," said Marissa. "How much do I owe you?"

"Twenty dollars," said Mr. Davis.

"My pleasure," said Marissa, pulling out a $20 note and handing it over.

She returned to her car and drove back towards Atlanta. She was pleased to have a goal, even if the chances of finding significant information were not terribly likely.

She made good time and was back in the city by 4 o'clock. Parking in a garage, she walked to the State House.

Marissa wanted to get whatever information she could as quickly as possible, and leave. Unfortunately, there was a long queue at the corporate division, and she had to wait.

"What can I do for you?" asked the clerk when it was finally Marissa's turn.

"I'd like some information about a corporation called Professional Labs, Inc., in Grayson, Georgia."

The clerk entered the name at a computer terminal. "Here it is," he said. "Incorporated just last year. What would you like to know?"

"Is it a partnership or a public corporation?"

"It's a limited partnership."

"Are the partners listed?" asked Marissa, excitement mounting.

"Yup. There's Joshua Jackson, Rodd Becker—"

"Just a second," said Marissa. "Let me write this down." She got out a pen and began writing.

"Let's see," said the clerk, staring at the computer screen. "Joshua Jackson, Rodd Becker, Sinclair Tieman, Jack Krause, Gustave Swenson, Duane Moody, Trent Goodridge and the Physicians' Action Congress."

"Can an organization be a limited partner?" She remembered the name Physicians' Action Congress from Markham's list of contributors.

"I think so, lady, or it wouldn't be here. There's also a law firm by the name of Cooper, Hodges, McQuinllin and Hanks."

"They're partners, too?" asked Marissa.

"No," said the clerk. "They're the service agent."

"I don't need that," said Marissa. "I'm not interested in suing the company."

Thanking the clerk, Marissa beat a hasty retreat and hurried back to the garage. Once inside her car, she opened her briefcase and took out the photocopies of Markham's contributors' list. Just as she'd remembered, the Physicians' Action Congress was listed as a corporate sponsor.

Curious, Marissa looked to see if any of the other partners of Professional Labs were on Markham's list. To her surprise they all were. The partners came from all over the country, and from Markham's list she had all their addresses.

Marissa sat back, trying to decide what to do next. She really didn't have much information, and she was getting rather far afield from the Ebola outbreaks. But her intuition told her that everything she had learned was related. And if that was the case, then the Physicians' Action Congress was the key. But how could she investigate an organization she'd never heard of?

Starting the car, Marissa had an inspiration: the American Medical Association! If she couldn't get information about a physicians' organization at the AMA, then it wasn't available. Besides, she knew that the headquarters of AMA was in Chicago, and Chicago sounded safe. She headed towards the airport.

JOSHUA JACKSON'S FURY MOUNTED with each mile he drove. He didn't want to visit the lab, but he had no intention of being seen in Atlanta with Dr. Arnold Heberling. The man was proving increasingly unpredictable. Asked to create minor confusion, he had resorted to atomic warfare. Hiring him had been a terrible decision, but there wasn't much they could do about it now.

Pulling up at the lab, Jackson parked opposite Heberling's Mercedes.

He walked up to the front of the building. There was a click, the door opened, and he stepped inside.

"I'm in the conference room," shouted Heberling. Jackson made his way there.

"I hope this is important," said Jackson when the two men sat facing each other.

"The Blumenthal girl was right here in the garden," said Heberling. "She didn't see anything, but just the fact that she was here suggests that she knows something. She's got to be removed."

"You had your chance," snapped Jackson. "Twice! And each time, you and your thugs made a mess of things. First at her house and then last night at the CDC."

"So we can try again. This time we'll give her Ebola. She's been exposed to it, so there'd be no questions."

"I don't want an Ebola outbreak in Atlanta!" shouted Jackson. "Leave the woman to us. We'll take care of her."

"Oh, sure," scoffed Heberling. "Like when you got her transferred out of the Virology Department. Well, she's still a threat to the whole project, and I intend to see that she's eliminated."

"You are not in charge here," said Jackson menacingly. "And when it comes to fixing the blame, none of us would be in this mess if you'd stuck to the original plan of using influenza virus. We've all been in a state of panic since you decided to use Ebola."

"Oh, we're back to that complaint," said Heberling disgustedly. "You were pretty pleased when you heard the Richter Clinic was closing. If the Physicians' Action Congress wanted to undermine the public's growing confidence in prepaid health clinics, they couldn't have done better. The only difference from the original plan was that I got to carry out some field research on Ebola."

Jackson studied Heberling's face. He'd come to the conclusion the man was a psychopath, and he loathed him. Unfortunately, the realization was a bit late. And to think that the plan had sounded so simple when the PAC executive committee had first suggested it.

Jackson took a deep breath, knowing he had to control his anger. "I've told you a dozen times the Physicians' Action Congress is appalled at the loss of life. That had never been our intention, and you know it."

"Bull!" shouted Heberling. "There would have been loss of life with influenza, given the strains we would have had to use. How many would you have tolerated? A hundred? Anyway, I don't believe any of this rubbish you and the PAC feed me about your concern for the negative drift of American medicine away from its traditional values. It's all an attempt to justify your own economic interests. All of a sudden there are too many doctors and not enough patients. The only reason I've cooperated with you is because you built me this lab." Heberling made a sweeping gesture with his hand. "You wanted the image of prepaid health plans tarnished, and I delivered. The only difference is that I did it my way for my own reasons."

"But we ordered you to stop!" yelled Jackson. "Right after the Richter Clinic outbreak."

"Half-heartedly," said Heberling. "You were pleased with the results. Not only did the Richter Clinic fold, but new subscribers to California health plans have levelled off for the first time in five years. The PAC feels a twinge of conscience, but basically you're happy. And I've vindicated my beliefs that Ebola is a premier biological weapon, despite the lack of vaccine. I've shown that it is relatively easy to contain and devastatingly contagious to small populations. Dr. Jackson, we are both getting what we want. We just have to deal with this woman before she causes real trouble."

"I'm telling you once and for all," said Jackson. "We want no further use of Ebola. That's an order!"

Heberling laughed. "Dr. Jackson," he said, leaning forward, "you're in no position to give me orders. Do you realize what would happen to your career if the truth got out? And I'm telling you that it will, unless you let me handle Blumenthal my way."

Jackson knew the man was right. "OK," he said reluctantly. "Do whatever you think is best about Dr. Blumenthal. Just don't use Ebola in Atlanta."

"Fine." Heberling smiled. "I give you my word. After all, I'm a very reasonable man."

SINCE THERE WERE so many flights scheduled on the Atlanta—Chicago run, Marissa only had to wait half an hour for the next available one. She decided to call Tad and attempt an apology. She dialled the lab, and as she had suspected, he was working late.

"Are you mad at me?" she asked when he answered.

"I'm furious. You took one of my access cards."

"Tad, I'm truly sorry. When I see you, I'll explain everything."

"You actually went into the maximum containment lab, didn't you?" Tad said, his voice uncharacteristically hard.

"Well, yes."

"Marissa, the lab is a shambles. All the animals are dead."

"Two men came into the lab and attacked me."

"Attacked you?"

"Yes," said Marissa. "You have to believe me."

"I don't know what to believe. Where are you?"

"I'm at the airport," said Marissa.

"If what you say about being attacked is true, then you should come back here and explain. You shouldn't be running away."

"I'm not running away," insisted Marissa. "I'm going to the AMA headquarters in Chicago to research an organization called the Physicians' Action Congress. Ever hear of them? I believe they are involved somehow."

"Marissa, I think you should come directly back to the CDC. You're in real trouble, in case you don't know."

"I do. But for the time being what I'm doing is more important. Could you ask the Office of Biosafety who else went into the maximum containment lab last night?"

"Marissa, I don't think that's possible. No one will tell me anything right now, because they know we're friends."

"Tad, I—" Marissa stopped speaking. Tad had hung up. She couldn't really blame him.

She had five minutes until boarding, so she called Ralph. In contrast to Tad, he was concerned, not angry. "Marissa! What is going on? Your name is in the evening paper. The police are looking for you."

"I can imagine," she said, thinking that she'd been wise to use an alias, Carol Bradford, and pay cash when she'd bought her airline ticket. "Ralph, have you found a good lawyer yet?"

"No, I'm sorry. When you asked, I didn't realize it was an emergency. Why don't you come over here? We can talk, and I can get you a lawyer in the morning."

"Have you ever heard of an organization called the Physicians' Action Congress?" asked Marissa, ignoring Ralph's offer.

"No," said Ralph. "Marissa, please come over."

Marissa heard her flight called. "I'm going to the AMA to find out about the organization I just mentioned," she said quickly. "I've got to run." She hung up and boarded the plane.

CHAPTER 9

Arriving in Chicago, Marissa decided to treat herself to a nice hotel and was happy to find the Palmer House had a room. She risked using her credit card and went straight upstairs to bed.

The next morning, while watching the television news, she heard the presenter mention Ebola. He was describing a new outbreak, at the Rosenberg Clinic on Upper Fifth Avenue in New York City. A doctor by the name of Girish Mehta had been diagnosed as having the disease.

Marissa shivered. She got the AMA's address and set out for Dearborn Street.

The woman at the information desk directed her to the public relations office. The PR director, a James Frank, passed by as Marissa was trying to explain her needs to one of the secretaries. He invited her to his office.

Mr. Frank reminded Marissa of her high school guidance counsellor. He was of indeterminate age, slightly overweight and going bald, but his face exuded friendliness and sincerity.

"Physicians' Action Congress," he repeated when Marissa asked about the organization. "I've never heard of it. But let me see what my computer says." He punched in the name. "What do you know! It's here." He pointed to the screen. "Physicians' Action Congress Political Action Committee. Let's see who they have been supporting."

"I can tell you one name," said Marissa. "Calvin Markham."

"Yup. Here's Markham's name along with a number of other conservative candidates. At least we know the political bent."

"Right wing," said Marissa.

"Probably very right wing," said Mr. Frank. "I'd guess they are trying to limit immigration of foreign medical school graduates, stop HMO start-up subsidies and the like." He tapped a few keys. "Let's see who is on the board of directors."

As Marissa looked at the screen the names appeared. The president was Joshua Jackson, MD; vice-president, Rodd Becker, MD; treasurer, Sinclair Tieman, MD; secretary, Jack Krause, MD; directors, Gustave Swenson, MD, Duane Moody, MD, and Trent Goodridge, MD. Opening her briefcase, she took out the list of partners for Professional Labs. They were the same names!

MARISSA LEFT THE AMA WITH her head spinning. The question that loomed in her mind was almost too bizarre to consider: What was an ultraconservative physicians' organization doing with a lab that owned sophisticated equipment used only for handling deadly viruses? Purposely, Marissa did not answer her own question.

Her mind churning, she began walking in the direction of her hotel. Trying to pick holes in her own theory, Marissa ticked off the significant facts: each of the outbreaks of Ebola had occurred in a prepaid group health-care facility, most of the index patients had foreign-sounding names, and in at least two cases the index patient had been mugged just prior to getting sick. She still believed that the one exception, the Phoenix outbreak, was food-borne.

A plan was forming in her mind. If her suspicions had any merit, if the previous outbreaks had not been the result of chance, then the index patient in New York was probably working for a prepaid health-care clinic and had been mugged a few days previously. Marissa decided she had to go to New York. Suddenly she was overwhelmed with fear. No wonder she'd been attacked in her home. No wonder the men in the maximum containment lab had tried to kill her. No wonder Markham had had her transferred. If her fears were true, then a conspiracy of immense proportions existed and she was in extreme jeopardy.

Up until that moment Marissa had felt safe in Chicago. Now everywhere she looked she saw suspicious characters. She ducked into a coffee bar and ordered a cup of tea to calm down. She sat at a window table and stared out at the street. It was then that she saw the businessman. It was the way he was carrying his briefcase that caught her attention—with his arm at an awkward angle, as though he couldn't flex his elbow.

In a flash Marissa was back in her own home, desperately fighting the unseen figure whose arm seemed frozen at the joint. And then there was the nightmare in the lab . . .

As Marissa watched, the man took out a cigarette and lit it, all with one hand; the other never left his briefcase. She remembered that Tad had said the intruder had carried a briefcase.

Marissa sat rubbing her eyes for a minute, praying she was imagining things. When she looked again, the man was gone. She finished her tea, then headed for the Palmer House.

She walked quickly, nervously. At the first corner she looked over her shoulder. The businessman was coming towards her. Immediately changing directions, Marissa crossed the street. She watched the man continue to the middle of the block and then cross after her. With a rising sense of panic she turned round and headed for the elevated train. Hurriedly she climbed the stairs, catching up with a large group.

Once on the platform, she felt better. There were lots of people standing about and Marissa walked a good distance away from the entrance. Her heart was still pounding, but at least she could think. Was it really the same man? Had he been following her?

As if in answer to her question, the man popped into her line of vision. He had large features and coarse skin, with a heavy five o'clock shadow.

Before she could move the train thundered into the station, and the crowd surged forward, taking Marissa along with the rest. She lost sight of the man as she was carried into the train.

Fighting to stay near the door, Marissa hoped she could detrain at the last moment as she'd seen people do in spy movies, but the crush of people hampered her, and the doors closed before she could get to them. Turning, she scanned the faces around her, but she did not see the man with the stiff elbow.

The train lurched forwards, forcing her to reach for a strap. Just as she grabbed it, she saw him again. He was right next to her. He was so close Marissa could smell his cologne. As she was looking at him, he turned and their eyes met. A slight smile formed at the corners of his mouth as he reached into his jacket pocket.

Losing control, Marissa screamed. Frantically she tried to push away from the man, but she was hindered by the crush of people. Her scream died, and no one moved or spoke. They just stared at her.

Then, to her utter relief, a transit policeman managed to shove his way over to her.

"Are you all right?" he yelled over the sounds of the train.

"This man has been following me," said Marissa, pointing. The policeman looked at the businessman. "Is this true?"

The man shook his head. "I've never seen her before. I don't know what she's talking about."

The policeman turned back to Marissa as the train began to slow. "Would you care to file a complaint?"

"No," yelled Marissa, "as long as he leaves me alone."

The screech of the wheels and the hiss of the air brakes made it impossible to hear until the train stopped. The doors opened.

"I'll be happy to get off if it would make the lady feel better," said the businessman.

A few people got off. The policeman kept the door from closing with his body and looked questioningly at Marissa.

"I would feel better," said Marissa shakily, suddenly unsure of her reactions.

The businessman shrugged his shoulders and got off. Almost immediately the doors closed and the train lurched forward once again.

"You all right now?" asked the policeman.

"Much better," said Marissa. She was relieved that the businessman was gone. She thanked the policeman and he moved on.

Realizing that every eye within sight was still on her, Marissa was acutely embarrassed. As soon as the train pulled into the next station, she got off. Descending to the street she hailed a taxi and told the driver to take her to the Palmer House.

Within the security of the taxi Marissa was able to regain a degree of control. She knew she was in over her head, but she had no idea to whom in authority she could go. She was presupposing a conspiracy but had no idea of its extent. And worst of all, she had no proof, just a few highly suggestive facts.

She decided she might as well continue on to New York. If her suspicions about that outbreak proved to be correct, she'd decide there whom to contact.

As soon as she got back to the hotel Marissa went directly to her room. She wanted out as soon as possible, criticizing herself for having used a credit card and, hence, her own name.

She opened her door and went in, tossing her bag and briefcase onto the desk. Out of the corner of her eye she saw a movement and ducked automatically. Even so, she was struck so hard that she was knocked forward over the nearest of the twin beds, ending up on the floor between them. Looking up, she saw the man with the stiff arm coming towards her. Frantically she tried to scramble underneath one of the beds, but the man got hold of her skirt with his good arm and yanked her back. Marissa rolled over, kicking furiously. Something fell out of the man's hand and hit the floor with a metallic thud. A gun, she thought, compounding her terror.

The man bent to retrieve it, and Marissa slithered beneath the bed closest to the door. The man got down on his knees, caught Marissa by an ankle and pulled her towards him.

Marissa screamed and kicked again, loosening the man's grip. In a flash she was back under the bed.

Tiring of the tug-of-war, he dropped his gun on the bed and came after her. But Marissa rolled out the other side. She scrambled to her feet and ran for the door. She had just wrenched it open when the man leaped across the bed and caught her hair. Whipping her round, he threw her against the chest of drawers with such force that the mirror fell with a crash.

The man checked the hall quickly, then closed and secured the door. Marissa ran to the bathroom, grabbing what she thought was the gun off the bed. She almost managed to get the bathroom door closed before the man reached it.

Marissa wedged her back against the basin and tried to keep her attacker from opening the door further. But his greater strength prevailed. The door opened a crack, enabling him to get the arm with the frozen elbow through.

Marissa eyed the wall phone but couldn't reach it without letting go of the door. She looked at the weapon in her hand and realized she was holding an air-powered vaccination gun, the kind she had used for mass inoculations in her old pediatrics clinic.

The door had opened enough for the man to move his arm more freely. He blindly groped until he got a grip on one of Marissa's ankles. Feeling she had little choice, she pressed the vaccination gun against the man's forearm and discharged it. The man screamed. The arm was withdrawn, and the door slammed shut.

She heard him run across the room, open the door to the hall and rush out. Going back into the bedroom, Marissa breathed a sigh of relief, only to be startled by a strong odour of phenolic disinfectant. Intuitively she sensed the gun contained Ebola virus, and she guessed that the disinfectant she smelled was part of a mechanism to prevent exposure to the operator. Now she was truly terrified. Not only had she possibly killed a man, she might also have triggered a new outbreak. Forcing herself to remain calm, she carefully placed the gun in a plastic bag that she took from the wastepaper basket and then got another plastic bag from the basket under the desk and placed it over the first. She knotted it closed.

Marissa looked out into the hall. It was clear. She carried her belongings, including the plastic bag with the vaccination gun, down to a housekeeping cupboard. There were no cleaning people in sight. She found a bottle of disinfectant and disinfected the outside of the plastic bag, then she washed and disinfected her hands.

In the lobby, she called the Illinois State Epidemiologist. Without identifying herself, she explained that room 2410 at the Palmer House might have been contaminated with Ebola virus. Before the man could gasp out a single question, she hung up.

Next she called Tad. His initial coolness thawed when he realized that she was on the verge of hysteria.

"What is going on, Marissa?" he said. "Are you all right?"

"I have to ask two favours. First, I need a phial of the convalescent serum you developed from the Los Angeles outbreak. Could you send it by overnight carrier to Carol Bradford at the Plaza Hotel in New York?"

"And just who is Carol Bradford?"

"Please don't ask any questions," said Marissa, struggling not to burst into tears. Carol Bradford had been one of her college room-mates.

"The next favour involves a parcel I'm sending you by overnight carrier. Please do not open it. Take it inside the maximum containment lab and hide it." Marissa paused.

"Is that it?" asked Tad.

"That's it," said Marissa. "Will you help me, Tad?"

"I guess," said Tad.

"Thank you. I'll explain everything in a few days."

Marissa hung up and called the Plaza and reserved a room for that night under the name of Carol Bradford. That accomplished, she scanned the Palmer House lobby. No one seemed to be paying her any heed. Trusting that the hotel would bill her on her credit card, she did not bother to check out.

The first stop was a Federal Express office. The people helped her pack her plastic bag in an unbreakable metal box when she said it was a special vaccine needed in Atlanta by the next day.

Back on the street, she hailed a taxi to O'Hare Airport. As soon as she was inside she began checking her lymph nodes and testing her throat for soreness. She'd been close to Ebola before but never this close. She shuddered to think that the man had intended to infect her with the virus. It was a cruel irony that the only way she'd escaped was by infecting him. She hoped that he realized the convalescent serum might have a protective effect if it was given prior to the appearance of symptoms. Maybe that was why the man had left so precipitately.

During the long taxi ride, Marissa began to calm down enough to think logically. The fact that she'd been attacked again gave more credence to her suspicions. And if the vaccination gun proved to contain Ebola, she'd have her first real piece of evidence.

The taxi driver dropped Marissa at the American Airlines terminal. After she had bought her ticket for New York, passed through security and walked to the gate, she found she had nearly half an hour to wait. She decided to call Ralph. She badly needed to hear a friendly voice, and she wanted to ask about the lawyer.

When Ralph answered, Marissa quickly explained that she was at the American terminal in Chicago, on her way to New York, but that she'd probably be back in Atlanta the following day.

"I made some discreet inquiries about a good lawyer," said Ralph, "and I think I have just the man. His name is McQuinllin. He's with a large firm here in Atlanta."

"I hope he's smart," said Marissa.

"He is," said Ralph. "But what's so important in New York? I hope it's not the new Ebola outbreak. Why don't you just fly back to Atlanta? I'm worried about you."

"Soon," said Marissa. "I promise."

After hanging up, Marissa kept her hand on the receiver. It always made her feel good to talk with Ralph. He cared.

As she boarded the plane Marissa was wondering how the man with the frozen arm had known she was in Chicago. And how had he known when she'd been in the maximum containment lab? To answer both questions, her mind reluctantly turned to Tad. When Tad had discovered the missing card, he must have known she would use it that night. Maybe he told Dubchek, to avoid getting into trouble himself. Tad had also known she was flying to Chicago, but she simply couldn't believe he had intentionally set a murderer on her trail. And much as she resented Dubchek, she respected him as a dedicated scientist. It was hard to connect him with the Physicians' Action Congress.

Thoroughly confused as to what was intelligent deduction and what was paranoid delusion, Marissa wished she hadn't let the vaccination gun out of her hands. If Tad was involved, then she'd lost her only evidence.

GEORGE VALHALA STOOD by the Avis Rent-A-Car counter and casually scanned the crowds. His information was that the girl would arrive on the 5 or the 6 o'clock flight from Chicago. The 5 o'clock had just landed, and a few passengers were beginning to appear.

The only minor problem George foresaw was that the description he'd been given was vague: a cute, short, thirty-year-old female with brown hair. Usually he worked with a photo, but in this case there hadn't been time to get one.

Then he saw her. It had to be her. She was almost a foot shorter than everyone else in the army of attaché-case-carrying travellers swarming in the baggage area. And he noticed that she was bypassing the carousel, having apparently carried her suitcase off the plane.

Pushing off the Avis counter, George followed Marissa outside, where she joined the taxi queue. He wondered how on earth this little woman had managed to overpower Paul in Chicago.

He crossed the street in front of the terminal and climbed into a taxi waiting opposite the taxi stand. The driver twisted round, looking at George. "You see her?" He was a skinny fellow with birdlike features, quite a contrast to George's pear-shaped obesity.

"Jake, do I look like an idiot? Start the car. She's in the taxi line."

Jake did as he was told.

"There she is," said George. Marissa was climbing into a cab. "Pull up a little and let her cab pass us, then follow it."

During the taxi ride into Manhattan, Marissa decided not to check into the Plaza as Carol Bradford. Instead, she'd stay at the nearby Essex House, using the name of her old school chum Lisa Kendrick. If the New York outbreak confirmed her theories about the origin of the Ebola outbreaks, she would go to Ralph's lawyer and let him and the police sort things out. She wasn't up to playing medical detective any longer. Not against a group who thought nothing of risking entire populations.

Forty minutes later Jake and George watched Marissa get out of her taxi in front of the Essex House.

CHAPTER 10

Marissa did not sleep well. After the incident in the room at the Palmer House she might never feel comfortable in a hotel again. Every noise in the hall made her fearful, thinking someone would try to break in.

She also kept imagining symptoms. She could not forget the feel of the vaccination gun in her hand, and each time she woke up she was certain she had a fever.

By morning she was totally exhausted. She ordered fresh fruit and coffee, which arrived with a complimentary *New York Times*. The front page carried an article about the Ebola outbreak in New York. The number of cases had risen to eleven, with one death—the initial case, Dr. Girish Mehta.

Starting at 10 o'clock, Marissa repeatedly called the Plaza to inquire about a parcel for Carol Bradford. If it arrived, she would be less wary of Tad's betraying her and would then go up to the Rosenberg Clinic. Just after 11 o'clock she was told that the package was there.

As Marissa prepared to leave the hotel she didn't know whether or not to be surprised that Tad had sent the serum. Of course, the package could be a ruse to get her to reveal her whereabouts. Unfortunately, there was no way for Marissa to be sure, and she wanted the serum enough to make her doubts academic. She would have to take a chance.

GEORGE VALHALA had been in the lobby of the Essex House since early that morning. When he saw Marissa get out of the lift, he dropped his *New York Post* and beat her out of the revolving door. Dodging Fifty-ninth Street traffic, he jogged across to the taxi where Jake was waiting and climbed into the front seat.

"You're sure that's Blumenthal?" asked a man in the back seat. He wore his blond hair in a Julius-Caesar-style cut, and his pale blue eyes were as cold as a winter sky. His name was Al Hicktman.

"She registered under the name of Lisa Kendrick, but she fits the description," said George. "It's her all right."

"She's either awfully good or awfully lucky," said Al. "We've got to isolate her without any slip-ups. Heberling says she could blow the whole deal."

They watched as Marissa climbed into a taxi and headed east.

Despite the traffic, Jake worked his way up to a position only two cars behind Marissa's taxi.

"LOOK, LADY, YOU GOT to tell me where you want to go," said Marissa's driver, eyeing her in his rearview mirror.

Marissa was twisted round, still watching the entrance to the Essex House. No one had come out who appeared to be following her. She was still trying to think of a safe way to get the serum. Facing forward, she told the driver she wanted him to stop at the Plaza and wait while she ran inside.

"There are plenty of cabs," pointed out the driver. "Why don't you get another?"

"I'll add five dollars to the fare on the meter," said Marissa, smiling at the cabbie. "I promise I won't be long."

The driver shrugged. He pulled up at the Plaza. The hotel doorman opened the door and Marissa got out.

She was extremely nervous, expecting the worst at any second. She watched as her cab moved ahead and stopped about thirty feet from the entrance. Satisfied, she went inside.

As she'd hoped, the ornate lobby was busy. No one seemed to notice her at all as she approached the porter's desk.

"I'll need to see your room key, madam," the porter said, when Marissa requested the parcel.

"But I haven't checked in yet," she said.

The man smiled. "Why don't you check in and then get your parcel? I hope you understand. We do have a responsibility."

"Of course," said Marissa, her confidence shaken. Recognizing that she had little choice, she walked to the reception desk.

Even that process was complicated when she said she didn't want to use a credit card. The receptionist made her go to the cashier to leave a sizable cash deposit before he would give her a room key. Finally, armed with the key, she got the package.

Tearing it open as she walked, Marissa lifted out the phial and glanced at it. It seemed authentic. She threw the wrapping in a rubbish bin and pocketed the serum. So far so good.

Emerging from the revolving door, Marissa hesitated while her eyes adjusted to the midday glare. Her cab was still where she'd last seen it. She descended the few steps to the street and ran the short distance to it.

Reaching the cab and grasping the rear door handle, she cast one last look over her shoulder at the Plaza entrance. No one was following her. Her fears about Tad had been unfounded.

She was about to slide inside when she found herself staring into the muzzle of a gun held by a blond man who'd apparently been lying on the back seat. The man started to speak, but Marissa didn't give him time. She swung herself clear of the cab and slammed the door. The weapon discharged with a hiss. It was some kind of sophisticated airgun. The cab window shattered, but Marissa was no longer looking. She took off, running as she'd never run before. Out of the corner of her eye she saw that the blond man was following her, pushing his way through the crowds.

People shouted as she crashed by them, but she kept going. The confusion she caused hampered the blond man, but not dramatically. He was gaining on her.

Running across the drive east of the Plaza, Marissa dodged taxis and cars, reaching the edge of the small park in front of the hotel. Frantically her eyes swept the park. Near the centre a crowd was seated by a fountain, watching her with studied indifference. Being New Yorkers, they were accustomed to any form of excess, including panic-filled flight.

As Marissa rounded the side of the fountain the blond man was so close she could hear him breathe. Pushing and shoving, she forced her way through the pedestrians. She finally broke into a clear space, then realized she was in the centre of a circle formed by a large crowd of people. Three muscular black men were break-dancing to rap music. Marissa's desperate eyes met those of the youths. She saw only anger; she'd crashed their act.

Before anyone could move, the blond man stumbled into the circle and came to a halt. He started to raise his gun, but he didn't get far. With a practised kick one of the infuriated dancers sent the weapon flying out of his hand. People began to move away as Marissa's pursuer countered with a kick of his own. The dancer caught the blow on his forearm and fell to the ground.

Three of his friends who'd been watching from the sidelines leaped to their feet and rushed the blond man from behind.

Marissa didn't wait. She melted into the crowd that had backed away from the brawl. Most of the people were crossing Fifth Avenue, and she did the same. Once north of Fifty-ninth Street, she hailed a taxi and told the driver she wanted the Rosenberg Clinic. Marissa sat back and closed her eyes. Instead of fear, she was suddenly consumed with anger. She was furious with everyone, particularly with Tad. There could be little doubt now that he was telling her pursuers her whereabouts. Even the serum that she'd gone to so much trouble to obtain was useless. With her current suspicions, there was no way she'd inject herself with it. Instead, she'd have to take her chances that the vaccination gun had been designed to protect the user adequately.

For a short time she considered skipping her visit to the Rosenberg Clinic, but the importance of proving, at least to herself, that Ebola was being deliberately spread won through. She had to be sure.

The clinic was a fancy renovated structure that occupied most of a city block. A TV truck and several police cars were parked in front, and a number of officers stood on the steps. Marissa had to flash her CDC identity card before they let her into the building, which was in the same state of confusion as the other hospitals that had suffered Ebola outbreaks.

She approached the information desk, and although it was unoccupied, it was loaded with printed literature. It only took a moment for her to learn that the Rosenberg Clinic was a prepaid HMO facility, just as she'd suspected.

Marissa then turned and watched the stream of people coming and going across the lobby until she worked out where the doctors' cloakroom was. She quickly crossed to it and opened the door.

Inside, she put on a long white coat and rolled up the sleeves. There was a name tag on the lapel that said "Dr. Ann Elliott". Marissa took it off and placed it in the coat's side pocket.

Returning to the lobby, Marissa was terrified of running into Dubchek, but she knew she had to find out more about the dead index case. She went over to the directory, saw that the Department of Pathology was on the third floor and took the next lift. Entering the department through a pair of double doors, Marissa found herself surrounded by secretaries, all busily typing. This was the centre of pathology, where all the reports were prepared.

"May I help you?" asked one of the women as Marissa approached.

"I'm from the CDC," Marissa said warmly. "Do you know if any of my colleagues are here?"

"I'll have to ask Dr. Stewart," said the secretary. "He's in his office."

"I'm right here," said a big burly man with a full beard. "And to answer your question, the CDC people are down on the second floor in our isolation wing."

"Well, perhaps you can help me," said Marissa, introducing herself.

"I've been looking into the Ebola outbreaks from the beginning, but unfortunately I was delayed getting to New York. I understand that the first case, a Dr. Mehta, has already died. Did you do an autopsy?"

"Just this morning."

"Would you mind if I asked a few questions?"

"I didn't do the autopsy," replied Dr. Stewart. Then, turning to the secretary, he said, "Helen, see if you can round up Curt."

He led Marissa to a small office.

"Did you know Dr. Mehta?" asked Marissa.

"Quite well," said Stewart, shaking his head. "He was our medical director, and his death will be a great loss."

"Do you know where he did his training?"

"In Bombay. Why do you ask?" said Stewart.

"I was curious if he was a foreign medical school graduate," said Marissa.

"Does that make a difference?" asked Stewart, frowning.

"It might," said Marissa vaguely. "Are there a large percentage of foreign medical school graduates on the staff here?"

"Of course," said Stewart. "All HMOs started by hiring a large proportion of foreign graduates. American graduates wanted private practice. But that's changed. These days we can recruit directly from the top residencies."

The door opened and a young man came in.

"This is Curt Vandermay," said Stewart. "Dr. Blumenthal has some questions about Dr. Mehta's autopsy."

"I'm interested in the external exam," said Marissa. "Were there any abnormalities?"

"For sure," said Dr. Vandermay. "The man had extensive haemorrhagic lesions in his skin."

"What about trauma?" asked Marissa.

"How did you guess?" said Dr. Vandermay, surprised. "He had a broken nose. I'd forgotten about that."

"How old?" asked Marissa.

"A week, ten days. Somewhere in that range."

"Did the chart mention a cause?"

"To tell the truth, I didn't look," said Dr. Vandermay. "Knowing the man died of Ebola haemorrhagic fever took precedence. I didn't give the broken nose a lot of thought."

"I understand," said Marissa. "What about the chart? I assume it's here in pathology. Can I see it?"

"By all means," said Vandermay. "Why don't you come down to the autopsy area. I have some photographs of the broken nose, if you'd like to see them."

"Please," said Marissa.

100

Stewart excused himself, and Marissa followed Vandermay.

Dr. Mehta's chart wasn't as complete as Marissa would have liked. And although there was a reference to the broken nose and the name of the doctor who had treated Mehta for it, there was nothing concerning the cause.

Vandermay suggested that they phone the physician who set it. While he put through the call, Marissa read the rest of the chart. Dr. Mehta had no history of recent travel, exposure to animals or connection to any of the other Ebola outbreaks.

"The poor man was robbed," said Dr. Vandermay, hanging up the phone. "Beaten up and robbed in his own driveway. What a world we live in!"

If you only knew, thought Marissa, now absolutely certain that the Ebola outbreaks were deliberately caused. A wave of fear swept over her, but she forced herself to continue questioning the pathologist. "Did you happen to notice a circular lesion on Dr. Mehta's thigh?"

"I don't recall," said Dr. Vandermay. "But here are all the photos." He spread them out.

Marissa looked at the first one. Despite the profusion of haemorrhagic lesions, Marissa was able to pick out the same circular mark she had seen on Dr. Richter's thigh. It corresponded in size to the head of an air-powered vaccination gun.

"Would it be possible for me to take one of these photos?" asked Marissa.

Dr. Vandermay glanced at them. "Go ahead. We've got plenty."

Marissa slipped the photo into her pocket. She thanked Dr. Vandermay and got up to leave. An intercom system crackled to life, informing Dr. Vandermay that he had a phone call on line six. He picked it up, and Marissa overheard him say, "That's a coincidence, Dr. Dubchek. I'm talking with Dr. Blumenthal right this moment."

That was all Marissa needed to hear. She began running towards the lifts. Vandermay called after her, but she didn't stop.

Facing the lifts and fire escape, she decided to risk the lift. If Dubchek had been on the second floor, he'd probably use the stairs. She pushed the "down" button.

A lift stopped, and Marissa squeezed in. The doors seemed to take for ever to close, but finally the lift started to go down, and Marissa began to relax. Turning to a grey-haired technician, she asked where the cafeteria was. He told her to get off at the ground floor, turn right and follow the main corridor.

She had decided it was too dangerous to risk the front entrance to the clinic. Dubchek could have told the police to stop her. Instead she ran into the cafeteria, which was crowded, and headed directly for the kitchen. The staff threw her a few questioning looks, but no one challenged her. As she'd imagined, there was a loading dock, and she exited through it.

Marissa walked briskly out onto Madison Avenue, where she hailed a cab. She told the driver to take her to the Essex House.

ONCE SAFELY ENSCONCED in her room, with the door bolted shut, Marissa contemplated what to do next. Now that her suspicions appeared to be true, the only thing she could think of was to go to Ralph's lawyer and tell him what she believed: that a group of right-wing physicians were introducing Ebola into privately owned clinics to erode public trust in HMOs. She could hand over the meagre evidence she had, and let him worry about the rest of the proof.

Feeling much better having come to a decision, she reached for the phone and dialled Ralph's office number. "Are you coming home today?" he asked as soon as he came on the line.

"That depends," said Marissa. "Do you think I can talk to that lawyer today?" Her voice wavered.

"No," said Ralph. "I called his office this morning. They said he had to go out of town but that he's expected back tomorrow."

"Too bad," said Marissa, her voice beginning to shake.

"Marissa, are you all right?" asked Ralph.

"I've been better. I've had some awful experiences."

"What happened?"

"I can't talk now," said Marissa, knowing if she tried to explain, she'd burst into tears.

"Listen to me," said Ralph. "I want you to come home immediately. Get the next flight. I'll come and pick you up."

The idea had a lot of appeal, and Marissa was about to say as much when there was a knock on her door. She froze.

"Just a minute," she said into the phone. "There's someone at the door. Stay on the line." Marissa put the phone down on the bedside table and warily approached the door. "Who is it?"

"A delivery for Miss Kendrick." Marissa opened the door a crack but kept the safety catch on. One of the uniformed bellboys was standing there holding a huge basket of flowers.

Flustered, she told the man to wait while she went back to the phone. She promised Ralph she'd call him back as soon as she knew what flight she was taking home to Atlanta that evening.

Returning to the door, Marissa called out, "Would you mind leaving the flowers? I'll get them in a few minutes."

"My pleasure," said the man, setting down the flowers.

Removing the chain, Marissa quickly picked up the basket and relocked the door. It was an arrangement of spring blossoms, with an envelope addressed to Lisa Kendrick.

Marissa pulled out a folded card. Her heart skipped a beat as she began to read:

Dear Dr. Blumenthal,
    Congratulations on your performance this morning. Obviously, we know where you are at all times, but we will leave you alone if you return the piece of medical equipment you borrowed.

Terror washed over Marissa. For a moment she stood transfixed in front of the flowers. Then, in a sudden burst of activity, she began to pack her belongings. But she stopped when she realized nothing was exactly where she'd left it. They had been in her room. Oh, God! She had to get away.

Rushing into the bathroom, she snatched up her cosmetics, dumping them into her bag. Then she stopped again. The implications of the note finally dawned on her. If they did not have the vaccination gun, that meant Tad was not involved. And neither he nor anyone else knew she was staying at the Essex House under an assumed name. The only way they could have found her was by following her from the airport in Chicago.

The sooner she was out of the Essex House, the better. After flinging the rest of her things into her suitcase, Marissa's eyes drifted back to the flowers. All at once she understood. The purpose was to frighten her into leading her assailants to the vaccination gun.

She sat on the bed and forced herself to think calmly. She felt certain that she would be followed. Undoubtedly her pursuers expected her to leave in a panic, making it that much easier for them. Well, she thought, they were in for a surprise.

Looking again at the magnificent flowers, she decided to use the same strategy as her enemies. She began to develop a plan that might provide the answers that would solve the whole affair.

Unfolding the list of officers of the Physicians' Action Congress, Marissa reassured herself that the secretary was based in New York. His name was Jack Krause, and he lived at 426 East Eighty-fourth Street. Marissa decided that she'd pay him an unannounced visit. Her appearance on his doorstep should spread a lot more panic than any bouquet.

Meanwhile, she decided to leave her suitcase and briefcase behind and to take some steps to protect her departure. Going to the phone, she called the hotel manager and complained that the desk had given her room number to her estranged boyfriend, who had been bothering her.

"That's impossible," said the manager. "We do not give out room numbers."

"I have no intention of arguing with you," snapped Marissa. "The fact is it happened. Since the reason I stopped seeing him was because of his violent nature, I'm terrified."

103

"What would you like us to do?" asked the manager.

"At least move me to another room," said Marissa.

"Fine," said the manager. "I'll see to it myself."

"One other thing," said Marissa. "My boyfriend is blond, with a Julius-Caesar-type haircut, athletic-looking, sharp features. Perhaps you could alert your people."

"Certainly," said the manager.

AL HICKTMAN HAD BEEN SURE that his note would send Marissa flying out of the hotel. Now, sitting in the taxi with George, across the street from the Essex House, he was mystified. She was either super-smart or super-stupid. The job was not going well, and Al hoped that Jake was properly situated in the lobby so that Marissa could not leave by a back entrance, unseen. Since the vaccination gun had not been in the woman's hotel room, his orders were to follow her until she retrieved it, but it was all too apparent that Dr. Blumenthal was not about to accommodate them.

Al watched as a group of revellers came stumbling out of the Essex House arm in arm, swaying, laughing and generally making fools of themselves. They were attending some convention, wearing plastic sun visors emblazoned with their company's logo.

The doorman signalled a group of limousines waiting just up the street. One by one they drove to the door to pick up their quota of conventioneers.

Al slapped George on the shoulder, frantically pointing towards the largest group to emerge through the revolving door. Among them were two men supporting a woman wearing a Sanyo visor who seemed too drunk to walk. "Is that Blumenthal hanging onto those guys?" he asked.

Before George could answer, the woman disappeared into a limousine. He turned back to Al. "I couldn't be sure."

"Damn!" said Al. "Neither could I." After a moment's hesitation Al jumped out of the taxi. "If she comes out, George, follow her." Al then dodged the traffic and raced across to get into another cab.

From the back of the limousine Marissa watched the entrance to the hotel. Out of the corner of her eye she saw a man alight from a parked taxi, run across the street and climb into another taxi. She turned to face forward. She was certain she was being followed.

When the limousine turned onto Fifth Avenue, Marissa asked the driver to pull over. He complied, figuring she was about to be sick, but before anyone knew what was happening, she had thrown the door open and jumped out, telling the driver to go on without her.

Spying a bookshop, she quickly ducked inside. From the shop window she saw the cab speed by and caught a glimpse of a blond head in the back seat. The man was sitting forward, staring straight ahead.

IN THE GATHERING DUSK the house looked more like a medieval fortress than a New York luxury town house. Its leaded windows were narrow and covered with twisted wrought-iron grilles, and the front door was protected by a stout iron gate. It was hardly a hospitable sight, and for a moment Marissa had second thoughts about visiting Dr. Krause. But somehow she could not imagine that he, a doctor, would be capable of harming her directly. Perhaps through an organization like the PAC, but not with his own two hands.

Casting one last glance up and down the quiet street, she rang the bell.

The door opened a crack. "Yes?" said a woman's voice.

"I would like to see Dr. Krause," said Marissa.

"Do you have an appointment?"

"No. But tell the doctor that I'm here on emergency Physicians' Action Congress business. I think he'll see me."

The door closed, but was reopened after a couple of minutes.

"The doctor will see you." Then there was the painful sound of the iron gate opening on hinges that needed oil.

"If you'll follow me, please," said the woman, who was dressed in a maid's black uniform.

Marissa was led down a corridor to a panelled library. "Wait here," said the woman. "The doctor will be with you shortly."

Marissa glanced round the room, which had a fireplace and was furnished with antiques. Bookcases lined three of the walls.

"Sorry to keep you waiting," said a mellow voice. "Please have a seat."

Marissa turned. Dr. Krause had a fleshy face with deep lines, but the eyes were those of an intelligent, sympathetic man.

"What can I do for you?" he asked when they were sitting.

Marissa leaned forward to watch the man's face. "My name is Dr. Marissa Blumenthal." She paused, but Dr. Krause's expression did not change. Either he was a good actor or her name was not familiar.

"I'm an Epidemic Intelligence Service officer at the CDC," added Marissa. His eyes narrowed.

"My maid said that you were here on PAC business," said Dr. Krause, a measure of hospitality disappearing from his voice.

"I am," said Marissa. "Perhaps I should ask if you are aware of anything that the PAC might be doing that could concern the CDC."

This time Krause's jaw visibly tightened. He took a deep breath, cleared his throat, and finally started to speak. "The PAC is trying to rescue American medicine from the economic forces that are trying to destroy it. That's been its goal from the start."

"A noble goal," admitted Marissa. "But how is the PAC attempting to accomplish this mission?"

"By backing responsible and sensible legislation," said Dr. Krause. "The PAC is providing an opportunity for more conservative elements to exert some influence." He stood up and moved over to the fireplace, his face lost in shadow.

"Unfortunately, it seems the PAC is doing more than sponsoring legislation," said Marissa. "That's what concerns the CDC."

"I think we have nothing more to discuss," said Dr. Krause. "If you'll excuse me—"

"I believe the PAC is responsible for the Ebola outbreaks," blurted Marissa, standing up herself. "You people have some misguided idea that spreading disease in HMOs will further your cause."

"That's absurd!" said Dr. Krause.

"I couldn't agree more," said Marissa. "But I have papers linking you and the other officers of PAC to Professional Labs in Grayson, Georgia, which has recently purchased equipment to handle the virus. I even have the vaccination gun used to infect the index cases."

"Get out of here," ordered Dr. Krause.

"Gladly," said Marissa. "But first let me say that I intend to visit all the PAC. officers.I can't imagine they all agreed to this idiotic scheme."

Maintaining a calm she did not feel, Marissa walked to the door. Dr. Krause did not move from the fireplace. "I'm confident that one of the PAC officers.I see will want to help stop this horror. Perhaps by turning state's evidence. It could be you. I hope so. Goodnight, Dr. Krause."

FOR A FEW MOMENTS Dr. Krause didn't move. It was as if his worst nightmare were coming true. Panic followed paralysis. He rushed to his desk and placed a call to Atlanta.

Seconds later Joshua Jackson's smooth accent oiled its way along the wires as he said hello and asked who was calling.

"Jack Krause," said the distraught doctor. "What the devil is going on? You swore that aside from Los Angeles, the PAC had nothing to do with the outbreaks of Ebola. That the further outbreaks sprang from accidental contact with the initial patients."

"Calm down," said Jackson. "Get hold of yourself!"

"Who is Marissa Blumenthal?" asked Krause in a quieter voice. "She just showed up on my doorstep accusing me and the PAC of starting all the Ebola epidemics."

"Is she still there?"

"No. She's gone," said Krause. "But who is she?"

"An epidemiologist from the CDC. But don't worry. Heberling is taking care of her. What did she want with you?"

"She wanted to frighten me," said Krause. "And she did a good job of it. She said she has the names and addresses of all the PAC officers, and she implied that she was about to visit each one."

"Did she say who was next?"

"Of course she didn't. She's not stupid," said Krause. "But if she sees us all, somebody's going to fold. Remember Tieman in San Fran? He was adamantly against the project."

"Try to relax," urged Jackson. "There's no real evidence to implicate anyone. I'll tell Heberling the girl plans to visit the others. We'll take extra precautions to keep her away from Tieman."

Krause hung up. He felt a little less anxious, but he decided he'd phone his lawyer in the morning. It couldn't hurt to inquire about the procedure for turning state's evidence.

As HER CAB WHIZZED over the Triborough Bridge towards Kennedy Airport, Marissa was mesmerized by Manhattan's night-time skyline. From that distance it was beautiful. She forced her eyes back to the list of names and addresses of the PAC officers, which she had taken from her bag. They were hard to make out as the taxi shot from one traffic light to the next.

There was no logical way to choose whom to visit after Krause. The closest would be the most obvious to her pursuers. For safety's sake, she decided to visit the man furthest away, Dr. Sinclair Tieman in San Francisco.

At the airport, Marissa was pleased to find that there was a convenient United flight to San Francisco. She bought her ticket and decided to use the few moments before takeoff to call Ralph. As she anticipated, he was upset she hadn't called him back sooner but was pleased to learn where she was.

Marissa chose her words carefully. "I wish I could see you tonight," she said, "but. . ."

"Don't tell me you're not coming," said Ralph, feigning anger to conceal his disappointment. "I made arrangements for you to meet with Mr. McQuinllin tomorrow at noon."

"It will have to be postponed," said Marissa, wondering why the lawyer's name seemed so familiar. "I must go to San Francisco for a day or two. I can't explain right now."

"Marissa, what on earth are you up to?" asked Ralph in a tone of desperation. "Just from the little you've told me, I'm absolutely certain you should come home and see the lawyer. Then, if Mr. McQuinllin agrees, you can still go to California."

"Ralph, the fact you care makes me feel so much better, but everything is under control. What I'm doing will just make my dealings with Mr. McQuinllin that much easier. Trust me."

"I can't," pleaded Ralph. "You're not being rational."

"They're boarding my plane," said Marissa. "I promise I'll call again soon."

She replaced the receiver with a sigh. Ralph might not be the world's most romantic man, but he certainly was sensitive and caring.

AL WAS SITTING with Jake in the taxi while George waited in the Essex House lobby. Something told Al that things were screwed up. He'd followed the limo all the way to a restaurant in SoHo, but then the girl he'd seen get in didn't get out. Coming back to the hotel, he'd had Jake check to see if Miss Kendrick was still registered. She was, but when Jake went up and walked past the room, he'd seen it being cleaned. Al's professional intuition told him that the girl had fled and that they were wasting their time staking out the Essex House.

Al's beeper went off. Reaching under his jacket, he turned the thing off, cursing. He knew who it was.

He got out of the taxi and ran across the street to the Plaza, where he used a pay phone to call Heberling.

Heberling did not try to hide his contempt. "The woman's only a hundred pounds or so. I'm not asking you to take out Rambo."

"She's been lucky," said Al.

"Do you have any idea where she is?" asked Heberling.

"I'm not positive," admitted Al.

"Meaning you've lost her," snapped Heberling. "Well, I can tell you where she's been. She's just seen Dr. Krause and scared him to death. Now we're afraid she's planning to visit the other PAC officers. Dr. Tieman's the most vulnerable. I'll worry about the other physicians. I want you, George and Jake to go to San Francisco. Whatever you do, don't let her get to Tieman."

CHAPTER 11

It was just beginning to get light as Al followed Jake and George into San Francisco's central terminal. They'd taken an American flight that first stopped for an hour and a half at Dallas, then was delayed in Las Vegas on what would have been a brief touchdown.

The more Al thought about the current situation, the more frustrated he became. The girl could be in any one of at least four cities. And it wasn't even a simple hit. If they did find her, they first had to get her to tell them where she'd hidden the vaccination gun.

Leaving Jake and George to get the luggage, he hired a car, using one of the several fake IDs he always carried. He decided the only thing they could do was stake out Tieman's house. That way, even if they didn't find the girl, she wouldn't get to the doctor. After making sure he could get a car with a phone, he spread out the map of San Francisco. Tieman lived in some out-of-the-way place called Sausalito. At least there wouldn't be much traffic; it wasn't even 7:00 yet.

The operator at the Fairmont Hotel placed Marissa's wake-up call at 8 am, as she'd requested. Getting up, she opened the curtains to a breathtaking view of the San Francisco Bay Bridge. She only wished that she was visiting under more pleasant circumstances.

By the time she'd showered and wrapped herself in the thick white dressing gown supplied by the hotel, her breakfast had arrived—coffee and an enormous selection of fresh fruit. Peeling a peach with the sharp knife supplied, she wondered if it would be better to visit Tieman at his office rather than at home. She was sure someone had contacted him after her visit to Dr. Krause, so she couldn't count on surprising the man.

The Yellow Pages was in one of the desk drawers. Marissa opened it to "Physicians and Surgeons", found Tieman's name and noted that his practice was limited to obstetrics and gynaecology.

To be certain he was in town, Marissa called his office. The receptionist told her Dr. Tieman wasn't expected until 3 o'clock. This was his day for surgery at San Francisco General.

Marissa decided to confront him in the hospital. It would be safer than his office if he had any idea of trying to stop her himself.

SAN FRANCISCO GENERAL was like any other large city hospital, with the same random mixture of old and modern. There was also that overwhelming sense of bustle and disorganization characteristic of such institutions. It was easy for Marissa to walk unnoticed into the doctor's locker room.

As she was selecting a scrub suit an attendant came over and asked, "Can I help you?"

"I'm Dr. Blumenthal," said Marissa. "I'm here to observe Dr. Tieman's operation."

"Let me give you a locker," said the attendant without hesitation, and gave her a key.

After Marissa had changed, she went into the operating area. In the vestibule she put on a hood and bootees, then stopped in front of the big scheduling board. Tieman was listed for a hysterectomy in room 11.

"Yes?" inquired the nurse behind the operating-room desk.

"I'm here to observe Dr. Tieman," said Marissa.

"Go on in. Room eleven," said the nurse.

"Thank you," said Marissa, starting down the wide central corridor. The operating rooms were on either side, sharing scrub and anaesthesia space.

Entering the scrub area between rooms 11 and 12, Marissa put on a mask and pushed into Tieman's operating room.

There were five people besides the patient. There were two surgeons, one on either side of the table; an anaesthetist; a scrub nurse, who was perched on a stool and a second nurse. As Marissa entered, one of the nurses came over and asked what she needed.

"Which one is Dr. Tieman?" asked Marissa.

"The one on the right," she said. "Who are you?"

"A doctor friend from Atlanta," said Marissa. She didn't elaborate. Moving round to the head of the table and looking at Dr. Tieman, she was surprised to see that he was black.

How odd, thought Marissa. She had assumed that all the PAC officers would be old guard, white and racially prejudiced.

For a while she watched the operation. Tieman was good. His hands moved with that special economy of motion that could not be taught. It was a talent, a gift from God.

"START THE STUPID CAR," said Al, hanging up the car phone. They were parked opposite a sprawling redwood house that clung to the hillside above the town of Sausalito.

Jake turned the key in the ignition. "Where to?"

"Back to the city."

"What did Tieman's office say?" asked George.

"That the doctor was in surgery at San Francisco General," said Al, almost white with anger. "His first operation was scheduled for seven thirty, and he's not expected at the office until three."

"No wonder we missed him," said George disgustedly. "The guy must have left his house an hour before we even got here. What a stupid waste of time."

"I think we should get another car," Al said. "Just in case we run into a problem and have to split up. Then we'll go to San Francisco General. The sooner we spot Tieman, the better."

FEELING CONFIDENT THAT she'd have no problem recognizing Dr. Tieman now that she'd seen him, Marissa left the operating room as his assistant was closing. She changed back to her street clothes, wanting to be able to leave straight after she spoke to Tieman. Then she went into the surgical lounge, where she found a seat by the window.

Half an hour went by before Dr. Tieman appeared. He immediately poured himself a cup of coffee.

Marissa walked over to him. "I'm Dr. Marissa Blumenthal," she said, watching him for a reaction.

He had a broad, masculine face with a well-trimmed moustache. He looked down at Marissa with a smile. It was obvious from his expression that he had no idea who she was.

"May I speak to you in private?" asked Marissa.

He nodded and took her into a small office near the lounge. There was one chair, and Dr. Tieman gestured for Marissa to sit. He leaned against a counter, holding his coffee in his hand.

Acutely conscious of her short stature and its psychological handicap, she insisted that he sit, since he'd been standing in surgery since early that morning.

"OK, OK," he said with a laugh. "I'm sitting. Now, what can I do for you?"

"I'm surprised you don't recognize my name," said Marissa. "Hasn't Dr. Jack Krause called you about me?"

"I'm not sure I know a Dr. Krause," said Dr. Tieman, directing his attention to his coffee.

The first lie, thought Marissa. Taking a deep breath, she told the doctor exactly what she'd told Krause. From the moment she mentioned the Los Angeles Ebola outbreak, he never lifted his eyes from his cup. She could tell that he was nervous.

"I haven't the slightest idea why you are telling me this," he said, starting to rise.

With uncharacteristic forwardness Marissa gently touched his chest, forcing him back in his seat. "I'm not finished," she said. "I have evidence that Ebola is being deliberately spread by the PAC. You are their treasurer, and I'm shocked that a man of your reputation could be connected with such a sordid affair."

"You're shocked," countered Dr. Tieman, finally rising to his feet and towering over her. "I'm amazed that you have the nerve to make such irresponsible allegations."

"Save your breath," said Marissa. "It's public knowledge that you are an officer of the PAC as well as a limited partner in one of the only labs in the country equipped to handle viruses like Ebola."

"You'll be hearing from my lawyer," warned Dr. Tieman.

"Good," said Marissa. "Call your lawyer. Maybe he will persuade you to come forward." She stepped back and looked up into his face. "Think about it, doctor. You don't have much time."

As she pushed through the swing doors Marissa realized she had forgotten to say she was planning to visit the other PAC officers. She decided it didn't matter; the man was terrified enough.

"THERE SHE IS!" yelled Al Hicktman. He and Jake sat in a parked car across the street from the hospital. George waited behind them in a second car. When Al turned to look at him, George gave a thumbs-up sign, meaning that he'd also seen Marissa.

Jake started the car, and as Marissa got into a cab he pulled out behind her, followed neatly by George.

About fifteen minutes later Marissa's taxi stopped at the Fairmont Hotel. Jake quickly parked across the street and, dodging the midmorning traffic, reached the front of the hotel before Marissa had got out of her cab. In the lobby he picked up a newspaper and positioned himself so that he could see everyone coming into the hotel.

Marissa walked right by him and down a hall lined with shops. Jake took off after her. Guessing she was headed towards the lifts, he beat her there and mingled with the crowd already waiting.

A lift arrived, which Jake boarded before Marissa, making certain there was plenty of room. Holding his newspaper as if he were reading, he watched as Marissa pressed 10.

When the lift stopped at the tenth floor, Jake strolled off, still absorbed in his paper, allowing Marissa and another guest to pass him. When she stopped in front of room 1127, he kept walking. He didn't turn and go back to the lifts until he'd heard her door close.

Back out on the street, Jake crossed over to Al's car. "Room eleven twenty-seven," he said with a self-satisfied smile.

"You'd better be right," said Al, getting out of the car. "Wait here. This shouldn't take long at all."

He then walked over to George's car and leaned on the window. "I want you to drive around and cover the back entrance. Just in case."

Feeling better than he had for several days, Al crossed the street to the posh red-and-black lobby. He headed for the lifts.

On the tenth floor, he searched for the housekeeping trolley. He found it outside a suite. Taking a towel, he carefully folded it on the diagonal, creating a stout rope. Gripping an end in each hand, he entered the suite where the maid was working.

She was on her knees, scrubbing the bath. A tin of cleanser was on the floor beside her. Without a moment's hesitation Al stepped behind her and, using the folded towel as a garrotte, strangled her. When he let up the tension on the ends of the towel, she slumped to the floor.

Al found the passkeys in her pocket. Back in the hall, he hung a "Do Not Disturb" sign on the knob and closed the door to the suite. Then he pushed the housekeeping trolley out of sight into the stairwell. Flexing his fingers like a pianist preparing for a recital, he started off for room 1127.

MARISSA PEELED THE LAST OF the breakfast fruit with the sharp knife. She was on the phone to Northwest Airlines trying to make a reservation to Minneapolis. She had decided PAC would think she'd probably go to Los Angeles, so Minneapolis seemed as good a bet as any.

The agent finally confirmed her on an afternoon flight. Flopping back on the bed, she was debating how she should spend the next hour or so when she heard a metallic click. It sounded like the door, but she knew she'd left up the "Do Not Disturb" sign. Then she saw the knob silently begin to turn.

Panic danced through her like an electric current. Pulling herself together, she reached for the phone. But before she could lift the receiver, the door burst open, splintering part of the jamb as the screws holding the chain-lock plate were yanked out of the moulding. A man slammed the door shut, then hurled himself at Marissa. He grabbed her by the neck with both hands and shook her like a mad dog in a frenzy. "Remember me?" he snarled furiously.

Marissa remembered him. It was the blond man with the Julius Caesar haircut.

"You have ten seconds to produce the vaccination gun," hissed Al, loosening the death grip he had on her throat. "If you don't, I'll snap your neck."

Barely able to breathe, Marissa fruitlessly clawed at the man's powerful wrists. He shook her again, and she fell back, hitting her head against the wall. By reflex her hands extended behind her to cushion her body. Her right hand touched the knife, and her fingers wrapped around the shaft. Holding it in her fist, she hammered it up into the man's abdomen as hard as she could. She had no idea if she'd penetrated anything, but Al let go of her and rocked back on his haunches, his face registering disbelief as he saw blood staining his shirt.

With the knife pointed at her attacker, Marissa edged towards the door. But before she reached it, he leaped at her like an enraged animal, sending her racing to the bathroom. It seemed as if only hours before she'd been in the same predicament in Chicago.

Al got his hand round the door before it shut. Marissa hacked blindly, feeling her knife strike bone. Al screamed and yanked his hand away. The door slammed shut, and Marissa locked it.

She was about to dial on the bathroom phone when there was a loud crash and the entire bathroom door crashed inwards. Al forced Marissa to drop the phone, but she hung on to the knife, stabbing at him wildly. Ignoring the knife, Al grabbed Marissa by her hair and flung her against the basin. She tried to stab him again, but he grabbed her wrist and bashed it against the wall until her grip loosened and the weapon clattered to the floor.

He bent down to pick it up, and as he straightened, Marissa grabbed the receiver that was swinging on its cord and hit him with it as hard as she could.

For a moment Al stood as if he were frozen. Then his blue eyes rolled upwards, and he seemed to fall in slow motion into the bath, striking his head on the taps.

As Marissa watched, she was torn between fear and her medical training. The man was obviously badly injured, the front of his shirt stained with blood. But terror won through, and Marissa grabbed her bag and ran from the room. Remembering that her assailant had not been alone in New York, she knew she had to get away from the hotel as soon as possible.

Once on the ground floor, Marissa avoided the front entrance.

Instead, she went down a flight of stairs and followed arrows to a rear exit. Standing just inside the door, she waited until a cable car came into view. Timing her exit to give herself the least exposure, she ran out of the hotel and jumped onto the trolley.

George Valhala blinked in disbelief. It was the girl. Quickly he dialled Jake's car and said, "She just came out of the hotel and jumped on a cable car."

"Is Al with her?" asked Jake.

"No," said George. "She's by herself."

"Something is weird."

"You follow her," said George. "I'll go in and check on Al."

Marissa looked back at the hotel for any sign of being followed. No one came out of the door, but as the cable car began to move, she saw a man get out of a car and run for the hotel's rear entrance. The timing was suggestive, but as the man didn't even look in her direction, she dismissed it as a coincidence. She continued to watch until the cable car turned a corner and she could no longer see the Fairmont. She'd made it.

As she relaxed and her fear abated, she became more aware of the pain where her hip had hit the basin, and her neck was exquisitely tender and probably turning black and blue.

"Fare please," said the conductor.

Without lifting her eyes, Marissa fished around in her purse for some change. That was when she saw the blood caked on the back of her right hand. Quickly, she changed the way she was holding her purse and used her left hand to give the money to the man.

When he moved off, Marissa tried to figure out how they had found her. She'd been so careful . . . Suddenly it dawned on her. They must have been guarding Tieman. It was the only possible explanation.

Her confidence shattered, she suddenly began to have second thoughts about having fled the hotel. Perhaps she would have been safer if she had stayed and faced the police. For all she knew, she'd killed two men. It was all too much. She decided not to go to Minneapolis. She would go home and turn everything she knew or suspected over to the lawyer.

The cable car stopped in Chinatown. Just as it was starting again Marissa swung off. No one got off after her. She looked around and was pleased to see that both sides of the street were crowded.

She came to a Chinese restaurant and went inside, heading directly for a pay phone in the rear. She called the Fairmont and reported that there was a man in room 1127 who needed an ambulance. The operator told her to hold on, but Marissa hung up.

JAKE HAD WATCHED Marissa go into a restaurant called Peking Cuisine. At least he hadn't lost her. He scrunched down in the driver's seat. The girl had just come out of the restaurant and was hailing a cab.

114

An hour later Jake watched helplessly as Marissa handed over her ticket and boarded a Delta Airways nonstop flight to Atlanta. He had thought about buying a ticket himself, but scrapped the idea without Al's OK. She'd spent the last half hour closeted in the airport's ladies' room, giving him ample time to try the mobile phone at least ten times, hoping for some instructions. But neither George nor Al answered.

As soon as the plane taxied down the runway Jake decided to try the mobile phone one last time. To his astonishment George answered.

"Where the hell have you been?" Jake demanded. "The girl is on a plane to Atlanta, and I didn't know what to do."

"There's been a problem," said George, subdued. "Al was knifed, I guess by the girl. He's at San Francisco General having surgery. I can't get near him."

Jake was speechless.

"He's not supposed to be hurt that bad," continued George. "What's worse is that apparently Al wasted a maid. He's being charged with murder."

"Unbelievable," said Jake. Things were going from bad to worse.

"Book us on the next flight to Atlanta," said George. "I think we owe Al a bit of revenge."

CHAPTER 12

Ralph Hempston was catching up on his journals when the doorbell rang at 9:30 pm. Glancing at his watch, he wondered who could possibly be visiting at that hour. He looked through the glass panel on the door and was shocked to find himself staring into Marissa's face.

"Marissa!" he said in disbelief, quickly opening the door. Behind her he could see a yellow cab pulling out of his driveway.

Marissa saw him hold out his arms, and she ran into them, bursting into tears.

"I thought you were in California," said Ralph. "Why didn't you call and let me know you were coming? I would have met you at the airport."

Marissa just clung to him. It was so wonderful to feel safe.

"What happened to you?" he asked, but was only greeted by louder sobs.

"At least let's go and sit down," he said, helping her to the couch. For a few minutes he just let her cry. "It's OK," he continued, eyeing the phone and willing it to ring. He had to make a call, and at this rate she was never going to let him get up. "Perhaps you'd like something to drink?" he asked.

She shook her head.

"I have a nice bottle of Chardonnay open in the refrigerator."

Marissa just held him tighter, but her sobs were lessening. At last she sat up. "Maybe in a little bit. Just stay with me a while longer. I've been so scared."

"Then why didn't you call me from the airport? And what happened to your car? Didn't you leave it there?"

"It's a long story," said Marissa. "But I was afraid that someone might be watching it. I didn't want anybody to know I was back in Atlanta."

"Would you like me to drive you over to your house to get some things?" asked Ralph.

"Thanks, but I don't want to show up there, for the same reason I was afraid to go to my car. If I were to drive anywhere tonight, I'd run over to the CDC and get a package that I hope Tad put away for me. But to tell you the truth, I think it all can wait until morning. Even that criminal lawyer, who I hope will be able to keep me out of jail."

"Good grief," said Ralph. "Don't you think it's time you told me what's going on?"

Marissa picked up Ralph's hand. "I will. I promise. Let me just calm down a little more. Maybe I should eat something."

"I've got some cold chicken in the refrigerator," he said.

"No, thanks. Maybe I'll just scramble some eggs."

"I'll join you in a minute," he said. "I have to make a call."

Marissa dragged herself through the house. In the kitchen she got the eggs out of the refrigerator, along with some bread for toast. Then she realized she hadn't asked Ralph if he wanted any. Putting the eggs down, she went over to the intercom and began pushing the buttons on the console to see if she could figure out how it worked. Suddenly she heard Ralph's voice.

"She's not in San Francisco, Jackson," he was saying. "She's here . . . I don't know what happened. She's hysterical. Listen, I can't talk now. I've got to get back to her . . . I'll keep her here. But get here as soon as you can. Bye."

Marissa clutched the countertop, afraid she was going to faint. All this time Ralph—the one person she'd trusted—had been one of *them*. And Jackson! It had to be the same Jackson she'd met at Ralph's dinner party. The head of the PAC, and he was on his way over. Oh, God!

Marissa had to force herself to go on with her cooking. She had just put the eggs on when Ralph appeared with some drinks. "Smells good," he said brightly. He put down her glass and touched her lightly on the back. Marissa jumped.

"Wow, you really are uptight."

Marissa didn't say anything. Although she was no longer the slightest bit hungry, she went through the motions of cooking the eggs and buttering the toast. Looking at Ralph's expensive silk shirt, the heavy gold cuff links, the tasselled Gucci slippers, she suddenly saw it all as a ridiculous affectation. It represented the conspicuous consumption of a wealthy doctor, now fearful of the new medical competition.

Obviously Ralph was a member of the PAC and a supporter of Markham. And it was Ralph, not Tad, who had been informing her attackers of her whereabouts. In fact, now that she knew Ralph was implicated, Marissa remembered why the name of the lawyer he'd suggested had sounded familiar: Cooper, Hodges, McQuinllin and Hanks had been listed as the service agent of the PAC.

Marissa felt trapped. The men pursuing her had powerful connections. She had no idea how deeply they had penetrated the CDC. Certainly the conspiracy involved the Congressman who exerted control over the CDC budget. Her mind reeled. She was terrified no one would believe her, and she was acutely aware that the only piece of hard evidence—the vaccination gun—was resting somewhere in the maximum containment lab, to which, she knew from painful experience, her pursuers had access. The only thing that was crystal clear was that she had to get away from Ralph before Jackson, and maybe more thugs, arrived.

Serving the eggs, she had a sudden vision of the blond man hurling himself through the bathroom door in San Francisco. She dropped the fork, again afraid she was about to faint, and put her head in her hands. She had to get herself under control.

"Not hungry after all?" asked Ralph.

"Not very," admitted Marissa.

"Maybe you should take a tranquillizer. I've got some upstairs."

"OK," said Marissa.

"Be right back," said Ralph, squeezing her shoulder.

This was the chance she had prayed for. As soon as he was out of the room Marissa was on her feet, snatching the phone off its hook. But there was no dialling tone. Ralph must have disconnected it. Replacing the phone, she rushed round the kitchen searching for Ralph's car keys. Nothing. Next she tried the adjoining family room. There was a tiny marble urn on the room divider with a few keys, but none for a car.

She went to to the little hall by the back door. There was a small chest, and she began opening drawers, finding a jumble of gloves and scarves.

"What do you need?" asked Ralph, suddenly appearing. In one hand he held a glass of water; the other was closed.

Guiltily Marissa straightened up. "I thought maybe I could find a sweater."

"I'll turn the heat on in the kitchen," said Ralph. "Here, take this." He dropped a blue tablet into Marissa's palm.

"Valium?" she questioned.

"It will relax you," explained Ralph.

Marissa pretended to take the Valium but dropped it into the pocket of her jacket instead.

"Now, let's try the food again," said Ralph as he guided her to the table.

Marissa shook her head. "I'm just not hungry."

"Well, let's go into the living room."

She was glad to leave the cooking smells, but the moment they were seated, Ralph urged her to have a drink.

"I don't think I should after the Valium."

"A little won't hurt."

"Are you sure you're not trying to get me drunk?" said Marissa. She forced a laugh. "Maybe you'd better let me fix the drinks."

"Fine by me," said Ralph, lifting his feet to the coffee table. "Make mine a Scotch."

Marissa went directly to the bar and poured Ralph a good four fingers of Scotch. Then, checking to see that he was absorbed, she took out the Valium tablet, broke it in half and dropped the pieces into the alcohol. They dissolved slowly.

"Need any help?" called Ralph.

"No," she said, pouring a little brandy into her own glass. "Here you go."

Ralph took his drink and settled back on the couch. Sitting beside him, Marissa racked her brains to figure out where he might have put his car keys. A horrible thought occurred to her. Of course, he had probably just put them into his trousers' pocket.

Distasteful as it was, Marissa forced herself to snuggle against him. Provocatively she placed her hand on his hip. She could feel the keys through the light gabardine.

Gritting her teeth, she tilted her face to his. As his arms encircled her she let her fingers slide into his pocket. Scarcely breathing, she felt the ring and pulled. The keys jangled a little, and she began to kiss him. Sensing his response, she decided to take the chance. Please God, she prayed, and pulled out the keys.

"Darling," she said, once the keys were safely hidden in her own pocket, "I hate to do this to you, but that pill is getting to me. I think I'm going to have to lie down." She pulled herself out of his embrace, and he solicitously helped her up the stairs to the guest bedroom on the first floor.

"Would you like me to stay with you?" he asked.

"I'm sorry, Ralph. I'm about to pass out. Just let me sleep." She forced a smile.

"Well, call if you need anything. I'll be downstairs."

The moment he closed the door, she tiptoed over and listened to him going down the front stairs. Then she went to the window and opened it. Outside was the balcony she remembered seeing above the front door. As quietly as possible she slipped out into the cool spring night.

Quickly she surveyed her position. There was no possibility of jumping. She was about fifteen feet above the asphalt driveway. The balcony was surrounded by a low balustrade, which separated it from the sloping roof of the porch. To the left the porch roof abutted on the tower, and to the right it swept round the corner of the building.

Climbing over the balustrade, Marissa inched her way to the corner. The porch roof ended about twenty feet away. The fire escape descended from the second floor, but it was out of reach. Turning, she started back for the balcony. She was halfway there when she heard a car turn into Ralph's driveway.

Marissa lay still on the sloped roof. She knew that she was in full view of anybody coming up the driveway if he happened to look up. Headlights swept across the front of the house, bathing her in light before the car pulled up to the front steps. She heard the doors open and several voices: They were not excited; apparently no one had seen her sprawled on the roof.

Marissa scampered along the roof and climbed back over the balustrade to the balcony. She ducked into the guestroom and eased open the door to the hallway. She started silently towards the back stairs.

She was halfway to the second floor when she stopped. She still heard voices, but she also heard footsteps. The problem was, she couldn't tell where they were coming from. With her heart pounding, she continued up the stairs, wincing at every sound. The door to the servants' rooms at the top was closed but not locked.

As quietly as possible she made her way across a dark sitting room and out onto the fire escape. Hesitantly she started down. By the time she reached the first floor, she heard excited voices and the sound of doors opening and slamming shut. They had realized that she had fled.

Forcing herself to hurry, Marissa rounded the first-floor platform and was stopped by what seemed to be a large jumble of metal. Feeling with her hands, she realized that the last flight of stairs had been drawn up to protect the house from burglars. Frantically she tried to figure out how to lower them. Then she noticed a large counterweight behind her.

Gingerly she put her foot on the first step. There was a loud squeak of metal. Knowing she had no choice, she shifted her full weight onto the step. With a nerve-shattering crash the stairs shot to the ground, and she ran down them.

As soon as her feet touched the grass she ran for the garage, praying it was not locked. It wasn't. As she raised the door she heard the back door of the house open. Desperately she stepped into the dark interior and moved forward, colliding almost immediately with Ralph's Mercedes sedan. Feeling for the car door, she opened it and slipped behind the wheel. She fumbled with the key until it slid into the ignition, and the car roared to life. She shifted to reverse and pressed the accelerator. The big car shot out of the garage, sending two men diving sideways for safety. She had certainly hit something—or someone.

Marissa jammed on the brakes and changed to forward gear. One of the men, taking advantage of her momentary halt, flung himself across the bonnet. She accelerated and the car shot forward, dislodging her attacker as she careered down the drive.

"DAMN," SAID JACKSON. "That woman lives a charmed life. Even if we go after her, we'll never catch her. She has too big a head start." He looked furiously at Arnold Heberling. "This probably wouldn't have happened if I'd come here directly instead of waiting for your goons to get in from the airport."

"Yeah?" said Heberling. "And what would you have done? Reasoned with her? You need Jake and George."

"I don't know how she escaped," said Ralph apologetically. "I'd just left her to sleep. She's had ten milligrams of Valium, for heaven's sake." He noticed that he felt a little dizzy himself.

"Any idea where she might go?" asked Jackson.

"I don't think she'll go to the police," said Ralph. "She's terrified of everyone, especially now. She might try the CDC. She said something about a package being there."

Jackson looked at Heberling. They had the same thought: the vaccination gun.

"We may as well send Jake and George," said Heberling. "We're pretty sure she won't go home, and after what she did to Al, the boys are most eager for revenge."

FIFTEEN MINUTES from Ralph's house Marissa began to calm down enough to worry about where she was. She had made so many random turns in case she was being pursued that she had lost all sense of direction. For all she knew, she could have driven in a full circle.

120

Ahead, she saw street lights and a filling station. Marissa pulled over, lowering her window. A young man came wearing a baseball hat.

"Could you tell me where I am?" asked Marissa.

The young man eyed the damage to Ralph's car. "Did you know that both your taillights is busted?"

"I'm not surprised," said Marissa. "Could you tell me how to get to the Centers for Disease Control?"

"Lady, you look like you've been in a stockcar race," he said, shaking his head in dismay.

Marissa repeated her question, and finally he gave her some vague directions.

Ten minutes later she was cruising past the building. It seemed quiet and deserted.

Although she still wasn't sure what she should do or whom she could trust, fear forced her to do what she felt was her only logical choice: she had to get the vaccination gun. It was the only piece of evidence she had. Without it she doubted if anyone would take her seriously. She still had Tad's access card.

Boldly Marissa turned into the driveway and pulled up just past the entrance to the CDC. She wanted the car handy in case anyone tried to stop her.

She got out, and looking in at the front door she saw the guard sitting at the desk, bent over a paperback novel. When he heard her come in, he looked up, his face expressionless.

Marissa walked deliberately, trying to hide her fear. She scrawled her name in the sign-in book. Then she looked up, expecting some comment, but the guard just stared impassively.

She went to the main lifts, pushed the button to her floor, then turned and looked at him.

He was still watching her.

The moment the doors shut, he snatched up the phone and dialled. As soon as someone answered, he said, "Dr. Blumenthal just signed in. She went up in the lift."

"Good work. We'll be right there. Don't let anyone else in."

"Whatever you say, Dr. Dubchek."

Inside the virology building, Marissa hurried to the steel security door. Holding her breath, she inserted Tad's access card and tapped out his number.

There was a pause. Then she heard the sound of the latch releasing. The heavy door opened, and she was inside.

After flipping the circuit breakers, she climbed into the next room and, instead of donning a scrub suit, went directly into the next chamber. As she struggled into a plastic suit she wondered where Tad might have hidden the contaminated vaccination gun.

121

DUBCHEK DROVE RECKLESSLY, braking for bends only when absolutely necessary, jumping red lights. Two men had joined him. The one in the front seat braced himself against the door; the one in the back had more trouble avoiding being thrown from side to side. The expressions on all three faces were grim. They were afraid they would be too late.

"THERE IT IS," said George, pointing at a sign saying "Centers for Disease Control".

"And there's Ralph's car!" he added, pointing at the Mercedes in the semicircular driveway. "Looks like luck is finally on our side." Making up his mind, he pulled into the car park across the street.

He drew his Smith & Wesson .357 Magnum and checked to see that all the chambers were filled. He opened the door and stepped out, holding the gun down along his hip. Light gleamed off the stainless-steel barrel.

"You sure you want to use that cannon?" asked Jake. "It makes so much damn noise."

"I wish I'd had this thing when she was driving around with you on the bonnet," George snapped. "Come on!"

Jake shrugged and got out of the car. Patting the small of his back, he felt the butt of his own Beretta semiautomatic. It was a very much neater weapon.

AIR HOSE IN HAND, Marissa hastily climbed through the final door to the maximum containment lab. She plugged into the central manifold and looked round.

The mess she'd helped to create had all been cleared away, but the memory of that other fateful night flooded back with horrifying clarity. Marissa was shaking. All she wanted was to find her parcel and get out. But that was easier said than done. As in any lab, there was a profusion of places were a small package could be hidden.

Marissa started on the right, working her way back, opening cabinet doors and pulling out drawers. She got about halfway down the room when she straightened up. There had to be a better way.

At the central island, she went to the containment hood that Tad considered his own. She searched the cupboards, but there was no package resembling hers. She was about to move on when she looked through the glass of the containment hood. Behind Tad's equipment she could just barely make out the dark green of a plastic rubbish bag.

Turning on the fan over the hood, Marissa pulled up the glass front. Then, careful not to touch Tad's set-up, she lifted out the bag. Inside was the Federal Express package.

At the central manifold, she hurriedly detached her air hose, then headed for the door. It was time to find someone in authority whom she could trust.

Standing under the shower of phenolic disinfectant, Marissa tried to be patient. Once in the next room, she struggled out of her plastic suit, pulling frantically each time the zip stuck. When she finally got it off, her street clothes were drenched with sweat.

DUBCHEK CAME to a screeching halt directly in front of the CDC entrance. The security guard was already holding open one of the glass doors as the three men piled out of the car.

Dubchek ran into the waiting lift, with the other two men on his heels, and pressed the button for the second.

MARISSA HAD JUST STARTED across the catwalk when the door to the main building opened and three men burst out. Spinning round, she ran back into virology.

"Stop, Marissa," someone yelled. It sounded like Dubchek. Oh, no. Was he chasing her, too?

She latched the door behind her. To her right was a lift, to her left a stairwell. There was no time to debate.

By the time Dubchek had managed to force open the door, all he could see was the lift light pointing down. She was already on the lobby level as the three men began pounding down the stairs. Knowing Dubchek was close behind her, Marissa knew she had no time to slow down to avoid alerting the security guard. He stood up as she streaked past him and out through the door.

Outside, she fumbled for the keys to Ralph's car, switching her parcel to her left hand. She heard shouts and then the doors to the CDC crashing open. Wrestling the car door open, she started to slide behind the wheel. She was so programmed for flight that it took a minute for her to realize that the passenger seat was occupied. There was also someone in the back. But worse was the sight of a revolver pointing at her.

Marissa tried to reverse her direction, but it was if she were caught in a heavy, viscous fluid. Her body wouldn't respond. She saw a face in the half light and heard someone start to say goodbye. Then the gun went off with a fearful explosion, and time stopped.

WHEN MARISSA REGAINED consciousness, she was lying on something soft. Someone was calling her name. Slowly opening her eyes, she realized she was on the couch in the CDC lobby. Flashing red and blue lights, like those in a tawdry punk discotheque, washed the room. She wondered what had happened to the men with the guns.

She saw Dubchek bending over her, his dark eyes black with fear. "Marissa," he said, "are you all right? I've been so worried. When you finally made us realize what was going on, we were afraid they'd try to kill you. But you never stayed still long enough for us to find you."

Marissa was still too shocked to speak.

"Please say something, Marissa," Dubchek pleaded. "Did they hurt you?"

"I thought you were part of it. Part of the conspiracy."

Dubchek groaned. "I was afraid of that. Not that I didn't deserve it. I was so busy protecting the CDC, I just dismissed your theories. But believe me, I had nothing to do with any of it."

Marissa reached for his hand. "I guess I never gave you much chance to explain either. I was so busy breaking all the rules."

An ambulance attendant came up to them. "Does the lady want to go to the hospital?"

"Do you, Marissa?" asked Dubchek.

"I guess so, but I think I'm OK."

As another attendant came up to help lift her onto a stretcher she said, "When I heard the bang, I thought I'd been shot."

"No. One of the FBI men with me shot your would-be killer."

Marissa shuddered. Dubchek walked beside the stretcher as they took her to the ambulance. She reached out and took his hand again.

EPILOGUE

Marissa was unpacking from a two-week vacation, taken at Dr. Carbonara's insistence, when the doorbell rang. She had just returned from Virginia, where her family had done everything they could for her, even giving her a new puppy that she'd immediately named Taffy Two.

As she walked downstairs she couldn't imagine who might be at the door. She hadn't told anyone the exact date of her return. When she opened the door, she was surprised to see Cyrill Dubchek and Dr. Carbonara, the head of the Epidemic Intelligence Service.

"I hope you don't mind our turning up like this," said Dr. Carbonara, "but we wanted to see how you were. And I wanted to thank you personally for your brilliant detective work."

"With no help from us," admitted Dubchek.

"I'm flattered," said Marissa, at a loss for words.

Dubchek cleared his throat. Marissa found his new lack of confidence appealing. When he wasn't making her furious, she could admit that he was actually very handsome.

"We thought you'd like to know what's been happening," he said. "The press has been given as little detail as possible, but even the police agreed that you are entitled to the truth."

"I'd love to hear everything," said Marissa. "But please come in and sit down. Can I get you something to drink?"

When they were settled, Dr. Carbonara said, "Thanks to you, almost everyone connected with the Ebola conspiracy has been arrested. Al Hicktman, the man you stabbed in San Francisco, was quick to implicate Dr. Heberling. Heberling is a former CDC employee. The authorities think he stole the virus and operated the lab in Grayson."

"By the way, the police think Hicktman *wanted* to be sent to jail so you couldn't find him again," said Dubchek with a hint of his old sardonic grin.

Marissa shivered, remembering the terrible episode in the Fairmont Hotel. Then, pulling herself together, she asked what had happened to Heberling.

"He'll be going before a grand jury on multiple counts of murder," said Dubchek. "The judge refused to set bail, no matter how high, saying that he was as dangerous to society as the Nazi war criminals."

"And the man I shot with the vaccination gun?" Marissa had been afraid to ask this question. She didn't want to be responsible for killing anyone or for spreading Ebola.

"He'll live to stand trial. He did use the serum in time, and it proved effective, but he came down with a severe case of serum sickness. As soon as he's better, he'll also be off to jail."

"What about the other officers of the Physicians' Action Congress?" asked Marissa.

"A number of them have offered to turn state's evidence," said Carbonara. "It's making the investigation inordinately easy. We are beginning to believe that the regular members of the organization thought that they were supporting just an ordinary lobbying campaign."

"What about Tieman? He certainly didn't seem the type to be mixed up in such an affair. Or at least his conscience certainly seemed to bother him."

"His lawyer has been making arrangements for a lighter sentence in return for his cooperation. As for the PAC itself, the group's bankrupt. The families of many of the victims have filed suit. Most of the officers are being prosecuted criminally. So they should be behind bars a good while, particularly Jackson."

"I guess Ralph will also go to jail," Marissa said slowly. She was still trying to come to terms with the fact that the man she had considered a protector had tried to kill her.

"I doubt that Ralph will be released for a long time," said Dubchek. "Aside from his connection with the PAC, he is directly linked to the attacks on you."

Marissa sighed. "So it's really over."

"Thanks to your persistence," said Carbonara. "And the outbreak in New York is definitely under control."

"Thank heavens," she said.

"So when will you be coming back to the CDC?" asked Dubchek. "We've already got you clearance for the maximum containment lab." This time there was no doubt about his grin. "No one relished the thought of your stumbling around there at night any more."

Marissa blushed in spite of herself. "I haven't decided yet. I'm actually considering going back into pediatrics."

"Back to Boston?" Dubchek's face fell.

"It will be a loss to the field," said Dr. Carbonara. "You've become a national epidemiological hero."

"I'll give it more thought," promised Marissa. "But even if I do go back to pediatrics, I'm planning to stay in Atlanta." She nuzzled her new puppy. There was a pause, then she added, "But I've one request."

"If we can be of any help . . ." said Dr. Carbonara.

Marissa shook her head. "Only Cyrill can help on this one. Whether I go back to pediatrics or not, I was hoping he'd ask me to dinner again."

Dubchek was taken off guard. Then, laughing at Carbonara's bemused expression, he leaned over and hugged Marissa to his side.

ROBIN COOK

"Why did I become a doctor?" Six foot tall, lithe and trim, with striking blue eyes, Robin Cook, MD, leans forward in his chair to respond. "Well, as a kid growing up in New York, I was good at science, but I was very interested in archaeology too. Then I spent a summer in Egypt and decided I'd missed a big archaeology career by a hundred years—all the good buried cities had already been found. So I turned to medicine; it seemed like a challenge."

Robin Cook likes challenges. At high school he was a basketball and swimming star, and he graduated with distinction from Wesleyan University in Connecticut. Then it was on to Colombia University's College of Physicians and Surgeons, in New York, where he supported himself by cleaning monkey cages and working in a lab. "It was a far cry from that high-tech CDC lab in *Outbreak*," he says, smiling. "There are only a few laboratories like that in the world."

After receiving his degree, Dr. Cook joined the navy. It was to escape the boredom of submarine duty that he began to write *The Year of the Intern*, his first novel. It sold fairly well, so he wrote another. That one he called *Coma*, and it soared to the top of the bestseller lists. Medical thrillers became his forte.

Today, Cook's career in ophthalmology is on "hold" while he addresses his predominant challenge—alerting his millions of readers to potential problems in the American medical world so that they will become more informed and more critical recipients of medical care. Cook, who lives in an 1830s town house on Boston's historic Beacon Hill, intends to "continue with medical issues for my novels until I run out of subjects". That doesn't seem likely to happen for quite some time.

THE COLLABORATORS

A CONDENSATION OF THE BOOK BY
Reginald Hill

ILLUSTRATED BY JOHN RAYNES

June 1940. While Parisians try to go about their business as usual, German troops march through the streets of Paris. The occupation has begun.

In the coming years, Frenchmen and women react in different ways to their new masters: some quietly shun them; some, fired with bravery and burning hatred, fight them to the death. Some collaborate.

One such is Janine Simonian, who waits anxiously for news of her Jewish husband, imprisoned by the Nazis. In her struggle to get him home, and in her fight to save her children, Pauli and Céci, from the death camps, she turns to the only person who will listen—a German officer called Lieutenant Mai.

Their story is a touching one: a tale of two people torn by loyalties which they both betray. Which one of them, in the end, is the collaborator?

PROLOGUE March 1945

She dreamed of the children. They were picnicking on the edge of a cornfield, Pauli hiding, his sister, Céci, giggling with delight as she crawled through the forest of green stalks. Now she too was out of sight, but her happy laughter and her brother's encouraging cries drifted back to their mother, dozing in the warm sunshine.

Suddenly there was silence, and a shadow between her and the sun, and a shape leaning over her, and a hand shaking her shoulder. She sat up crying, "Jean-Paul!"

"On your feet, whore. You've got a visitor."

It was the fat wardress, who pulled her upright off the palliasse. A man in a black, badly cut suit was standing before her. Without hesitation she sank to her knees and stretched out her hands in supplication. "Please, sir, is there any news of my children? I beg you, tell me what has happened to my children?"

"Shut up," said the wardress. "Here, put on this hat."

"Hat?" She was used to cruelty but not to craziness. "What do I want with a hat? Is the magistrate bored with the sight of my head?"

"Your examination's over, woman. Haven't you been told?" The man spoke with bureaucratic irritation.

The wardress shrugged and said, "She'll have been told. She pays little heed, this one, unless you mention her brats. Now, put on the hat. See, it's like one of them Boche helmets, so it should suit you."

She was holding an old cloche hat of dirty grey felt.

"Why must I wear a hat? This is lunacy!"

131

"Janine Simonian," said the man, "the examining magistrate has decided that your case must go for trial before the Court of Justice set up by the provisional government of the Republic. I am here to conduct you there. Put on the hat. It will hide your shame."

Janine Simonian was still on her knees, as if in prayer. Now she let her arms fall slowly and leaned forward till she rested on her hands, like a caged beast. "My shame?" she said. "Oh no. To hide *yours*, you mean!"

Impatiently the wardress dropped the hat on her skull, but Janine tore it off and hurled it at the official. "No! Let them see what you've done to me. Let them see me as I am!"

"That will be the purpose of your trial," said the official, retrieving the hat. "Now, if you please, madame."

She screamed as the wardress twisted her arms behind her and locked them together with handcuffs so tight that they crushed the delicate wristbones beneath the emaciated flesh.

"Now, on your feet," said the wardress, ramming the hat down over her brow with brutal force. "And follow the nice man, though it's a waste of time and money, if you ask me. Straight out and shot, that's the way for your kind. I don't know how they missed you."

"Keep your mouth shut, woman," ordered the court officer. "You're a government employee. Show some respect for the law."

The wardress glared resentfully.

She got her revenge twenty minutes later, as they paused outside the courtroom. Janine suddenly lunged her head at the door jamb. She gave her skull a sickening crack, but she dislodged the hat. The official stooped to pick it up, and before he could retrieve it the wardress had pushed Janine through the doorway.

From the crowded public benches, voices rose in a ripple of expectancy, surged momentarily into a chorus of abuse, then almost instantly faded into an uneasy silence.

They had been expecting to see a woman they could hate. Instead they found themselves looking at a creature whose pale face, eroded by hunger and cold, was completely dehumanized by the high, narrow dome of the shaven skull. In the six months since the first punitive shaving, her head had been razored three times more, as an anti-vermin measure. Now the shadow of regrowing hair, and the scars and sores where the razor had been wielded with deliberate savagery, gave her skull the look of a dead planet. Even the jury, selected for their unblemished Resistance records, looked uneasy.

Janine, indifferent to their reaction, fixed her gaze on the single presiding judge and cried, "Please, your honour, I don't care what you do to me, but if you have any news of my children, please tell me. Surely I've a right to know, a mother's right?"

For a moment the plea touched almost every heart, but at the same time it made her human again and therefore vulnerable, and they had come to wound. "Probably the little bastards've gone back to Berlin with their dad!" a voice called out.

Eager for release from the confusing sympathy that they were feeling, the majority of those present burst into laughter. But this died away as a man on the witness bench leaped to his feet and cried angrily, "Take that back! The father of this whore's children was a hero and a patriot. Don't slander him or his children. He couldn't help his wife, and they can't help their mother."

Again the courtroom was reduced to silence under the contemptuous gaze of the speaker, a man of about thirty with a face almost as pale and intense as the prisoner's. On the breast of his smart black business suit he wore the ribbons of the Médaille de la Résistance and the Croix de l'Ordre de la Libération.

This time the judge, a grey-faced, tired man of perhaps fifty, broke the silence. "Monsieur Valois," he said, "we are delighted to see you restored to health, and honoured to have you in court, particularly as your testimony is, I understand, essential to the prosecution of the case. However, you must remember that during the course of this trial you are as much subject to the discipline of our country's laws as the prisoner herself. Therefore I would respectfully ask that you offer your testimony in due order and form."

Christian Valois sat down slowly and the judge let his weary gaze move over the public benches. He had lost count of how many of these cases he had had to deal with since the Courts of Justice had finally creaked into operation here in Paris last October. Justice required that those who had betrayed their country's trust should be brought to account, and the people demanded it. But it was well for the people to know too that the days when the Resistance wrote its own laws were past.

Satisfied that his point was made, he said, "Now, let us proceed."

In an intense silence, the charges were read: "Janine Simonian, born Crozier, you are accused that between a date unknown in 1940 and the time of your arrest in August 1944 you gave aid and comfort to the illegal occupying forces of the German army; that during this same period you acted as a paid informant of the secret intelligence agencies of the said forces; that you provided the enemies of your country with information likely to assist them in defeating operations and arresting members of the Resistance; and, more specifically, that you revealed to Captain Mai, counterintelligence officer of the German *Abwehr*, details of a meeting held in June 1944; and that as a result of this betrayal the meeting was raided, several *résistants* were captured, tortured and deported, and your own husband, Jean-Paul Simonian, was brutally murdered."

The official reading the charges paused, and the spectators filled the pause with a great howl of hatred.

"Janine Simonian, how do you plead? Guilty or not guilty?"

She looked slowly round the room as if searching for someone.

Finally her eyes came to rest on the pale, drawn features of the man called Christian Valois. He would remember, as she did so clearly, the way it had all begun.

PART ONE   June - December 1940

1

The poplar-lined road ran arrow-straight from north to south. At dawn it was empty. The rising sun barred its white surface with the poplars' shadows so that it lay like an eloper's ladder against the ripening walls of corn.

Then a car passed down it, fast. A few minutes later there was another. Both had their roof racks piled high with luggage.

The sun climbed higher, grew hotter. By ten there was a steady stream of southbound traffic. By eleven it had slowed to a crawl.

It no longer consisted solely of cars. There were trucks, buses, taxis; horse-drawn carts and pony-drawn traps; people on foot pushing hand-carts, prams and trolleys; men, women and children and babes in arms; soldiers in blue, priests in black, ladies in high heels, peasants in sabots; and animals too.

By midday the stream was almost static, setting up a long ribbon of heat haze which outshimmered that which rose above the ripening corn. Cars broke down and were quickly pushed into the ditch by those behind. Janine Simonian sat in her tiny Renault, terrified that this would soon be her fate. She glanced at her two small children and tried to smile reassuringly. Then she returned her gaze to the dark green truck ahead of her and concentrated on its tailboard, as if by will alone she hoped to be towed along in its wake.

Her lips moved in prayer. She'd done a lot of praying in the past few weeks. So far it hadn't worked at all.

THERE WERE FOUR of the green trucks, still nose to tail as they had been since they set off from Fresnes prison.

In the first of them, unbeknown to Janine, sat her cousin, Michel Boucher. It was to his sister, Mireille, living in what seemed like the pastoral safety of the Ain region east of Lyon, that Janine was fleeing.

Boucher himself wasn't fleeing anywhere. Rattling his handcuffs behind him he said, "Hey, do we have to have these things on? If them Stukas come, we're sitting ducks."

"Shut up," commanded the warder.

"Know what this lot looks like?" said another prisoner, a thin bespectacled man called Pajou. "A military convoy, that's what. Just the kind of target Stukas like. We'd be better off walking."

"You think your mates would be able to spot you then, at a couple of hundred miles an hour, Pajou?" said the warder viciously. "No, my lad, you'll be getting your Iron Cross posthumously if the Boche come!"

Pajou looked indignant. He'd been a charge hand at a munitions factory near Metz. A year before, he had been sentenced to eight years for passing information about production schedules to German military intelligence. He had always loudly protested his innocence.

Before he could do so now, Boucher rattled his handcuffs again and pleaded, "Come on, chief, you know it's not right. If them Stukas come, we're staked out for execution."

The warder opened his mouth to reply, but before he could speak Pajou cried, "Listen! Look!"

Two black spots expanded like ink stains in the clear blue sky, in a crescendo of screaming engines; then came the hammering of guns, the blossoming of explosions; and the long straight river of refugees fountained sideways into the poplar-lined ditches, as the Stukas ran a blade of burning metal along the narrow road.

Boucher saw bullets ripping into the truck behind as he dived over the side. With no protection from his arms he fell awkwardly, crashing down on one shoulder and rolling over and over. Then he lay half stunned.

All round him he heard cries and moans. How long he lay there he did not know, but it was that other sound, heard only once but now so familiar, that roused him. The Stukas were returning.

Staggering to his feet he plunged deeper into the field which lay beyond the roadside ditch. What crop it held he could not say, being a Parisian. But the sea of green and gold stems gave at least the illusion of protection.

Rising again, he found he was looking into Pajou's pallid face. The man's spectacles were awry and one lens was cracked, but an elastic band round his head had kept them in place.

"You all right, Miche?" Pajou asked.

"Yeah."

"What now?"

Why the man should offer him the leadership, Boucher did not know. He hardly knew Pajou and didn't care for what he did know. Robbing the rich was one thing, betraying your country quite another. But he knew people often deferred to him simply because of his appearance. Over six foot tall, titian-haired, he had the kind of piratical good looks which promised adventure. Also, if his easygoing manner made anyone doubt his capacity for violence, his sheer bulk inhibited them from testing it.

But Pajou's question was a good one. What now? Run till they found a friendly blacksmith who would cut off their handcuffs?

"Hold on," said Boucher. He retraced his steps to the roadside. Lying in the ditch, just as he had remembered, was the warder. There was no sign of a bullet wound, but the man was unconscious. Squatting down, Boucher undid the warder's belt, then fumbled along it till he came to the ring of keys. It slid off easily.

It took ten minutes, working back to back, to unlock the cuffs from Pajou's wrists, two seconds then to release Boucher.

Released, Pajou was a different man, confident of purpose. "Come on," he said, massaging his wrists.

"Where to, for God's sake?"

"Back to Paris, of course," said Pajou in surprise. "With the Germans in Paris, the war's over."

"Tell that to them back there," said Boucher, curtly gesturing towards the casualties on the road.

"They should've stayed at home," said Pajou. "There'll be no fighting in Paris, you'll see. Once the peace starts, it'll be a German city."

Boucher considered the idea. He didn't much like it. "All the more reason to be somewhere else," he growled.

"You think so?" said Pajou. "I think there'll be work to do, money to be made. Stick with me, Miche. The *Abwehr* will be recruiting likely lads with the right qualities, and they're bloody generous, believe me!"

"So you *did* work for them," said Boucher in disgust.

"It didn't harm anybody," said Pajou. "If anything, it probably saved a few lives. The Boche were coming anyway. Whatever helped them get things over with quickest was best for us, I say. It's them military men who went on about the Maginot Line that should've been locked up. We must've been mad to pay heed to a pathetic old man like Pétain ..."

Boucher seized him by his shirtfront and lifted him up till they were eye to eye. "Careful what you say about the marshal, friend," he growled. "He's the greatest man in France, maybe the greatest since Napoleon."

"All right, all right," said Pajou, "he's the greatest. Come on, Miche, let's not quarrel. Like I say, stick with me, and we'll be all right. What's the difference between robbing the Boche and robbing our own lot? What do you say?"

For answer Boucher flung the smaller man to the ground and glowered down at him. "Go and work for the Boche, you traitor. I'll stick to honest thieving. I may be a crook, but at least I'm a French crook! Go on, get out of my sight, before I do something I probably won't be sorry for!"

"Please yourself, friend," said Pajou, scrambling out of harm's way. "If you change your mind, you know how to find me! See you, Miche."

He got to his feet, and next moment he was gone.

Michel Boucher sat alone by the field of waving cereal. It was peaceful here, but it was no place for him. He was a creature of the city, the city of Paris. Pajou had been right in that at least. There was nowhere else to go.

The difference was that he would return a Frenchman, ready to resist in every way possible the hated occupiers. Feeling noble, he rose to his feet and, ignoring the path trampled by Pajou, began to forge his own way northwards through the ripening corn.

JANINE SIMONIAN had dived into the ditch on the other side of the road as the Stukas made their first pass. Like her cousin, Michel Boucher, she had no arm free to cushion her fall. The left clutched her two-year-old daughter, Cécile, to her breast; the right was bound tight round her five-year-old son, Pauli. They lay quite still, hardly daring to breathe. Finally the little girl began to cry. The boy tried to pull himself free, eager to view the vanishing planes.

"Pauli! Lie still! They may come back!" urged his mother.

"Maman, why do we have to go to Lyon?" asked Pauli.

"Because we'll be safe down there," said Janine. "We'll stay with your Aunt Mireille and Uncle Lucien. They've got a farm way out in the country. We'll be safe there."

"Why won't we be safe in Paris?" asked the boy.

"Because the Germans are in Paris," answered his mother.

"But Gramma and Granpa stayed, didn't they? And Bubbah Sophie."

"Yes, but Granpa and Gramma have to look after their shop."

People were beginning to return to the road. There didn't seem to have been any casualties in this section of the long procession, though from behind and ahead drifted cries of grief and pain.

Pauli rose and took a couple of steps onto the road, where he stood shading his eyes against the sun. "They *are* coming back," he said in his quiet, serious voice.

Janine was busy comforting her daughter, and it took a couple of seconds for her to realize what he meant.

"Pauli!" she screamed, but her voice was already lost in the first explosion of a stick of bombs only a couple of hundred metres ahead, and the blast from the next bowled her over back into the ditch.

Then the screaming engines were fading once more.

"Pauli!" she cried, eyes trying to pierce the smoke and dust which enveloped the road, heart fearful of what she would see when she did.

"Yes, Maman," said the boy's voice from behind her.

She turned. Her son, looking slightly surprised, was sitting in the cornfield. "It flew me through the air, Maman," he said in wonderment. "Like the man at the circus. Did you see me?"

"Oh Pauli, are you all right?"

He rose and came to her. He appeared unscathed. Céci was crying again and the boy said gravely, "Let me hold her, Maman."

Janine passed Céci over. She often reacted better to the soothing noises made by her brother than to her mother's ministrations.

Turning once more to the road, Janine took a couple of steps towards the car. Now the smoke cleared a little. The bomb must have landed on the far side of the road. There was a small crater in the cornfield and a couple of poplars were badly scarred.

"Quickly, Pauli, bring Céci. Get into the car!" she shouted.

"I think it's broken," said the boy.

He was right. A fragment of metal had been driven straight through the engine. There was a strong smell of petrol. It was amazing that the whole thing hadn't gone up in flames.

Opening the car door she pulled two suitcases onto the road. She doubted if the long procession of refugees would ever get moving again. If it did, it was clear her car was not going to be part of it.

"Pauli, take Céci into the field!"

"Are we going back home, Maman?" she asked.

"Yes. I think so," she said wearily.

"Will Papa be there?"

"I don't think so, Pauli. Not yet."

If there had been the faintest gleam of hope that Jean-Paul would return to Paris before the Germans came, she could never have left. But the children's safety had seemed imperative.

She looked at the bomb craters. So this was safety! And in common with many others who had found a despair beyond terror, she set off with her family, back the way they had come.

2

Under the Arc de Triomphe, a cat warmed herself at the Eternal Flame. Then, deciding that the air on this fine June morning was now balmy enough to be enjoyed by a sensitive lady, she set off down the Champs-Elysées. Sometimes she sat in the middle of the road and washed herself. Sometimes she wandered from one pavement to the other, hoping to find tasty scraps beneath the café tables. But no one had eaten here for at least two days. Finally she decided that she'd better start fending for herself, and bounded away among the chestnut trees where the beat of a bird's wing was the first sign of life she'd seen since sunrise.

Christian Valois too was reduced to getting his own breakfast, in his family's spacious apartment in Passy. Four days earlier the government had packed its bags, personal and diplomatic, and made off to Bordeaux. With them had gone Valois's parents, his young sister, Marie-Rose, and the maid-of-all-work. Léon Valois was a member of the Chamber of Deputies and a fervent supporter of Pétain. A lawyer by training, he reckoned there weren't many things, including wars, which couldn't be negotiated to a satisfactory compromise. His son, though a civil servant in the Ministry of Finance, was a romantic. To him the move to Bordeaux was a cowardly flight. He refused to leave Paris. Neither his father's arguments nor his mother's hysterics could move him. Only Marie-Rose's tears touched his heart, but they couldn't melt his resolve.

At work, his superior had simply smiled wearily and said, "Try not to spill too much blood on my office carpet."

For three days Christian Valois had conscientiously gone to work, even though he had nothing to do and no one for company. The ministry occupied part of the great palace of the Louvre. What was happening in the museum he did not know, but in his section, overlooking the Rue de Rivoli, it was eerily quiet, both inside and out. This morning, as he arrived at the Louvre, the thought of his silent dusty room revolted him, and his feet took him with little resistance down towards the river.

Was he merely a fool? Christian asked himself moodily as he strolled along. Perhaps his father was right: with the army in flight, the time for heroics was past. It was time for the negotiators to save what they could from the debacle. Perhaps the Germans wouldn't even bother to send their army into Paris. Perhaps as an ultimate act of scorn they would occupy the city with a busload of clerks!

At least I should feel at home then, he told himself bitterly.

He crossed to the Ile de la Cité. When he reached the Pont du Change he headed for the right bank again, half resolved that he would waste no more time on this foolishness. If he truly wanted to be a hero he should have fled, not to Bordeaux but to England, and looked for a chance to fight instead of merely making gestures.

So rapt was he that his feet were walking in time with the noise before his mind acknowledged it. It was the crash of marching feet, powerful and assured, striking sparks off the paving stones as if they made an electrical connection between conquerors and conquered. He stopped and leaned against the low parapet of the bridge.

Suddenly he could see as well as hear them, and the reality was devastating. In columns of three they were striding towards him, trio after trio of strong young men, their faces beneath their heavy helmets grave with victory. Past him they strode with never a sideways look. He turned to follow their progress, saw the leaders halt before the Palais de Justice, saw them turn to face it, saw the great gates swing open and the gendarme on duty stand aside as the first Germans entered.

It was essential he should be at his desk. He walked as fast as he could without breaking into an undignified trot which might be mistaken for fear. By the time he reached the Louvre the Rue de Rivoli had come to life, but what a life! No colourful drift of shoppers and tourists, but a rumbling, roaring procession of trucks and tanks and cars and motor-cycles; and above all, of marching men, an endless stream of grey, like ash-flaked lava flowing through the streets of Pompeii.

Seated at last at his desk, he realized he was shaking. Minutes passed, perhaps an hour.

Suddenly, without hearing anything, he knew they were in the building. He'd grown used to its emptiness, its sense of sleeping space.

Noise soon confirmed his intuition. Footsteps: steel on marble; regular, swift, certain.

He tried to control the trembling in his body, but couldn't, and prayed, not out of fear but shame, that they would not find him.

But now the footsteps were close. Doors opening and shutting. And at last, his. In that self-same moment the trembling stopped.

It was the young soldier who looked in who showed shock at his discovery, clearly taken aback to find anyone there.

"Yes?" said Valois testily.

The soldier levelled his rifle, turned his head and called, "Sir! Here's someone!"

More footsteps, then a middle-aged officer came into the room, pushing the soldier's rifle aside with irritation.

"Who the hell are you?" he said, in execrable French.

"Valois. Junior Secretary, Ministry of Finance."

"Ministry of Finance, eh? Don't suppose you keep any money here, though!" the man laughed.

Valois did not reply.

"All right. Don't go away. Someone may want to talk to you."

Turning to the soldier, the man commanded, "Stay on guard outside!"

The soldier left. The officer gave a mock salute. "Carry on with your work, Monsieur Valois," he said, smiling. Then he was gone.

Valois slowly relaxed. The trembling was starting again, but less violently now. He felt a sudden surge of exultation through his body. He had seen the enemy face to face and had not flinched.

But best of all, he had felt such a powerful hatred that it must surely spring from a reservoir deep enough to sustain him through the long, bitter and dangerous struggle that lay ahead. He'd been right not to flee to Bordeaux, or even England. Here was where the real resistance to the Boche would start. Whatever the future held for France, the worst it could hold for Christian Valois was a hero's death.

3

There was no getting away from it, thought Günter Mai. Even for an *Abwehr* lieutenant who was more likely to see back alleys than front lines, it was nice to be a conqueror. Nice to be here in this lovely city, in this elegant bedroom in the luxurious Hotel Lutétia which for the next five? ten? twenty? years would be the headquarters of military intelligence in

Paris. He gazed out across the sun-gilt rooftops to the distant Eiffel Tower and saluted with his pipe. "Thank you, Paris," he said.

Behind him someone coughed, and when he turned he saw it was his section head, Major Bruno Zeller.

"Good morning, Günter," said the elegant young man. "I missed you at breakfast. Can my keeper be ill? I asked myself."

"Morning, sir. I wasn't too hungry after last night's celebrations."

"You mean you *ate* as well as drank?" said Zeller, lounging gracefully in a chair. "You amaze me. Now tell me, do you recall a man called Pajou?"

Mai's round, amiable face lengthened into a scowl. A hangover reduced his Zeller-tolerance dramatically, although he had long got over the irritation of having to "sir" someone several years his junior. Such things happened, particularly if you were the son of a mere customs officer in Offenburg and "sir" was heir to some turreted castle overhanging the Rhine.

"Pajou. Now, let me see," said Mai. Yes, of course, he remembered him well. But it suited him to play the game at his own speed. From his dressing table he took a thick black book. It was an old *Hitler Jugend Tagebuch* which he'd never found any use for till he started in intelligence work. Now, filled with minuscule writing, it was the repository of all he knew.

He saw Zeller's long, manicured fingers beat an impatient tattoo on the arm of the chair. The movement caught the light on his heavy silver signet ring, reminding Mai of another source of irritation. The ring bore the family's heraldic device, a zed crossed by a hunting horn. On first noticing it, Mai had remarked unthinkingly that he had seen a similar device on some brass buttons on a coat belonging to his grandfather. Zeller had returned from his next visit home with the news that there had once been an underkeeper called Mai working on the Zeller family's Black Forest estate, till he'd gone off to Offenburg to better himself. "And here's his grandson, still working for the family in a manner of speaking! Strange how these things work out, eh, Günter?"

Thereafter he often jokingly referred to Mai as "my keeper". Mai took it all in good part—except when he had a hangover. Basically he liked the young major.

He began to read from the book: "Pajou, Alphonse. Worked for the National Armaments Company. I recruited him in Metz in thirty-eight. No political commitment, in it purely for the money. Jailed just before the war. So, what about him?"

"It seems he got an early release, and would like to re-enter our employ. He's not very trusting, however. The duty sergeant says he insisted on dealing with you when he rang earlier this morning."

"Why didn't he put the call through, then?" asked Mai.

"The sergeant says that you left instructions last night that you weren't to be disturbed by anything less than a call from the Führer."

Mai grimaced behind a puff of smoke. "Look, sir, I'm not sure Pajou's the kind of man we want just now. He's a nasty piece of work, and he's not even a native Parisian. What we ought to be doing now, before the first shock fades, is establishing a network of nice ordinary citizens who'll feed us with intelligence just for the sake of reassurance that the dreadful Hun is a nice ordinary chap like themselves."

"Clever thinking, Günter. But in the end we'll doubtless need the nasties, so we might as well recruit Pajou now. If we don't, no doubt the SD will when they arrive."

The *Sicherheitsdienst* was the chief Nazi intelligence-gathering service, closely allied to the SS. With France under military control, the SD ought not yet to have a presence, let alone a function.

"*When!*" said Mai. "I heard the bastards are already settling in at the Hôtel du Louvre. And I'm sure I saw Fiebelkorn in the restaurant last night—in civvies, of course, not his fancy SS colonel's uniform."

"Let's hope it was a drunken delusion," said Zeller with a shudder.

"One thing's certain. If they've started showing their faces, it means the fighting's definitely over. Right, sir, I'll talk to Pajou if he rings back."

"No, you'll talk to him face to face," said Zeller, rising from his chair. "He left word that he would look for you by the Medici fountain at ten thirty this morning. Let me know how you get on."

With a smile and a salute, Zeller left.

Mai had been looking forward to his favourite hangover cure of sweet black coffee and half a dozen croissants, but it wasn't worth the risk of irritating Zeller.

He clattered through the lobby of the hotel trying to look brisk and businesslike, but once out into the gentle morning sunlight he slowed to strolling pace, taking deep breaths of the rich, enchanted air. Pajou could wait. What was more, he *would* wait. He wasn't selling information today, he was applying for a job!

Half guided by memory, Mai wandered into the Rue d'Assas. It ought to lead him roughly towards the Luxembourg gardens.

Eventually he reached a narrow crossroads, and looking left he could see down to the gardens. But his nose was turning him away to the right, and he followed it along the narrow street till his eyes could identify the source of the rich, warm smell.

It was a baker's shop, not very big, but dignified by the words *Boulangerie Pâtisserie* above the windows, in ornate lettering. On the glass of the door was engraved "*Crozier Père et Fils depuis 1870*" underlined by a triangle of curlicues. The shop window was fairly bare, but the smell of baking was rich and strong.

Mai pushed open the door and went in. There was one customer, one of those Frenchwomen of anything between fifty and a hundred who wear black clothes of almost Muslim inclusiveness. She was being served by a stout woman in middle age with the kind of flesh that looked, not unfittingly, as if it had been moulded from well-kneaded dough.

The black-swathed customer looked in alarm at Mai's uniform, said abruptly, "Good morning, Madame Crozier," and left.

"Good morning, Madame Duval," the stout woman called after her. She turned to Mai. "Monsieur?" Her attempt at sangfroid failed miserably.

He set about allaying her fears. "Madame," he said in his rolling Alsatian French, "I have been drawn here by the delectable odours of your superb baking. I would deem it an honour if you would allow me to purchase a few of your croissants." The woman's doughy features stretched into a simper. "Claude!" she shouted.

The door behind her opened, admitting a great blast of mouth-watering warmth and a man cast in the same mould as his wife. When he saw Mai his face, which would have made him a fortune in the silent movies, registered fearful amazement.

"Good day, monsieur," said Mai. "I was just telling your wife how irresistible I found the smell of your baking."

"Claude, are there any more croissants? The officer wants croissants," said Madame Crozier peremptorily.

"No, I'm sorry..."

"Well, make some, Claude," she commanded. "If the officer would care to wait, it will only take a moment."

The man went back into the kitchen and the woman brought Mai a chair. As she returned to the counter the door burst open. A good-looking woman of about twenty-five with dishevelled fair hair and a pale face rushed in. She was carrying a child of about two and at her heels was a boy a few years older.

"Janine!" exclaimed the woman. "What are you doing back? Why aren't you in Lyon? Oh, the poor baby! Is she ill?"

The little girl had begun to cry. Madame Crozier reached over the counter and took her in her arms with much cooing.

"No, she's just hungry," said the young woman, then broke off abruptly as she noticed Mai sitting quietly in the corner.

Mai got to his feet. "I'm sorry, madame," he said. "Please do not let me disturb this reunion."

"No, wait," cried Madame Crozier. "Claude! Where are those croissants?"

"They're coming, they're coming!" was the reply, followed almost immediately by the opening of the bakehouse door. Once again Mai had the pleasure of seeing that cinematic amazement.

"Janine!" cried Crozier. "What're you doing here? Why've you come back?"

"Because the Boche dropped bombs and fired bullets at everyone on the road," cried Janine vehemently. "They could see we were a real menace. Men, women, children, animals, all running south in terror."

Sighing, Mai put on his cap. Not even the best croissants in the world were worth this bother.

"But you're not hurt, are you? Claude, the officer's croissants!"

The man put the croissants in a bag and handed it to Mai, who reached into his pocket. The woman said, "No, no. Please, you can pay next time."

A good saleswoman, thought Mai approvingly. Ready to risk a little for goodwill and the prospect of a returning customer. The young woman was regarding him with unconcealed hostility. As he took the croissants he clicked his heels and made a little bow, just as Major Zeller would have done. She might as well have her money's worth.

He left the shop, pausing in the doorway as if deciding which way to go. Behind him he heard the older woman say, "Oh, look at the poor children, they're like little gipsies. And you're not much better, Janine."

"Mother, we've been walking for days! We slept in a barn for two nights. Has there been any news of Jean-Paul?"

"No, nothing. Now come and sit down and have something to eat."

Mai left, smiling but thoughtful. These French! Some of his masters believed that they could be brought into active partnership with their conquerors. With the baker and his wife it might be possible. Offer them a fair armistice and business as usual; yes, they might grumble, but only as they grumbled at their own authorities. They'd cooperate.

But alas, not all the French were like Monsieur and Madame Crozier. Take that girl, so young, so childlike, but at the same time so fierce!

He turned left at the *bassin* in the Luxembourg gardens. As he skirted the lush green lawn before the palace, he saw two German soldiers on guard duty. They were looking towards him and he remembered he was still in uniform. The sooner he got out of it the better. One of the joys of being an *Abwehr* officer was the excuse it gave for frequently wearing civilian clothes. The sentries offered a salute. He returned it, realized he was still clutching a croissant, grinned ruefully and bore right towards the Medici fountain.

Slowly he made his way alongside the urn-flanked length of water to take a closer look at the sculpture. In the centre of three niches a fierce-looking bronze fellow loomed threateningly above a couple of naked youngsters in white marble. Us and the French! he told himself, crumbling the croissant for the goldfish.

A hand squeezed his elbow. He started, turned and saw a thin bespectacled man showing discoloured teeth in a smile which was at once impudent and ingratiating.

"Hello, Lieutenant. Didn't use to be able to creep up on you like that!"

"Hello, Pajou," said Mai coldly.

"I was really glad when I realized you were in town, Lieutenant. That

Mai's a man I can trust, a man I can talk to, I thought. So here I am, reporting for duty. Do you think you can use me?"

Mai returned his gaze to the sculpture.

"Yes, Pajou," he sighed. "I very much fear we can."

4

Sophie Simonian was praying for her son when a knock at the door and a voice calling, "Bubbah Sophie, it's me, Janine," made her hope for a second that her prayers had been answered.

Leaning heavily on a silver-topped cane, she went to the door, opened it, and saw at once that there was no good news in her daughter-in-law's face. On the other hand, there was no bad news either, thanks be to God for small mercies.

"Bubbah, how are you? You look well," said Janine, embracing her. "Is there any news of Jean-Paul?"

"Nothing. No news at all. Sit down, my dear. Where are the children?" In sudden alarm she added, "There is nothing wrong with them? Why are you back in Paris?"

"No, they're fine, really. I'll bring them round soon. But I thought I'd come myself first so we can have a good talk."

Quickly she described her abortive flight, her slow return. Unlike her parents, her mother-in-law had approved her decision to leave, though refusing Janine's offer to take her too. Nearly seventy, with an arthritic knee, a return on foot would have been quite beyond her. Besides, she'd done her share of being a refugee almost forty years before, after the great pogrom of 1903 in Kishinev, in Russia. France had offered a new life in every sense. It was here in Paris that she had given birth to a son. Iakov Moseich he was named, after his father, and Jean-Paul, to tell the world he was a native-born Frenchman.

Her husband had died of a heart attack in 1932. Jean-Paul had wanted to abandon his university place and get a job so as to look after his mother. She had told him scornfully that it was time to start acting like a real Frenchman and not a joke-book Jewish son.

He certainly took her at her word, she later told herself ironically. During the next few years he abandoned his religion, declared himself an atheist, flirted with the Communist Party, and announced that he was going to marry Janine Crozier. This last was perhaps the biggest shock of all. Some left-wing intellectual *shiksa* from the university she could have understood. But this wide-eyed child of parents whose attitudes were as offensive to his new political religion as to his old racial one, was a complete surprise.

When she asked, "Why? *Why* do you want to marry this child? She isn't even pregnant!" he had given her the only reply which could silence her: "Because whenever I see her, I feel happy."

Six years and two grandchildren later, Sophie was completely converted, and during this trying time she had derived much comfort from her daughter-in-law.

As Janine finished her tale, there was a knock at the door and a man's voice called reassuringly, "It's only me, Madame Simonian. Christian."

Janine opened the door. Christian Valois was standing there, with a ginger cat in his arms.

"Janine!" he said. "Is there news?"

Janine shook her head. "No. Nothing. Hello, Charlot, you're fatter than ever!"

The cat purred as she scratched him, and then jumped out of Valois's arms and bounced onto Sophie's lap.

"You've heard nothing either, madame?" said Valois, kissing the old lady. "Why doesn't he write to one of us?"

His voice was full of concern, which slightly irritated Janine. True, he was an old friend of Jean-Paul's, but this hardly entitled him to put his concern on a level with that of a wife or a mother.

"We are going to have some tea, Christian. Will you stay?" said Sophie.

"Just for a moment. I have to get back."

"Back where?" asked Janine in surprise. "Surely there is no work for you to do. I thought everyone in the government had run off to Bordeaux?"

"I stayed," said Valois shortly. In fact, his gesture in staying on at the ministry was proving rather a strain. It hadn't taken the Germans long to realize that he had neither authority nor function.

"That was brave," said Janine sincerely.

Valois's thin sallow face flushed. "Thank you."

As they drank their tea, Janine told her story once more. Valois frowned as she told of the German planes attacking the refugee column.

"It's war," said Sophie. "What do you expect? Stopping the war is the only way to stop the killing."

"Only the war will not stop, will it?" said Valois.

"But the marshal is talking with the Germans about a truce," cried Janine. "It was on the wireless."

"Truce? Defeat, you mean. Is that what you want?" demanded Valois.

"No! I mean, I don't know. I hate the Germans, I want to see them thrown out of France. But the only way for Jean-Paul to be safe is for the fighting to stop! I mean, it's stupid, he's out there on the Maginot Line and all the Germans are here in France behind him! I mean, it's just so stupid!" She was close to tears. Sophie put her arm round her and frowned accusingly at Valois.

"I'm sorry," he said. "You know I'm worried about Jean-Paul too.

Listen, there will be a truce, something like that, I'm sure. He'll be safe. But that's not what I mean when I say the war won't end. De Gaulle's going to England. I heard him on the British radio saying that he would fight on no matter what happened here."

"De Gaulle? Who's he?" asked Janine.

"He's a general, a friend of the marshal's."

"But the marshal wants a truce, doesn't he?"

"That's right."

"Everyone says the Boche will be in England soon too. There's nothing to stop them. What does this de Gaulle do then? Go to America?" asked Janine scornfully.

"At least there's someone out there who's not giving up," said Valois. He finished his tea and stood up. Janine saw his gaze drift round the room, coming to rest on the large silver seven-branched candelabrum on the windowsill.

"Are the other apartments still occupied?" he asked casually.

Sophie said, "A lot of people went. They'll be back when it's safe, no doubt. Madame Nomary, the concierge, is still in the basement. And Monsieur Melchior is still upstairs."

"Melchior?"

"You must have seen him," said Janine. "The writer. Or artist. Or something like that. At least, he dresses that way. You know, flamboyantly. I think he's..."

"He likes the men more than the ladies is what she doesn't care to say in front of silly old Bubbah," mocked Sophie. "But he's a gentleman and very quiet, especially since the war. I think he's been hiding up there, poor soul. Why so interested in my neighbours, Christian?"

"No reason. I must go, Madame Sophie. Take care."

"I'd better go too, and rescue my mother from the kids," said Janine, jumping up. "Bye, Bubbah. I'll bring Pauli and Céci next time."

"Be sure you do, child. God go with you both."

Outside in the Rue de Thorigny they walked in silence. Finally Janine said, "What's worrying you about Sophie, Christian?"

He shot her a surprised glance, then said, "I thought I was a better actor! I was just wondering how I could suggest that it might be politic not to, well, advertise her Jewishness. You must have heard how the Boche treat Jews. Some of the stories..."

"But that's in Germany," protested Janine. "They wouldn't dare do anything here, not to Frenchmen. The people wouldn't let it happen!"

"I hope so," he said doubtfully.

"I'm glad you didn't say anything to worry Bubbah."

"It wasn't just her I was concerned about," said Christian gently.

"Me? Why should it worry ... oh, my God. Jean-Paul, you mean? If they capture Jean-Paul..." She stood stricken.

"I'm sorry," he said. "It probably won't happen. And he'll be a prisoner of war in any case, under the Geneva Convention. Where are you going?"

She'd set off at a pace that was more a trot than a walk. Looking back over her shoulder she cried, "I've got to get back to the children, see they're all right. Goodbye, Christian."

"Goodbye," he said. "I'll call . . ."

She was out of earshot. He walked on with his shoulders hunched, his head down, and did not see, or at least did not acknowledge seeing, the huge red and black swastika banners which fluttered everywhere, like prospectors' flags marking out what the Germans were claiming for their own.

5

"Hey kid, what's your name?"

Pauli looked up at the man who'd just appeared in the doorway of the little courtyard behind the bakery. He was big, with long red hair, a longer beard and a strong curved nose. He looked as if he'd been living rough, and as he moved nearer, Pauli realized he smelt that way too.

"Pauli," he said. "Well, Jean-Paul, really. But Maman calls me Pauli."

"Pauli, eh? Maman, you say? Would that be Janine?"

"Yes, that's Maman's name," said the boy.

"Well, I'll be blowed! And look at the size of you! Little Janine's boy! Well, I'm your Uncle Miche, Pauli. Not really your uncle, more your half-cousin, but uncle will do nicely till I've stood out in the rain long enough to shrink to your size."

This reversal of the usual adult clichés about growing up into a big boy amused and reassured Pauli. He stood his ground as the big man moved forward and rested a hand on his head. He noticed that this new and fascinating uncle did indeed seem to have been standing out in the rain. His shapeless grey trousers and black workman's jacket were damp.

Michel Boucher shivered. "Why don't we go inside and surprise Uncle Claude?" he said. "I bet it's nice and warm in the bakehouse!"

It was. There were two huge ovens, one on either side of the vaulted ochre-bricked building, and both were going full blast. Claude Crozier was removing a trayful of loaves from one of them to add to the morning's bake, already cooling on the long central table. Boucher looked at the regiments of bread with covetous eyes and said, "Morning, Uncle Claude. How's it been with you?"

The baker almost dropped his tray in surprise.

"Michel! What the blazes are you doing here?"

"Just passing, Uncle, and I thought I'd pay my respects."

"Kind of you, but just keep on passing, eh? Before your aunt sees you."

Crozier was not a hard man but his nephew was an old battle, long since lost. The baker had been more than generous in the help he gave his widowed sister to bring up her two children. But when, within the space of a year, she had died of TB, her daughter Mireille had married a farmer and Miche had got two years' juvenile detention for burglary, Louise broke her disapproving silence and said, "Enough's enough. Not a penny more of our hard-earned money goes to that ne'er-do-well."

Now here he was again.

"You can't stay," said Crozier urgently.

"Oh, I won't stay, Uncle," said Boucher. "Just long enough for a bite of breakfast, eh?"

The baker's consternation at this prospect changed to terror as the door to the shop opened and his wife came out. She stopped dead at the sight of Boucher.

"Morning, Auntie Lou," he called cheerfully. "Just dropped in to pay my respects. And have a bite of breakfast." He took a couple of steps nearer the tray of new-baked bread as he spoke.

"My God!" cried the woman, peering closely at him. "You're wet! You're dirty! You're unshaven! And you smell!" Her tone was triumphant as well as indignant. There were few pleasures dearer to her bourgeois heart than being justified in a fit of moral indignation.

"Yes, well, I've been down on my luck a bit," said Boucher.

Suddenly, Pauli moved forward to the table, picked up a roll and presented it to the man.

"Thanks, kid," he said, shedding crumbs with every syllable.

"Pauli, what are you doing! How dare you?" thundered Louise.

"Maman, what's going on? Why're you shouting at Pauli?" Janine, attracted by her mother's bellow, had appeared in the doorway.

"I just gave Uncle Miche a roll," explained the little boy tearfully.

"Hello, Cousin Janine. This is a good lad you've got here," said Boucher. He stuffed the rest of the roll into his mouth. "Delicious! Well, I'll be on my way. Don't want to outstay such a generous welcome. Cheers, kid." He patted Pauli on the head again and left.

Pauli ran to his mother and said, "Maman, he was all wet. He says he stands out in the rain to shrink."

"You'll have to do something about that boy," said Louise, annoyed at feeling in the wrong. "The sooner he gets off to school, the better."

Janine glared at her mother, then turned and ran back to the shop. A moment later they heard the street door open and shut.

Janine met her cousin as he came out of the passage which led into the rear yard. "Here," she said, stuffing a note into his hand. "It's not much, but I haven't got much."

"Thanks, cousin," he said, looking at the money.

"What *are* you doing, Miche?"

"I'm not sure," he said. "I thought somehow, when this lot started, I'd be fighting the Boche, slate wiped clean sort of thing. But the first flic who recognized me came charging after me waving handcuffs! So I've had to keep my head down. It's been a bit rough, but I'll get sorted sooner or later I don't doubt."

"Haven't you got anywhere to stay?" asked Janine sympathetically.

"No. Well, I was all right at first. I shacked up—I mean lodged—with an old friend. Arlette la Blonde, a dancer. Well, that was all right, only a few days back the club opened up again and well, late hours and that, it wasn't convenient, you know these show people . . ."

"You mean she brings friends back for the night and they don't care to find your head on the pillow already!"

"Yeah, that's it," he said, grinning. Then he stopped grinning. "I could have hung on there, only I found she was bringing back Krauts! That really got up my nose!"

"You won't have to be so choosy, Miche. Not now they're our friends."

"Friends? What do you mean?"

"Haven't you heard? An armistice was signed yesterday."

"Armistice? Signed by who? Not the marshal?"

"Yes," said Janine. "Pétain signed it. At Compiègne."

Boucher shook his head in bewilderment.

"Janine!" called her mother's voice from inside.

"I'd better go." She smiled, pecked his cheek and went in.

Boucher turned and walked away, not paying much attention to the direction. Despite his experiences, he'd gone on hoping that somewhere in this mess there was going to be a chance for redemption. But now it was over before it had really begun and he was still a wanted man.

He paused to take stock of his surroundings. He'd almost reached the Boulevard Raspail. There was a car coming towards him. It didn't look official, but any car you saw on the streets nowadays was likely to be official. He coughed, covering his face with his hand, just in case.

The car was slowing. It pulled in to the kerb just in front of him. His head still lowered, he quickened his pace as he went by. The car door suddenly opened. His legs tensed, ready to break into a run.

"Miche? Miche Boucher? It *is* you!"

He paused, glanced back, turned. "Bloody hell," he said. "Pajou."

6

Maurice Melchior carefully examined his black velvet jacket for dust or hairs. Satisfied, he slipped his slender arms into it, spent some time adjusting the angle of his fedora, then stood back from the mirror to get the total effect.

Stunning, was the verdict. He was at that ideal point in his thirties where youth still burned hot enough to melt the mature, and maturity already glowed brightly enough to dazzle the young.

He tripped, light as a dancer, down the rickety staircase. On the floor below he met Charlot, the ginger cat belonging to old Madame Simonian. Charlot wanted attention. It was hard to resist those appealing eyes, but, "Not when I'm wearing the black velvet, my dear," explained Melchior.

A few moments later he was out in the sunshine.

This was not the first time he had been out since the Boche came, but his previous expeditions had been furtive, at dusk, well wrapped up, to buy a few provisions and scuttle back to his lair. Really, a man of his sensibility should have fled as soon as the invasion became a certainty, but as usual he'd put off the decision till the sight of all those jostling refugees made it quite impossible.

And what had happened? Nothing! Life, he had gradually been reassured, was going on much as before for those courageous souls who had refused to be panicked into craven flight. Today he was going out in broad daylight, and not just round the corner to the grocer's shop. Today he was strolling south, heading for where he truly belonged. To the Left Bank! Saint-Germain-des-Prés!

After his first exhilaration at being back in his old haunts, a certain uneasiness began to steal over him. Everything was so quiet. Not many people about and next to no traffic, except for the odd German truck which still sent him diving into the nearest doorway. He found himself thinking of going home. Then he drew himself up to his full five feet seven inches and cried, "No!" Whatever this day brought forth, Maurice Melchior, intellectual, wit, not to mention homosexual and Jew, would be there to greet it.

Overcome with admiration for his own courage, he stepped unheeding off the pavement. There was a screech of brakes and a car slewed to a halt across the road. It didn't actually touch Melchior but sheer shock buckled his knees and he sat down. Out of the driver's window a man in a grey uniform began to shout at him in German.

"Be quiet," said an authoritative voice. "Monsieur, I hope you're not hurt."

Maurice Melchior looked up to see a Nordic god stooping over him with concern in his limpid blue eyes.

"My name is Zeller. Major Bruno Zeller. You must allow me to buy you a drink."

They went to a café on the Boulevard Saint-Michel where Melchior used to meet student friends. It was empty at the moment and the patron was delighted to have their custom, greeting Melchior by his name, a fact which seemed to impress the German.

"Yes. Melchior's my name! Magus that I am, bearing gifts of gold, from the East I come!"

It was a little verse from a nativity play with which he used occasionally to tease his Christian friends. Zeller laughed.

They spent the next hour chatting and Melchior idly reminisced about the past. His conversation was liberally laced with references to great figures of the worlds of art and literature. Nor was his familiarity altogether feigned. He'd been fluttering around the Left Bank too long not to have been accepted as a denizen.

Zeller was clearly impressed. Melchior soon had him placed as an intelligent and reasonably educated man, by German standards, but culturally adolescent. Paris was to him the artistic Mecca which held all that was most holy. He needed a guide.

"Major Zeller. I thought it was you." A black Mercedes had drawn in at the kerb close to their pavement table. A man was looking out of the open rear window. He had a florid face with watery eyes in which little black pupils glistened like beads of jet. Melchior felt something unpleasantly hypnotic in their gaze.

Perhaps Zeller felt it also for he rose with evident reluctance from his chair and went to the car. "Ah, Colonel Fiebelkorn. On leave? I hope you have long enough to take in all the sights."

Melchior recognized insolence when he heard it.

"The interesting ones." Fiebelkorn's cold eyes slipped to Melchior. "Why don't you introduce me to your friend, Major?"

"This is *Abwehr* business," said Zeller coldly. But Melchior came forward. He examined Fiebelkorn with interest. In his fifties, a powerful personality, he guessed. In the lapel of his civilian jacket he wore a tiny silver death's head. Too, too Gothic!

"Maurice Melchior," he said.

"Walter Fiebelkorn," said the German. "I'm glad the security of the Fatherland is in such safe hands, Major. Monsieur Melchior. Till we meet again."

As the car drew away, Melchior said testily, "Nice man."

"If you can think that, you're a fool."

"Oh dear. And that will never do if I'm to be a secret agent, will it?"

Zeller laughed and took his arm.

7

As autumn began, Pauli caught measles. Soon afterwards Céci went down with it too. It was a worrying time but at least it focused Janine's mind outwards from her daily increasing fears for Jean-Paul.

There were all kinds of rumours about French prisoners, the most popular being that now the war was over they'd be sent home. But the long trains had rolled eastwards since then, carrying millions into captivity, and only the sick and the maimed had returned.

At least most families with a missing man had learned if he were dead or alive. But Jean-Paul Simonian's name appeared on no list.

It was to her father that Janine turned for support. She had never forgotten the terrible look on her mother's face when she'd announced joyously that she and Jean-Paul were to be married. It had been her father then who had comforted her and made her understand just how many of his wife's prejudices had been roused in a single blow. By being an anti-clerical, intellectual, left-wing, Jewish student, Jean-Paul was offensive to her in every particular.

Louise Crozier's attitude to the Germans was soon another point of conflict.

"That nice lieutenant from the Lutétia was asking after the children this morning," said Madame Crozier one lunchtime.

"The fat Boche? What business is it of his?" said Janine.

"He was only being polite," retorted her mother. "Politeness never hurt anyone. He always comes in on pastry day and asks for three of your brioches. I told him you hadn't done any. He wasn't at all put out but asked, very concerned, how the children were. I think he's charming."

"He's a pig, like the rest of them," said Janine, who was tired and irritable. "I don't see why you encourage them to come into the shop."

"Don't talk stupid!" said her mother. "The war's over, so who's the enemy now? All right, the Germans are here in Paris, but they've behaved very correctly, you can't deny that. All that talk about burning and looting. Why, the streets are safer now than they've ever been!"

"How can you talk like that!" demanded Janine. "They've invaded our country. They nearly killed me and the kids. They've probably killed my husband. And you talk as if they've done us a favour by coming here!"

"Listen, my lady, we run a business here. We don't pick our customers, they pick us. And we don't have to like each other either. But I tell you this, there's a lot of our French customers I like a lot less than Lieutenant Mai."

"Maman," said Pauli at the door, "Céci's crying."

"Shall I go?" offered Louise.

"No thanks," said Janine, "she doesn't speak German yet." She left the room, pushing her son before her.

"She gets worse," said Madame Crozier angrily to her husband.

"It's a worrying time for her, what with the children being ill and no news of Jean-Paul," said Claude Crozier.

"If you ask me, she'll be better off if she never gets any news of him," said the woman. "It was a mistake from the start."

"He's a nice lad," said Crozier. "And there was never any fuss about religion. The children are being brought up good Catholics, aren't they?"

154

"That's no credit to him," replied Madame Crozier. "You can't respect a man who doesn't respect his own heritage, can you? There's someone come into the shop. Are you going to sit on your backside all day?"

With a sigh, Crozier rose and went through into the shop. A moment later he returned, followed by Christian Valois.

"Janine's upstairs with Céci," Crozier said. "I'll tell her you're here."

"Thank you. Hello, Madame Crozier."

"Hello, Christian," she said. "How are your charming parents?"

She'd never met them but knew that Valois senior was an important deputy.

"They are safe and well, madame," said Valois. "My father continues to look after the country's interests in Vichy." He spoke with a bitter irony which was lost on Madame Crozier.

Janine came in. "Christian, is there news?"

"Nothing, I'm afraid. But I've written to my father asking for help."

She turned away in disappointment. He looked at her with exasperation. Clearly she regarded his efforts on Jean-Paul's behalf as at best coldly bureaucratic, at worst impertinently intrusive. His sacrifice of pride and principle in writing to his father for assistance meant nothing to her. He said brusquely, "There's another matter."

"Yes?" said Janine indifferently.

"Perhaps, a word in private?"

"Come through into the shop," said Janine after a glance at her mother, who showed no sign of moving.

In the shop, Valois said, "Have you seen Madame Simonian lately?"

"Not for a while. I usually take the children on Sundays, but they've been ill. Why?"

"I went to see her earlier. The concierge said she'd just gone down to the greengrocer's so I went after her. I found her having an argument with a German sergeant who'd seen her pulling down the JEWISH BUSINESS poster the greengrocer had put in his window."

"What poster's that?" asked Janine.

"It's been decreed that all Jewish shopkeepers have to put up these posters. Fortunately the sergeant clearly thought there weren't many medals to be won for arresting an old woman who threatened him with a bunch of celery, so he was glad to let me smooth things over."

"Yes," she said, taking in his neat dark suit and his guarded bureaucratic expression. "You'd be good at that, Christian. Personally, I think you'd have done better to join in bashing the Boche with the celery. If we all did that, we'd soon get things back to normal!"

"All? Who are these *all?*" exclaimed Valois.

"People. You don't think any real Frenchman's going to sit back and let the Boche run our lives for us, do you?"

He said, "Janine, it's real Frenchmen who are putting their names to these decrees. I'll tell you something else that real Frenchmen have done. It's been *suggested* to publishing firms that they might care to do a voluntary purge of their lists, to get rid of unsuitable authors such as German exiles, French nationalists, and of course Jews. They've *all* agreed! No objections. Not one!"

"Oh, those are intellectuals with their heads in the clouds, or business-men with their noses in the trough," said Janine wearily. "It's the ordinary people I'm talking about. They won't let themselves be mucked around by these Boche, you'll see. But thanks for telling me about Sophie. I'll keep an eye on her."

Behind Valois the shop door opened and a German officer came in. He was a stocky fellow of indeterminate age with an ordinary kind of face, were it not for a certain shrewdness of gaze which made you think that every time he blinked, his eyes were registering photographs.

"Good day," he said. "I hope the children are improving. I was asking after them when I talked with your excellent mother earlier. I thought perhaps a few chocolates might tempt their appetites back to normal..."

He proffered a box of chocolates. Janine ignored it and glanced furiously at Valois. She was angry that after what she'd just been saying, the civil servant should see her on such apparently familiar terms with this Boche. Feeling herself close to explosion, she took a deep breath and said, "No thank you, Lieutenant. I don't think they will help."

"Oh," said Günter Mai, nonplussed.

He regarded her assessingly, placed the box carefully on the counter and said, "Forgive the intrusion. Perhaps you or your mother might enjoy them. You'll be doing me a favour." He patted his waistline ruefully, touched the peak of his cap in the shadow of a salute and brought his heels gently together in the echo of a click.

It was the gentle mockery of these gestures, plus the diplomatic courtesy with which he'd received her rejection, that finally triggered off the explosion. She pushed the chocolates back across the counter with such force that the box flew through the air, struck him on the chest and burst open, scattering its contents all over the floor.

"We don't want them, do you understand?" she shouted. "I can look after my own kids without any help from the likes of you."

The door from the living quarters burst open. "What's going on?" demanded Madame Crozier.

"It's nothing, madame. The young lady is upset. Just a little misunder-standing," said Mai.

"I've been telling your Boche friend a few home truths," cried Janine. "You talk to him if you want, Maman. I've had enough!"

She pushed her way past her mother and disappeared.

"Janine! Come back here!" commanded Madame Crozier. "Lieuten-ant, I'm so sorry, you must forgive her, she's overwrought. Excuse me."

156

She turned and went after her daughter. Soon angry voices drifted back into the shop where Mai and Valois stood looking at each other.

"And you are . . . ?" said Mai courteously.

"Valois. Of the Ministry of Finance."

"Ah. Not in Vichy, monsieur?"

"Finance remains in Paris."

"Of course. Good day, Monsieur Valois."

No salute or heel-clicking this time. Mai turned and left the shop. Christian Valois went to the door and watched him stroll slowly along the pavement. His back presented an easy target. With a shock of self-recognition, Valois found himself imagining pulling out a gun and pumping bullets into that hated uniform. But if he had a gun would he have the nerve to use it?

Behind him, Louise Crozier re-entered, her face pink with emotion. She sank to her knees and began collecting chocolates. Janine came in. Ignoring her mother, she said, "Christian, no need to worry about Sophie. Soon as the children are well enough, I'll be coming to stay with her. Will you tell her that, please? I'll be round later to sort things out."

"It's a very small flat," said Valois. "You'll be awfully crowded."

"Not as crowded as we are here, knee-deep in Boche."

"Listen to her. She'll get us all killed," muttered Louise, crawling around in search of stray chocolates.

Stepping gingerly over Louise, Christian Valois left the bakery. As he walked along the empty street, he began to smile, then to chuckle.

Unobserved, in a doorway on the other side, Günter Mai smiled too.

8

In October, a census of Jews was announced.

At the police station there was a long queue. When she reached its head, Sophie Simonian filled in her registration form with great care. Only at the "Next of Kin" section did she hesitate. Something made her look over her shoulder. Behind her, winding round the station vestibule and out of the door, stretched the queue. Conversation was low, most didn't speak at all but stood with expressions of stolid resignation, every now and then shuffling forward to whatever fate officialdom had devised for them.

"Come on, old lady," said a gendarme. "What's the holdup?"

She put a stroke of the pen through "Next of Kin".

"What? No family?"

"A son. Until the war."

"I'm sorry. Now, sign your name and be on your way."

It felt good to be out in the street again and her confidence rapidly returned as she walked home as briskly as her arthritic knee permitted.

When she reached the apartment building, Maurice Melchior emerged, resplendent in a long astrakhan coat. "Good day, Madame Simonian. And how are you? Taking the air?"

Piqued at being accused of such unproductive activity, Sophie said sharply, "No, monsieur. I've been to register."

"Register?" He raised his eyebrows. "How quaint! Good day, madame."

Melchior set off at a brisk pace, eager to put as much distance as possible between himself and this silly old Jewess who'd gone voluntarily to put her name on the official census list. How desperate people were to convince themselves that everything was normal. Normal! All they had to do was stroll along the boulevards and look in the shop windows. Everything had gone. Rationing had been introduced the previous month.

The forecast was for a long, hard winter, and Melchior had more immediate and personal worries. Bruno Zeller was close to dumping him.

The trouble was, as life returned to something like normal it had grown increasingly difficult to maintain his claim to be at the heart of things. Name-dropping was only successful if the names dropped kept a decent distance from the city. But many had returned, and even when they were polite, they made it very clear they were not intimate with him.

Zeller had been furious. "Melchior, you haven't been honest with me, have you? It seems that far from being the celebrity you claim, you're a nobody. Worse, you're a laughing stock. That's your bad luck, but by your idiocy, you've got me involved in it too. I don't care to be made to look ridiculous. Recruiting you was a mistake. Some people can forget mistakes. I can't. I need to correct them."

"What do you mean, Bruno?" Melchior had demanded nervously.

"You're going to have to start earning your pay," said Zeller bitterly. "From now on, if you want protection—and the alternative, let me assure you, is persecution—you're going to have to come up with some hard information."

Melchior was more than willing to oblige, but the kind of gossip he was so expert at collecting was not, alas, the kind which held much interest for the guardians of military security.

Then at last, a break came. There were rumours everywhere that, angered by the complacent acceptance by their elders of the German occupation, the university students were planning a demonstration on November 11, Armistice Day. Melchior spent all his spare time in the cafés on the Boul' Miche. The youngsters were happy to let him pay for their drinks, but laughed behind his back at his efforts to draw information from them. However, there were others who noticed and did not discount his efforts so scornfully.

On November 10 he was sitting disconsolately in the café where he'd taken Zeller on their first meeting. The owner no longer greeted him by name now that his usual clientele were back. Finishing his coffee, Melchior rose and left. As he walked along the rain-polished pavement observing with distaste the spattering of his mirror-like shoes, footsteps came hurrying after him. He looked round to see a youngster he knew as Emile approaching. He was a sick-looking boy, and shabby even by student standards. When he caught up, he glanced behind him furtively, then drew Maurice off the boulevard into a doorway.

"Monsieur," he said, "I need a thousand francs."

Melchior looked at him sharply. "Even if I had such a sum, which I don't, why should I loan it to you?"

"Not loan. Pay. Look, monsieur, everyone knows you're interested in the plans for our demo tomorrow. Well, I can tell you it's not going to wait till tomorrow. It'll be at midnight tonight."

"But that'll mean breaking the curfew."

"It's not the only thing that will be broken," said Emile. "Come on. Are you in the market or not?"

"I'd need proof," Melchior said.

"For God's sake, what's proof? I've got a copy of the plan, with timings and locations, if that's what you mean."

"I'll tell you what," said Melchior who, despite everything, was quite enjoying getting into his role as an agent, "you give me the plan. If it works out, I'll pay you five hundred francs tomorrow."

"You don't imagine I'm going to trust someone like you!" said Emile angrily.

Melchior smiled and said significantly, "It wouldn't be me you were trusting, Emile. Your payment would be guaranteed, believe me."

The youngster weighed this up. Strange, thought Melchior. He knows I mean the Germans and he'll doubtless decide he can trust them more than me. He was right.

"OK," said the student reluctantly. "Payment tomorrow morning, nine sharp, the Tuileries gardens, by the Orangerie, all right?"

"Agreed," said Melchior, holding out his hand.

A folded sheet of paper was put into it, then Emile hurried away into the gathering dusk.

Melchior walked along, studying the paper. There were going to be torchlight processions starting in the Place de la Bastille at 11:30. And once the authorities' attention had been concentrated on the processions, the German embassy in the Rue de Lille and the Hôtel de Ville were going to be the objects of the main demos, at midnight. Melchior practically danced along the pavement. This would be a real coup for Zeller.

But now, as quickly as it had come, his joy faded as a sense of revulsion swept over him. What the hell was he doing? Giving this to Zeller meant hundreds of youngsters could be walking into a trap. No! He wouldn't do it. He walked on, feeling incredibly noble.

Then he heard the sound of breaking glass. He turned a corner and saw a tobacconist's with its window shattered. Pasted on the door was a now familiar sign saying JEWISH BUSINESS. Two youths with the armbands of the *Parti Populaire Français* were standing laughing on the pavement. They fell silent as he walked past. Then he heard their footsteps coming after him. Faster and faster he walked, till he was almost running.

Finally, exhausted by effort and fear, he stopped and turned. He was alone. But he had left his feeling of nobility far behind.

NOVEMBER 11 DAWNED. A German corporal was growing very irritated. He'd been up since before midnight, lying in wait to quell an assault on the embassy which never happened. Then, when at last he was stood down, he'd just had time to stretch out on his bunk before he was ordered here, to the Place de l'Etoile, to deal with some real demonstrations. All was quiet now, and he could be thinking of getting back to his bunk if this funny little twerp would stop babbling at him in broken German about some abortive ambush last night.

Maurice Melchior had woken up earlier that morning to a terrifying silence. No one was talking about midnight marches and assaults on the embassy. He was supposed to meet Zeller to collect Emile's payoff, but he had the sense not to keep that appointment. He did go to the Orangerie, however, hoping Emile might turn up with an explanation, but he hung around in growing despair till news of disturbances at l'Etoile had brought him hurrying here, hoping against hope that somehow *his* disturbances had moved on in space and time.

The corporal grew angry. Only his eagerness to get to bed stopped him from arresting Melchior. He turned away. The Frenchie grasped his shoulder! That did it. He turned and hit him. Melchior sank to the ground.

"No," said a voice from a staff car which had drawn up alongside.

Through tear-clouded eyes, Melchior recognized a face. No. *Two* faces. One, looking at him through the window, was Colonel Fiebelkorn's. The other, less frightening but more incredible, belonged to Emile, who looked at Melchior and smiled.

"Monsieur Melchior," said Fiebelkorn, opening the door. "Won't you join us?"

9

It was Christmas Eve.

"You must go to your parents tonight, for the children's sake especially, but for your own sake too," said Sophie firmly.

"But what about you?" said Janine. "Why should you be left all alone at Christmas time?"

Sophie laughed merrily. "What are you saying? An old Jewess alone at Christmas? What's Christmas to me, darling?"

"All right, I'll go," said Janine.

"I knew you would," said the old lady laughing. "You're a good daughter. To me, as well as to Madame Crozier."

The welcome they received at her parents made Janine ashamed that she could have dreamed of staying away. Louise burst into tears of joy at seeing them and later, while she was putting the children to bed, Claude said confidentially to his daughter, "If you'd not come here, we were going to come round to see you tomorrow."

"Maman too? But she said she'd never visit Sophie's flat." *Never set foot in that heathen temple* had been the precise phrase.

"I told her it was Christmas and she'd have to swallow her pride," said Claude. "She shouted at me a bit, but deep down she wanted to be told."

The truce lasted all that evening, and even survived until the next morning, when Janine was amazed at the way in which rationing and growing food shortages did not seem to have affected her mother's preparations for Christmas dinner. Probably all over Paris housewives were performing similar miracles, she assured herself. But she had a feeling this miracle had started with a bit more than a few loaves and fishes.

Just on midday, with the house rich with the smell of baking and boiling and roasting, the door burst open to admit a tall, broad-shouldered, red-bearded man, resplendent in a beautifully cut suit, a silk shirt and a flowered necktie fastened with a diamond-studded gold pin. He had the look of a pirate king dressed up for his bosun's wedding. On his arm was an elegantly furred woman with tight black curls, a great deal of make-up, bright red nail varnish and a good figure.

"My God, Miche, is that you?" said Janine.

"Cousin Janine, how are you, girl?" Boucher cried, stooping to give her a kiss. "I hoped you'd be here. I've brought a few things for the kids. Hey, this is Hélène, by the way. She dances at the *Folies*. Now where are those kids? And where's the old folks?"

"I think they're in the bakehouse," said Janine. "I'll go and tell them..." Warn them, she meant. But it was too late.

The door opened. Madame Crozier stopped dead in her tracks. Then, spreading her arms, she cried, "Michel, my dear. You've come!"

And, amazed, Janine saw those old antagonists embrace.

It soon became clear that the reconciliation had taken place some time before and obviously it had much to do with Cousin Michel's new affluence. He presided over the feast like a red-bearded Father Christmas, commanding Pauli's help to fetch in from his car bottles of champagne, a smoked ham and a whole wheel of Camembert. In addition there was a huge fairy doll for Céci and a penknife for Pauli.

Janine demurred at the knife. "He's far too young. He'll cut himself."

"Nonsense!" said her cousin. "I was carrying daggers and knuckle-dusters at his age!"

Pauli said, "Maman, it's not all a knife. It's got all kinds of things." He demonstrated, pulling out a corkscrew, a screwdriver, a gimlet. "I can't cut myself with these," he said earnestly. "If I promise not to open the blade till I'm old enough, can I keep it? Please, Maman?"

He fixed his unblinking wide-eyed gaze upon her, beseeching her to retreat before the logic of his argument.

As usual, there seemed nothing else to do. "All right," she said. "Only, Pauli, *I'll* decide when you're old enough, you understand?"

"Yes, Maman."

"Isn't it lovely to see them opening their presents?" said Hélène. "I just long to have children of my own, Janine. You're so lucky to have this beautiful pair."

She sounded as if she meant it and Janine found herself warming to her. Soon they were deep in conversation, while Madame Crozier busied herself being the perfect hostess. One thing that no one mentioned was the immediate past or the foreseeable future. The Paris that lay outside the door might not have existed. Christmas, always a game, was being played with extra fervour this year.

Only a child, to whom all play is reality, would not grasp the rules of this game. Pauli ate his dinner silently, and drank his wine and water, and looked after his little sister. And all the time he hardly ever took his eyes off Michel Boucher. But Janine knew, and the knowledge wrenched her heart, that it was his father he was seeing.

And now her own father, as if catching the thought, broke the rules too and said quietly when Pauli had taken his sister to the lavatory, "Any news of Jean-Paul?"

Janine shook her head. Boucher said, "That man of yours not turned up yet? That's lousy. Have you tried the Red Cross?"

"I've tried everything," said Janine dully.

Then Louise came in with brandy and chocolates and the subject was shelved.

When the time came for the visitors to go, Janine showed them out. After he had put Hélène in the car, Miche came back to the shop doorway. "It's been great today," he said.

"That's good, Miche. And it was lovely having you and Hélène here."

"Yeah. Surprising too, eh?" He laughed. "I saw your face! Thing is, I've always liked your dad. He's been good to me over the years. You're all the family I've got, you Croziers. It was meeting Hélène that made me realize a man needs a family. So when I started doing well enough to get round Auntie Lou, I thought, what the hell. I can put up with her funny little ways."

"I'm glad, Miche. You and Hélène are serious then?"

"Serious enough," he said. "Look, Jan, about Jean-Paul, if you like I'll have a word with my new boss, see if he can help."

"Your new boss. Who's that, Miche?" asked Janine suspiciously.

"Doesn't matter, if he can help, does it?" laughed Boucher. "And if he can't, then it doesn't matter either. I'll be in touch. *Wiedersehen!*"

As Janine frowned her displeasure, he smiled, shrugged and said, "When in Rome, sweetie, do like they do in Berlin. *Leb'wohl!*"

10

So the year drew to its close. Winter, like the Germans, came swiftly, hit hard, felt as if it was here to stay.

A glittering New Year reception was held at the embassy. Günter Mai stood in the most obscure corner of the huge reception room, feeling itchy and uncomfortable in his dress uniform. All round him were the richest, most influential members of the Parisian ruling classes. Women in elegant billows of silk and satin, necks gleaming with gold or diamonds; men in tailcoats smiling, drinking, joking with their conquerors.

Major Zeller appeared at Mai's side. "Enjoying yourself, Günter? The perfect end to a perfect year, wouldn't you say? Triumph after triumph? I never thought it would be so easy."

"Victory, you mean?"

"Not victory in the field. It was always possible that *that* would be easy. No, the remarkable thing is the degree to which we have made ourselves accepted. More than accepted. Welcomed! I actually feel at home in this city, a visitor rather than a conqueror."

"It's early days, sir," said Mai. "You knock a man down, he may be concussed and in shock for a long time afterwards. He may even believe that he didn't really mind being knocked down. But you'd better wait till he's fully himself again before deciding if you really want him holding the ladder while you're cleaning windows."

Zeller regarded him curiously. "Cleaning windows? How quaint you sometimes are, Günter. I do hope you will not put your quaintness forward as official *Abwehr* thinking, tonight. The SD are keen enough to undermine us without giving them ammunition."

Suddenly a voice drifted across the room. "Zeller! I thought it was you."

Zeller swung round to confirm with his eyes what his ears found incredible. "What in the name of God are you doing here?" he cried, bewilderment as yet stronger than rage.

Maurice Melchior raised his eyebrows. "I'm having a really delightful time, that's what."

He turned round, his elegant silk dinner jacket giving a quick flash of its brilliant scarlet lining.

"Walter, I told you he'd be here. Zeller, my dear chap, do you know my friend Walter? No, we'd better be formal, I know how much protocol matters to you military boys. SS Lieutenant-General Fiebelkorn, may I have the honour of presenting you to Major Bruno Zeller?"

Mai saw the fury that held Zeller stiff, his fists clenched so tight that the silver signet ring stood out like a weapon. Zeller was still being ribbed by officers put on alert for the non-existent midnight disturbances. Mai was now convinced that the SD had been behind the fiasco, to make the *Abwehr* look ridiculous.

Melchior might live to rue the day he had made an enemy of Major Zeller.

But as Günter Mai looked at the SS colonel's impassive face and unblinking, watery gaze, he felt a sudden certainty that it had been a far more dangerous day for Melchior when he had made Fiebelkorn his friend.

Across the room, a gorgeous French film star complained how warm it was. A gallant Panzer officer immediately drew back the heavy brocaded curtains and began to wrestle with a window.

"Remember the blackout!" called someone.

"The blackout?" said the officer. "There's no danger up there unless Churchill starts sending trained pigeons from Trafalgar Square!"

There was a burst of laughter which became general as his shaft of Aryan wit was passed round the room, and for a while the open curtain was forgotten, allowing the brilliance of the many chandeliers to spill their diamantine glory into the darkness outside.

A crowd had gathered in the Rue de Lille earlier, to see the notables arrive, but as midnight and the New Year approached, most of the watchers had drifted away.

A few remained, however. Among them was Janine Simonian. She had felt compelled to get out of Sophie's tiny flat that night. She'd let herself drift towards the university quarter, to which Jean-Paul had often brought her. Finally, the memories had become too much and to escape them she had joined the watchers in the Rue de Lille.

"What's happening?" she asked someone.

"It's a ball, just like the old days," was the reply.

At that moment the curtain was drawn back and the spectators could see right into the reception hall. It was a scene of assurance and power; it stated more forcibly than marching troops or rumbling gun carriages that we, here inside, are the conquerors and will be for ever; while you, outside, are for ever the conquered.

A flurry of snow left flakes on her cheeks like tears. The last watchers began to depart. Someone said, "Happy New Year."

Janine said, "Jean-Paul, wherever you are, Happy New Year, my love."

Then she too turned and walked slowly away.

PART TWO   February – December 1941
1

If it wasn't the coldest February in years, to most Frenchmen it felt like it.

Monsieur Edouard Scheffer of Strasbourg sat in the Café Balzac and shivered. Not even two thicknesses of overcoat, a homburg hat and frequent sips of coffee could keep him warm. The patron, who valued his custom, was apologetic. He and Monsieur Scheffer had done a few small black-market deals in the couple of months since Miche Boucher had introduced them, so he was sure that monsieur would appreciate the problem of fuel shortage.

The seated man nodded, and thought of his warm room at *Abwehr* headquarters in the Lutétia. Bruno Zeller, he was sure, would never undertake assignments which involved freezing to death. In fairness, it was difficult to imagine Zeller being able to pass himself off as anything other than a German officer, but just now Günter Mai didn't feel like being fair.

Two figures entered the café. One was Boucher, the other was the girl. Boucher peered down the long shadowy room in search of Mai, who always sat at the furthermost end, near the kitchen door, partly for security, partly to avoid the draught.

Now Boucher saw him. Spoke to the girl. Pointed.

She looked, saw, recognized.

In that instant he could see she'd had no idea whom she was going to meet. He'd assumed Boucher would have told her, and he'd been surprised when nevertheless the redhead had confirmed that the meeting was on. But then, the girl was desperate, and desperate people made easy recruits.

She was trying to leave but her cousin was hanging on to her arm. Mai willed him to let her go. If she was forced to confront him now his cover could be blown, and he found Edouard Scheffer very useful.

She was coming. Damn. He signalled the patron to bring more coffee. The girl arrived and glowered down at him. Angrily she sat down in the chair he pulled out for her.

"I didn't know it was you," said Janine, after the patron had retired out of earshot.

"You wouldn't have come?" asked Mai.

She shook her head, then added, "Not because of the shop, what happened that time, but..."

"Because I'm not a general, someone important? I take your point."

She was much calmer now. It didn't surprise him. This was what he was noted for—baiting, hooking, playing, and not so much landing the little fish as persuading them to jump out of the water.

He produced his pipe and, as he lit it, he studied her. On her entry to the café he had thought she was plumper than he remembered. Now he realized that like himself she was wearing several layers of clothes against the cold, and was in fact rather thinner than he recalled. It was a good face, not beautiful but intriguing, full of life and mobility.

"So, have you managed to track down Corporal Jean-Paul Simonian?"

She went red with shock and anger. "Miche shouldn't have told you," she said. "He had no right."

"He didn't tell me anything," said Mai. "I got the details elsewhere."

For a moment she looked puzzled, then it dawned. "*Maman!*" she said. "She's been talking to you, hasn't she?"

He was right. She was no fool. He nodded. "Mothers like to talk about their children. She told me you were on edge because you'd no idea what had happened to your husband. So when Miche said you had a problem, I guessed."

"Very clever," said Janine. "What else did Maman say? That I'd be better off if Jean-Paul never came back?"

Mai shrugged, a good French shrug. "He might not come back, you know that? In fact it's the likeliest outcome."

"Of course I know that."

Her anger had faded. He could see she was building an equation, checking what it meant. At last she shook her head. "This is a waste of time. For both of us. I'll be honest with you. Since Miche arranged this meeting, I've been wondering why any German should even think of helping me. There's only one possible reason. He'd want me to agree to be an informer, a spy, something like that."

She paused. He asked, "And what had you decided?"

"I decided anyone who got me as a spy would have made a bad bargain," she said with unexpected humour. "Though I suppose, now that I know Miche's boss isn't a stranger, there could be another possibility."

It took him a couple of seconds to work it out. He had to make an effort to keep the surprise out of his face, but Janine put his thoughts into words. "Though I daresay German officers have easier ways of getting girls. Anyway, the fact is, now I've met you there's no point. I can't see a mere lieutenant being any more useful to me than the Red Cross or a Vichy deputy." She rose to leave.

He didn't try to stop her.

She walked straight past Boucher at the bar without saying a word.

"Hey, Janine," he cried, going after her. "What's up?" he demanded as he overtook her in the street. "Won't he help?"

"He's a lieutenant, Miche. What can someone like that do?"

"You're probably right," he said, walking fast to keep up with her. "Except that my mate, Pajou—he's the one who got me the job—he reckons old Günter really runs the show at *Abwehr* HQ."

She stopped and turned to face him. "This job of yours, what is it exactly?" she asked.

"It's all aboveboard. We help the authorities recover things. Food that's been hoarded, valuables that have been hidden—illegally, I mean."

"You help the Boche to loot!"

"No," he said with genuine indignation. "It's just recovery. People abandon their houses, make no proper provision for storing delicate antiques, so the authorities take care of them."

"Rich Jews' villas, you mean? And what do you know about delicate antiques, Miche?"

He grinned and said, "Not much. But they have experts to deal with things like that. And it's not just Jewish stuff either. I reckon it's a lot of rubbish this stuff about the Boche being down on the Jews."

It struck Janine that her cousin was trying to justify his working for the Germans. And it struck her also that she was feeling rather holier-than-thou for someone who had lain awake all night debating just what she would agree to, in return for information about Jean-Paul.

But it had all been a waste of time. She was running out of hope.

2

It was an April evening, but the wind that met Christian Valois head-on as he cycled back to the family apartment in Passy was full of sleet. He carried his bike up the stairs and into the apartment with him. Cars had practically vanished from the streets. There was little petrol to be had and, in any case, you needed a special *Ausweis* from the Germans to use one, so bikes were now pricey enough to attract the professional thief.

As he took off his sodden coat, the telephone rang.

The line was poor and the female voice at the other end was faint.

"Hello! Hello! I can't hear you. Who is that?"

Suddenly the interference went and the voice came loud and clear. "It's me, your sister, idiot!"

"Marie-Rose! Hello! How are you?"

"I'm fine. Listen, quickly, in case we get cut off. Are you coming down this weekend? Please, you must, it's my birthday, or had you forgotten?"

She was seventeen on Saturday. Seventeen. A good age, even in awful times. But could he bear to go to Vichy? His parents had urged him frequently to come for a visit. So far he had refused. But Marie-Rose's birthday was different. His sister adored him, and he adored her.

"I'll see," he said. "I won't promise, but I'll see."

Shortly afterwards they were cut off.

The next morning, spring finally exploded with all the violence of energy too long restrained. On the Friday afternoon, he caught the train to Vichy.

At the crossing point into the Free Zone, they were all ordered out to have their papers checked. Valois had had no difficulty in getting an *Ausweis*. When your father was a Vichy deputy and you were a respectable civil servant, you were regarded as quite safe, he thought moodily.

As the train pulled into the station at Vichy, Christian caught sight of his sister, long black hair streaming behind her, running down the platform to greet him.

They embraced. Since he'd last seen her she'd become a young woman, and a very beautiful one. She tucked her arm through his in delight and led him to where their mother was waiting.

"Where's Father?" asked Valois as they approached.

"Busy. He sends his apologies."

"No, I understand. Without his constant efforts, the country would be ground down under the conqueror's heel."

"Shut up and behave! I don't want my birthday spoilt."

He just about managed to obey her injunction during the weekend, but there were difficult moments. Vichy disgusted him, with its opulent façades all draped with tricolours. He preferred the stark truth of those swastikas he could see from his office window flapping lazily over the arcades of the Rue de Rivoli. The people, most of them, were the same. "Like characters on a film set," he told his sister.

"I agree," said Marie-Rose. "It's so boring here. That's why I want to come back to Paris with you!"

He looked at her in alarm. This was the first he'd heard of this idea, and the more he thought about it the less he liked it. In Paris his decisions only concerned himself; it was a time of danger and it would get worse. He tried to explain this to Marie-Rose and they quarrelled. But by way of compensation, he found an area of common ground with his father, who was absolutely opposed to any such move.

Indeed he and his father kept the peace till the time came to part. His mother presented him with a bag full of "goodies" and his father with a piece of paper.

"It's a permit to use the car, the Renault. I'll want to use it myself whenever I come to Paris and it's absurd for it to stand in the garage all the time, so I got a permit for you too."

His instinct was to tear the paper in half. "Father, have you any idea what it's like in Paris? The kind of people who're still driving around in cars, well, they're not the kind of people I want to be associated with. There's still a war on, Father, believe me!"

"No, there's an armistice on, *you'd* better believe *me!*" snapped Léon Valois. "Face up to reality, even if you don't like it. The facts are that the Germans are in control and likely to stay that way. With or without us, they'll rule. Without us ... well, I dread to think how it might be. With us, we can restrain, influence, perhaps eventually control! They're a rigid race, good for soldiering, poor for politics. Believe me, Christian, my way's the only way to build a future for France!"

He spoke with passionate sincerity, but there was no place for them to meet. The one good thing about their quarrel was that it reunited Christian with his sister, just as their row had temporarily brought him closer to his parents. She kissed him tenderly at parting and asked, "Is it really so awful under the Boche? I worry about you."

"Oh, it's not so bad really," he assured her.

"No? Well, no matter what you say, one day I'll surprise you and come and see for myself!"

She grinned in a most un-seventeen-like way and hugged him once more, with a childish lack of restraint, before he got on the train.

He leaned out of the window and waved as long as he could see her on the platform. As he turned to sit down, the compartment door opened and a man entered. Christian recognized him. "It's Maître Delaplanche, isn't it?" he asked.

"You recognize me?" The lawyer's face, which was living proof of his Breton peasant ancestry, screwed up in mock alarm as he took a seat.

"You're often in the papers, and I attended several meetings you spoke at when I was a student."

"Did you? Ah yes. I seem to recall you now." The face screwed up again in an effort of recollection. "Valois, isn't it? Christian Valois. I knew your father when he practised, before politics took him over."

Delaplanche was well known in legal circles as a pleader of underdog causes. Whenever an individual challenged the state, his counsel would be sought, and he had spoken on a variety of socialist platforms.

"Nice to meet you," said Valois.

"Was this your first visit to Vichy?"

Christian nodded.

"Well, what did you think?"

"I'll tell you what I thought," Valois said savagely, and Delaplanche listened in silence as the young man vented his anger at the way in which men like his father were cooperating with the enemy.

Finished at last, Valois waited for approval.

"I hope you're not always so indiscreet," was all the lawyer said. "Especially with strangers."

"Strangers? But..."

"What do you know of me?"

"I know your reputation. I know you're a man of the people, a socialist, some even say a..."

"Communist? Yes, some do say that. Of course, if I were a Communist, that would put me in the German camp, wouldn't it?"

"No! On the contrary..."

"But Russia and Germany have a non-aggression pact."

169

"Yes, but that hardly means the Communists support the Nazis."

"No. But wasn't it enough to stop you from joining the Communist Party just when you were teetering on the edge?"

The rest of the journey passed in silence, with the lawyer reading his paper and Valois brooding on the man's apparently detailed knowledge of his own background.

Their farewells in Paris were perfunctory. Valois felt tired, yet restless. It had been an unsettling weekend and it was with a sense of relief that he entered his apartment building. Perhaps his outrage at the idea of the car permit ought to extend to his use of his parents' large, well-appointed flat, but he was glad to find his mind could accommodate this as comfortably as the flat accommodated him.

Christian headed for the staircase, ill-lit by a shrouded bulb to comply with the blackout regulations. The apartment was one floor up.

As he reached his landing, fatigue and melancholy vanished in a trice, replaced by terror. There was a man crouched in the shadow of his door with a submachine gun under his arm. It was too late to retreat. The waiting man had seen him. "Monsieur Christian Valois?"

"Yes."

"I've got a message for you."

The man moved forward into the dim light. The machinegun became a wooden crutch under his left arm and the lurking assassin became a haggard, grey-haired man in a baggy suit.

"A message? Who the hell from?" demanded Valois, trying to cover his fear with aggression.

"A friend," said the man. "Jean-Paul Simonian."

3

"But he's alive?" demanded Janine for the sixth or seventh time.

"Yes, yes, yes, how many times do I have to tell you?" said Christian Valois with growing irritation. "He was shot in the head. He was critically ill for a long time but now he's recovering. He's in a military hospital near Nancy, and soon he'll be shipped off to some camp in Germany. But he *is* alive, he *is* all right."

"Why didn't he get in touch earlier? Why doesn't he write instead of sending messages by this man Pivert?"

Janine knew how absurd all these questions must sound, but they forced themselves out against her will. The truth was, at first she didn't believe it, *couldn't* believe it, when Valois, unnaturally flushed with suppressed excitement, had burst in, crying, "He's alive! Jean-Paul's alive!"

Then the door had opened and Pauli, attracted by the noise, had rushed in crying, "Maman, what's the matter? Are you ill?"

"No, Pauli. It's your father. He's alive!"

For a moment the little boy had stood perfectly still. Then he sat on the floor and began to cry, not the silent, half-concealed tears she had grown used to, but howling like his little sister.

"Pauli!" she said, kneeling beside him and hugging him close. "It's all right, my love. It's all right. Daddy's alive! Daddy's alive!"

And suddenly it *was* all right. Her sobs joined the child's and at last her emotions flowed as freely as her joyful tears.

"I'm sorry, Christian," she said a little later, as they sat and drank a glass of wine. "I didn't dare to believe you. Do you understand that? Now, quickly, before Sophie comes back from shopping, tell me it all again so I can break the news to her the best way possible."

Corporal Major Pivert's story had been told with an old soldier's rough directness. He had been second-in-command of the section in which Jean-Paul was serving. They had held out against a ferocious onslaught.

"Most of the Boche just went round us," he had told Christian, "leaving half a company to mop us up. Well, we showed them! Mind you, we took a pounding. It brought us real close together. We'd been a tight-knit group before, but being under heavy attack together, that really binds you close as cement. It's a grand feeling, but oh! the pain of it, when one of your mates gets hit. Do you know what I mean?"

Christian said, "I think so, I'm trying..."

The old soldier regarded him keenly and said, "You've had no service, have you, sir? You can't understand, without knowing it for yourself."

Valois flushed and said, "Go on."

"Finally the lieutenant decided to call it a day. Simonian was keen to go on fighting at first, but the lieutenant persuaded him for the sake of his mates to give it up. So we made a white flag, but before we shoved it up, the lieutenant said, 'Hold on. Simonian, let's have a look at your passbook.'

"'What for?' asks Simonian.

"'You'll be better off if you don't have the name Iakov Moseich Simonian in your passbook when the Boche get round to checking prisoners,' says the lieutenant. He takes it and he scratches and tears it, then hands it back, looking right scruffy but no worse than many another after what we'd been through. 'There,' he says. 'You've been christened in every sense!' And I glanced at the book and saw that all that remained of his name was Jean-Paul Simon!

"Now he waved the flag. The only trouble was that the Boche seemed to be a bit shortsighted. Or a bit short-tempered. They just shot the flag to pieces and us with it. There were only four of us left alive, and only me and Simonian lasted long enough to get to hospital, me with one foot shot off and him with a bullet in his head.

"And that was it. I didn't even know Jean-Paul was still alive till a month or so back when I ran into him. He didn't seem to recognize me at first, but when we got to talking I could see it all gradually coming back to him. The thing was, he was still down in the books as Jean-Paul Simon. I asked one of the nurses about him. She said it was sad, he never said anything about his past life and there didn't seem to be any next of kin to inform. Well, I guessed that he was just playing dumb because, having changed his name, he could hardly start talking about a family called Simonian, could he? And from what I heard people saying, the lieutenant had been right. Iakov Moseich is not a good label to wear in the heart of Bocheland, which is where he'll likely end up.

"As for me, well, there was no use sending a one-legged man to a POW camp. So they decided to discharge me back home. When I told Jean-Paul, he asked me to get in touch with you, Monsieur Valois, and tell you he was alive and well. He didn't want to risk putting anything down on paper in case I got searched. So here I am and that's my message!"

"By the time he'd finished it was nearly curfew or I'd have come round last night," Valois said when he'd concluded the story.

"Can I talk to him?" demanded Janine.

"Of course," said Valois. "Though not straight away. I'll fix it up later. There's still a slight risk now, and it's best not to take chances."

This wasn't the real reason, but Janine in her joy was easily persuaded to accept it. The truth was that Valois had another reason to feel uneasy about a meeting between Pivert and Janine. He'd censored all references to the mental scarring left by Jean-Paul's wound.

"I knew he was married, with kiddies," Pivert had said. "You talk about these things when you're under fire like we'd been. But first time I mentioned them in the hospital, he just looked blank. Another time he talked about them like he was talking about something in a dream.

"But you he seemed to remember, sir. You and his old mother. He said to contact you first so you could break it to the old lady."

When Sophie returned from shopping, Valois diplomatically withdrew. They needn't have worried, however. She short-circuited Janine's tentative approach to the subject with a crisp, "You've got news of Jean-Paul, haven't you? Well, praise be to God, he's alive!"

"Bubbah! How did you know?" demanded Janine, amazed.

"Know? I've always known! And how did I know you were going to tell me? Well, I've not seen your eyes sparkle like that for over a year, so I didn't think you were going to tell me he was dead! Come here, child!"

Laughing and crying, Janine fell into the old woman's arms.

AFTER JOY CAME DECISION. There was now a future to be planned. Janine wanted to write a long loving letter to Jean-Paul straight away but found herself at odds with Christian.

"You can't just write," he said. "Letters are censored. I don't know how much danger Jean-Paul would be in if they discovered his background, but they'd certainly sit up and take notice if they found out he'd been misleading them about his name. So it can't help him if suddenly out of the blue he starts getting letters from his family, can it?"

To Janine's surprise and disappointment, Sophie supported Valois. "If my son is soon to go into one of these prisoner camps, better he go as Jean-Paul Simon, Catholic, I think."

"But we have to let him know that we're all well, Bubbah, you, me and the children!" cried Janine. "And if we don't contact him straight away, how will we ever know where they send him? Oh, don't let's lose him again so soon after finding him! Couldn't I travel to Nancy to see him?"

"Please, I beg of you, Janine. Do nothing without consulting me first," Christian urged. "The Germans have got themselves a prisoner, an ordinary soldier of no importance, called Jean-Paul Simon. The only danger is from us, if we draw their attention to him in any way."

Suddenly all Janine's other emotions were blanked out by a single memory. Up to now she'd completely forgotten her interview with the *Abwehr* lieutenant. Now Valois's warning brought it all back. Just how much had her mother told Mai about Jean-Paul? She shook her head. The *Abwehr* were hardly going to concern themselves with one French soldier.

"Are you all right?" asked Valois.

"Fine. It's just the excitement. What *do* we do?"

"Here's my idea. The only person who can contact Jean-Paul without drawing undue attention is Pivert. So let's send a parcel through the Red Cross with a note, allegedly from Pivert, saying that he's safely back in Paris and has found his own family, Sophie, Janine, Pauli and Céci, safe and well. And he can tell Jean-Paul to write to him, care of my address. It's a risk, but not much of one. How does that sound to you?"

Janine considered. It sounded cautious, reasonable, well-planned. It sounded so many things she found it hard to be but which she knew she was going to have to learn to be. "It sounds all right," she said.

When Christian left she accompanied him to the street door. He was quiet and she guessed he was still worried that by some impulsive act she might endanger Jean-Paul. The thought annoyed her. Didn't he know that while there was an ounce of strength in her body she would fight for Jean-Paul?

"I'll be in touch then," he said, leaning forward and kissing her cheek.

"Thank you, Christian," she whispered, "for being such a good friend."

4

Maurice Melchior was bored with his job.

He was bored with bumping around in a smelly army truck. He was bored with his companion, SS Sergeant Hans Hemmen, who had no conversation whatsoever. And he was beginning to get a little bored with his new boss, Colonel Walter Fiebelkorn.

It was of course Fiebelkorn who'd got him attached to the SS's so-called Art Preservation Section. Everyone was at it, the SS, the *Abwehr*, not forgetting visiting notables like Goering. Melchior had eased his early pangs of conscience by assuring himself there was real preservation work to be done in places where the owners had been too concerned with packing everything portable to worry about protecting what wasn't. But in the end it came down to looting.

This was brought home to him beyond all doubt one glorious June day in a villa on the Hauts de Seine. The usual anonymous informant had told them that the owner had gone for a long "holiday" in Spain. The tip-off must have come from someone who was very keen for the house to be "preserved", as he had evidently informed the *Abwehr* preservation group too. Melchior recognized one of them, a big piratical redhead who occasionally visited old Madame—or perhaps young Madame—Simonian in the flat below. He seemed an amiable fellow, which was more than could be said for his mate, a nauseating little man called Pajou whose eyes, behind their thick spectacles, never stopped moving.

It was Pajou who said, as the argument between Hemmen and an *Abwehr* captain reached its height, "Look. We're all in the same game, aren't we? Spin of a coin, winner takes the lot."

Melchior retired in disgust. All in the same game indeed! Whatever game he was in, it certainly wasn't that little rat's. His indignation led him to temptation. There was a beautiful piece of Nevers *verre filé* in a niche, a tiny figurine of a young girl strewing flowers from a basket. Its intrinsic value was not great but it gave him great pleasure to look at. What would its fate be if it fell into the hands of either set of looters? And if preservation really was their job, who would preserve it more lovingly than he?

Checking that Hemmen was too immersed in the row to keep his usual distrustful eye on him, Melchior slipped the figurine into his pocket.

Five minutes later a staff car drew up outside the villa and SS Colonel Walter Fiebelkorn got out.

Now there was no contest. But Fiebelkorn seemed ready to be a good winner. "We both look after our fatherland's security in our different ways," he said to the *Abwehr* captain. "This is not something to sour a friendship over. Why don't we simply divide the spoil? You take the ground floor, we'll take the rest."

It was not an offer the *Abwehr* man could refuse, even though it was clearly based on Hemmen's report that the ground floor had been almost entirely cleared, the upper floors much less so.

It didn't take Pajou and Boucher long to remove what little remained downstairs. Fiebelkorn watched with an impassive face.

"All done?" said the disgruntled *Abwehr* captain.

"Not quite," said Pajou. "If we are to have everything from down here, what about the figurine that little fairy's got in his pocket?"

All eyes turned to Melchior. He felt no fear, only irritation that in his eagerness to be sure he was unnoticed by Hemmen, he'd ignored Pajou's shifty gaze.

"Oh, this?" he said, holding out the little figurine. "Sorry."

"This is a serious offence, Colonel," said the *Abwehr* captain, delighted to have captured the initiative from the SS. "Theft of works of art sequestered to the state is punishable by death."

"You want him killed?" asked Fiebelkorn indifferently.

"No," said the captain. "I just want to be sure the SS will take the serious view I think this case demands. Examples should be made."

"I agree," said Fiebelkorn. "Sergeant."

Hemmen approached Melchior, his eyes alight with pleasure. In his hand he held his machine pistol. For a terrible second, Maurice felt sure he was going to be shot. Then the figurine was swept out of his outstretched hand by the gleaming barrel. Before it hit the floor, the gun had swept back, catching Melchior along the side of his face. He felt no pain, only a warm rush of blood down his cheek. Then the barrel came back, laying open his temple this time, and now he collapsed sobbing to the ground, as kicks were aimed furiously at his chest and stomach.

Melchior rolled this way and that in his effort to avoid the blows, finally ending up at Fiebelkorn's feet.

He looked up into that blank face and choked, "Walter ... please ..."

Perhaps something moved in those dead eyes, but the voice was perfectly calm as the SS man said, "Well, Captain, is this sufficient to satisfy the *Abwehr?*"

"Yes. Enough," said the captain unsteadily.

"Good. Rest assured, if our friend here troubles us again, we will not be so merciful."

To Melchior, remembering that moment later, the most horrifying thing was to recognize that Fiebelkorn had been utterly sincere. In his eyes this beating had been an act of mercy. But just now Melchior had no thought of anything but pain. He lay very still, heard footsteps leaving the room, heard them mounting the marble staircase. Then silence. Then a hand on his shoulder. He screamed in terror.

"Come on, my little hero," said Michel Boucher's voice. "You've got a lot to learn about thieving, my friend. Now, can you stand? We'll get you out of here before Attila returns."

Unsteadily Melchior rose. The little figurine crunched beneath his feet.

"TODAY," SAID GÜNTER MAI, "is the twenty-first of June, the longest day. Hereafter begins the darkness."

"I hope I don't detect a metaphor," said Bruno Zeller sardonically.

"Why? Can they arrest you for metaphors now?"

Mai was rather drunk, but it had seemed ungracious not to take full advantage of the major's unexpected hospitality, particularly when it involved the Tour d'Argent's superb duck, with wine to match.

"Tell me, Bruno, sir, what precisely am I doing here?"

"In Paris, you mean?" said Zeller, deliberately misunderstanding.

"No. I know what I'm doing in Paris. There's a war on, remember?"

"Really?" Zeller looked round the crowded room. "Hard to believe, isn't it?"

"Not if you look out of the window. Out there, under every roof, there's at least one person who knows he or she is fighting a war."

"So you do have X-ray vision! It explains a lot."

Günter laughed. "Even here I can look towards the kitchen and see them spitting in the soup."

"How fortunate we avoided the soup then," said Zeller, suddenly impatient. "But you're right. There is of course a reason for our little tête-à-tête. I have a serious question for you. What do you think is the greatest danger to the *Abwehr*'s work?"

"Easy," said Mai. "The *Sicherheitsdienst*, the SD."

"Explain."

"A military occupation with a *Wehrmacht* chain of command is not to their taste. To them, security is not just a means of keeping the peace but of putting their ideology into action. Where our areas of work overlap, their best way to gain complete control is to discredit us. Also, men like Fiebelkorn honestly believe that the only safe condition for an occupied country is one of constant terror."

"Don't mention Fiebelkorn to me," said Zeller. "That trick of his, feeding that runt Melchior with false information last November, was just a beginning. Listen, Günter. I've been unofficially authorized to organize a small section to keep an eye on whatever the SD are getting up to. I'd value your assistance."

Mai sipped his wine and said, "Of course. Though, as doubtless you know, our workload's going to be increased quite a bit after tomorrow."

Zeller nodded. A slow smile spread across his face and he signalled to a waiter. "Cognac," he said. "Günter, you may be an impudent peasant, but by God, you're one of the best men we've got!"

THE FOLLOWING MORNING the news was broadcast. The German army had invaded Russia. The civilized world was invited to applaud, and to join in the great crusade against Communism.

It was a Saturday morning and Christian Valois was drinking his morning coffee when the bell of his apartment sounded.

He found the lawyer Delaplanche on his doorstep.

"Heard the news?"

"Yes." Christian had no need to ask which news.

"The case is altered, I think. Like to talk?"

"Come in. Let me get you some coffee."

The lawyer sat down and looked round the luxuriously appointed room.

"Nice place," he said.

"It's my parents'," said Valois curtly, pouring the coffee.

"No need to be defensive," laughed Delaplanche. "There's no harm in enjoying comfort, as long as you fight for other people's right to enjoy it too. You will fight, I take it?"

"Let's get one thing straight. Are you a Communist, Monsieur Delaplanche?"

"I'm a Frenchman and a patriot, isn't that all that matters?"

"What do you want with me?"

"Nothing. I thought you might like to join a celebration party," said Delaplanche. "Or if you prefer, an anniversary party. Don't you remember? A year ago today the armistice was signed. For a year we've been citizens of the Third Reich. Anyway, come if you like. The Café Carvallo, Rue Saint-Honoré, you know it? No need to wear cloak and dagger. It really is a celebration. My secretary is getting engaged. But there will be a couple of people there I'd like you to meet. Seven o'clock. These things start early because of the curfew."

He emptied his coffee cup, rose, shook hands and made for the door. As he reached it the bell rang. When Valois opened the door, he found Janine on the step, her face flushed.

"Christian, I must talk to you. Oh, I'm sorry."

She had spotted Delaplanche. The lawyer smiled at her, said, "Madame. Goodbye, Monsieur Valois," and left.

"Wasn't that Maître Delaplanche?" said Janine, when Valois had closed the door.

"You know him?"

"I've seen his photograph in the paper. Christian, I'm sorry to bother you, but something's happened."

She flopped down in a chair, her face crumpling with worry.

"You've had some news about Jean-Paul?" he guessed, full of concern.

"Yes. No. I mean, indirectly. Perhaps. Oh, I'll have to tell you."

Wretchedly she told him of her earlier meeting with Günter Mai.

"It was my idiot cousin's idea. I should never have listened. Then to find Maman's been blabbing all my business to this Boche. And all the time Jean-Paul's been trying to keep his real name quiet!"

"No harm done," Christian soothed her. "If Jean-Paul fooled the Boche in the hospital, no mere *Abwehr* lieutenant's going to work it out, from Paris!"

"I know. But then why does he want to see me again this afternoon?"

Miche had brought her the message, grinning like an ape, expecting thanks.

"I had to talk to you, Christian. I can't go, I can't!"

She put her hands to her face, which was wet with tears. He caught her wrists and drew her hands away. Leaning close, he said urgently, "You must go, Janine. You must hear what he has to say."

"Must I?" she said, looking at him like a child eager for guidance.

"Yes. You must. And never fear! Soon the *Abwehr* and the secret police are going to have other things to worry about."

"What do you mean?"

"Haven't you heard? Hitler's attacked Russia. He's set the French Communists free."

"Is that good?"

He looked down at her and found himself smiling. He knew in that moment that whatever proposals Delaplanche was about to make to him, he would accept. Janine and all those like her represented the raw emotional energy of France which without direction and protection would burn itself out uselessly, or be blown out by the Boche.

"Yes," he said softly. "That is very good indeed."

5

By four o'clock that Saturday afternoon, Günter Mai was just about recovering from his excesses at the Tour d'Argent. He had woken to a horrified mental rerun of all his indiscretions of the night before. Had he really told that joke about Hitler? And should he be consoled by the memory of Zeller laughing so much he almost choked on a piece of Roquefort? If he had been indiscreet, so had Zeller, and each was the other's only witness.

He arrived at the Café Balzac half an hour early.

Miche Boucher was there. Mai frowned. He quite liked Miche, but he didn't want him hanging around while he talked to Janine.

"Hello, Monsieur Scheffer," the redhead greeted him.

They sat and talked for a little while. Mai used the opportunity to pump Boucher about his work with the *Abwehr* Purchasing Section. It was always useful to know what one's colleagues were getting up to.

Gradually it became apparent that Boucher had deliberately sought him out. Finally he got to the point. "The thing is," he said, "Pajou's been going on about making a move. He's got his fingers in every pie, and he's evidently been talking to the Gestapo. He reckons he can get a better deal there, more freedom of action, a wider brief. He wants me to move with him. He says things like . . ."

He hesitated, then went on with a rush, ". . . like, the *Abwehr*'s on its way out and this time next year it'll be all Gestapo and we'd better be in on the ground floor. Now, I'm a bit bewildered by all this. I mean, you and the Gestapo, you're all Boche, right? So what's he getting at? I'm happy with Purchasing. It's easy work and there's plenty of perks. Pajou says that in this new job, there'd be more perks, though. Because we'd be dealing mostly with people, not things. I don't get that, myself. I mean, you can't cream off people, can you?"

Mai smiled to himself at the man's naïve openness. He said, "I think what Pajou means is, if you're bringing in a hundred crates of champagne, you can perhaps 'lose' four or five for yourself. But if you're bringing in a man, and he happens to have a hundred crates in his cellar, you can probably help yourself to the lot."

Boucher digested this. "Yes," he said. "I thought it was something like that. Bringing men in, I mean, not things."

"That would bother you?" asked Mai.

"I don't know," said Boucher honestly. "Depends who it was. Look, what do you think? Pajou's not often wrong. I mean, this business of the *Abwehr* being on the way out. What's that mean?"

"I really don't know," said Mai, his mind racing. "There are admittedly some rivalries, bound to be. I'll tell you what, Miche, I'd like to help you. You've helped me a lot. So why not go along with Pajou? At the same time, tell me what you're up to, and I'll give you the benefit of whatever inside knowledge I have. All right?"

Boucher considered this, then began to smile.

If Mai had had any thought of recruiting an unconscious spy, that smile removed it. Boucher knew exactly what he was being asked to do.

"You want a scout in the opposition dressing room, is that it?" he asked. "All right, you're on. Now I'd best be off before Janine gets here." He lifted his great length out of the chair and, with a cheerful wave, departed.

Mai sipped his coffee and reflected on the happy knack he seemed to have of turning up aces. He had wanted a nose in SD operations and almost immediately one had turned up.

"Monsieur Scheffer?" It was Janine, who'd arrived unnoticed.

"Sorry," he said, half rising. "Please sit down. Patron, some coffee."

He looked at her thoughtfully. She was nervous. Perhaps in the expectation of news; perhaps simply because Boche officers, even in civilian clothes, made her nervous.

He said, "How is your family?"

"The children are fine. I expect you see more of my parents than I do."

The sudden jibe amused him. Even in her nervousness she couldn't control her dislike of himself and of her parents' conciliatory attitude towards him. He wondered how he might use her.

"And your friend, Monsieur Valois? How is he?"

This clearly came as a surprise. There was something like alarm in her face. That was interesting. "You know Christian?"

"I met him at your parents' shop, remember? When you had the accident with the chocolates."

"Yes," she said, flushing, "I remember. He's well, I think. Now, please, why have you asked to see me?"

"Why? Because you asked for my help and I felt it only polite to offer a progress report. But if you'd rather we didn't proceed any further..."

He let his hurt tone fade away into a hurt expression. He could see that a need stronger than her dislike and resentment was keeping her in her seat.

"No. Go on. Now I'm here..." The words emerged with difficulty.

"All right. As you requested, I made certain inquiries as to the whereabouts of your husband, Iakov Moseich Jean-Paul Simonian."

He paused. She felt faint but held herself perfectly still. He knew Jean-Paul's full name. Surely her mother wouldn't have told him that? Miche...? But Miche didn't know Jean-Paul's full name.

The lieutenant's next words confirmed her worst fears.

"I obtained from French military records a full list of those in your husband's unit. Then I circulated a request to all POW camps for information on prisoners from the unit and in particular one called Iakov Moseich Jean-Paul Simonian. It's an unusual name, that, madame. For a Frenchman. But that made it all the easier to check." He paused, then went on. "I'm sorry to report that all responses were negative."

She tried desperately to conceal her relief, or to let it emerge as disappointment. "You mean there's no trace?"

"None. I'm sorry."

"Yes. Well, thank you, Lieutenant."

She was being polite, now that he couldn't help her! He watched her prepare to go.

Then he said, "However, I did encounter one odd thing. A military hospital in Lorraine had a couple of patients from your husband's unit."

Slowly she sank back into her chair. "Yes?" she said.

"One of them was on the unit roll I had. But for some reason the other wasn't. A man called Jean-Paul Simon."

He spoke the name as if he was savouring the syllables on his tongue. She sat perfectly still, trying to keep all emotion from her face, fearing that her very lack of expression would in itself be a giveaway. She felt his eyes on her, his will pressing her to speak. She could think of no words that would not be a betrayal, and yet her silence too seemed vibrant with guilt.

Then Günter Mai laughed. "Which just goes to show how useless official records are! I'm sorry I haven't been able to help, Madame Simonian, truly sorry. But don't give up hope. I checked casualty lists too, and there's no sign of your husband's name there either. Now, let's have some more coffee, shall we?"

6

"Come on," snapped Maurice Melchior. "I haven't got all day. Let's do business." His hand went up to the still pink scar on his cheek, a gesture he found hard to control when feeling nervous.

Silently the café owner handed over an envelope. It allegedly contained fifty thousand francs, but Melchior slipped it under his waistcoat without counting. When you were an accredited agent of Miche Boucher's black-market business, you didn't need to count.

At last things were going right for Maurice Melchior. Working for Boucher had begun a period of unprecedented contentment and prosperity. Miche seemed to be able to get his hands on almost anything, and Melchior had discovered in himself an unsuspected talent for judging what the market would bear and then squeezing a little extra.

"Same order next month," said the proprietor.

"We'll have to see," said Melchior doubtfully. "The booze should be OK, but I don't know how long we can keep spuds down to eight francs the kilo. As for the steak ...!"

The owner looked sullen, then said, "Filthy Boche!" which was the nearest he dared come to a protest against his supplier.

Melchior left. Outside he paused. He felt he was being watched. He looked at two soldiers at a pavement table. No danger there. It must all be in the mind.

Then he saw him, only a few feet away, almost hidden by a lamppost, his face expressionless, his calm unblinking gaze fixed on Melchior.

It took a couple of seconds for full recognition. Then he stepped quickly forward and said, "Hello. It's Pauli, isn't it! From the old lady's flat? What are you doing here? Run away from home, have you?"

Pauli Simonian slowly shook his head. The truth was, he was a great wanderer and spent a large part of his time, while his mother thought he was just round the corner playing with friends, exploring interesting quarters of the city.

"I have to meet Maman," he said. "She's shopping."

He spoke very convincingly. To his surprise, the little man laughed out loud. "Good try, Pauli, but your maman's not the type to come shopping in this squalid area. No, you're on the loose, doing a bit of exploring, aren't you? I used to like that myself when I was a boy. But I think maybe you've come far enough today. I'd better get you back home."

Taking Pauli firmly by the hand he led him towards the métro station. As they walked, Melchior chatted away. Pauli listened, fascinated even when he didn't understand.

They entered the metro station and Melchior bought tickets. The platform was crowded and soon Melchior was holding forth on the injustice of having to travel like a bullock being transported to market. But Pauli was no longer listening. His attention had been caught by a young man a few feet away whose face was set in an expression of ferocious concentration.

Close to the young man, a little nearer the edge of the platform, was a German officer. He had a fresh, open face and his lips were pursed to whistle some tune or other which Pauli could not hear, for the train was here now, decelerating noisily as it emerged from the tunnel. As it halted, the waiting travellers surged forward to the unopened doors. The young Frenchman too stepped forward, bringing his hand out of his jacket pocket. Clutched in it was a small pistol. Pauli saw him raise it to halfway up the officer's spine. The pressure of his finger on the trigger was visible through the whole length of his arm, yet he did not seem to be able to bring himself to release the hammer. A small stout man suddenly lurched forward and grabbed at the gun. When his hands closed over the younger man's he added his strength to the trigger finger. The gun fired. And fired again as the small man renewed his pressure.

A woman shrieked. Blood spurted out of the officer's tunic, spattering the hands of both his assailants. The German fell slowly forward. The small stout man turned away, dragging the younger man with him. The crowd surged away from the falling body like water driven from the centre of a pool by a heavy stone. The fleeing men came straight past Pauli. Melchior turned to see what was happening and was pushed aside by the fugitives as he took in the twitching body only a few feet away.

"Oh, my God!" he cried, raising his hands to his face to block out the sight. Then he screamed in greater horror as he saw there was blood on his jacket sleeve where the assassins had brushed against him.

Two German soldiers from further up the platform forced their way to the body. A gendarme came clattering down a stairway, blowing his whistle. People were shouting, gesticulating, pointing. It seemed to Melchior they were pointing at him. In a blind panic he turned and began forcing his way towards the staircase up which the killers had vanished. The flight was instinctive but not illogical. He had under his shirt fifty thousand francs in dirty notes which he had no way of explaining.

Almost at the staircase, he heard a clicking noise behind him and a German voice called, "Halt, or I fire!"

He halted, turned; a German soldier with his rifle at the ready came running towards him. Behind him was a gendarme. The soldier thrust the muzzle of his weapon into Melchior's belly. The gendarme cried breathlessly, "Is this one of them?"

Melchior regarded them helplessly and speechlessly.

Then a small figure pushed between the gendarme and the soldier and rushed up to him, crying, "Uncle! Uncle! I'm here! I lost sight of you, I was so frightened!"

Lowering his half raised arms, Melchior clasped Pauli to his breast and said, "There, there, it's all right, it's all right," and, raising his eyes to the gendarme, "I lost him in the crowd, there was such a panic. I thought he'd run away."

The gendarme rolled his eyes in exasperation. "Come on!" he said to the soldier. "This way!" The two of them ran off up the stairs.

The journey home was silent. But as they walked towards the apartment house Melchior said, "Perhaps we'd better not say anything to your mother, Pauli. You know how mothers worry."

As they parted outside Sophie Simonian's door he gravely offered the little boy his hand. "Thank you, Pauli," he said, "thank you very much."

THAT EVENING as his mother tucked him up in bed, Pauli said in a low voice, so as not to disturb his sister who was already fast asleep, "Maman, is there still a war on, like when the Boche bombed our car?"

"No!" said Janine, taken aback. "Not here, anyway."

"Are the Boche our friends then?"

"No!" said Janine, with even more vehemence. "You can trust a friend, can't you? You must never trust a Boche!"

It was guilt that made her so vehement. Since her last interview with Mai, she'd debated in her mind what he'd said a thousand times. Had he been laughing at her, knowing full well who Jean-Paul Simon was? Or was he really too stupid to make the connection?

Whatever the truth, she'd decided not to tell Christian what had happened, merely assuring him that Mai had confirmed there was no trace of Jean-Paul in any official records. This decision was based on fear that Christian might advise against attempting further contact with Jean-Paul if he thought the Boche were on to him. Not that there'd been any contact yet. Christian had sent a letter, allegedly from Pivert, telling Jean-Paul in veiled terms that all was well, but there'd been no reply.

"Is Monsieur Valois not coming tonight?" asked Pauli.

Valois's visits were regular and this was one of his nights.

"Yes, he is late," said Janine smiling. Christian nearly always brought the children something, a precious sweet or an apple, whatever he could get hold of. "Don't worry. If he comes, I'll send him in to see if you're awake! Goodnight now."

She left the room. Pauli lay in the dark. His eyelids were pressed tight in pretence of sleep, but his ears were straining to listen, and it wasn't until the clock in the living room struck eleven and his mother tiptoed into their shared room that he really fell asleep, persuaded at last that there was no chance now of opening his eyes to find Christian Valois leaning over him, offering him a red-skinned apple with the same outstretched hand Pauli had last seen in the métro, stained with the blood of the German soldier he had just shot.

7

There was a poster on the wall of the bakery. Günter Mai recognized it from some distance away. Everybody was now familiar with the black-and-red edged notices printed in parallel columns of French and German on a dull biscuit-coloured background. They were notifications that more executions had taken place.

This one, he saw as he got nearer, had been defaced. Someone had scrawled across it in thick blue letters, GERMAN BUSINESS.

Clever, he thought. An accusation against the authorities and also a parody of the notices which Jewish-owned shops had to display.

He found Madame Crozier in a state of mixed indignation and apprehension. "I really don't know what to say, Lieutenant," she protested. "I know your boys have to put their notices up somewhere, but I hardly feel my shop is the proper place. Then when it was defaced, well, of course my natural instinct was to take it down, but that would make me to blame, wouldn't it?"

She was right. Removing or defacing official posters was a serious crime.

He said, "I'll have a word about it."

"Thank you, I knew I could rely on you."

He accepted the usual invitation to step into the living room and take a cup of coffee with madame while Crozier put together his order.

"I went to the exhibition at the Berlitz the other day, have you been, Lieutenant? You must go, it's really fascinating."

The exhibition was called *Le Juif et la France*. Mai had seen the advertising poster. It showed a caricature Jew, bearded, hook-nosed, digging claw-like fingers into a huge globe of the world.

"I was telling Madame Pascal about it, and she said that she couldn't see the point of the exhibition, we were all French together, and wasn't Jesus a Jew. Well, I ask you! Jesus a Jew! Excuse me, that sounds like the shop door."

She went out. Mai produced his *Hitler Jugend Tagebuch* from his pocket and made an entry. He was a collector of trivia, a sower of tiny seeds. From the shop he heard a voice whose words he could not catch but which he recognized. Then Madame Crozier spoke, in a low tone just audible to the sensitive ear. "Lieutenant Mai is here."

He listened for the sound of the street door opening and shutting. It didn't come. He smiled and put away his book. Sometimes the tiny seeds took root.

The door opened and Madame Crozier re-entered. "Here's my daughter, Lieutenant. I think you've met."

He stood up and bowed. "Good day, Madame Simonian."

"Good day, Lieutenant," murmured Janine in a low voice.

She wants to talk to me, he thought. He'd guessed it when she didn't immediately walk out of the shop. He knew it now he saw her.

It hadn't been difficult to confirm that the patient "Simon" and Iakov Moseich Jean-Paul Simonian were one and the same person. He'd arranged with the hospital for any correspondence for "Simon" to be intercepted, and a letter now lay in his files. He'd checked Pivert's alleged address and discovered it was Valois's. So far he had found nothing against the young man, but he had one of his feelings...

He felt no guilt about keeping all this to himself. He could see no advantage in letting the warped minds which organized farces like the Berlitz exhibition know that one of their POWs was a Jew; on the other hand, the knowledge might be useful in recruiting another pair of ears and eyes to help his job here in Paris.

He finished his coffee and said, "Now I must go. Thank you for the coffee. Good day, Madame Simonian."

He left swiftly. Janine wouldn't talk to him in front of her mother, he knew that. She would need an excuse, so he'd provided her with one. And he smiled to himself a few seconds later as he heard her voice calling, "Lieutenant! You forgot your cakes."

He stopped and turned. Faintly flushed, she ran up to him, carrying a small white box.

"Thank you," he said. "That was kind. Though it might have been kinder to my waist to let me forget."

She smiled. It was an effort, but she managed it.

He said, "Are you walking my way, by any chance?"

"Yes, I think I am," she said.

They walked in silence a little way.

"How are your children?" he asked, seeking a means of prompting her request for help.

"They're very well, thank you."

"They must miss their father," he said sympathetically.

"Yes. They do. We all do." A pause, then it came out with a rush. "I was wondering if perhaps your inquiries, you were kind enough to help, if anything else..."

The rush declined to a stumble.

"I have learned nothing more than I knew last time we talked," he said carefully. "Nothing has changed."

He could feel her scrutinizing his words, desperate for significance. She was hooked, but he would need to play her very carefully. He recalled her suspicion that it might be her body, not her loyalty, he was after. Which would a woman find it easier to contemplate—betraying her husband or betraying her country?

He said, "He has my sympathy, your husband, wherever he is."

"What do you mean?" she demanded.

"It is a lonely business, being far from home, in a strange country, whatever the reason," he said with a sigh. "I know that from experience. You long for a little sympathy, a little kindness."

He reached out and took her cold, unresponsive hand in his. "I hope," he said softly, "wherever he is, your man is finding a little kindness."

For a moment he thought he'd overdone it. Then her hand squeezed his and she said, "I hope so too."

He raised her hand slowly to his lips and kissed it. She lowered her head so that her hair fell in a fringe over her face, he guessed to hide her look of revulsion.

She said in an almost inaudible voice, "The poor man you were telling me about, the one in hospital whose name did not appear on any official unit list . . ."

"Yes. I remember him."

"He must be very lonely, if no one knows where he is."

"Yes," said Mai. "He's often been in my mind."

"I could sense you were sympathetic," said Janine with a flash of savage sarcasm. "Perhaps it would be a kindness to find out how he is, what is planned for him when his treatment is finished."

"You would be interested in that, madame?" he said. "Then I'm sure I can find it out for you. Perhaps you would do me the honour of dining with me one night. Then I could report what I've managed to discover."

"Yes, I would like that," she said, trying for brightness.

"On Friday then? Seven o'clock at the Balzac, shall we say? I look forward to that very much," said Mai, letting his face break into a smile.

She nodded, turned and ran off, in haste to put distance between them before he should recognize her loathing and self-disgust.

He watched her go. Poor child, he thought. All upset because she thinks the big, bad Boche wants to bed her! She'll chatter like a chipmunk in her efforts to postpone the awful moment. And by the time she realizes it's only the chatter I'm after, she'll be so relieved, and so used to the idea of cooperating with the enemy, that the rest will be easy.

He resumed his walking. He knew he ought to be feeling pleased that yet another of his little schemes was working out so well, but somehow he was not.

"Christian," said Delaplanche, "you are an imbecile. May I come in?"

Valois stood aside and let the lawyer pass by him into the flat. He'd been expecting the visit. Delaplanche had been away in the Free Zone at the time of the shooting in the métro.

Valois had been ill for a week afterwards. The prospect of seeing Delaplanche had not made him get better any quicker.

Delaplanche held up a paper-wrapped parcel. "A gift," he said. "From your mother. I met her in Vichy. We knew each other when your father and I were young lawyers. She asked if I could deliver it to you. I was only too pleased. It's such an excellent justification for my presence here."

"Thank you," said Valois, taking the parcel.

Delaplanche sat down and raised his eyebrows invitingly.

"I'm sorry," said Valois wretchedly. "It was a mistake, I see that now. They've taken hostages, they're threatening to shoot them. I never thought the Boche would react like this."

"Didn't you? I did!" said the lawyer. "It's the best thing that could happen for us."

"That innocent Frenchmen should be shot?"

"That the most innocent of Frenchmen, or women, or even children should not be able to feel safe!"

Valois sat down opposite the lawyer. "Why burst in here calling me an imbecile, then?"

"Well, for a start, you don't seem to have been very good at it, do you? Oh, don't look so affronted! I understand you were all cut up about the killing. Now you take offence at not being complimented on a nice job! I'll give you the same compliment I gave Théo, shall I?"

Théo was the Resistance cell leader. He was also the man who'd had to help Valois pull the trigger.

"Don't blame Théo! It was my choice! My responsibility!"

Delaplanche said softly, "I told Théo he was stupid, unfit for our work. And I tell you the same. Choice? Responsibility? What have they got to do with it? Listen, Christian. I didn't recruit you to run around the métro killing the Boche. All right, so you succumbed to some childish need to prove yourself—don't interrupt!—well, I take the blame for that. I'd forgotten what it is to be young and untried while the old men are boasting. I shouldn't have put you anywhere near Théo."

"He's not being punished on my behalf, is he?"

"Such self-importance!" said Delaplanche. "On the contrary, he's a great success, a first-class organiser, and he kills a lot of the enemy. No, he's going onward and upward, don't worry about Théo. It's just that you're going in different directions. By the time the war is finished you could well be in just the kind of position we need to help us rebuild the country. In the meantime, you'll be a pair of eyes and ears for us in the Ministry of Finance. Make yourself popular. No need to collaborate actively with the Boche, I don't want you tainted with *that* brush, or some ambitious killer may rub you out! But be nice to people. Make up your differences with your father, for instance. Visit him more often. There's all kinds of useful little things to be picked up in Vichy!"

"You want me to spy on my father? For God's sake, that's a Nazi trick, isn't it?"

Delaplanche said quietly, "I hope no one ever has to die because of your sentimentality, Christian."

JANINE WAS LATE for her dinner date with Günter Mai at the Café Balzac.

"I'm sorry," she said breathlessly, tumbling into her chair. "I was held up, the métro, some trouble..."

"It's all right," he said, amused. "You're only a quarter of an hour late. That's punctual in French terms, surely? Now, I thought we would just eat here, if that's all right?"

"That's fine," she said.

He had expected her to be too impatient for news of her husband to wait more than a few moments, but she seemed content to exchange small talk and to tuck into the meal without questioning him. She was, he guessed, delaying the moment which would put her in his debt.

His guess was partly right. The other part was that Janine was determined to eat her fill. The more she ate here, the less hungry she would be when it came to sharing out the rations at home.

At last she had finished. "All right, Lieutenant," she began, but paused as Mai put his finger to his lips.

"Not lieutenant. Not here," he smiled.

"What then?"

"Edouard. Let us act like friends."

"As long as we remember it is an act," she said. "What have you to tell me about my husband?"

So, she was determined to start by throwing aside all pretence. It was a good move. "He is well, almost well enough to be discharged," he said, accepting her change of rules.

"Discharged? Will they send him home?" she asked with sudden hope.

"I doubt it. If it had been a permanently crippling wound, probably yes. But when there is a complete physical recovery..."

He stressed the word physical, but she did not take him up. Instead she said gloomily, "But to keep him in hospital such a long time, it must have been a terrible wound."

"The head wound was very serious," admitted Mai. "There was a fragment of metal lodged inside the skull. They did not dare try to remove it till his other wounds had healed and the body was strong enough to risk the operation."

"You've gone into this pretty deeply," she said.

He had in fact received a copy of "Simon's" full medical record. What he'd said about the soldier's physical health was true, but there'd been more. The patient suffered from bouts of severe withdrawal, and his recollection of the past was disturbed and fragmentary.

189

He poured more wine into her glass. She was consuming it greedily. Perhaps she was trying to anaesthetize herself against whatever payment she was expecting him to exact? He studied her face over his glass. She met his gaze squarely. How did she see him? As the ruthless spymaster, or a lecherous Hun? How did he see himself?

She said flatly, "How can you help me?"

Good girl! he thought. She was at least going to try to extract from him a promise of something more positive than silence.

"Alas," he said, "only with advice."

"What advice?" Her voice, now slightly blurred by the wine, had a note of desperation in it. It wasn't just fear. This was the despairing voice of a woman alone, living with problems she did not dare to share with anyone.

He'd been intending to underline his power over her with a couple of gentle threats disguised as advice, and then to start leading her inexorably into the role of *Abwehr* informer. But now he found himself wanting to ease the pain he heard in her voice with some real advice.

He said, "You must be patient. It's clear your husband is using another name because he fears what might happen if it came out he was a Jew."

"Is he right to be fearful?" she asked with a calm dignity which took him by surprise.

He met her unwavering gaze, thought of all the reservations he could make, the assurances he could offer; then he thought of his opposite number in the SD and said quietly, "Yes, he is right to be fearful."

She shook her head disbelievingly and said, "There must be something I can do?"

"Get it into your head," he said. "Any kind of fuss endangers your husband and perhaps even your family."

"My family?" she said in alarm. "What danger can there be to us? Bubbah Sophie's a Jew, yes, but she's an old lady. The children and I are good Catholics. As for Jean-Paul, he hates all religion."

In exasperation Mai snapped, "Being an old lady is no protection, and saying you've been converted is no protection, and being brought up Catholic is no protection." His vehemence at last frightened her.

"Protection against what?" she demanded.

He sat back wearily and wondered how to answer. He had seen plenty of anti-Semitic violence in Germany before the war. Here in France it was just starting. The anti-Semitic press was growing ever more abusive. And, of course, the Nazi intelligence-gathering service, in its battle to take over effective control of the city from the Military Command, would see the pogrom both as a means and an end.

"Listen, Janine," he said earnestly, "I don't know what's going to happen, but prepare for the worst. Make sure all your papers are in order. Here in France bits of paper can still protect you to some extent. Friends in high places are useful too."

190

"But why? What's all this to do with me?" she asked in bewilderment. "I don't have any friends in high places."

"Monsieur Valois must know important people," Mai suggested. "Isn't his father a deputy?"

"Yes, but they don't get on," she said. "Though, come to think of it, Christian does know Maître Delaplanche, and he's important, isn't he?"

It was enough to make you believe in God, thought Mai, but a God of malicious irony rather than loving kindness. Here he was enjoying helping this girl, having put aside (for the moment, anyway) all thought of using her, and instantly those lovely pale lips had coughed up this pearl. *Delaplanche*. Almost certainly a Communist, but too clever to have his name recorded on any list and too well connected to be easily touchable. He'd been on the *Abwehr*'s list of men to be watched for a long time.

"Never heard of him," he lied easily. "He's well known, you say?"

"Oh yes. He's been in the papers a lot, helping ordinary people in trouble, so maybe someone like him could help Jean-Paul."

"Perhaps," said Mai. The effort of changing back from friendly adviser to *Abwehr* officer was surprisingly hard.

"You've met this lawyer fellow, have you?" he asked.

"Yes, in a way. I saw him at Christian's flat."

Mai said, "Bear him in mind. Some time in the future you may find him useful, after you've got your husband home. For the time being, the less you say to anyone, the better, family or friends."

She seized upon the bait he offered. "When I've got Jean-Paul home? But you said there was no hope!"

He smiled. "No *official* hope. But who knows..."

He'd done this sort of thing a thousand times, manipulating contacts with half promises, veiled threats, hinted bribes. It had never felt degrading before. Then he thought of that German soldier who had been assassinated in the métro. The link between Valois and Delaplanche might be nothing. On the other hand it could lead right into the middle of a Resistance group.

Janine set down her glass with a bang. "All right," she said decisively. "But you're not getting me body *and* mind. If it's information you want, I'll try. If it's me you want, you can have me. But don't hope for both."

She was missing the point, but they nearly all did. They thought of one-off bargains, not appreciating that the initial exchange was merely the planting of the hook. It didn't much matter what form it took. In Janine's case, bedding her would be as good as anything. With that family-destroying evidence against her, he could probably play her for evermore.

He looked at her and for a moment was tempted. She saw it in his eyes and looked away to hide whatever was in her own. No, that wasn't the way, he told himself, shocked that he could have entertained the idea for even a second.

Before he could say anything, the patron appeared at the table and stopped to whisper in his ear. "The flics are outside, Monsieur Scheffer. They'll be raiding us any second, to check papers."

Mai didn't have to feign alarm. Not that there'd be any trouble from the police if he showed his *Abwehr* identification, but he didn't want to lose a well-established cover.

He said, "Can we get out the back?"

"No. They'll have someone there. But you can hide upstairs. Second door on the right. Lock it after you."

Mai rose, pulling Janine with him, and went through a door behind the bar. They went up a flight of rickety stairs and into the room indicated by the patron. It was small, almost totally filled by a huge metal bedstead with a feather mattress. What light there was filtered through a threadbare curtain over the tiny window.

"Here?" she said in a small voice.

He took a second to get her meaning. She thought he'd made his choice and opted for payment in flesh rather than information. He opened his mouth to tell her about the police raid but suddenly she moved forward and pressed herself against him. It was the leap of the timid swimmer plunging into the icy pool before her nerve completely fails. Mai put his arms round her and kissed her passionately. There was little response from her lips, but his body responded with all the fervour of long deprivation. His mind was still protesting that this was wrong, professionally, morally, emotionally. If she'd cried out in rejection, if he'd been able to see the contempt on her face, he might still have had the will to back off. But the room was dark and Janine was silent except when she said desperately, "He will come home, won't he?"

"Yes," he promised, pulling her down onto the bed.

THAT SAME NIGHT six synagogues were blown up. In the collaborationist press the outrage was reported as the protest of ordinary Frenchmen indignant at the slowness of the anti-Jewish reforms promised by their new military leaders. In fact, it had been an SD operation, and Boucher had tipped Mai off a few days earlier.

"I told you what was going to happen!" fumed Günter when he met Zeller the following morning. "Why wasn't it stopped?"

"How? By putting a permanent *Wehrmacht* guard on all the synagogues in Paris? Think how that would have looked back in Berlin!"

"At least we could have used the advance warning to make sure everybody knows who really organized this."

Zeller sighed wearily. "You disappoint me, Günter. Of course everyone knows who really did it, but private knowledge and public acknowledgment are very different things. No, the SD have done very well for themselves here. They've put the military governor in an impossible position either way. So, despite your excellent advance intelligence, it's one in the eye for the *Abwehr* too."

Later that week, Mai was sitting having a drink with Michel Boucher, debriefing him about the aftermath of the synagogue burning.

"Fiebelkorn's going around with a huge smile on his face," Boucher said. "They all are. I don't get it. What's so clever about letting off a bit of dynamite?"

"I can't say, Miche," said Mai, who found Boucher's political thought processes at once naïve and impenetrable. "We'll keep in touch, eh?"

"Sure. Talking of which, Auntie Lou was wondering if she'd offended you somehow. Says you've not been into the shop for ages."

"I've been busy."

"That's what I said. I expect she's just worried she'll not get her next lot of extra flour. I told her I'd fix her up if you let her down. Cousin Jan was asking after you too. I think she's still hoping you might be able to help with finding Jean-Paul."

So at least the girl had had the sense to keep the news of her husband's survival to herself. "It's not easy," he said.

"I didn't reckon it would be," said Boucher. "Might cost a bit, I told Janine a while back. Only make sure you get value for money."

He knows, thought Mai. Or at least, he's guessed!

Mai had avoided meeting Janine since the night he'd raped her. Yes, that was the right word; the act had been brief, brutish and against her will. The memory of the encounter filled him with shame.

And yet, amidst the shame, he had to acknowledge desire. He found himself thinking of Jean-Paul Simonian with furious resentment. For God's sake, it was almost like being jealous of the man.

The only way he could get Jean-Paul released officially was either to confide in or lie to Zeller, and process an official *Abwehr* request. The dangers were too great, to Jean-Paul as well as to his own career. Or was it simply that he didn't want Simonian released?

After ten days of intermittent soul-searching, it occurred to him that he could do one thing at least. There was no need to withhold Simonian's mail. Having once made up his mind, he acted swiftly, authorizing a direct telephone call to Erhard, the doctor in charge of "Simon".

"Give him the letter, you say? About time. It's an act of sadism, keeping it from him. More Gestapo than *Abwehr*, I would have said."

"Yes, I'm sorry," said Mai. "It was necessary. But no longer."

"Good," said Erhard. "Pretty soon we're going to have to make our minds up, and his reaction to the letter might help."

"Make up your minds about what?"

"About where he goes next."

"And what are the alternatives?"

"POW camp or medical repatriation, of course. Not that there's much

choice in this case, whatever I say. Unless there's some vital part missing, our admin chief is impossible to convince, so it's the long road east for this poor soul."

"He'll surely review the evidence first," said Mai mildly.

"You would say that," snorted Erhard. "You're two of a kind. Bureaucrats under the skin! This fellow keeps on trying to get transferred to Intelligence. That's where the real work's done, he says. Same bloody work, as far as I can see. Gathering information you don't know what to do with."

Mai now knew that by promising the admin officer a transfer to *Abwehr* intelligence, he could secure, in return, Simonian's release.

"I wonder if you could get this call transferred to your admin officer?" he said.

Ten minutes later it was done. No official forms, file records, or signed requests. Just hints, hesitations and half-promises of rewards, the dialect of deception.

"You're looking pleased with yourself, Günter," said Zeller, entering the room. "Up to something wicked?"

"On the contrary, Major," said Mai with a smile.

9

On the last day of the year, a train from the east pulled into the rain-lashed station at Compiègne. The platform was crowded with hopeful relatives and helpers from various voluntary agencies.

Janine scanned every window as the train decelerated past her. "I can't see him," she said wretchedly to Christian Valois. "He hasn't come."

"Don't be silly!" he said confidently. "Of course he's come. You can't have seen everyone!"

Uncomforted, she leaned against him and pressed her face into his shoulder. Valois watched the line of bandaged and limping figures being helped from the train.

Then he saw him.

He held his breath and didn't speak for a few moments till he was sure. Then he let it out with a sigh. "He's here," he said.

"*What?*"

"He's here."

She turned her head slowly as if fearing a deception. And when she saw Jean-Paul, she fixed her eyes on him with a desperate intensity as though fearful that even a single blink would wash him away.

He was much thinner, and they must have shaved his head for the operation, for his black hair was still only stubble. She could see the scars. One for the bullet at the side of his left temple, the other where the surgeon's scalpel had probed. But it was still Jean-Paul, unmistakable, unbelievable, Jean-Paul. Her heart swelled with love. She'd hated Günter Mai in the days after he had taken her, but now she forgave him. More, she laughed at him and mocked him for having asked so little of her in return for this dearest of treasures.

Jean-Paul hadn't seen her yet. He was walking slowly along the platform, not like an invalid, but with the slowness of uncertainty.

And now suddenly he smiled, the smile which turned his dark face from ascetic scholar to Sicilian shepherd boy. He came running towards them, heedless of the people between. She stood quite still, frozen by joy. And now for the first time in nearly two years she heard her husband's voice.

"Christian!"

Suddenly his arms were round Christian Valois's neck and his joyous face pressed hard against his shoulder.

"Jean-Paul, it's so good to see you," cried Valois. "But hold on a bit. I don't think you've quite got your priorities right."

Disengaging himself from Jean-Paul, he twisted him round so that he faced Janine. For long, silent seconds the young wife and the returned husband looked at each other and the smile faded from both faces.

Jean-Paul turned to Valois and said in a puzzled tone, "Who's she?"

PART THREE   February-November 1942
1

Janine woke. For a moment she did not know where she was. The room was full of frosty radiance as dawn broke through the high sash window. Jean-Paul always slept with the curtains pulled wide.

Jean-Paul. She turned. There on the bolster beside her was his dear head. In the month since his return his hair had grown to a fledgling's fluff, obscuring much of the scarring, and his face had lost something of the wasted pallor that had turned him into his own ghost.

He turned in his sleep, stretched out his arm, draped it round her. She held her breath. He opened his eyes, saw her face so close to his and smiled. It was a smile that drew back years, the smile of a young man who knows that already he has got all that he needs to guarantee his happiness.

The door burst open. Céci rushed in crying, "Maman, Maman, Pauli's hid Mimi!" Janine looked at her daughter with unusual irritation. These first moments of the day when sleep had thrown a fragile membrane over Jean-Paul's inner wounds were her most precious possession, her greatest hope for his healing. He was sitting up in bed now. The smile had gone and with it the carefree boy, as his face took on its now more normal expression of puzzled watchfulness.

"All right, Céci. I'll be out in a minute," she said.

Disappointed with her mother's lack of sympathy, the little girl turned to her father. "Papa, Pauli's very naughty," she chimed.

Jean-Paul looked at her; then he smiled, not the same smile he had woken up with but undoubtedly a smile. Janine felt a flood of relief. Though her old Jean-Paul was rarely with her for more than a few waking moments, there were at least two new ones. This one acknowledged formally who she was and was able to smile at his daughter. The other, the one she feared, was a grim, intense figure who clearly inhabited a world of darkness and pain.

"Let's go and see Pauli, shall we?" he said, swinging his legs out of bed and picking up the delighted child.

Janine followed them out of the bedroom. She was always worried at any confrontation between Pauli and his father. Of all the renewed relationships this was the worst. Even at his darkest, Jean-Paul recognized his mother and Christian. Céci he had no recollection of, but she had none of him either. This was her papa, she was told, so that's how she treated him, leaving him no choice of response. As for Janine herself, her days swung between the joy of that morning recognition and the pain of subsequent rejections. But the real problem was Pauli.

She saw it now as she watched through the door of the children's room.

"Come on, Pauli, give Céci the dog. Big boys don't play with toys like that, do they?"

Jean-Paul was making an effort, but he couldn't hit the right tone. The trouble was that Pauli did remember him, and had missed him, had been almost ill with excitement at the prospect of his return, and now found it impossible to understand the changes in him. Despite Pauli's apparent maturity in so many matters, she could see that all he felt was a small child's hurt at being rejected. He withdrew into his pain just as his father so often withdrew into his. And neither of them emerged far enough to grasp the other's reaching hand.

Now Pauli threw the dog at his father's feet. Jean-Paul's face set. Then he put the little girl down and, pushing his way past Janine, re-entered his room.

"Pauli, hurry up and get ready for school," Janine said.

She turned and almost bumped into Christian Valois. He was dressed in his dark business suit.

"Christian, I'm sorry. I should have been getting breakfast ages ago. We've slept in."

"Don't be sorry. How's Jean-Paul this morning?"

"All right. You know, not black."

"Good. I must rush. See you tonight."

She watched him leave and thought, soon we must get out of this flat. It was marvellous of Christian to have put them up. Sophie's flat had been impossible. It was all right for her to share with the children, but not for the four of them to sleep in the same room. The boulangerie offered more space, but the problem there was Louise. She and Jean-Paul had never got on well. Now, their proximity might be positively dangerous. There was a violence in Jean-Paul which hadn't been there before and she did not know when or where it might come out.

But staying here was not a long-term solution. In fairness to Christian they ought to move on. But where? To find a decent place they could afford was not going to be easy. The Boche set the price of things with their inflated exchange rate, and property ran high.

She went to get dressed. Jean-Paul had got back into bed. His face was turned away from her but she could tell by the set of his shoulders that he was drifting into that dark solitary world where no one else could follow. She knew that if she walked round the bed she would find his eyes wide and staring, totally devoid of recognition.

2

There was a queue outside the Crozier boulangerie. The customers looked defeated and depressed.

Günter Mai turned up his collar and slipped round the back to enter via the bakehouse, where he found the baker removing a lightly loaded tray from the right-hand oven. The bigger oven on the left wall hadn't been lit for almost a year now, due to the shortage of fuel and flour.

"Bread ration day, is it?" he said.

"That's right," said Crozier gloomily. "And there's not much to go round. I hate to see the poor devils' faces when we're short. Come on through while this lot cools, and we'll have a coffee and croissant."

"Thank you," said Mai, smiling. "How's Janine? And your grand-children?" he asked.

"Fine," said Crozier, face brightening.

Mai sat and listened to the baker talking proudly of Pauli and Céci, and let his thoughts drift to their mother. He hadn't seen Janine since that night at the Balzac, but of course had been kept up-to-date by her parents on his visits to the bakery. He would really have liked to wash his hands of Janine, but God was still pushing her into his professional path. Why did she have to take her family to stay at Christian Valois's apartment? Zeller assured him he was getting obsessed by that young man, but the more Valois became a model citizen, the less Mai liked it. He'd felt the man's resentment bordering on hatred the only time they had met, and there was no way he could square this with Valois's reported reconciliation with his Vichy father or with his unquestioning acceptance of the collaborationist aspects of his work at the ministry.

198

The one flaw in Valois's otherwise unblemished front was his acquaintance with Delaplanche. Even that had been explained away by Zeller. "He's an old acquaintance of Valois *père* from their law-student days, and Delaplanche knows the value of not making unnecessary enemies. So when he returns from a visit to Vichy, what more natural than that he should bring back a gift from Madame Valois for her much-missed son?"

Zeller might be right. But Mai didn't think so. And now he had in Christian Valois's flat a potential agent ready to be activated. So far he'd been able to justify his inaction on the grounds that Delaplanche was still in the south, doing God knew what. But word was that he was on his way back to Paris. So what now? And what kind of agent would Janine make anyway, especially when she felt the price had already been paid?

Crozier's rambling chatter was interrupted by his wife's arrival from the shop.

"Hello, Lieutenant," she said. "Crozier, isn't that next batch ready yet? Two lots of forged tickets I've had today. I think it's the Gelicot family. Wasn't the son apprenticed in the printing trade?"

Mai made a mental note. Any hint of an illicit press was of interest these days. He wondered how conscious Madame Crozier was of what she was saying.

As he rose, Crozier said in excuse, "We were just chatting about the children, dear."

"I wish I had time to chat. They're fine children, which is saying a lot when you consider their father. Doesn't know his own wife half the time."

"He's been through a lot," said Crozier mildly.

"Has he?" snorted Louise. "Well, I hope you'd have to go through a lot more, Crozier, before you forgot me."

The two men's eyes met for a moment and Mai was still smiling a few minutes later as he left through the bakehouse door.

"You're looking very happy, Lieutenant."

It was Janine, who'd just come into the yard. She had her daughter in her arms, but the little girl was struggling to get down. Set on the ground, she ran instantly to Mai and waved a little bunch of winter jasmine at him.

"Are these for me?" he asked, bending down.

"No," said Céci scornfully. "For Gramma. I want donkey."

"I'm sorry," said Mai, "I seem to be out of donkeys."

"I want donkey like Uncle Chris," cried the little girl.

Mai looked at Janine who said, "Her Uncle Christian gives her donkey rides on his back. Céci, don't bother..."

"No bother," said Mai. "I work like a horse, so I might as well look like one."

He swung the laughing child onto his shoulders and stood upright.

"She's growing fast," he said. "How old is she now?"

"Four. It was her birthday last week."

"They soon grow up," he said. "How are you, Janine?"

"I'm fine." She was looking at him warily. "Lieutenant, I'd like to thank you," she said abruptly.

"Oh yes?" he said gruffly. Gratitude was salt to his still raw guilt.

"For getting Jean-Paul home to me," she said. "I can never thank you enough. Except ... I can't do *that* again. Not now Jean-Paul's home."

She still thinks I'm capable of forcing myself on her again, he thought desperately.

"*That* will not be required again," he said stiffly. "But I should like to meet and talk sometimes. As friends."

He saw her expression and laughed without amusement. "You'll never make the Comédie-Française," he said. "All right, as friendly enemies. Tonight for instance?"

She shook her head.

"Sunday then?" he pressed.

Her awareness of having no real choice shadowed her face. "Sunday," she said. "But not in the evening. I take the children out for a trip on Sunday afternoons. The Jardin d'Acclimatation in the Bois. The Porte de Sablons entrance. Two, or just after."

Reaching up, Mai plucked Céci from his shoulders and swung her to the ground, ruffling her hair as she ran back to her mother. The little girl waved her flowers, and shouted "Bye-bye, donkey!"

Mai strolled slowly back towards the Lutétia. He'd done everything right. Every clandestine meeting she agreed to added another filament to the web she was tangled in. But he found himself wishing he'd left the bakery earlier, or that she'd come later.

3

Though Mai did not know it, Janine had been avoiding him just as keenly as he had been avoiding her. Whenever she visited her parents she always listened at the door to make sure he wasn't there.

Now she was glad to have got the meeting over. But in its place there was this new worry. He wanted to see her again. Why? His request filled her with suspicion and fear. A mere lieutenant, yet he was far from powerless. He had managed to get Jean-Paul released.

These thoughts ran through her mind as she got ready for her rendezvous on Sunday. Things had fallen out well. Jean-Paul had gone to have lunch at his mother's. The two had always been very close even after Jean-Paul's abandonment of his religion. Janine prayed that the time they spent together would speed up his healing. The doorbell rang. She heard Pauli's voice and came out of the bedroom. Standing on the threshold looking down at the boy was Maître Delaplanche.

She gave him a big smile and said, "Christian's in the kitchen, I think. Just go through. Pauli, are you ready? I'll be with you in a couple of minutes. See that Céci is all right, will you?"

She was still worried about Pauli, but the solution seemed simple. Jean-Paul's relative normality this morning had extended to giving his son a casual peck on the cheek as he left. This unthinking act of affection had lit up the boy's face. That was all he needed. Love.

When she came out into the hall, Pauli and Céci were standing hand in hand, ready to go. She went to the living room to say goodbye to Christian but paused at the sound of quarrelling. The lawyer's voice rose loud and clear.

"He's a Jew? And he was in hospital under a false name? For God's sake, Christian, what are you thinking of? You're risking everything for a self-indulgent impulse. Get rid of them!"

Janine turned away, forcing herself to smile at the children. "Let's go and see the monkeys, shall we?"

Valois and Delaplanche heard the door open and shut. The lawyer went to the window and watched till they emerged on the pavement.

"Listen, Christian," he said, "the reason I've been away so long is that I got a message in Vichy inviting me to visit some friends further south. It turned out de Gaulle has sent an envoy to coordinate resistance. It makes sense to pull together. We're all being picked off too easily. So for now I'm going along with this fellow. But if de Gaulle imagines this is a step towards putting him on top when the war's over, he's a fool. The future belongs to us, the Communists, so long as we have men like you willing to sit and wait."

"I'd rather stand up and fight," said Valois.

"I know. But what you've got to do takes a special kind of courage. That's why you mustn't take foolish unnecessary risks like harbouring a mentally deranged Jew!"

"He's not mentally deranged," protested Valois. "All right, what he went through has done something to him. In particular, it has made him want to kill Boche. He's desperate to get an active Resistance job. If someone doesn't use him soon, I'm scared he'll just go off by himself and kill Germans with his bare hands. Couldn't Théo use him?"

"No. Théo's too valuable now to be landed with a wild man. Jean-Paul could join one of the peripheral groups perhaps, but not till he's gone from here. Tell him anything, but get him out."

There was the sound of a key in a lock, a door opening and shutting.

"You tell him," said Valois.

The lounge door opened.

Delaplanche's first impression was of a slight, almost boyish, figure who stood very still in the doorway. But when his eyes met the man's unblinking gaze, the stillness seemed to grow vibrant with menace.

"Well," said Jean-Paul. "You're Delaplanche, aren't you?"

"That's right. You know me?"

"Only what everyone knows."

"What's that?"

"Nothing."

"I gather you were a guest of our German friends for over a year."

"Oh, yes. They cared for me and healed me and sent me home," sneered Jean-Paul. "Christian, where are Janine and the children?"

"They've gone for a walk. The Jardin d'Acclimatation, I think."

"I'll see you later," said Simonian. He turned abruptly and left.

"And that's the man you want me to employ," said Delaplanche drily.

"I tell you, he hates the Boche!"

"Oh yes. I could feel the hate. I hope it's for the Boche! Christian, I'm all the more certain now, he's got to be moved out of here. All right, I'll see if we can use him. But he's not for you, my boy. The chances of that one surviving the war are minute, but you, Christian, you're the whole future of France!"

JANINE WAS LATE. It was a chilly afternoon, not actually raining, but with the gusty wind damp as well as cold against any exposed flesh. There weren't many people about, just a few hardy souls whose Sunday promenade in the Bois wasn't going to be interrupted by either war or weather.

Mai glanced at his watch. Perhaps she wasn't coming. Then he saw her in the distance and his heart leaped as if he was a lover waiting for his lass, instead of an *Abwehr* intelligence officer waiting for a woman whose body he'd abused and whose loyalties he was planning to corrupt.

She greeted him as if it were a chance meeting, presumably for Pauli's benefit. After they'd entered the Jardin d'Acclimatation Pauli said, "I've promised to show Céci the monkey house, Maman."

"All right," said Janine. "But come straight back to the parrot house."

"Yes, Maman," said Pauli, and the children set off hand in hand.

"Will they be all right?" asked Mai anxiously.

"I thought you'd be pleased to be rid of them for a while."

"Yes, but . . . they're so young."

"I sometimes think Pauli's older than me," said Janine moodily. Then she smiled and added, "But thanks for being concerned. Honestly, they'll be all right."

"Will they mention me?"

"What if they do? An acquaintance met by chance. Anyway, Jean-Paul doesn't spend much time talking to the children. Nor to me either."

"To Monsieur Valois then?"

She seemed to take this as an implied reproach. "Christian's his oldest friend. Jean-Paul's memory has been affected, you know that. He remembers the fighting and what happened after that. And the further back he goes the more he recalls. It's just the bit between..."

"The bit with you and the children in it?"

"Yes."

"You must be very grateful to Monsieur Valois. For letting you share his apartment, I mean. Do you plan to stay there long?"

Mai wanted to establish some kind of timetable for his campaign, but her reply intrigued him. "I knew we couldn't rely on staying for ever, but I thought we would see the winter out. Now, I don't know."

"Oh. Why's that?"

"Why do you think?" she said indignantly. "It's you people, of course. Christian's a civil servant. And of course it's the Boche that really run the government. So if they found out he had someone like Jean-Paul staying in his flat, it could mean trouble for him."

There was no denying this was true, but it had been true from the start. What had made it an issue now?

He asked, "Did Monsieur Valois say this?"

"No. He's far too generous to say anything like that. I overheard one of his friends spelling it out to him today."

"One of his colleagues, you mean?" he said casually. But suddenly she was alert.

"I expect so. I didn't know the man."

He smiled. Alert she might be, liar she wasn't. All he had to do was check with the man he had watching Valois's apartment. If it turned out that Delaplanche, just back from Vichy, had dropped in...

He felt impatient to be off, but a sudden departure would confirm any suspicions she might have. Besides, it was more important than ever to keep the line on which he was playing this woman taut. It was good to feel himself in such a purely professional relationship with her.

They were in the parrot house now. It was crowded with visitors, both French and German, looking at the bright-feathered, beady-eyed birds. He turned to whisper to her that here was not a good place to continue their conversation, but before he could speak, Pauli's voice called excitedly, "Maman, Maman, Papa's here!"

Without looking round, Mai moved slowly away. After a few moments, he pulled out his pipe, and under cover of lighting it he looked towards the doorway. Standing there was a slim dark man. The resemblance between him and Pauli would have marked him out even if he hadn't been carrying Céci in his arms. Janine and the boy joined him. Even at a distance it was possible to see Janine's joy at meeting him. Mai felt a crazy urge to go across and introduce himself.

"Hey, no smoking," said an attendant, pointing at a sign.

"Sorry," said Mai. Involuntarily he had spoken in German. It didn't matter. The attendant had moved away and no one else paid any attention. Mai searched his mind for the source of this slip, a sudden, incomprehensible urge to blow his cover.

It wasn't hard to find, but finding it brought little comfort. It had been the sight of Janine going with such obvious joy to that man.

It had been jealousy.

4

In an empty apartment off the Rue Monge, Jean-Paul Simonian and Christian Valois were quarrelling.

"You want to be rid of us," said Jean-Paul flatly.

"Nonsense. As I say, a friend mentioned this place. It's roomy, it's handy for Janine's parents, and Sophie's place is just across the river. And it's cheap."

"You're quite a salesman, Christian," said Jean-Paul unpleasantly.

Valois grew angry. "Look, do you want it or not? You can't stay in Passy for ever. My apartment belongs to my father. He comes back to Paris from time to time and won't take kindly to finding he can't use it."

"Very touching," mocked Jean-Paul. "There was a time when you'd have filled the flat with Hottentots to *annoy* your father! No, something has turned you into a hypocrite. Delaplanche wouldn't happen to be this friend who just happened to mention this place, would he?"

"Don't be stupid," said Valois, aware of how unconvincing he sounded. He'd forgotten just how sharp Jean-Paul's mind was.

"Stupid? I don't think so. I'll tell you what I do think. Delaplanche has recruited you, right? And he's given you the kind of job you like, which is sitting around doing nothing till the great revolution comes!"

Valois was filled with fury. "At least I've made a choice, an intellectual decision. Who the hell do you think you are? What have *you* done since it started?"

"At least I got this *fighting*," said Jean-Paul, his hand flying up to the livid scar on his temple. "And I lost friends, true friends."

"Did you now! And what did these 'true friends' do for you, tell me that?"

"They died for me," said Jean-Paul dully. "And before they died they killed Germans for me. Can you match that, Christian?"

Valois, by now more hurt than he cared to admit, said with an effort at casualness, "Well, I'm not dead, so you've got me there. But you don't have to be a soldier to kill the enemy, you know. As a matter of fact, I've killed my Boche. Oh yes. And not blazing away out of a trench either. I waited, and picked him out, and stood behind him, and let him have it!" He pretended his hand was a gun and made a banging sound.

"You did that?" said Simonian, incredulous.

"You think I'm a liar as well as a hypocrite and a coward?"

"No. Of course not. I know how honest . . ."

To his dismay, Valois saw his friend was crying. Tears glistened on his cheeks. "Jean-Paul . . . please . . . I'm sorry."

"What? Am I crying again? Sometimes it just happens."

He wiped away his tears, then lit a cigarette and said seriously, "Let me explain what it's like being me just now, Christian. It's like there's another me, the *real* me, the *essence*, walking around in my mind, like a man strolling in wooded countryside by a river on a misty day." He drew on his cigarette. "Sometimes the mist clears a little and I see people and places. Sometimes I recognize them instantly. As with you. Sometimes I know I know them, but I'm not sure *how* I know them. But I study them and it all comes back. But it comes back as knowledge, not feeling. I can remember everything about Janine. Above all, I remember that she made me happy, the sight of her, the sound of her. And I remember the children too—well, Pauli anyway—but I can't believe that they're anything to do with me. They're part of another, unreachable world."

He paused. The two men looked at each other, one face pale with horror, the other dark with despair.

Then the darkness vanished from Jean-Paul's features to be replaced by a serene, childlike smile. "And there are times when the mist rises completely and I see everything in brilliant sunshine. Oddly enough, those moments usually occur when I'm confronted by a German in uniform and I know that what would make my happiness complete would be to kill him! The trouble is, I need a gun and I need help. I hear talk of the Resistance and I read about acts of terrorism. But how do I join?"

"Advertise?" said Valois grinning.

"That's what I'm doing, I think," said Simonian, returning his grin. "I may be ideologically shaky, but I can take orders. And I'm ready to kill. Tell Delaplanche that."

"I don't know what you're talking about," said Valois, still smiling.

"Of course you don't. And it occurs to me that Maître Delaplanche won't want to know either, not while I'm sharing a flat with his little Mister Clean. So, thank you, friend. This apartment looks very nice. Very nice indeed. I think, after all, we will take it. As long as there's a bar within two minutes' walk."

Valois glanced at his watch. "Let's find out," he said.

5

Winter slowly turned to spring and Parisians observed all the old "firsts"—the first crocus, the first chestnut blossom, the first swallow.

Towards the end of May, Maurice Melchior saw his first yellow star.

He was sitting outside the Deux Magots feeling at one with this sunlit world. Then an old woman with a yellow star sewn to the breast of her threadbare coat walked by. It was like a shadow crossing the sun. Five minutes later he saw another on a middle-aged man.

Hastily paying his bill, he jumped up and followed, overtaking the man just beyond the church of Saint Germain.

"Excuse me, monsieur," he said, but did not need to complete his question. Across the middle of the star was printed *Juif*.

"You haven't heard the new ordinance?" said the man, observing him keenly. "You must be one of the clever ones who didn't register. Won't do you any good, monsieur." With a harsh laugh the man walked on.

It was nothing to do with him, Melchior assured himself. He was safe. Unregistered, anonymous. It was just another bit of Boche bureaucracy. But whatever his mind said his stomach was telling him that everything had changed. Police registers, notices in shop windows, these were fleabites; but labelling people in the streets was the beginning of the plague the fleas carried. Nervously, Melchior made his way home.

How pleasant everyday things looked. A woman passed, pushing a pram; an old man scuttled by, clutching to his chest three carrots in a string bag; some small boys were playing a ball game; everything was lemony in the early evening sunlight, so calm, so ordinary.

One of the boys looked up from his game, saw Melchior, and crossed the street to block his path before he reached the corner. It was Pauli Simonian. They hadn't met since that ghastly day in the métro.

"Hello, Pauli," Melchior said. "Visiting your grandmother?"

"Yes, monsieur. Bubbah said if I saw you while I was playing, to give you a message."

Melchior had been edging slowly past the boy, but now he stopped and returned. The steady, unblinking brown eyes still disturbed him.

"Yes?" he said irritably.

"Bubbah says there's a man, a German soldier, waiting to see you."

Melchior backed away in horror. He grasped the boy's shoulder for support. "Thanks, Pauli, I'm running up a big debt to you."

He turned on his heel and walked swiftly back the way he had come.

Behind him, Pauli watched his departure with an expressionless face.

JANINE SAT SILENTLY watching her mother-in-law sewing a yellow star onto her coat. She'd come to the flat ready to pour out her own woes, but when Sophie had told her the meaning of her task, she'd been unable to begin.

"Why should you have to wear such a thing at all?" demanded Janine.

"Rules," said the old woman calmly. "There, how does that look?"

She held up the old coat on which the star, with the word *Juif* picked out in black thread, glowed like an exotic decoration.

"Boche rules!" exploded Janine. "God, how right the Resistance are to shoot them."

"Bullets kill people," said Sophie. "That can't be right. But how can a piece of yellow cloth harm me?"

"You obviously thought it might harm Monsieur Melchior," said Janine, rather irritated by Sophie's unjustified complacency. "Otherwise you wouldn't have asked Pauli to warn him about the soldier who's waiting."

"Monsieur Melchior has broken their rules," said Sophie sternly. "He is a lost soul, I think. But he's also one of our own, so I will help him. But it is his own fault, certainly not that young German's, sitting on the landing up there. He seems a nice boy. I gave him some tea and he showed me a photo of his family. His mother looked nice. I'm sure she would show kindness to a French boy away from home."

Janine took a deep breath. This seemed like a good cue. "Bubbah Sophie, I wonder ... I mean ..." She hesitated. It was hopeless. She couldn't do it.

Sophie Simonian folded the coat up so the star didn't show and laid it beside her chair. "I wondered when you would ask me about my son," she said. "I admire you for not coming rushing to me to weep about how changed he is. You've given it time and that's good, that's right. Also, though, you should admire me, a Jewish mother, for keeping her mouth shut all these months! Women have won medals for less."

She laughed as she spoke and Janine smiled with her. Suddenly it became easy, or at least easier. "I've been wanting to talk to you for weeks," she said. "But there are times when, well, he seemed to be almost his old self. But always he drifts off again..."

"Drifts off?"

"Yes. It's as if everything close around him fades away and he slips off into somewhere else. There are times when he just sits and stares at nothing for an hour or more. There is a lot of hate in him. I can feel it sometimes when we're out and we see some Germans. It's as if he needs it, as if it feeds him somehow. Does that sound stupid to you, Bubbah?"

The old woman shook her head sadly and said, "No. Such a need, such a drive has always been in him, even as a child. He turned away from religion, I think, because it was not pure enough, too much emotion, too much giving of himself. In the same way, when he was wounded in the head, his mind closed off the section with you in it. That got rid of another weak part in him."

"Weak? You think our love was weak?"

"The memory of happiness can weaken a man *in extremis*, I think," said Sophie seriously. "Perhaps he needed to concentrate his strength as he lay near to death. And his strength comes from something stern and strong and unremitting, like hate."

JEAN-PAUL SIMONIAN stood in a doorway in a narrow side street which ran alongside the Golden Gate Club.

Further down the street a rubbish truck was moving slowly towards him, its loaders exchanging loud abuse above the noise of their work. Simonian ignored them. His thoughts were concentrated entirely on the Golden Gate, and he trembled in anticipation.

Out of the main door of the club burst a couple of young women in a fanfare of laughter. They were closely followed by two German soldiers, flushed with drink. As the girls turned into the side street the soldiers caught up with them, one on either side, and putting their arms round their shoulders, formed a chorus line across the narrow pavement.

They were almost opposite the doorway when Simonian stepped out. At point-blank range he fired twice into the soldiers' gaping mouths. The men remained standing but it was only their dying grip on the women's shoulders that kept them upright. Screaming, the girls dragged themselves free and at last the soldiers fell. A hand grasped Simonian's arm. He was pulled up onto the rubbish truck, which accelerated noisily away.

A few minutes later, the truck came to a halt in what looked like a timber yard, and Jean-Paul was led into a workshop which smelt of glue and woodshavings. A man was working at a foot-operated lathe. He was middle-aged with a farmer's high colour and a Mexican bandit's droopy moustache.

"OK Henri," the woodworker said to the truck driver. "Better get the truck back to the depot. You get paid today, don't you? Mustn't be late for that."

With a cheerful wave, Henri left.

"Who are you?" demanded Jean-Paul.

"Call me André. I'm in charge."

"I thought Henri was in charge."

"Henri's in charge of entrance tests," replied the other with a smile.

"Did I pass?"

"You'd not be here if you hadn't! But don't kid yourself you passed with flying colours. You were told to shoot them in the back after they'd passed you. Henri tells me you stepped out and shot them in the head."

"I'm sorry. They were my first. I wanted to see them face to face. From now on, I won't need that."

"That's nice to know! Also, Pierre here got the impression you were tempted to shoot the girls."

A tall lugubrious man in his twenties who was standing alongside nodded confirmation.

"Yes," admitted Jean-Paul. "Whores! If anything, they're worse than the Boche!"

"You think so? Then what stopped you shooting them?" asked André curiously.

208

"I had orders not to," said Simonian flatly.

"Wrong!" laughed André. "What would have stopped you shooting them was Pierre, who'd have blown your head off if you'd tried! Look, here they are now. The blonde's Arlette. She's Pierre's girlfriend. The little brunette's Mathilde. She's my daughter. So you did well to obey orders, monsieur!" André went to a cupboard, produced a brandy bottle and poured three drinks.

"Simonian," he said. "You won't get much in the way of romantic, heroic gestures from us. We're serious businessmen, just remember that, and our business is getting rid of the Boche. But on the other hand, we never miss an excuse for a drink, so here's to you, Jean-Paul. Welcome aboard!"

He tossed back his drink and then said seriously, "And now you're aboard, how do you fancy a bit of real work?"

6

"To tell the truth, I'm getting a bit worried, Lieutenant," said Michel Boucher.

"About our little arrangement, you mean? I shouldn't like to think I was causing you a problem of loyalties."

"What? Oh no! I mean, what's telling one bunch of you lot what another bunch is doing got to do with loyalties?" inquired Boucher with no irony whatsoever. "No, what I mean is, well, you Germans are not going to be here for ever, are you?"

It's a real puzzle, thought Mai. Does the fact that Boucher feels able to talk like this mean that I'm very good at my job, or hopeless at it? They were sitting outside a café with the sun at its height crushing the shadows of the chestnut trees into pools of black round their boles. Most of the tables were full; there was a buzz of casual talk, a clinking of glasses, a flutter of white-coated waiters, and the world strolled past along the pavement of the Champs-Elysées. It was difficult not to feel relaxed and confidential and full of goodwill towards Boucher, particularly as the man had supplied him with some excellent pipe tobacco.

"What then, friend Miche? Is it the thought of what your countrymen might do to you after we've gone that's bothering you?"

"*Do* to me? Why should they do anything to me? They can't blame a man for earning a living, can they?" said Boucher lugubriously. "Let's have another drink."

Mai drank again. It wasn't yet midday and here he was, supping brandy and feeling very inclined to sit here till dark! But there was work to be done. He said, "All right, Miche. What's new?"

"Nothing much. Since Eichmann dropped in from Berlin last month,

209

they've been chuntering on about rounding up the Yids, but you probably know more about that than I do."

Mai nodded. Not that he knew much except that some big operation was being planned by the SD from their offices on the Avenue Foch.

"What are you working on at the moment?" he asked.

"Nothing much," said Boucher. "In fact, I've been neglecting my patriotic duties a bit recently. Pajou's been moaning like mad. Threatening to take me off the payroll. Oh, don't look so worried. I'm off to the Avenue Foch in a couple of minutes to show my face. My job's safe. Pajou may be more to their taste, but he doesn't know Paris like me. He's a nutcase, Pajou. Always speaks highly of you, though."

"Does he now?" said Mai without much enthusiasm.

Boucher laughed. "Talking of old friends, there's someone else mentioned you. Seemed to think you were OK too."

"Oh? Who's that?"

"Little poof called Melchior. Maurice Melchior."

Mai nodded and said, "Yes, I remember him. Didn't he get friendly with one of your new bosses? Colonel Fiebelkorn, wasn't it?"

"For a bit, so I gather," said Boucher. "Melchior worked for me too, in a manner of speaking. You know, essential supplies, nudge, wink. He was rather good at it too, only that's all behind him now."

"Why?"

"Well, he's screwed things up. For a start he's a Yid but he's not registered and he's not running around with a yellow star, which is all right if the Boche don't know you're a Yid, or don't care. But in his case they know *and* they care. What he needs is a long holiday in the Free Zone. So I wondered if you could fix him up with an *Ausweis*?"

The man was quite incredible. His mind dealt with issues in the most pragmatic fashion. He judged people and situations as they impinged upon him personally. He found no contradiction in being a patriot, a collabo and a crook. Like Janine, he saw things clearly and simply. The difference was, of course, that Boucher's judgments related to his own interests first and foremost, while Janine's concern was all for her family.

The thought of Janine made him prickle with anticipation. After several weeks without seeing her, he had suggested another meeting, and she hadn't demurred. This time the rendezvous was in the Jardin des Plantes, which was very handy for her new apartment, and it was scheduled for this afternoon. He tried to think of a good professional reason for the meeting, but he was hard pushed. So what? he asked himself.

"Sorry, Miche," he said firmly. "I don't see how I can help. I'm going home on leave in a couple of days."

"Hey, that's good. I'm pleased for you," said Miche benevolently. "No sweat. I'll be away myself for a few days. So Maurice will just have to keep his head down. Hey, I must go. I'm late already!"

A clock had struck twelve. They could hear a band playing martial music, and soon they could hear the tread of marching feet and see the eagle perched on the swastika, as the standard of the Paris garrison was borne on its triumphant daily parade down the Champs-Elysées.

A couple of minutes later Boucher's car roared away up the Champs.

It wasn't just the extra burden of commerce thrust upon him by Melchior's need to stay out of sight that was bothering Boucher. His girlfriend, Hélène, was putting pressure on him too. How was it that a glamorous dancer could suddenly become a bourgeois housewife just because she was pregnant? She would like to live in the country, she'd announced. It was better for bringing up children. Coincidentally, Boucher had the chance of buying a very nice little property near Moret from a black-market contact. The price was right, but Boucher hesitated. It was such a commitment.

He was still debating internally as he entered SD headquarters in the Avenue Foch.

"Pajou?" he said to the man on duty in the vestibule.

"Top floor. Interrogation room," said the man.

Boucher ran lightly up several flights to the top landing.

He could hear the splashing of water and a voice slowly counting. He pushed open the door and looked inside. The curtains were drawn to cut out the sunlight. Directly beneath a bare light bulb a tin tub full of water had been placed. Crouched over it was Pajou. With both hands he was pressing the head of a kneeling figure into the water. "Eighteen, nineteen, twenty ... hello, Miche. Damn! You've made me lose count. Where was I?"

Two young SS men, who were lounging against the wall with tunics removed and sleeves rolled up, laughed appreciatively.

"Let's say twenty-seven. Twenty-eight. Twenty-nine. Thirty. Now, let's see if that's dissolved the blockage in your throat, my dear."

He dragged the head up by the hair, which Boucher now saw was long and golden; the white, water-puffed face was a woman's.

"Hey, Pajou, I think you've killed her," said one of the SS men anxiously, glancing towards the shadows at the far end of the room. Boucher became aware of Fiebelkorn sitting on a stool in a corner.

"No," said Pajou, "she's all right. Watch."

He pressed his hand slightly into the woman's stomach and doubled her up. Suddenly she began to cough and retch water into the tub.

"There!" said Pajou triumphantly. "What did I say?"

The woman groaned terribly and tried to fall to the floor, but Pajou held her up. Her eyes fixed on Boucher.

The return of animation to her face, far from reassuring Boucher, brought fresh horror as, incredibly, the bloated features merged with another very different image. "Oh no!" he exclaimed. "Is that little Arlette from the 'Golden Gate'?"

"The very same. She talked too much one night to one of our boys. Dead proud she was of how her boyfriend was murdering Germans. Funny, once we got her here, she stopped being so gabby. I thought a good gargle might clear her throat."

Boucher looked down at the distorted face and desperate eyes. She was a tart, who had sheltered him when he had no money and nowhere to go. He said, "Does it have to be like this?"

"If you've got any better ideas, tell us, Miche."

Boucher didn't reply, but turned abruptly and left. As he walked along the landing, Pajou came after him, water still dripping from his arms.

"Miche, what the hell's the matter? Too strong for your stomach, is it? You amaze me, I'd have thought you were just the lad for the rough stuff."

"Rough stuff? Don't lecture me about rough stuff, Pajou," snarled Boucher.

"Look, mate, don't take it so hard. There's no lasting harm done, she'll be back on the job tonight. She doesn't know all that much. Bait for Boche soldiers, that's her game. But she's picked up from her boyfriend, some bloke called Pierre, that his gang's planning a raid on some canal barges soon, and I reckon if she can squeeze the details out of him, we can scoop up the lot."

"You mean she'll betray her man?" said Boucher.

"No," laughed Pajou. "She's done that already. He's the only one whose name she knows. Now we get her working for us so she can *save* him! Clever, eh? We promise he'll come to no harm if she cooperates."

"She didn't look like she was cooperating in there."

"Just a taste of what she can expect if she double-crosses us," said Pajou. "Love and fear, that's how you tame 'em, old Fiebelkorn says. I'd better get back." Whistling cheerfully, he turned and re-entered the room.

It wasn't so bad, Boucher reassured himself. Arlette was going to be all right. All the same, if this was the way things were going, it wasn't going to be so easy to kiss and make up after the Boche had gone. And they *would* go, of course. Suddenly he made up his mind. He would buy the house at Moret. Not in his own name, though. In Hélène's name. He would be her respectable businessman husband, working all week in the city. For once in his life he'd look to the future.

NOT FAR AWAY, in the Jardin des Plantes, Michel Boucher was the topic of conversation.

Mai had offered the subject as one of neutral common interest, and Janine had gladly accepted it. "He's got a good heart," she said, "but he doesn't think. Working for you people could bring him a lot of trouble one day."

Mai sucked deeply on his pipe, and glanced sideways at her.

She interpreted his glance as the comment it was. "Yes. I know it's incongruous, me sitting here saying things like that. That's the trouble with life, isn't it? It's all mixed up, instead of being clear-cut and simple. Miche is kind and generous, but he's also a Géstapiste. Maman is prejudiced and grasping, but she's still my loving mother. You're the enemy, yet somehow I feel quite willing to be here, talking to solid, reliable Monsier Scheffer from Alsace, whose company I almost enjoy."

The pleasure Mai felt at hearing these words was far from professional, but inside him the *Abwehr* officer, the enemy, was telling solid Monsieur Scheffer, "She's vulnerable. She wants to talk. Work on her."

Sadly, he listened. But where should he push her? Now that she was out of Valois's flat (definitely at Delaplanche's instigation; he'd established a link between the lawyer and the owner of the new apartment), what was the best way to use her?

He said, "Yes, I see what you mean. And your husband too..."

"More than anyone, he's two people," she agreed sadly. "Loving husband, loving father. And the other, the cold, distant man your bullets turned him into."

"How does Jean-Paul pass his time?" asked Mai casually. "Does he see much of his friend, the one whose flat you stayed in?"

"Christian? No. Not since we moved out. To tell the truth, I don't know what he does or where he goes ... sometimes I think..."

She shook her head, not in denial, but in exasperated self-reminder that this was not some old family friend she was talking to, but a German intelligence officer. She must be on her guard.

By her side, Mai caught her hesitation, and guessed its cause. Jean-Paul returned late, ignored her questions. Normally the answer would be obvious—another woman. But the man and the times suggested other possibilities, and Günter Mai's heart sank as his professional mind computed the likelihood that a Boche-hating former soldier like Simonian would be recruited by the Resistance.

And if he had been, it was *his* job to pursue and destroy him.

7

It was a bright, clear July night, with a moon lighting up the poplar-lined towpath like a stage spot.

The canal, like the majority of the waterways in and around the city, was lined with fishermen most weekends and evenings. That day André's group had used their fishing as a cover for concealing weapons and explosives along the banks, to be picked up that night.

There were eight of them in the team; André, Pierre and Jean-Paul plus four others were the attack force, while Henri was providing backup in a wood two kilometres to the east. The plan was for the raiders to join him there, pass the night in the open, then filter into the great Sunday rush of hopeful anglers and so get back to the city unnoticed.

Personally, Jean-Paul thought it was all too clever, and that they'd have been much better advised to head straight back to Paris under cover of darkness. But he had resolved to take orders till he felt sufficiently accepted to voice opinions.

Fifteen minutes later his fears about the complexity of André's plan had been partially allayed. They'd successfully picked up all the weapons and explosives and were now approaching the main waterway where the three supply barges were moored above the lock.

"There they are!" whispered André. "What did I tell you?"

They were attacking two to a barge, with André in support with his Sten gun wherever he might be needed. This part of the operation had been meticulously rehearsed. Timing was of the essence. The German deck guards had to be gunned down simultaneously so that the attack on one barge wouldn't alert the next. Four Germans to a barge, two on watch, two below, sleeping. The deck secure, the next move was to get below and take the other two before they were fully awake. Pierre was all for dropping a couple of grenades down the hatch first, but André said, "No. The crew are French lads, doing their job. What's up with you, Pierre? Arlette giving you a bad time?"

"She had bad feelings about this job," admitted Pierre. "She didn't want me to come."

Now they were in position, crouched behind the low wall which separated the towpath from the plantation of plane trees they'd just come through. Pierre was checking his watch, mouthing figures as he counted them down to the agreed deadline. Jean-Paul focused his gaze on the familiar yet fearsome silhouette of the nearest German guard. The other German joined his comrade, offered him a cigarette. They lit up. Their faces looked young, almost childlike, in the glow of the match.

"... three ... two ... one ... GO!"

Pierre's shout took Jean-Paul by surprise, and he was a second behind him in going over the wall. He had his pistol ready, however. There was nothing like the rattle of gunfire to spread fear and alarm, so as he ran forward he let off a couple of shots. Or tried to.

He was pressing the trigger but nothing was happening. Jammed, perhaps? But that explanation was crowded from his mind by the awareness that neither to left nor right was there any sound but running feet and the clicking of useless hammers on unresponsive cartridges.

Then the moon came out. No, not the moon. These were lights, blossoming from either side of the towpath and now joined by beams from the barges themselves, as the grinning soldiers pulled back tarpaulins from searchlights and machineguns.

"Hands up! Stand still!" called a voice in fluent French.

214

The wise thing was to obey, to stand still, to wait for the triumphant Germans to herd them away to a cell where they could sit and ponder on who had betrayed them. That is probably what they would have done. But from somewhere behind them in the plantation came a pathetic flurry of shots from a handgun. One of the searchlights shattered, but there was still more than enough light for the machinegunners to mow down the line of attackers as they turned to flee. Jean-Paul was already diving for the ground. A bullet clipped his shoulder as he fell, but he felt no pain. Pierre too was down and hit. "Arlette ..." he breathed, whether in accusation or simple farewell Jean-Paul had no way of knowing.

He pushed himself to his feet with his right arm, aware that the left was useless. The German guns had for the moment swung towards the plantation, in a blind effort to destroy their unexpected assailant, who must be André.

Jean-Paul ran in the only direction possible, towards the water. He had surprise on his side, but not for long. The soldiers on the barge missed him with their first two shots, but the third caught him in the side and the fourth burned through his thigh. He fell forward into the cold black water. He'd reached his goal, but with one leg and one arm out of action his success looked likely to be his death also.

Deep down he went. Instinct sent him reaching up in search of light and air, but each time he tried he crashed against an obstacle as long and solid as a coffin lid. He was under a barge, moving with the slow current down its whole endless length. He kicked out with his good leg and arm but felt no responding surge of speed. Slowly he tumbled and turned, feeling long tongues of weed lick and caress him. His mouth and nose and lungs and belly were full of water but still that fire of fear and hatred would not be quenched.

He screamed, "*No!*"

It wasn't much of a scream, which was a good thing, he realized, for the waters had parted above his head. He looked back and was amazed to see how very far past the barges he had come. The gunfire had stopped. He turned over and with an awkward sidestroke made for the bank. When he reached it, he saw instantly that he might have spared his effort. The bank here was steep and crumbly. Even if his good hand could have pulled his body up, the shallow-rooted grasses lacked the strength to support it.

He clung to the bank one-handed. Suddenly his wrist was seized and someone was pulling him, dragging his sodden body up the bank.

"For God's sake, make an effort!" hissed a voice.

Weakly he dug his good leg into the clay and pushed. Next moment he was out of the water and lying beside the towpath.

"I thought it must be you making all that noise," said André. "I saw you go in the water."

"The others?" Jean-Paul gasped.

"Dead, I think. I hope so, for all our sakes," said André grimly. "Come on. We can't stay here. The Boche are still searching the plantation, but one of them may decide to wander down this way at any moment. Can you walk?"

Jean-Paul consulted his body. "I can hop," he said.

Leaning heavily on the older man, he let himself be led away. His wounds and the tangled undergrowth made progress painfully slow, though from time to time they were helped by the moon's brief appearance.

"This is crazy," Jean-Paul gasped. "You can't lug me along like this. We'll both end up dead."

André didn't waste his strength arguing. "I'll hide you here," he said. "Then I'll try to get Henri. We've got contacts in the area, if you can just hang on."

"Don't worry about me," said Jean-Paul. "I'm good at hanging on."

They were moving parallel to a small stream which ran towards the canal. With André's help, Jean-Paul slid down almost to the water's edge and pulled a tangle of low-growing bushes across his body.

"I'll be back as soon as I can," said André.

Jean-Paul heard him move away, then he was alone, as he'd been alone in the German hospital, concentrating all the resources of his heart and mind on simply staying alive, from minute to agonizing minute.

8

When Christian Valois reached his flat, the telephone was ringing. It was impossible to say, of course, but he had a feeling it had been ringing for a long time, and immediately found himself thinking, It's Mama, she's ill; it's Marie-Rose, she's had an accident; it's . . .

It was Janine. He recognized the voice at once and with considerable irritation, as though she had got him to the telephone by a confidence trick. "What do you want?" he said angrily.

"It's Jean-Paul . . . Oh Christian, he's gone," she cried wretchedly. "I'm so worried. He's been gone since Saturday. I asked him where he was going, and he just laughed and said, 'Fishing.'"

"Fishing? Does he fish?"

"Not that I know of. He seemed very excited. I was very unhappy. I imagined all kinds of stupid things . . . even another woman . . ." Christian Valois shook his head. To him, this kind of secretive behaviour meant only one thing. Delaplanche had carried out his implied promise and, once Jean-Paul was out of the apartment, had made sure he was recruited into an active Resistance cell. He felt a pang of pure envy.

"But I don't think it is a woman," Janine continued. "It feels more like . . .

something sinister. Oh Christian, I think he may have got mixed up with the Resistance! The house is being watched."

"What? Are you sure?"

"Oh yes. Last night there was a man. Pauli noticed him. He was there for hours. Oh God, Christian. What can I do?"

"Nothing," he said, immediately businesslike. "I'll ask around, see if I can find out anything. And I'll call round to see you tomorrow night, all right? If anything happens in the meantime, ring me."

IN THE NEXT TWENTY-FOUR HOURS Christian discovered nothing of comfort. An accidental encounter with an old acquaintance working in the Ministry of the Interior elicited the news that there'd been an abortive Resistance attack on some canal barges at the weekend.

"Happily, they were expected. I gather some tart betrayed them."

"They were captured, you mean?"

"Killed, my dear chap. Our Gestapo friends don't mess about, you know."

What was it Jean-Paul had told Janine he was going to do? Fishing? The link between that reply and the canal attack was too strong to be ignored.

He went round to Janine's flat that evening, uncertain what to tell her. It was a desire to postpone the moment as much as natural circumspection which made him check the neighbouring streets thoroughly for signs of surveillance. There was nothing. He went in and rang the bell.

The door opened. Janine stood there, her face pale. There was a mark on her brow, like a circular weal.

"Janine!" he said, stepping forward, his arms outstretched.

He never reached her. His right arm was seized at the wrist, twisted downwards so that he spun round, screaming in pain. Then he was dragged into the room and hurled forward onto a sofa. A pistol muzzle stamped its cold circle onto his brow. Behind it stood a square-faced, middle-aged man in stained and smelly overalls who looked ready to kill him.

"It's all right! Please, it's my friend," Janine cried. "The one I told you about. Christian, are you all right?"

Valois nodded uncertainly as the gun was slowly withdrawn.

"This is Henri, Christian," babbled Janine, both frightened and excited. "He's been with Jean-Paul. He's hurt, but he's alive, thank God!"

Valois pushed himself upright. "Where . . . where is he?" he stammered.

The man called Henri described what had happened swiftly and succinctly. "Everyone bought it, except André and Jean-Paul. Our whole group wiped out, just like that!"

"Then there's still the three of you left," urged Valois.

"Two."

"What . . . ?"

"No. Not your friend, *my* friend," said Henri dully. "André. Our boss."

They'd got a local doctor to look at Jean-Paul, and he'd transferred them to a house in the area whose owners were sympathetic, but who said both men would have to be moved out by Friday.

"Their son-in-law's a gendarme; he'll be visiting this weekend. They're not sure how he'd react. I came back to work on Monday. I'm with the Sanitation Department, and I didn't want my absence to be noticed. They were checking us very carefully, I noticed that. I didn't know why, but it bothered me. Still, there was no sign of activity round my house, so I thought it might be all right. I checked André's place and that seemed all right too. Then I came on here, just to be sure."

"My son spotted you," said Janine.

"Did he? Not so bloody good, am I? I wish he'd been with me when I checked André's place! Anyway, I told André it was OK. So he came back yesterday. I didn't try to see him. Act normal, he said. That meant a day with my in-laws. So I didn't go back to André's till this evening. You should've seen it! Everything smashed up, blood everywhere. They'd been waiting for him!"

"What about his family?" demanded Janine, aghast.

"A daughter. She was away, thank God. I've sent a message to the poor kid telling her to stay away. After that, all I wanted to do was find out who'd betrayed us."

"So you came round here!" exclaimed Valois indignantly, understanding the mark on Janine's brow.

"Yes. I'm sorry. I soon realized it couldn't be her. Then you came, Jean-Paul's best friend, the lady said. People often confide in their best friends."

"And they often confide in their tarts!" said Valois. He passed on what he'd gleaned from his friend in the Ministry of the Interior.

"Arlette," said Henri wearily.

"You know her? Then why haven't you been arrested?"

"Because André was the only one whose address she knew. She'd known me as a dustbin man, nothing more, and there's hundreds of us. As for Jean-Paul, she'd know nothing at all about him as he was so new to us."

"But André knows all about you, and Jean-Paul too!" cried Janine in alarm.

"André won't talk," he said sadly. "I saw the blood, remember? I doubt if they got him to Gestapo headquarters alive."

There was a moment of silence, intense as prayer.

Then Janine said, "Please. What about Jean-Paul?"

"He'll live, but he has to be moved. We need transport."

"I can get a car," said Valois quietly.

"What? With a proper permit, you mean?"

"Oh yes. A proper permit. Very proper."

He'd never used the car since his father got him the permit. Despite his pretended reconciliation he balked at openly joining the small privileged bunch of private drivers.

"You must be important," said Henri, regarding him distrustfully.

"He is," said Janine. "Christian, you can't get mixed up in this. It could ruin you. Lend us the car and the permit. If we get caught, we'll say we stole it."

"It's in my name," he said flatly. "I can get away with it. You can't."

"He's right," said Henri. "We've no choice."

"All right," said Janine. "When do we go? Tonight?"

"We?" said Valois.

"I'm coming too," she said coldly. "No argument."

"But you mustn't!" he said. "The children..."

"I'll leave them with Sophie," she said. "I'm coming, Christian, and there's an end to it."

Henri laughed and said, "Not married, are you, monsieur? Thought not, else you'd know you were wasting your breath."

The altercation seemed to have persuaded him to trust Valois and he now outlined his plan for picking up Jean-Paul.

THE PICK-UP WENT PERFECTLY.

The middle-aged couple who'd taken Jean-Paul in were at the same time relieved and apologetic. "We would have kept him longer," explained the woman, "but our son, Jacques..."

"No names," said Henri. "The less we all know the better. How is he?"

"The doctor's been today. He's very weak still but he can be moved."

Janine went into the room first. On the journey out she had convinced herself that Jean-Paul would have regressed to complete amnesia, and now she steeled herself for a heart-tearing lack of recognition.

Instead, the pale face raised itself from the pillow, broke into a joyous smile, immediately replaced by a look of concern, and he said, "Janine, you shouldn't be here!"

"She's come to take you home, so shut up and be grateful," said Henri.

"We're using Christian's car, he's got a permit," said Janine, covering her emotion by being very businesslike.

"Christian. You too. God, what risks you're taking," said Jean-Paul.

"No risks," said Valois. "First sign of trouble and you're out in the ditch."

Jean-Paul laughed and gripped Valois with his good arm.

The light was beginning to fade as they got him into the car. He didn't cry out or even wince, but Janine felt his pain in the tension of his body. At last the car was ready to depart and Janine embraced his hosts with tears in her eyes. "Thank you, thank you," she said.

With the light fading fast, they drove slowly so that they didn't need headlights. Janine sat in the back with her arm round Jean-Paul. Soon after they set off he said in a low voice, "How are the children?"

"Fine. They're with your mother. They missed you."

"Does she know about this?"

"No."

He smiled his approval, then slipped into silence.

In the front, Valois drove while Henri navigated. It was almost dark now as they penetrated further into the unlit suburbs. Suddenly Henri said, "Wait. Slow down, turn left here."

"What's up?" said Valois, obeying.

"Didn't you see? Up ahead there was a roadblock. Right in about two hundred metres should bring us back on course."

"Where are we?" asked Janine, trying to hide her fear.

"On the edge of the tenth *arrondissement*. Right here, I think. Hell, there they are again! Left, *left!* Just turn off, but don't hurry!"

This time they were close enough for them to see quite clearly the activity ahead. Two police cars. Half a dozen gendarmes.

"All right. Straight on. Fast as you can," commanded Henri, twisting round to look for signs of pursuit. There were none.

They were heading east and Valois kept going till they hit the Boulevard Davour, where they turned south. Several times when he was contemplating turning west towards the city centre again he glimpsed gendarmerie cars parked across roads intersecting the boulevard.

"Henri, what's going on? We can't be that important!"

"Don't flatter yourself, we're not!" said Henri. "They're not interested in us. What the hell's that?"

A convoy of three green and white Paris Transport Company buses went speeding by. Their interiors were dark, but they seemed to be packed.

It was pitch dark by now and Valois was forced to use his sidelights. They crossed the Seine by the Pont National. Once on this side of the river, all signs of a police presence seemed to evaporate and they crawled west to the Quartier Mouffetard without further alarm.

"Jean-Paul, we're home," whispered Janine.

The words seemed to act like a reviving injection, as if he had deliberately lapsed into semi-unconsciousness to preserve his strength for this final effort. Even so, Valois had to carry him up the flight of stairs, and when they laid him on the bed he was quiet and still.

Henri checked his dressings. "He'll be all right," he assured Janine. "Peace and quiet are what he needs. I'll fix for a doctor to call. He's good with bullet wounds and even better at keeping his mouth shut. We'd better be off now."

Valois turned to Janine. "Look, I'd stay, only I have to get the car back in the garage. Out there, it could attract attention."

220

"Yes, of course. Thank you, thank you both for what you've done."

She embraced them, then accompanied them down the stairs to the front door. "Take care," she said anxiously. "Those gendarmes will probably still be about."

Valois nodded, kissed her cheek and got into the car.

Henri grinned. "Don't worry, without your husband we're just a couple of good citizens in a car with a permit. Besides, whatever the flics are up to tonight, one thing's for sure; it's nothing to do with us!"

THE KNOCK AT THE DOOR came just after Pauli had got into bed.

Sophie Simonian twitched, more in irritation than alarm. It was probably that idiot concierge complaining once more that Charlot was howling outside her kitchen window. Then a movement on the sofa told her that the cat was still sleeping there, in his favourite spot.

"Who's there?" she called at the door.

"Gendarmerie, madame," replied a courteous voice. "Please open the door."

She obeyed.

There were two of them, a sergeant and a younger constable. The constable smiled apologetically, but the sergeant wore the stern face adopted by stupid people who are happy to accept instructions as a substitute for independent thought. Outside on the landing, Sophie could see two more men, wearing blue shirts, with cross-straps and armbands.

· The sergeant was consulting a printed sheet. "You are Madame Sophie Simonian of this address?"

"Yes, monsieur. I have my papers here if you wish to see them."

She moved towards her old bureau but the sergeant said impatiently, "No, don't show them to me. But bring them with you. They will be checked."

"*Bring* them, monsieur?" said Sophie. "When?"

"Now, of course." He flourished his sheet of paper at her. It was a list of names and addresses, headed *Census of Jews and Foreign Nationals 1941*. She recalled her visit to the police station to register.

"I have done nothing wrong."

"No one's saying you've done anything wrong," he said impatiently. "It's just the law, madame. Now, please get ready. Bring some clothes with you."

"Clothes? You mean I shall be away all night?" she said in alarm. She could trust Pauli to look after his sister for an hour or two, but all night! She was opening her mouth to say something of this when the constable cried, "Hey sarge! In here!"

He had wandered through into the little bedroom. Céci was still fast asleep, but Pauli was sitting up, wide-eyed, regarding the policemen with his disconcerting gaze.

The sergeant consulted his paper. "There's nothing about them down here. Here, lad," he said to Pauli. "What's your name?"

"Paul Simonian."

"Oh, I see. So this lady is . . . ?"

"She's my grandmother," said Pauli. "Is something wrong?"

"No, sonny, it's all right. Nothing to worry about," said the constable.

Sophie ushered them back into the living room. She saw that the two other young men had ventured through the front door in the meantime and were examining her ornaments and giggling together. She could see now that their armbands bore the initials PPF. *Parti Populaire Français*. She knew little of politics but she knew that this party were virulently anti-Semitic.

"With your permission, Sergeant," she said quietly, "I will ask the concierge to keep an eye on the children."

The gendarme was blocking her way to the door. "Their parents, where are they?"

"Not here. I'm looking after them for a little while."

"Oh yes. It's your son who's their father, right? I don't see his name down here."

"He is not Jewish."

"Not Jewish?" the sergeant exclaimed. "What do you mean?"

"He abandoned the faith many years ago," she explained.

"It doesn't work like that, madame, as you know," said the sergeant with grave stupidity. "We'll check on him, never fear. Now, get yourself ready, quick as you can."

"Shall I see the concierge about the kids?" offered the constable.

"No, you get yourself upstairs. That special case we've got noted, the one who isn't registered, see if there's any sign of him. And take this pair of delinquents with you in case he's locked himself in."

"Yes, sarge. But what about the kids?"

"They'll have to come," the sergeant said grimly. "They're family, aren't they? It's no use making a fuss, madame. I've got my job to do."

"But these are *children!*" protested Sophie.

"Yeah, sarge. They're only kids," echoed the constable.

"*Jewish* kids," said the sergeant. "Or have they given it up too, madame? Didn't I give you an order, constable!"

"Yes, Sergeant." The constable left with the two PPF youths.

The sergeant said, "Now, get yourself packed, and those children too, madame. Fifteen minutes, that's the most I can give you."

Sophie obeyed. She recognized the kind of man the sergeant was. There was no point in arguing with such people.

She went through to the children. They were both awake now. Pauli had his arms round Céci and was talking to her in that low-pitched incomprehensible buzz which was still their private form of communication.

"Children," said Sophie, "we're going out now with the gendarmes. Don't worry, it won't be for long, but the night air can be chilly even in summer, so you must dress up warm. Pauli, will you help your sister while I pack a few things together?"

"Yes, Bubbah," said the boy.

From upstairs came a violent crash and the sound of splintering wood. Céci began to cry. Sophie said, "There, there, child. It's nothing. They're here to protect us, the gendarmes, you know that, don't you, Pauli?"

Their eyes met. Hers moved away. "Yes, Bubbah," he said.

Swiftly they made preparations, to the accompaniment of footsteps and banging from above. Finally they were ready, their belongings crammed into an old carpetbag. The PPF bully boys were back in the flat, their faces flushed with the joy of vandalism. At the door, Sophie produced her key and stood and stared at them. There was a long pause.

The constable said, "Right, you two, out! The lady wants to lock up."

The youths came out with very ill grace and Sophie locked the door. She had scribbled a note to Janine and left it on the stove where she'd be certain to see it. In her heart she was beginning to have grave misgivings. These grew when she got down into the street and saw several other little groups being shepherded along by uniformed policemen. There were old men with paper parcels, old women with sticks, whole family groups, all of them neat and tidy despite the unexpected summons and the late hour, all silent or talking only in low murmurs.

By the time they'd crossed the little Place de Thorigny and were walking down the Rue Elzevir, they had become a procession. "Where are we going?" someone asked. "Only to the Rue des Rosiers," someone else said reassuringly.

There were spectators now, one or two on the pavement, several at open windows. Someone made a remark, there was a laugh. At another window a woman was sobbing uncontrollably. Most just watched in silence.

When they turned into the Rue des Rosiers, Sophie saw a long line of buses. The sight of these everyday green and white vehicles in this most familiar of streets, where she had shopped and chatted for thirty years, should have been reassuring. It wasn't. Everything seemed transformed by the hour and the atmosphere into something terrifying, like an evil dream.

The queues of people slowly shuffled forward into the gaping doors of the buses. Finally, the Simonians' turn came. The bus was jam-packed, but a man rose and gave Sophie his seat. She drew Céci onto her lap and the little girl promptly fell asleep. Pauli leaned against her shoulder with his arm round her neck. Elsewhere on the bus children were crying and mothers were making comforting noises.

The bus sped swiftly through the deserted streets. Sophie was vaguely aware that they crossed the river, but otherwise she had little sense of where they were going. Her mind was going back to when she had lain on the floor of a crowded train with her husband Iakov Moseich, her head pillowed on this very bag now jammed between her legs, being carried westwards to their long-dreamed-of new and better life.

The bus stopped. A gendarme yelled at them to get out. They found themselves standing before a huge building she didn't recognize.

"What is this place?" she asked no one in particular.

"It's the Vél d'Hiv," said Pauli, whose secret wanderings had familiarized him with the far corners of Paris.

"What?"

"The Vélodrome d'Hiver," he expounded. "Fifteenth *arrondissement*. It's a cycling stadium, Bubbah."

Another youngster, recognizing the place, said seriously, "Are we going to see a race, Papa?"

Once more they filed forward in an orderly fashion. But once they were inside the huge open-air stadium all sense of order vanished. There were people everywhere and more pouring in by the minute. Sophie was instantly aware of the first great danger which was separation. From all sides there came voices calling out the names of those they'd lost and, most piteous of all, the voices of children calling simply, "Maman! Papa!"

"Pauli," Sophie said sharply. "Here, you must carry the bag. Can you manage it?"

"Yes, Bubbah," he said.

"Good. Now put your other hand in my pocket. There. Clench your fist. And don't take it out, you hear me now? Good."

She stooped and picked up Céci, who was fully awake again, staring round-eyed at this mad, crowded world she suddenly found herself in.

"Now, let's try to find ourselves somewhere to sit."

They made their way across the arena. It seemed a long walk: they stumbled over unseen obstacles in the dark and people were continually colliding with them. Finally Sophie halted out of sheer exhaustion.

"This will do nicely," she said, as if she had been searching for just such a spot, and they all collapsed to the ground.

"Want to go home," said Céci plaintively.

"Yes, darling. You shall go home, shan't she, Pauli?"

"Yes, Bubbah," said Pauli, and he murmured into his sister's ear. Finally she closed her eyes and fell asleep, resting against his arm.

"Bubbah," said Pauli, "how soon shall we go home?"

"Oh, tomorrow I expect. Tomorrow when it's light the authorities will come and sort this chaos out. Now, get some rest, Pauli."

"Yes, Bubbah." He closed his eyes, but their lids became a screen on which memories of that strange night flickered like images cast from a magic lantern. And when sleep finally came, he bore the images into its shallow depths with him.

And still the buses drew up outside and still the people poured in.

9

Janine woke up. She found herself lying in Pauli's bed and for a moment was filled with a paralysing panic. *Where were the children?*

Then she remembered, and sighed with relief. And remembering why she was sleeping in her son's bed, she rose and went through the open door into her own room.

Jean-Paul lay as if he hadn't moved all night. With the beginnings of terror she reached out to touch him.

He opened his eyes. There was no recognition there, only blank bewilderment. Then he tried to sit upright and his face crazed with pain and his head fell back on the bolster.

"Jean-Paul, are you all right?" cried Janine, hovering helplessly.

He stretched out his good arm and she took his hand in both of hers.

"You came for me," he said. "Thanks."

It was a good moment. Then she felt his hand pull away from hers and he clutched his side and grimaced. "I feel hot," he said. "Could I have some water?"

She went to fill a glass. When she returned he was in a high fever.

The next few hours were an agony. The doctor who'd treated him had left him a few tablets. For a while there seemed to be an improvement, then the fever flared up again, bearing Jean-Paul into a confusion of other worlds. He slipped in and out of childhood, student days, marriage, the war, hospital, and his contact with the Resistance.

By midday, Janine was in despair. Where was Henri's doctor? If he didn't come soon she would have to take the risk of sending for someone else. An hour later she had made up her mind.

She ran to the door, opened it, and almost screamed. A man was standing there, heavy-jowled, badly shaven. He wore a crumpled black suit and carried a scuffed attaché case. "Henri sent me," he said. "How's the man?"

She took him through without question or demur. He looked down at Jean-Paul for a moment, then said, "Where can I wash my hands?"

When he returned, he opened the old attaché case. In it were crammed the essentials of his trade. He began removing the dressings, assuming without question that Janine would act as nurse. The arm and thigh wounds were clean and dry but the wound in Jean-Paul's side was red and angry.

"There's your troublemaker," he said with satisfaction.

He worked swiftly and efficiently despite the fact that, as Janine had soon realized, he was dog-tired.

"There," he said. "With luck that ought to do the trick." He smiled ruefully and added, "A few days in hospital is what he really needs, but with three bullet-holes in him, someone's bound to ask questions. I'll call again in two or three days."

He left. She went back to look at Jean-Paul. He was sleeping peacefully. She went out into the living room and sat down and wept, long and silently, for fear of disturbing the patient.

Then she thought, Oh God! The children!

She ran down the stairs to the telephone in the hall. Three times she tried to call the concierge's number at Sophie Simonian's building but the line was clearly out of order. This was annoying but not unusual.

She returned to her husband's bedside.

At six o'clock that evening, Christian Valois appeared. His thin, handsome face looked tired and worried.

She greeted him with a smile, saying, "Henri sent a doctor like he promised. Isn't he marvellous? Jean-Paul had a fever, but he seems much better now. Come on through. I'm sure seeing you will cheer him up."

Her uncomplicated delight should have been contagious, but Valois seemed untouched by it and not in too much of a hurry to see his friend, either. He stood in the living room doorway and looked round.

"Children not here?" he said.

"No. I told you. They're with Sophie. I haven't had time to go round there and collect them, as you can imagine. Besides, I wonder if it mightn't be a good idea to let them stay with their grandmother a bit longer. I don't want them to see Jean-Paul while he's ill again."

Valois said, "That's OK, is it? I mean, for them to stay? You've talked with Sophie on the telephone?"

"No. The line's out of order again."

She was looking at him closely. Open natures might find evasion difficult to contrive, but they are quick to spot it. "What's up, Christian? There's nothing wrong, is there?"

"No, no. I'm sure not," he said unhappily. "It's just that, well, you remember as we drove back last night we kept on hitting those road-blocks? I found out the reason for that this afternoon. It seems they weren't roadblocks to stop traffic getting in, they were to stop people getting out. The police sealed off half a dozen *arrondissements* north of the river, last night."

"But why?" asked Janine.

"They were rounding up Jews."

"Jews? But ..." She was puzzled, till visibly her mind moved from the general to the particular and she cried out, "Oh God! Which *arrondissements*? The fourth? Was one of them the fourth?"

He nodded and said, "I believe so."

"But why? You say it was the police? No Germans?"

"That's what I was told. Over a thousand of them. All French."

"Then that must be all right, mustn't it? If the Boche weren't involved?"

Her eyes fixed on his as though she hoped to mesmerize reassurance out of him.

He said, "The Boche *were* involved, of course they were involved! Who do you think organized the whole thing? They just think it looks better if they can get us to do their dirty work."

As he spoke, Janine was struggling into a light summer coat. Now she ran into the bedroom to look at Jean-Paul.

"He's asleep," she said to Valois, "but he'll wake up soon. There's some soup to heat up." She made for the door.

"Wait!" cried Valois. "Where are you going?"

"To Sophie's. I've got to see about the children."

"Wait! I'll come with you."

"No," she said, as if talking to a simple child, "someone has to stay with Jean-Paul. I'll be back as soon as I can."

AS SHE CYCLED through the evening streets, Janine forced her mind away from what might lie ahead. She kept up speed till she was across the river, but as she turned along the Quai des Célestins she was already flagging and her breath began to burn in her chest. It was dark in the canyons of the north–south streets, a darkness accentuated by the explosions of sunlight at east–west intersections. Rue Malher, Rue Payenne ... and now at last Rue de Thorigny and Sophie's house.

Too tired and too fearful to go through the usual ritual of chaining up her bike, she let it slip into the gutter and went inside.

There was no sign of Madame Nomary, the concierge. She went upstairs, each step requiring a real effort of strength and will. The apartment door was ajar. "Sophie?" she called. "Pauli? Céci?"

She pushed open the door, fearing the silence.

"Oh, God, help me!" she said.

The room was in chaos, with furniture overturned, curtains ripped down, and every drawer and cupboard door flung open. She ran through into the bedrooms. A movement beneath a tangle of coverlets set her heart pounding, but what emerged was the head of a cat, wide-eyed and fearful.

"Charlot!" she said, reaching out her hand.

The animal snarled, struggled out of the bedding and dashed past her through the door. She turned to follow it and stopped dead at the sight of a woman in the doorway. "Madame Nomary!" she cried. "What happened here? Where are my children?"

"The police came last night," said the old woman. "They took everyone away. Everyone who is Jewish, that is."

"The police did *this?*" exclaimed Janine, gesturing at the wreckage.

"No. That was the young men, the PPF they call themselves. They did some damage upstairs, but no one was there. Here they did nothing till your mother-in-law and the children were taken away. Then they came back without the police and asked for my key. I told them I would not give it, but they broke my phone and said they would break my arm too. I had to give in . . ."

Janine realized that the old woman was trembling. "Please, Madame Nomary, don't upset yourself," she said. "But the children . . . is there nothing you can tell me?"

"Madame Sophie left a note. I found it on the floor."

Janine recognized Sophie's writing at once, though it showed every sign of haste. "*Janine, two policemen are taking us away. The sergeant won't let me leave the children. Don't worry. Sophie.*"

"Where? Where have they taken them?" cried Janine.

The old woman could only shake her head helplessly.

"Oh God," moaned Janine. "Oh God!"

10

"Pauli," whispered Céci. "I want to do pi-pi."

Pauli Simonian sat up. Beside him, his grandmother stirred but did not wake. They were huddled close together, partly for warmth, but mainly because of the sheer lack of space. Everywhere he looked the dim starlight showed him people, vague outlines against the greyness of the night.

He stood up carefully. He was dressed in his outdoor clothes plus a thick cardigan of his grandmother's, worn like an overcoat. She didn't feel the cold, she assured him. Old people had less sensitivity.

"Careful," he admonished his sister as she too got up. He took her hand and gingerly they picked their way among the recumbent bodies towards the distant lavatories beneath the stand. The stench hit them long before they got there. The lavatories had packed up within the first twenty-four hours, under sheer pressure of use, and they were now like open sewers.

"Pooh," said Céci wrinkling her nose. "Like Charlot when he got shut in. Oh, sorry, madame."

The woman she had stumbled against didn't protest or move, not even when Pauli, close behind, made the same error and almost fell on her, putting his hand on her shoulder to steady himself.

"Come on, Céci," he said. "Over here. Hurry up."

They reached the lavatory door. It was pointless to go in. The room was literally overflowing. Céci squatted down and quickly relieved herself. On their way back, she said, "I'm hungry."

"We'll get some food soon."

Sophie Simonian had packed a little food in her old carpetbag. She eked it out to them in dribs and drabs once she realized that no one seemed interested in feeding them. Already they'd been here in the Vél d'Hiv three, or was it four nights? Dysentery was already rife. There'd actually been a doctor in the place yesterday. She'd heard him respond angrily to a woman demanding more of his attention. "There are two of us, madame, two for all these people. What can I do?"

You can go home at night, thought Sophie. Go home and sit with your family and put us out of your mind.

That was the hardest thing to bear, the knowledge that out there within only a few yards of them there were French families eating, drinking, laughing, playing. The sense of abandonment was the worst thing of all.

Sophie woke from her fitful feverish half-sleep and realized the children were no longer with her.

"Pauli!" she cried. And sobbed with relief as a voice answered instantly, "Here, Bubbah."

They were back. "Céci wanted pi-pi," explained the boy.

Sophie glanced at her grandson, her old eyes somehow sharper in the dark than they had been when she was a girl. He seemed preoccupied.

"What are you doing, Pauli?" she asked.

"Just cleaning my hands, Bubbah," he explained.

"Good boy. That's good. You have to keep clean," she approved. "Then go back to sleep."

Satisfied, she let her own head sag back and soon the shallow waves of sleep lapped around her again. While in the darkness by her side her grandson, Pauli, tried to cleanse his hand of the blood that had stained it ever since he stumbled on that woman and steadied himself with his fingers against her deep-gashed throat.

NEXT MORNING they were woken by a voice calling, "Up! Up! Up! Hurry! Hurry! Hurry! Come on there!"

Sophie Simonian rose slowly, leaning heavily on Pauli's shoulder. She took a step forward, swayed and almost fainted.

"Bubbah, are you all right?" said Pauli anxiously.

"Yes, my dear. Fine. I think I've forgotten how to walk, that's all. Never mind. I'll soon learn again."

"Can you really forget things like that? How to walk, I mean?" asked Pauli.

"Of course you can! You can forget your head if you're not careful. You can forget anything."

"I don't think I'll ever forget this place, Bubbah," said Pauli seriously, as he helped his little sister up. "Céci, you'll have to walk. Bubbah can't carry you and I've got to carry the bag. Take Bubbah's hand."

"Where are we going, Pauli? Are we going home?" Céci asked.

Pauli looked up at his grandmother. "I don't think so," she said. "Later, perhaps. But not today. Come on, children. Come on."

Slowly they joined one of the long shuffling queues winding towards the stadium exits.

11

"Günter. Back already? Isn't it strange how other people's leave seems to pass even more quickly than one's own?" said Bruno Zeller.

Mai was sitting in the Lutétia's lounge enjoying a cup of coffee, which he'd found almost unobtainable at home. He'd just got back, having travelled overnight. "Has anything interesting happened since I've been away?" he asked, lighting his pipe. "Before I went there was a rumour about our friends planning a big anti-Jewish operation."

"Oh yes. Operation *Printanier*. It missed its target by fifty per cent I gather, but they still locked up fifteen thousand."

"Good God! And how did the French authorities react?"

"React? It was the French who did it. Not a single German in sight. Operation Spring Wind! A thousand French cops using French census lists to gently waft French Jews into French concentration camps guarded by French guards."

"And once in the camps, what then?"

"A trainload went east earlier in the year. No doubt there'll be more."

"What a waste of time, manpower, transport!" exclaimed Mai indignantly. "Forced labour I can just about understand. But this locking them up and guarding them for evermore, it's just crazy! Don't you agree?"

"My dear fellow, who wouldn't agree? But what else I've heard makes 'crazy' an ... understatement."

A mess orderly approached and clicked his heels.

"Begging the major's pardon, a telephone call for the lieutenant. A French lady, I think."

"Good Lord, Günter, hardly off the train and already they're after you!"

"Excuse me," said Mai, rising.

He moved over to the telephone and picked it up. "Hello? Günter Mai."

"Hello! It's Janine Simonian. Lieutenant, can I see you? *Please?*"

The voice was urgent, pleading. She sounded desperate. Best to suggest delay, stretch her nerves to the point where she'd make any bargain for his help. That was what she wanted, he was in no doubt. "I'll come at once. No. Give me ten minutes to change. Where?"

She said, "I can't go far. The Jardin des Plantes, by the big cedar."

The telephone went dead.

He made his way to the switchboard and asked, "I've just had a call from a woman. I wondered, has she perhaps rung before?"

The operator looked at his log. "Yes, sir. There's been some woman trying to get hold of you several times in the past couple of days."

"Thank you." He'd guessed from the sound of her voice that she was far past the stage of a first call. Perhaps it hadn't after all been kindness that made him agree instantly to meet, but a professional awareness that she'd done all the necessary nerve-twisting for herself.

Or is that what I want to think? he wondered.

By the time he had changed out of uniform, he was late arriving at the Jardin. A sudden fear came upon him that she would not have waited. Not the fear of a professional who dislikes having his time wasted, but something much more irrational. He broke into a trot without thinking. As he turned up the track towards the cedar, he saw her slim figure standing beneath the magnificent spread of summer-heavy branches.

She started speaking rapidly as soon as he arrived, but he waved her words aside without even looking at her and collapsed onto the stone bench round the trunk of the tree. "All right, all right, give me a minute," he said. He took out his pipe, filled it and put it in his mouth, saying, as he struck a match, "Now you can begin."

He looked up at her as he spoke and his voice faltered as he saw more closely the face which matched the desperate voice. Sunken cheeks, bloodless skin, deep-shadowed eyes, all combined to make her look more like some spirit of the underworld than the lively young woman he remembered.

For four days Janine had begged for news at the police station and wandered desperately in the streets outside the Vélodrome d'Hiver, hoping for a message, a glimpse. Four days of this, with fear in her heart that to press too close, to make too much fuss, might draw the attention of the authorities to Jean-Paul, unregistered, unstarred, lying between life and death with three German bullet holes in his body.

"Madame Simonian, please, won't you sit down? You're ill."

"No, no, I'm not ill," she said, sitting by him. "Please, listen to me, you must help me. There's no one else."

The story came pouring out—the arrest of Sophie and the children, their imprisonment in the Vél d'Hiv, her vain attempts to see them, and then her discovery that they'd been moved out of the stadium.

"I can't find out where to. Some say it's somewhere in the Loiret. Are there camps there? What *can* you want with little children? People near the stadium said you took them away in cattle trucks. It's monstrous, monstrous! Oh please help me, Lieutenant! Please, please, you've got to, I beg you—I'll do anything!"

Her tone switched from bitter accusation to desperate pleading and back again as she spoke. Tears ran down her cheeks. Mai put his arm round her shoulders and said helplessly, "Please ... Janine ... I beg you ..."

She leaned against him and sobbed without restraint. "I've tried everything ... asked everyone ... Christian tried to get his father to help but he said he couldn't interfere ... *interfere!* ... Miche tried to find out, but the people he works with won't help ... they hate Jews, he says ... it was their idea ... but he suggested you ... and I rang and they said you were away ... but I kept on ringing ... because I don't know what else to do ... please ... help ... me ..."

He said, "Of course I'll help. Believe me; trust me. I'll do everything in my power. Now, give me all the details please. Everything will be recorded. But I must have the details."

It was the right approach. For a second she threatened to be as devastated by her joy at his promise as she had been by her despair at her loss. But his businesslike manner as he produced the black *Tagenbuch* and questioned her, and made tiny illegible notes about the children's age, history and description, brought her back to something like normality.

Only when he mentioned her husband did he immediately sense a reticence. "He must be desperate, the poor man," he said casually. "His mother *and* his children. How's he taking it?"

The hesitation. "He doesn't know," she said.

"What?"

"I haven't told him. He's been ill, very ill. The wound he got in the war, it's been bothering him again."

Liar, he thought tenderly. You shouldn't try to lie, better still, you shouldn't need to lie.

She was looking at her watch in alarm. "I have to get back to him," she said. "I left him sleeping. When will you know something? When shall we meet?"

Her impatience touched and amused him. It was tempting to fuel her joy at his promise of help by saying tomorrow. But it would be a selfish suggestion. "Seventy-two hours," he said. "Three days."

Her face showed dismay. "Three days? So long?"

It was too short. The bureaucratic machine was efficient, but it could also be very slow. "Three days to our next meeting. And there's no guarantee that I will know anything by then."

Now she surprised him. "Oh but you will, Günter, I know you will," she cried. "Thank you, thank you so very much."

She kissed him on the cheek, then began to hurry away down the hill. After a few yards she turned, still moving backwards, and cried, "Same place, same time, by the cedar!" and waved and was gone.

He remained for a little while, relighting his pipe and sending curls of pungent smoke into the branches above.

And when he finally moved off, he didn't go straight back to the Lutétia, but strolled round the garden, gently nursing the image of Janine running away down the hill and turning to call and wave, like any young woman parting from her lover. He smiled. There were worse places to be than Paris on a summer day.

And wherever Céci and Pauli Simonian were was certainly one of them. It was time to get the search under way.

232

12

"You smiled, Bubbah," said Pauli. "What did you smile at?"

So my smile has become such a rare thing that this grandson of mine instantly spots it, thought Sophie sadly. Bending over Céci's hair which she was combing for lice, she plucked one out, held it up and said, "I was just thinking, there's such a one! Must be the grandfather of a whole family! Crack, and there's an end to him."

Her lie seemed to satisfy the boy. What she had actually been smiling at was a sudden memory of Iakov singeing lice from the seams of his clothes with a candle and accidentally setting his shirt on fire. Such memories were precious sustenance for the soul, here in Drancy.

For Drancy was an abomination. The food was vile beyond description. They slept like animals on straw infested with parasites. Every day new arrivals poured in, including vast numbers of children, many separated from their parents. When she saw them herded out of the trucks, Sophie wanted to rush to comfort them, pressing to her as many as possible.

But she did not dare to do it. All her energy was directed to keeping Pauli and Céci with her. She'd seen families ripped apart after dawn roll calls when those picked out had been marched away to the train station.

She concentrated her attention on Céci's hair.

"Bubbah," said the little girl idly, "when will it be our turn to go to Pitchipoi?"

"Pitchi-what? Where's that, my little cabbage?" she asked.

"Pitchipoi!" repeated Céci. "When are we going?"

"Pauli?" said Sophie, turning to the boy, as always when she couldn't grasp what Céci was meaning.

"It's the name some of the children give to the place they're going to send us," said Pauli, who was trying to repair his worn and torn trousers. It would be much easier if he had a needle or even a knife. He thought with regret of the super knife that Uncle Miche had given him. He'd left it at home the day his mother had suddenly decided they should stay with Bubbah. He wished he had it now. Even though he'd promised Maman he would never open the blade till he had her permission, there were still all those other bits and pieces which would have been so useful.

"It's an awful place," announced Céci, happy to be forthcoming now that her brother had shown the way. "It's a dreadful place, where they make stew out of the little girls and steak out of the little boys."

"Céci!" exclaimed Sophie, almost choking in alarm. "That's silly."

"No it's not," said the child indignantly, "everyone knows. It's an awful, awful place and it's miles and miles from home and you never, never ever come back, 'cause if you try to run away there's big dogs like wolves to eat you. Isn't that right, Pauli?"

233

Her brother looked up at his grandmother, then looked away. Céci took the silence as assent and cried triumphantly to Sophie, "See, Pauli knows it's true!" and in the very moment of her triumph, the implication of having her worst fears confirmed by her infallible brother hit her.

Bursting into tears, she squeezed tight against Sophie and sobbed, "I don't want to go, Bubbah. I don't want to go to Pitchipoi."

"There, there, cabbage, there's no such place, it's just a silly game," crooned Sophie, rocking the child to and fro. "We're not going to go anywhere."

"DRANCY!" JANINE did a jig of delight. "Near Le Bourget Airport! Oh, thank God they're still in Paris."

Mai looked at her gloomily. It had been in little spirit of celebration that he had brought his news. He had obtained it through a friend on the staff of the military governor.

"Tell me about Drancy," he had said to the officer.

"The camp, you mean? It was a building project, apartment blocks mainly, only half finished when the war started, but it was perfect for a camp. Easy to fence off, plenty of accommodation for the prisoners, but not too comfortable! Good communications, east and west..."

"East and west?"

"West to the city centre. And east to wherever you like. There's a railway station just round the corner. They've started sending this latest lot east for resettlement. What's your interest?"

"It's just that an agent of mine got picked up and I'm anxious to help. Good agents are hard to come by."

"Is that it? And I bet you believe the SD did it deliberately? I wouldn't put it past them. But no problem, Günter. Just pop round here with the details some time and we'll fix up an *Ausweis*."

"I'll do that," said Mai. "Incidentally, this resettlement, where is it, precisely?"

"If you're thinking about asking for your agent back if he's already gone, forget it!" laughed the officer. "They're sending them off to some godforsaken hole in Upper Silesia. Auschwitz, I think they call it."

Mai pulled his mind back to the present and was disconcerted to find Janine looking at him as if he had just given her champagne, her eyes sparkling with hope.

She said confidently, "What do we do now, Günter?"

He could detect nothing premeditated in the use of his name. It slipped out as naturally and easily as any friend's.

"I can get them out," he said.

If he expected a dance of joy he was disappointed. But what he got was more disturbing. She merely nodded with serene confidence.

"But there's a price," he added harshly.

Again she surprised him. "Of course," she said. "Do you think I imagined you were doing this out of the goodness of your heart?"

If she'd chosen deliberately to strike at him she could not have aimed a better weapon. Pain rose in Mai and must surely have shown in his eyes.

She fixed her clear, candid gaze on him and said, "Please, don't think I can't see that you *do* have much goodness of heart. But you'll also do your job. I don't think you want sex with me, not this time. I'm not sure how much you wanted it last time."

He flushed and said, "More than I realized. But not like that."

"No? How then? No, don't answer that. What I imagine you want this time is the help I can give you professionally. I've no idea what that may be, and I'm not sure if you have. I think perhaps deep inside, you hope it may not be very much. So do I. But I'll give you what I can, and I know you will not refuse what I can give. You've got me in a trap, Lieutenant, but I half suspect you're in there with me."

He shook his head slowly, not in denial but in admiration, and in self-exasperation too.

"What's the matter?" she asked.

"I've been stupid," he said. "I have misjudged you. I should have grasped that your husband was not a man to make such misjudgments."

The mention of Simonian cast a veil over her expression.

He said, "So we understand each other. To get an *Ausweis* for your children and the old lady, I shall need to affirm that you are a valued agent of the *Abwehr*, and your name will appear in our files. As you say, anything you can tell me, I shall not hesitate to use. Anything I think you can do for us, I shall not hesitate to ask."

He had never contemplated so open an approach. He had always thought of himself as the manipulator, the puppet-master. But now, with this woman, in these circumstances, he could see that nothing else was possible.

"When can you do it?" she cried. "When can I have them home?"

"I should have the *Ausweis* by tomorrow. Then I have to arrange for a release order to be sent to the camp."

"Tomorrow? Can't we go for them tonight?"

He said brusquely, "Tomorrow at the earliest. It takes time."

She said, "Of course. I'm sorry, I'm just so impatient. Günter, thank you, thank you more than I can say."

She leaned forward and kissed him lightly on the lips. "Till tomorrow." Once again she turned and waved as she ran lightly down the hill.

THE NEXT MORNING in the corpse-light of a grey, drizzling dawn, their names were called out in the list for departure.

Sophie tried to protest, but all she did was draw attention to herself. "Quickly, over there! Do as I say, old woman!"

They collected their pathetic scraps of belongings. The old carpetbag was long gone. Now what they had was contained in a ragged square of cloth tied together at the corners.

"Over there! Get on the bus!"

The old green and white buses were being used today. There was a large number of unaccompanied children being deported and it was felt there was a risk that the sight of them being herded along the rain-soaked pavements to the station might provoke some kind of protest.

On the bus Sophie sat near the door and pulled Céci and Pauli close to her. They didn't speak but sat by the rain-spattered window, fearfully watching the confusion outside.

Whatever system there had been had clearly broken down. Harassed French officials with lists were trying to check names. A German officer appeared, and began to shout angry instructions, adding to the confusion. A girl of about ten ran from one of the detention blocks and spoke to him. She gestured towards the buses. The officer spoke to a French official who studied his list and shook his head. The officer pointed back to the block, the girl persisted, and finally the official dragged her, screaming, back into the building. It was like watching a vision of madness, then realizing you were no spectator but a part of it.

Céci said, "Bubbah, are we going to Pitchipoi now?"

"No, of course not," said Sophie, but her voice carried no conviction. She had to do something. She closed her eyes in prayer for a moment, opened them again and saw the young girl, who was desperate to get on a bus, being driven back by the angry official once more.

"Pauli," she said, "don't ask questions. Take Céci to the block. If anyone stops you, tell them you *want* to go on the bus because there's a nice lady there who's been kind to you. But don't tell them your name. Can you do that, Pauli?"

He looked straight into her eyes with that unblinking gaze he had inherited from her son. Then he nodded. "Yes, Bubbah," he said, and flung his arms round her neck and kissed her.

Then he took Céci by the hand. Their bus was full and their guard was round in front, smoking a cigarette. The door was slightly ajar. Pauli pushed it so it slid just wide enough for them to squeeze out.

Sophie watched them walk away. They looked so small, so defenceless. The old woman half rose from her seat to call them back. But she slumped down again without calling. In her mind she was seeing that sad, already defeated queue, shuffling forward to register what no civilized state could have any reason for wanting them to register. Even then she had known, but not been able to admit, where that queue led to.

Now it was her fate to travel east at the end of her life just as she and Iakov had travelled west at its beginning. But for the children any delay must increase their slender chance of rescue from this nightmare.

They had almost reached the nearest detention block, but just as it seemed they had made it, a gendarme planted himself in front of them and pointed back to the buses.

Sophie felt her old frail body ready to collapse at this last disappointment. She sank back and put her hands over her face.

Pauli looked up at the man and began to yell, "We *want* to go! We *want* to go! But he won't let us! He won't let us!"

At last the gendarme realized what was being said. "What do you mean? Who won't let you?"

"The man on the bus! We want to go with the lady, but he said we can't!" He now screwed his face up and made himself cry. Céci had no idea what was going on, but tears are infectious, so she joined in, "We want to go with the lady!"

"Shut your row," ordered the gendarme. "What's your name?" He had a list.

Pauli thought desperately. All names except his own vanished from his mind. Then he saw his grandfather's shop, and smelt the fresh-baked bread. "Crozier," he said. "I'm Claude Crozier and this is my sister, Louise."

The gendarme studied the list. Suppose there was someone called Crozier on it? Pauli clasped his sister's hand so tight she squealed in pain.

"Poor kid. You really are upset, aren't you?" said the gendarme, paying attention to Céci for the first time. Men were always delighted with the little girl's wide-eyed, appealing face framed in blonde curls, and even in her present state, the charm still worked. Suddenly, Pauli foresaw a new danger: success. He flung himself forward against the gendarme. "Let us go with the lady! Let us go with the lady!" he cried, beating his fists against the policeman's thighs.

"Yes, you've got to!" yelled Céci, adding her tiny fists to the tattoo.

The gendarme doubled up with pain. "Get out of here before I break your neck! Go on, you nasty little Yid! Get out of here!"

In the bus, Sophie took her hands from her eyes. She saw the gendarme straightening up, saw Pauli and his sister disappear back into the detention block. Thank God! she thought, certain beyond reason that somehow the children would now be freed completely from Drancy. Thank you, dear God. Now I can die.

13

Three months after Sophie Simonian's journey to the east, the rescued children stood on a cold, windswept platform of the Gare de Lyon and prepared once more to journey to the home of their Aunt Mireille in the Ain. This time the journey made even less sense to Pauli than it had in 1940. Then, at least their mother had been going with them.

Towering over the children on the platform, one huge hand resting on each small head, was Michel Boucher. To protect Janine, not to mention his own interests, Günter Mai had suggested that Boucher be given the credit for obtaining the Drancy release order, and it had made sense to maintain the deception when it came to the children's permit to travel into the Free Zone.

While Boucher had been delighted to play the role of benevolent provider, he hadn't omitted to use the occasion to his own advantage. The children needed an escort, at least as far as Lyon where his sister would meet them. He knew just the man. And there was no need for Mai to worry. He, Boucher, would supply all the necessary identification papers if the German could arrange *Ausweis*. Mai finally agreed, and the result was Monsieur Roger Corder, commercial traveller, who stood there, wan-faced, anxious-eyed, in a grey fedora and an astrakhan coat.

Boucher said, "For God's sake, Maurice, dump that coat! It's a dead giveaway."

"Do you know how much this coat cost me?" replied Melchior passionately. "*Nothing!* Do you expect me to give up so easily something which was a gift from God?"

Janine had been more than relieved to learn that Melchior was travelling with the children on such a long trip. She had been tempted in many ways to obey Jean-Paul's harsh instructions and Mai's gentler urgings to go with them herself. But her fear was that if she made the trip, she would not have the willpower to come back.

She looked at her husband, standing beside her on the platform. She'd kept the news of his mother's deportation from him as long as possible, waiting till he got some of his strength back. The night she told him, he rose from his sickbed and went out, returning hours later with no explanation. But she noticed that the toes of his heavy boots were stained brown and the backs of his hands were scored with scratches such as a woman's long nails might make trying to loosen a strangler's grip.

Next day there were red and black notices everywhere announcing heavy reprisals for the brutal murder of a German sergeant. Not mentioned in the notices was the fact that he had been killed at the apartment of a blonde prostitute from the Golden Gate Club, and that the woman had been throttled so violently that every bone in her throat was shattered.

Since then Jean-Paul seemed to have become a creature of stealth. Janine and the children he either ignored or looked at with baffled despair, like a man watching birds through a barred window.

There was danger here, she could feel it. For herself, she did not mind. But the thought of having the children brought into peril again became too much, and finally she opted to send them away.

Now at last the time had come for the train to leave. Whistles blew, flags waved, smoke billowed up. Slowly, the great locomotive began to move.

From a distance, a pair of eyes observed the scene. They saw Janine run helplessly a little way from the train, saw the small pale faces of the children, their arms outstretched and waving; saw above them a long adult arm languidly flapping a pale pink kerchief; saw Jean-Paul turn away and march towards the barrier; saw Janine squeeze Boucher's arm and set off after her husband.

Günter Mai turned away also because he did not wish to see the pain that must be etched on Janine's face.

He didn't go far, however, and when Michel Boucher came off the platform, Mai fell into step beside him.

"Lieutenant! So you did come. Hey, listen, come and have some champagne. I'm a father! How about that? The loveliest little girl you ever saw. We're calling her Antoinette. Classy, eh?"

"Very," said Mai. "Congratulations. How was everything? On the platform, I mean."

"Oh, it was fine. That Pauli's cool as a butcher's slab and as long as he's OK, the little girl will go anywhere."

"And Janine?"

"Well, what do you think? Upset naturally, but she'll be OK. She's got strength, that one. No, the only fly in the ointment was that husband of hers. I reckon that Boche bullet's left a permanent hole in his head, poor devil. Now, what about that drink?"

"Later," said Mai. He hesitated, then added, "Perhaps a lot later. Look, Miche, I've got to leave Paris. I've been posted."

"Not to the Russian front?" said Boucher with alarm.

"No. I'll still be in France. And I hope to get back here eventually. I just wondered if you'd mention it to your cousin. Tell her the file is closed. She'll understand."

It was self-interest not sentiment that had made him erase Janine's name from his records, he assured himself. If his successor got interested in what this female agent was doing for the Reich, explanations would not be easy, whereas anyone could explain a gap in the files.

"Good luck," said Boucher. "I'm going to miss you."

They shook hands and he walked quickly away.

There, it was done. Perhaps after all it would be better in Toulouse.

Toulouse. That was why he didn't wish to give the news of his posting to Janine himself. She was bound to ask why it was that he was being posted into the so-called Free Zone, to which, with his aid, she'd just dispatched her children for safety.

He hadn't the courage to give her the news which he himself had only learned the previous day. Four days hence, on November 11, a second army of occupation would sweep south to secure the Africa-threatened Mediterranean shore. The Free Zone would cease to exist.

PART FOUR March–December 1943

1

Day broke, grey and cold.

Janine watched it as she had watched many days break that winter. This was her time of despair. Recognizing that it was going to destroy her, she had ceased to flee it and had started instead to face and embrace it. It was far from easy, especially on days like this when there was little promise of sunlight. She lit a cigarette.

These days Jean-Paul slept soundly, like a man satisfied with his day's work. Outwardly their relationship was now fairly stable, but in the months since the children's departure, she had realized just what a softening effect they had had upon their father, just how much of a buffer they had been between herself and Jean-Paul. From the start she had sensed that there was no path back to the way things once were, but even now the gleam of his old smile could set her heart pounding with renewed hope and give her the strength to hold on till dawn when next her terrors roused her early. Such a moment came unexpectedly this morning.

"Got one of those to spare?" said his voice behind her.

She turned. He had come silently into the kitchen where she was sitting. She had no idea how long he had been watching her.

"Of course," she said, passing over the packet. "You're up early. I've put some coffee on. Like some?"

"Please," he said. "I've got to go out shortly, that's why I'm up. I was watching you sitting there. You looked, I don't know, as if you were ... well, you certainly didn't look happy."

"Didn't I?" she said lightly. She felt at the same time full of happiness and full of tension.

"What were you thinking about? The children?"

"Yes," she said, to keep things simple. "I miss them so much."

"I miss them too. And I worry about them."

"You don't think they're not safe?" she said, fearful that he had heard some news she'd missed about the situation in the Ain. There'd been a period of rage and fear when the Boche had occupied the Free Zone so soon after the children's departure. Günter Mai would have suffered if she could have got near him at that moment, and when Miche told her of his posting, it had seemed to her like flight. At first she had wanted to fetch the children home, but had been dissuaded. Whatever happened in the old Free Zone, the dangers in Paris hadn't changed and next time things went wrong there would be no Günter offering help.

"I'm sure they're safe," Jean-Paul said. "It's just that they must miss you. Why don't you join them?"

Here it was again, the pressure. She felt her moment of happiness slipping away. "And would you come too?" she asked quietly, pouring the coffee with a steady hand.

"I can't," he said. "I have work to do here."

"Your precious Fishermen, you mean?"

"What do you know about the Fishermen?" he demanded.

"Nothing specific. But I've heard you and Henri talking. Am I supposed to be deaf or something? Or stupid? Or not to be trusted?"

The thought flashed unwanted across her mind that it was easy for her to wax indignant about trust with Günter Mai safely out of the way. She stared defiantly at her husband, expecting anger.

"I don't want you involved in this," he said.

"I'm your wife. While I live with you, of course I'm involved."

"Yes," he said, nodding as if she were agreeing with his argument. "You see what I mean then. Jan, when all this is over there'll be a time to sit and mend things. Just now there's no time for *personal* relationships. We can't afford to divert our energies."

Before she could respond he looked at his watch and said, "See what I mean? I've got to go. You'll think about what we've said?"

He was gone with a swiftness which was typical. Well, at least it had been a real conversation. Perhaps he would be safer in Paris by himself, while she took care of the children at Mireille's.

These thoughts stayed with her as she set off for the boulangerie. After the children had gone she had begun to help in the shop and the bakehouse first thing in the morning. There was very little to do there, and she knew it was simply a device by which her parents could subsidise her. Jean-Paul seemed to have other sources of subsidy. *Les Pêcheurs.* The Fishermen. She could only guess the kind of work they did. Sabotage, theft, disruption. Perhaps it needed to be done but it seemed to have precious little effect on the stranglehold the Boche had on Paris.

She was on foot. Jean-Paul had taken the bicycle they shared. Despite the fact that spring was officially here, the morning was gloomy. Normally she would have walked to the shop but today the weather drove her into the métro. She emerged from the station nearest to the bakery, into the Boulevard Raspail, not far from the Lutétia.

She thought again of Mai. There was no reason why they should ever meet again, so she could look objectively at the relationship. On balance she had profited from it, there was no doubt of that. On one side, her husband and her children safe; on the other, one act of sex and the threat, since removed, of having her name on an *Abwehr* agents' list.

"Janine!"

Alarmed, she halted uncertainly. She was just off the boulevard in a side street. A man was standing in a doorway. He leaned out of the shadows and was instantly recognisable as Miche Boucher.

"Miche. What are you up to?"

"Saving your life," he said. "Do you always wander round in a dream?"

"I'm on my way to the bakery," she said. "What are you hiding from, Miche?"

"I'm on watch," he corrected. "We've had a tip that a Resistance group are planning to hit a staff car." He opened his expensive jacket dramatically and showed her a Luger in a shoulder holster.

"Why don't you just warn the men in the car?"

It was a good question and one which Boucher had put to Pajou.

"Because one of the guys in the car is Major Zeller," Pajou had said. "Basically old Fiebelkorn doesn't mind how many *Abwehr* officers get hurt so long as we sort out these Resistance people afterwards. Why do you think it's us lot on this job? Whatever happens, Fiebelkorn gets all the credit and none of the blame."

In a window overlooking the boulevard a man struck a match. It was the signal. The staff car was in sight. Grabbing hold of Janine, Boucher drew her roughly into the doorway. "Keep back," he ordered.

As the car approached, a cyclist wobbled out of a narrow entry on the other side of the road. He looked like a workman on his way to work. His dirty old raincoat was sodden wet and over his shoulders was a canvas toolbag.

He seemed to be having trouble with his brakes, and slid sideways on the greasy road right into the path of the German car. It skidded to a halt alongside the fallen cyclist. The driver leaned out of the window and began shouting. The two officers in the back looked unconcerned. The cyclist rose from the ground and started yelling back at the driver.

And then another cyclist appeared, a gendarme. Attracted by the commotion, he halted on the other side of the car, saluted the officer and started asking questions.

"What the hell's that idiot doing?" groaned Boucher.

The gendarme addressed the workman, who grumbled, stooped and picked up the bicycle. Another salute to the officers and the two cyclists moved away alongside each other. The car set off in the opposite direction.

"Trust the flics to mess everything up," said Boucher, stepping out of the doorway and looking desperately for some signal to indicate the next move. And then in the same instant two things struck him.

The workman no longer had his toolbag. And there had been something dragging along beneath the car.

He opened his mouth to yell, but his words were drowned by a huge explosion, followed by the scream of tearing metal and a second flash as the petrol tank went up.

The two cyclists raced away up the boulevard. But now the trap was sprung and Pajou's men came out of a building ahead of them and began blazing away with machine pistols. The gendarme was hit instantly and went flying over the handlebars. The workman wrenched his bike round, the front wheel rearing as though he were riding a horse. He held himself low and bumped up onto the pavement to give himself the protection of the lampposts. Windows shattered alongside him as the stream of bullets whiplashed in pursuit.

Boucher's Luger was out. The fugitive was being driven straight towards him. Janine had come out of the doorway and was standing close behind, watching with horror.

Boucher raised his gun.

Janine cried, "Miche! No!" and flung her arms round his body as the cyclist went hurtling past them, down the side street and out of view.

Shaking himself free, Boucher turned to Janine and said disbelievingly, "That was your husband."

She nodded, hardly able to speak from the shock.

"Did you know?" demanded Boucher.

She shook her head, gasping, "No, Miche, I swear it."

Men came running up, among them Pajou. "What the hell are you playing at, Miche? You must have been within spitting distance of him."

"Bloody gun jammed," said Boucher.

"Yeah? Did you get a look at his face?"

"Not much. He was all muffled up."

"Great." Pajou's eyes turned suspiciously towards Janine. "Who's this?"

"My cousin, Janine. She works close by. I saw her and told her to keep her head down."

Another man joined them. "The one we got's dead," he reported. "Also the car driver and one of the officers. The other one's still alive, the major. But he's all smashed up. Burned too. He'll be lucky to make it."

"That should please the boss anyway," said Pajou. "Better get back and report. Coming, Miche?"

"I'll catch you up."

He waited till his companions were out of earshot, then said, "Look Jan, are you sure you had no idea what Jean-Paul was up to?"

"Of course I had *some* idea," she retorted. "But I didn't realize ..."

"That it involved blowing people to pieces?" Boucher completed the sentence for her. "One thing's sure: he'll get caught or killed sooner or later. Get out while you can. The Gestapo won't believe you're not in it too. Join the kids at Mireille's place, that's the wise move."

Of course it was the wise move. But now more than ever she knew she had to stay. It wasn't the slaughter, shocking though it was, that had appalled her. It was the sight of Jean-Paul's face as he raced past. Fear she would have expected to see there, and perhaps even excitement. But all she had seen was wild exultation, a glow of sheer joy.

There was no way that she could think of leaving him now.

2

"Hey, Paris-piglet!"

Pauli Simonian ignored the cry. He was sitting on a stone by the pond watching a flotilla of ducks.

"Are you deaf as well as stupid, Yid?"

It was Christophe calling, the youngest of "Aunt" Mireille's three sons. The two older boys had accepted the arrival of the newcomers with indifference, but Christophe, a burly nine-year-old, had been antagonistic from the start. Somehow, he'd picked up the fact that their father was a Jew and he'd taken to calling Pauli "Yid".

"See if your dirty ears can hear that then!"

A stone struck the water in front of Pauli, splashing droplets in his face. Another larger one followed. Céci, playing a few yards away, looked up in delight at this new game and laughed merrily. But the next stone hurled by Christophe went astray and sent a spray of cold water over her. Laughs turned to sobs. Pauli rose, fists clenched. Christophe, seeing that he had at last found a way of stinging his unwanted "cousin", now began to aim at Céci. Pauli ran towards the other boy, who regarded his approach with pleasurable anticipation. A year older, two inches taller and a stone heavier, Christophe didn't doubt he could put the Paris-piglet in his place. He planted his feet firmly and raised his already brawny arms to ward off the expected frontal onslaught.

Instead, Pauli came to a halt in front of him, then with great force and accuracy kicked his cousin just beneath the left kneecap.

Christophe screeched with pain and hopped on his right leg, which Pauli's foot immediately scythed from under him. He fell on his back. Pauli dropped both knees into his belly and proceeded to beat him about the chest. Finally, still not having uttered a word, he rose and, leaving his blubbering cousin prostrate on the dank grass, went to collect Céci and take her back to the farmhouse to get dry.

After that, things got much better. Pauli often went off alone, and was soon almost as familiar with the surrounding countryside as he'd been with the streets of Paris.

Mireille was at first unhappy about his long absences. "Janine said he was a bit of a wanderer, but that was in the town where he knew his way around."

"Less chance of coming to harm in the country," said her husband.

"Well, keep an eye out for him in your wanderings. There's too many wild men with shotguns up in the hills for my liking."

Since the Occupation there'd been a steady trickle of men taking to the hills and woods. Their reasons varied, but their cause was common: hatred of the Boche. These were the Maquis. As their organization improved, they began to prick the Germans with acts of sabotage and there had already been reprisals against the families of men known to be involved.

"I promised you, I'm not going to join," said Laurentin wearily. "I'll not put my family at risk for a gesture. But I'll not turn my back on them either. Dropping them the odd sack of vegetables is the least I can do."

"As long as it stops at that," said Mireille.

"I'm going up today," said Laurentin bluntly. "Old Rom will be working in the barn if you want anything."

Rom was the farm labourer, a taciturn man of unguessable years.

Despite the burden of a sack over his shoulder, Laurentin made his way rapidly up into the hills which rose gently on all sides of the farm. After half an hour he stopped for a breather, resting against the vegetable sack.

Twenty yards behind, Pauli halted too, his heart pounding with excitement. He guessed where his uncle was going and was longing to glimpse these wild outlaws that the boys at school talked of. He lay on the cold earth and watched the outline of the knobbly sack against which his uncle was reclining in the long grass. Above, grey clouds played with a pale sun, alternating patches of dark and bright across the rolling landscape.

He lay in sunlight, but then a shadow swept over him, more intense than a cloud's shadow, and he screamed in terror as the nape of his neck was seized by a strong hand and he was dragged roughly to his feet.

"Watch the beast, not the burden," said Laurentin's voice in his ear. "Next man you follow may reckon it's safer to blast away with his shotgun than come crawling back here to trap you alive."

He released the boy, whose legs felt so weak he almost collapsed back onto the ground. But he forced himself to stay upright and stood looking silently at his uncle, waiting for his verdict.

"Straight back to the farm," ordered Laurentin. "Don't mention this to anyone, least of all your aunt. Understood?"

"Yes, sir," said Pauli.

"Then go. I want to see you run."

Twenty minutes later a breathless Pauli came running down the long meadow which sloped towards the farmhouse, just as an old truck spluttered into sight round the bend of the farm track.

Non-military vehicles were rare enough to bring Mireille to the door and old Rom out of the barn. The truck halted noisily. There were two men in it, one round and gross and untidy, the other small, slim and dapper. This one got out first, leaping nimbly to the ground.

"Madame, how pleasant to see you again," he said, walking up to Mireille. "How are you? Do you hear from that brother of yours?"

As recognition struggled into Mireille's face, Pauli arrived, driving his flagging legs into a sprint. "Monsieur Melchior!" he cried.

"Monsieur Corder, you mean," said Melchior reprovingly, but he smiled as he swept the delighted boy up into his arms.

Minutes later, he was seated in the kitchen drinking coffee with his companion, whom he introduced as his business partner, Octave Timbal.

"But monsieur, when you left the children with me at the station last year, I thought you said you were travelling on to Marseille?"

"Such was my plan," said Melchior. "But first I needed rest. My nerves were quite ragged. I took a room in the Hôtel Terminus just across from the station. A short respite of perfect peace, then on I would go to Marseille. Can you imagine how I felt a few days later when I heard the dreadful din of grinding engines and marching feet and looked out of my window to see the fearful Hun? How it took me back to nineteen forty! Naturally I tried to leave, but all travel was restricted."

"So what did you do, monsieur?" asked Mireille.

"Happily, I make friends easily. Also I had a few sous set aside for emergencies. So eventually I decided to set up in business with my dear friend Octave here."

Mireille had been eyeing Timbal with some misgiving. "And what is your business?" she asked.

"Retailing," said Melchior. "We bring surpluses and shortages together, particularly of fresh comestibles."

"You mean you're in the black market," said Mireille.

Melchior spread his hands and smiled. "We are suppliers."

"And you thought we might have something to sell, eh?" said Mireille.

"Good Lord, it never crossed my mind. I simply recalled that you lived somewhere in this vicinity, and I thought how nice it would be to see my young friends again." He ruffled Céci's hair and winked at Pauli. "But of course if there should happen to be anything ... a ham perhaps, some fresh vegetables ... we would offer the very best price."

Mireille began to laugh. Melchior joined in. Soon the children, not knowing what they were laughing at but with spirits lifted by this visitor from their previous life, were laughing too.

Now Mireille lowered her voice and said, "All right. But I'll want a favour. Janine's coming to see the children soon. She says she'd rather see them in Lyon than come out to the farm. Something about getting more time with them that way, but I reckon ... well, that's family business. But if you could find somewhere for them to stay for a few days ..."

"My pleasure," said Melchior.

"Thanks," said Mireille rising. "Now, let's see what we can find for you to buy."

They went out into the yard. Most of the clouds had cleared now and the sunshine was beginning to have some warmth in it.

Céci had taken Melchior's hand and as he stood and enjoyed the sun on his face, he felt his other hand grasped too. He looked down and smiled.

"You see, Pauli, everything works out for the best. Bearing gifts of gold, that's me, my boy. I think I've fallen on my feet at last!"

3

Early in the summer Gunter Mai returned to Paris.

The *Abwehr* chief at the Lutétia said, "I'm sorry if you feel mucked around, Mai, but Bruno Zeller was adamant that you knew as much about the work in his section as he did. He wants you to take over."

"How is the major?" Mai asked.

"Lucky to be alive. Or perhaps not. He's lost his right arm and the best part of his left foot and he was badly burned about the face and the upper torso. They've shipped him back home for treatment."

"Anything special I ought to know, sir?" Mai asked.

"It'll all be in the files," came the reply. Mai doubted it.

"And our friends in the Avenue Foch, how are they?"

"Cock-a-hoop that they caught Moulin," said the chief.

Jean Moulin had been de Gaulle's emissary, given the task, which he'd almost accomplished, of coordinating the various branches of the Resistance. He'd been caught in Lyon and had died under interrogation.

"Caught and killed," said Mai. "Before he told anything, I gather."

"It still comes out as a triumph. We'll have to be alert, Mai, or they'll steal all our thunder."

Was the man a fool? wondered Mai as he returned to his room. The battle with the SD was long lost. All they could do now was fight a rearguard action.

His conclusions about the way things were going were confirmed as he slipped back into his old work. Paris was now definitely the capital of a conquered country and the techniques of persuasion had been abandoned in favour of the threat of terror. The pretence of partnership had gone; they had lost France and were losing Italy. News of external defeats had had its inevitable effect upon the great passive majority of the people. Now the good burghers of Paris were cautiously moving some of their eggs into the Resistance basket.

THIS GENTLE SHIFT had made Christian Valois even more unhappy with his role. In obedience to Delaplanche, he had almost broken off contact with the Simonians, but he knew that Jean-Paul had cobbled together his own group out of what was left of André's after the canal fiasco, and every reference to *les Pêcheurs* still filled him with envy. The memory of his one piece of action, the shooting in the métro, now seemed like an adolescent daydream.

He visited his parents for a few days. Vichy was now a dead and dispirited place. Since the occupation of the Free Zone its function was manifestly an empty pretence. He found his father silent and depressed, his mother drinking too much, and even his lovely sister, Marie-Rose, seemed offhand and self-absorbed. He pressed her to tell him what was the matter but all she replied was, "I've just got to get away from here."

"Come and see me in Paris," he said.

To his surprise she shook her head. "I can't," she said. "Not yet. Soon perhaps."

"Why? Is there something the matter?" he asked.

She shook her head and laughed but as he sat on the train home the sense that Marie-Rose was hiding something from him was a further cause for depression.

As he came off the platform in Paris, a man collided with him and forced him into an embrace.

As Christian tried to pull loose, Jean-Paul's voice hissed in his ear, "It's me, idiot. Head for the old bistro by the Cluny." Then he was gone.

There was no doubting where he meant. The bistro near the Cluny Museum had been a favourite haunt in their student days.

When Christian got to the rendezvous, Jean-Paul was there already with two drinks in front of him.

"What's happened?" asked Valois, sitting down and trying to conceal his anxiety.

"They've taken Théo Laffay."

Théo was the Resistance group leader who'd helped Christian to pull the trigger in the métro.

"What happened?"

"There was a meeting. It was blown. Théo got taken."

"Théo won't talk," said Valois certainly. "He'd die first."

"Everyone talks," said Simonian contemptuously. "Twenty-four hours is what we usually expect. Hold out for twenty-four hours, then spill your guts out. Trouble is, the Gestapo know this as well, so they do everything possible to start the talking earlier. In this case I reckon they've got Théo's family. I rang to warn them. There was no reply. His wife screaming in the next room may loosen Théo's tongue ahead of schedule."

"Good God! I'd better warn Delaplanche!"

Valois began to rise. Simonian grabbed his arm and pulled him down.

"Delaplanche can look after himself. He's a big man, too big to go under easily. No, it's you I'm here to warn. Théo knows about you, right?"

"He's met me," said Valois, suddenly cautious.

"He knows you killed a Boche, doesn't he? He was there!"

"But we only met briefly. In his eyes, I'm not important at all," protested Valois.

"Perhaps not. But he'll be grabbing for scraps to feed those bastards by the time they finish with him. If he mentions that you killed one of them...!"

Valois picked up his empty glass and attempted to suck the last few drops out of it. "What shall I do?" he asked desperately.

"Lie low. Ring your office, tell them you've had to stay in Vichy—sick relative, anything. Come and stay at my place for a couple of days. We'll watch and wait. Perhaps it will blow over."

Simonian grinned. He looked young, carefree, like the student who had so often sat in this very bistro those few, short, lifelong years ago. Valois felt a small surge of hope.

VALOIS SPENT A WHOLE WEEK closeted in the Simonians' apartment before Jean-Paul confirmed it was safe for him to return home. "Poor old Théo's heart gave out three days ago," Jean-Paul told him. "There's been no sign of the Gestapo round at your place. So it looks as if everything's clear. You can go home and resume the even tenor of your ways!"

His apartment felt cold, unused. He closed the blinds and put the lights on. It was just as he'd left it. A half full coffee cup stood on the telephone table reminding him that as usual he'd left in a rush.

He poured himself a drink and walked around. It was good to be back, he decided. Good to get out of that poky little flat in the Quartier Mouffetard. The telephone rang, startling him.

He picked it up but did not speak. His mouth was dry.

A voice said, "You all right?"

It was Jean-Paul. "Yes, I'm fine. Look, I didn't really say how grateful I was . . ."

"That's OK. Go to bed." The telephone went dead.

Bed. It was good advice. Suddenly he realized he was exhausted.

He woke later that night to darkness and the sound of rain lashing the windowpanes and wind rattling a badly closed door. He glanced at the luminous dial of his watch. It was five am. Gestapo time.

He pushed the unpleasant thought from his mind and rolled over.

In a corner of the room a torch flashed on.

He sat up, holding his hand against the jet of light.

"Monsieur Valois, so you've come home," said a soft, friendly voice. "I said you would. Don't go crashing into his flat, I said, smashing up his nice things, tearing up the floorboards. What would a nice young man, son of a deputy, be hiding there, anyway? No, watch and wait, watch and wait, I said. When all seems safe, he'll come wandering home."

"Who are you? What do you want?" demanded Christian fearfully.

"Come now. You can answer both those questions yourself."

Valois struggled out of bed. The torch was his enemy. He plunged towards the disc of light. A forearm caught him round the throat. His mouth gaped wide, gasping to take in air, to let out screams. A gloved hand fastened on it and squeezed so tight he thought his cheeks would tear. His nostrils sucked in air, but not enough.

"Now, let us go quietly," said the soft voice. "No need to disturb the neighbours, is there?"

4

Mai sat under the great cedar in the Jardin des Plantes and filled his pipe for the third time. The few people who had passed him in the last hour had glanced at him with amusement, thinking he was a lover who'd been stood up. Good cover, except that that was just what he felt like.

Since his return to Paris he had only seen Janine distantly, but he had been kept up-to-date by her cousin, Miche, with whom he'd resumed the old working relationship.

Miche had passed on a problem. "That stuck-up mate of hers, Valois, he's gone missing it seems. She seems to think he might have got himself arrested. Would you mind asking around?"

"Did she ask you to ask me?"

"No, that was my idea."

"You've got a cheek!" said Mai. But inside, he had been suddenly hit by a powerful desire to see Janine again.

He had said, "All right. I'll see what I can do. But she'll have to come herself. Tell her tomorrow afternoon, three o'clock, the usual place."

"The usual place?" Boucher raised his eyebrows and grinned. "We'll make a Frenchman out of you yet!"

A fool was all that had been made out of him, thought Mai gloomily, looking at his watch. It was four.

He got up stiffly and set off down the steep path. As he turned the corner at the bottom of the slope, there she was, standing by the railings.

"You're late," he said shortly.

"This wasn't my idea. I didn't have to come."

"Why did you?"

She thought of the answers she wasn't going to give. She was worried sick about Christian. Her attempts to join the hunt for information had been dismissed by Jean-Paul, and she was expected to be available in the kitchen at all hours to provide *les Pêcheurs* with coffee and food. They'd moved out of the Quartier Mouffetard as soon as they realized Christian had vanished, and were now living in a dilapidated flat in Clichy. It had seemed clever to try to steal a march on the men by asking Miche for help, but her reaction when he told her about Mai had been anger. She didn't want to get involved there again.

But today, furious at being left alone after an urgent message had taken Jean-Paul out of the flat without explanation, she had gone out herself. In direct contravention of her husband's instructions, she had headed back to the old apartment to pick up some of her things. Then, though she'd resolved not to keep the appointment with Mai, finding herself so near the Jardin she'd come anyway.

She said, "Curiosity. And to find out about Christian."

"Your friend was arrested by the Gestapo. He is at present in Fresnes prison, unharmed as far as I can ascertain."

Taken aback by the ease with which she'd got the information, she stammered a thankyou.

"What for? It's not good news. And please don't tell me he's innocent. Even more, don't tell me he's guilty. I know that already."

"If you're so sure, why are you helping me?"

"Why do you think?"

"I don't know. Because you still hope you can turn me into a collabo like Miche?"

He laughed to hide his absurd hurt. "That would require surgery," he said. "So, you're convinced Germans aren't capable of altruism?"

"I'm not sure what Germans are capable of," she said in a low voice.

"Just Germans? It was your gendarmes who rounded up your kids and put them in Drancy."

"There are always idiots who will follow orders," she said dismissively. "But you've got to be sick or evil to give those orders."

"And which am I?" he asked. "Sick or evil?"

"Not evil," she replied at once. "But to be part of it, even on the edge of it, you must be a little sick, I think."

"You do, do you?" said Mai, feeling himself driven into a corner by the simple intensity of her reasoning. "And what does Nurse Simonian prescribe as the cure for this sickness?"

"Simple," she said. "I would prescribe a long, long rest. At home."

He opened his mouth to destroy her with some fine German metaphysics but instead he let out a huge roar of laughter. And after a moment, seeing that it was her joke he was laughing at, and not her, she joined in.

"Thank you for coming to give me this consultation," he said, still chuckling. "I'll pass your recommendations on to my superiors. Now, how are the children? Miche tells me you went to see them."

She stared at him resentfully. She could hardly bear to think about her short visit. The way Céci's face had crumpled as she got on the train ... and Pauli's eyes ...

"Yes. It wasn't easy arranging it but Miche helped. Mireille brought them to Lyon and we stayed a few days in a boardinghouse. They were fine, really fine."

He could tell it was painful for her to talk about them.

"Why didn't you go to the farm?" he asked.

"It seemed better. This way I could have them to myself ..."

Also, he guessed, she'd wanted to avoid the additional pressure likely to be put on her at the farm to make her stay permanent.

Could this fellow Simonian have any idea of the demands he was making on her love and loyalty? Obviously not. From what Boucher reported, he seemed as keen as anyone for his wife to join the children.

252

"I'll stay at the farm next time," she went on. "I'd like to go at Christmas."

"Let me know," he said. "I'll fix the travel papers. And before you ask, no conditions."

They passed through the exit from the Jardin. A car was parked at the kerb. Two men got out. Mai's attention was focused on Janine and he scarcely registered them until one of them stepped in front of Janine and said, "Madame Simonian!"

"Yes?"

"Come with me."

The man seized Janine's arm. She turned on Mai with an expression that was something between an appeal for help and a Medusa-stare of accusation.

"Hold on!" cried Mai. But before he could take more than half a step forward, his left arm was seized from behind, twisted round and forced between his shoulder blades till he doubled forward in pain.

Mai drove his heel hard beneath his captor's right knee, then stamped viciously on his left toe as he hopped about in pain. The man crashed to the ground, needing both hands to break his fall. Mai straightened up. His impulse was to go to Janine's aid, but a third man was emerging from the car and in his hand was a pistol.

"You idiots!" shouted Mai in his best parade-ground voice, "You blockheads! I'll have you on the Russian front for this!"

The man with the gun looked at him in bewilderment.

Mai reached inside his overcoat, and brought out a leather wallet. He opened it, took out his card of identity, and handed it over. The gunman examined it, returned it, put the gun away and, stiffening momentarily to attention, spoke in a conciliatory voice. Mai replied in kind. The gunman gestured towards Janine and spoke again. Mai's reply this time was emphatic and urgent. The gunman looked dubious. Mai returned to his earlier, frighteningly authoritarian manner. This seemed to do the trick. A few more words and some rudimentary salutes were exchanged. Janine's captor released her. The men got into the car and it accelerated away.

Mai watched them go. As he stood there he felt Janine's hand take hold of his arm. "Günter," she said. "Who were they? What's going on?"

"Gestapo," he said. "They were going to arrest you." He paused, then went on, "No, not arrest you in the legal sense. If they'd had a formal warrant with the signature of a high-ranking officer on it, nothing I said would have stopped them. They were just going to take you in for a little unofficial questioning."

"But why? What have I done?"

He turned, looked into her eyes and said sadly, "Janine, stop playing the innocent. There's no protection from us, nor from your own people."

"My own people? Why should I need protection from them?"

"You're standing here talking to a German officer, for a start. Don't you imagine there'll be Frenchmen willing to believe what I hope those Gestapo hoodlums believe?"

"What's that?"

"How do you think I got rid of them? I told them who I was and said that you were one of my best agents. Janine, I'm afraid you're back on my books again."

She showed neither gratitude nor surprise. Her mind was still occupied with working out what had happened. Why her? Why here? They must have been on watch near the flat in the Quartier Mouffetard.

She felt faint at the thought of what would have happened if she'd abandoned the rendezvous with Mai entirely and headed straight back to Jean-Paul. The Gestapo agents must have decided that while one was worth following, two were worth picking up. Thank God the other had been Mai.

Impulsively she leaned forward and kissed him on the cheek. "Thank you," she said. "Now I've got to go."

Rushing off to warn her precious husband, thought Mai. And why should he need warning?

Alarm bells were sounding in his mind. He'd been right in his suspicions about Christian Valois. Simonian was an even more likely member of the Resistance, and not in any passive capacity either. How deep was he willing to plunge in his increasingly ambiguous relationship with Janine? Mai asked himself. When did he reach the point where protecting her meant protecting men whose aim was to kill Germans?

Meanwhile, talking of protection, he'd better set about protecting himself. The Gestapo men were probably reporting in already.

Janine was turning to go.

He said, "Hold on. If you want to see me, ring the Lutétia and leave a time. I'll meet you an hour earlier at the Balzac the same day."

"An hour earlier?" she said, puzzled.

"Just so you won't keep me waiting," he joked. Then, because it was no joking matter, he spelt it out. "For security. You're one of my best agents, remember?"

He watched her run away along the damp pavement towards the métro. Slim-hipped, she ran with an athlete's grace, like a winning runner.

"One of my best agents," he repeated, without irony.

5

"Where the hell did you hear that?" demanded Jean-Paul Simonian.

She'd been full of her news. It might not be good but she'd got it herself despite their attempts to keep her out. Now all her elation drained away.

"Miche found out," she said. It was a believable lie. She hadn't been able to think of one to cover her close escape from the Gestapo, so she'd kept quiet about that.

"That treacherous bastard! I've told you to keep away from him."

"At least he can find things out which none of your patriotic friends can manage," she retorted.

"You think not," he said, looking pleased with himself. "Well, at least we can confirm that for once your Géstapiste cousin is telling the truth."

He sat beside her, his outburst of temper forgotten. "Yes, he's in Fresnes prison. We found out from a warder there who wants to keep on the right side of the Resistance for the day he's called to account. He says Christian's in the German section of the prison. He looks a bit bruised about the face but otherwise all right. The word is, that Vichy father of his pulled strings before the Gestapo really got to work."

"Will his father be able to get him out?"

"No. Once Théo talked, Christian was a dead man. Old Valois can hold things up for a bit, but the Gestapo will be given a free hand eventually. Once that happens Christian will tell everything he knows."

"Is that all you're worried about?" she cried. "That Christian may break and tell them something about your precious group?"

"Look, Christian's been my friend, my dearest friend, for years. I know the risks he took to get me back home after the canal raid. I know that if I were in Fresnes, he wouldn't rest till he got me out. Don't tell *me* what my reasons are for wanting to rescue him," he said, in a voice low with restrained anger.

"Rescue him? From Fresnes? Surely it's impossible!"

"That's a word the Boche like to use," he said. "They haven't realized yet that it doesn't mean the same here as in Berlin."

"And what does it mean here, Jean-Paul?" asked Janine.

He let out a joyful laugh. "It means that Christian will be back safe with us tomorrow!"

THE DUSTCART COUGHED its way under the arch of the main entrance to Fresnes prison. It slowed almost to a halt so that the guard could scan the driver's familiar face. They exchanged greetings, then the truck accelerated across the courtyard, following the familiar route to the kitchen block where the rubbish was stacked.

The man next to the driver got out, stretched, and wandered round to the back of the truck. After glancing casually round, he rapped on the tailboard. A moment later a man slipped down from the back. He was dressed in the uniform of a warder. He stood chatting casually to the dustman, as if he'd just come out to supervize the loading.

"How do I look?" asked Jean-Paul Simonian.

"Not bad," said Henri, eyeing him critically.

A great respect had grown between these two since the debacle at the canal. "He's mad and he may get us all killed yet," Henri would declare to other members of *les Pêcheurs*, "but not without getting himself killed first, trying to save us."

"Don't forget your parcel," Henri added.

"I've got it." Jean-Paul reached into the truck and extracted a neatly wrapped box with the name of a well-known patisserie on it. "Back in twenty minutes," he said.

"Make it fifteen," said Henri. "This is one place we don't want to hang around on the job. Good luck."

He watched Jean-Paul stride boldly away. "Good luck," he repeated to himself. They were going to need it.

Simonian had no such doubts. It was at moments like this that he felt most truly in control, most passionately alive. For the moment he felt that he actually was a prison warder who'd just taken delivery of a cake addressed to the commandant of the German prison block at Fresnes.

He burst through the door with a suddenness which had the corporal at the desk leaping to attention before he spotted the uniform. "A cake," he announced, banging the box onto the desk.

"A cake?" said the corporal. "Oh, yes. It's his birthday."

"Is it?" said Simonian, who'd obtained this and much more information about layout, procedure and timing, not to mention his uniform, from the warder who'd first revealed that Christian Valois was here.

"He must have rich friends," he continued. "Ask me when I last had a decent slice of cake. Shortages, they say. This doesn't look very short to me." He shook the box.

"Careful," said the corporal. "He'll play hell if you muck it up."

"No. It's all right, I'm sure. Let's take a look."

He undid the elegant bow, lifted a corner of the box, smiled his approval and then, to the corporal's round-eyed horror, inserted his hand into the box as though to scrape at the icing.

"Here, none of that!" said the corporal. "None of . . ."

He stopped speaking as a second, more powerful shock stifled his voice. The hand had come out of the box with a revolver in it.

"Open up," ordered Jean-Paul. "Take me to the prisoner Valois. Resist and I'll put a bullet in you. Move."

The corporal rose, took his keys and began unlocking the door to the cells.

Using the cake box to conceal the gun, Simonian followed close behind him. They passed a couple of German guards coming the other way but the men paid no heed to the common sight of a French warder's uniform.

The corporal stopped and opened a cell.

"Get in," snarled Simonian.

The man entered. Simonian followed. As the corporal's leading foot

256

touched the floor of the cell, the gun barrel came down on the nape of his neck. He slumped to the floor and Christian Valois, squatting on the end of his trestle bed, had to leap out of his way.

"What the hell ... Jean-Paul!" he exclaimed in alarm

The two men embraced. When they drew apart, there were tears in Valois's eyes. "But Jean-Paul ..." he began.

Jean-Paul shook his head testily. "No time. Put this on."

Simonian opened the box fully and took out of it another warder's tunic, which Christian quickly put on.

Jean-Paul lifted the corporal onto the bed, gagged him with a length of cloth, then pulled his arms together and joined them with a pair of handcuffs taken from his pocket.

"That should keep him quiet," he said, throwing a blanket over the body. "Now, let's go. Just look as if you owned the place!"

In fact they left the block without encountering a soul, and though they saw one or two other guards on their way towards the kitchens, no one spared them a second glance.

Henri was just emptying the last bin. "In you get," he said.

With a glance round to make sure they were unobserved, Valois slipped over the tailboard.

"Now you," said Henri to Jean-Paul.

The kitchen door opened and a man in a cook's apron appeared, yawning in the cold sunlight. Jean-Paul was just clambering over the tailboard.

He paused and stared at the cook, who grinned back. "Think they're escaping in the rubbish, do we?" he called mockingly.

Jean-Paul dropped to the ground. "Maybe," he said.

Henri coughed. He could see round the side of the truck. Jean-Paul stepped forward and followed his gaze. On the far side of the courtyard, a prison officer and a German soldier had come out of a building and were talking together. Jean-Paul willed the cook to go back inside. Perhaps he was OK, but their driver was looking very unhappy, and if he didn't trust the fellow, then certainly Jean-Paul wasn't going to.

The officer and the soldier split up, the soldier heading away, the officer walking towards the kitchen block. There was little time left.

Jean-Paul went up to the still smiling cook, pulled out a long-bladed knife from its sheath in his belt and drove it unhesitatingly into the man's ribcage.

"Henri, help me," gasped Jean-Paul.

They tipped the dead man into the rubbish. Simonian plunged in after him and covered up the body, then himself. Valois stirred. Jean-Paul whispered, "Lie still."

The truck set off towards the main gates, which opened as they approached, and they were waved through without an inspection.

6

As soon as he'd got back to the Lutétia from the Jardin, Mai had composed a formal complaint to send to the SD in the Avenue Foch. He'd decided that if a fuss was going to be made, he'd better do the lion's share, as the injured party.

When news of the daring rescue of Christian Valois reached him the next day, he was stricken with guilt and fear. The guilt was soon disposed of. His reason told him that merely telling Janine where Valois was imprisoned couldn't have had anything to do with his escape just twenty-four hours later. But if the Gestapo decided to make an issue of his interference in Janine's arrest—as, enraged by the humiliation of losing Valois, they might—then anything could happen, to him and to her.

There was nothing to do but wait.

A few days later, as he sat in his office, the door opened and he rose swiftly to his feet as Major Nebe, the head of Records, appeared, ushering in Colonel Fiebelkorn who wore a smile like a hangman's.

"Heil Hitler!" said Mai smartly.

"Heil," replied the colonel. "How are you, Captain Mai?"

"I'm well, thank you, sir."

"Excellent." Gold teeth glinted in another smile. You could almost hear the mouth muscles creak in protest at this unusual activity. But not even gold could glitter brightly enough to touch the dark, dead eyes. Suddenly, he became businesslike. "I am here on a small matter of shared interests, exchanging information. We should do more of this, don't you think?"

"Yes, Colonel."

"Yes. Then perhaps if we did, embarrassments like trying to arrest each other's agents would be avoided!"

"Yes. I'm sorry, Colonel . . ."

"No, no," said Fiebelkorn holding up a pale pudgy hand in remonstrance. "There is nothing for you to be sorry about. I can understand your anger. I have been glancing at the woman Simonian's record, with Major Nebe's permission of course, and I can see how much you must value her."

Mai had worked on Janine's file all night after the incident outside the Jardin to give her real substance as an agent, expecting the row to explode almost immediately. Instead of which, he could have taken his time. In any case, far from a row, he was getting an apology!

"So let's say no more about it," said Fiebelkorn. "But let us try to be more sharing and cooperative in the future. We need to unite our strength against all the enemies of the Fatherland. Agreed?"

"Agreed, Colonel," said Mai.

"Good. And should you ever wish to restructure your career, Captain Mai, give me a ring. There's always room in the SD for any man with the skills to persuade a woman to stay with her terrorist husband so she can keep on betraying him!" He laughed as he spoke.

Later, alone, Mai sat down heavily and soon had the room foggy with tobacco smoke; but for once the fumes brought no compensating clarity to his thoughts. He realized now that he had made a mistake in not insisting that he had some means of contacting Janine. He wanted to see her, to make sure she was safe. No. He just wanted to see her.

Two days later, the telephone rang when he was out. A woman, the message simply, *Two o'clock.*

He got there at ten to one. At two he was still sitting in the Café Balzac with the patron making sympathetic grunts every time he bought another drink. At two forty-five, he gave up. This was absurd. He tried to feel annoyance, but all he could feel was terror.

He stood up, looked down the café for the patron. And there she was. Standing in the doorway. She came to him and sat down.

"You're late!"

"No I'm not!" she replied indignantly. "Don't you remember, you said I should say a time an hour before the real time? I'm early."

He began to laugh, but the laughter didn't sound right. So he stopped laughing and clasped his hands together in an effort to control their sudden trembling.

"Are you ill?" she asked with real concern.

"No, not at all. Just relieved," he said. "I was so worried."

"About me?" She sounded surprised. But concerned too. And perhaps even, though this might have been his imagination, pleased.

"Let's walk, shall we?" he said.

"If you like."

Mai paid his bill and they left the café. As they walked along he asked, "What happened when you got back home that day?"

"I told Jean-Paul that I'd learned from Miche where Christian was."

"*Was* is the operative word."

"The escape had nothing to do with our conversation."

"I worked that out for myself."

Relieved, she moved away from that delicate topic. "What about you? What happened about those Gestapo thugs?"

"Is that why you rang? To find out?"

"Yes. I got more and more worried."

For the sake of that precious husband, no doubt, thought Mai. He told her briefly of his visit from Fiebelkorn. Ahead lay the Tuileries gardens. Mist seemed to hang in the leafless trees like some ghostly decoration. There were a few people about, stick-figures with little plumes of breath trailing behind them.

The grey tendrils of mist curled round them, weaving a curtain which shut them off not merely from sight and sound of the great city but from time and circumstance too. He took her hand as they walked, and was not surprised when she did not pull it away. Why should she? They were in a state of suspension. What was said and done now didn't count.

Or rather, it might count more than anything they had ever said or done before.

She said gently, "What can you tell me that justifies the Germans being here? That justifies the things you've done?"

He found himself swinging her hand like a child as he wrestled with the problem. "Humiliation, perhaps. You humiliated us at Versailles back in nineteen-nineteen. That's what made this war possible."

"That's a cause, not a justification. And I hope you're wrong. Because you're going to be humiliated again." She spoke with such certainty that he halted and peered into her face as if hoping to see there the source of such firm prophecy.

"Why do you say that?"

"Because you boast so proudly and behave so meanly," she declared. "Everybody knows what empty boasts they are! You were going to destroy England, weren't you? Well, it's still there. Half of Paris listens to its broadcasts every night and every night we hear British and American planes droning away overhead. It's the sound of our victory, your defeat. And it won't be a noble defeat either, when the full story of your barbarity comes out."

He spoke, trying to keep his voice as even and controlled as hers had been. "I can't argue with you. But we've had our job made easy in France. When the world finds out that the Germans have got more than their fair share of madmen, they'll also learn that France had its fair share of collaborators!"

She said, "Do you count me as a collaborator?"

"No," he said, recognizing the truth as he spoke.

"Then, if I'm not, you must be."

He was surprised only for a moment. He turned his head away and strove to force his sight through the mist back to the real world, back to the Rue de Rivoli where the crimson swastikas still flapped lazily in a triumph as empty as the shops beneath them. But it was no use. He said slowly and with effort, "I'm not a collaborator. I'm in love with you."

Immediately he felt a vast sense of relief. He was still holding her hand. He raised it, played with her fingers, kissed them gently.

She said sadly, "Yes. That's what I was afraid of."

"Afraid?" He wanted to laugh. "You mean you'd rather I was the enemy manipulating you to betray your country?"

"No. Of course not, Günter, what I meant was I'm afraid for you." Her voice was soft with sympathy. How clearly she saw things, he realized.

There was no place in her life for him other than as a source of help in the enemy camp. By his declaration of love, he had removed all threat from that help and transferred it to himself. She had been right after all. Being in love did make him a collaborator.

He drew her towards him. She did not resist, but bowed her head away from his lips and he buried his face in her mist-damp hair.

"I love you," he said, taking pleasure from speaking the words again.

"Poor Günter," she murmured, almost to herself. "Poor Günter."

7

In the days that followed his rescue, Christian Valois was moved around so much that he began to lose track of place and time.

"For God's sake," he protested, as they moved yet again, "is this really necessary? I mean, if *I* don't know where I am, the Boche are going to be hard put to trace me, aren't they?"

"Someone's put the bastards on to me," said Simonian grimly. "And with relatives like my wife's cousin I'm taking no chances."

"Boucher helped get the children away safely, didn't he? That shows he's still got some scruples."

"Sentimentality is not a moral quality," said Jean-Paul.

"But he got papers for that Jew, Melchior, too," protested Valois.

"You're very defensive of this traitor, Christian," said Jean-Paul.

"It's just that . . . I know he's a collaborator, but that doesn't mean he'd betray everything. And he *is* Janine's cousin."

When they reached the new safehouse, there was a reminder of the past waiting for Valois.

"Christian, good to see you!" said Delaplanche, rising from a chair.

"And you!" said Valois, surprised and pleased. "I'm sorry . . . all your plans for me—*kaput!*"

"It wasn't your fault," said the lawyer. "Théo pointed the finger. Don't blame him. I heard what the bastards did to him. It was enough to make a man betray his own mother."

"So he gave them Christian but he didn't give them you. Odd, that," said Jean-Paul, staring at Delaplanche speculatively.

"He gave them everyone he knew, including me," said the man calmly. "We got the others safely hidden as soon as we heard the news. When I heard Christian had gone to ground, I guessed he'd been warned too."

"So why didn't the Boche pick you up?"

"They did. They interrogated me. They let me go."

"Just like that?" said Jean-Paul incredulously.

"Not quite. There were telephone calls, in and out. Angry scenes. Threats on both sides. Then they let me go."

"Why?"

"Because, so far, I've managed to confuse the issue. I can't work underground like you, Monsieur Simonian. I'm a public figure. I must move publicly. When this war started and I saw what my role must be, I planned for it. If I could not rise above suspicion, I would smother myself in it! From the very beginning I've had accusers. Not an act of terrorism occurs without a stream of anonymous accusations against me pouring into SS headquarters. Men like Théo have instructions if they are caught and questioned about me, to babble out agreement with whatever suggestions the Boche make. Thus, by being innocent of ninety per cent of what I'm accused of, I've so far managed to keep my head above water.

"I've also got friends. And there are people in power on both sides that I know enough about for them to value my silence. But perhaps the Gestapo's patience will finally snap and they'll simply send a bunch of their French friends round to blow my head off," he concluded, and watched for Jean-Paul's reaction with a faint smile.

"You're a brave man, monsieur."

"Am I? If so, it's a finite quality and I think I've almost drained the barrel."

"I think not. You've been frank with me. Now I'll be frank with you. What plans have you got for Christian?"

"Plans? All my plans for Christian are ruined, since his capture."

"So you have no plans? Good. Then you'll have no objection if he transfers his allegiance to my group?"

"Agreed. He's yours. Now, I must go. I've been here too long already. Christian, goodbye. I hope we'll meet in happier times very soon. Any message for your parents?"

"You'll be seeing them?" said Valois eagerly.

"Yes. I saw them a couple of times when I was in Vichy recently. I was able to advise them how best to react to the news of your disappearance, where to put pressure on, how to delay energetic interrogation from the start. It seems to have worked."

"Are they well?"

"Concerned, naturally. A double concern, as it happens. Your sister . . ."

"What about my sister?" interrupted Valois fearfully.

"It's all right! Nothing's wrong. She just ran away from home, that's all. She's bored by Vichy, it seems. Well, who can blame her? And there was an attachment to an 'unsuitable' young man, someone who supported the Resistance. Your parents broke it up. She disappeared. They've had a postcard from Besançon. She knows someone there, I gather?"

"An old school friend," said Valois.

"Well, let's hope she stays there and doesn't try to get into Switzerland. But she sounds a determined young lady. Goodbye, Christian. Take care. When next I see your father, I'll tell him you're well."

·He shook hands and left. Jean-Paul followed him out of the room. When he returned he found Valois slumped forward with his head in his hands. "Christian! Cheer up! You're alive and free. Your sister too. And your parents. So why so sad?" asked Jean-Paul.

Valois said, "My parents. What do you think will happen when the war ends, Jean-Paul? To people like my father, I mean. Men who've gone along with the marshal and collaborated."

"It depends how far they've gone, I'd say. But they must pay something, you can see that, can't you, Christian? And as for rubbish like my wife's cousin, I wouldn't even waste a trial on them!"

Valois laughed humourlessly. "So, token trial or summary execution for everyone tainted with collaboration, eh? I hope no one's in a hurry to rebuild France after the war, Jean-Paul. From the sound of it, for the first year or so one won't be able to move for bodies in the streets."

"Perhaps," said Jean-Paul. "Let's hope that for the last year of the war we won't be able to move for German bodies. Talking of which, are you really interested in joining us? Or would you rather let your tally stop at one?"

For a second Valois looked at him without comprehension. Then he said, "Yes, of course, that's what I want more than anything."

"Good," said Simonian. "Then it's back to school for you."

He went out and returned a moment later with a gun in his hands.

"This is what they call a Sten gun," he said. "Let me show you how to strip it down."

Two hours later they were sitting surrounded by a confusion of weapons Jean-Paul watched critically as his friend assembled a machine pistol, loaded the magazine and rammed it into place.

"I think I've been underestimating you, Christian," he said. "You know, it wouldn't surprise me if by the end of the year you are even better known to the Germans than your father!"

Valois looked at him closely, a slight frown on his face, and then began to laugh.

Soon both men were laughing together. But it was not a very harmonious sound.

8

"You said you had news of my son?" Léon Valois asked Delaplanche.

"He hasn't been in touch direct? No, he wouldn't want to risk getting you involved, would he? Well, I haven't seen him for some time, but I've heard from reliable sources that he's in good health."

"And safe? Is he safe?"

Delaplanche laughed. "Don't be silly, Léon. Your boy has left safety far

264

behind. He is a highly effective and highly wanted *résistant*. I must say I'm surprised. I didn't really think he had it in him, to be a successful man of action, I mean. Depending on who wins the war, you've fathered a very great criminal or a very great hero, Léon. How does this make you feel?"

"All his mother and I want is that he should stay alive," said Valois, gripping the table in front of him so tight that his knuckles were as white as marble.

"Yes, I know," said Delaplanche, touched by the intensity of the other's feelings. "In case I get the chance to pass a message to Christian, what can I tell him about the family? You don't look too well, Léon."

"Don't tell him that!" urged Valois. "I'm in good health, really. His mother too. Excellent health."

"And his sister, Marie-Rose?"

Valois passed his hand wearily over his face. "Almost as much a worry as Christian," he admitted. "But for God's sake, don't tell him that either."

"No, but I have to say something. Is she still in Besançon?"

"So her cards say. But I know it's not true. A friend visiting Besançon went to the house and found it shut up and empty. Evidently the family left almost a year ago. I think she may have done something crazy like joining the Maquis."

"I've got a lot of contacts," said Delaplanche. "Perhaps I can find something out. After all, what are old friends for?"

A WEEK LATER it was New Year's Eve. Delaplanche sat in his apartment overlooking the park. He was alone, but an open bottle of Saint Emilion and two glasses showed that he was expecting company. While he waited he studied some papers with the care of a lawyer who knows on how fine a point matters of life and death can depend. In this case, Marie-Rose's life.

There was a single knock at the door. He didn't move. There came a double knock, another pause, then a quadruple knock, all evenly spaced.

Satisfied, he unlocked the door.

"Come in," he said to the muffled figure outside. "I've got something very interesting for you. About your friend Valois ..."

"Have you now?" said Alphonse Pajou, pressing the trigger of his Mauser automatic pistol. "Happy New Year!"

Twenty minutes later, Jean-Paul Simonian arrived. He found the lawyer's bullet-riddled body lying by the door in a lake of blood. He glanced briefly round the flat. No one else was there. The glasses and the wine bottle still stood on the table, but the papers had gone.

He stepped carefully back over the corpse, closed the door behind him and ran down the stairs.

PART FIVE January–August 1944

1

"For God's sake, woman," said Mireille Laurentin. "Why don't you give him his marching orders!"

It was New Year's Day. The two women were sitting alone at the kitchen table. A glass of wine had set all the fumes from the previous night's celebrations stirring and Janine, urged by her cousin to extend her stay permanently, had spoken more freely of her situation than she had intended.

"He's my husband," she said. "I love him. He needs me."

"Funny way he has of showing it," said Mireille. "Your fellow doesn't seem to consider anything but himself, from what you say."

"So Lucien decided not to join the Resistance?" said Janine, wanting to be reassured that her children weren't staying in an endangered home.

"With a bit of help from me, he decided," grinned Mireille. "Oh, I don't say he doesn't drop the odd sack of vegetables to those maquisards up in the hills. But as for going around shooting people and blowing things up, Lucien's got more sense than to get mixed up with that. But from what you say, your Jean-Paul's gone a lot further! If he gets caught, that's you and the kids dropped right in it."

"Perhaps he won't get caught," said Janine unhappily.

Now the children came in, wet with snow. They'd been sledging. Céci was red with exertion and excitement, full of tales of thrills and spills.

Pauli took his coat off and sat quietly in a corner from which his dark eyes were able to watch everything else in the room. He looked so like his father, self-contained, watchful, assessing.

Janine said, "Pauli, come here and give me a kiss for the new year."

He rose instantly, and came and embraced her. She tickled him and he threw back his head and laughed, and that happy laughing face was again so like his father's, that her heart contracted and she felt hot tears burning her eyes. She knew then that she had to go back. She was no longer sure if the old Jean-Paul was retrievable, but while there was the faintest chance, she could not abandon him.

NOT ALL THE RESOLVE in the world could render the final leave-taking any less painful. Céci cried her heart out until Pauli took her aside and assured her that all was well and Maman would soon be back, and there were honey-cakes for tea. But there was no one to do the same comforting service for him, and more than anything else it was the sense of tight control in his slim body as she kissed him goodbye that almost persuaded Janine to change her mind, even at this stage.

At last she was on the train. She waved from the window, smiling, till her cousin and the two little heads on either side of her dwindled to nothing. Then she cried, quietly but passionately.

But there was one consolation. At least the children were safe.

2

Paris in the springtime. Of all the clichés about the city, this was the one Günter enjoyed most.

1941 had been best: triumph still tasted sweet and there'd seemed to be some correspondence between the blossom on the trees and the shape of things to come. 1942 hadn't been too bad, the daffodils and lilac speaking of a second chance to remedy lost time and opportunities. In 1943 he'd hardly noticed the spring.

From Boucher he had news of Janine, though he never asked directly for it. He'd seen her distantly from time to time, arriving at or leaving the boulangerie, where he still enjoyed a croissant and coffee. He knew she used the house as a poste restante for the regular postcards from the Ain, which confirmed the children were well. They had never exchanged more than a formal greeting since that day he had declared his love.

From time to time he updated Janine's "agent" file, to be on the safe side, in case the Gestapo had their plant in the Lutétia just as he had his in their offices in the Rue des Saussaies. It wasn't for her sake he was doing this, he assured himself. It was for his own safety. Also the children's. If he'd done nothing else worthwhile in this war, at least he'd helped two innocent kids to a place of safety where the sounds of spring could still fall without distortion upon responsive ears.

ALL AFTERNOON there had been the crackle of distant gunfire in the hills.

Hunters, Mireille told herself. But she had lived too long in the country not to know the difference between hunting rifles and automatic fire.

And there was no sign of Lucien.

She went into the living room and looked at the old clock. It was time to eat. In fact, as she well knew, it was rather late. The table was set, the food was ready. Céci had been sitting there impatiently for some time. Mirelle went to the door and called, "Boys!"

They came at their own pace as boys do, the elder pair first, then Christophe, all red-faced and hot from their exertions.

"Where's Pauli?" she asked.

"Don't know," said one of the older boys.

"And don't care," added Christophe with the surliness he still showed at the mention of Pauli's name.

"He's here now," said one of the others. His sharp young ears had caught what Mireille heard a moment later, Pauli's voice calling, "Aunt Mireille! Aunt Mireille!"

She went to the window. The boy was in the farmyard, running past old Rom, whose weatherbeaten face was provoked to something like surprise, and tumbling through the kitchen door.

"The Boche are coming, the Boche are coming!" he gasped.

Even as he gave his news, the noise of vehicles could be heard and Mireille could see a covered truck and a German staff car bumping down the track towards the farm.

"Stay inside, children," she commanded.

She went out, shutting the door behind her.

"Pauli, what's going on?" demanded the eldest boy.

"They attacked the Maquis," said Pauli, beginning to regain control of his breathing. "They killed some of them, captured the rest. They captured Uncle Lucien."

"Papa? Why did they capture Papa?" The boy's voice was shrill.

"He was up there. He'd taken some vegetables I think. He often did."

He sat down by Céci and putting his arm round her said, "Eat your meal, little one. Eat it all up." And seizing a hunk of bread himself, he began to chew vigorously.

Outside, the vehicles had come to a halt. Two soldiers sprang from the back of the car, one of them knelt with his gun aimed at Rom, the other ran past the old man, kicked open the kitchen door and went inside.

A little while later he emerged. "Just some kids, Captain," he said to the officer in the car, who now got out. Mireille's heart contracted even further as she recognized the SS insignia on his tunic.

He saluted her and said, "Madame Laurentin?"

"Yes."

"Wife of the terrorist, Lucien Laurentin?"

"What do you mean? My husband's no terrorist!"

"You must come with us, madame," said the captain.

"Please, monsieur, it's all a mistake. My husband's not a maquisard. A few vegetables he gave them from time to time, that's all. What's the harm in that? They're local boys, we've known them for years..."

"In the truck!"

He turned away, she caught at his arm; he pulled it free, then swung the back of his hand into her face with a force that broke her nose.

She screamed. The kitchen door opened and her sons tried to come out, but old Rom blocked their way.

"No, no," she cried to them, "I'm all right. I'm all right. Stay inside. I'll be back soon."

She held her hand over her face in an effort to conceal the blood. One of the soldiers took her arm and said, "Come on, missus. Let's get you in the truck."

There were more soldiers in the truck. They dragged her over the tailboard and now she saw they were not alone. There were half a dozen men lying on the floor, most of whom she recognized. At least two were unconscious. All had blood soaking their clothes.

The engine started. She went to the tailgate; the soldiers grabbed her arms but she thrust her head out and cried, "Rom, take care of the children!" Then the truck was grinding round the bend and out of sight of the house.

Back in the farmyard, one of the soldiers said, "What about him, Captain?" pointing his weapon at Rom.

"Him? Of course not," said the officer with distaste. "We're not in the business of collecting scarecrows."

The soldier laughed and went on, "And the kids?"

"They'll be sorted out later. Corrective schools most likely, so they don't grow up like their terrorist parents. You didn't notice such a thing as a bottle of wine in there, did you? It's been thirsty work."

"I'm sure we can find you something, sir," said the soldier.

They went into the kitchen, the three Laurentin boys and the old man retreating before them. Pauli and Céci were seated at the table. Pauli was still eating.

"Hello, more of them," observed the captain. "Surely our information was three, all boys?"

He took out some papers and examined them. "Yes. So, we have two over. Is that you two, the hungry ones?"

His French was excellent. Pauli nodded.

"And who may you be?"

"We're visitors, monsieur. Madame Laurentin is my mother's cousin."

"I see," said the captain. "Then what stories you'll have to tell when you get back home, eh?"

He smiled as he spoke. His friendliness to Pauli, his casual reference to their return home combined with all the other sources of resentment in Christophe: bursting from the restraint of Rom's long arm, his face red with terror and fury, he burst out, "It's all their fault! It wouldn't have happened if they hadn't come! They're Jews, they're filthy Jews, that's why this happened."

The soldier appeared with a bottle of wine and a glass which he filled. The captain took it and drank.

"Not too bad," he said. "Jews, you say, boy? But they're your relatives. Does that mean you too are Jews?"

Christophe's fury was spent. Only the terror remained. And increased. He shook his head but couldn't speak.

"Well, boy, what's your name?" The question was to Pauli, who was thrusting pieces of bread into his pockets.

"Paul Simonian, monsieur."

"Simonian? Now, that has a flavour, certainly. And are you Jewish?"

The boy's eyes met his unblinkingly. "We're Roman Catholics, sir, like Maman."

"Ah yes. But your father, what about him?"

Before Pauli could reply, Céci piped up, reassured by the captain's relaxed manner, "Bubbah Sophie is Jewish, she told me so. The bad men took her away to Pitchipoi."

"Bubbah Sophie? Your grandmother?"

Pauli put some more bread into his pocket but didn't reply.

The captain finished his wine. "Time to go," he said. "Fetch the children."

"All of them, sir?" asked the soldier.

The officer hesitated, looked at the brothers.

Pauli said, "Madame Laurentin is my *mother's* cousin, monsieur, not my father's."

The captain laughed. "No wonder we need to deal with you people!" he said. "Even the children are cleverer than half of our own adults! No. Just the young professor here and his sister. Quickly!"

Pauli and Céci were seized and dragged to the car.

"Hello. What's this?" said the captain languidly.

An ancient truck had come creaking into sight down the farm track. It shuddered to a halt as its driver saw the staff car. Then, realizing that retreat was impossible, he set the vehicle bumping slowly forward again. It stopped by the barn.

The passenger door opened and out climbed Maurice Melchior. He strolled across, his sharp eyes taking in the frightened children at the farm door and the young Simonians in the car. He tried to send a warning to Pauli and it got through. But Céci was too young for warnings. Delighted to see a familiar adult face, she cried, "Hello, Monsieur Melchior." Melchior ignored her. "Good day, Captain," he said.

"Who are you?" asked the officer, lighting a cigarette.

"Corder. Roger Corder. My partner and I do a little business with these good people. We're privileged to help keep many of your brave fellow officers in Lyon supplied with the fresh produce they deserve."

"You mean you're a black marketeer. Why did this child call you Melchior?"

"A childish nickname. She thinks I come bearing gifts of gold."

The officer smiled. "Go back to your truck, monsieur."

"But of course. If I can ever be of service?"

"Trooper," called the officer from the car. "Get in that truck with those gentlemen and accompany them back to camp. If they lose their way or if the truck breaks down, shoot them. Driver, move on."

The car pulled away. As they climbed the track, Pauli got a last glimpse of Melchior, pale but still smiling.

3

Janine woke up. The bedroom was full of sunlight. She glanced at her watch and saw that it was only five forty-five. These nights of early June were short. Too short. She rolled over, realized that Jean-Paul was not by her side, and suddenly knew what had woken her. Voices in the next room. Five o'clock in the morning. This was Gestapo time.

She jumped out of bed, rushed to the bedroom door and flung it open. The living room was full of smoke. She saw at once that the full council of *les Pêcheurs* was here, including Henri and Christian Valois.

"I'm sorry," she said, "I thought it was a raid!"

To her surprise Jean-Paul laughed. Interruptions of meetings of *les Pêcheurs* on any pretext usually filled him with irritation. Something must have put him in a good humour.

"Shall I make some coffee?" she asked.

"Yes, if you would," said Jean-Paul.

Christian came into the tiny kitchen to drink some water to ease his talk- and smoke-roughened throat. Dressed in a baggy old suit, with a heavy moustache and a fringe of beard, the once elegant civil servant now looked like a character from Hugo's *Les Misérables*.

His manner had changed too, over the months. There was an alertness about him, a sense of command. He was *les Pêcheurs'* mouthpiece, their linkman with other members of the Resistance council.

"What's happened?" Janine asked him.

"Hasn't he told you? The message was broadcast from London last night. *The dice are cast.*"

"Meaning?"

"He doesn't tell you much, does he? It means the invasion's close! We've got to do our bit to tie up the Boche from behind. There'll be high-level conferences later on, but you know Jean-Paul. He'll want to be sure *les Pêcheurs* get their fair share of the action."

He went back to the meeting. The invasion! thought Janine. She was filled with hope, with fear, and also with some resentment. Jean-Paul's use of her in connection with *les Pêcheurs* was almost solely on the domestic level. Like now. She occasionally carried low-key messages, made telephone calls, left signs chalked on doors or walls. She didn't object. The less she knew, the less she could betray. But he might have come to her himself with this tremendous news.

She shook the thought from her head and went in with the coffee. Afterwards she went back to the bedroom and left them to their planning.

At eight thirty she re-emerged and said to Jean-Paul, "I'm going to my parents'! There should be a card from Mireille soon."

"OK," he said with a wave.

As she stood in the crowded métro carriage, she wondered how many of those around her had heard and understood the BBC message.

There was a smell of baking coming from the boulangerie when she reached it, but nothing like the rich perfume which used to make mouths water two streets away.

Louise Crozier was in the shop. They embraced and Janine said eagerly, "Any card from Mireille?"

"No," said Louise, "but there's a letter for you. It was posted through the door the night before last."

"Where is it?" asked Janine.

They went into the living room. The envelope was addressed simply to Madame Simonian. Janine ripped it open and began to read the single sheet of paper it held:

Madame Simonian,

Monsieur Laurentin's farmhand, Rom, who cannot read, has brought me your cards from the farmhouse. It is my sad duty to tell you that Monsieur Laurentin and his wife have been arrested on charges of terrorism. Their sons are being looked after by neighbours, but your children, I regret to say, were taken into custody, I believe on the suspicion that they are Jewish. Since their arrest, I have been unable to discover anything further of their fate.

It was signed by the curé of the local village.

Janine read it once. Read it twice. Then she turned her stricken face to her mother and said, "Oh, *Maman!*"

"Child, what is it? Oh God!" She caught her daughter as she fell. "Crozier!"

Crozier came in from the bakehouse, wiping his hands on his apron, and froze with horror in the doorway. "What's happened?" he cried.

"Shut up and help me. Quickly, quickly!"

Together they eased Janine onto the sofa. Louise loosened her clothing and raised her feet. "Fetch the smelling salts. Hurry."

Crozier rushed away, and, with her arm supporting Janine's head, Louise read the letter. "Holy Mary, Mother of God!" she exclaimed, letting the single sheet flutter to the floor.

Her husband returned with the smelling salts. She held the bottle under her own nose for a second before administering it to Janine, while Crozier stooped and picked up the letter. Through tear-filled eyes, Louise saw his pasty face go even whiter.

Janine coughed and rolled her head away from the salts. With consciousness came memory, and she started to sob wildly.

"There, there, child," said Louise, pulling her daughter's head onto her bosom. "It'll be all right, you'll see. It's just a mistake, a dreadful mistake."

Freeing herself from her mother's embrace, Janine sat upright, her gaze fixed on her father as if trying to force some reassurance from him. His face was full of love and pain as he said, "We'll find them, never fear. We'll take advice, get a lawyer, don't worry, we'll find them . . ."

But Janine knew that they had all moved beyond the world in which love, and shared pain, and protest, and promises, could deter monsters. Jumping up she cried, "I have to tell Jean-Paul. He'll know what's best."

"Wait!" cried Louise.

But it was no use. The next moment they heard the front door slam.

How Janine got back to the flat in Clichy, she did not know. The meeting was still going on, but her entrance was so sudden and violent that all talk stopped instantly. Jean-Paul regarded her with cold irritation at being interrupted. Henri tried to lighten the moment by saying, "God, you nearly gave me a heart attack, coming in like that."

She opened her mouth to speak but all that came was a torrent of sobs.

Jean-Paul, his face twisted with alarm, took her in his arms, but this only made things worse. Pushing herself away from her husband's embrace, she told them what had happened as plainly as she could. These men devoted their lives to fighting the world that was trying to destroy Pauli and Céci. Here, surely, she would find help.

Jean-Paul seized the letter and read it with a scowling intensity.

Henri swore softly. "The bastards, I heard they'd blitzed the Maquis down there. Didn't you know that your cousin was . . . I'm sorry . . ."

"It's all right, Henri. No, I didn't know. Mireille said that Lucien dropped them the odd sack of potatoes. If I'd thought there was any real risk, do you think I'd have . . ." She was close to sobbing again. She took a deep breath.

Valois took her hand. "It'll be all right," he assured her. "They're running out of time. The invasion force will go through France like a knife through butter, you'll see."

"But if they've been sent to Germany . . ."

"They won't have fuel and transport to spare to send kids to Germany," he said.

She looked to Jean-Paul for confirmation of this theory.

He said bleakly, "They had fuel and transport for my mother."

Henri took Christian's arm and gestured with his head towards the door. Jean-Paul caught the gesture and said, "No. Don't go yet. We'll go in here." He took Janine's hand and led her into the bedroom.

They sat on the bed and for a minute or more they simply held each other, in silence. She was the first to speak. "What are we going to do?" she asked. "Should we go straight to Lyon? That's where they're likely to be, isn't it?"

"Perhaps. But they could be anywhere. There are plenty of camps. They could even be back in Drancy by now."

"Drancy?" Her eyes lit up with sudden hope. Drancy was vile but it was close. And she'd already got them out of there once.

"Don't worry, I'll check," he said, with the quick confidence she'd been looking for. "And I'll get word to the network in Lyon to see if they can find anything out."

"You don't think we should go there, then?"

"Jan, the invasion's just about to start, there's going to be chaos . . ."

She drew away from him now and said incredulously, "You're not saying that you're going to be too busy to look for your children?"

"Don't be stupid!" he said angrily. "What I'm saying is, the Boche will be expecting an upturn in Resistance activity and it'll mean a clampdown on travel, a tightening of security checks. Anyone vaguely suspicious is bound to be taken in. That's probably all that's happened to Pauli and Céci. Just some kind of protective custody."

"The letter said that Mireille's own kids weren't taken, just ours," said Janine. "Why should the authorities be so concerned about Pauli and Céci?" She was trying to stop herself from growing angry.

"The letter! Some senile country priest taking dictation from a half-witted peasant. No, let's find out what's really happened first." Jean-Paul was sounding angry too.

"Jean-Paul," she said quietly. "What are *you* going to do?" No longer *we*. *You*.

He turned to her, took her head in his hands and looked straight into her eyes. "Jan, I'm going to do everything possible, believe me," he said with a fierce intensity. "And one thing you can be certain of, if any harm comes to the children, the bastards who did it will pay a thousand times over."

She stood up and looked down at him. "And you take some consolation from that thought, do you?" she said thoughtfully.

"Yes, I do," he answered, not flinching from her gaze. "But, Jan, I'm not saying I believe anything's happened to the kids, far from it. I'm ninety per cent certain we'll find they're OK . . ."

"No," she interrupted. "No, you're not. I understand you now, Jean-Paul. What you're ninety per cent sure of is that the worst has happened, that there's nothing we can do. Or perhaps you simply have to believe that because that's your way of dealing with life now."

"For God's sake," he said angrily.

"Jean-Paul, they've got our children again. Last time I had to face it alone. This time, help me, please, I beg you."

"I will," he cried, in an anguish almost matching her own. "But I can only do what seems best . . ."

"Like carrying on with your meeting, you mean?"

"*Yes!* That's one of the ways, yes. Everything we can do to help the invasion brings everybody's freedom closer . . ."

"I don't give a damn about *everybody*, or *anybody* except Pauli and Céci," she said harshly. "The worst thing those German bullets did to you was to make you forget how to love your children. You must have forgotten, or else you'd know that there was nothing more important in the world." She turned and marched through the living room, where *les Pêcheurs* were sitting with the embarrassed expressions of men who'd heard every word.

Jean-Paul came into the room a moment later and sat down heavily.

"For God's sake, go after her, man," urged Henri.

"Why? You heard what she said. She was right. Inside I do fear the worst. Later, I'll talk with her later. Now, there's work to be done."

Valois shook his head and said softly, "Janine was right. Those bullets really changed you, didn't they?"

"They taught me to face up to the truth," said Jean-Paul. "They taught me there are no short cuts to winning."

"I see. It's the *Cause* that's all important! And you wouldn't betray that Cause, not even to save your own flesh and blood, would you?"

"No!" came the reply.

"I don't know whether to admire or despise you," mused Valois.

But Henri said softly, "From the bottom of my heart, I pity you."

4

Günter Mai also received a letter that morning. The envelope bore Zeller's hunting horn emblem and, as required by military law, had the sender's address on the back. Nevertheless, it had been opened. Censorship of officers' mail was unusual, especially from such an influential source. Was it because of me or because of him? wondered Mai uneasily.

It was a relief to find the contents were not subversive. Zeller, now promoted colonel and, he modestly noted, awarded the Iron Cross, said the doctors had finally finished with him. He'd returned from Berlin to the family estate on the Rhine, where he was convalescing. He hoped Mai would spend a few days of his next home leave visiting him.

Had it not been for the censorship, Mai might have jokingly replied that he'd possibly look in as the whole army retreated across the Rhine. He too had been told of the BBC's message the previous night. "*The dice are cast*" merely confirmed what had been anticipated for weeks. The only question was, where would the landings be?

"Excuse me, Captain," said a corporal, sticking his head round the door. "There's a woman to see you."

"A woman?"

"Yes. She just walked in, bold as brass, and asked to see you. They're holding her downstairs."

"I'd better take a look."

He ran down the stairs into the sumptuously decorated vestibule of the Lutétia. Standing quietly by the desk with an armed guard in close attendance was Janine Simonian.

He said to the guard, "It's all right," and to Janine he said, "Come."

He led her into the lift. As they journeyed upwards he said, "What is it? The children or Jean-Paul?"

He knew that it must be some grave family crisis which had caused her to walk so openly into *Abwehr* HQ. When she said, "The children," he was relieved. To tangle with the Gestapo over Simonian, a terrorist Jew, was more than he could undertake. Yet he feared that if she'd asked him, he might have tried.

They went into his office. "Sit down," he ordered, going round his desk. When he turned, she was still standing.

"You look different in your uniform," she said.

She'd grown used to seeing him in civilian clothes, perhaps had even half grown to think of him as Edouard Scheffer, the dubious Alsatian businessman. Here, in uniform, he was indubitably the enemy, and she was beginning to believe she must be crazy to have come.

"Janine, sit," he said gently. He undid his tunic, removed it, rolled up his shirtsleeves, lit his pipe.

"Thank you," she said and sat down. Silently she handed him the curé's letter. He read it without comment and handed it back.

"Find them," she said. "Get them released. You helped me last time."

"Last time," he echoed. He marshalled his thoughts. He should be telling her that last time they had been held in Paris and there had still been some semblance of military control of internal security; he should be telling her that last time the children had been picked up because they were staying with their Jewish grandmother, not arrested because they were illicit members of a terrorist household.

"I'll see what I can do," he said.

"Thank you," she said rising. "I'll be at the boulangerie."

"You're living with your parents again?"

"I shall be, from today," she said, heading for the door.

He summoned the corporal. "Please escort madame to the street," he ordered.

When she had gone, he reached for the telephone and asked to be connected with Lyon. The exchange operator told him there was very heavy traffic that morning and also that several lines were out of commission, meaning, he guessed, cut. It had started already, the Resistance back-up to the invasion. The operator wanted to know his priority so that she could fit him into the order of precedence. He hesitated, then gave the highest *Abwehr* priority he was authorized to use.

When his call got through, about midday, he kept it short. Two children, Paul and Cécile Simonian, had been taken from the house of an Ain farmer called Lucien Laurentin, some time in May. What had happened to them? Where were they now? Top priority.

He hadn't heard anything by midnight. He'd felt a strong urge to walk round to the bakery earlier, but the picture he had of hope lighting up that pale, thin face, then fading as she realized he brought no news, kept him from such foolishness. Besides, he was very busy. Everybody was. There was an electricity in the air. Everyone, French and German alike, knew it was coming, knew it was close. Rumours multiplied.

But Mai knew it was no rumour that made his corporal shake him awake in the early hours of the following morning, June 6.

"Sir, it's started," he said. "We've just had a signal."

Mai rubbed his eyes, stretched. "Where?" he asked.

"Normandy."

"Thanks," he said and went back to sleep.

Next morning, as Mai sat in the Café Balzac waiting for Michel Boucher, the atmosphere had changed from electric to explosive. He wondered if the big redhead would turn up. News of an allied invasion must have sent tremors of fear through the more blatantly collaborationist community.

But Boucher turned up, dead on time. "How are you, Edouard?" he asked.

"I'm fine. How's your family?"

"Great!" said Boucher, his face lighting up. "Hélène loves it down in the country. And she's having another! It'll be a boy this time."

"It must be great to be so certain of the future. Congratulations."

"Thanks. The future's what you make it, Günter. That's the one thing I've learned these last few years," said Boucher with confidence.

Mai smiled ruefully, almost enviously. "How're *they* taking things?"

"Blaming your lot for not knowing where the landings were coming."

"They may be right. Any action?"

"They're going after the terrorists with a heavy hand," said Boucher. "They reckon this invasion will trigger off all the loonies, so they're going to pull in everyone they know."

"Anything specific?"

"There's some meeting tomorrow morning, a Resistance council or some such thing. They're going to take it. They've got the address, timing, everything. I got details." He passed over a piece of paper.

Mai studied it. "Good intelligence," he said with professional admiration. "Are you on the raid?"

"No. Germans only. They're not even letting Pajou in on this. They must want some of these fellows alive!"

Mai slipped Boucher his money a little later. The redhead didn't put the envelope out of sight with his usual speed.

"What's up?" said Mai rather sharply. "Not enough?"

"What? No!" laughed Boucher. "No, the thing is, Günter, the way I'm placed, I've got more than enough cash. I don't need this."

"You mean you want to break our connection?" said Mai.

To his surprise, Boucher said, "No! I mean, it's not much of a connection really, professionally speaking. I never have much to tell you. And in any case, it's no contest any more between your lot and the Avenue Foch boys. They're in charge, aren't they? No, I enjoy meeting you, having a chat. I hoped maybe you felt the same."

Mai was at first amazed. Then, as he examined what the other had said, he was forced to acknowledge its truth. Partly it was Boucher's relationship to Janine that kept him coming to these meetings; but also it was because he enjoyed relaxing for a friendly chat with this amiable, uncomplicated collaborator!

"Yes, I do, Miche," he said. "Where does that leave us?"

"Same place, same time next week," said Boucher cheerfully. "But keep your money to spend on booze."

He tossed the envelope back and left.

The next morning Mai's telephone rang at last.

"Mai! Bruch here." It was his opposite number in Lyon. "They're in Montluc. At least, they've got two Jewish terrorists called Simonian listed, so I presume that's Gestapo longhand for the kids. The Gestapo here seem to have taken the invasion personally. They're rounding up everyone. Montluc's bursting at the seams, but the only way they know of releasing anyone is down a gun barrel into a grave. I thought they were going to take *me* in! So next time I hear from you, it'd better be with a written order with a big, *big* signature. Otherwise, my hands are tied." The telephone went dead.

Mai sat unmoving for several minutes. Then he picked up the receiver once more.

Ten minutes later he went round to the office of his *Abwehr* chief.

"This had better be important, Captain Mai," the man warned.

"I think it is, sir," he said, producing the paper Boucher had passed him. "One of my agents, a woman, she's always been most reliable in the past, well, she's just come through with information about a high level Resistance council meeting this afternoon. I've got everything—timing, location, security, escape routes, the lot. This could be a real coup for us, sir. All my agent wants in payment is..."

Half an hour later he got two copies of the release order. One he delivered personally to Gestapo HQ with a request that they expedite the release. The other he dispatched to his *Abwehr* counterpart in Lyon.

Mai felt exhausted. It wasn't surprising. This had all started at nine thirty that morning. It was now three. But he hadn't finished yet. As he stood up, the telephone rang. It was the chief.

"Mai, that intelligence you got."

"Sir. Nothing wrong, I hope?"

"No, it's all fine. The trouble is, the SD have it already. They got a hint somehow that we were setting up an ambush operation and rang to request us to hold off."

"I'm sorry, sir," he said, "I didn't know..."

"How could you? Not your fault." With a brusque goodbye, he rang off.

Mai sighed with relief. If for one moment the man had suspected how he'd been manipulated... There were still tracks to be smoothed over before he could feel safe.

And best of all, there was the good news to pass on!

When he reached the bakery, however, his heart sank with disappointment. The shutters were up and there was a "Closed" sign on the door.

Disconsolately he rapped on the glass. After a couple of minutes he was just turning away when the blind twitched. Next moment it had flown up and he saw Janine pulling at bolts and twisting at keys in her desperate haste to open the door.

"What happened?" she was demanding, even before he'd got across the doorstep. "Is there news? Please, please!"

"It's all right," he said. "They're alive and well."

"Oh, thank God!" she said, swaying forward into his arms.

He held her for a moment, then she broke away and taking his hand pulled him from the open doorway into the living quarters behind the shop. "Please, please, tell me everything," she begged.

"Are you alone?" he asked.

"Yes," she said impatiently. "There's no flour, so Maman and Papa have gone to visit friends. Please, tell me!"

He told her what he knew, what he'd done.

"And they'll let them go, you're sure?" she demanded.

"Absolutely," he said, with more confidence than he felt. With the Gestapo, who could be sure? But he could do no more.

"Oh thank you. Thank you," she said. She was aglow with relief, with joy. He could have sat and watched her for the rest of the day. But there were still things to do.

He said rather brusquely, "One more thing. To get this release, I've had to make out you're one of my top agents. Only this time, I had to claim you'd given me details of an important Resistance meeting. It would be useful to have this supported by written evidence in your file. I've jotted down the details."

He handed her his jottings and a blank sheet of paper.

She said, "You want me to copy this and sign it."

"Yes."

"And that will help the children?"

"The children's release is already on the way. This will help me, in the not unlikely event that the Gestapo decide to check my files again."

"So it's just to help you?"

He thought he was being accused of selfishness and said sharply, "Yes, but if you don't want to copy it, I'll understand."

"No, no," she said shaking her head, taking up the pen he'd given her and beginning to scribble. "But tell me, why didn't you bring this to me first? Wouldn't that have been the clever thing, to make sure you had your cover-up fixed in advance?"

"The release form was the important thing," he said. "Time might be of the essence."

She scrawled her name at the bottom of the sheet. When she passed it over to him, he folded it without looking at it, thrust it into his tunic and stood up. "What will you tell your husband?"

"I don't know," she said. "The truth perhaps."

"I'd avoid the truth," he said uneasily. "Can't you give Miche the credit for finding out that the children are alive?"

"OK, I'll tell him that. When I can find him. And if it happens he's not too busy." Her bitterness was unmistakable.

Mai said, "I'm sorry."

"Why?" She rose now and stood before him, studying him curiously. "You said in the Tuileries gardens that you loved me."

"Yes."

"I didn't know what to believe. Now you've put yourself at risk again for me, and only thought later of how you'd cover yourself."

He tried to turn away, thinking he couldn't stand much more of this, but she caught at his arm and pulled him back to face her. Now she stepped so close to him that he could feel her warmth.

"I don't want a *reward!*" he cried.

"Don't you?" she said. "That's your affair. What I want is to be held by a man who loves me and puts that before everything."

Her face was raised to his. "Janine . . ."

"No words," she said quietly. "No nationalities. No deals, no rewards. Just love."

5

Christian Valois struck the table so hard that a glass fell off it and only Jean-Paul's instant reflexes prevented it from hitting the ground.

"Calm down," he said, replacing the glass. "You'll get us arrested and then neither of us will get to the meeting."

They were sitting outside a café on the Avenue d'Italie. Christian was furious because during a last-minute briefing before an important meeting

280

at which he'd thought *he* was to be *les Pêcheurs'* accredited representative, Jean-Paul had casually announced that he was coming along as well.

"What's the matter?" he demanded. "Don't you think I can argue our point of view?"

"Better than me, probably," said Jean-Paul. "Only, I've got things to say which I have to say myself."

"They're only expecting one. They won't want two," argued Valois. "It's not democratic, it's not good security."

"All right. Then I'll go by myself," said Jean-Paul equably.

Christian shook his head. "No," he said. "I'm the delegate."

"So you are. The delegate of *les Pêcheurs*. But I'm *le Pêcheur* himself, Christian, never forget that. What I say goes!"

The friends locked gazes.

"Right, shall we go?" said Jean-Paul suddenly.

"It's not for an hour. We'll be early."

"Then perhaps we'll arrive at the same time as the Gestapo, if they happen to be coming!"

"For God's sake, this is no joking matter," snapped Valois. "There's always danger, especially if people start changing the arrangements."

Jean-Paul looked at his friend curiously. "Don't let it get to you, Christian," he said. "I've noticed you showing the strain a bit lately. Look, I'm sorry I've upset you, but I really do think I should attend this one. And we'll take extra care, I promise."

In fact, so cautious was the approach mapped out by Jean-Paul that they needed almost the full hour, even though the house where the meeting was being held was only ten minutes' walk from the café.

As they entered the shadowy hallway, a man confronted them with his hand in his coat pocket. Hastily Christian gave the password.

"There's only supposed to be one of you," said the man.

"He's our group leader," said Christian.

"The Fisherman? Well, I suppose that'll be all right."

"Kind of you," said Jean-Paul.

They climbed to the second floor. It was the waiting room of a dentist's surgery. This was the cover, in case of interruption. The dentist and a "patient", both *résistants*, would be in the surgery next door.

The last representative arrived on the stroke of three and the meeting got under way. Below, in the hall, the guard peered through the peephole he'd poked in the curtain. He saw a couple walking along the pavement, the woman with a piece of towel held against her mouth, the man with his arm round her shoulders.

"Damn," said the guard as the couple paused uncertainly. Deciding that positive action was best, he opened the door and stepped out. Glancing at the woman, he said, "Not looking for the dentist, I hope? He's away. All shut up. Won't be back for a week."

"Bloody hell!" said the man. "It's just about killing her. Is there another dentist round here?"

"Well," said the guard, "I've seen a sign, but whether there's anyone still working there ... If you go down the street, take the first left..." He turned to point. Something hard rammed into his spine.

"Keep quiet," hissed the man.

He said in as loud a voice as he dared, "Now what's all ..."

The woman hit him in the belly with amazing strength, so that he doubled up as he was forced back through the doorway. He was dimly aware, now she'd dropped the towel, that the woman needed a shave. He was also aware that at least two more men had slipped into the hall.

"Let's go," said one, in German.

They went, quiet as snakes, up the stairs.

Some instinct for danger made Jean-Paul begin to rise a single second before the door burst open and the armed men rushed in crying, "Gestapo! No one move!" He stared at them like a cornered animal, his body tensed to leap. But Christian cried, "Jean-Paul, no!" and, grabbing his arm, pulled him down.

"Let's get them downstairs," said the Gestapo leader. He seized Christian by the collar and hurled him towards the door, where one of the others spun him onto the landing and pushed him down the stairs. Valois didn't stop, but flung himself out of the street door. A car was coming to a halt just outside. He turned and ran in the direction it had come from. The passenger door opened and a man got out without haste, drawing a pistol from his pocket. But before he could aim, he screamed with pain as another figure rocketed out of the house and crashed the car door against his legs. It was Jean-Paul.

Christian had reached a corner. He glanced back as he rounded it. For the first time he became aware that Jean-Paul was behind him.

And behind Jean-Paul two—no, three—of the German raiders were bringing out their guns.

Christian screamed, "Jean-Paul! *No!*"

The guns fired. A rackety volley like an old motorbike trying to start. Ten yards from the corner, Jean-Paul threw up his arms. But he kept coming, his heart pumping blood to desperate straining muscles, three yards, two, and he flung himself into Christian's arms. Valois felt the blood spurting out against his hands before his friend's body became a dead weight in his arms.

He looked back towards the house. The gunmen were still standing there, guns outstretched, as though frozen in a movie frame. Then the reel jerked into life again and they came running towards him, shouting.

Gently he laid Jean-Paul Simonian on the pavement. The face looked young again, and the scar from that hopeless battle back in 1940 was almost invisible.

The Gestapo men were closing fast. Christian reached inside his jacket and pulled out an automatic pistol. The Germans seemed nonplussed to find him armed, and he had killed the first two before the third managed to get a retaliatory shot in. It ripped into Christian's left shoulder, but his right arm was steady as he shot the man through the head.

Now there were more men in the street, running, firing. He dropped his gun into the gutter, clutched at his wounded shoulder, and ran. He had no conscious idea of where he was going but his brain knew where he had to go, so it was no surprise to find himself approaching the Crozier boulangerie.

The shop door was open. He walked in and through to the back. There was no one there, but he thought he heard a noise above, so he went to the foot of the stairs and called, "Janine."

There was silence. "Janine!" he called again. "For God's sake!"

A door opened and she appeared at the head of the stairs. She had pulled a cotton wrap about her body and was tying it at the waist. Her hair was loose and trailed like sun-bleached silk over her shoulders.

"Christian! What is it? I was asleep."

He pushed himself away from the wall as his swimming mind sought the words to convey his terrible news. Janine let out a cry of horror and he realized that his palm had left a bloody imprint on the wall.

"You're hurt," she said, starting down the stairs towards him.

But her cry had reached other ears. Through pain-filled eyes Christian saw another figure appear behind her on the landing. He recognized the man buttoning up his grey tunic as the *Abwehr* officer who was always hanging round the bakery.

Janine reached him. He swung his good arm with all his strength and struck her across the mouth.

"Whore!" he cried, as she fell back on the stairs, her lips bloody.

Mai started to descend, shouting angrily, his hand plucking his gun from its holster, but Janine half rose to block his way. "For God's sake, what's happened?" she asked thickly.

"Jean-Paul's dead," said Valois with vicious clarity. "Our meeting was raided. They shot him down in the street!"

Then with one last contemptuous look at the stricken woman, he turned and staggered out of the house.

Mai put his hands on Janine's shoulders and turned her towards him, flinching away from her accusing gaze. "I didn't know. I swear I didn't know," he said urgently.

She shook her head in disbelief. "Go! Just go."

He had no resources for dealing with this, he, Günter Mai, captain of military intelligence, master of agents, manipulator of men. He could find nothing to do but fasten his buttons and put on his cap and sneak away like any squalid philanderer caught in an act of betrayal.

Betrayal of whom? he asked himself that night as he drank alone in his room. There had been a wanted man, a *résistant* who had been involved in the murder of many Germans, standing wounded and unarmed within easy reach of him, and he had done nothing. That was betrayal, surely?

He was drinking schnapps by the tumblerful, but drunkenness was a long time coming, and at eleven o'clock he had a telephone call which put it completely beyond reach.

"Mai? Walter Fiebelkorn here. Look, I've just been dining with your chief. We were amused that we'd both wanted to ambush the same terrorist meeting today. I thought you might like to know that it went fairly well. We got a good haul. The interrogation's been going on while I've been having dinner and I'm sure they'll begin to break soon."

"Congratulations, Colonel. Thank you for calling."

"Wait. A moment more. The dead man was called Simonian, also known, I believe, as the Fisherman. I was interested to learn that it was this man's wife who gave you the information! Excellent work, Mai. Didn't you once rescue her from us before? It just shows how right you were! Also, I gather, as a reward and an incentive, you were trying to get this woman's children released. Quite right. A couple of Jewish children for an agent like this would be a bargain."

Now Mai was as sober as he ever had been in his life. "That's right," he said. "There's a release order on the way. I left a copy at Gestapo HQ."

"Yes, yes. I have it before me now. I took the liberty of ringing Montluc myself to ensure your order was executed. Captain Mai, I'm sorry to tell you this, but I was too late. Alas, these miserable children have already been put on a transport."

"When? Where to?" shouted Mai.

"Who knows? With such large numbers as are dealt with daily, there is always some vagueness. But their ultimate destination is certain enough. To Auschwitz, Captain Mai. To Auschwitz camp, in Poland."

6

"Pauli," whispered Céci. "Is it Christmas yet?"

"No. Not yet."

"It's just that we've been here such a long time, I thought maybe it was nearly Christmas."

"No, but don't worry. I'll tell you when it comes."

Pauli knew exactly how long they'd been in Montluc. He kept a count of the days, scratched in his sandal leather with his thumbnail. He could have scratched more efficiently if he'd wanted, for deep in the lining of his trousers he had the knife which Uncle Miche had given him. They had only been perfunctorily searched on arrival, nothing like the thorough body searches given at Drancy, where every item of value had been stripped from the inmates.

There were three buildings in the fortress of Montluc: the main cell block; a block referred to, though not used, as the refectory; and a building made of yellow-painted wood where the Jewish prisoners were housed. It was into this that the Simonian children had been pushed. A mutter of protest went up at the sight of the youngsters, but it was stilled by a man called Stern who seemed to have some authority.

"Let 'em be," he growled. "Draw attention to them and God knows what may happen. Each day we sit quietly here is a day nearer the end of the war."

Somehow, contact was kept with the outside world, and the fever of anticipation of the expected invasion had touched even these men who were least likely to benefit from it. The Gestapo guards sensed this traffic of news in and out and did everything they could, by way of punishment and infiltration, to halt it. The inmates always required any new prisoner to give a full account of himself, to convince them he was not a German spy.

Not even the clear evidence of recent beating visible on the face of the thin little man hurled into their midst a couple of days later was enough. "What's your name, friend?" inquired someone.

"Now that's a matter of some small dispute," said the newcomer, massaging his bruised jaw. "Magus I am, but I fear my gifts of gold have been knocked from my teeth. Let me tell you my most melancholy story."

But before he could start his narration, he felt a small hand slip into his. Looking down, he met a gaze whose steadiness was more disconcerting here than ever before. "Good morning, Monsieur Melchior."

"What? Pauli? Is it you? And Céci. Oh God, have they thrown you two in this awful place, my dears?"

Maurice Melchior knelt down and embraced the children, with tears streaming down his face.

"You know this man, kids?" said Stern.

"Yes, sir. He brought us from Paris to Lyon. He lived upstairs from Bubbah Sophie, my grandmother in Paris."

That established Melchior's credentials. Now he told his story without embellishment, conscious of Pauli drinking in every word.

"Even then, I might have persuaded them I really *was* Corder if Octave, my business associate, had not decided he could save his own skin by offering them mine," he concluded. "Since this war began, I have not been fortunate in my choice of friends. But at least it has brought me in touch with these unfortunate children again. I owe Pauli at least two debts. We must get them out, and ourselves too!"

Stern shook his head. "Forget it. There are only two ways any of us are leaving this place. *Avec bagages* or *sans bagages*."

"I'm sorry?" said Melchior puzzled.

"If your name is called *avec bagages* it means you're on your way to a concentration camp in Germany," said Stern.

"And *sans bagages*?"

"Shorter journey. Quicker end," said Stern laconically.

"Oh God." Maurice Melchior closed his eyes.

Céci moved against his chest and whimpered. He opened his eyes and adjusted her head so that she was once more comfortable.

He glanced at Pauli and tried to smile. His purpose was to offer hope and encouragement, but the smile would not come. It was strange, but if there was any reassurance in that brief eye-contact, it passed not from him to the boy, but from that steady, thoughtful gaze into his frantic mind.

DAYS PASSED, BECAME WEEKS. It was good when they were allowed to pass in utter passivity. A world of stinking air, overflowing toilet buckets, vile food and the complete and uncontrollable infestation of person, clothing and bedding with every kind of crawling, burrowing and flying vermin imaginable, made itself bearable only when the mind was anaesthetized into accepting this as the best, and the worst, there was. But there were disturbances, prisoners dragged out for interrogation, or for deportation or, worst of all, the four am *appels sans bagages* which were followed a short time later by the rattle of rifle fire.

Then, late one night, the guard opened the door and cried, "Simonian: Paul, Cécile. Out!" The guard looked down at his list again and rattled off some more names. Last among them was Melchior. "*Avec bagages*, if you've got any."

"Where are we going? Is it to Drancy?" Melchior asked.

"No. Usually you lot go to Drancy first. But this time you're privileged. Straight to Germany or, should I say, straight through Germany?"

Behind him Melchior heard Stern's voice calling, "Good luck! Remember, there's no way out from within!"

If that was a hint it ought to have come with a printed diagram, thought Melchior bitterly, as they were herded by soldiers armed with submachine-guns across the short distance which separated the prison from a complex of railway sidings. Here a line of cattle-wagons awaited. They were driven into them.

The wagons were crowded, but it was possible for everyone to squat, though not to stretch out. The children were accorded a corner and Melchior, by asserting his status *in loco parentis*, joined them.

"Let's get comfortable," he said, trying for cheerfulness. "I daresay it will be a longish journey."

"Let no one wish it shorter," said someone with gloomy foreboding.

Melchior tried to sleep, but his mind seemed to have been jerked into frenetic and useless activity by the move, like an old clock whirring into life for a little while when shaken. Also, there were too many noises, among them a gentle scratching, perhaps the least of all the sounds that disturbed him, but the most regular and certainly, he decided, the closest.

He finally tracked it down to Pauli, who lay almost doubled up, apparently sleeping.

He touched the boy gently and he opened his eyes. "Monsieur?"

"Pauli, that noise..."

The boy shifted his leg slightly and looked down. Melchior followed his gaze. His eyes rounded as he saw in the boy's hand a knife.

"I promised Maman I wouldn't use the blade until she said I could," said Pauli guiltily.

"I think, if she knew, she wouldn't mind at all," said Melchior.

The boy was scratching away at the floorboards. To Melchior it looked like a hopeless task. The boards were thick, close-laid and solidly nailed. "Let me know when you're tired," he said.

And now the long wait was on their side. Inevitably, it seemed like no time at all before they felt the jolt of a shunting locomotive being attached, and then the movement of the wagons beginning to roll.

They only went a few miles, however, before they came to a halt again. Melchior guessed they were being linked with another train, possibly a supply train. They wouldn't want to waste a precious locomotive on a few Jew-filled wagons.

But even with these hours of delay, the impression made on the floorboards still seemed little more than a scratch when, after another series of bangs and jerks, they at last started up once more. Matters weren't helped by the need to keep their efforts secret. Melchior knew there was no guarantee that they wouldn't find their fellow prisoners more terrified of reprisals than interested in possible escape.

The train stopped again. They heard a guard on the roof of their wagon call, "What's happening?" and the distant reply came, "It's the line. Some *résistants* have blown it up!"

The work went on, more carefully and therefore more slowly when there wasn't the sound of the train to cover the scratching. But the extra time was invaluable and shortly after the train started again Pauli gave a little cry, and when Melchior looked, he saw that the knife was moving quite freely at one end of a deep groove.

Blowing the woodshavings aside, he pressed his eye to the slit and saw the railway sleepers rushing by beneath the wagon.

All this had attracted attention. A middle-aged man who'd been sitting close by reciting prayers for most of the journey, suddenly said in a frightened whisper, "What are you doing?"

"Sh," said Melchior, putting his finger to his lips.

"Are you crazy?" said the man who'd now glimpsed the knife and the damage to the floorboard. "You'll get us all killed, you know that?"

"All the more reason to keep your mouth shut!" said Melchior.

Another thirty minutes had the break extended across the whole width of the floorboard. Now they picked a point about twenty inches along the same board, and set to work again. Surprisingly, though his strength was greater than Pauli's, Melchior lacked the boy's stamina, and they soon evolved a system of thirty minutes' steady scratching from Pauli followed by a quarter of an hour's hard assault by Melchior.

The train began to slow again, and came to a halt. It was dark outside. They'd been on the train for at least twenty-four hours with nothing to sustain them but a couple of buckets of dirty water. These were long since empty and one was being used as a toilet bucket. Suddenly the wagon door slid open. Bright lights shone in. Melchior shifted his position to give Pauli, who was working at the floorboard, maximum cover. The man who had objected moved as if to stand up, and even began to speak. Then he changed his mind and sat down, silent once more.

Melchior waited in fear for the order to get out.

Instead, a couple of new water buckets were dumped on the wagon floor and a cardboard box containing several hard German loaves.

Just before the door slid shut again, Melchior glanced towards the man to show his gratitude. In the glare of the electric light he saw that Pauli was sitting, blank-faced, with the point of the knife pressed against the man's kidneys. Then the door closed and darkness returned.

Melchior crawled towards the bread and water and by calling out, "The children! The children!" he managed to get a reasonable share.

Refreshed, they worked even harder, and as the grey light of dawn began to seep through the gaps in the side of the wagon, the blade of the knife slipped completely through at one end of the second groove. Another ten minutes and all that held it in place was a thin splinter. Carefully Melchior sawed through this and withdrew the knife. The section of floorboard remained in place. Impatient, he stood up and drove his heel down hard. The wood vanished and there, a couple of feet beneath them, was the stone-filled track, rushing by like a pebbly torrent.

By now almost everyone in the wagon was aware of what was going on. Men crowded round the aperture and peered down. It took some time for someone to voice the general thought. "Who's going through *that*? A rubber dwarf?"

It was true, now it was finished the aperture looked remarkably small. Eighteen inches by twelve perhaps. And even if it were possible to squeeze through, to drop onto that rushing track looked like certain death.

"We're slowing down again," someone said.

"What is it? A station?"

One of those peering through the slats in the side of the wagon said, "No. It's a bridge. I can't see much. It's dark. But there's a river. Yes, definitely a river. It must be the Rhine! We must be in Germany."

The news chilled their hearts. They were in the beast's own terrain.

Some time later, the train came to a halt. Again, not a station, the man at the spyhole reported. Nothing but trees were visible. A couple of guards stretching their legs stopped outside the wagon, and their conversation could be heard clearly. "What a stink from these wagons!" one of them said.

"Not to worry," said the other, "we'll get 'em out and have a bit of fun with the hoses when we reach the station!"

Laughing, they moved away. Maurice, whose German was excellent, translated their words. "That does it," he said. "It's now or never."

He sat down, thrust his skinny legs through the hole and slid downwards. When he reached his hips, he stuck. The others in the wagon pressed his shoulders but it was in vain.

Finally he said, "This is wasting time. Get me out."

They pulled him upwards, not without difficulty. He turned to the children. "All right, Pauli. Down you go."

The skinny boy got through without difficulty. Next he passed down the little girl, her eyes wide at this latest extraordinary game she and Pauli were having to play.

"Right, Pauli. Lie down between the tracks. Don't move till the train has gone right away. Understand?"

"Yes, monsieur. Please, Monsieur Melchior, can't you come too?"

Whether the appeal was based on concern for the adult or the child, Melchior didn't know. Either way, it moved him greatly. "I'm sorry, I can't," he said. "All this rich living has made me fat. Now if I had some nice goose grease, I might slip through!"

He saw the direction of the child's eyes. With a child's clarity, Pauli had identified the only possible source of lubrication in that wagon. Melchior rose and looked down into the slop bucket. His stomach turned over. But it came to him then that there could be a time when he would recall his squeamishness and weep.

He began to slip off his clothes and toss them through the hole to Pauli. Naked, he bent with a handful of straw; retching, he plunged it into the bucket and then began to anoint his hips.

"Stand aside, Pauli," he said. He stepped into the hole. The vile lubrication worked: a shove from above and he was through.

Melchior felt the train beginning to lurch forward. He flung himself down. Pauli was already lying between the tracks, almost covering his sister. A foot from his head a huge wheel strained round, lost its grip and slithered, sending a stream of sparks into the boy's hair. He didn't flinch. If this child can bear this, what cannot I bear? Melchior asked himself, as he buried his face in the gravel between the sleepers. On either side, the wheels found traction; the train began to move, gathering speed; the ground trembled beneath his belly.

The trio lay still a little longer. Then Melchior and Pauli rolled over on their backs and looked up at the dawn-grey sky. After a while Melchior rose and, stepping off the track, began to pull handfuls of dewdamp grass to clean the evil-smelling lubrication from his body.

"What do we do now, Monsieur Melchior?" asked Pauli.

"We walk," said Melchior, pulling on his clothes. "Back that way, towards the Rhine. Then we cross it and get back into France and go home. How does that sound, little prince?"

The boy didn't speak but nodded noncommittally and turned to help his sister. You're right, thought Melchior. That's how it sounds to me too. Hopeless! But he had managed without hope before.

7

It was more than a month since Mai had been to the Balzac.

Michel Boucher greeted him with undisguised pleasure. "Hey, I was beginning to think you were avoiding me."

"No," said Mai sharply. "Pressure of work."

"Yeah? The Resistance has certainly been busy, since the invasion. Auntie Louise was saying you never get down to the bakery now. I think she'd have liked to ask your advice about the kids. Ask! I think she'd have got down on her knees and begged. Janine said there was nothing you could expect a German to do. Only she wasn't as polite as that."

"She asked if I could help. I couldn't," said Mai.

"That's what I reckoned. But I knew you'd do your best, Günter."

"And how is Janine?" asked Mai in a voice only just under control.

"How do you think? The kids. Then Jean-Paul. I wanted to get her out. You know how it is with the Gestapo. Once they get their hands on a *résistant* or his body they usually go looking for the rest of the family. But she wouldn't. And they didn't. Funny, that."

"Yes, funny," said Mai.

"People said some nasty things. I had to slap a couple of mouths."

It occurred to Mai that Boucher was not the most convincing champion a woman accused of collaboration might select.

He said, "Is she ill?"

"Ill? She ought to be dead by the look of her," said Boucher bluntly. "But she'll keep going till she finds out something. She's been wandering round everywhere. The Kommandatur, Avenue Foch . . . she even goes to Drancy, stands and waits for convoys to leave. Günter, are you sure there's nothing you can do for her?"

"I've done all I can," he said. "There's nothing more I can do."

He must have sounded desperate, for Boucher patted him sympathetically on the arm and said, "Don't take it to heart. It's not your fault. You look a bit run-down to me, Günter. Why not come and stay with us in Moret for a couple of days? We keep very quiet down there. To tell the truth, no one knows anything about me in Moret."

Intrigued at this glimpse of a new domestic and discreet Boucher, Mai thought, Why not? The invasion forces were still being held, though at great cost. Perhaps he could sneak a day or two...

"You'll love it," said Boucher. "Peace, booze, and lots of lovely grub. Hélène's a marvellous cook. So, what do you say?"

"I'll come," Mai said. "Next week, if that's OK?"

"That's great," enthused Boucher. "You'll have a wonderful time."

For once the redhead's assurances proved totally reliable and Mai enjoyed his stay even more than he had expected.

It was only thoughts of Janine which darkened the sunlit days. He found himself imagining her in Hélène's place and himself in Boucher's, with Pauli and Céci playing on the grass, and he would drift so deep into these reveries that it often took a vigorous shake of his shoulder to bring him back to the painful reality.

Boucher was no great intellect, but it didn't take him long to fathom the cause of his guest's distraction. Over a bottle of Armagnac on the last night of his stay, Mai found himself confiding in the man. Boucher's response was both comforting and devastating in its directness.

"I've always seen you were sweet on her," he said. "And she fancied you too, even if she didn't want to."

"Did she?" said Mai, amazed.

"Oh yes. I reckon I saw it before she knew it herself."

THE NEXT MORNING Mai was woken by a loud knocking at the main door. He glanced at his watch. It was still very early. He heard Boucher's door open further along the landing and his voice booming to Hélène, "It's all right, go back to sleep."

Mai went to the window. There was a long black car parked across the drive. Two men leaned against it. Both were armed.

He ran out onto the landing to warn Boucher, but looking down the stairs into the hall he saw it was unnecessary. Boucher was already moving quietly towards the door with a machine pistol in his hand.

There was a spyhole fitted on the door. The big man put his eye to it, and let out an exclamation. Then he stepped back, undid the bolts and the lock and flung the door open.

"Pajou!" he said. "What the hell do you want?"

The weedy little Géstapiste stepped inside uninvited. He didn't seem to be armed. He wore an ingratiating smile but his eyes behind the wire-rimmed glasses were darting glances everywhere.

"Miche," he said. "Morning. Sorry to disturb you. Hey, it's a lovely place you've got here!"

"How the hell did you know about it?" demanded Boucher angrily.

"It wasn't a secret, was it?" said Pajou, with mock surprise. "Well, you know me, Miche. Sharp eyes, sharp ears. But if it was supposed to be secret, then I'm glad I came myself."

"What do you mean?"

"It's just that there's a bit of a flap on among our Boche mates. They want Captain Mai in a hurry, and I happened to know he was down here enjoying a spot of leave, so I offered to fetch him."

Pajou never looked directly up the stairs but Mai knew he'd been seen, and that the contemptuous reference to "our Boche mates" had been dropped in for his benefit.

But what could have happened to make this little rat so impudent in the presence of a *Wehrmacht* officer? It was time to speak.

"Pajou, what the hell's going on?" he demanded.

"There you are, Captain," said Pajou, advancing to the foot of the stairs. "You haven't heard? Well, how could you, down here, enjoying your leave? That's a mark in your favour. You see, there's bad news and good news. The bad news is, someone tried to blow up the Führer."

"What?" exclaimed Mai, knowing as he saw Pajou's cynical smile that he didn't sound surprised enough. Why should he? Anyone with half a mind had known that it was only success that had made the old military families like Bruno Zeller's put up with vulgar little Adolf so long. With the invasion forces advancing, some kind of revolt was inevitable.

"*Tried*, you say?" said Mai.

"Oh yes. That's the good news. The Führer was uninjured. A little annoyed, so they say, but completely safe!"

"Who sent you, Pajou?"

"Well, Colonel Fiebelkorn, sort of. I'll explain in private, shall I?"

Uninvited, he came running up the stairs. Mai led him into his bedroom and quickly got dressed.

"Civilian clothes, eh? And no doubt you've got Monsieur Edouard Scheffer's identification somewhere about you? That could be useful."

Did this little bastard know everything? "All right, Pajou. Spit it out," he said brusquely.

Pajou soon made his purpose clear. There'd been several hours during which it was believed Hitler was dead. The *Militärbefehlshaber* had ordered the arrest of senior SS and SD officers to prepare the way for the expected assumption by the army of all powers, political and military. But the Führer's survival had changed everything. Released, the SD were bent on revenge. The high ranking officers involved would be returned to Berlin to be dealt with there. Smaller fry would be disposed of locally.

"I was at the Avenue Foch when some *Wehrmacht* chaps were invited in for a chat," said Pajou. "That's when I realized Colonel Fiebelkorn was keen to see you, and as I happened to know where you were . . ."

He was here under his own steam, that was clear. And his reasons were soon clear too. For a "consideration", he would give Mai a running start to disappear into the countryside.

When Mai packed his bag and announced his intention of returning to Paris, Pajou's ingratiating manner ceased. "You're an idiot," he said. "All right, in the car! Sooner we get you back the better."

"Pajou," said Mai softly. "You forget yourself. To talk to a *Wehrmacht* officer in that insubordinate tone is a criminal offence. Men have been shot for less."

This was the real test. For a moment Pajou looked uneasy and Mai felt triumphant. But when he turned to Boucher and said, "Right, Miche. Let's go," Pajou said, "Oh no, Captain. With me, not him."

"I prefer to choose my own transport," retorted Mai.

"There may be less choice than you think. Eh, Miche?"

Boucher was sitting on a sofa with Hélène, whose face was heavy with apprehension. Her grip on Boucher's arm visibly tightened. The redhead's gaze met Mai's then slipped away. "I'm sorry, Captain," he said.

"Never mind, Miche," said Mai, smiling. "I understand."

Pajou's keen nose must have sniffed out Boucher's special arrangement with the *Abwehr*, as well as his country hideaway, so poor Miche was in no position to make gestures on behalf of a German officer in trouble.

As they approached Paris, Pajou renewed his offer. Mai didn't respond. Why should he become a fugitive? Whatever he had guessed, he had *known* nothing about the assassination plot. At worst he might now find himself under officer's arrest in the Lutétia, and he could use the time to weed out his files before the withdrawal from Paris—a withdrawal he now accepted as certain. An intelligence officer had loyalties to his agents. Some, like Boucher, were too prominent in their activities to be protected. But others, more clandestine in their work, did not deserve betrayal by their employers.

And there was one more, whose name must be expunged completely. He'd kept Janine's file on record so that her alleged *Abwehr* status could protect her from the SD. Now, suddenly, he wished he'd anticipated matters and destroyed it before his trip to Moret.

He wished it even more a little later. "Where are we going? I want to go to the Lutétia!"

But Pajou only smiled at him, as the car came to a halt a few minutes later before the SD HQ in the Avenue Foch.

"Wishing you'd made a deal now, eh, Captain?" said Pajou, opening the door. "Sorry, but it's too late." Pajou seized his arm in a grip which was close to the point where friendly directive pressure became arresting force. They went in. An NCO led them down a flight of stairs and opened a door into a brightly lit though sparsely furnished room in which Colonel Fiebelkorn was talking to a Gestapo man.

"Captain Mai! So here you are," said Fiebelkorn. "Sorry that your leave has been interrupted. Thank you, Monsieur Pajou, for your assistance. Though if you'd told us you knew where to find the captain, we could have saved you the trouble."

There was a threat vibrating unmistakably behind the words and Pajou retreated before it, smiling ingratiatingly.

"You must know what has happened?" said Fiebelkorn, turning to Mai.

"Yes. I learned of the assassination attempt from Pajou. It was a terrible shock. I was of course delighted to hear the attempt had failed. What I don't understand is why I have been brought here?"

"There are certain necessary investigations. I hope we can rely on your aid."

"Of course, sir."

"Good. Now, for a start, you can perhaps point out the code phrases in this and tell us what they mean."

He tossed a piece of paper onto the desk.

Mai examined it briefly and said in surprise, "But that's a letter I got recently from Colonel Zeller."

"Yes. What we want to know is its significance."

"It's just a letter. He was badly hurt, he's been convalescing..."

"It's a very friendly letter for someone of Zeller's background to be writing to a subordinate like yourself, wouldn't you say?"

"Perhaps. But as I didn't write it, I don't see why I should need—"

Fiebelkorn cut across him brutally. "Are you saying it was just coincidence that you decided to bury yourself in the countryside on the day of this assassination attempt?"

"Of course. What other reason—"

"A prudent man might think it best to keep his head down till he saw which way things were going."

"A prudent man who knew what was going to happen, yes! But I didn't. Colonel, I demand to see someone from the *Wehrmacht*'s legal department. If I'm going to be cross-questioned, I want it to be at a properly constituted Board of Inquiry."

"Someone from the *Wehrmacht* ..." mused Fiebelkorn. "Have a look through there, see if there's anyone you fancy."

He pointed to a door behind him. Günter Mai approached it, then hesitated. Something in him resisted going through that door. The Gestapo man reached past him and turned the handle.

The room beyond was not so brightly lit, but bright enough. Three meat-hooks had been screwed into a beam. From them stretched wires so fine that the men hanging from them seemed to be supporting themselves, like performers in some grotesque ballet on the very tips of their toes.

Mai looked at the naked bodies in shocked disbelief. The bleeding flesh, the gaping lips and protruding tongues. What could it mean? he wondered dully. When men could do this to other men, *any* men, let alone their fellow soldiers, what could *anything* mean?

"And now, Captain Mai," said Fiebelkorn's distant, echoing voice, "let the Board of Inquiry begin."

8

Four days after their escape from the train Maurice Melchior and the children woke, high on a forested slope, and found themselves looking down on a broad river gleaming in the midday sun.

"Is it the Rhine?" asked Pauli incredulously.

"Of course, my child," replied Melchior casually.

He thought he concealed his own delight and amazement very well. They had travelled only at night. Mercifully, the weather had held fine. They had drunk spring water and eaten whatever of the midsummer vegetation Pauli's recently acquired country lore pronounced safe. They'd made one large diversion to avoid an encampment of soldiers but, that apart, they had seen no one. Each morning as the moon faded, they had chosen a hiding place and snuggled up together to get what sleep they could.

In Melchior's mind they were completely and irretrievably lost. Thus to wake up this morning and find that by some miracle he had done what he had promised and brought them to this mighty river, gave him a greater joy than he could recall. It seemed a guarantee of their safety.

"Don't move!" came a harsh command from behind him. "Hands up!"

He couldn't believe it, not here, not now, with the Rhine in sight. A man moved slowly by him, keeping a safe distance away. He was dressed in a grey-green tunic which, for a moment, Melchior thought despairingly was *Wehrmacht* uniform. Then he realized that soldiers didn't wear old feathered hats, nor did they carry shotguns, nor were many of them, except generals, in their seventies.

"Good day," Melchior said in his best German. "The children and I were having a little picnic. I do hope we're not..."

"Foreigner?" said the man accusingly.

"Yes, but a friend," said Melchior disarmingly.

"Move," the man commanded. When Melchior stood still, he raised his shotgun menacingly.

Apart from the man's age and his weapon, there was something else about him which tugged at Melchior's attention and kept his mind off their destination, as they marched uphill through the forest. The children walked ahead. Pauli held his sister's hand and she chatted quite happily as she trotted along.

After about twenty minutes they stepped out of the trees and there ahead of them was a castle. It wasn't a big castle as Rhine castles go, but it had all the usual absurdly romantic turrets and towers.

There was another old man, who seemed to be pruning some bushes. Their captor shouted at him. He came and peered in amazement at the prisoners, then turned and lumbered off towards the house. He too was wearing a sort of uniform tunic. Melchior identified it as the source of his mental irritation. He stopped and turned. The gun came up.

"No, no," said Melchior soothingly. "I just want to look at your buttons." He looked. They bore a heraldic device—a zed crossed by a hunting horn—that he had last seen on a heavy silver signet ring.

"And what have we here?"

The voice sounded familiar. When Melchior turned he saw a man standing on the steps leading up to the open main door. He looked as if something rather terrible had happened to him. He was leaning heavily on a stick, his right sleeve was empty and pinned to his breast, and as for his face ... it was heavily muffled, but what Melchior could see had the burnished, purpureal look left by severe burning...

And then he saw the eyes and recognized their recognition of him. He took a step forward. "Zeller? Is it you? Oh God. Bruno Zeller ..." He felt tears damp on his cheeks.

9

Janine Simonian looked in her bedroom mirror and wondered why she hadn't gone mad. Her reflection showed what could easily have been the likeness of a madwoman. Thin by nature, emaciated by malnutrition, her face was now positively cadaverous through grief, and her neglected hair hung in knots and tangles over her shoulders.

But she knew she was sane. As long as the children were alive she would shun the tempting path down into madness. And the children *were* alive. She knew it with the same certainty she had felt about Jean-Paul during those long months of silence.

But even the firmest faith requires a sign.

During the past weeks she had gone everywhere, confronted everyone, in search of this sign. The fact that the Germans did not seem interested in arresting or even harassing her, the widow of a notorious Jewish *résistant*, was not going unnoticed, except by herself. She had no time for any distraction from her search for information, for hope. She went everywhere, even to the Lutétia, where she demanded to see Günter Mai. They told her that Captain Mai had been transferred.

Michel Boucher, when she told him this, looked grim. "Transferred, is that what they're calling it now?"

No one, not even Pajou, knew precisely what had become of Mai but there were plenty of stories of the horrific treatment of other suspects in the July conspiracy. What Miche told her of his conversation with Mai at Moret persuaded her that she had probably misjudged him.

"Poor Günter," she said.

But she could not get out of her mind that being in bed with him had had some kind of link with Jean-Paul's death.

August came and sunny days succeeded each other, and Paris listened to the news from the west, and some watched to see what the occupiers would do, and others made their own preparations.

"They're leaving! They're going! Oh God, Crozier, is it ending at last? Is our ordeal over?"

Madame Crozier burst into the shop where Claude was leaning on the counter talking to some customers.

"We may survive after all," she went on. "Thank God I kept my head and did my duty as a French citizen!" Louise Crozier's conversion to a flamboyant patriotism had gathered pace rapidly since the Normandy landings.

"So, it's happening, eh?" said Crozier.

The German exodus had started the previous day, and now it had swollen to flood proportions. But there was not yet any cause for rejoicing. Informed opinion pointed out that this wasn't retreat but a clearing of decks for the battle to come. It was the administrators who were leaving, the bureaucrats and the petty officials.

"I heard that the Gestapo are pulling out too," said a customer.

"What do you expect? No stomach for a real fight, those bastards!" growled someone else.

"Don't worry, friend. It's the *Wehrmacht* that's staying. You'll get your real fight!"

"Fighting? I hope there's going to be no fighting round here," said Madame Crozier in alarm. "Crozier, get the shutters up. Janine, dear, where are you going?"

Silence fell in the shop as Janine entered. "Out," she said. "I'm going out. If the Germans are leaving, there may be some news."

Claude Crozier had at first tried to steer her gently to an acceptance that perhaps the children were lost for ever. But soon he had given up.

Janine was recognized by several people in the immediate neighbourhood. Familiarity with her haggard looks had dulled what sympathy they had initially aroused, and today her passage was marked by contemptuous glares and taunts. She gave no sign that she saw or heard anything.

But when she reached the main streets, then she became animated, eyes darting glances everywhere, ears strained to hear everything. The streets were jammed with German traffic: staff cars, armoured vehicles, supply trucks, ambulances, buses, lorries, all of them packed with personnel, equipment and luggage.

Suddenly, Janine's mind was back on that other refugee-crowded road in 1940. She saw the long traffic jam between the poplars, felt the children by her side, and burst into tears. A man by her side, mistaking her grief, put his arm round her shoulders and said, "Take it easy, lady. The Boche will pay, be sure of that."

She shook him off and began to push through the spectators, peering closely into every vehicle. It seemed possible, indeed likely, that somewhere in this confusion she would glimpse those longed-for heads, hear those yearned-for voices.

A truck had broken down near the Madeleine. The driver had got out and, urged on by a middle-aged Gestapo officer, was peering uncertainly beneath the bonnet. It was an open truck and there were several SS officers sprawling among the luggage in the back. Their passage had been marked with a perceptible heightening of hatred among the spectators.

A young man detached himself from the crowd and strolled forward. "I'm a mechanic," he said, smiling. "Here, let me take a look."

He gently edged the driver aside and stooped to probe deep into the engine. After a moment he stood up, wiped his hands on a handkerchief and said with a shrug, "*Kaput!*" then walked slowly away.

The driver looked back into the engine, spoke to the Gestapo man and pointed. The officer looked, turned round, pointed after the Frenchman, opened his mouth to call.

The front of the truck blew up. The driver and officer were hurled to the ground by the blast. Flames rolled back from the cab and, screaming, the other SS officers began to scramble over the tailboard, beating at their smouldering clothes.

The alleged mechanic had halted and turned. From his jacket he produced an automatic pistol and taking steady aim he began to pump bullets into the burning men. German soldiers, attracted by the noise, began to leap off other trucks and the crowd scattered in panic as the bullets began to fly.

Christian Valois paid no heed. When his clip was empty, he turned and walked away at the same steady pace, till his arm was seized and he was forced into a run. It was Henri, who'd transferred his allegiance wholeheartedly to Valois after Jean-Paul's death, but who had soon found that his new leader was even more dangerous than the old.

Once out of range of the Germans he forced the younger man into a café and made him sit down, while a quick-witted waiter rapidly provided them with two half full cups of coffee, to give the impression they'd been there for hours. Sensitivity to the needs of the Resistance had never been higher.

"Right," said Henri. "What the hell do you think you're playing at? I thought Jean-Paul was bad. He didn't give a damn if he got killed or not. *You* look as if you *want* to!"

Valois smiled coldly and drank his coffee.

Henri said earnestly, "Don't mess it up for the rest of us. Another week, we'll be free or we'll be dead. I know which I prefer. The future stretches a long way beyond getting rid of the Boche."

"What future?" said Valois.

"Christian, I know it hit you hard, Jean-Paul's death. And then the news about your sister."

He saw the other's grip tighten on the cup till it seemed the handle must break. The news that Marie-Rose Valois had been executed for Resistance activities had been released six weeks earlier, but no one had dared talk to Valois about it. He seemed to have decided that single-handed he would kill every German in Paris. It was a miracle he had survived so long.

"She's gone, Christian," Henri urged. "Accept it. Never forget it, but accept it."

10

And now at last Paris began to rouse herself. This was the best of times, the worst of times. The police occupied the Préfecture, the FFI fortified the Hôtel de Ville. Citizens took to the streets too. Fired by a vision of justice, or a lust for revenge, they hunted down, judged and sentenced their errant fellows. Some were beaten, humiliated; some were executed; some were thrown into jail to await a formal judgment.

Meanwhile, other jails were being opened, other prisoners set free. At Fresnes prison, on the southern approaches to the city, a pitched battle took place. It cost the Free French 2nd Armoured Division five tanks to overrun this strongpoint on their way to the Porte d'Orléans.

An American medical team took charge of the inmates, transferring them to a nearby civilian hospital. The Americans looked aghast at the evidence of torture they observed on the bodies of some of their new patients. In some cases there seemed little hope. In others, proper medication and nourishment plus, above all, the news of the imminent liberation of Paris brought rapid improvement.

And in one case all these, plus a night's rest, seemed to produce a really remarkable recovery.

"Hey, Doc," said one of the orderlies early the following morning, "we've lost a patient. One of those guys from the jail."

"Well, they were pretty badly hurt, poor devils."

"No, I don't mean he died. He's just up and gone!"

"Perhaps he didn't want to miss the celebrations! Which one was it?"

The orderly consulted his list. "Scheffer," he said. "Edouard Scheffer."

GÜNTER MAI made his way back into Paris in the wake of the 2nd Armoured Division. It was remarkably easy even for a man in his condition. As the liberators drove through the suburbs, the empty streets of early morning suddenly exploded with life. From every doorway, every window poured shouting, singing, laughing, weeping people. Mai had never seen, never heard such joy. Under the cloudless summer sky, this turmoil of flags and banners and cheering and thrown blossoms and spurting wine looked like some great artist's living realization of the spirit of joy. He recalled the stillness, the emptiness, the sense of cold eyes dully watching from shuttered houses that had greeted the invading Germans four years before.

He was slightly delirious, he realized. Somehow he'd scrambled up on the back of a half-track where he clung, unremarkable in a convoy festooned with men, women and children, kissing the soldiers, waving their flags, singing the "Marseillaise". He had to get back to reality.

"What's the date?" he asked a young woman who clung by his side, almost hysterical with joy.

"August the twenty-fifth. You'll never forget it, none of us will!"

She was probably right. What it meant to him was that he'd been in Fresnes for about three weeks. Fiebelkorn's men had worked on him in a leisurely way, pushing him often to the edge of confessing to complicity in the plot, for that way surely peace and rest lay. But some stubbornness at his core refused to let him lie. "I knew nothing. Nothing!" he had repeated.

And finally Fiebelkorn believed him. Or got sick of him. Or simply forgot him. He was transferred to Fresnes. "We'll be back for you tomorrow," promised his SS escort. But they never came. And he'd lain on his prison bed, and slowly he'd started to explore his ferociously abused body. Cuts, bruises, missing teeth, a broken nose, even cigarette burns he catalogued as minor inconveniences. Cracked ribs and mangled fingertips were more lasting sources of pain, but these too would pass. What had worried him most was his left eye which, even when he forced the bruised and swollen flesh around it apart, admitted no light.

Three weeks' rest had worked no miracles, though what the American doctor had hidden beneath the dressing on his eye he did not yet know. Perhaps he should have waited to find out. In fact, why hadn't he? What was he doing in his condition clinging precariously to this enemy vehicle? Was he trying to escape?

The thought made him smile. It was the oddest escape route imaginable! No, it was some basic instinct that was taking him back into Paris. If there was a last chance to see Janine, he had to grasp it. And if there was a last chance to protect her, he had to take it. He prayed that all his files at the Lutétia had been burned or removed or that he could get to them in time to destroy all reference to Janine.

"Here, don't fall off," said the girl next to him, grabbing his arm.

He hadn't realized he'd been slipping. "Thanks," he said.

She looked closely at him and said, "My God, you've been through the mangle, haven't you? Did the Boche do this?"

"Yes," he nodded. "Yes. The Boche."

"But this is the day they get their comeuppance! Think of that! Death to the Boche! Death to the Boche!"

Others took up the chant. And after a while, for the sake of verisimilitude he told himself wryly, he joined in.

And so, on the back of a liberator's half-track, with tricolours flying round him and flowerpetals in his hair, Günter Mai returned to Paris.

11

They'd come for Janine Simonian the previous night.

She put up no resistance. Her father wasn't in the house and her mother had screamed and run and locked herself in the bakehouse when she saw the mob, thinking they were after her.

But once she realized it was Janine they wanted, she reappeared and flung herself into her daughter's defence, both verbally and physically, till two of the men had to restrain her.

They dragged Janine out into the street. By the time they reached their destination, a café a couple of streets away, their number had doubled. The interior of the café was already packed. In better times they would have a singer or a musician there, on a small stage at the back.

Tonight the stage was the focus of attention. Huddled together on it were half a dozen women. Their heads had been shaved and their bare feet trod on their own tresses. At the front of the stage a fat man in a blue apron stood over a woman seated on a wooden stool. He was cutting her hair with a large pair of scissors, flourishing each tress triumphantly before throwing it over his shoulder. The audience clapped and cheered, but fell silent when he put the scissors aside and took a cutthroat razor to perform the final shaving.

Janine closed her eyes wearily. That too she could bear.

Now she was up on the stage. She heard her name called to the audience: "... Janine Simonian who fornicated with a Boche officer while her husband was being murdered"—the crowd howled their hate—"and who stayed in Paris to indulge her lusts while her children were sent out into the country to be picked up and deported by the Boche..."

"No!" she screamed.

The change from corpse-like indifference to vital, struggling indignation was so electrifying that for a second it reduced the mob to silence. Then they began to urge the barber on, but his was no easy task. She had to be held down while he used the scissors. Twice she overturned the chair, twice was forced upright with increasing violence. And when the blue-aproned man came to take the razor, he looked with great unease at her wildly jerking head.

"Be still!" he hissed. "It's only hair, woman!"

He put the razor to her skull. She flung her head from side to side. Next moment there was blood streaming from a long cut on her brow. Now the barber seemed bent on proving that, far from being an accident, this drawing of blood had been deliberate. Ferociously he hacked at the stubble and when the razor pierced the skin he did not draw back.

They dragged Janine back through the streets and put her in the boulangerie doorway and left her there, banging at the door.

No one came. Louise Crozier was too terrified, not knowing what madmen might be roaming the streets to avenge imagined wrongs, and Claude Crozier was not yet home. She might have stayed there all night, if Michel Boucher hadn't turned up an hour later.

He too was not in the best of condition. There was blood on his face and his clothing was torn and dusty. But his bruised and swollen knuckles showed that he'd inflicted as well as taken damage.

"Janine, what are you doing out here? Oh, my God! You too! Let's get you inside. Come on, open up! Auntie Louise! Uncle Claude! It's Miche! Hurry it up! Oh, Janine, Janine, you poor kid. They've gone mad. What have we done, eh? I've tried to earn an honest living, nothing more. For that they tried to hang me! Would you believe it? And that Pajou! He'll wish someone had hanged him when I get hold of him. I should've been long gone, but when I went for my car, it wasn't there. Pajou! He stole the car, and everything else he could lay his hands on! I'll tear his head off. Come on, Auntie Lou! Can't you see it's me?"

And at last Louise Crozier, trembling and terrified, unlocked the door and let them in.

IT WAS ESSENTIAL for Günter Mai to get to the Lutétia and check what had happened there.

But he didn't need to get within more than a hundred yards to see he was too late. The Resistance had got there before him.

So: the boulangerie. For what purpose? To see Janine once more before he met whatever fate was awaiting him? What he was hoping for from the encounter he couldn't say.

At the bakery, the noise of fighting from the direction of the Luxembourg gardens was loud. He pushed the door open and went in, passing through the bare and empty shop with the familiarity of use. Last time he had been here, Janine had taken his hand and led him up these stairs ...

He paused and looked up them. At the top stood Madame Crozier. "You!" she said. "You dare come here? You!"

"Madame," he said, "where's Janine?"

"You've come to see what they've done to her? Perhaps you should! It's your fault!"

He ran up the stairs, all pain and weakness forgotten, pushed open the door and looked at the bed where he and Janine had lain.

Now she lay there alone.

"Oh, God!" said Mai. "What have they done to you?"

He advanced towards the bed but a voice behind him said, "She's sleeping. Leave her."

He turned. It was Claude Crozier speaking, his voice firmer, more commanding than Mai recalled. And in his hands, with the hammer cocked, was a large revolver. "Downstairs, please, Captain."

He urged Mai ahead of him. Behind, Louise Crozier went back into the bedroom and shut the door.

"What have they done to her?" demanded Mai.

"Punished her for associating with you, what do you think?" said Crozier.

"You sound as if you almost sympathized with them!"

"They're Frenchmen. It's a sense of their weakness not of their virtue that makes them act like this," said Crozier wearily.

"Tell me, Claude, how have you and your wife managed to escape? Why did these brave supporters of French justice pick on Janine?"

"Because of you. Because they couldn't stomach her sleeping with you while Jean-Paul was being shot. If I'd been here, perhaps I could have intervened, kept them off her. Perhaps."

"Like you kept them off your wife? She's fifty times more of a collaborator than ever Janine was!"

"Yes," agreed Crozier, "you're right. But croissants aren't embraces. And she is my wife." He glanced at his watch. "I have some friends arriving shortly. We'll be going out on a matter of business. It's probably best that they don't see you. Come this way."

He motioned Mai towards the bakehouse.

As they went through the door, Crozier said, "I don't know why I should bother about you. Except that I came to think of you as honest."

He gestured towards the left-hand oven, the bigger one, the one which shortage of flour and fuel had caused him to keep unused for more than three years.

"Get in there," he said.

"In the oven? What the hell for?" demanded Mai.

"Don't worry. I'm not going to bake you. And you should be reasonably comfortable, at least by Resistance standards. I've had plenty of time to pad it out."

"Pad it out . . . ?" Mai's professional mind was suddenly back at work. He knew what Crozier must be telling him, but he couldn't believe it. How many times had he been in this bakehouse? Leaned against this very oven door? Chatted to Crozier, and his wife and thought of himself as the great manipulator!

"That's right," said Crozier, allowing himself a brief smile of triumph. "I've had a lot of interesting people in there. Allied airmen, *résistants*, escaped prisoners—and not a single search in all these years, for which I've got you to thank, I believe, Captain Mai."

"Madame Crozier too?" said Mai disbelievingly. "Was she . . . ?"

Crozier shook his head. "No, I'm afraid not. She provided such good cover, I could hardly take her into my confidence. And I made my friends promise she wouldn't be touched afterwards. But Janine . . ."

He fell silent, then sighed and said, "All right. In you get. My wife will release you in an hour. What you do then, where you go, is your business. Both of you."

"Both?" said Mai, puzzled.

"Oh yes. You've got company."

He swivelled the iron bar which held the oven door shut and swung it open. "Hello, Günter," said Michel Boucher.

12

There was fighting yet to do; there was blood still to be shed. While to the south of the river they were dancing in the streets, troops were still fighting for victory on the Rue de Rivoli.

There were ordinary Parisians here too, many of them simply spectators, eager to see the final act of this epic drama. But there were others who weren't content to watch, but who, unasked and sometimes unwanted, rushed forward to join the Allied soldiers in the last battle.

An American infantry section, pinned down by fire from a pillbox close to the Orangerie, settled to wait for the arrival of a tank to remove the obstacle.

A young man with an automatic pistol joined them. He reached out to the grenades which the section leader had dangling from his belt. "You permit?" he said.

"It's your party, friend," said the American.

Taking two grenades, the Frenchman stood up and walked towards the pillbox. Perhaps his casual mien baffled the German gunners, or perhaps they thought he came bearing a message of truce.

When he got close enough to throw the grenades, they opened fire. But it was too late, for them and the Frenchman alike. The pillbox rocked, cracked, fell silent. And the Frenchman slid to the ground.

When the Americans reached him, they thought at first he was dead. So did he. It was with a profound sense of disappointment that Christian Valois opened his eyes to see the anxious faces peering down at him.

GENERAL CHOLTITZ, the German commander, surrendered early in the afternoon. General de Gaulle entered the city at four thirty. On his way in, he may have passed Michel Boucher and Günter Mai on their way out. When Louise Crozier released them from the oven, Mai asked to see Janine again. Her mother refused, and threatened to call for help. Boucher seized Mai's arm and said, "Come on, Günter. If they get hold of you today, they'll lynch you! Look what they tried to do to me!"

"Where are we going?" demanded the German as he was dragged, weak and bewildered, into the street.

"We'll get a few things together, pick up some transport. You leave it to me. Then we'll head off to my house at Moret. Hélène will be worried about me. We'll hole up there till things quieten down. Just do what I tell you, OK?"

So they left, the *Abwehr* officer and the collaborator, while Janine lay, her eyes open, staring sightlessly at the cracked, uneven ceiling.

THEY CAME FOR HER again in the first month of the Liberation, not a mob of them this time but two gendarmes in neat clean uniforms. They brought an official warrant.

"Can't you leave her alone?" demanded Crozier. "Look at her! You can see what they've done already."

"Sorry," said the policemen, "but she's got to come. She'll be safer with us anyway, when the news of the charge gets out."

"What charge? That she was friendly with a German officer? Who wasn't? You lot did more toadying than anyone, everyone knows that. Just because you decided to do a bit of fighting in the last few days doesn't mean we've forgotten the years before."

The gendarme had difficulty in keeping his temper, and spoke sharply.

"They've been going through the files the Boche left behind. They say your daughter was a paid agent of the *Abwehr*. They're saying it was her who gave away the meeting when her husband got shot!"

Janine hardly seemed to notice her arrest. In a state close to catatonia, only once did she show any sign of emotion. When the enclosed police van into which she was put came to a halt and she was urged out, she stood blinking in the sunshine. Then it registered where they had brought her, and something like a smile floated across her thin, bruised face, but not a smile of hope or of humour. It was more an acknowledgment of what she had known instinctively for a long time. This world her husband had fought and died for, this world she had lost her children and her liberty for, was not too different from the world it replaced. Oppression and blood, revenge and hate: the basic materials were much the same. Even the locations clearly weren't to be very different.

They'd thrown her, with the other thousands arrested since the Liberation, into the prison camp at Drancy.

PART SIX   March 1945
1

On the face of it, the Simonian trial had everything, even in those days when the Courts of Justice had been resounding to tales of death, deceit and betrayal for several months. But somehow, after the first day, it never took off.

The trouble was the prisoner herself. She stood there like a pillar of salt, absorbing all emotion like moisture from the atmosphere. She denied nothing, admitted everything. Yes, she had been on the *Abwehr* officer's list of agents; yes, she had accepted favours from him; yes, she had slept with him; yes, she had signed the letter found in his files in which she betrayed her husband's last meeting.

The only time the proceedings came to life was when the prisoner pleaded for news of her children. The judge had felt enough pity for her distress to have their fate checked, but nothing was known except that they had been put on a train carrying several hundred Jewish prisoners from Lyon to Germany.

The verdict was, of course, inevitable. All that was still debatable was the sentence. The prosecutor would certainly demand death, but so far de Gaulle had commuted every death sentence passed on a woman. So it was jail. But for how long?

For the woman's defence, there was only her father, who was, it seemed, a Resistance hero. Was there anyone who wasn't? wondered the judge. From the biographical stuff the father gave, it didn't seem likely that the woman would deliberately set out to get her husband killed. And the larger part of her association with this German seemed to spring from concern for her family. Perhaps twelve years would be enough?

So the trial drew to its close. This final morning should see it over well before lunch.

The defence lawyer was talking with, or rather listening to, the father. Now, with evident reluctance, he approached the bench.

Another defence witness? To character? No, to fact!

The judge was doubtful. The prosecutor was scornfully, almost imperiously, dismissive.

"By all means, let us hear him," said the judge finally.

The man was brought in. He was down-at-heel, with clothes that were manifestly too large for him. But he had an honest, open kind of face.

"Your name, monsieur?" the judge asked.

"Scheffer. I'm known as Edouard Scheffer."

For the first time, at the sound of his strong Alsatian accent, the woman's head rose and she turned her eyes to the witness stand.

"You say you're *known* as Edouard Scheffer?" said the judge. "That implies a *sobriquet*."

"Yes sir," said the witness. "My real name is Mai. Günter Mai. Captain Günter Mai, late of the *Abwehr* counterintelligence unit stationed at the Hôtel Lutétia in the Boulevard Raspail."

Now the pall of boredom lifted from the courtroom like a morning mist.

GÜNTER MAI had spent the past months at Boucher's house near Moret. That it should prove such a safe place of refuge, so close to Paris, seemed unlikely, but the care which Boucher had taken in establishing this retreat for his family was soon revealed. To the few locals he had had any contact with, he was merely a businessman whose work kept him in Paris a good deal. He had complete sets of papers for himself and his wife under the name of Campaux. He shaved off his beard, trimmed his hair and set about giving the appearance of a man taking a rest till the turmoil had settled enough for him to resume his work.

"I thought you didn't think anyone could wish you harm," said Mai ironically.

"There's always some mad fool," said Boucher. "For myself, I reckon I can take care of anything. But there's Hélène and the kiddies to think of. That's why I set up here in the first place."

"And very well you've done it."

"Yes. Foolproof, I'd say."

"But not Pajou-proof," reminded Mai.

Summer browned into autumn, blackened into winter. So certain was Mai that each day must be the one when they came looking for Boucher, or when his own thin pretence was pierced, that he felt no sense of time passing or of time stretching ahead.

"I should try to get away," he said to Boucher one night.

"Where to?"

"Switzerland," he said, without conviction.

"Yes," said Boucher eagerly. "Switzerland, that's what I thought. But it's too dangerous on your own, Günter. Wait till the baby comes and Hélène gets her strength back. Then we'll all go."

So he stayed, needing no persuading. The only place he really wanted to be was in Paris, to find out what had happened to Janine.

"She'll be all right," Boucher assured him. "Like me, tough as old rope."

"But the children. If she hasn't heard anything about the children..."

Boucher pressed his little daughter to him, but did not reply.

The new baby came early in January, a boy. Boucher wanted one of his names to be Günter but Mai advised against it.

"Edouard, then," said Boucher. "He shall have your French name at least." So the child became Michel Edouard Boucher.

At the end of January there was a second arrival. Pajou.

The little Géstapiste was in a pretty run-down condition, unkempt, unshaven. The left lens of his spectacles was cracked and there was a suppurating scar down his cheek.

"Why've you come here? To apologize? Where's my bloody car?"

"Miche, I'm sorry. Sorry for everything, sorry to disturb you now. But God, you've no idea how relieved I am to find you still here. My last hope! If anyone will help an old mate, it's Miche. I mean, look at the way you're helping the captain here. This is a real surprise, Captain, but I'm glad to see you looking so well . . ."

"Talk," Boucher said.

Pajou talked. It seemed he'd decided that Spain was the best place for him and had headed south in the stolen car with as much loot as he could carry. After narrowly evading the American and Free French forces who'd landed on the Mediterranean coast and were rapidly driving their way north, he'd reached the Spanish border, paid a large sum to a guide to take him over the Pyrenees, spent an exhausting and bewildering couple of nights on the mountain paths, woken on the second morning to find himself abandoned and all his baggage missing, and descended to the valley below to find himself not in the Basque country that he'd been promised, but back in Gascogny where he'd started. He'd returned to Paris because it was there that he'd left hidden the bulkier items of his war loot. But when he went to the warehouse he'd hidden it in, he found it was too late, it had gone. Worse, his presence had been reported, and so for the last week he'd been on the run, living rough, with his description in the hands of all the gendarmerie units.

"They're saying dreadful things about us, Miche," he concluded indignantly. "But we're innocent, aren't we?"

He stressed the we, making his meaning unambiguous. He wasn't asking for help and sanctuary. He was stating quite bluntly that if he didn't get it, Miche might as well give himself up too.

If Boucher had decided to slit Pajou's throat there and then, Mai would not have intervened. But the big redhead had no stomach for murder, and so the house at Moret got another guest, but one who had to remain hidden, for there was no explanation to cover his presence.

He was not good company. He drank everything he could lay his hands on and when in his cups he gave up his pretence at innocence and boasted of the disgusting things he'd done with nostalgic glee. "Oh yes, the day they try to put me on trial they'll hear some things about their precious heroes they'd rather not hear! No, they'll send me to Switzerland with a pension rather than risk putting me up in open court!"

"They won't bother with the expense of a trial," said Boucher. "They'll kill you in the streets."

"For what? For doing a job?" said Pajou, suddenly fearful. "I tell you,

Miche, they're trying everyone in Paris. Everyone! They've even got that skinny cousin of yours under arrest, the one you used to meet in the Balzac, Captain, and in the Jardin des Plantes."

He leered and winked at Mai, delighted to show off his intimate knowledge of everything that had gone on.

Mai couldn't speak. Boucher said, "Janine? She's arrested? For what?"

"She's been under arrest for months," said Pajou dismissively. "They've accused her of getting her husband killed, of betraying all his Resistance plans to the Boche, mainly you, Captain. Funny files those ones you kept, it seems!"

"They have the files?"

"Oh yeah. You should've burnt them, Captain. Better still, you shouldn't have written them in the first place."

Later, alone with Boucher, Mai sat in deep silence drinking more than his usual share of brandy.

"Give us a week," said Boucher suddenly.

"A week?"

"A week's start before you go back to Paris."

Mai made no effort to deny his intention. "I'd not say anything about you, Miche, you know that."

"Of course. But Pajou will, and you'll be taking him with you, I think. So. A week. And we'd better sort him out now. Once he gets wind that we're moving on, he'll be like a rat in a trap."

They went for Pajou at Gestapo hour the next morning. He sat up in bed, blinking shortsightedly at the sudden light.

"What's up?" he asked fearfully. "Are we being raided?"

"You are, Paj," said Boucher. "On your feet. No need to bother getting dressed."

The little Géstapiste obviously thought they were going to kill him. His face turned grey and his legs could hardly support him. Mai felt little sympathy. Pajou must have roused hundreds of his own countrymen at this hour. And Mai hadn't forgotten that it was Pajou who had delivered him into Fiebelkorn's hands.

When he realized they were only going to tie him up, his first reaction was relief. But once he grasped Mai's purpose he went wild.

"They'll lynch me," he screamed. "They'll lynch us both. We'll never see a court. And if we did, do you think I'm going to say anything?"

A few hours later the house was in turmoil as the Bouchers prepared to leave.

"Has anyone seen Antoinette?" asked Hélène.

"She's upstairs," said her husband. "Antoinette!"

He ran lightly upstairs to the nursery, but as he passed the door to Pajou's room he saw that it was slightly ajar. Carefully he pushed it fully open.

Pajou had managed to get one arm free and he had it locked tight around little Antoinette's neck. "A knife," he snarled. "Give me a knife, else she stops breathing."

"Sure, Paj," said Boucher easily. "Don't get excited. Here you are."

From his pocket he took a clasp knife like the one he'd given Pauli for Christmas. He pulled out the blade, then he proffered it, handle first. For a second the grip on the child's neck relaxed as Pajou's free hand reached out to take it. Then Miche spun the knife round in his fingers, and plunged it into Pajou.

A moment later he came out of the room nursing the little girl in his arms. Mai came up the stairs and took in what had happened in a glance. "Is she all right?" he asked anxiously.

"Oh yes, fine, aren't you, my love? But Pajou's dead. What will you do now? Will you still go back?"

"Oh yes," said Mai. "I must."

THEY TRIED TO STOP the trial. The prosecution wanted Mai arrested. The crowds wanted him lynched. The judge summoned the gendarmerie to restore order, and then came to his decision. The trial would go on.

"Where have you come from, Captain Mai?" he began courteously.

"I cannot say," said Mai.

"Let us leave that for the moment. Much has been said of your relationship with the prisoner. Can you explain what it was?"

"At first, I intended to use her as an agent. Later I changed my mind."

"Why?"

"I didn't think she would make a very good agent. She was—is—too open, too direct, too honest."

There was harsh laughter and incredulous whistling.

"I notice you don't say too patriotic?"

"She attacked me and abused me in our early meetings," said Mai. "Yes, I'd say she was patriotic. But I brought pressure to bear. I offered to help her get her husband released from imprisonment."

"In other words, Captain, you hoped to blackmail her into working for you?"

"Yes."

"But you changed your mind because you didn't think she could be of use?"

"Yes."

"Yet you continued to see her?"

"Yes. Accidentally. Incidentally. And I grew ... fond of her."

"Fond? Did she become your mistress?"

"No! Not in any real sense," said Mai.

"In what sense then? You slept together?"

"Only twice," he said in a low voice. "I forced her."

"You raped her, you mean?"

"No. Not physical force. By threats, promises. Blackmail, you called it."

"Once," said Janine. She'd been almost forgotten since Mai took the stand. Now every eye turned to her.

"Once it was against my will," she said in a listless voice. "The other time, not."

"I see," said the judge. "Apart from helping to get her husband released, what else did you do for the accused, Captain Mai?"

"I helped get her children out of Drancy," said Mai.

"Günter, where are the children? Do you know anything about the children?" demanded Janine, suddenly agitated.

"I don't know anything," said Mai sadly. "I'm sorry."

"Carry on, please, Captain Mai," said the judge.

"I helped get the children into the Free Zone, as it was then. And I protected Madame Simonian from arrest by the Gestapo."

"You did all this for two encounters, one forced, one willing, in four years?" said the judge incredulously. "You do not look like a romantic to me, Captain Mai. Surely there must have been some other consideration. Information? Betrayal?"

"No! Never!" said Mai emphatically.

"But your files ... these *are* your files? Would you like to examine them?" He pointed at the files before the State Prosecutor.

"No," said Mai. "I'm sure they're mine."

"They state categorically that the prisoner was your agent. What is more, in the matter of the betrayal of the meeting when her husband was shot down, there is a letter giving every detail of the arrangements—place, time, security—and it is signed by the prisoner, who *admits* she signed it. Is this true?"

"Yes, she signed it. But she had no idea that the meeting had anything to do with her husband. Neither had I." He looked at Janine and repeated with emphasis, "Neither had I."

"So why ... ?"

"Her children were imprisoned once more, this time by the Gestapo in Lyon. I wanted to get a release order. To do this, I needed incontrovertible proof that she was a valuable agent of the *Abwehr*. The Gestapo would not be easily convinced."

The judge consulted his notes. "It is my understanding that this meeting was in fact raided by the Gestapo. If you were on such bad terms with them, why did you cooperate with them in this operation?"

"I didn't. They got the information independently."

"And you, Captain Mai? If, as you say, the prisoner did not give you the information, where did you get it?"

"I got it from the Gestapo," he said wearily. "Unofficially."

312

There was a burst of contemptuous laughter.

The judge shook his head and said, "How unfortunate. I thought at least you were going to offer us an alternative traitor, someone you couldn't name, perhaps, or someone who was dead."

"No," said Mai, "I'll stick to the truth. I got the information indirectly from the Gestapo. When I got it, I had no idea how *they* had obtained it in the first place. I only found out the truth about that a short while ago, from a man called Pajou."

There was a stir in the courtroom.

"Alphonse Pajou, the Géstapiste?" said the judge. "This man is high on the state's wanted list. If you have information as to his whereabouts..."

"He's dead," said Mai.

"Dead? So this man who you claim told you the truth of how the Gestapo got their information is not available for questioning?"

"I said, he is dead."

The judge frowned. He'd bent over backwards to be fair, but now was the time to point out a few legal realities.

"You must see, Captain Mai, whatever you claim Pajou said, it can really put us very little further forward. The court has been patient..."

"*He* told the Gestapo," said Mai. His finger pointed without emphasis or histrionics towards the witness benches. "Valois. It was Christian Valois."

There was a second of silence, then a howl of outrage went up. Valois didn't move, but he turned deathly pale.

Mai looked towards Janine and saw what his accusation had done to her. She was leaning forward towards Valois, her head shaking, her features twisted in disbelief. Mai in his turn instinctively reached his arms out to her but she did not see him. Perhaps to the spectators the gesture looked like one of defiance, for suddenly half a dozen men came rushing forward. Before the court officers could protect him Mai was hurled to the ground. As kicks drove into his ribs and belly, he heard the judge crying, "Clear the court!"

Then a steel-capped boot, swung with all the strength of four years of hate, crashed against his head, and judge, Janine, court and all went spinning away to a single point of light.

2

It was Spring.

A detachment of Americans mopping up small pockets of resistance on the east bank of the Rhine came under fire as they emerged from the shelter of a pine forest. They hit the ground and looked for their target. Ahead was a castle like an illustration from a children's book. An old man stood before it with a smoking shotgun. Before the soldiers could make up their minds whether to kill him or not, a woman's voice called imperiously in German, and the old man threw his weapon down.

The woman was not as old as the man but her face was worn by suffering. One of the soldiers who spoke German talked to her, translating for his sergeant.

"She says she owns the joint. She says this guy here is her gamekeeper. She says all her other servants are long gone. She wants to use our radios to seek news of her son. She says the Gestapo took him away last summer saying he'd tried to kill Hitler or something."

The sergeant shook his head and began to laugh.

"Sarge. Over here!" cried a soldier urgently. He was standing by the open door of what looked like a stable block.

"What's up? Trouble?" called the sergeant, hefting his submachine-gun.

"No, sarge. You'd best come and see."

CHRISTIAN VALOIS sat in his room, cleaning a Luger machine pistol. He had been heroic, there was no denying that. He'd finally overcome that degrading physical fear and become a real hero. Now there was nothing he could not do.

For a while after the Boche's intervention at the trial, he had found his old trembling had come back again, but now . . . he held up the gleaming barrel. Steady as a rock.

It had been good to see the way in which the Boche's accusations had driven the people into a fury of indignation. Even those appointed to question him had been deferential and apologetic. And the judge had ordained that it should be done privately, to spare him the indignity of a public examination.

He'd told them the truth, that he loved Jean-Paul like a brother. As for the rest, his scars and his medals surely attested to the absurdity of calling him a collaborator! They had seemed satisfied.

And he himself, was he satisfied? He should be. A long and illustrious career lay ahead of him. If Marie-Rose's death had not been expiation enough, then a lifetime of service to France must surely be. What did he have to reproach himself for? He'd been forced to work for the Germans by their promise to kill Marie-Rose if he didn't. When he stopped working for them, they kept their promise. He had done all he could to stop Jean-Paul from going to that meeting, just as he had made sure that, whoever else he betrayed, Jean-Paul's operations always went unreported. It had been his friend's own arrogance which had put him in the firing line. And Delaplanche, if only he had stuck to his revolutionary plots and not diverted to check precisely what had happened to Marie-Rose.

Which left Janine. There was no doubt she was the one who had really betrayed Jean-Paul. Lying in bed with that Boche's hands upon her while her husband ... Perhaps even if he, Valois, hadn't told the Gestapo about the meeting, the *Abwehr* would have been there to arrest and kill.

No, there was very little to reproach himself for, he thought as he reassembled the gun with practised ease. He had tried to die and his sacrifice had been refused. All that remained now was to return to the court when the trial recommenced, and give his evidence, and then he could begin his life's work once more. And Janine?

That was for the court to decide, not him.

The machine pistol was assembled now. His finger pulled the trigger almost absently.

THERE WAS BLUE SKY and the promise of a glorious day on the morning that they brought Janine back to the court for judgment.

Janine was indifferent to the climate. Mai's intervention, far from comforting her, had cast her down into the absolute depths of depression. How could she take comfort from what was impossible to believe anyway—that Christian had been a traitor and betrayed the meeting where Jean-Paul was killed? Even when her father assured her that there had been talk in Resistance circles that someone like Christian, whose sister ended up in Gestapo hands, had to be regarded as a risk, she was unconvinced. But all speculation had ended with the terrible news of Christian's death.

"At least be grateful you have a man who loves you so much that he is willing to sacrifice his own liberty and risk his life for you," said Claude, desperate to pull his daughter back from the edge of the pit she was staring into.

"Günter, you mean? If he had stayed away, Christian would be alive and all this would be over. And what have I got to do with love any more?"

Sharing his fears with his wife, Claude got the reply, "It's the children, can't you see that? She's stopped talking about them. She's finally given up hope."

Now Janine stood in the gloomy courtroom and looked with vast indifference towards the judge. It was a very different atmosphere from her last time there. Determined not to risk a repetition of those disturbances, the judge had denied admission to all except Claude and Louise Crozier.

He didn't waste any time.

"Janine Simonian, on the principal charge of supplying information to the *Abwehr* which resulted in the capture or death of many members of the FFI, it is the judgment of this court that you are not guilty."

There was a shriek of relief and delight from Louise, choked off as the judge glared at her angrily. But sounds of a more distant disturbance outside the door continued. The judge checked his exasperation and continued with his judgment.

"With regard to the subsidiary charge that you gave aid and comfort to the illegal occupying forces of the German army, it is the judgment of this court that you are guilty."

He had to raise his voice to make himself heard above the growing level of noise outside.

"It is the sentence of this court that you will undergo five years national degradation. In case you do not know, let me explain what that entails, if I can make myself heard above this din. Officer, would you step outside and arrest whoever is causing that disturbance?"

The gendarme on duty before the big double door turned and began to unlock it.

The judge went on, "During this period you will be deprived of all civic rights, the right to vote, the right ..." but for the first time Janine's attention had moved from him. Slowly she turned her head towards the back of the court.

The gendarme had got the doors partly open, admitting a shaft of brilliant sunlight and a voice which demanded admission. There was the sound of a scuffle, voices raised in anger, a cry of pain, and suddenly the gendarme was thrust aside as a man burst into the court.

Once inside he skidded to a stop and peered uncertainly towards the judge, obviously finding the gloom within blinding, after the dazzle outside.

"And who the devil are you, monsieur? What is your business here?" demanded the judge furiously.

The man did not answer straight away. He was a strange-looking figure, not very tall, with a long black rabbinical beard and dressed in American army fatigues which were several sizes too large for him. He screwed up his bright eyes as they focused on Janine, as if in an effort to recognize her.

She moved her head, suddenly feeling faint with an emotion she did not dare name. The movement seemed to act as confirmation, for now the strange newcomer laughed and, turning to the judge, bowed and said, "Your honour. Melchior's my name. Magus that I am, bearing gifts of gold, from the East I come!" And with a wave of his hand which was indeed oriental, he directed their eyes to the doorway.

Janine looked and could see nothing but the glow of diffused sunlight. She closed her eyes, shook her head and tried again. Her heart was beating so fast and so loud that it drowned all other noise.

And now for the first time she saw a movement in that golden glow, a shape, two shapes, two small shapes advancing uncertainly, hand in hand. She felt as if she were drawing them forward with her eyes, that one flicker, one blink, could send them drifting back into the dark once more, beyond all hope of recall.

But at last they stepped shyly into the solid world of the courtroom, and sound came back to her ears, breath to her lungs, and life to her heart once more.

316

3

They brought Günter Mai out of the hospital as dawn was breaking. His head was still heavily bandaged and beneath his shirt his cracked ribs were swathed so tight that breathing was not so much painful as almost impossible.

In the vestibule, two military policemen were waiting to escort him to a POW camp. There was a great deal of form-filling before he was satisfactorily transferred from civil to military custody. Then he was briefly in the open air before being helped into the back of a truck.

The truck moved towards the gate.

"Are we going far?"

"Far enough. But it'll be nice for you to be back with your mates, won't it? Sort of a homecoming."

He seemed to mean his comment to be friendly. Mai tried a smile, but he felt depressed. What kind of homecoming was possible for him when all that he wanted lay in this city he was now leaving?

As the truck passed through the gates and swung across the road to turn left, the sergeant pulled open the canvas flap over the tailboard.

"Some people were keen to see the back of you," he said enigmatically.

Mai glanced out of the truck. It was true. There was a small group of spectators on the pavement outside the gate. Four people: a man, a woman, two children. His mind fought against what it was sure was the madness of recognition. He blinked his eyes as though he had stared into the sun. They were still there, the illusion as strong as ever.

He tried to speak but couldn't. The truck was already beginning to move away. He let his gaze run swiftly over Claude Crozier's amiable features, stern now in the dawn light; down to little Céci's round face, her mouth open wide in a yawn; across to Pauli's sallow oval, his eyes unblinking and wary; and finally up to Janine. Her face was thin, so very thin. Even the scarf bound tightly round her head couldn't disguise the ravages of assault and imprisonment.

But there was life in her features now, life triumphing over the deathly despair he had seen in court. He recalled her running down the path in the Jardin des Plantes and turning to wave like a young girl leaving her lover.

She smiled now and as the truck gathered speed, she raised her hand briefly from Pauli's shoulder and waved.

He waved back. It didn't feel like waving goodbye.

Now they were tiny, anonymous figures in a long empty street. And now they were gone altogether. But still he peered out of the truck, like a tourist anxious not to miss any of the sights. The route took them across the city, empty at this hour. They crossed the Seine, they passed beneath the gilded Victory on the Colonne du Palmier, they passed the Louvre where

Christian Valois had made his first act of resistance. And then they drove past the Tuileries gardens where he, Günter Mai, had made his first declaration of love to Janine Simonian. They climbed the Champs-Elysées, passing the café where he had sat and talked with Michel Boucher, till they reached the Arc de Triomphe and the Eternal Flame.

He took one last look out over the city. It was coming to life now after the long dark night. God knows what these Frenchmen would make of the future. He'd never been able to understand them. But this was nothing to the problems of understanding he feared his own countrymen might be setting the Allied armies as they drove deeper into Germany's dark heart. He shuddered and let the flap drop.

"Seen enough?" said the sergeant.

"For now," said Mai.

"For *now?* You mean you're planning to come back? I'll say this for you Fritzes. You don't know when you're beaten!"

"Oh yes, we do. It's knowing when you've won that's difficult," said Günter Mai.

REGINALD HILL

"I wanted to write a book about war that wasn't just about fighting," Reginald Hill told us when we interviewed him about his latest novel. "I was also very interested in the moral dilemmas that collaboration poses."

He first began researching *The Collaborators* when Klaus Barbie had just been captured and there was much talk of what was going to come to light at his trial. "It was thought that all sorts of cats would be let out of the bag—but in fact they never were. What surprises me is the extent to which the French are still reluctant to talk about collaboration."

While writing the novel, Reginald Hill spent several days in Paris checking up on historical facts, getting to know the layout of the streets, and generally soaking up the atmosphere. "You never really know what you're looking for until you get to a place," he confided. "In the Resistance Museum I found interesting accounts of the trials of French citizens suspected of collaboration."

Famous among these were the two trials of French *résistant* René Hardy. "Hardy was captured by the Gestapo then released, but he was later suspected of having gained his freedom by betraying the resistance leader Jean Moulin. Though he was acquitted twice he remained a controversial figure right up to his death in 1987."

Hill stresses that there was at least as much heroism as collaboration in wartime France, and that his purpose in writing *The Collaborators* was not to show the French in a bad light. "It was the drama of betrayal that interested me—the ways in which the instinct for sheer survival can make people collaborate. It's a problem we haven't had in this country." Does he think he might have collaborated? "I would have been much too young at the time, so fortunately I wouldn't have had to face that question!"

Hill also writes under the name Patrick Ruell, as he did in the case of *The Long Kill*, a previous Condensed Book selection. He's already at work at home in Doncaster on a new book, but says he is superstitious, and won't reveal plots ahead of time . . .

A BOY CALLED
BRACKEN

A CONDENSATION OF THE BOOK BY
Elizabeth Webster

ILLUSTRATED BY TED LEWIN

Bracken, a gipsy boy, is a wizard with animals, especially sick ones. Anything wild, lost or injured, ends up in his careful hands.

Perhaps that is why he understands Jake Farrant, a world-weary reporter who has come to a cottage in Gloucestershire to reconcile himself to the fact that he has only a few months left to live.

In Bracken's wise and thoughtful company, Jake's dull acceptance of his fate begins to evaporate like the morning dew. He discovers the fragile beauty of the world around him—and the hope that lies in its constant renewal.

CHAPTER ONE

The leaf twirled down and fell at his feet. He stooped and picked it up, and held it between his fingers. Even a tree must die, he thought. Then he looked at the leaf—young and new and green—torn off by some passing bird or a small, tugging breeze. It must be spring, then, he thought. Not autumn at all. Not the dying year.

He realized suddenly that he never really noticed the seasons—dashing about across the world chasing after news, then coming home here to the busy London newspaper office. Was it really spring? The seasons were different out there in the field. Rain fell for months on end, or the sun burned on endlessly in an unforgiving sky. He certainly never had time to stop and look at a leaf.

But here? Here the sky was soft, and the leaf in his hand was green.

He moved on, and his feet took him automatically to Fleet Street. He climbed the stairs to the busy newsroom, nodding to the doorman as he passed. "Morning, George," he said.

The doorman smiled. "Morning, Mr. Farrant, sir." He liked Jake Farrant. Most people did. Although he was such a famous television personality, covering each new crisis as it came along, he never forgot to greet George by name when he came home from an assignment.

Jake paused inside the newsroom, looking round with a curious sense of unreality. Phones rang; teleprinters clacked; heads stooped over desks. No one really noticed him—they were too busy.

He gave a rueful shrug and went on across the big, noisy room towards the inner sanctum of the news editor, Bob Harris. He could see him beyond the open door, directing a stream of angry words to some unfortunate recipient at the other end of the telephone line.

Jake cocked an eyebrow in the editor's direction and inquired of the harassed journalist at the end desk, "Bob busy?"

Bill Franklyn, one of Jake's closest friends, gave a despairing grin. "When isn't he?" Then, seeing something strange in Jake's face, he added, "He'll see *you*, though. Anything I can do?"

Jake shook his head. "Not now. Come for a drink after?"

"After what?" asked Bill.

But Jake had already gone inside and shut the door.

"Morning, Jake," said his editor, finishing his decisive tirade and slamming down the phone. "Did I send for you?"

"No, I'm here of my own free will. Bob, I want to resign."

"Resign?" said his editor. "You can't be serious!"

"Perfectly."

"But"—he sounded nonplussed—"you're my most senior foreign correspondent, the best I've ever had! What is it? More money?"

"No. Nothing like that." Jake stood looking down at Bob Harris with affection and regret. "It's just ... I need a breather."

"Writing another book?"

He hesitated. "Maybe."

Bob looked at him searchingly. Something in Jake's face disturbed him. It was as good-looking as ever—perhaps a little thinner than usual? And his eyes, which Bob knew from past assignments saw an awful lot, were as steady and clear as ever, and as deep a grey—or were they even darker? He couldn't put his finger on it, but there was something about him, something almost fragile.

"So what's biting you?" Bob Harris asked abruptly.

Jake shrugged. "I just want to go away and think."

"Go away where?"

"I don't know. Just away. I need some time alone." Time, he thought. I need time.

"You can take as long a leave as you like, but your resignation I won't accept! You can stay on full salary till you know your plans."

Jake looked embarrassed. "I may not have any plans."

"Don't be absurd," said Bob briskly. "Everyone has plans. In any case, what would you do for money?"

"Live on my savings, and maybe write a new book. I don't need much."

Bob snorted. "A likely story!"

Jake turned to go. "I'll be in touch," he said.

For some reason that he could not explain, Bob got to his feet and grasped Jake by the arm. "Take care of yourself!" he said.

In the main newsroom Bill Franklyn took one look at Jake's face and sprang up and followed him outside. They were joined on the way by

Manny Feldman, another of Jake's closest colleagues, and they all went down together to the pub, where everyone met at lunchtime. Greetings were hurled at Jake from all sides as he pushed his way past the crowd to a small snug at the back.

"Quieter here," he said, and bought drinks all round.

Bill settled his long legs under the table and said, "What's all this about, Jake?"

"All what?" asked Jake, trying to sound casual and innocent.

"All this about resigning." Bill's voice was flat. "Walls have ears, you know."

There was silence for a moment. How can I tell my friends I am going to die? Jake was thinking. It sounds so absurd. How can I say I'm not good old Jake any more, resourceful in danger and reliable in a crisis? Jake, the experienced campaigner, the good companion everyone can trust. It isn't true any more. I've got to leave my work now to someone else, someone who isn't going to die on their hands. But I can't tell them, he thought. It would only embarrass them profoundly.

"I'm going away," Jake said.

"Going away *where?*" asked Manny.

"I don't know. Somewhere quiet." He suddenly felt a little dizzy and took a gulp of his beer. "I must find a place."

"My sister's got a cottage she doesn't use," said Bill slowly. "You're welcome to it."

"Where?"

"Gloucestershire, in some valley in the Cotswolds."

"Hills," murmured Jake dreamily. "And an English spring!"

"You're going soft at the edges!" said Manny.

Jake laughed.

"I'll give you the address," went on Bill severely, "on one condition. You keep in touch. You hear?"

"Oh, I will," agreed Jake. "I will."

When he left them, with the address of the cottage in his pocket, his two friends looked after him with concern.

"What's on his mind?" asked Manny, his long, mobile face looking greatly troubled.

"I don't know," answered Bill, sounding even more troubled than Manny looked. "But I suppose he'll tell us in his own good time."

THE COTTAGE STOOD halfway down the valley, with its back to the beech-woods, facing southwest. It was small and square, built of honey coloured stone, and its windows reflected the setting sun. Below its overgrown garden and a broken boundary wall was a steep grassy slope leading down to the valley floor. Here, threading through sedges and flowery meadows, was a meandering stream that flowed into a small reed-fringed lake. The brown water was so still that the moorhens and coots chugging across it made little arrows on the surface. Around it the hills climbed in springy rises of turf and wedges of beechwood. It was very quiet and very beautiful.

Jake put down his bag and sighed with pleasure. Such stillness and peace! Surely here he could come to terms with what he had to face?

He had left his car at the top of the lane and walked down the stony path to the cottage gate. Even that small walk had tired him, and he closed his eyes for a moment in silent rebellion. He wasn't used to weakness. Until now his body had always accepted challenges and hardships without complaint. But now?

Resolutely he opened his eyes and found himself looking into the face of a merry brown boy who was perched on the gate, swinging a leg and smiling.

"Hello," said the boy. "Staying long?"

"Maybe," said Jake in surprise.

"Could get you some milk?" suggested the boy. "And eggs?"

Jake nodded. "Good idea."

The boy looked pleased. He slid off the gate and cast a practised eye at the clear sky above the westering sun. "Be fine tomorrow."

"That's good," said Jake, picking up his bag and pushing open the gate. When he turned round, the boy was gone.

Inside, the cottage was very simple. There was a big living room with rough stone walls, and a small kitchen at the back. The furniture was dark oak, and there were two rag rugs on the polished wood floor. Upstairs were two smallish bedrooms, both looking out over the sloping hillside down to the little lake below. Behind the head of the stairs, along the slanting roof wall, was a bathroom.

Jake looked round approvingly, and chose the bedroom with the widest view from its window. It was furnished sparsely with a bed, a chest of drawers, a chair and a soft brown wool rug.

There was running water in the cottage, but no electricity. However, there was a small gas cooker in the kitchen, and the bathwater appeared to be heated by the living-room fire. What happened in summer? he wondered. Cold baths, he supposed. In any case, he might not be there by the summer.

Before his thoughts could progress further down that unprofitable track, there was a knock at the open door.

The brown boy stood there, smiling. He was carrying a can of milk, a loaf of homemade bread and a basket of eggs. "Farmer's wife, Mrs. Bayliss, says pay at the end of the week."

"Good," Jake said, nodding.

"Firewood's in the shed," added the boy. He seemed all brown and gold, standing there in the setting sun. His hair was tousled and brown, his eyes were brown flecked with gold, and the freckles on his nose made a light dusting of brown-gold on his tanned skin. Even his clothes were a faded earthy brown.

"Could show you the swans," he said as he turned to go. "Tomorrow?"

"I'd like that," agreed Jake. Already, he thought, I'm looking forward to something. He smiled to himself and went indoors.

HE WOKE EARLY the next morning, just as a few sleepy birds were beginning to murmur. He didn't know all their voices, but wasn't that a drowsy wood pigeon? Then a different, more wide-awake bird tried out some clear, fluted notes and whistles. A blackbird, he was sure. As he lay listening, a small shower of pebbles hit his window. He got out of bed, trying not to notice his growing slowness, and went to peer out of the window.

Below him, looking up with a grin of welcome, was the boy.

"Come on," he said. "Best time of day!"

Jake dressed and went outside into a newly washed world. Dew lay on every leaf, and his feet made silver footprints on the grass.

"That's my blackbird," said the boy, with a jerk of his thumb towards the top of a pear tree. "Fell out of the nest last year. Everyone told me to wring his neck. But he lived! I gave him bread and milk at first, then chick feed. He'd sit on my shoulder and put his head in my hair and go to sleep."

"In your *hair?*"

The boy rubbed a hand over his brown curly head. "Thought I was his mum, I expect. One day I came back and found him banging to and fro against his cage, trying to get out. I knew it was time then, so I let him out, but he'd come down to eat if I banged a spoon on a cup. Still does." He looked up into the creamy blossoms on the pear tree and whistled at the bird. It whistled back.

"See? He knows me still. Kept him alive all through the winter. Lived in your garden shed. We'd a lot of snow come January. Real hard on the birds, it was. Nothing to eat. I'd bring him something every day." He took some stale bread out of his pocket, crumbled it and tossed it on the ground. "Got a mate now ... and a nest with five eggs."

The blackbird in the pear tree cocked a beady eye in their direction and let out a joyous trill of song. Then it flew down and started to investigate the scattered crumbs.

"Tame, he is," commented the boy. "Morning, Beaky. You're right, it's a grand old day." He gave a skip of delight and went on across the turf, with Jake beside him.

I must be bewitched, Jake was thinking. I don't know this boy, not even his name, and here I am at five in the morning being led into mischief like a child. And, what's more, I'm enjoying it!

They went on down the slope. The lake was still—not a ripple stirring.

The boy put a finger to his lips and motioned to Jake to crouch down beside him on the grassy bank.

"Wait," muttered the boy. "The swans'll be here soon."

Jake's eyes moved to the curious, untidy clump of twigs at which the boy was gazing so intently. Suddenly the whole quiet world of the lake was disturbed, and a host of wild duck rose up from the reeds. Jake was enchanted. The air seemed to be alive with wings.

"Listen," whispered the boy. "They're coming!"

And then Jake heard them. At first it was the faintest thrum in the wind, but it grew and grew until the great wingbeats were a whole symphony of glorious, throbbing sound. The noise of their passing washed over him, and he looked up and saw them against the morning light—four great white swans, their slender necks outstretched, their wings beating in perfect unison.

He and the boy stayed there a long time, spellbound, until the swans had gone and tranquillity had returned to the little lake.

At last the boy stirred and reached out a hand. "Come on," he said. He pulled Jake to his feet and they wandered back through sunlight and slanting shadow to the cottage gate.

"Coming in to breakfast?" asked Jake.

The boy shook his head, an expression almost of regret crossing his face. But then he grinned cheerfully. "Not today. Gotta go now. I could come tomorrow, though?"

Jake nodded, smiling too. He wondered how he could thank the boy for the miracle he had shown him. But before he could think of a way, the boy had gone.

THAT FIRST DAY Jake spent his time getting in stores for the cottage and exploring his small domain. He walked up the path and took his car to the village shop. He didn't feel like eating much these days, but there was the boy to consider. He looked like being a frequent visitor, and boys were hungry creatures.

He loaded up his car, smiled at the village postmistress who was also the shopkeeper, and drove slowly home along the sun-dappled, leafy road.

He spent a peaceful afternoon laying out his books and setting up his typewriter on a table near the living-room windows. He had brought a radio with him, and he put it on for the news. But already those world-shaking events in which his old life had been so embroiled seemed far away and unimportant. Outside the cottage the evening sun was shining and the blackbird was calling.

He went out to have a look at his tangled garden. It was spring. Maybe he should try to clear the ground and grow something? His fingers itched to get at that jungle of greenery. He would probably not be there to see the results, but all the same . . .

"I could scythe that old grass for you," said the boy's voice at his elbow. "And we could clear a bit for veg, but I like flowers best." He tugged at Jake's sleeve. "Look! The snowdrops is over, but there's primroses under the leaves, and wild daffs, see? And the bluebells is just coming."

Jake stopped to look at the pale creamy stars of the primroses. "So young," he said obscurely.

The boy grinned. "They're young, all right. Only just come up. It's a terrible old world they've come into. Feet trampling all over the place. Tractors and sprays everywhere. But they're safe enough here."

He spoke as if the flowers were people he knew, Jake thought, innocent people looking for a safe, quiet place to live. He remembered the long lines of refugees struggling down the roads from the last battle he had seen. But this was a different battle on a different battleground, and he was part of it.

"It's worse for the creatures, though," said the boy. "Hounded to death, most of 'em." Sparks of anger flickered in his eyes. "Like the badgers. They're nearly all gone from here now. Gassed or dug out."

"Why?" Jake asked.

"It's an old idea that they can give TB to cows." The boy snorted. "If you ask me, it's all rubbish. Badgers were here long before dairy herds, and no one's been able to prove that the poor old badgers is to blame. Anyway, they does a lot of good, badgers does."

Jake nodded soberly. "You're a good champion."

The boy kicked a stone with his foot and went on reminiscently, "I had a fox cub last year. Found him curled up in a barn, half dead with cold. I s'pose someone shot the vixen. I kept him till he was strong enough to manage on his own. You can't keep wild creatures too long, you know, or they can't ever go back."

"What happened to him?"

The boy shrugged. "I let him go when he was ready. He may've survived, if the hunt didn't get him, or one of the farmers. He was bound to pinch a chicken sometime. Can't blame him, can you? Everything would be fair game to him, see?" His voice did not sound particularly sad. It was the way things were, and you had to accept it. "Things live and things die," he added philosophically. "When I was little, I used to cry about it. I don't any more."

Jake had been looking at him strangely. Now he asked, "Do you have a name?"

The boy laughed. "Two or three, but you couldn't pronounce them. We're Travellers, you see."

Travellers, thought Jake. I've been a traveller too for most of my working life, though not in your sense. Aloud, he said, "Romanies, you mean?"

The boy hesitated. "We come from the Rom, yes, so our grandfather said. We came down from Hungary—or it might have been Poland—a long, long time ago. We were called the Musicians then."

"When did you come to England?"

"A long time ago, even before my da was born. We still go south for the winter, after the hop picking."

"South? Back to Europe?"

He nodded. "Spain, or sometimes Africa, where it's warm. And we come back in the spring. We follow the sun like the *vadni ratsa*, the wild geese."

"But you stayed here last winter, through the snow? You told me about the blackbird in the shed."

"Yes. One of us was too sick to travel, so we stayed. It was terribly cold." He shivered, remembering more than the hard winter. "And then our grandmother died. We had to burn her *varda*, her wagon. It was the last of the old *vardas* in our family. They was too rickety and slow for travelling, though I liked the horses better than motorcars! My da still keeps a few *grais*, horses, cos he likes them best too!"

For a moment the brown, gold-flecked eyes were sombre and far away. But then he was his laughing self again. "Anyways, now it's spring, and we have a new trailer, and the sun is shining!"

"Yes," persisted Jake, fascinated, "but what do they *call* you?"

"Sometimes it's Kazimir, like my da, sometimes it's Jerczy. The boys at one of the schools I went to called me Jumper—because of Jerczy, see? And because I could jump high." He gave a little leap into the air.

Jake grinned. "So you do go to school occasionally?"

"Sometimes—when we're in one place long enough, and if they've got room for us. Or if there isn't a horse fair. Or it's a wet day!"

A conspiratorial grin passed between them. Jake was escaping from something too. But he told himself that he ought to make responsible noises about the boy's future. "You could learn things that might be useful."

The boy stared out beyond him at the wide countryside, suddenly quite serious. "I can read books and I figure better than my da. But where would I learn more than this?" He swept a brown hand around from horizon to valley floor.

Where indeed? thought Jake, and resolved to say no more. "You still haven't told me what to call you."

"Our family name is Bracsas—it means a viola player. The people round here call me That Bracken Boy. It's the nearest they can get to Bracsas." He grinned at Jake with sudden mischief. "And my da says as I was born in the bracken, it suits me very well!"

Jake laughed. Then he tried it out, almost shyly. "Bracken?"

"That's me!" The boy gave a delighted little twirl on his toes and cast a practised eye over the tangled wilderness that had once been a cottage garden. "I'll fetch the old scythe from your shed," he said. Then he paused and looked at Jake. "You better just watch, this time. You can rake tomorrow. You done enough today."

Jake's eyebrows shot up in astonishment. "What—?"

The boy smiled and laid his brown fingers on Jake's arm. "When a creature is tired, it rests," he said gently. "Stands to reason. Besides, I got a lot to show you yet!"

Before Jake could answer, Bracken had darted off to the shed and returned with a rickety wooden chair and an ancient scythe. In a dream, Jake allowed himself to be settled in a small island of green while the boy worked round him in ever widening circles.

At last most of the jungle lay flat in pale, cut swathes, and the sweet scent of drying grass filled the air. "Gotta go now," said the boy. "We're moving the *grais* tomorrow, but I'll come the morning after, if that's all right?"

"Bracken," said Jake, "thanks for all this." He waved an arm to include the cut grass, the sunny hillside and the darkening lake below.

Bracken's smile grew strangely adult and tender. "Might as well enjoy life while you can," he said, and went off into the twilight without another word.

THE NEXT TIME, Jake was awake before the shower of pebbles. Pain had assailed him in the night, and for a while he had been occupied with trying to master it. He knew that there would come a day when it would get worse, but he didn't want to think about that yet. He had other things to occupy his thoughts, and they were strangely comforting.

There was Bracken, for instance. His infectious joy of life, his deep love of the countryside, the revelations Jake was experiencing in his company. *Things live and things die*, said his tranquil voice in Jake's ear. Being with him, Jake began to realize that he was part of the pattern too, and that death was not something terrible and final but a natural sequence in the long, long life cycle of the world around him. I don't believe I'm so afraid of it any more, he said to himself with wonder. It will happen when it happens—and meanwhile, Bracken is right, I might as well enjoy myself while I can!

He fell to wondering about the boy himself. Where did he live? Hadn't he said something about a new trailer? A caravan, then. How many people were there? What did they all do? And then there was Bracken's voice— light and lilting, certainly not Gloucestershire, but not foreign, either. Jake spoke a smattering of a few languages picked up on his travels, including a little Polish and Hungarian. But, he suspected, Bracken and his family would not speak either nowadays, if they ever had. They had probably left those countries behind generations ago. Romany was their second language, he supposed, and even that was dying out. And yet there was something a little strange about the boy's voice—the way he spoke, which was sometimes quite educated and adult and sometimes carelessly childish; that gentle, laughter-laced voice, too quiet to frighten any creature, too full of music to be ordinary, sometimes speaking tranquilly of things that Jake had scarcely dared to put into thought himself . . .

When I was little, I used to cry about it. I don't any more.

No, thought Jake. No tears. I'm going to live every day to the full. I'm going to look at everything, see everything, do everything while I can, and be thankful. The shower of pebbles came then, and Bracken's lilting voice called up from the garden, "The light's growing; come on out!"

This time, Bracken did not take him to the lake. They went side by side into the beechwoods, where the new young leaves were just beginning to unfurl. The light was still dim among the tall silver-grey trunks of the trees, and the air smelled of moss and last year's leaf mould and fungus. Above them the birds were already trying out their morning songs.

Bracken and Jake did not stay in the woods but began to climb—past the tall rows of beeches, past ivy-covered stumps of old, fallen trees and high sandy banks. Bracken paused often to give Jake time to breathe, and always covered it by pointing out some new thing for him to look at. And though Jake wasn't fooled, he didn't mind.

"Nearly there!" said Bracken at last. "Just in time for sunrise!"

Jake could see that the trees were thinning. Beyond them was a grassy rise leading to the top of the hill. The sky was awash with pale rose, and a few flamingo clouds were drifting high above the horizon.

Swiftly Bracken pulled Jake after him to the crest of the hill and stood beside him on the highest point, looking out. Around them lay fold on fold of Cotswold hills, blue in the distance, brown and green and golden on their nearer flanks. Jake seemed to be standing on the edge of the world, and he could see the whole curve of the sky and the whole round bowl of the earth as it fell away from the rolling hills to the deep, mist-filled valleys below. Great dark beech woods gave way to gently swelling pastures with clusters of white sheep upon them, and far away to the west he caught a glint of the silver Severn River winding its way down to the sea.

"Look over there," breathed the boy, pointing towards a tall rounded hill facing east. As he spoke, a thin, brilliant line of light seemed to touch the smooth curve of the hill's brow. Then the sky above it flamed with fire, and the line of light grew ever more vivid until the eye was dazzled . . . and the sun's bright disc rose over the rim of the world.

Jake had seen many sunrises on his travels, but somehow never one like this. The pure air, the blue, sleeping valleys, the white mist wreathing the lower slopes of the beech woods, the vibrant green of the new turf under his feet, the sound of an early lark spiralling upwards and, above all, the great wash of fiery colour—all this untouched, unspoiled beauty left him breathless and enraptured. He felt like the lark, still climbing on beating wings, still pouring out ecstasy to the sky—except that he could not sing.

But Bracken seemed to know his mind. He knew it was hard to come down from the skies, and after a while he sat down cross-legged on the grass and drew Jake down beside him. "We can watch the valley waking up. It'll be warm in the sun."

Jake suddenly remembered something and felt in his pockets. "I brought some bread and cheese, and some apples." He glanced at the boy. "I get hungry in the mornings."

"So do I," said Bracken, and they sat together on the scented turf, happily munching and looking down at the valleys and little hills below them, while the sun climbed in the sky.

CHAPTER TWO

Back in London in the busy newsroom, Bill Franklyn got up from his desk and went to see his editor. "Bob," he said. "Manny and I are worried about Jake."

"I don't think there's anything we can do," said Bob Harris. "He's made up his mind to go off on his own. We've got to respect that."

"Yes, but ... he may need help." Bill's kindly, worried eyes met his editor's in mute anxiety.

Bob nodded. "So he may. But we can't force him to accept it."

Bill was not convinced. "D'you know who his doctor is?" he asked bluntly.

The editor thought for a moment. "It used to be Lawson, in Harley Street. They are old friends, I believe." His face reflected Bill's grave concern. "Let me know what happens," he said. "Maybe we can do something useful."

ANDREW LAWSON was a famous and busy specialist, but he had been friends with Jake Farrant since his houseman days, and he agreed to see Bill and Manny informally over a drink.

"I must warn you, though," he said gravely when they met, looking at them over the top of his glass of sherry, "I'm not at liberty to discuss a patient's condition with anyone, however well intentioned!"

"We know that," agreed Manny. "It's just that we're worried about Jake. He was so good at his job, and he loved it. But he's suddenly chucked it all, gone off and buried himself in the country."

"What we want to know," said Bill, attempting to discover the truth without asking the forbidden question, "is ... is he likely to need help in the near future?"

The specialist's grave look softened. "Yes, I'm afraid he is."

"H-how soon?" asked Bill.

"I should say within the next three months," said Lawson, his voice suddenly deep with compassion. "I'm afraid our friend Jake left things until much too late. But, of course, there are things like remission. One never knows what may happen."

There was a small, heavy silence, and then Bill said awkwardly, "Well, at least now we know where we are."

"You will treat what I have told you with the strictest confidence, won't you?"

"Of course," said Manny, and Bill echoed it.

"But"—Manny was pursuing his own line of thought—"how will we get him to let us be any help?"

"Jake is a very proud and self-contained man," said Andrew Lawson. "Still, I'm sure you'll be able to get round him somehow. But remember, sometimes a man's independence and privacy are all he has left. One must allow him to keep that final dignity."

"Yes," agreed Manny sadly. "But he might be glad of some support from a couple of old friends?"

"He might indeed." Lawson nodded at them very kindly. "Why don't you give it a try?"

"Oh, we'll try all right!" said Bill.

IT WAS TWO EVENINGS after his last visit that Bracken came back to Jake's garden. The blackbird was sitting in the pear tree singing, and the evening sunlight lay like gold on the brown earth as Jake turned it with his spade. He had raked up most of the long grass, and it stood now in two sweet-smelling heaps at the end of the sloping lawn.

"I brought you a few plants," Bracken said, reaching into the leather pouch he always wore on his belt. "Farmer gave 'em to me. I was planting for him all day. These spindly dark ones is cabbage and brussels. Those floppy pale ones is lettuce. You'll get some of those ready quite soon if you plant 'em now. Those with two grey leaves is broad beans, and those is runners."

He showed Jake how to plant each fragile seedling in the newly turned earth. Then, after working for a while in silence, he said suddenly, "Do you sleep much, nights?"

Jake looked at him, surprised. "Not a lot, no. Why?"

"I just wondered if you'd like to come badger-watching."

"I'd love to." Jake sounded really pleased.

"Not tonight, though; you done a lot today." His quicksilver smile shone. "You have a lay-in tomorrow. We'll go out in the evening."

Jake felt a lurch of absurd disappointment: He loved those early morning wanderings. "Oh, but—" he began. Then he remembered that the boy already gave up a lot of his spare time on his account. "Yes," he said lamely, "that'll be fine..."

Bracken looked at him consideringly, head on one side. He was not taken in one bit. "All right then," he said, smiling. "We'll just go a short way in the morning, but you gotta rest in the daytime, mind!"

Jake found himself laughing, not at all annoyed at being bullied.

It was almost dark now, and the first stars were winking between the branches of the pear tree.

"A cup of tea?" asked Jake.

Bracken hesitated. "Can I sit out here on the step?" He didn't say, I don't like houses, they make me feel shut in. But Jake understood,

Jake went inside and boiled some water. Presently he carried two mugs of tea outside and sat down on the step beside Bracken to look out at the night.

He found himself gazing intently at the dried seed heads of some of last year's cow parsley, illuminated by the lamplight from the doorway. He realized suddenly that he was looking at things with entirely new eyes since meeting the boy. Everything seemed clearer and more vivid—and extraordinarily beautiful. It was as if each day of his increasing weakness made him more aware of the world around him, so that even his illness brought him unexpected gifts.

"I like nighttime," said Bracken softly. "You see shapes clearer against the dark."

Against the dark, thought Jake, and turned to smile at Bracken.

But the empty mug lay on the step, and the boy had gone.

IN THE NIGHT Jake was woken by a piercing scream right below his window. For a moment his mind jumped with thoughts of muggings and murder, but then he remembered he was in the countryside, not the dark streets of London.

The scream came again, harsh and wild in the night. Then he heard the answering sharp, metallic bark of a dog fox in the woods beyond. It's a vixen calling, he thought. I know about that, but I've never heard one before. It's a dreadful, eerie sound.

The vixen screamed again, and he got up to have a look. Bright moonlight lay on the sleeping fields and dappled the garden with silver. He was just in time to see the vixen's long, slender body slide gracefully over his wall and go across the field like liquid shadow.

Jake knew now when a bout of pain was coming. He took a couple of painkillers and went downstairs. A sheet of paper, half typed, stuck out of the typewriter. He stooped to read it, and found that his account of the course of a foreign war seemed meaningless to him. What am I writing this stuff for? he thought. It all seems so far away now. Who will care what I say about violent happenings on a distant shore?

He took a new sheet of paper and wrote swiftly and decisively: "Today I saw the sunrise, and in the night I heard a vixen scream."

I will keep a diary, he thought. Each day I will set down the marvels I have seen. Each day I have left will be a new voyage of discovery. I will record each day, each living moment, as it comes.

He looked out once more at the moonlight in the garden, and then he went back to bed and fell asleep.

THAT MORNING it took two handfuls of gravel to wake him. He was deep in a heavy, drugged sleep and it seemed impossible to drag himself out of it. He felt slow and stupid, and there was an ache in all his limbs that seemed to hold him down.

But outside the light was growing and the blackbird was practising a new bit of song, and Bracken's voice came to him clearly through the window.

"Tea's up. I brought a flask today! It's a pearly old morning... you coming out?"

Jake struggled to his feet and went to the window. Below him the garden lay bathed in dew, and the lower slopes of the valley were swathed in translucent wisps of mist, veils of shimmering light. It was indeed a pearly morning.

"Hang on," he called down to the boy. "I'll be there in a minute." When he stepped outside, Bracken took him firmly by the hand and perched him on the garden wall, then busied himself with the flask. "Try this."

"What is it?"

"Herb tea. We dry the herbs ourselves. Makes you feel all fresh, like the morning."

They shared the fragrant tea companionably in the still before the dawn. Bracken waited for the startling pallor to recede from Jake's skin as the warm tea revived him. To the boy, Jake was just another sick creature who needed caring for until he was strong enough to manage on his own. Many of the creatures who came through Bracken's gentle hands were bewildered and frightened, as well as injured. But this one was not frightened now, not even very bewildered any more.

The cuckoo was calling insistently from the woods. Bracken looked at Jake's peaceful face as he sat sunning himself on the wall, and judged him to be about ready to wander off into the bright morning.

Bracken did not take Jake as far as the lake that day. He turned off along the stream and followed its course back up the hill till its shallow banks grew steeper and it came out into a small, hidden pool with a little waterfall at one end. Here, the boy cast a swift glance round the stooping willows and alders that leaned over the water, and then sank quietly to the ground and drew Jake after him.

"We might see the kingfisher, if we wait," he said.

At first all they saw was the gently tumbling waterfall and the widening ripples it made on the quiet surface of the pool.

In the pool itself, Jake saw the speckled lissom body of a fish, turning lazily among the weed, moving with a flick of its tail.

There were flowers all round this hidden sanctuary. Jake recognized most of them now—kingcups, pale lilac cuckoo-flowers, blue speedwell and creamy primroses. And there were the first bluebells under the skirts of the beechwoods on the slope above. Dog violets grew in little purple clumps at his feet, and the grass was starred with golden celandine.

They were like friends waiting to welcome him.

"Look!" whispered Bracken, and clutched his arm. "There he goes!"

Jake held his breath. Was it gone already? Was that brilliant, heart-stopping glimpse all he would ever see?

But the kingfisher came again, speeding low over the water like blue fire, and dived suddenly in a diamond sparkle after a shadow swimming below the surface. Almost at once it was out of the water and perched on a willow branch, with something small and silver caught in its razor-sharp beak. The sun glinted on its bright plumage—a blue so dazzling that it almost hurt his eyes, and a glowing orange-chestnut on its smooth, trim breast. The fish vanished in a single gulp, and the little bird sat there quite still, sunning itself above the quietly moving water.

Look thy last on all things lovely every hour said the treacherous voice in Jake's head. But he shook it from him and looked at the brilliant little bird with delight.

At last the kingfisher took fright at a sudden movement in the reeds and darted off, flashing blue lightning as it went, till it was lost among the trailing willow branches.

Jake and Bracken walked back across the springy hillside. When they got to the garden gate, Bracken said gently: "You gotta rest now, see? So's you'll be ready for tonight. I'll come just before dark."

"I'll be ready," said Jake.

HE HAD MEANT to do as he had been told and rest, but it seemed such a waste of the day. So he decided to drive to the village. He needed a few things, and he knew that he ought to locate the village doctor. So far, he reflected, he had been singularly impractical in his deliberate isolation. But now that the initial spate of shock and despair was over ... Over? he thought, astonished.

He realized yet again how much Bracken's gentle company had already done for him. Grief and rage and towering pride had sent him away from his friends. Now he could scarcely remember what had driven him to be so fiercely solitary, except that he had run like a wounded animal for cover, for sanctuary and peace. And he had found it.

In the village, he called on Mary Willis, proprietor of the general store and post office. She was a round little woman with a cheerful face, and she was quick and light on her feet, like a bird.

"Aren't you Jake Farrant?" She smiled at him rosily. "I've seen you often on the telly. Staying at Mrs. Cook's cottage, aren't you?"

"That's right," Jake said. "Bill Franklyn, Mrs. Cook's brother, is a friend of mine." A sudden wave of nostalgia came over him for the hard, bright days in the field. I miss my work, he thought, and the brave, unspoken loyalty of my friends.

"I hear you've been out exploring with our gipsy boy, Bracken?"

"Yes," admitted Jake. "I suppose everyone here knows him?"

Mary Willis smiled even more cheerfully. "Bless your heart, course we do. He's a wizard with animals, that boy, especially sick ones. All the villagers take their pets to him, and anything wild or lost or injured lands up in his hands."

Yes, thought Jake, so it does.

"What about the rest of his family?" he asked.

"Oh, they're all right too, as gipsies go. They work on the farms come spring and summer. And they go up Hereford way in August for the hop picking. They don't seem to steal nothing, and the boy's father is very good with horses, can cure anything. Mind you"—she leaned over the counter to wag a finger at Jake—"there's still some as won't have a gipsy near the place, set the dogs on them, even. But this lot never did anyone any harm, and they'll be off again come winter."

Jake's heart gave a curious lurch of dismay. Off again come winter?

"But there I am, running on! What can I get for you, Mr. Farrant?"

He gave her his list, and inquired about the doctor.

"Dr. Martin lives over in the next village, Sheepwick, and he has a surgery there every day. But he has one here twice a week for people as can't get over there." She looked searchingly into Jake's face. "Been a bit under the weather, have you?"

"A bit," said Jake. Then, taking a deep breath, he added, "Mrs. Willis, I'd be grateful if you didn't let on to everyone who I am. I've come down for some peace and quiet, you see."

"Of course, my dear. Nobody'll bother you here." She paused. "And the Bracken boy'll take good care of you, I'm sure."

Jake went out of the shop with his purchases and stood looking down the single village street at its little stone houses. Sunlight lay like a charm on the golden stone of the cottage walls, and daffodils nodded golden heads in the little gardens. Peace, thought Jake. Why do I feel my life increasing? What strange spell has this place cast on me?

"I thought you were supposed to be resting!" said a laughing voice at his elbow. Jake turned to look into Bracken's smiling, upturned face. The boy had a wicker cage swinging from his hand. Inside it, Jake could see a ruffled bird looking at him with a glazed and baleful eye.

"What have you got there?"

"It's a young kestrel, winged with lead shot. But I think I can make him

338

well." He looked down at it, frowning and angry. "People with guns . . . they never give a thought to what they hit!"

They strolled towards Jake's car. "Want a lift?" Jake asked.

"Good idea," said Bracken, and then, as an afterthought, "Maybe you could help me with the bird."

"Maybe," agreed Jake, "though you'll have to show me how."

"Don't worry," said Bracken, climbing into the car, "I will!"

BACK AT THE COTTAGE, the boy asked for a bowl of water, a sponge and some disinfectant. "Though I've got some herbs with me—self-heal and comfrey and sorrel and some nettles. They'd probably be better."

They sat together on the step and Bracken set down the cage between them. "You'll have to hold him," he said, taking the bird out gently. "Like this. Both hands round his wings, so he can't flap."

Jake laid his hands round the rumpled feathers and felt the warmth of the bird's body against his fingers. He could feel its frantic heart beating unevenly as it struggled to overcome its fright.

"Hold still now," the boy said to the bird, "and let me look at you. That's it . . . gently does it. You see? That didn't hurt a bit."

Talking softly to it all the time in his caressing voice, he began to clean the matted feathers and the small bleeding holes where the shot had entered the frail body. Jake held the bird firmly, but not too tight, he hoped. Its bright yellow-rimmed eyes were alert and open, and it turned its head from side to side trying to see what the boy was doing. It made no attempt to attack Jake with its sharp, curved beak.

"There now," said Bracken. "That's got you clean. I don't know about the shot, though." He reached into his pocket and brought out a curious, long thin probe. "This here will do the trick if anything can." Using the fine steel blade, he worked very fast and presently he had got out quite a row of small lead shot, which he laid on the step beside him. The bird was still now, its golden eyes half closed, but the brave, tired heart still laboured on.

"That's the best I can do," muttered Bracken. "Daren't do any more; I'll kill him else. He's scarcely a year old yet, I should think. Only just got the white tips on his black tail feathers—look!"

He stroked the damp feathers back into place. Then one brown finger stroked the chestnut mantle, lingering lovingly on the blue-grey head. "We can put him back in the cage now. We'll try feeding him a bit later on, when he's got over the shock."

Gently Bracken laid the limp bundle of feathers down on the floor of the wicker cage. "If you don't mind," he said, "I'll leave him here with you for today. I don't want to move him about too much."

"But I shan't know what to do!" protested Jake.

"You needn't do anything," said Bracken. "We'll put him in the shed, where it's dark. He'll sleep. If he's going to live, he'll wake up hungry, and I'll be back by then."

So they carried the cage into the shed and placed it on top of a wooden bin. Bracken covered it with a piece of old sacking.

"Have a nice sleep," he said. "I'll be back to see you soon."

IN THE LATE EVENING, when the twilight was deepening in the valley, Jake went out to have a look at the bird.

Its body lay still, and Jake's heart misgave him as he peered into the cage. Was it dead? But as he got closer he saw the speckled breast still heaving. The golden eyes suddenly opened to look at him.

"So you're alive!" Jake said. "Congratulations!"

The bird seemed to listen to his voice but did not try to rise.

Jake went out of the shed and stood looking down the field beyond his garden wall. A movement caught his eye, and he realized it was Bracken approaching.

"Brought the bird some supper," said the boy as he reached Jake's side. He held up a cone of bloodied paper containing a few lumps of raw mince. "He can't tackle much yet, but we'll try."

When they got to the shed, the bird was sitting up and feebly pecking at the bars of its cage. Bracken put a couple of pieces of the mince in the cage. But the wounded kestrel didn't seem to see them, so Bracken picked up a piece in his fingers and held it just in front of the bird's head. The curved beak opened automatically, and Bracken dropped the meat inside the pulsing throat. Patiently he did this with every morsel. The bird swallowed each mouthful with increasing eagerness.

"That's it for now," he said. "You'll burst, else! Next time you'll be strong enough to pick it up yourself." He turned away and wiped his fingers on the side of his ancient brown jersey.

Leading Jake outside, he looked up at the sky and said, "The moon'll be up soon. We'd best get into position first, then we won't scare the badgers off. You ready?"

"Yes," said Jake, "I'm ready."

Bracken led him through the beechwoods, climbing higher and further from the cottage with every quiet step. The woods seemed very still and dark. Behind them Jake could hear the thin voices of the lambs in the hillside meadows, and a late thrush was finishing his evening song in one of the tall beeches. Even the cuckoo called a couple of times in the deepening dusk as it flew home to roost. But presently they were all silent, and Jake became aware of other sounds—rustlings and comings and goings—all around him in the woods.

At length they came to a clearing where a steep bank thrust upwards, displaying the gnarled roots of tall grey beech trees. The bank was a miniature quarry, sandy and scarred, with loose stones and golden yellow shale in between the clinging roots, and various holes and heaps of scratched earth and trampled grass all over it.

"Here," murmured Bracken. "This is what I call Frith Wood Badger Sett. It's still occupied. You can see the droppings over there, all in one place—see? Very clean creatures, badgers is. There's the old bedding thrown out. See them balls of grass and such? They've probably pulled in new beds today—the grass looks all torn up."

Jake stood gazing at the holes in the sandy earth of the bank, and wondered what hidden tunnels and passages lay beneath them.

"Best get under cover," whispered Bracken. "Very keen scent, badgers have. They'll never come out if they smell you." He and Jake hid in a clump of green alder bushes, then settled down to wait.

It was a male badger, a boar, who came out first. He spent a long time sniffing suspiciously about, then sat down to have a good scratch. That done, he had another sniff around, decided all was safe and began to clean his fur. He was very meticulous about this, although he looked pretty spruce already with his neat black-and-white markings. Soon his mate arrived behind him, and the two turned towards each other, nose to nose, grunting and speaking in close communication.

All this time a growing radiance was spreading through the trees from behind the hill, as the moon rose in the sky. Soon it was light enough to see the badger sett quite clearly. Black shadow and white moonlight lay in bars on the forest floor, and black-and-white fur gleamed on the sleek heads of the badgers as they rooted and scratched and talked. At last the boar trundled off, leaving the sow behind. Now the young cubs came tumbling out of the sett and started to play, rolling over, chasing each other, wrestling and squalling. Presently a couple more adults appeared and got mixed up in the cubs' infectious spring fever on this heady, bluebell-scented night.

Jake and Bracken watched for a long time, until their limbs were cramped and all the badgers had disappeared.

"Gone a-hunting," murmured Bracken, and took Jake's hand and helped him to his feet. "Are you cold?"

"No," he said. "I'm not cold. I'm completely enchanted!"

When they got back to the cottage, Bracken went into the shed to fetch the sick kestrel. "I'll take him home now," he said. "He'll need a lot of care yet, and it's not fair to leave him with you. But I'll bring him back to see you before I let him go."

Jake nodded, suddenly realizing that he was very tired.

"A long rest," said Bracken judicially, looking down at the bird in its wicker cage. "That's what you need."

Jake did not answer. He had his eyes closed and was trying to stop the world from spinning.

"And dream of growing strong," added Bracken softly.

AFTER CONSIDERABLE THOUGHT and anxious consultation with Manny, Bill Franklyn decided to go and see his sister, Carol, whose cottage Jake had rented. Carol was a widow who lived in a sunny flat in West Kensington with her twin boys, Matthew and Mark. The household was turbulent and busy, but she was always glad to see her brother. It was the twins' birthday, and she was putting the finishing touches to a cake when he arrived.

"Hi, Bill," she said. "Sit down, if you can find a place. I'm trying to get this cake done before the twins come home."

"Where are they?"

"Playing squash. They'll be ravenous. Are you staying to supper?"

"I might," Bill said cautiously. "Depends on what you've got."

Carol laughed. She was a bit like Bill, with clear hazel eyes and ready laughter, but her hair, the same kind of hazel brown as her eyes, had two startling wings of silver at each side of her forehead. And her mouth, when it was not laughing, had a saddened downward curve.

Bill, observing the laughter and the sadness it covered, spoke abruptly. "How's things? Money all right?"

Her eyes softened. "Brother mine, you'll kill me with kindness! Yes, the rent's paid; my teaching salary's just about enough to cover most things, and we have enough to eat. So what is there to worry about?"

"Holidays?"

Carol's smile faded a little. "Yes, well ... I thought I might send the boys on a pony-trekking holiday in Wales. It's not too expensive." She looked at Bill severely. "And you're not to come up with any more prepaid miracles!"

It was Bill's turn to laugh. "Well, anyway, what's for supper? Shall I go down to the takeaway?"

"No, not yet anyway. You can tell me first what is on your mind."

Bill sighed. "Never could hide much from you, could I? All right, then. It's Jake."

"Jake Farrant? The one who's got my cottage?"

"Yes. Thing is, he's ill. I want to find out how he's managing, but I don't want to appear to be intruding or fussing unduly."

"How ill?" asked Carol.

Bill was silent for a moment. Then he shook his head faintly and said, "I think it's about as bad as it could be."

"I see ... " She was looking at Bill with compassion and much kindness. "Where do I come in?"

"You're his landlady. Could you drop in to see how he is?"

"Bill, dear, it's a hundred miles! I can't just 'drop in'."

Bill looked a trifle crestfallen. "Well, then, stay the night."

"At the cottage? With your reluctant friend Jake who has gone away to *escape* from people? No, thanks!"

"You were talking about the boys going to Wales. Well, stay a night at the Farmer's Arms on the way. You could surely find a reason to call and see him just for a few moments? *Please?*"

Carol sighed. "You know I can't say no to you! All right, I'll go."

Before either of them could say any more, the twins burst energetically into the room, squash rackets in hand.

"Hi, Mum; hi, Uncle Bill," they chorused. "What's new?"

They were both fairer than their mother, but their eyes were the same light-filled hazel. Only the set of their heads and the shape of their mouths were like their father's—firm and courageous, as Robert's had been, till the day six years ago when he had been killed in a motoring accident.

"New?" Bill said. "Your birthday, for a start. I brought one of you a camera and the other some binoculars. You'll have to fight it out between you. Shall we go down and get something special to eat?"

"Great!" they said. "Can we get Chinese?" All at once it was a party. It almost made Bill forget about Jake.

CHAPTER THREE

Jake stayed in bed a long time the morning after visiting the badger sett. There seemed to be no strength left in his body at all. This won't do, he thought. I can't go out with the boy if I'm going to collapse on his hands. I've got to overcome this somehow.

After a while his legs felt firm enough to carry him downstairs to make a cup of tea. It was a beautiful morning again. The sun was well up, and the garden looked very inviting. The apple tree near the shed was suddenly a mass of pink blossoms. Even his lettuces were growing in the newly burned earth of his vegetable plot. He carried his mug of tea in one hand and went to sit on the step.

For a time he just dreamed in the sun, waiting for his strength to return. He reluctantly decided he ought to walk up the lane to his car and make an attempt to see the local doctor. But when he stood at the bottom of the lane, it seemed to stretch for ever, and its curve was frighteningly steep.

I can't get up there! he thought. It's much too far! All the same, he started walking slowly up the path. Suddenly his strength gave out. The trees, the hedgerows and the stony path seemed to spin into a whirling spiral of colour and then rise up and hit him.

Jim Merrett, the postman, was coming down the lane on his bicycle when he saw a dark heap lying ahead of him on the path. He leaped off his bicycle and stooped over Jake, saying anxiously, "Are you all right, Mr. Farrant, sir? Mr. Farrant! Can you hear me?"

Dimly Jake heard the voice. "All right in a minute," he muttered.

"Take your time," said Jim. "Here, let me help you up. Gently does it. Feeling a bit groggy, were you?"

"A bit," said Jake faintly. "The lane . . . too steep!"

"All the pitches around here are too steep, leastways for a bicycle. Shall I give you a hand back to the cottage?"

"Thanks." Jake was on his feet but weaving. "Better now."

"Course you are. Tell you what, you sit on my bicycle and I'll wheel you down! You don't look fit to walk yet, to me!"

So they progressed unsteadily, wobbling from side to side, until they got to the gate. Here, Jake almost fell off the bicycle, and Jim put a sturdy arm round him and helped him into the cottage.

"You'd better sit down," he said, lowering Jake into the nearest chair, "and rest awhile. Should I fetch the doctor?"

Jake shook his head. "No, thanks. I'll be fine. Just overdid it a bit. Silly of me. There's a can of beer in the larder, if you'd like one."

"Not me!" said Jim, grinning. "Not on my rounds. I'd soon be falling off my bike on all the corners. That reminds me, I was bringing you a letter. Here you are."

Jake took it from him and looked at it curiously. Only Bill Franklyn knew where he was, and this was not Bill's writing.

"I'll be off now, then," said Jim, "if you're sure you're all right?"

"Yes, perfectly," Jake assured him. "And thanks for all your help."

"You know," said Jim as he turned to the door, "I was just thinking. That's your car at the top of the lane, isn't it?"

"Yes."

"Well, if you brought it down to the farm lane beyond the field, it's not so steep and not half so rough. You'd only have to walk across that one field, just beyond your garden wall. I'm sure Stan Bayliss wouldn't mind."

"Is he the farmer?"

"Yes. I'll ask him, if you like. I'm going on there now."

"Would you? That'd certainly save me a lot."

Jim winked at Jake. "No point in wasting energy," he said. Then he went out, climbed on his bike and rode away.

But when he got back to the village after his rounds, he told Mary Willis at the sub-post office all about it, and she agreed with him that Dr. Martin ought to be told.

THAT EVENING, when Jake was feeling a bit stronger, there was a knock on his door, and a cheery voice called out, "Can I come in?"

Dr. Martin was nearing sixty, and had been looking after his wide-spread country practice for most of his working life. He loved this countryside and the slow-moving, quiet people who lived in it. He was a squarish, patient, bluff kind of man, with keen blue eyes and a warm, firm voice that instilled confidence.

"Dr. Martin," he said, holding out his hand. "I hope I'm not intruding? Jim Merrett was worried about you."

Jake got to his feet and grasped the outstretched hand. "It was good of you to come." He gestured to a chair. "Please sit down."

The doctor sat in the chair opposite Jake and fixed his bright blue eyes on him. There was knowledge in them already, and sympathy.

"Dr. Martin," Jake began, "I must explain. I already know what's wrong. There's nothing much anyone can do. I've come to terms with that by now. This countryside has already taught me a lot about acceptance."

The doctor nodded. "Yes, it does that."

"I came down here expecting to shut myself away and let things take their course. But now I'm enjoying myself so much that I want to keep active as long as I can! I've discovered I'm lucky to be alive and living here. The only question is, can you help me to keep going . . . just a bit longer?"

Dr. Martin considered. "Hadn't you better tell me where you stand?"

"A couple of months ago I collapsed in the street. I was in London at the time, so I went to see my doctor and he took me in for tests. I have advanced leukaemia. It's only a matter of time now."

Dr. Martin nodded. "Much pain?"

"A bit. It comes in bouts, and the painkillers keep it within bounds. But it's this sudden weakness that defeats me. There's so much I want to do, so much I want to see. I just wondered if there was anything I could take when I feel weak."

Dr. Martin sighed, wishing—not for the first time—that he could work miracles. "Well, before I make any suggestions, could I see your medical records?"

"Of course." Jake got up, and found them lying on the table by his typewriter, beside the unopened letter that Jim Merrett had brought. He had felt so weak and faint after Jim had gone that he had laid it down and forgotten all about it. "Here you are," he said.

David Martin began to leaf through the records, and Jake took the opportunity to read his letter.

Dear Mr. Farrant,

First let me introduce myself. I am Bill Franklyn's sister, Carol—and your landlady. I am writing to say that the boys and I are coming down to Gloucestershire for a night on the way to a holiday in Wales, and I wondered whether you would mind if I called to collect a few things I put away in the spare room? If you would rather be left in peace, please say so, and we will not trouble you. We will be at the Farmer's Arms for the night of April 26. A message there will be sure to find me. I do hope you are enjoying the cottage.

Yours sincerely,
Carol Cook

Jake looked up from the letter to find Dr. Martin studying him with a look of compassion in his eyes. "You do seem to have been through the mill," he said. "What I suggest is this: I'll take a blood sample with me now, and I'll let you know the results. In the meantime, I'll send you down some pills via Jim Merrett. As for practical precautions: you must be careful of infections; try to avoid falls of any kind—you'll bruise much too easily, and you may set up internal haemorrhaging; don't do anything too strenuous; don't take unnecessary risks; don't walk too far." He stopped, seeing Jake's mutinous expression. "Yes, I know you must hate the idea of being so cautious. But you may give yourself a little longer that way. I wish I could be more optimistic, but all I can really say is, rest as much as you can and enjoy yourself in between! If things get really bad, we'll help you through. You know that."

Jake nodded. "I'm not afraid of that part. It's just staying mobile. I looked up that lane today—it looked enormous—and I thought, I can't do it! I've never thought that before, and it scared me. I didn't know I was such a coward."

"You're no coward," said Dr. Martin. "I hope I'd face your future with as much courage and equanimity. Roll up your sleeve, will you?"

Jake obliged.

When David Martin was ready to go; Jake said suddenly, "Do you know the owner of this cottage?"

"Carol Cook? Yes, why?"

"This letter says she's coming down. I was just wondering what she was like."

"She's a very nice woman, and a brave one. She has twin sons. Her husband was killed in a car crash some six or seven years ago. She's a teacher, and she's bringing up those boys on her own. I think you'll like her. She won't fuss." Dr. Martin smiled. "I'll let you know the results of the blood tests. In the meantime, take it easy!"

"Yes," agreed Jake dutifully, "I will."

THE NEXT AFTERNOON the weather broke. A grey pall of rain swept over the valley, drenching the trees and drowning the young flowers in the grass. Jake watched, fascinated, from the cottage windows as the light changed and grew dimmer and a silvery nimbus seemed to clothe every dripping leaf and blade of grass.

As suddenly as it had come, the rain ceased about teatime, and a small, brilliant rainbow clung to the hills when the sun came through the clouds. A cuckoo called in the wet woods, and a chorus of birds started up, including the blackbird, who sat on the topmost branch of the pear tree declaring his approval of the newly washed world.

I must go out, thought Jake. It looks so green and untouched—all the colours are brighter ...

He was standing in his garden gazing out at the green beechwoods when Jim Merrett came up the path.

"Evening, Mr. Farrant. Dr. Martin sent these down from the chemist for you. And I had a word with Stan Bayliss at Wood End Farm. He says it's quite all right to use his lane, and if you give me the keys and trust him with your car, he'll run it down for you this evening and leave the keys in it for you to collect."

"That's wonderful," said Jake. "I'll fetch them for you."

When he came back, he also had an envelope in his hand. "I wonder, do you go near the Farmer's Arms on your travels?"

Jim laughed. "Most days! And most nights, when I gets the chance!"

"Could you leave this there for Mrs. Cook, so she has it when she comes this weekend?"

"Course I will."

Later that evening Jake decided to stroll across the field and see if his car had arrived. He climbed the gate at the end of the field and found himself in a leafy lane like his own, but with a gentler slope and less stony surface. And there, parked on a patch of grass at the side, was his car. On the driver's seat was a package and a note that said: "Hope this will be all right for you. It won't be in the way if you leave it here. The missus sent you some homemade cheese. S. Bayliss."

Jake was touched. He had done nothing to deserve all these kindnesses, yet the quiet people of this valley seemed determined to help him. He felt ashamed of his self-centred pride and independence. He ought to be grateful, not afraid of kindness. Or pity.

That was it, of course. He was afraid of pity. That's why he had run from all his friends and hidden himself away in this solitary place. Only, it wasn't solitary at all—especially if Bracken had any say in the matter!

When Jake got back to the cottage, Bracken was in his garden hammering away at a wooden frame. He looked up at Jake, and then said a little shyly, "Will you mind? I'm making a flying cage for the kestrel up here. He needs to exercise that damaged wing. He can't go free yet. He'd never last a day without something attacking him."

"Why here?" asked Jake, not at all put out. "Why not at your camp?"

"It's the dogs," said Bracken. "Their barking scares him to death."

Jake looked at the bird, who sat sullenly in his cage glaring at him with a fierce, angry eye. Yes, my friend, thought Jake, you hate your captivity. And you are proud and independent too, aren't you? You hate people trying to help you. I know just how you feel.

The bird scowled at him and blinked his yellow eyes.

"Have you given him a name yet?" asked Jake.

"Yes," said Bracken. "Sky, because he belongs there."

"Sky?" said Jake to the bird. "Yes, it suits you. Don't worry, my friend. It won't be long now. Poor, grounded Sky. Be patient!"

Bracken had brought a roll of chicken wire with him, and now he erected the wooden frame he had been making, fixed it to the four tall posts he had already driven into the ground near the apple tree behind the shed, and began to stretch the wire over the top and round the sides.

"Here, let me give you a hand," said Jake.

Together they worked on the long cage until it was safe and enclosed. Bracken had arranged it so that one gnarled branch of the apple tree was inside the wire, and he had put an old twisted tree trunk inside for a perch and scratching post. There was also a wire-covered frame door, so that he or Jake could enter the enclosure.

"It's a regular little aviary, nice and high too," said Jake. "I hope he likes it."

"He won't," said Bracken. "But it's better than nothing. At least he can fly about a bit. I want that wing to get strong. He's got to be able to ride a storm and lie on the wind before he goes."

"How long will that be, do you think?"

"Dunno, maybe a couple more weeks." He turned to Jake, still shy about having brought the bird up to the cottage. "I'll come up morning and night to feed him, and I'll leave you some food for midday. He likes raw meat, or a mouse or two. He ought to have a bit of fur and bones soon, for roughage, like. Don't you worry, though. I'll see to his supplies."

"I'm glad of that!" said Jake. "I don't think I'd be much good at catching mice."

Bracken carefully picked up the wicker cage. He turned to Jake and said, "Would you like to let him out into the flying cage?"

Jake looked at the boy, knowing that yet another gift was being given. "How shall I do it?"

"Just go inside. Put the cage down, open the door, then come out fast. He won't attack you. He's still too sick and scared."

Jake did as he was told; then he and Bracken watched to see what Sky would do. At first the injured kestrel sat staring at the open door of his wicker cage as if he did not believe in even partial freedom any more. But then he took one hesitant step forward on his thin, scaly yellow legs, and then another—a curious, nervous, uneven hop, with the damaged wing dragging a little and a desperate hope beginning to dawn in his golden eyes. Then he was out. Suspiciously he turned his head this way and that, and then he made a scrabbling, ungainly dash for the upright tree stump, his wing still dragging pitifully along the ground. But he managed to lift himself in a fluttering heave of long wing feathers onto the top of the tree-trunk perch, where he sat very still, upright and wary, surveying his new, wider world.

Suddenly he uttered a strange, fierce *kee* and hurled himself across the open space to the branch of the apple tree at the other end of the enclosure. For one awful moment Jake thought the bird was going to dash himself to pieces against the wire itself, but his lurching, unsteady flight just upheld him till he reached the tree.

"That's it," said Bracken. "Try again; you'll soon get stronger."

Then he went quietly into the enclosure and laid some pieces of meat on the tree stump. "There you are," he said, and retreated, closing the door behind him and fastening it with a twist of wire.

Sky uttered another harsh *kee* and flew lopsidedly down to his tree stump and stood over his food, wings forward protectively.

Satisfied, Bracken turned away. "He'll be all right now for a bit. Will you be able to feed him like that, midday?"

"Yes, I think so."

"I thought"—the boy was suddenly shy again—"I thought maybe he'd be company for you?"

"Yes," said Jake. "I shall enjoy watching him get better. Look, Mrs. Bayliss sent me some cheese. Why don't we sit down and eat it?"

He fetched them both a hunk of bread, and at the same time put on his kettle and made tea.

"It's hard when things is hurt and you don't know how to help them," said Bracken, with his eye on the bird.

"Yes," murmured Jake, busy pouring tea. "It is."

"But letting them go is harder." Bracken's voice was soft as spring rain.

THE NEXT MORNING Jake got up without feeling exceptionally weak and went out to look at the bird.

It was still very early, but Sky was awake, sitting alert and belligerent on his perch, looking out at the world with the same angry stare.

"I know," said Jake aloud. "You want to be free and away. It's hard to wait."

Sky turned his proud head in Jake's direction. He seemed to be listening to his words.

"Never mind, Sky, my friend," Jake went on comfortingly. "One day, when your wing is strong again, you'll find the door open, and you'll be away up there, soaring and hovering, flying free on the wind ... " He looked up, dreaming, at the limitless spring sky.

The bird looked at him fiercely, as if to say, What do you know about it? How do you know what it feels like to be cooped up in here, weak and useless, when all the wide sky is above me, taunting me with its wind-driven spaces where I used to fly free—free as thistledown?

But Jake knew ... yes, he knew ... and he sighed because he could not make the bird understand that it would soon mend and fly free. Even though Jake would not.

"There's ways and ways of flying free," said Bracken's voice softly at his elbow.

When Jake turned to look at him in astonishment, the boy only smiled and added, "Look, I've brought him his breakfast, some meat and a mouse."

They watched Sky fly across to the food, and fancied his wing was stronger already: the crumpled feathers looked smoother and glossier in the morning light.

"He's mending," said Bracken. "Let's go and look at the morning."

THAT DAY they did not go far. Bracken took him to a little hill, where they sat in the spring sunshine admiring the view. "Over there," Bracken said, waving an arm at distant beeches below yet another hill crest, "is an old quarry where the kestrels nest. I expect Sky will go there when he's older, looking for a mate."

"What's it called?"

"Hawkswood Quarry. And that's Hawkswood—the big wedge of beeches yonder."

Jake was getting used to the lie of the land a bit by now. "Isn't that the wood where the badgers' sett is, over there?"

Bracken nodded. "The one we went to, yes. There's another big one the other side of Hawkswood." He looked troubled.

"What's the matter?"

The boy was gazing intently out at the furthest beechwoods, frowning a little. "I dunno—something one of the farmers said. Over there, t'other side of the hill, there's one of them rich dairy herds, and the owner doesn't like badgers. Says they're a risk to his cows." He paused. "We used to work for him once. Before we lived on Mr. Bayliss's land, we had our encampment—we call it our *hatchintan*—on his land, but he threw us out."

"Why?"

The boy shrugged. "He said he wanted the pasture, but it was only scrub, and he never touched it after we left. I looked. I guess he just didn't like gipsies. And he said the *jukels*—our dogs—were sheep killers. But they're not!"

Jake was silent. He could see the pattern of the age-old war between the caravan dwellers and the settlers. It never came to an end. "So?" he said at last. "What's worrying you?"

Bracken hesitated. "I think the badgers is threatened. You can't make that man see reason. I think they're in for trouble."

"What will he do? Dig them out?"

"Probably, or put the dogs in. Or drive them out and club them to death, or shoot them. Poor things, they're never safe for long, and there's nothing much I can do about it, either." He sounded fierce and upset. "I wish there was!"

He stayed still for a while, brooding and silent, looking out at the countryside with sombre eyes. But then he turned back to Jake, full of cheerful energy. "Come on," he said. "It's time to be heading home."

They clambered down the little hill and strolled back towards the cottage. "There's a horse fair at Stow tomorrow," said Bracken, as they approached the gate. "So I'll be wanted all day. I'll come up to feed Sky tonight, though. D'you think you could manage him yourself tomorrow? I'll be back the day after."

Jake nodded, pleased that Bracken would entrust Sky to him.

"By the way," added Bracken with seeming carelessness, "can you ride a *grai*?"

"Yes," said Jake. "I used to ride a lot at one time."

"Bareback? We don't use saddles on ours."

Jake paused, smiling. "Yes. I've ridden bareback. Horses, mules, donkeys. I even rode a camel once or twice, but that was horrible!"

Bracken grinned, but his eyes were thoughtful. "Wonderful with *grais*, my da is," he murmured. "Can tell what they're thinking, almost."

"Like you can with birds."

He glanced at Jake. "You can usually tell what creatures is thinking," he said, "if you cares about them enough!"

Jake was silent, realizing how close his thoughts marched with the boy's these days. "Yes," he said at last, "so you can."

THE NEXT MORNING, when Jake came down he found that Bracken had been and gone. There were two packages on the step, and a note written in a clear, painstaking hand: "I've fed Sky and left you some for 2 more feeds. The cake is for you. Back tomorrow. B."

Jake opened the first packet and found a screw of paper containing some chunks of raw meat and two small mice. The other package held a wedge of golden sesame cake. He carried both packets inside and put Sky's food away on the larder shelf.

He went out to feed Sky at midday. The bird watched him, head on one side, seeming as angry and unapproachable as ever. When Jake had left the cage, the young kestrel let out a sudden sharp *kee* and flew across to the new supply of food with an almost balanced swoop.

"That's better," said Jake. "Keep trying!"

Sky stood with his two feet clutching the chunks of meat, his wings hunched forward, looking at Jake with the same baleful stare. Then he lowered his head and tore at the meat with his cruel beak. For the first time he looked what he was—a wild, savage bird of prey, compact and deadly, and somehow beautiful in his fierce, unbending pride.

Yes, thought Jake, you're getting better. Your self-respect is coming back and you really look like a fighter now.

He went away and left the bird alone, sure somehow that it preferred to eat in solitude.

Returning to the cottage, he lay back in an armchair and dozed. There were things he ought to do, papers he ought to deal with before it was too late, but he was tired. Things would have to wait.

He was roused from a confused dream about the kestrel by a knock on the door. He struggled to his feet and went to see who was there. Standing outside on the step was a woman with two cheerful-looking boys beside her.

Jake's hazy mind did a swift double take. Of course! It was Carol Cook and her twins. He must have forgotten the day.

"I'm sorry," he said. "I'm afraid I was dozing. Do come in." He crossed from the living room to his kitchen to put the kettle on. "Could you do with a cup of tea? I know I could."

Carol Cook spoke in a warm, friendly voice. "Jake—I can't call you Mr. Farrant after Bill's been going on about you so much—are you sure you don't mind us coming?"

"No, of course I don't," said Jake, busy with the teapot. "And anyway, I'd like to hear news of Bill."

Carol was looking at him quietly. She recognized the lean, ardent, good-looking face she had seen often on the television screen, reporting from some battlefront or disaster area, talking to soldiers, to refugees, to victims of flood, earthquake and famine. He had always looked as if he cared about those people.

It was the same face now, but thinner and sadder, and terribly transparent. But no, it was not really sadder; there was a strange calmness and serenity about it. It was almost as if he were watching some other event in some other place. And yet she felt she knew him somehow, had always known him, and that this meeting was full of recognition. Recognition? How could it be? Nonsense! It's only because I've seen his face so many times before and Bill has talked of him so much, she thought.

Jake, for his part, when he looked up from his tea-making, saw a tallish, slender woman with a face like Bill's, only distinctly more attractive, and a smile that lit her up and made sparks in her eyes. A face he could almost trust, almost felt he knew already, somehow.

Then he looked at the boys, who had been hovering shyly in the background, and thought, They are like their mother—tallish and friendly, same brown hair, same eyes, the same incandescent smile.

"I'm a rotten host," he said. "Tell you what. While the tea's brewing, would you like to come and help me feed the kestrel?"

"What kestrel?" chorused the boys. They turned to Carol with easy deference. "Can we?"

"If Jake says so, of course!" She smiled. "Can I come too?"

They all went along the path to the kestrel's pen. But there Jake made them stand a little way back in case they frightened the bird. He opened the door, went inside and laid some meat and one of the mice down on the tree stump. "Cheer up," he said. "Your dinner's arrived. Why don't you try those wings?"

As if Sky had understood him, the bird suddenly flexed his wings and let out his harsh, fierce cry, *kee-kee-kee*, and flew straight down the length of the pen and back before settling on the tree trunk.

"That's wonderful!" said Jake approvingly. "You're getting stronger!"

Sky glared at him, guarding his food like a stiff, angry sentinel.

"All right," said Jake. "I'm going! Bracken will be here tomorrow. You'll feel better then." He slipped out of the pen and closed the door.

"Who's Bracken?" asked one of the twins.

Jake took them back to the cottage, gave them some tea and some of Bracken's sesame cake, and explained.

They listened, spellbound. Carol heard the enchantment in his voice as he told them about the marvels he had seen in Bracken's company.

Presently the boys decided to go to have a look at the lake. When they had gone, Jake said, "You love this countryside too, don't you?"

"Yes. We used to come down to this cottage a lot when my husband was alive. But somehow, since he was killed, I couldn't really face it. The boys were only six when they came here last, but they still remember it." She sighed. "I was wrong, of course."

"Wrong? About what?"

"Shutting things out. It isn't any good."

"No," said Jake slowly.

"I've come to terms with it now." She spoke quite naturally, but Jake knew she was not only talking about herself. "I wouldn't see anyone, not even Bill, and I wouldn't admit I needed any help."

There was silence between them for a moment, and then Jake said quietly, "Why exactly did Bill ask you to come here now?"

Carol's hazel eyes were clear and unembarrassed. "Simply to find out how you were—if you needed anything. And I think he'd dearly love to come down to see you, but he's afraid of bothering you."

Jake sighed. "You're very good to be so honest about it."

"Remember, I've been through this too, though in a different way. I was terrified of pity; I snubbed all my friends!"

He grinned at her. "You're very clever! You've undermined my defences already."

They were both laughing when the boys came back, muddy and dishevelled but very happy.

"It's great down there," said Matthew. "So quiet."

"And everything smells green," added Mark.

Carol got up to go. But her eyes were on Jake's face. "You've been very patient with us. What shall I tell Bill?"

"Tell him ... " Jake hesitated. "Tell him I'm managing very well, and that my life is richer and happier than it's ever been."

Carol nodded. "And ... ?"

"And tell him he's a scheming old devil, and I'd love to see him."

She smiled her relief. "And Manny?"

"And Manny, of course!"

She went over to him and patted his arm affectionately. "Well done! You're learning much faster than I did!"

Jake turned to the boys and said, "I hope you'll come and see me on the way back from Wales."

They all paused to look at him.

"Do you want us to?" asked Mark, speaking for them all.

"Yes," said Jake, smiling. "I do!"

CHAPTER FOUR

Bracken did not come the next morning. Jake told himself that the boy had every right to stay away if he liked, but even so, he found that he was absurdly disappointed.

He had been exhausted last night after Carol and the boys had left. It was as if the warmth of their visit had been almost too much to bear, and their going had taken some of his strength away with them. He had fallen into a heavy sleep, and dreamed wildly. He could remember his dream now. It was full of dark shadows, and his feet were sliding helplessly as they tried to climb impossible slopes on shaley mountains. He had reached out his hand to grab at a fragile tree growing out of the rock. A real anxiety dream, he told himself, and not to be taken seriously.

This morning he was still tired, but he made some tea, then went out to feed Sky. He had only enough food for the bird's breakfast, so he decided to go to the village and get more supplies, in case Bracken did not turn up.

It was another pearly morning. He found himself smiling as he thought of Bracken's upturned face and his voice calling from the garden. *Come on out ... It's a pearly old morning.* He walked across the meadow to his car. Overhead a lark was singing. A pearly old morning, and yet, somehow, he didn't feel easy. The edge of his dream still clung to his mind, a shadow he could not quite dispel.

In the village, he bought a few things at the store, and then he went on to the butcher's shop and explained his dilemma about Sky.

The butcher was as cheerful as Mrs. Willis, and turned out to be her brother, Ted. "What you need is some rough ends," he said. "I've dressed a couple of rabbits this morning; you can have the remains. The bird'll like those!"

After leaving the butcher, Jake drove off down the farm lane, parked his car on the grass and strolled home through the field. A wave of dizziness caught him halfway across, and he sat down for a few moments on a nearby stone to let it pass.

From here he could hear Bracken's blackbird singing in the pear tree, as joyous and carefree as ever. But Jake did not feel carefree today. Something was wrong. Some hawk's-wing shadow still hung over his mind.

Back home, he gave Sky a morsel of rabbit, then retreated to the cottage and sank into a chair to rest.

In the evening Bracken still had not come, and Jake gave up expecting him. He had just settled down to read when there came a quiet knock at the door. He got up and went to see who it was.

A man stood on his doorstep, a brownish, sturdy-looking man wearing brown corduroys, a cloth cap on his head and a red kerchief round his neck.

"Sorry to bother you, sir," he said in a warm and lilting voice. "I was wondering—have you seen the boy?"

Jake's heart seemed to make a sudden stop and then go lurching on too fast. "The boy? You mean Bracken?"

The man was looking at him keenly with assessing brown eyes. Now he relaxed a little and smiled briefly. "That's what folks like to call him round here, yes."

"I haven't seen him since the day before yesterday, though he left some food for the bird on my step yesterday morning. Is he missing?"

The man nodded. "Hasn't been home since last evening."

"Has he ever stayed out all night before?" Jake asked anxiously.

"No," said the gipsy. "Not all night. Not without saying."

"Let's get it straight," said Jake, trying to be practical. "Didn't he go with you to the horse fair at Stow?"

"Yes. Brought the *grais* home, tethered them near the trailers, then slipped off. Thought he was coming to see you, but he didn't?"

"No, he didn't," said Jake slowly, his mind heavy with dread. "When you were over at Stow, did anything happen that might've upset him? Did anyone talk about any animals in trouble or anything?"

"I see what you mean," said the man. "That would set him off! But I can't say as I heard anything special."

Jake sighed. "You know this country better than I do. He might be anywhere. I'll come with you if you're going to look for him."

The gipsy laid a kind, restraining hand on his arm. "No, don't do that, sir. We know you've been a bit poorly. The boy told us. Besides, we can take the *grais* across country and cover more ground. You'd best stay here. He might turn up here yet, to see after his bird."

"I suppose he might," said Jake. But he looked so uncertain that the gipsy was moved to say, "Don't worry, sir. He can take care of himself, like all us Romanies. He'll turn up soon."

Jake said, suddenly recognizing that lilting voice and the brown, firmly chiselled face, "Are you his father?"

"I am that."

"He's a good boy," said Jake. "You must be proud of him."

A glimmer of a smile passed between them, and the gipsy turned away into the darkening evening. Jake saw then that a shaggy grey pony was tied up at the gate.

"We'll send to let you know when he gets back!" said the gipsy as he swung himself up onto the pony's back.

IT WAS WHILE BRACKEN was holding the horses for his father that he had heard the farmers talking.

"Better dig 'em out," said one. "Don't feel inclined to leave 'em, with all my stock involved. Do you?"

"No," grunted the other. "Did you organize anything?"

"Got a few blokes together."

"When?"

"Tonight would be as good as any. There's a moon."

"I'll bring the dogs and the guns. May take a while; there's several entrances. Got to stop them first."

They moved off, still talking. Bracken stood looking after them, cold with the knowledge of what they were planning to do.

It was the far beechwood badger sett they would be after, he knew, the one in Hawkswood. One of those two farmers was the man who owned the rich dairy herd, the one who had turned Bracken and his people off his land. What can I do? he thought. How do you warn a whole colony of badgers that their lives are in danger? Even if he got there first, he would never be able to drive the badgers out of their setts alone before the farmers and their dogs came to destroy them.

Unless ... unless he could smoke them out? Sometimes, he knew, the farmers would lay smoking rubbish in the entrances and wait for the badgers to emerge. Then they would set the dogs on them, or shoot them, or hit them over the head with shovels till they were dead.

He might, if he hurried, be able to get them out first. But there was the horse fair to be got through, and it was late before he got back from Stow to the *hatchintan*. The family was settling down to eat by the open campfire when he slipped away into the blue-grey dusk.

He covered a lot of miles that evening, arriving at the badger sett before moonrise. There was no one about yet, although he thought he could hear more farm dogs than usual barking in the distance.

Frantically he cast about for twigs, dried grass and leaves to burn. He had brought a few oily rags from the camp, and he put one of these with every pile of leaves and placed them inside each sett entrance he could find. Then he took a box of matches from his pocket and carefully lit each heap.

The smoke curled outwards into the evening air, and the boy ran wildly from pile to pile, shoving the burning debris further into the holes with a long hazel stick.

At first nothing happened, but then, pushing and grunting, the badgers began to emerge. First came the boars, scenting the air for danger, sneezing and spluttering in the smoke, suspicious and slow to move. Behind them came the sows and their cubs, lining up at the entrances, waiting to get out when the boars said the coast was clear.

Bracken didn't know what to do. If he started to shout and wave his arms, the badgers would retreat back into the setts. If he stayed still, they would sit about snuffing the breeze and wait for the smoke to subside. Either way, they would be doomed.

He decided to work his way round behind them and appear, shouting, above the bank of the sandy hollow where the tree roots were. That way the whole bunch might take fright and run off together.

He moved silently, keeping downwind as long as he could, hoping that when he crossed over behind them, the drifting smoke would cover him from the nearsighted badgers. Wriggling through the beechnuts and bluebells, he arrived at the top of the bank and suddenly got to his feet and began to shout and wave his arms.

And then pandemonium broke loose. From a spinney at the side came the sharp yelping of eager dogs on the scent, and from beyond the drifting smoke came the furious shouting of men.

"Quick!" yelled one. "Someone's smoked 'em out! Bring up the guns!"

"Put the dogs in!" shouted another. "Come on, Spot! Get down there!"

"Get the shovel!" bellowed a third. "Hit 'em over the head!"

The bewildered badgers looked this way and that, and then, with one accord, they broke out together and dashed away into the woods as hard as they could go. A flurry of shots and shouts broke out, and one beautiful sow fell in a heap. The rest seemed to vanish into the shadows of the woods.

For a moment the men and dogs were left in the clearing, not knowing which way to go. Then Farmer Deacon's big bull mastiff, Boley, began to give chase.

"Dig out the sett!" ordered a voice. "Then they can't come back! I'll go after the dogs. We might get another shot."

But Bracken was ahead of them, driving the badgers on, shouting, tripping over roots, trying to destroy the scent and increase the distance between the badgers and the dogs. A full-grown badger, he knew, would be a match for any dog, but what about the cubs?

"Run!" he panted. "Get away! Run!" He ran himself until he could run no more. In front of him the silent badgers ran on, deep into the woods. Behind him the sounds of men and dogs grew fainter.

I believe we've done it! he thought.

But then his foot caught against something soft, and he stooped down and found two badger cubs huddled close together, panting, lost and alone. "You can't stay here!" he said. "The dogs'll get you. Come on!" He picked up both the squirming cubs, thrust them inside his anorak and ran on. Close behind, Boley, the fastest of the dogs, came crashing through the undergrowth at his heels.

Terrified for the cubs, Bracken ran on blindly, crossed a moonlit clearing and came to a flat verge of scrubby grass and a dark, unseen edge of sandy soil. Without a glance he plunged on ... and found himself falling over and over, down and down, bumping and bouncing from boulder to tree stump, from grass to scree and shifting shale, down the steep side of the ancient disused quarry where the kestrels came to nest.

JAKE COULD NOT SLEEP. He kept telling himself that the men of Bracken's family would be perfectly capable of finding him, and anyway, he was probably not lost but only helping someone or some animal. But however much he argued with himself, Jake could not shake off the feeling of foreboding that had been growing in him all day.

Something was wrong. He could still feel that hawk's-wing shadow pulling him. Hawk's wing? Suddenly, vividly, he remembered his dream: he had been trying to climb the shaley side of a mountain, and every time he took a step forward, the crumbling surface had given way and started a landslide of falling stones, and sliding, cascading streams of pebbles and sand. His feet sank into loose gravel and could not be pulled out. He struggled and heaved, and the yellow sand fell on him, choking him so that he could not breathe.

And then he remembered Bracken saying, *Over there is an old quarry where the kestrels nest.* And he remembered too the boy's troubled face as he said, *I think the badgers is threatened.* And, last of all, he remembered the name Hawkswood. Not a hawk's-wing shadow—his mind had been playing tricks all day. It was Hawkswood!

Swiftly, Jake pulled on his anorak and boots, picked up his torch and went out into the garden. Driven now by a fearful sense of urgency, he walked as quickly as he could to his car in the moonlight. When he reached it, he sat with the door open and the roof light on while he spread out his map of the district. He shone the torch down on the mass of fine lines and names. There was the lake—Sedgecombe, it was called. There were the beechwoods across the valley. And yes, there it was—Hawkswood Quarry, about two miles from the top road across the woodlands marked Hawkswood.

Jake laid the map beside him on the seat, snapped off his torch and drove away fast uphill into the deepening shadows of the lane. He guessed it must be about two o'clock in the morning.

He drove on, skirting the woods and following the contours of the hills until he came to the crest of a rise that overlooked the wedge of beeches known as Hawkswood. The quarry, he thought, should be a couple of miles through the woods and out on the other side.

He parked the car, picked up his torch and started the long walk through the woods. All was silent except for an owl that hooted sadly far down in the lower slopes of the wood.

All this time he had not stopped to consider the implications of what he was doing. Now, sudden doubts assailed him. What had made him so certain he knew where Bracken would be? Why was he following the dictates of a dream? But even as he argued with himself, he knew he was not wrong. Somewhere ahead Bracken was waiting for him, in trouble and alone in the night.

His torch picked out the path fairly well, and at last, after walking for what seemed like a very long time, he came out of the trees into a moonlit clearing near a sandy verge, with a yawning blackness beyond. I'm here! he thought. This is Hawkswood Quarry, and Bracken is here somewhere. I'm sure he is.

He went to the edge and looked over. It was very dark, but he could discern the broken, shaley sides of the quarry and the few stunted bushes leaning outwards. It was just like his dream.

"Bracken?" he called. "Are you there?"

There was no answer.

But wait, he thought. In my dream I was climbing *upwards*. If I go over the top here, I shall be climbing down, and I'll bring the whole quarry side down with me, and he might be underneath. I'd better go round the edge and look for a way down.

With the beam of the torch glimmering ahead of him, he saw a path that seemed to circle the quarry's flanks until it reached the valley floor. He followed the path down into the darkening shadow, going deeper into pitch-black night with every step. The moonlight could not reach down there.

At the bottom of the path he found he was actually standing on the quarry floor, looking up at the sandy, flaking sides as he had in his dream. This is where it was, he thought. I must begin climbing *here*.

He called again once, "Bracken!" But his own voice mocked him with echoes round and round the stones.

He began to climb. The ground shifted under his feet; his boots filled with gravel; but he knew where he had to go. There was a small tree growing out of the rock somewhere above, and if he could hold on to that and pull himself up, he would be there.

He was light-headed with exhaustion, but he did not even notice it. Something was driving him, pushing him faster with every step. The beam of light ahead of him wavered to and fro in his unsteady progress, and then settled firmly on the little tree. Yes! There it was! Waiting for him. His hand reached the tree and pulled. It was very steep here, and he inched his way up, clinging to the tree's pliant stem. And then ... the little tree came out of the ground and sent him toppling backwards. He slewed sideways in a shower of stones and dust and landed in a heap on top of something warm and soft.

"Bracken?" he said. "Is that you?"

He pulled himself into a sitting position, and in the beam of the torch saw the boy spread out before him in a tangle of limbs. His eyes were closed. There was a deep gash in his head, and there was blood all over his clothes. For one awful moment Jake thought he was dead, but then he saw that he was breathing quite naturally and that the blood came from a dead badger cub in his arms.

"Bracken?" he said again, and shook him gently. "Wake up! Can you hear me? I've got to get you home!"

The boy sighed, and Jake took the limp body of the dead badger cub away and laid it down on the stones. Then he loosened Bracken's coat and found a second cub, apparently unhurt, cowering in terror against the boy's warm side.

"Wake up!" said Jake again, and then he remembered that Bracken usually carried a flask in his leather bag. He found the pouch under the boy's back. The flask inside was filled with herb tea.

He cradled Bracken's head in one arm and held the plastic cup to the boy's lips, tipping a little tea into his mouth. Bracken coughed and tried to sit up.

"Take it easy," said Jake. "You've had a bang on the head. Rest awhile."

"I knew you'd come," said Bracken. "What about the cubs? I tried. The others got away, but they shot one of the sows."

"Never mind," said Jake. "You're safe, and one of the cubs is too."

"It was my fault," said Bracken, and he suddenly began to weep.

Jake understood then that in some way he felt to blame for whatever had happened. "Don't worry about it now," he said. "Have a drop more of this magic tea. We've got to get you out of here!"

Bracken laid a dusty, tear-streaked face against Jake's arm and said, "Sorry. I was too late, you see, just too late."

"No, you weren't!" said Jake. "You just told me—the other badgers got away. And we've got this little fellow here to take care of, see? Come on now, you're the one who knows his way around. What's the best way to get out?"

"Down first," said Bracken. "We could never climb up there!"

For a while they sat still, waiting for Bracken to feel stronger. Jake didn't know whether he himself felt strong or weak; he only knew he had to get the boy home safely somehow. He was wondering whether he could carry the boy and the cub if Bracken could not stand.

But in the end he helped Bracken to his feet, and, moving cautiously, step by careful step, he managed to guide him down to the bottom of the quarry. Here they began to climb the circling path. Bracken refused to let Jake carry him, but he allowed him to take the cub and tuck it inside his anorak.

They paused frequently to get their breath, but at last they reached the head of the path by the quarry and sat down to rest in the grass. "It's about two miles to the car," said Jake. "D'you think you can make it?"

Bracken smiled at him. "If you can, I can."

They began the slow walk through the woods. The moonlight seemed to be paling now, and the east was beginning to lighten in the translucent way of a spring sky before dawn.

"I'm tired," sighed Bracken suddenly, and sank to the ground. Jake sat down beside him, trying to think what to do. I could leave him here and go for help, but I might not remember exactly where he is. Anyway, he's hurt; I've got to get him back somehow.

Jake picked up the boy in his arms and staggered on. Bracken seemed strangely light in his grasp, but even so, the small weight made a sudden, deep ache in his chest. He was not at all sure whether he would ever reach the road, but he had to try. The trees round him seemed to close in and weave up and down before his eyes.

And then, all at once, there was the sound of voices calling, the clip-clop of hooves, a swinging circle of lights, and willing hands came out to take the boy from his arms.

"Be careful, he's hurt," Jake said very distinctly. Then he fell in a heap on the woodland floor.

JAKE CAME ROUND to find himself lying on a pile of soft quilts beside a bonfire. There were four neat modern trailers drawn up in a circle round him, and to one side a bunch of horses grazed peacefully. Bracken was lying fast asleep on another pile of quilts near him. Someone had washed the blood off his face and bandaged his head.

"It's all right," said a lilting, musical voice close beside Jake. "The boy's not much hurt, nothing a good sleep won't cure. You brought him back to us, and we thank you. *Devlesa avilan*. It is God who brought you."

Jake turned and found himself looking into the face of a handsome, dark-haired gipsy woman who was sitting on the ground nearby, patiently weaving a basket out of thin, pliant twigs.

"What happened to the cub?" he asked.

"The little one is safe. We put her in a box in the dark."

Jake nodded, satisfied. Then another thought struck him. "I have to feed the boy's kestrel."

The woman smiled at him. "One of us went up to see to him, and there was still some food on the ground. The bird is all right."

Jake sighed. Everything was all right except that he was so tired.

"I have made you some tea," said the woman. "You will feel better soon." She handed him a cup full of fragrant, amber-coloured liquid.

Jake, looking into the brown farseeing eyes, knew he was talking to Bracken's mother. He sipped the tea gratefully, then said, "Tell me what happened."

"The men found your car on the top road. They were working their way across on the *grais*, so they knew you must be somewhere in Hawkswood. When they found you and the boy, they put you both in the car and drove it down here." She pointed across the grass to a stone wall. "It's just over yonder."

"Thank you," said Jake. "I can drive it home."

The woman looked at him with a hint of reproof. "You've got to rest first. They've gone for Dr. Martin to look at you and the boy."

"I don't need—"

She laid a hand on his arm. "We don't hold with doctors mostly. We do our own medicine. But Dr. Martin's different. He's a friend."

"Yes," Jake agreed, "he is."

It didn't seem necessary to talk, so Jake lay back and dreamed, while Bracken's mother sat quietly beside him, weaving her basket.

Presently Dr. Martin arrived. He squatted down next to Jake, seeming quite at home in the gipsy encampment, and took his pulse. "Hm," he said. "Might be worse. I thought I told you to take things easy!"

Jake pointed to Bracken, lying asleep close by. "There's your casualty. I'm just an also-ran."

"That's what I'm complaining about," said Dr. Martin severely. "You walked five miles or so, and you *also ran!* I want you to stay here and rest today. The gipsies can keep an eye on you. They need to do something for you today. Saving a gipsy's life makes you someone special to them. So let them fuss over you; it'll do no harm. You're privileged, you know. Not many outsiders—*gorgios*—get to see the inside of a *hatchintan*, and they're going to have a *patshiv* tonight when the men get home from work."

"A what?"

"A *patshiv*, a ceremonial party in honour of a special guest." Dr. Martin grinned at Jake. "I ought to order you home to bed, but I won't! All the same, I want to warn you. All this activity and the fall you had may have set up internal bleeding. If you start feeling cold or faint, send someone up for me at once, do you hear?"

Jake nodded.

"Rest now," said Dr. Martin as he turned to go. "And enjoy yourself! I'll see you later."

So Jake remained the whole day at the gipsy encampment, idling and resting. The women came and went, bringing small gifts of tea and saffron cakes. In the afternoon, when both he and Bracken were feeling better, the

363

boy took him to see the ponies, introducing them one by one with conscious pride. Then he took Jake to see two yellow ferrets in their cages and a tame rabbit with an injured leg, who hopped peacefully about under the trailers, cropping the grass. And he showed him the two lurcher dogs, Gambol and Streaker, tied up by the leading trailer, grateful for any kind word and the scraps of food Bracken had in his pockets for them.

Last of all, they went to look at the badger cub, curled up asleep in a cardboard box in a dark corner under one of the trailers. Bracken now told Jake everything that had happened on the night of his fall, and ended up by saying again, "I was just too late. If I'd got there earlier, all of the badgers would have escaped."

Jake shook his head. "Most of them did. Don't blame yourself. Only one sow and one cub lost isn't bad from a whole sett, is it?"

Bracken sighed. "No, but I'd rather it was *all* of 'em!"

"Do you think you can rear this cub?" Jake asked.

Bracken looked thoughtful. "Depends if she'll take food. She must be nearly weaned; she looks big enough. The trouble is"—he looked round at the *hatchintan* doubtfully—"I can't really leave her here. It's too noisy, and the dogs'll worry her. She ought to have a kind of sett of her own, only sort of protected, till she's ready for the wild."

"We could build one for her up at the cottage."

The boy's face was suddenly joyous. "Could we? It would mean you'd have to do part of the feeding, like you do for Sky."

"Well, why not? I've nothing better to do."

So they planned it together, and went back to sit by the fire, discussing tunnels and underground chambers and old drainpipes.

The gipsies had decided among themselves that both Bracken and Jake needed time to recover, and that the festivities would not begin until the evening, when the men came home. Meanwhile, the women were busy cooking over their campfires. Finally, the sun began to sink in a muted blaze of apricot fire. The men returned from work, and the women disappeared into their trailers to change from their dullish working clothes into their brightest and best. Soon scarlet and blue and green and a flash or two of gold shone in the firelight. The men donned brilliantly coloured shirts and kerchiefs, and the vivid colours of the costumes helped create a sense of excitement and gaiety.

The air was now full of the smell of woodsmoke and roasting meat, and Jake quickly lost count of the special dishes the women brought from their cooking fires for him to try. Each one seemed to taste richer and more aromatic than the last.

The men had brought out a huge barrel of beer, and they kept filling Jake's mug, as fast as he emptied it. I'm going to feel terrible tomorrow, he thought, but it's worth it.

Bracken almost never left Jake's side. He saw that he had the best space near the fire, and watched him covertly in case he began to look too exhausted. Presently the boy's father sat down next to Jake.

"I wanted to ask you—" began Jake, and glanced round to see if Bracken was listening. But he appeared to be ladling food onto his plate from a pot on the fire. "Is there likely to be any trouble over the badgers?"

"Shouldn't think so," said Kazimir. "The boy says they didn't see him. In any case, I been over there again today, shoeing a horse, and I asked around. They told me Deacon—that's the farmer that threw us off his land—is hopping mad, but there isn't a lot he can do about it. Besides, that sett in Hawkswood isn't really on his land at all."

"Isn't it?" Jake was interested.

"No. Hawkswood belongs to a farmer named Thornton, so Deacon can't say too much about digging out badgers there, can he? Let alone boast about letting one of his dogs run the boy over the edge, if he were to find out." Kazimir Bracsas looked very troubled. "It could have been a lot worse, you know, running straight off the edge like that. He could have been killed."

Jake nodded soberly. "Well," he said, "let me know if anything comes of it—if he needs any help, I mean."

"I will that!" said the gipsy warmly. "Drink up! The singing will begin soon!"

Bracken came and handed Jake a plate of food. "I've brought you a *bokoli*," he said. "It's a pancake with meat inside. See if you like it."

"I'm sure I shall," said Jake.

While he was eating it, the singing began. Someone brought out a guitar, and someone else had a mouth organ. They sang songs, sad and fiery, from far away, and the circle of people round the fire clapped and stamped in rhythm.

I can see where the Hungarian influence comes in, thought Jake. These wild, dark, nostalgic songs are full of Magyar yearning and melancholy, and the long, long wanderings of the Travellers.

Suddenly the mood changed, and a couple of the younger men got up and began to dance. The music swung faster, and the hands clapped with mounting excitement as the young men showed off in the firelight— spinning, leaping, snapping their fingers, tapping their heels. When the music had pushed them on to a final frenzy, they collapsed in a panting heap and a couple of the older men took over. The dance was slower now, and more deliberate. It reminded Jake of dances he had seen in Greece— quiet, held back until the tension suddenly broke into the wild, insistent beat of real abandon. But here the music did not break; it stayed serious and restrained, while the men circled gravely, repeating the intricate steps of long ago.

Then the guitar quickened its thrum, and it was the girls' turn. Jake noticed that the men and women never danced together—always separately. The bright skirts swung, the heels clicked and the gold-coin necklaces clashed as the girls moved to the mounting beat.

After the dancing Bracken's father emerged from his trailer carrying an old, shiny viola. A small cheer went up, and he tucked it under his chin, lifted his bow and began to play.

"I told you Bracsas meant viola player," said Bracken. "The viola is a *sumadji*, a family treasure. It belonged to my great-grandfather."

The men and women round the fire sat enraptured as Kazimir's viola sang out, deep and lamenting, in the night.

When he had finished, there was a silence for a moment. Then the clapping broke out again, and laughter and talk filled the air.

Jake was feeling very strange by now. The bruises from his fall in the quarry were beginning to hurt, and he was ominously cold. He closed his eyes, summoning strength to cope with the curious feeling of vagueness and unreality that was creeping up on him. He must not pass out at the party.

Suddenly a voice seemed to be whispering to him from far away. He opened his eyes and realized that it was Bracken's mother. "Dr. Martin will be here soon," she was saying quietly. "We asked him to the *patshiv*, only he was on duty. But he is coming for a bit, and then he will take you home."

"I can—" began Jake, and then stopped. It was silly to protest. He knew he was not fit to drive. The world looked strangely grey and misty somehow, and this quiet woman with Bracken's gentle smile knew all about him.

"How do the Romanies look on death?" he asked her suddenly.

She did not seem surprised. "It comes to us all; it is natural," she answered tranquilly. "We like to die out of doors, with the sky above us, if we can, like Bracken's creatures do. We believe in honouring the dead. We keep them in our thoughts, and we use special words that remember them. We say, '*Te avel angla tute*'—we do this in your memory—and that keeps them with us. As for ourselves, one day we will know what death is like, so we don't worry about it very much before. God will look after us."

It was what Jake expected—simple, natural and strangely comforting.

Then he felt a hand slip into his, and Bracken's lilting voice said confidingly, "I was thinking we might call the little cub Zoe. My da says it means life."

CHAPTER FIVE

Dr. Martin did not take Jake home. Instead, he took him straight to the local hospital, where they gave him a blood transfusion and did some tests. Jake could see by everyone's exceptional kindness that the results weren't good. He was not surprised, nor was he very troubled. His whole mind was set now on willing himself to be strong enough to go home. The rest would follow when it would.

After ten days Dr. Martin decided that Jake was stable enough to be released. He took a local taxi back to his cottage, and was deeply touched to find quite a row of small offerings on his doorstep. There was a homemade game pie from Mary Willis, together with a small box of groceries. There was cheese from Mrs. Bayliss at Wood End Farm; a scented packet of herb tea, a slab of sesame cake and a bunch of bluebells from the *hatchintan*; two lamb chops and some "rough ends for the bird" from Tom, the butcher; and a book about Gloucestershire from Jim Merrett, the postman, who had also left a note that read: "If you want anything, just leave a list on the step."

Jake carried his presents indoors and made himself some herb tea from the gipsies' packet. When he had rested, he struggled up his garden path to have a look at Sky. Jake found the young kestrel sitting on his tree stump, patiently grooming his long flight feathers.

Jake scattered a few of the butcher's rough ends on the ground near the far end of the pen. Sky looked round at him, then flew across to investigate. His wings were clearly stronger. "You look a lot better," Jake said. "Won't be long now."

The next morning there was a note on the doorstep from Bracken: "Sky is getting strong. Hope you are. The badger cub is still alive and eating. I brought you a chrysalis. I think it is a hawk moth. B." Beside the note was a glass jam jar full of leaves with a brown, casket-shaped chrysalis on the bottom. Jake carried it into the living room and set it down on the table. I wonder when it will hatch out, he thought.

He was still too weak to venture beyond his garden, although he promised himself he would manage it tomorrow...

But tomorrow came, and with it Carol and the boys returning from their holiday, and still he had not been able to summon enough strength to get beyond his garden gate. Through the open cottage door, he heard their voices in the lane and decided reluctantly to stay put in his chair rather than appear at the door weaving on his feet.

The twins came down the lane running, but slowed as they approached the cottage. Finally, they stood by his door, looking in anxiously when they saw Jake in his chair. "Are you all right?" they chorused. Then Matthew added, "We heard in the village about you rescuing Bracken!"

"What happened to Sky?" put in Mark. "Is the badger cub still alive?"

"Wait, boys," said Carol from behind them. "Give him a chance."

She came past the twins and stood just inside the doorway, looking at Jake. Her smile was open and affectionate, and there was the same almost unwilling sense of recognition in her eyes as there was in Jake's. But she was inwardly dismayed to see Jake's unmistakable frailness.

"Jake," she said. "We should have warned you, but we met Bracken up the lane, and he said you would want us to come."

"Of course I do!" said Jake, his face alight with welcome. "Put the kettle on, boys, and ferret about in my larder. I've been given all sorts of presents. There's lots to eat!"

Before long, the boys had spread a feast on the living-room table and were telling him all about pony-trekking in Wales. And Jake told them all about Bracken and the badgers and the gipsy *patshiv*. When they had exhausted their news, the twins went out to look at Sky.

There was silence for a little while after they had gone. Then Carol said gently, "How has it been?"

"Full of excitement," said Jake, wilfully misunderstanding her. "And since the badger rescue, everyone's been extraordinarily kind!"

"I should think so." She shook her head at him with reproach. "You know I didn't mean—"

"I know what you meant," interrupted Jake swiftly. "I'm fine."

She sat down on a stool close to him, where she could look out of the doorway at the garden. "Jake, while the boys were off on their ponies, I used to walk along the beach every morning on my own, and I found myself thinking of you a lot."

"Did you?" He too had his eyes on the garden and carefully avoided looking at her.

"You see, Jake, I've been living in a kind of cold-storage limbo since Bob died. It's only recently, really, that I've even been able to let the twins come close. They felt shut out at first—they've told me so—but we're all fully operational now!" She smiled a little, and glanced at Jake.

He did not speak.

"I know you're happy here," she went on, "and this countryside has come to mean a lot to you. But Jake, human affection matters too. Life's awfully barren without it. For a long time I've felt like a figure behind glass. It was cold in there, silent and lonely. But now"—she fixed her candid gaze on him—"since I met you the thaw has set in. The world is suddenly full of warmth and colour again. It's almost like being reborn, and I wanted to thank you."

"Thank *me?*" Jake sounded astonished and shaken.

"Yes, you. I don't know quite what you've done, but I'm alive again. I think it's something to do with—"

"Immediate joy," murmured Jake.

"What?"

"It's what Bracken's been teaching me. They say the gipsies live in a perpetual 'now', and in a way its true."

Carol understood him. "Seeing you here, so delighted with each small thing..."

"Sky isn't a small thing," said Jake obscurely.

369

"No. Giving back life and freedom to another creature isn't small!"

He smiled. "The boy Bracken does it all the time."

"Well, so do you, now. And I'm your first success!"

He looked at her, the smile dying in his face. "Carol—"

But she would not let him issue any warnings. She laid a hand on his arm. "This is your gipsy 'now', Jake. I'm not talking about the future. I'm not even talking about close companionship. You've chosen the way you want things to be. I respect that. But Jake, I could walk by the sea and think of you and feel warm again and full of unexpected joy. I want you to be able to feel the same. Just an extra source of—of strength?"

"Now?" he said incredulously, his eyes very bright and strange. "*Now*, when it is so much too late? How can I feel this now?"

"Time doesn't come into it," she said softly. "I've said an awful lot, I know. But, dear Jake, there are many kinds of love."

He said, "Yes, there are."

"And we ought not to refuse to recognize them?"

"No," he said, suddenly throwing off doubt and smiling at her with radiant certainty. "No, we shouldn't!"

And he bent towards her and kissed her very gently.

They looked at each other in wonder, but they did not touch again. Instead, they sat talking quietly in the falling twilight until the twins came back from visiting Sky.

Carol saw that Jake was tired, so she got up to go, sending the boys on ahead in a scatter of farewells and laughter.

Jake got to his feet then and gently put his arms round her.

"I haven't given you an extra burden, have I?" she asked.

"No. An extra dimension, perhaps."

"You will be all right?"

"I will be more than all right ... now!"

She kissed him tenderly. "I won't say goodbye. Can we come down again during the summer holidays?"

He hesitated. "Carol, I may—"

"And meanwhile," said Carol firmly, "you can give my love to this valley *every day!* Keeping some for yourself, of course!"

She left him then, and ran down the path after the boys. He heard their voices receding into the distance, and then there was only the quiet night and an owl calling from the trees. Carol, he thought. Now, when I know I am watching death approach day by day, yet I feel my life increasing, not diminishing. He put his hands over his face, trying to shut out the longings he must not have and concentrate on present happiness.

IN THE MORNING there was another note from Bracken that said: "There is a present for you in the garden."

Intrigued, Jake went down the path to have a look. When he got to the little strip of grass under the tree, he saw—placed carefully at the best viewpoint—a brand-new wicker garden chair with a high sloping back and a footrest. The willow basketwork still looked fresh and pale, and it was faintly scented like new-mown hay.

"How lovely!" he murmured, and went to sit in it and admire the view.

Then he heard Sky shouting, "*Kee-kee! Kikikik! Kee-kee!*"

He got up and went rather unsteadily to Sky's pen. The young kestrel seemed to have gone berserk. He was flying to and fro, screaming and crashing into the wire mesh at the end of every flight.

"Stop it, Sky!" Jake said, horrified. "You'll kill yourself."

But Sky would not stop. He went on flying up and down, up and down, fighting his prison at every turn. His wings seemed strong and balanced. He was flying true.

You're ready, then, Jake thought sadly. The time has come, and you know it. What shall I do?

"I told you he'd let us know when he was ready. I'm glad you're here to see him go."

Jake turned and saw Bracken perched on a branch of the apple tree above the pen, unfastening the staples that held the wire.

"It will be better for him to fly straight up," the boy said. "So I'm going to roll the top wire back."

"Let me help," said Jake, forgetting his weakness. Bracken climbed down from his perch, and together they furled the wire slowly back until the top of the pen was open to the free air above.

Then Bracken scrambled back up onto the branch and called to Sky, trying to make him stop his frantic horizontal flight and look up. "Sky," he said. "Look up! You're free now, Sky, you're free!"

For a moment the desperate bird continued its headlong dash at the wire; then it paused in midflight, as if sensing a change in the air above. The smooth blue-grey head looked up; the golden eyes cleared from their unreasoning panic and saw not wire but empty space above. With one swift thrust of those powerful wings, Sky was through the gap, up above the shed and lifting, lifting—flying straight up into the clear morning light, higher and higher until he was only a speck, a mote in the wild, free air of heaven. Jake and Bracken stood together looking up, until there was nothing left to see.

"Goodbye, Sky," said Bracken. "Fly safe, fly free."

Jake found that there were tears in his eyes, and he could not speak at all. That's how I should like it to be with me, he thought—sudden and swift and free.

WHEN HE CAME DOWN the next morning, he found that Bracken was hard at work constructing the sett for little Zoe. He had taken down most of Sky's pen and was cutting the wire in half horizontally, so that he could

371

enlarge the size of the enclosed area. He planned to use the dry-stone wall at the end of the garden as one of the barriers.

"She won't need anything too high," he explained. "But she'll need to be stopped from going too far. Zoe's not ready to fend for herself yet, though I expect she'll try to dig her way out! I thought we could make the sett over here."

Jake saw that he had already dug out two long trenches in which he had laid some old bits of drainpipe. Jake was feeling much better this morning, and he insisted on helping Bracken. They worked together, absorbed and happy in the morning sun.

Before long, they had finished the wire enclosure and adjusted the drainpipes in the trenches in such a way that the open ends came out in two different places in the middle of the grassy cage.

"What will we use for her bedroom?" asked Jake.

Bracken went over to the shed, and came back carrying an old wooden beer barrel. "I brought this up," he said. "If we lay it on its side and line it with grass, it should be nice and snug." Then he picked up his saw. "But I'm going to saw it in half lengthwise so's we can take the top off to have a look at her. She might need dealing with, and she's got to be kept warm. Then we'll make two holes in the barrel and line up the drainpipes with them."

Jake nodded. "What are you feeding her on?"

"Watered-down milk and some chick feed. It'll be worms and grubs soon. I'll bring her up this evening, if that's all right?"

"Of course," agreed Jake. "I'm looking forward to it. Does she mind people much?"

"Not now, when she's so small. And she'll need brushing and combing at first, because her mother would have done it for her. I expect she'll let you do it—she doesn't mind me. But we oughtn't to handle her too much, I s'pose, or she'll never go back to the wild. Just like Sky. I never dared to get too friendly!"

Jake smiled, thinking that it would be almost impossible for Bracken *not* to be friendly. "Come and have some tea," he said. "I'm going to sit in my brand-new chair and admire the view."

Presently they sat side by side, with Jake in the chair and Bracken perched on the wall, and looked out over the sunlit valley.

"Next week," said the boy dreamily, "my da says we can borrow two of the *grais* if we like."

"Really?" Jake knew that was a signal honour from a gipsy horse dealer.

"The quietest two!" said Bracken. Then, suddenly pointing across the valley, he said, "Look! There's a kestrel. I wonder if it's Sky."

"Would he come back?"

"Perhaps. It might smell like home to him." The boy looked at the

372

steady, hovering shadow. "Still, there are lots of kestrels round here. He's old enough to be looking for a mate soon, I should think."

Bracken got down from the wall now and stood looking gravely at Jake. "Will you rest a bit? I'll be back this evening."

"I will. I'll sit in this beautiful chair and dream."

"We all helped to make it," said Bracken. "My father cut the withies. My mother boiled them and stripped them; the sun dried them; I made the frame, and the others wove the basketwork round it." He paused and looked at Jake. "In the old days, my da says, the Romanies used to put a blessing on everything they made, even clothes pegs! I hope it still works!"

"I'm sure it does!" said Jake.

HE MUST HAVE BEEN DOZING in his chair, for he didn't hear the voices and footsteps in the lane. But he sensed a shadow fall across him, and he opened his eyes to see Bill and Manny standing awkwardly beside him on the grass.

"Well, I'm damned!" he said, feeling a rush of warmth at the sight of his old friends. "Come on in and have a beer!"

He led them both inside and went on talking easily until he had them sitting down in his living room, each with a glass of beer in his hand.

Bill was looking at Jake with disbelief, almost with awe, for he seemed so changed. He was much thinner now, and the planes of his face had sharpened. It was clearly the face of a man who was mortally sick, but also a man who was entirely tranquil, entirely happy.

"Well?" said Jake, grinning. "What do you think of me?"

"I think you're fantastic!" said Bill, lifting his glass.

"Oh, I am!" agreed Jake. "You don't have to worry about me. I've found a good life here, an amazing life, really. I couldn't be happier, so drink up. I've got lots to tell you, and you can bring me up to date on all the office gossip."

Filled with a strange mixture of relief and sadness, the two men relaxed, and the three of them began to talk and exchange news. Jake told them about his adventures with Bracken and the saving of Sky.

"And then there's Zoe. If you stay long enough, you'll meet her," he said, eyes dancing with mischief. "She's coming tonight."

"Who's Zoe?" asked Manny with a wild hope in his eye.

"A badger cub, actually," said Jake, and then related the dark happenings of Hawkswood Quarry.

When all seemed said on each side, Bill looked at Jake with a tentative gaze and said, "You got on well with Carol, didn't you?"

Jake's smile was full of warmth, and something more that Bill did not quite understand. "Got on well? She simply took me by storm! I shall never be the same again! I liked the boys too. They're all coming back to see me during the summer holidays—all being well, that is."

Bill was surprised and pleased. "She didn't tell me that!"

While they were talking, there was a light tap on the door, and Bracken's voice said, "I've brought Zoe up. Come and see!"

He did not show any surprise when three men, not one, came outside. He just said quietly, "Go softly; she's still scared of loud noises."

They followed him out to the wire enclosure, and there, in a cardboard box on the ground, was the tiny badger cub. She was curled up asleep, surrounded by wisps of hay and pieces of woollen cloth to keep her warm. The small black-and-white face was perfectly marked, but the fur on her back was brindled and scrappy and stuck up like tangled wire. Jake's fingers instantly itched to have a brush between them and to start smoothing down the rumpled fur.

"How old is she?" asked Bill.

"About three months, we think," said Bracken. He busied himself measuring out some food—a handful of chick feed moistened with milk and water, a drop of fish oil and half a chopped-up worm.

"You'd better watch me," he said to Jake, "so's you can manage if I can't come."

"Don't you dare not come!" said Jake. "I'd be terrified!"

Bill and Manny laughed, but Bracken went on, unperturbed, "She's got to get used to you too. Have a go at feeding her." He handed Jake a small metal spoon. "She'll wake up in a minute," he added. "It's getting near dusk."

Sure enough, the small body uncurled and stretched, the questing snout with its clean white blaze came up to sniff the air, and the little nearsighted eyes opened and looked round with distrust.

"There now," said Bracken, crooning to the cub. "See, Zoe, we've made you a new house. Come on out and have a look round. It's your dinnertime as well."

He lifted the little cub out of her box and put her on the ground. She sat still for a few moments, quivering all over, but then she began to look about her and to snuff along the ground. She came up against the bowl of food with a bump and sat down again on her haunches to look at it and smell it.

"Now!" said Bracken. "Hold some up in the spoon!"

Jake scooped up some food and held it towards the twitching nose. The little cub stared at the approaching spoon with deep apprehension and then butted it violently with her snout.

"Try again," said Bracken.

Patiently Jake began again. This time Zoe inched forward, sniffed the spoon and took the food.

Absurdly pleased, Jake offered her another spoonful. Again, the cub came forward and sought the food with her sensitive nose. The two men stood watching Jake, so absorbed and happy, and did not say a word.

"Now," said Bracken, "try holding the spoon near the dish."

Before very long Zoe had discovered that a dish held more than a spoon, and was eating tranquilly from the bowl. She ate all the food and then began to explore her new home in earnest. Bracken had left Sky's tree trunk for her to climb over, and now he arranged two extra logs as climbing obstacles in her playground. She tried to clamber over these, fell over backwards and waved her feet in the air. Then she scrambled up and darted round in circles, playing with a leaf or a twig or a pebble, pouncing like a kitten, then backing away in mock terror, gambolling cheerfully in her newfound freedom.

Last of all, Bracken tossed a furry baby's ball, quartered in brown and black, into Zoe's path. She was delighted with it, rolling it, jumping on it, chasing it and finally settling down with it pressed close to her side in a corner of the pen.

"I thought she might like it," said Bracken. "She misses her brothers and sisters, you see. We'd better put it in the box with her when she goes to sleep."

Fascinated, the watchers stayed there admiring Zoe's antics until she began to tire, and Bracken put her back in her box together with her woolly ball. He made sure the opening in the end of the box was clear for her to go in and out. Seeming perfectly content, the cub curled herself into a second woolly ball and went to sleep.

"She'll come out again later," whispered Bracken, placing the lid on the box. "She's at her most active just after dark. We can leave her now."

Everyone tiptoed away. Manny and Bill stopped on the path and looked at Jake in the falling dusk. Neither of them knew how to say goodbye. But Jake took a step forward and grasped them each by an arm. "I'm glad you came down so you could see for yourselves I'm all right!"

They seemed to see something reassuring in his face, and Manny said, "I hope we haven't worn you out."

"No," said Jake, smiling, "I've enjoyed it very much."

Jake thought perhaps Bracken had slipped away unnoticed, but he reappeared at this moment carrying a swinging storm lantern and said, "It's a dark old night. Shall I light you up the lane?"

Bill and Manny followed him gratefully, turning to wave to Jake from the gate, and made their way up the stony track to their car.

As he left them Bracken said very softly, "I'll look after him, you know, while I can." And before they could answer, he had gone into the shadows, the lantern swinging in his hand.

WHEN JAKE WOKE the next day, it seemed much later than usual. The sun was high, half hidden behind slow-moving clouds. When he went outside, he found Bracken up at Zoe's pen, tinkering about with some further additions.

"She's fast asleep," he said by way of greeting, and lifted the lid of the box for Jake to see the little cub. She looked small and lonely, curled up with the woolly ball close beside her.

"Her fur needs brushing," said Jake. "When ought I to do it?"

Bracken considered. "I tried it when she was eating. She didn't seem to mind too much. I think she might even come to like it."

He put the lid back on the box and left Zoe to her daylong sleep.

"I brought some tea up today," he said, and led Jake over to the new wicker chair.

They sat peacefully, looking out at the awakening valley. Jake found that it was not so very late after all. It was well into May now, and he had forgotten that the sun got high in the sky quite early.

Bracken looked at Jake's face and caught the longing in his eye. "We could go just a little way," he said to that saddened gaze.

Jake stirred and laughed. "I must be very transparent!"

"Yes," agreed the boy, laughing too, "you are!"

So they wandered out into the cool morning and drifted slowly down the sloping valley to the lake where the wild swans lived.

"We mayn't see anything special," said Bracken, looking up to watch a cuckoo fly across the valley.

"Everything's special to me," murmured Jake, also watching the cuckoo.

They arrived by the reedy fringe of the lake and settled down to watch the ordinary everyday life of that small enclosed world. Swifts were darting low over the water after insects, their high, thin voices echoing in the still morning air. Little coots and moorhens chugged fussily in and out of the bulrushes, and there were muted quacks and sudden watery flourishes from the mallards hidden in the thick reeds.

"There goes a dragonfly!" said Bracken. "Doesn't he look new?"

The darting, transparent wings flashed in the sun, and the long, delicate body seemed to gleam with fresh paint, the speckled browns and greens were so bright. Jake watched it, breathless, and presently it skimmed quite near to them and settled on a lily leaf to dry its gauzy wings. So beautiful, so fragile, thought Jake.

"I don't think the swans are coming," said Bracken. "They're usually earlier than this."

But even as he spoke, two of the great white birds came pulsing overhead. They landed far down the lake in a skidding stop, sending up a sparkle of spray, and sat there quietly floating, their snowy, graceful outlines meeting their two reflections in perfect symmetry.

"Only two?" said Bracken, sounding anxious. "Where are the others?"

And then Jake pointed, too enchanted to speak. For out from the willow shadows came their two mates, proudly gliding like ships in full sail, and with them came six small grey cygnets, swimming gallantly, small legs cleaving the water in their efforts to keep up with their two noble mothers. The four adult swans met in midwater, each cob greeting his mate with grave courtesy, dipping his long neck, touching beak to beak and then turning to swim tranquilly beside her, his pearl grey downy offspring following behind.

Jake and Bracken dreamed and idled a while longer. High above the lake a solitary kestrel swung and hovered, its wings outspread, leaning on the wind. "It might be Sky," murmured Bracken, lying back on the grass and gazing up into the clear blue air.

Sky, thought Jake. I believe I miss him. I miss his fierce, angry independence, the tameless golden eyes and arrogant head. But I'm glad he's up there somewhere in those wild spaces, flying free.

A small breeze stirred the willow leaves and lifted a thistledown head into the air. It sailed by, and Bracken reached out a lazy hand and caught it. He held it in his brown palm and offered it to Jake.

"Next year's flowers," he said, smiling his strange, tender smile.

Jake looked down at the perfect shape, the intricate filigree stars and minuscule feathery halos round each tiny seed head, the fine, hair-thin threads of stalk. So beautiful, so fragile, with a world of summers in its keeping.

"When I die"—Bracken's voice was as soft and light as the thistledown—"just think! I'll be part of a dandelion puff, or a dragonfly's wing, or a worm!" His smile grew luminous with unexplained joy. "I'll be part of Sky!"

Jake did not answer. He knew what Bracken was telling him. There were tears in his eyes, but he wasn't sure if they were from grief or some of Bracken's immediate joy.

He lifted his hand and let the thistledown blow away on the wind. It hung for a moment in the air above his head, shimmering in the sun, and then it drifted upwards on the merest breath and sailed away across the valley.

CHAPTER SIX

In the afternoon, when Jake was alone, he had a visitor. The man who stood at his door was solid and friendly, with a bluff, weather-worn face and the quiet blue eyes of a countryman. He wore an old pair of cords tucked into wellington boots, and a battered tweed jacket. His smile was calm and kind.

"Sorry to disturb you, Mr. Farrant," he said. "I'm Bayliss, of Wood End Farm. I wonder, could I have a word?"

"Of course," said Jake. "Come in."

The farmer followed Jake into the cottage.

"Have a chair," said Jake. "A glass of beer? Or tea?"

"A cup of tea would be more than welcome," said Stan Bayliss, settling into a chair as Jake went into the kitchen. In a few minutes he came back, bringing Bayliss a mug.

"Now," said Jake, "what's on your mind?"

Stan Bayliss took a gulp of tea and came straight to the point. "It's about the gipsies," he began. "I thought, maybe, a word of warning from you might come less amiss than one from me."

Jake's heart gave a lurch of fear. "Warning? About what?"

The farmer shifted in his chair. "It's the dogs. At least, I don't rightly think it's *their* dogs, but I'm having pressure put on me by Ralph Deacon."

"Deacon? The boy told me that Mr. Deacon threw the gipsies off his farm. But what's the trouble now?"

"Sheep worrying," explained Bayliss. "Something's attacked some of Deacon's lambs. He says it's not a fox, and he's seen something running the sheep. But he was too far off to recognize it."

"I see," said Jake.

"Now, I'm a peaceable man myself, Mr. Farrant. The gipsies never did me any harm, and they're good workers. They've been useful on my land, and I've no reason to turn them off. Live and let live, I say." He stopped and looked hard at Jake. "But Deacon's a powerful man. If there's any chance of proving that one of their dogs was a wrong 'un, he'd have 'em off and out. D'you see what I mean?"

"Yes. But I think they keep their dogs tied up at the camp."

"So do I," agreed Bayliss. "But could they prove it? People aren't that good about taking a gipsy's word."

"What do you suggest I do?"

"Just warn 'em. I've got sheep myself. I don't want any trouble. And if you could see your way to having their dogs up here for a day or two, at least till the varmint's caught, it wouldn't do no harm."

Jake nodded. "You're a man after my own heart, Mr. Bayliss."

"Stan. Call me Stan. Everyone does round here."

"Well then, Stan, I wish there were more like you!"

The farmer got up to go, and Jake went with him to the gate. "I'll do what I can about the dogs."

"Knew you would," said Bayliss. "I'll let you know if I hear anything more." He paused, then went on, "It's good country this, you know. Gives you more than you can put back."

"Yes," said Jake, smiling, "I know."

IN THE EARLY EVENING, well before dark, Zoe came out. Jake was up there alone as the little cub wandered about her grassy pen, sniffing and rooting among the leaves and the gnarled claws of the old apple tree. Jake

378

noticed too that she musked a couple of times round the edges of her territory, as if to declare her ownership.

He mixed her food, putting some in the bowl and a little on the spoon. She ate what was in the spoon, then lowered her beautiful, clever little head to look for the food in the bowl. "That's right," said Jake. "You're a fast learner, aren't you?"

Her roughened fur still bothered him, so he went down to the cottage and fetched an old clothes brush and began to brush Zoe's back. At first she shied a little, but then she seemed to get used to the feeling, and even began to rub herself against the soft bristles as if she liked it. "Good," said Jake. "We'll soon have you looking like a beauty queen."

When he was finished, he pulled a small paper bag from his pocket and brought out various titbits for her to try—a carrot, a raisin or two and a piece of apple. But a bit of bread smeared with honey was obviously best of all. "That's enough, now," he said severely, "or you'll get too fat to climb over your logs. Go and take some exercise!"

Zoe didn't need telling. She scrambled round, investigating corners and bushes and even the bottom layer of the dry-stone wall.

Jake watched her and thought to himself, She's not a bit afraid. It won't be long before she's over that wall! Or under it!

He decided to introduce her to the barrel and drainpipes that formed her homemade sett. Would she discover how to crawl out of the drainpipes into the grassy enclosure?

She had begun collecting small stones and carrying them back to her cardboard box, so when she was engrossed in arranging these, Jake picked up the box with her inside it and set it down with the opening leading directly into the warm, grass-lined interior of the barrel.

After a moment's pause at the sensation of being lifted, Zoe's inquisitive nature got the better of her. She came out of her box and went unhesitatingly into the mouth of the barrel.

Jake waited, breathless.

She rooted about inside, turning round and round and rearranging her bedding until she found herself facing another dark hole leading into one of the drainpipes. She sniffed at it, peered vaguely round with her nearsighted eyes and then disappeared into the pipe.

Jake went silently over to the other end of the pipe and laid a morsel of bread and honey by this exit. Sure enough, the pointed, questing black-and-white snout came through. The nose twitched, alert for danger; then the whole agile little body came through, and the bread and honey rapidly disappeared.

"Well done!" said Jake. "But can you find your way back?"

He went over to the barrel and this time put a small item of food beside the drainpipe opening.

For a while the cub played near the edge of the drainpipe, but then she

379

found a small treasure—a shiny piece of bark—and took it with her into the pipe and back to her bedding in the barrel.

There was still one more opening to explore, a drainpipe that led from the barrel to a place further down the enclosure, coming out near the wall. When Zoe was ready, the way over the wall would be cleared and made easy. She would be off down the long hedge and into the woods beyond.

"Put this by the pipe," said Bracken, appearing by Jake's side. "Let's see what she makes of a frog." He handed Jake a very small limp bundle of legs and bright green skin, and Jake laid it down by the wall. Emerging into the garden through this new way out, Zoe found the frog and sat down to consider it. Presently she got up and stood on it, beating it to pulp with her feet. Then she swallowed it whole.

"Ugh!" said Jake. "Rather you than me, Zoe!"

A sudden wave of dizziness assailed him, and he clung for a moment to the apple tree. Then the world righted itself, and he looked at Bracken and said, "Can we leave her out here on her own?"

"Oh, yes. We'll come back in a bit and see how she's managing with the barrel. She seems to know already what to do. I should think we could cover it; she'll probably feel safer if we do."

"Come on, then," said Jake. "I've something to tell you."

He took Bracken back to the cottage and sat on the step with him. "Stan Bayliss came to see me today," he began.

When he had finished, Bracken said, "It's always the same. We think we're safe, in a nice friendly place, and then trouble starts."

"It hasn't started. That's the point. Bayliss wants you to stay on his land, but he wanted me to warn you. Shall I have the dogs up here for a bit? Then if anything goes wrong with the sheep, I can swear blue that they were here."

Bracken nodded seriously. "Our *jukels* wouldn't touch a lamb or run the sheep. I'm sure they wouldn't."

"No," agreed Jake. "Stan Bayliss didn't think they would, either. But *something* has, and Deacon says it wasn't a fox."

Bracken thought for a bit. "I'll talk to my da," he said at last. "I'll bring the dogs up tomorrow."

"Not tomorrow," said Jake. "Now! A fox—or anything else—could get at those sheep tonight."

Bracken turned to look at Jake in surprise. "I've never heard you sound so fierce before! All right, I'll go down there now." He put a hand on Jake's arm. "Thanks!" he said, and went swiftly away.

Jake went back to the badger's pen to see how little Zoe was doing. At length he heard Bracken and his father in the lane with the two lurcher dogs. Jake went to meet them at the gate.

"This is good of you, Mr. Farrant, sir," said Kazimir Bracsas.

"That's all right," answered Jake. "It was Stan Bayliss who thought of it. You've got a good, fair-minded boss there!"

The man nodded. "Yes. We're lucky. Not too many of 'em about."

"Let's hope they catch the dog or whatever it is," said Jake.

"If there *is* a dog," murmured the gipsy.

Jake looked at him. The thought had occurred to him too. "You think it could be a put-up job? Out of spite?"

"Could be. I've known people do worse where us gipsies were concerned."

"We'll just have to sit it out, then," said Jake.

"I was going to say—before this happened—you could have two of the *grais* to ride tomorrow. I shan't be using Sheba and Ambler. You can go further that way, and it'll take a weight off your feet."

"That's very kind of you," said Jake, smiling.

"Right, then." Kazimir Bracsas turned to his son. "Choose a good route tomorrow for Mr. Farrant!" With that, he lifted his hand in a friendly gesture of farewell, and departed.

Bracken was stooping over the two dogs, fiddling with the chains on their collars. "You'll have to be good up here," he told them. "No barking, or you'll frighten Zoe. I'm going to chain you to the gate." The dogs, peaceful and content, lay down on the path.

"Listen!" said Bracken suddenly. "I thought I heard ... yes, there, it is! In that tall tree by the edge of the field. Can you hear it?"

Jake listened. And the night was all at once filled with throbbing song. Trill after trill of pulsing notes poured out into the still, scented air. "A nightingale!" he whispered.

"Yes! Never heard one so far up the valley as this before. Listen! Isn't he lovely? Sounds like moonlight turned into notes." The liquid silver song poured out of the sky, quite close above them now, from the topmost branches of the pear tree.

They stood there, spellbound, until the tireless bird caught the echo of a silver-throated answer from the woods and flew off to meet it.

The two listeners stirred, as if out of a dream, and Bracken said, "I'll be up in the morning with Ambler and Sheba. I hope the dogs don't keep you awake." Then he added, with a faint jerk of his head, "He's still singing out there somewhere. If you listen, you just might hear him!" And he disappeared quietly into the dark.

THAT NIGHT Jake could not get to sleep. The pain was worse than usual, but even more terrifying was the feeling of panic and anxiety that seemed to engulf him. He wandered out into the garden again to see what the little cub was doing. He found her sitting quite still in the middle of the grass, her neat white head with its two black bars pointed towards the distant fields beyond the wall, as if she were listening for something. She looked very small and lonely all by herself in the dark night, and Jake wondered if she consciously missed her mother and the other cubs or if she was simply caught by the scents and sounds of the night, longing for freedom. Something about that tense, listening head reminded him of Sky.

Jake was still not ready to go to sleep, so he returned to the cottage, wrapped himself in his thickest coat and came back to sit in his wicker chair. It was better out here. He could breathe again, and the panicky fear was gone. Out here in the calm, receiving night he forgot to be afraid. Presently, as the first faint glimmer of dawn grew in the east, he fell asleep.

THE NEXT MORNING Jake opened his eyes to find Bracken beside him and two inquisitive ponies looking at him over the gate.

"Must have overslept!" Jake said, confused. And then, looking at his view of the valley, he added, "A grand morning too! Wait while I put my kettle on." And he struggled indoors to shave off his midnight beard while the kettle sang on his stove.

Bracken, meanwhile, walked the two dogs in the lane. When he had run them up and down as much as he could manage, he returned them to their post by the gate and went to have a quick look at Zoe's pen. She was not to be seen, so he assumed she was asleep in her barrel.

"Tea!" called Jake from the doorway. "And currant buns. Mary Willis sent them!"

Bracken was looking at him a little anxiously. "Did you stay out here all night?" he asked as he took his usual place on the wall.

"Well, not exactly," said Jake. "I started off indoors, but I couldn't sleep, so I sat in my chair and sort of drifted off."

Bracken laughed. But he was not fooled. His friend Jake looked desperately pale this morning. He'd better not take him for too long a ride.

Jake, on the other hand, had taken a painkiller and was determined not to spoil this morning by being weak. And I'm not going to put the boy at risk by passing out, he thought sternly to himself.

When they had finished their breakfast, Bracken led Jake out through the gate to the ponies. "You'd better have Ambler," he said. "He takes my da everywhere. Sheba's all right too, but she's lazy. You have to kick her a bit."

Jake climbed on the grey pony's broad back and felt instantly at home. Bracken leaped up onto Sheba, gave her a dig with his heels, and the two of them moved off up the steep, sun-dappled lane.

"Where are we going?" asked Jake.

"I thought we'd go up to a hill called the British Camp," said Bracken, waving towards a ridge of hills ahead of them. "You can see for miles from the top. Feels almost like being up above the world."

They did not hurry. The ponies clip-clopped along the road and then turned off up a long, grassy track skirting the edge of the beechwoods.

Presently the track led into the woods, and they went on climbing steadily through the soft brown carpet of last year's leaves. The woods seemed full of birdsong, full of golden sunlight and shadow.

Eventually they came out of the trees onto the curving brow of the hill and went on upwards till they reached the first circle of the British Camp.

"There were soldiers here once," explained Bracken, "fighting off the Romans. They used to light beacons on the tops of all the hills to tell each other when the enemy was coming." He pointed up to the next grassy ridge. "And when things got bad, they went on up to the next level, and then to the top, and the Romans came on up after them and circled all round them, until they were done for."

"Where did you learn all that?"

Bracken smiled. "They told us a bit of it at school once when I was there, and afterwards the school lady gave me the book. It tells you all about this place, and where the burial chamber is, underneath that mound over there."

By now they had reached the smooth crown of the hill. They dismounted and tethered the two ponies to the only tree nearby, a stunted hawthorn, then sat on the grass to take in the view.

"I often think of those soldiers up here," said Bracken dreamily. "Fighting on and on until they died. They must have loved this land. It was theirs, and they didn't want it taken from them." He had picked up a stone and was turning it round in his fingers. "Look!" he said. "Long before all that, this land was all covered in sea," and he held out the small fossil of a perfect shell for Jake to see. "The earth is awfully old," he said.

Jake took the stone and marvelled at the fluted indentations still visible in it. Awfully old, he thought—millions of years old, like this shell in my hand, and here I am worrying about a few short weeks.

He looked out at the vista. Before them lay the wide, rich plain of Gloucestershire, with the silver Severn River threading its way down towards the sea. Beyond that lay the far blue mountains of Wales, and to the right of them stood the dramatic ridge of the Malvern Hills.

"So much space," he murmured. "It makes the sky look huge."

"Mm," Bracken said drowsily. "And there's a kestrel up there. I do believe Sky's keeping an eye on us!"

Jake smiled. He would like to think so too. Up there, he thought, sailing in airy freedom, with all high heaven to play in. It won't be long now. I shall be with you soon.

But something was troubling him, and he wondered how to explain it to Bracken, who resolutely never let him think more than one day ahead. How much did the boy know—or guess? Ought he to warn him? Had he the right to go on enjoying these marvellous expeditions, with his own hawk's-wing shadow hanging over him?

"If I was one of them soldiers," said Bracken, still apparently dreaming, "and I saw the enemy coming, creeping up the hill..."

"Yes?" said Jake strangely. "What would you do?"

Bracken did not look at him. His eyes were fixed on the faint wing shadow. "I'd say to myself, If I can't beat 'em, I'll go down fighting. But if this is my very last day, I'm going to enjoy it first! And I'd turn my back on them creeping up, and look at the view."

Jake's breathing was uneven. Then he said steadily enough, "But suppose you were looking at the view and an arrow struck you, and your comrades had to come out into danger after you?"

Bracken looked at him then with incredulity. "Don't be daft," he said. "What are comrades for?"

WHEN THEY GOT HOME, Bracken tied up the *grais*, and Jake went—a little shakily—to rustle up some bread and cheese and tea. He came out carrying a tray, and went to set it down on the wall by his willow chair. Then he straightened up to look at the view.

But something about the distant green hillside opposite made him pause. There was movement over there, a flicker. The white dots of the sheep seemed to bunch together, then run, scattering across the grass. "Bracken!" he called. "Come here a minute!"

Bracken came running. "What is it?"

"Look over there! Do you see what I see?"

Bracken looked. Then he turned back to Jake swiftly. "Something's after those sheep. What shall we do?"

"Whose sheep are they?"

"Farmer Bayliss's. That's his top pasture."

"Then go for Bayliss—*quickly*. I'll stay here with the dogs. Run, Bracken!"

"I'll take Sheba," said Bracken. "It'll be quicker." He sprang onto the pony's back, leaped the dry-stone wall and raced off towards the farm lane beyond.

Jake looked back at the hillside. The sheep were running crazily in circles, and something dark was running with them. There were one or two ominously still white blobs on the grass.

Jake made up his mind that he might be needed too. It was pointless to take the car—it would not cross those grassy slopes—so he got up onto Ambler's stolid back and plodded up the lane and across the ridge of hillside towards the green slope he had seen from his garden.

Meanwhile, Bracken had arrived in Stan Bayliss's yard in a scatter of mud and hens, flung himself off Sheba's back and run to the farmhouse door. Stan was just sitting down to breakfast.

"Quick!" said Bracken. "The top pasture. There's something chasing after the sheep!"

Stan Bayliss seized his gun and ran for his Land-Rover. "Tie up your horse. Come on."

They roared out of the yard, scattering the hens once more as they went. When they arrived at the head of the sloping hill, Stan parked on the grass verge, climbed the wall and went running downhill, with Bracken close beside him. And there, below them, an awful sight met their eyes. Several lambs lay dead, their throats torn out. One sheep lay upside down in the ditch, its feet waving feebly in the air, and another was caught in the brambles of the hedge. The rest were still milling and weaving in frantic terror, and a dark, brindled body was circling round them, closing in with every stride.

Bracken, with a cry of outrage, outdistanced Stan Bayliss and ran swiftly over the grass to get between the nearest terrified lambs and the snapping jaws of the dog.

"No, boy!" shouted Stan. "How can I shoot? I'll hit you! Look out, he's gone wild. He'll bite!"

But Bracken did not heed the farmer. He went on running, and scooped up the first two frightened stragglers in his arms. The dog's furiously snapping jaws met in his arm. A shot rang out, and the big heavy dog stopped in midstride and fell in a heap on the grass.

Stan came running, his gun still unfired in his hands. "Are you all right? You might've got yourself killed!"

"I'm not hurt," said Bracken untruthfully. "You shot him!"

"Not I!" said Stan. "It came from over yonder! D'you know whose dog it is?"

Bracken looked down at the bull mastiff at his feet. "It's Boley. It's Deacon's."

From across the field a man came out of the shadows, carrying a gun. He walked towards them, and stopped when he saw the dog.

"Well, Deacon," said Stan Bayliss, sounding as grim as the other man looked. "D'you recognize this dog?"

Deacon nodded. He had been fond of his old hunting companion, Boley. It was a shock to see any dog go wrong like this, let alone one of his own. He knelt down and sadly turned the dog over. It was quite dead. Then his eye fell on the carnage in the field. "I'm sorry about this."

"It's a bad business," said Stan. "Looks like I've lost several lambs."

Bracken, meanwhile, had put the unhurt lambs down on the grass, and had one hand tightly clasped round his arm where the dog had bitten him. "Hadn't we better pick up those poor sheep?" he said.

Deacon glanced at him sharply. "I might've known you'd be here!"

From behind him Jake's voice spoke very crisply and clearly. "If he hadn't been, Mr. Deacon, there would have been much more damage done." He turned to the boy. "We'd better get that arm seen to. A dog bite can be nasty. You were lucky not to get shot as well."

"You take the Land-Rover and see to the boy," Stan said to Jake. "I'll stay and clear up with Deacon. I'll bring the horses back later."

Jake nodded. "All right. Come on, my young friend. You've done all you need to here . . ." Bracken was gazing down with tears in his eyes at the dead lambs and the strong, sturdy body of the dog.

"What a waste," he murmured as Jake led him away up the hill. "What a stupid waste."

After Dr. Martin had cleaned and dressed the boy's arm and given him an injection, Jake invited Stan Bayliss, Ralph Deacon and Kazimir Bracsas to his cottage. He had decided that this stupid feud had to end before more damage was done.

He handed out beer and cake all round in his front garden and then addressed himself to Ralph Deacon. "As you probably know, I came down here for a rest!" he began. "I've seen too much of wars and disasters, Mr. Deacon. It seems to me that life's too short for needless disputes; there's trouble enough in it already! It's not my business, of course, but this young fellow here saved you a lot of extra expense today. Things could have been much worse. Shouldn't we all let bygones be bygones and call it a day?"

Jake knew he sounded a bit pompous, but he felt that what he had to say was important.

"I could keep my eyes open for a new dog," said Bracken's father, speaking quietly but with intent. "I see a lot on my travels."

For a moment it looked as if Deacon was going to utter a sharp refusal. But he caught the gleam in Jake's eye, and something about this man's pallor and obvious frailty made him ashamed. "Good idea," he said gruffly. "I'd be obliged if you would."

Bracken let out a sigh of relief, and Stan Bayliss gave Jake a wink.

"That's good," said Jake, lifting his glass. "I'm going to drink to this marvellous countryside, and everyone in it who's been so kind to me!"

Solemnly they all lifted their glasses in response. They ate some more cake, and then the little party broke up.

CHAPTER SEVEN

The next few days passed in a haze of weariness for Jake. He knew he had overdone it and he was bound to feel the consequences. But pain and weakness took over to such a degree that he was scarcely aware of what he was doing. He was ashamed of this and did his best to disguise it when Bracken came. By day he spent a lot of his time lying back in his wicker chair.

Bracken's arm was healing nicely, and each evening when he came up to see to Zoe, he told Jake firmly that he could manage alone. But Jake had become mysteriously attached to the little badger cub, and he could not resist going with the boy to have a look at her, even though it seemed to take a long time to get back up his garden path.

It was late dusk one evening after a week or so of his malingering, as Jake privately called it, when he decided he felt well enough to walk on his own to feed Zoe. The first stars were just beginning to appear in the primrose sky, but the shapes of the trees were still visible, and the white moon daisies in the field seemed to be filled with light.

He reached the wire enclosure and let himself in. Zoe was rooting about in a corner, and she came galloping across to meet him, grunting and squealing with pleasure.

"All right," said Jake, "I've got your dinner. I know it's late."

He set the bowl of food down on the grass, and Zoe's snout was into the dish before he could turn round. She concentrated on her food until the bowl was empty. Then she began to play.

Jake had found the woolly ball lying in the grass near one of the drainpipe exits—she must have brought it out from her bed—and he began to roll it for her. She immediately began pouncing on it and chasing it. But presently she seemed to grow tired of playing, and went up close to the wall, where the hedge began and the first tall ash tree beckoned and whispered in the night, about wild woods and secret paths and old tree roots and hidden sandy banks.

Zoe's small face was lifted to the night air, and her sensitive nose was wrinkling and twitching with the heady scents of summer.

"What is it?" asked Jake softly. "Do you want to go already? You're a bit small yet, you know, to manage on your own."

But the little cub still sat there, listening and scenting the night air, her whole small body filled with yearning to be wandering those silent, leafy paths.

"It won't be long now," he said, as he had said to Sky. "Soon, we will be able to let you go."

Jake walked slowly back to his chair in the garden. He had just reached it when he fell in a quiet heap on the grass.

He came round dizzily to find himself lying back in his wicker chair and Bracken walking towards him, carefully carrying a mug of tea.

"Sorry," Jake murmured. "Overdid it again." Then he suddenly realized. "Bracken!" he said, amazed. "You went inside the cottage! You've never done that before."

Bracken looked a trifle confused. "Well, you needed your tea." He held out the mug and made sure Jake's hands were firmly round it before he let go. "It's a lovely night," he said, perching on the wall. "Soft as milk."

Jake sipped his tea, saying nothing, waiting for the stars above the pear tree to stop spinning. In a little while they did, and he reached for one of the pills in his pocket.

"Shouldn't you be home by now?" he asked Bracken. "It must be quite late."

"Doesn't matter," said the boy. "They know where I am."

Bracken sat there for a long time in the scented dark, waiting for Jake to fall asleep.

Presently he did.

Jake woke the next morning to find himself warmly wrapped in the blanket from his bedroom and his wicker chair turned a little sideways to catch the morning sun. He felt rested and at peace.

"I brought some tea today," said Bracken, standing beside him in the sunlight. "And I thought we might make Zoe's pen bigger, so's she can try a bit of the wild hedge on the other side of the wall before she goes. She'll be ready soon. She's getting restless."

Soon, Jake thought sadly, and resolved to make sure that he did not collapse on Bracken's hands again. I must take more care, ration myself, so that I don't risk getting too tired. I hate being cautious, but soon I must say to him that I can't go on any more morning jaunts.

"I think when we first let her go, she'll want to come back to sleep here," said Bracken thoughtfully, "and she'll probably want you to go a little way with her, just to make sure she knows the way back."

"Do you think so?"

"Mm ... She'll find the world a big old place, a bit frightening, I shouldn't wonder." He paused. "So it'll be night wanderings, not mornings. Only short ones, mind!"

Jake gazed at Bracken, speechless, while the boy poured out some tea from his flask and gave Jake a bit of the gipsies' sesame cake.

"All the same," continued Bracken, rightly judging the expression in Jake's eyes, "I think we could go out a couple more mornings before she gets too restless. We'll enlarge the pen today, then we might have a look at those closest beechwoods tomorrow and see where she's likely to go first. What do you think?"

"Sounds like a good idea," said Jake, smiling radiantly.

The next day they explored the beechwoods, marking the high, sandy banks and hidden hollows under the ancient tree roots where Zoe might want to make another sett. Bracken also looked for signs of other badgers, and found one clearly occupied sett near the far end of the woods. There were piles of scraped earth and old tufts of bedding outside, and in one corner was a tidy dung heap among the brown covering of beechnuts and last year's leaves.

"She might make friends here," said Bracken cheerfully. "At least she won't be alone in the woods."

"They wouldn't attack her, would they—being a stranger, I mean?"

"Oh, no," replied Bracken, shocked. "Badgers is friendly creatures, even to each other! I expect they'll adopt her."

That evening Zoe went rooting in the grass and seemed very busy and happy. Jake thought she seemed to be finding quite a few earthworms and grubs on her own, but he still put out her food in her usual bowl, and she came to eat it eagerly.

After she had eaten, she scampered about the grass again, and often returned to Jake to nudge at his hand or tug at his boots. But in between she sat by the wall, her head tilted wistfully towards the distant woods, clearly longing to clamber over and explore the green world beyond.

The following day Bracken brought up another piece of old drainpipe and dug a way out of the garden between the wall and the hedge. For the moment, he covered the end that came out into the hedge with a piece of wire netting. "We can take it off when we're there, to see what she does," he explained. "We'd better bring a few extra titbits tonight, then we can bribe her to come back!"

When Zoe came out that night, Jake and Bracken introduced her to her larger domain. She found a piece of delectable bread and honey by a new hole close to the wall. She sniffed at the food and decided to eat it there and then. Then her inquisitive nose led her into the hole. Jake held his breath. She was going, then. Little Zoe was almost free, though she didn't yet know it.

The striped head came through the other end. It halted while she sniffed the wind for danger. Nothing seemed to threaten, so she went out of the drainpipe into the open field by the wild hedge. For a few moments she sat there, seeming puzzled by all that space around her. Then she began to forage in the hedge. She ventured a little further, and then turned round and came back again.

"Put another piece of food down," whispered Bracken, "so she can find her way back."

Jake laid it by the hole in the garden and stood there, waiting. The questing nose came closer to the drainpipe; then she plunged in again and emerged in the garden. Once again she ate the waiting food, and then came galloping up to Jake.

Jake gave a sigh of relief. He had been afraid she would run off, never to return. Now it looked as though her emancipation would come slowly. She could go and come as she pleased, but she would probably not venture too far afield at first.

This pattern was repeated for several evenings. Each time Zoe went a little further, but she always returned of her own accord. Jake still put food down for her, but Bracken said he ought to cut it down soon so that she would have to forage for herself. Jake and Bracken went into the woods after her on her first few wanderings, keeping track of her whereabouts, but not staying too close. She would often come gambolling back to them, as if pleased to see them, and never seemed to resent their being there.

"She will go soon," said Bracken one evening. "She's getting much more independent now. She's even begun to dig out a new sett in one of those old ones in the woods."

"Yes," agreed Jake a little sadly. He knew he would miss the little cub, just as he missed Sky. But he knew he must not say so.

AND THEN IT WAS HALF TERM, and Carol and the boys returned. They came down the path together, and all flung their arms round Jake and hugged him, laughing and exclaiming over the change he and Bracken had wrought in the overgrown garden. It is like a homecoming, thought Jake, and they are like my family, the family I never had.

Then he saw Carol looking at him searchingly, and he smiled and tucked her arm through his and said, "Come on. We'd better visit Zoe before she goes out on her rambles. You've only come just in time, you know." Then he saw the shock on Carol's face, and went on hastily. "She'll be going off on her own very soon now, Bracken thinks."

They all went down to Zoe's enclosure. She was already out in the summer dusk, rooting about. When she saw Jake coming, she came galloping across the grass to meet him. He sat down on the tree stump to talk to her, and she actually stood on her hind legs and reached up to put her front paws on his knee while she burrowed in his pocket for titbits.

"All right, all right," he said. "Your dinner's over there. Extra hungry tonight, aren't you? Been a long way, have you?"

Zoe grunted. She had found a very interesting collection in Jake's pocket—a piece of cheese, a walnut, a few crumbs of sesame cake and a radish. All these went down very well.

But Bracken had come earlier and laid out a little cache for her near the exit to the field, and this was even more exciting, for it contained two worms, a small dead shrew and a large black slug. After demolishing these, Zoe decided to play for a while before she went off exploring, and for a time she tumbled and rolled and lay on her back, kicking her feet in the air.

"Oh!" murmured the twins. "Isn't she beautiful!"

And Carol whispered, "Hush!" in a voice as enchanted as theirs.

At last, however, the scents of the summer night reminded Zoe of sweet, damp woods beyond the garden wall. She slid swiftly into the drainpipe and came out on the other side, a black-and-white shadow in the deepening twilight.

"She's going out," exclaimed Mark. "Can we follow her?"

"Yes," said Jake, "but don't get too close. You might frighten her."

The two boys were off in a flash. Carol and Jake turned back and walked slowly arm in arm through the garden to Jake's chair under the ancient

pear tree. There they stopped and stood side by side looking out at the valley.

"How have things been?" asked Carol.

"Pretty good," said Jake. "In fact ... marvellous."

"I had awful doubts after I left you last time."

"About what?"

"About whether I said too much."

"You did not!" He turned a smiling face in her direction.

Carol sighed, and feeling his exhaustion as he stood beside her, she said gently, "Won't you sit in your wicker chair? I want to picture you there when I'm snowed under with teaching in London!"

Jake submitted gracefully, and Carol sat on the wall beside him, gazing out at the deepening night. She wondered if she could ask him if he needed anything, or whether there were things he wanted done... but she supposed not. Better let it alone. He seemed happiest not to talk about it.

"Carol," said Jake, sounding tentative but determined, "I want to tell you something, but I'm not sure I know how."

She looked at him, serious and attentive. "Go on."

"It's about how things are for me down here. I mean, Bracken and his simple acceptance of the natural world have well and truly put me in my place. So that, even before you came, I had plenty to rejoice about. There was no need to be concerned over me, and now ... I think I'm a bit delirious, one way and another!"

Carol tried vainly to match his smile.

"What I'm trying to say is, Bracken told me he'd be part of a dragonfly's wing or a worm, or part of Sky. I feel the same. It's the continuity that counts, the marvellous, ceaseless life cycle of the earth. Do you follow me?"

"Yes, Jake."

"So you see, everything is perfectly all right." He reached out a hand and touched her quietly. "Especially now."

She nodded, keeping her eyes very wide in case the tears should spill over.

But Jake knew they were there. His fingers reached up and brushed them off her eyelashes. "No," he said, his voice full of compassion. "That's why I'm telling you all this. I want you to feel as I do, enriched and secure in love."

She blinked, as if his words had struck her like an arrow. "Enriched and secure in love," she repeated. "That's beautiful!"

"I'm anxious about you," Jake continued. "I know how it was for you before, and I'm trying to say it's all right. Your Bob is still part of all this"—and he waved an arm at the dusk-filled valley—"just as I will be. It was you, after all, who said there are many kinds of love, remember?"

She nodded again, silently.

Jake smiled at her in the falling twilight and murmured, "Now maybe I'm the one who's said too much!"

"No!" she said in swift protest. "You haven't."

"You will be happy?"

She drew a long breath of resolve. "Yes. I will."

"I'd like to think you'll come back to the cottage now and then? Not run away from it any more?"

"Yes. I'll come."

His smile was now luminous, but also full of mischief. "I shall be here, in every leaf! You'd better watch out!"

He had brought her safely out of tears towards laughter, he thought. He was silent for a while, waiting for her to grow calm again.

Presently he said, "Do you still feel as if everything is new?"

"Yes," agreed Carol. "I do."

"So do I. New wonders at every turn." Suddenly he leaned forward, framing Carol's face with his hands, and said very softly, "As for me, I feel more alive every minute—especially now." He kissed her quietly, still smiling in the summer night.

Above their heads Jake's nightingale suddenly let out a crystalline trill of sound, and as they looked up into the branches of the pear tree they saw the golden, smoky summer moon come up behind the hill.

They sat there a long time, listening to the tireless bird, hands clasped in perfect accord, until they heard the twins returning.

The boys chatted on about Zoe and the exciting sounds in the woods. But Jake and Carol, a little dazed and unable to free themselves from the spell of the nightingale, were strangely silent.

At last Carol got up to go. The parting was very hard this time, in view of the knowledge she saw in Jake's face. But she did her best to sound cheerful and normal, especially as the twins were standing beside her, still full of excitement at the night's adventures.

"Goodnight, dear Jake," she murmured. "Go on feeling new!" She put her arms round his neck and kissed him once more.

Jake's arms tightened about her for a moment, and then he let her go. I must not hold on, he thought. I must let her go.

The boys reached up and hugged him too, and then they all went up the path together, leaving Jake alone by his chair in the moonlit garden.

I hate partings, thought Jake. I don't want to watch them leave. I'd rather remember the boys clambering over the wall, and Carol looking up at the nightingale in my pear tree.

So he did not turn to see them wave. And they, looking back, saw only a tall, quiet figure gazing out at his darkening valley, with the moonlight clear on his face. But then, all at once, he turned round, lifted his hand to them and called out, "Goodnight! God bless!"

CHAPTER EIGHT

Jake was very tired the next morning, so he got up late. When he finally came down and went out to look at the morning, he found Bracken already in the garden, waiting for him.

"I was thinking," said the boy, his eyes alight with welcome. "Little Zoe's not going to need us much longer in the evenings. She can manage on her own now." And then, as if recognizing Jake's sudden sense of loss, he went on, "So we can go out again, mornings. You rest today, and we'll go out tomorrow."

"Yes," said Jake, his eyes on the golden summer morning. "Tomorrow." But then some shadow seemed to touch him, the faintest nudge. "No," he said suddenly. "Let's go today."

Seeing his face, Bracken said tranquilly, "All right. Today."

When Jake went inside to get his boots, he heard a curious, muffled thumping and whirring sound coming from the table by the window. His eye fell on the glass jam jar with the chrysalis inside that Bracken had given him. Only it wasn't a chrysalis any more. It was a big, beautiful, newly painted moth, trying desperately to escape from its glass-walled prison.

"Oh!" he said, enchanted. "Aren't you handsome!" And he carried the jam jar outside. "Bracken," he called. "Look what I've got! Come and help me let him go!"

Together they admired the vivid velvet-bloom colours of the freshly hatched moth. His front wings were a glowing cinnamon brown, shading from pink to buff, with intricate darker waves and delicate markings. His back wings began with an even brighter pink close to his body, and shaded towards the outer tips into pale, finely striped gold. But on the lower edge were two perfect eyes, blue circled with black.

"An eyed hawkmoth," said Bracken, awestruck. "I thought it might be. Isn't he beautiful!"

"How shall I let him go?"

"Just open the lid. He'll go. He'll soon smell the morning."

Jake did as he was told and held the jar up to the sun. The moth climbed slowly out and perched for a moment on Jake's fingers. Then he stretched his wings, flexed them once or twice, and suddenly lifted into a swift thrum of flight. He circled the garden, and then he flew over the wall and into the fields beyond.

"There he goes," said Jake. "Let's do the same!"

They did not go far that day. They wandered through the summer fields until Bracken led him out onto a grassy ridge looking down at the long brown lake below.

"I call this my listening post," he said, smiling at Jake in the sun.

"Why?"

394

"You'll see. It's something about the shape of the valley, the way the hills stand round it in rings. All the sounds seem to come up here extra clear—magnified, almost. Listen!"

Jake listened. He could hear a lark singing somewhere above his head, and the voices of the ducks on the lake below came up clear and crisp. There were the coots and moorhens too, calling sharply to one another. He could hear the thrash of wings on water, even the plop of a fish as it jumped at a passing mayfly. There were the white sheep on the hillside, the lambs grown big and woolly now, but still calling to their mothers in plaintive voices. And down at the bottom of the valley there was a farm dog barking, and the unhurried deep voices of the cows he was rounding up in the meadows below the lake.

Jake saw how the great wedges of green beechwoods sloped down the hillside. That was where the badgers were; that was where little Zoe would go looking for her friends.

"Look!" said Bracken, pointing. "The swans are still there."

Down on the brown lake four white stately forms sailed out across the water, gliding smoothly over the surface. And behind them came the six cygnets. Jake watched their quiet progress across the lake.

It was like a plan laid out before him, he thought. The lake, full of busy growing life; the secret woods above; the scented stretches of grassy turf leading the eye up to the horizon; the wide, strong shoulders of the hills and the steep rings of the British Camp beyond. The whole of it set before him in a perfect arc.

Bracken brought out his usual flask of tea. Jake patted his pockets and produced cheese and apples, and they sat there a long time, eating and dreaming in the sun.

"Bracken," murmured Jake, gazing up at the sky, "when I first came, you were there waiting for me. How did you know?"

"Sometimes," Bracken said, "things tell us when we're needed. No sense in asking why."

Jake nodded. Bracken was right. No sense in asking why. "It's been the happiest spring and summer of my life," he said softly. "Did you know?"

Bracken did not answer at once. Then he said, his eyes on the green, growing world around him, "All days are happy ... if you let them be."

Yes, thought Jake. All days are happy. What am I worrying about?

"Sky's up there somewhere," said Bracken. "I expect he's happy too."

I'll be part of a dragonfly's wing, a worm. I'll be part of Sky, sang Bracken's voice joyously in Jake's mind.

"Have you ever got lost?" Jake asked suddenly.

Bracken looked at him in surprise. "I mostly know where I am." But there was something about Jake's voice that made him pause and look at him oddly. "Once or twice, though, in the night, I've gone too far and it's been a bit hard to find my way back. Why?"

Jake fumbled in his pocket and drew something out. "This is my old pocket compass," he said. "I've had it for years, through all sorts of adventures when I was working. It's got my initials on it, see? And oddly enough, it's got a kestrel stamped on the leather case—or it may be a hawk. I think it's because kestrels always know where they are!"

Bracken laughed and bent to examine it.

"It's luminous in the dark," continued Jake. "It always got me home." He laid it in Bracken's hands. "There's a magnifying glass in the middle. Look, it swivels out, like this. It's for reading maps, really, but you can use it to look at fine things, like a moth's wing or a feather. And there's a barometer on the back, not that you need telling what the weather's going to do."

"Me?" said Bracken with incredulity.

"Yes, you," said Jake. "I want you to have it."

Bracken stayed still, still as stone. Then he raised his head and said in a fierce, strange voice that Jake scarcely recognized, "I don't need nothing to remember you by! I'll remember anyway. But I'll keep this till I die."

He sat there, clasping it in his hands, staring at Jake. Then the fierceness in his eyes died, and he began to smile again, the old, joyous upspringing of light that Jake had come to know so well.

"Better get home . . . before I burst!" he said, pulling Jake to his feet. "I told you all days are happy . . . if you let them be!" He carefully put the old, battered leather case in his pocket. "We'll go up to see our Zoe once more tonight, shall we? And then we must leave her be."

"Yes," agreed Jake.

"But first, you better rest. All right?"

"All right," said Jake. And he turned to look once more at the lake and the swans, before Bracken led him home.

THAT EVENING when they got to Zoe's enclosure, she was not there. They searched the corners and lifted the top off the barrel to have a look inside the sett. But they knew in their hearts that she had gone.

Without consulting each other, they climbed over the wall, went down the length of the hedge by the field and on into the woods.

Jake called out softly, "Zoe? Zoe? Are you there?" But there was no sign of her.

"Try again," said Bracken.

He called again, just a little louder, and waited . . . and called once more. Then, disappointed, he began to walk on through the much too empty woodlands. Little Zoe had gone, gone for good.

Bracken kept close beside him, saying nothing.

But all at once a black-and-silver shadow detached itself from the darkness and trotted confidently towards them along the path.

"It's Zoe!" breathed Jake. "She's come back to see us!"

The cub came straight up to them and rubbed against their legs with every sign of affectionate recognition. Jake's hand went to his pocket. Then he hesitated and looked at Bracken.

"Should I?"

"Don't see why not," said Bracken, hearing the note of longing in Jake's voice. "It won't do no harm for her to know she can come back for a titbit now and then."

Jake produced her favourite—a sticky honey sandwich—and a few nuts. Zoe reached into his hand with her long, striped nose and took the food happily.

For a while she remained near them, prancing and pouncing in her old playful manner. But then she sat up with her head pointing westwards into the heart of the wood and seemed to be listening or scenting something a long way off. She got up, circled them once and headed off into the shadows. Just before she disappeared from sight down into a leafy hollow among the trees, she paused and looked back at them. Then she was gone.

"Goodbye, little Zoe," Jake said. "Godspeed!"

"She'll be all right now," Bracken said. "We've done right to let her go. She's where she belongs, out there in the dark."

They wandered back through the woods to the garden. Jake went to put his kettle on, while Bracken perched on the wall under the pear tree and waited for the moon to rise behind the black curve of the hill. It was almost the last of the big summer moon. Tomorrow it would be waning, and rising late, and Bracken fancied the weather might be going to change. But now the sky was clear and pure—still golden in the west but deepening into true azure as the night came down.

They sat together, drinking tea and admiring the night and not talking very much, and presently the nightingale came back to the pear tree and poured out his silver song.

This evening Jake had felt a change within him. Something had seemed to give and settle, as if one more strand of the rope that held him tethered to earth had broken. He had not understood it then, only he had felt cold, cold, and the leaden weakness seemed to grow heavier and drag at his heels. But now, strangely, out here with Bracken, he felt all this weariness fall away, leaving him curiously light and untroubled in the beguiling summer night.

At last the bird ceased singing. Bracken leaped down from the wall. "Time you was resting," he said. And then, looking at Jake half shyly, he added, "I said all days are happy, but this one's been special!"

"Yes," agreed Jake. "It has."

Bracken was still looking at him, head a little on one side. "Why did you say 'Godspeed' to Zoe?" he asked.

Jake smiled. "Yes. I suppose we do say it too lightly, without thinking what it means. But I should think a kindly God would care about animals too?"

"Oh, yes!" said Bracken, full of certainty.

"Well then?" Jake prompted him gently.

"I just wondered ... if you could say it about people too?"

Jake drew a deep, unsteady breath. Then he said quietly, "Yes, Bracken. Of course you can."

The boy's voice in the darkness was reflective and slow. "We say, *Te avel Devlesa*. Go with God."

"That's almost better." Jake was smiling again. "You wouldn't feel lonely then!"

"Oh, you wouldn't be *lonely*," said Bracken, "not at all!"

Jake murmured, half to himself, "No. You're right."

"I like your word 'speed', though." The boy's voice was full of quiet dreams. "It reminds me of Sky."

Jake nodded. "In any case, they mean the same thing, really."

Bracken smiled at him in the darkness. Light seemed to spring into his face and flow upwards till Jake was dazzled.

"That's all right," the boy said softly. "So I can say Godspeed to you!"

AFTER BRACKEN HAD GONE, Jake could not sleep. The summer moon burned on, luring him out. Sighing, he reached for his jacket, picked up his torch and went out again into his garden.

His feet took him towards the old wire enclosure near his shed. There was no one there, of course. The silvered grass lay empty and silent, but as he turned away, something caught his eye—a shape, a shadow, a more dense patch of darkness. Something was sitting motionless on top of Sky's tree-trunk perch, something strong and slender, with furled wings and a smooth, unmoving head.

"Sky?" said Jake incredulously. "Sky? Is that you?"

For answer, the dark shadow unfurled its wings and launched itself upwards, circling over Jake's head. "*Kee!*" it called urgently. "*Kee!*" Then it let out the kestrel's brittle alarm call, "*Kikikik, kikikik, kee!*"

"It *is* you!" said Jake. "What's the matter?"

"*Kee!*" shouted Sky, circling overhead, then dropping to almost touch Jake's upturned face with his long flight feathers.

"What is it?" asked Jake. "What can I do?"

For answer, Sky called once again and began to fly away from Jake in widening circles, but always returning to hover overhead.

"I see," said Jake, quite sure now what Sky wanted. "All right. I'm coming. Lead the way."

He had been very tired all day, but now he followed Sky without hesitation, putting aside his weariness and the strange, increasing cold in all his limbs.

Above him Sky circled on impatient wings. "*Kee!*" he called. "*Kikikik! Be quick! Be quick!*"

Jake did not know how far he walked in the dark, with the kestrel's shadowy wings just ahead, leading him on. They went across fields, through small copses and clumps of elder and willow, skirting the edge of the great beech woods, up one hill and down another. He walked in a white trance, losing all sense of time and distance, moving from moonlight to shadow until they came to a steep, sloping field. And here Sky uttered one more fierce "*Kee!*" and sank down onto the grass. Jake stumbled forward, hearing a desperate thrashing of wings that grew louder in his ears. Then he saw a strange-shaped thing on the grass that glinted like dull metal in the moonlight.

When he got near, he saw that it was indeed metal, and in its wicked, gleaming jaws was another kestrel like Sky, only he fancied her head was brown, not blue-grey, and she was struggling wildly, trapped in those dreadful teeth of sharpened steel.

Sky called "*Kee!*" again and flew up and hovered, then came down and stood anxiously beside his terrified mate.

"So you brought me to her," said Jake, looking in pity at the wounded bird by the light of his torch. "I'll try, Sky. I'll do my best, but she's badly hurt. I may not be able to save her."

He heaved and pulled at the steel jaws of the trap, but he could not muster enough strength to open them. If I could get a solid piece of wood to lever it up, he thought, and cast around for something. At last he found a broken branch wedged against a stone wall at the edge of the field, and carried it back to the trap.

Sky was standing patiently beside his mate, and he spread out his wings and called "*Kee!*" as Jake approached. But he did not fly away. The female bird gave another convulsive heave and thrashed with her wings, and then lay still again. There was agony in her eyes.

Riven by her suffering, Jake struggled with the trap again. He felt dizzy and faint, and his heart began to thump wildly, but he fought on, forcing the jaws of the trap apart and inserting the tree branch inch by inch, until he had enough solid wood inside to act as a lever. Then he leaned on it with all his weight, and wrenched the deadly clamping teeth apart.

But the wounded kestrel was too feeble to move and did not seem to know that the trap was sprung.

Groaning with frustration, Jake gripped the piece of branch under one arm and leaned down to grab the bird. He seized her by her feet and flung her aside just as the branch snapped under his arm, unable to sustain the crushing weight of the spring. The steel jaws clashed together with a snap, trapping Jake's hand. The end of the branch rammed itself into Jake's side with a sickening blow, and he fell forward onto the bloodstained grass.

A great wave of pain came over him for a moment and then receded, leaving him in a floating mist of weakness. So it is now, he thought. Well, I'm glad I'm alone. I didn't want Bracken to have to face this with me. This is how it should be.

He thought he heard wings then, beating about his head—a great strong rush of wings all round him, circling and soaring. He thought he heard a kestrel's cry, growing fainter on the wind . . .

His body felt light now, and it was not cold any more. He lay on the dewy, moonlit grass, and an enormous sense of peace and tranquillity came over him. It was entirely right, and he was ready. This calm, serene acceptance of rest was all that was required of him. At last he was safe.

The wings still seemed to soar all round him. Swans' wings and kestrels' wings, swift and strong and free. Their music seemed to pulse right through him. He was part of their lifting, soaring flight.

Sky? he said, though no words came. Are you safe? Is your wounded mate flying free?

He thought he heard Carol's voice, then, close to him, full of warmth and comfort, saying, "*Enriched and secure in love.*"

And then Bracken seemed to come, all luminous with welcome, and take him by the hand, saying, "*Godspeed!*"

Smiling, Jake laid down his burden on the grass, and went out to join those soaring, swift, strong wings.

IT WAS BRACKEN who found him the next evening—Bracken, who had been searching for him through the woods and fields all the long day from very early in the morning when he had found him missing.

He was still smiling when Bracken came to him, serene and at peace in the summer grass. The two kestrels were gone, but there was blood on the ground and in the trap, where Jake's hand was still caught, and a scatter of long wing feathers on the grass.

No one could understand how Jake could have walked so far—more than fifteen miles from home, over very rough country—or why he had gone out like that, alone in the night.

But Bracken knew. He looked at those torn wing feathers and thought, Yes. He came here to help something. His last act on earth was to set something free. To Bracken, standing alone in the tumbled grass, this seemed entirely right.

Jake's friend Bill made all the arrangements, and he took charge of the diary Jake had been writing, which had a note on top of it saying: "For Bill and Carol."

He saw everyone in turn who had been concerned with Jake, even Bracken's father, and last of all he asked to see Bracken himself. He sat with him beside Jake's empty chair. He explained, very gently, that Jake had left him some money to use for his animals and birds.

"You could use it now if you wanted to. But your father agreed with me that maybe it would be better kept in trust for you till you're ready for it. What do you think?"

Bracken shook his head fiercely. "I don't want his money!"

"Not now," said Bill, understanding the boy's fierceness all too well. "But one day you might want to set up some kind of sanctuary for your birds and animals, like the one you made for Sky and Zoe, only bigger. I know money isn't important to you, and I know it can't bring Jake back, but he wanted you to have it. He thought you might find a use for it later on. You mustn't refuse him, must you?"

Bracken turned to him then, the gold-flecked eyes dark with grief. "All right, if he wanted it. But I'd rather have him back than all the money in the world!"

"I know," said Bill sadly. "I know, Bracken. So would we all."

Bracken looked at Jake's chair, standing empty on the grass. "It's a good thing he was a *gorgio*. If he was a Romany, we'd have to burn that chair—and everything else." He sighed. "I've never understood why we have to. I'd rather be reminded." He glanced at the chair again. "Can we leave it here? I'd like to think he could find it if he wanted to."

Bill nodded.

"Besides, the nightingale needs someone to sing to," he said obscurely, and walked away from the cottage and Bill without looking back.

THERE WAS A SURPRISING NUMBER of people at the funeral in the little village church. Bill and Manny were there, and Carol Cook and her boys came, looking somehow both sad and proud at once. There was someone called Bob, who they said was editor of foreign news on a famous newspaper, and there was a Harley Street doctor called Andrew Lawson.

But besides these strangers from London, almost the whole village seemed to be there: Mary Willis and her brother Tom, the butcher; Jim Merrett, and, of course, Dr. Martin and Stan Bayliss; and not far behind them in one of the pews was that dour man Ralph Deacon. And Bracken's father, twisting his best cloth cap in his hands, was sitting alone at the back.

Bracken did not go into the church. He sat outside on a tombstone and listened to the singing. The gipsies had their own ceremonies when an old friend died. His father would arrange it, he knew. There would be speeches made; they would praise famous men, and Jake in particular, and say, "*Tel avel angla tute*," and then there would be singing and drinking in the firelight. But Bracken would not feel part of it, any more than he felt part of this ceremony in the church.

In any case, the gipsies were moving on after today. His father, perhaps thinking it would be best for the boy now, had decreed that they should go. The whole *hatchintan* was packing up to move down Hereford way for the hop picking.

But the thought of moving on did not comfort Bracken. He had lost a friend who could never be replaced, and he had to find his own way out of this grief he did not understand. He knew he had done all he could for Jake. He had shown him all the wonders he knew, and cared for him when he was tired, as best he could. Hadn't Jake said it was the happiest spring and summer of his life? Well, then, it ought to be all right. He ought not to feel this aching sense of loss, here in the bright summer sunshine when every leaf and flower shone with life.

But he did. Brightness was gone from the day, because there was no longer a loved companion beside him to gaze and admire when he pointed to something new and said, "Look! There's a dragonfly!"

Then he began to remember the conversation about thistledown. He had been intent on comforting his friend then, and he had known, quite clearly, what to say to him. *I'll be part of a dragonfly's wing, or a worm. I'll be a part of Sky,* he had said, telling Jake what he knew to be true. So why was he letting this sadness dim the bright day? Jake was there, as he had said he would be, in every leaf and flower, in every blade of grass and every singing bird.

The people were coming out now and walking round to the new grave in the grass. Only four of them stopped to talk to Bracken—Dr. Martin, Manny and Bill, and Carol. And Bill, speaking for all of them, put a hand on his shoulder and squeezed it tight and whispered, "Thank you!"

When they had gone, he went over to the graveside and looked at the flowers. There were a lot of them, all expensive and stiff from the shops in the town.

But Bracken stooped and laid his own offering among the pile—a handful of kestrel feathers and a shell fossil millions of years old.

Then he walked away alone, and climbed the highest hill and stood on the topmost point, looking out at the wide valleys and rolling hills beyond.

He looked up into the summer sky and thought he saw a faint speck hovering there. Far and clear there came to him on the wind the cry of a bird, the call of a swift wild kestrel flying free.

ELIZABETH WEBSTER

Gloucestershire, which provides the lovely setting for *A Boy Called Bracken*, is also where Elizabeth Webster and her husband have made their home—in an old Cotswold stone house which overflows with books, manuscripts, theatrical costumes, musical instruments, and young people wanting help with anything from housing to A-levels and job interviews.

Elizabeth Webster has worked with young people all her life—which explains why she writes about them so well. Apart from having been a teacher of music and drama, she is well-known and much loved in the West Country for having founded the Young Arts Centre of Cheltenham, where the creativity and dreams of the young are encouraged and respected. To successive generations of new talent, Elizabeth has been a pied piper figure, leading young minds to new worlds.

She turned to writing in 1983, at the age of sixty-five—a time when most people are thinking of retiring. Daily, she rises at five in the morning and goes down to a little summerhouse at the bottom of her rambling garden to do her writing. "I have about four hours' work done before anyone else gets going," she says. "The early mornings are so beautiful, when the world is quite new and clean."

And how did *Bracken* come about? She explains, "Many people are frightened by the prospect of death, so I wanted to write a book that dealt with the world of nature around us, and showed how the simple patterns of birth, life and death are a comfort in themselves. I chose a city man who had forgotten what it is to live quite simply, and then I made him meet the gipsies, who are still the people most in touch with the natural world today."

Her research into Romany was difficult, since it is not a written language, but there are gipsies who turn up in Gloucestershire at harvest time. And undoubtedly the author's three children, five grandchildren, and the hundreds of youngsters whom she still works with daily, have helped her to create so lovingly the memorable gipsy boy, Bracken.

The Churchill Diamonds

A CONDENSATION OF THE BOOK BY

BOB LANGLEY

ILLUSTRATED BY EDWARD MORTELMANS

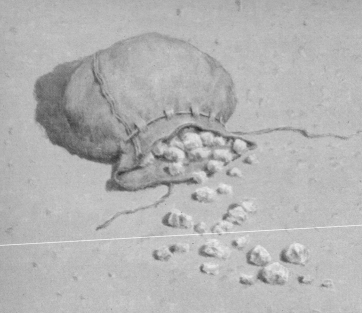

The Sudan, 1898. Lieutenant
Coffey is chosen from his regiment
to undertake a highly reckless
mission. When the dashing young
officer sets out with three
companions to rescue a girl and her
father from wild dervishes, he cannot know
that it will lead him to a hoard of
diamonds, a fortune on which he will later
build a business empire.

Decades later, those same priceless
diamonds have been stolen from the Coffey
Foundation in London. Who stole them?
And why? The answer lies in that daring
rescue back in 1898—and in the surprising
secret of the diamonds' final resting
place . . .

Prologue

Sergeant MacAngus lay where he had fallen, blood from his hip oozing into the coarse desert sand. He was flanked on one side by a narrow defile, a long bow-shaped scar in the earth where streams would flow when the rains came, and on the other by the flat pebble-strewn plain of the empty *reg*. Several feet away, its sorrowful face grinning incongruously, sprawled Sergeant MacAngus's camel. It was an ugly brute with a series of ancient knife wounds on its neck, and for eight days MacAngus had driven it to the point of exhaustion until, its last vestiges of strength now depleted, it lay in the dust, spittle oozing in long shiny strands from its blubbery grey lips.

MacAngus knew there was water in the leather-skinned *guerba* strapped to the camel's saddlehorn, but he doubted seriously if he could reach it because, several minutes earlier, at half past two in the afternoon of 19 July 1898, in the desert region known as El Gezira of the central Sudan, a dervish bullet had entered the front of MacAngus's abdomen and emerged through the *erector spinae* muscles in his lower back.

He felt no pain, which surprised him, only a strange numbness which dulled the feeling in his legs and feet. His lips were cracked and raw in the sun and his cheeks, baked red and covered with bristly beard stubble, looked hollow and ravaged.

He was not wearing the khaki uniform of his regiment, the 10th Westmorland Lancers, but the blue *gandoura* and *chech* of the Kel Ahaggar Tuareg, a tribal people who inhabited the Hoggar Mountains of the Sahara nearly a thousand miles to the northwest. His loose-fitting robes were ragged and sweat-stained, and at the point where the bullet had entered his body there was a rapidly widening circle of scarlet, coated with a thin film of orange dust from the desert floor. His right hand clutched the ribbed handle of a heavy Navy Colt revolver. His left, the fist tightly clenched, was pressed against the side of his chest.

Several yards away, the body of a man clad in metal armour and chain mail lay huddled on its side. His helmet had come off with the impact of his fall and his dark face, earringed and bearded and frozen into the glassy rigidity of death, contrasted strangely with the protective shell of his medieval-style apparel. Nearby lay two more corpses, both clad similarly in armour and chain mail, both clutching shields and lances from which pennants fluttered in the dry desert wind.

Vultures hovered overhead. They did not approach the corpses, for they sensed that the sergeant was still alive and therefore waited with the timeless patience of their species for death to take its natural course.

Sergeant MacAngus did not notice the scavengers, nor did he hear the soft clinking of accoutrements, or the shuffle of approaching hooves, as a reconnaissance patrol of British and Egyptian cavalry picked its way through the clumps of mimosa and spindly acacia trees. They moved slowly, riding in almost perfect formation, their brown jerseys, sand-coloured trousers and dark blue puttees etched sharply against the sky, their rifles glinting in the sunlight. Far to the right and left trotted their outriders, four blacks mounted on camels.

The troop was led by a young British subaltern whose nose had skinned in the heat and whose hair was bleached white by the sun. Accompanying him was an Egyptian sergeant from the 14th infantry battalion.

"Look, *bimbashi*," the sergeant said, spotting MacAngus and the corpses lying in the defile.

The young British officer was not a *bimbashi*, he was a lieutenant, but it pleased the sergeant to flatter the Englishman, who reined in his mount, peering curiously across the sand. "Tell your men to wait here," he ordered in a crisp voice, and, kicking his horse into a trot, rode through the mimosa clumps to where the first of the bodies lay sprawled in the dust.

"Good Lord!" he exclaimed, as he realized for the first time that the bodies were dressed in armour. "What have we here, the Knights of the Round Table?"

The sergeant followed him, and drawing his horse to a halt, spat on the ground. "They are dervishes from Agaiga," he said.

"But that armour they're wearing, it must be centuries old."

"Oh yes, *bimbashi*. Their Saracen ancestors took it from the Crusaders in the thirteenth century. They, and their fathers before them, have worn it in battle ever since."

"Incredible," the officer said, dismounting.

He moved forward, pistol drawn, studying each of the corpses in turn. When he reached MacAngus he said, "This one's different. I think he's still alive."

The sergeant frowned as he slid from his saddle and joined the young officer. "This man is not a dervish," he said. "The clothes he is wearing are the clothes of the Kel Ahaggar, the people of the Hoggar Mountains."

"Tuareg?"

The sergeant nodded.

"Is he dying?" the officer asked.

The sergeant knelt down and examined MacAngus carefully. "He is losing blood," he announced, "but the bullet has not lodged in his body. If we take him back to camp, he may yet survive."

The sound of voices made MacAngus stir. He turned his head and squinted up at the figures crouching above him. Though his vision was clouded, he was able to discern, framed against the sun, the pale outline of the officer's face, and he realized that he was not in the hands of dervish savages, but by some unaccountable miracle had been discovered by members of his own race.

"Wha's the time?" he whispered hoarsely.

The sound of MacAngus's voice speaking English made the young officer start. He leaned back on his haunches, frowning curiously. "Who are you?" he demanded. "What are you doing dressed like this?"

MacAngus coughed. It was a painful racking cough that lodged stubbornly in his throat. "The diamonds," he whispered.

The officer frowned. "What diamonds?"

"Ye must tell Coffey about the diamonds."

"Who on earth is Coffey?"

"He's at the river. Hurry. Mebbe ye'll still be in time to save him."

"What are you talking about, man?"

MacAngus struggled to speak again, but his eyes were glazing. His features slackened, then his head lolled back.

"He has fainted, *bimbashi*," the sergeant said.

The young officer nodded, still frowning. Leaning back, he noticed for the first time a stone caught in MacAngus's belt. He bent down and prised it loose with his thumb. It was roughly the size of a walnut, its corners jagged, its surface greasy to the touch. An uncut diamond.

"Now, look at this," the officer breathed, whistling as he held it to the light. "Why, it must be worth a fortune."

He glanced again at MacAngus's camel, his eyes narrowing as he studied the bulging saddlebags. "Strap those pouches to my pony's bridle," he ordered, "then call your troop and get this man mounted. God knows who Coffey is, but if we don't want this poor beggar to bleed to death we'd better get him medical attention as quickly as possible."

Several minutes later, with MacAngus lashed to the hump of a baggage camel, the patrol rode back the way it had come, the young officer keeping a wary eye on the sergeant's wound for any sign of haemorrhaging. Four hours later he delivered MacAngus and his possessions to the British forces on the River Nile.

It was not a significant episode in the young officer's life, nor one he was particularly disposed to remember. His name was Winston Spencer Churchill, future prime minister of Britain. Although he mentioned the incident in a letter to his mother, postmarked Khartoum and dated 11 September 1898, he did not include it in his published dispatches of the Sudanese campaign, nor did he ever refer to it publicly again.

Chapter One

A light rain was falling as the TV crew, three young men, casually dressed, sober-faced, carried their equipment across the white-pillared lobby of the Coffey Foundation headquarters in London's West End, registered at the reception desk and took the lift to the building's basement. They were met as the doors opened by a man in a dark grey uniform. "BBC?" he asked.

They nodded silently.

"My name is Johnson, chief security officer. You do understand that all visitors to the basement must go through our screening procedure?"

"That's already been explained," the TV director told him.

"Then you will please use these cubicles and remove your clothing. Just leave your equipment on the floor."

Without a word the three men swiftly undressed and submitted themselves to a stringent examination. They were photographed from three different angles, their fingerprints were recorded on sensitized tape and their physical statistics, including scars and birthmarks, were fed into a computer.

Thirty seconds later, the computer gave them clearance. Their equipment was then placed on a moving conveyer belt which carried it through an electronic X-ray machine. Only when the officer tried to include their can of unexposed film did the director object. "You'll ruin our stock," he complained.

Smiling apologetically, the officer returned the can untouched. When the examination was over the three men put on their clothes. After a few moments a new man appeared. He was middle-aged and athletic-looking. "I'm Webster," he smiled, sticking out his hand. "Welcome to the Coffey Foundation. Mr. Cray is waiting for you at the vault. Will you please follow me?"

Carrying their equipment, they walked through a series of corridors. At three different checkpoints, guards in security uniforms scrutinized Webster's ID card before waving them on. The guards were completely enclosed in metal cages protected by wire grilles. It was clear no one could pass the checkpoints undetected.

Webster stopped at a door marked "Maximum Security. No entry under any circumstances without authority of Foundation Director".

He slipped his ID card into a slot in the wall and the door slid open with a muffled click. The TV crew stepped into a room which looked at first glance like a computer centre. Around the walls a myriad dials and instrument panels hummed softly.

A second man came towards them, smiling.

"This is Mr. Cray," Webster explained, "our Class One manager."

Cray was short and slender. His hair was grey and combed upwards from the parting to hide a bald patch on the centre of his skull.

"It was good of you to admit us, Mr. Cray," the TV director said as they shook hands.

Cray chuckled. "You don't realize how privileged you are. This is the first time in the Foundation's history that outsiders have been allowed to set foot on the basement floor."

Cray indicated a heavy steel door set into the adjacent wall. Fixed on its surface was a clock dial with a single hour hand. "This is the vault," he said. "It's on a time clock, so we'll have to wait for it to open. We estimated your time of arrival and set it accordingly."

The TV director studied the dial with interest. "Supposing you tried to open it early?"

"Then the entrance chamber would seal itself off and we'd have hell's own job getting out of here. These walls are built of reinforced concrete, fifteen feet thick. You'd need an atomic warhead to blast your way through."

He paused as a click sounded deep inside the vault's mechanism. Stepping forward, he pulled hard on the metal wheel and, with a gentle creak, the massive door swung slowly open.

The interior of the vault was dim and claustrophobic, the walls lined with padded upholstery. In the centre of the floor stood a metal dais supporting a heavy steel container. Cray beckoned to Webster, who hurried in to join them.

"The container can only be opened by Mr. Webster and myself inserting separate keys at precisely the same instant," Cray explained. "If anyone attempted to force the lock, the doors would automatically shut and the alarm would sound at the security desks outside."

The two men slipped their individual keys into openings at opposite sides of the dais and the lid of the container slid back with a gentle buzzing sound. Lying on a shallow tray at the bottom of the container the

TV director was able to discern, dimly, a cluster of precious stones, each roughly the size of a small plum. They were cut and polished into a variety of different shapes, and as their textures caught and refracted the light, they glittered fiercely under his gaze.

"Beautiful," he breathed at last, studying them intently.

Cray nodded in agreement. "Apart from the cutting and polishing, they are exactly as Sir Stephen Coffey discovered them during the reconquest of the Sudan in eighteen ninety-eight."

"How many are there altogether?"

"One hundred and eighty-two. There were originally one hundred and eighty-three, but the most extravagant stone now forms part of the Crown Jewels. This is the first time they've ever been filmed for television, by the way. Company policy has always been to resist unnecessary public attention whenever possible. I can only assume someone at your office has a very persuasive tongue."

The director glanced quickly round the vault. "We'll have to rig up some lights in here. Got any plugs in the immediate vicinity?"

"You'll find some in the corridor outside."

"Excellent. We'll run in leads through the outer room. See to it, will you, Andy?" The director's bearded assistant nodded wordlessly and moved into the exterior chamber.

"In the meantime," the director added, grinning apologetically, "I think I'll have to go to the washroom."

Cray gave a short laugh. "I know how you feel. The first time I saw the diamonds they had the same effect on me! You'll find it at the end of the corridor, on the right."

Still clutching his film canister, the director walked casually along the passageway until he reached the lavatory door. Once inside, his air of composure vanished completely. Beads of moisture glistened on his temples and pallid cheeks. For a long moment he stood with his forehead pressed against the wall mirror, savouring its coolness. Then, with trembling fingers, he took out of his pocket a phial of yellow tablets. Thrusting two into his mouth, he scooped a palmful of water from the washbasin tap between his lips. He felt better as the drug infiltrated his bloodstream.

Locking himself in a cubicle, he took the can of unexposed film from under his arm and carefully prised open the lid. Taped to the tin base was a Walther 9mm P.38 automatic pistol with a heavy metal silencer. The director tugged the weapon loose and screwed the silencer to the barrel. Then, with the gun in his hand, he stepped from the cubicle and walked back to the vault where his TV crew were busy laying in cable from the wall sockets in the corridor. Cray and Webster were standing just as he had left them, laughing at some joke or other. When they saw the Walther, their laughter froze.

"There is no need for trouble," the director said icily. "And there is no need for anyone to get hurt. Do exactly as I say and you will both come out of this unharmed. Try to resist, or refuse to cooperate in any way, and you will both be killed immediately, is that understood?"

The two men nodded slowly.

Turning, the director gestured to his film crew and one of the men stepped into the tiny vault carrying a leather satchel which had previously contained pieces of sound equipment. He handed the satchel to Cray.

"Place the diamonds inside," the director ordered.

Cray stared at him aghast. "If I touch those diamonds, it will trigger the sensor devices. The alarm will sound at the security checkpoints along the corridor, and the outer door will automatically seal itself shut."

"I am aware of that," the director answered evenly. "Please follow my instructions."

"You're mad," Cray whispered. Glancing at his companion, he leaned forward and began to scoop the diamonds into the leather satchel. Dimly, along the corridor, they heard the furious clatter of the alarm bell. With a gentle buzzing sound the door to the outer chamber began to slide shut, but to Cray's surprise it suddenly stopped short with a little jerk, leaving a gap nearly a foot wide. With a small tremor of shock, he realized what had happened. The heavy TV cable which the raiders had so carefully run in from the outside corridor had jammed the door's progress.

He finished gathering up the diamonds and looked at the director questioningly. The director nodded to his assistant who took the satchel and fastened the metal clasps.

"Now," the director said, "in a moment the guards from the security desks will come to investigate. You will persuade them that in setting up our lights we disturbed the diamonds accidentally. It will be up to you, Mr. Cray, to put their minds at rest. Act sensibly and both you and Mr. Webster will be able to return to your families this evening unhurt. Attempt to be heroic, and it will be the last act you ever perform."

They heard footsteps clattering along the passageway outside. The director slipped the Walther into his jacket pocket and jerked his head towards the vault entrance. Cray stepped past him and raised his hands in a placatory gesture as the three uniformed guards burst into the room beyond.

"Sorry," he declared, trying hard to smile. "False alarm, I'm afraid. We were setting up the lighting gear and one of the leads fell into the diamond container. It must have triggered the sensor device."

"Are you sure everything's all right here, Mr. Cray?" one of the guards asked.

"Of course. Just a little slip on our part. Nothing at all for you to worry about."

The guard frowned and studied Cray shrewdly, noting the tautness of the jawline, the sickly pallor of the narrow cheeks.

"I'll just check everything's in order," the guard said, moving towards the vault door.

Deliberately, Cray blocked his way. "That's hardly necessary. I've already explained what happened."

"It'll set our minds at rest, Mr. Cray."

"Let him look," the director ordered quietly, his hand still resting in his jacket pocket.

Without a word Cray moved aside. The guard strolled to the container and peered down at the metal tray. They saw a tremor ripple through his body as his brain registered the fact that the diamonds were missing. When he moved back to the vault doorway he found his two companions standing with their hands in the air. The director was covering them calmly with the Walther automatic.

"Step forward three paces," the director ordered. "Keep your hands where I can see them and do it slowly and easily."

The guard joined his two companions.

"Everyone in the corridor," the director instructed. "You three"—he pointed his gun at the motionless guards—"remain where you are."

He moved back, dragging the heavy TV cable behind him, grunting with satisfaction as the door slid shut and the lock engaged with an audible click. He pushed the pistol back into his jacket pocket. "Now we are going to walk out of here," he said, "the five of us together. We are going to go through the checkpoints and take the lift to the roof. It will be your job, Mr. Cray, to placate any security guards we may encounter. Should anything happen to prevent us reaching the roof, or should the guards become suspicious and decide to investigate, I will kill you both before turning this pistol on myself and my companions. Is that understood?"

The two men nodded, their features deathly pale.

"Then let's go."

Down the corridor they strode, Cray and Webster walking side by side, the bogus TV crew following half a pace behind. They went through the three empty checkpoints and crossed the marbled lobby towards the lift. A solitary guard stood by the line of call buttons. He looked apologetic as he saw Cray approaching. "I'm sorry, Mr. Cray," he said, "but something's activated the security system. Probably a false alarm, but nobody's allowed to leave the floor until the police arrive."

Cray did not answer. He realized that his only chance of stopping the raid was probably this moment. Calmly, and with the full realization of what he was doing, he said, "It's no false alarm, officer. These men are impostors. They have stolen the Churchill Diamonds which they are carrying in that leather satchel there. I estimate you have about one second to use your mini-radio and alert your companions upstairs."

Unfortunately for Cray, the guard's reactions were slow and confused. He was still staring at Cray with a startled expression when the TV director hit him hard in the pit of the stomach. The man slammed back against the marble wall. The director swung his pistol in a savage arc, and as the guard instinctively lifted his arm to protect his face, the second blow shattered his wrist. Screaming with pain, he staggered back against the lift door and the director, following, hit him on the side of the skull. The man tumbled to the ground.

Livid, the director turned to face Cray. "You idiot," he hissed, "I told you not to do that." He brought the pistol round in a dizzy blur. Cray saw it coming and tried to jerk back but the barrel caught him across the face, breaking his nose with an audible crack. He howled and clutched with both hands at his face, blood welling between his fingers. The director hit him again, and Cray crashed to the ground.

The director seized Webster by the throat, jamming the Walther's muzzle against his lower ear. "Do exactly as I tell you," he snarled, "or I'll blow the top of your head off. Which one is the express lift to the boardroom on the top floor?"

Weakly, Webster indicated a door with a red light gleaming above it. The director pushed him into the narrow lift cabin and jabbed the button on the side wall. They sped silently upwards and the doors slid open onto a thick carpeted landing with a sign saying "Boardroom" and an arrow pointing to the left. The director ignored it and, turning to the right, opened a door leading into a narrow passage lined with empty buckets and rows of cleaning mops. Beyond lay a flight of concrete steps. Jostling Webster ahead of them, the raiders galloped up the stairway to the roof. Webster heard a roaring sound and as they burst into the open he saw a helicopter hovering just above, its giant rotor blades creating a vicious down draught which tore at his hair and clothing. From its open doorway, a cable dangled.

The director's bearded assistant scurried across the rooftop and hooked his arms through a canvas harness fluttering at the cable's end. Still clutching the leather satchel, the man was winched briskly into the aircraft's interior. One by one each member of the raiding team took his place on the cable and vanished into the gleaming fuselage. For a moment the helicopter continued to hover, then with a thunderous roar it banked sharply into the sky and sped off in the direction of the River Thames. Only when it had vanished from sight did Webster hear the mournful wailing of police cars in the street below.

ITN Newsflash, 18 June, 2.10 pm: We have just heard, within the last few minutes, that the legendary Churchill Diamonds, reputed to be the most valuable collection of their kind in the world, have been stolen in a daring daylight robbery by a gang posing as a television film crew. According to eyewitness reports, the raiders made their escape by helicopter from the roof of the Coffey Foundation building in London's West End, after locking three security guards in the vault chamber. One guard and a company executive were hurt.

The diamonds, said to be worth approximately one hundred and forty million pounds, derive their name from Sir Winston Churchill, who stumbled across them during the reconquest of the Sudan in 1898, but they were never owned by the Churchill family. It was the Foundation's creator, Sir Stephen Coffey, who successfully claimed them from the military authorities, using them to finance his multibillion-dollar business empire. The Coffey Foundation is famous for its charitable enterprises and extensive relief programmes in underdeveloped countries. Sir Stephen was knighted for his services to humanity in 1936. A Foundation spokesman described the diamonds as an integral part of Britain's heritage, and said the theft was a tragedy, not only for the owners, but for the entire nation.

Chapter Two

The limousine pulled into Baymont Avenue. Sitting in the rear, Thomas Kengle, fresh-faced, stockily built, forty-four years old, peered out at the rain sweeping the London streets and tried to think about nothing. He had a capacity for switching his brain into neutral at moments of great crisis; it gave him a clarity of vision which helped enormously in his decision-making, and making decisions was something Thomas Kengle was noted for. Six years earlier, at the remarkably young age of thirty-eight, he had taken over the presidency of the powerful and influential Coffey Foundation, running it with a flair and vision that astonished his many virulent critics.

In some respects the Coffey Foundation was too complex for any one individual to encompass completely, spreading as it did across a vast network of interests ranging from oil and motor cars to pharmaceutical products and heavy engineering, but so devoted was Kengle to his job that no part of his empire was too intricate or too trivial to escape his assiduous attention. Today, however, his customary confidence was dulled, and when the limousine slowed to a halt outside the chrome-and-glass facade of the Coffey Foundation headquarters, he groaned as he spotted a cluster of newspaper reporters waiting patiently beneath a canopy of umbrellas.

Beside him, his escort, Ben Crowley, cursed under his breath. "Damned press."

Crowley was a heavy-set Irishman in his early sixties. He had worked for the Coffey Foundation for as long as anyone could remember and was now responsible, not only for the safety of its president, but for the security of its entire worldwide operation.

Kengle's aide, Norman Elkins, sitting beside the driver, said, "I'll get Pembroke to sneak us round the back."

"No," Kengle said.

Ben Crowley looked at him with surprise. "Do you really want to talk to them?"

"Somebody'll have to, sooner or later."

The driver clambered out, opening the rear door for Kengle to alight, and seeing him the reporters came clattering down the steps. Kengle held up his hand, stilling the barrage of questions before it could begin. "Gentlemen," he said, "I must warn you I only have a couple of minutes. I've just returned from New York and I heard the news myself barely an hour ago."

"Any word from the police yet, Mr. Kengle?" a man inquired.

"I expect to talk to them later in the afternoon."

"What is your personal reaction, as president?" a woman asked.

"Shock, naturally. We thought our security system was impenetrable."

"How would you assess the importance of the Churchill Diamonds?"

Kengle considered for a moment. "I would say that for the better part of a century they have symbolized the adventurous spirit upon which the Foundation has been based. To a certain extent they have also helped to maintain public confidence, though today of course the Coffey Foundation is too vast to be affected in any real financial sense."

"Is it true the diamonds were discovered by Winston Churchill himself?"

"Not entirely," Kengle declared. "It's true Churchill figured prominently in their discovery, but the title 'Churchill Diamonds' is one given to the collection in more recent years by the British press."

"Is it true," a man queried, "that the Sudanese government has been trying to claim the diamonds back?"

Kengle looked at him sharply. "I understand so. However, it's unlikely we would have agreed to give them up."

At this point Ben Crowley stepped forward and took Kengle's arm, pulling him gently away. "Sorry, gentlemen," he said, raising one hand, "we're already ten minutes late. We'll issue a full statement at the end of the afternoon."

He hustled Kengle up the steps and through the glass swing doors, Norman Elkins scurrying along in their wake. They took the lift to the fifth floor and made their way to the corporation boardroom. A number

417

of directors were seated round the polished conference table, and they rose to their feet as Kengle entered.

"Gentlemen," he said, "I'm sorry we're late."

As usual the proceedings were being conducted by the board chairman, Henry Silvers. "Hello, Tom," he smiled. Then, turning, he indicated a good-looking man in his early fifties. "You know Commander Webber, who used to be with the Serious Crime Squad."

Kengle shook the detective's hand. "It was good of you to come, Commander."

As Kengle took his customary place at the table's head, the other executives settled back in their chairs. "Anything new?" Kengle demanded.

Henry Silvers shook his head. "Nothing concrete, Tom. It was a sound professional job, probably planned weeks—maybe months—in advance. We'll have to give the police a little more time, I'm afraid. At the moment they've got the basement sealed off and they're pulling the place to bits."

"Whose decision was it to let the TV people in?"

"Freddie Richardson's. He thought he was acting in our best interests. They said they were making a documentary on Britain's heritage."

"For God's sake, we've always resisted publicity in that direction."

Silvers said soothingly, "Freddie thought he was doing the right thing, giving the public a chance to see what the diamonds look like. And the TV people's credentials appeared to be above suspicion."

Kengle sighed. "Well, gentlemen, any ideas?"

A man with a sallow face said, "It's not the end of the universe, Tom. With or without the diamonds the Foundation will still survive."

"I appreciate that. But those diamonds have provided a financial bulwark for this organization since the beginning of the century. Losing them is like losing our right arm. In financial terms it may mean very little, but it puts a tremendous dent in our reputation. It shows the world the Coffey Foundation is vulnerable."

"I think everyone appreciates that, Tom," Silvers said.

"Good," Kengle nodded. "Then everyone will appreciate why we've got to get them back."

"How?" a man asked. "Surely that's up to the police?"

"I don't know how. But I have no intention of leaving this entirely in the hands of other people. That's why I invited Commander Webber to join us today. He retired from the Serious Crime Squad two years ago and he knows how criminals act, how they think. He will be our guide and counsellor."

Sitting at Kengle's side Commander Webber looked slightly discomfited. "Let me point out from the beginning that I'm here in a private capacity only," he insisted. "However, I'm happy to offer whatever

418

advice I can. My first instinct is that the job was a commissioned one. In other words, it's unlikely the thieves who carried it out intend keeping the diamonds for themselves."

"Why do you think that?" Kengle asked.

"Several reasons. Their professionalism suggests they're probably men with extensive criminal records, yet they were quite happy to leave their fingerprints and photographs on your company computer. That could suggest someone's promised them a new identity, possibly in a different part of the world."

"Who?" Kengle persisted.

"Well, the gems themselves might offer a clue to that. Unlike gold and silver, diamonds have no standard of value. Each stone depends upon its individual characteristics. The Churchill Diamonds are extraordinary first of all because of their greenish colour, and secondly because of their size. Even the smallest is as large as a pigeon's egg. Since diamonds are cut along the grain, it will not be possible to recut them without destroying their intrinsic value. Therefore, bearing in mind the fact that their peculiarities would be instantly recognized by a professional *diamantaire*, the stones cannot be resold on the open market."

"So in other words, whoever stole them is now stuck with them?"

"Correct. Now, the raiders used a helicopter for their getaway, and that kind of transport costs a lot of money. Also, they had cast-iron credentials and they knew the security system inside out. So, the raid was risky and it was expensive. Which means it had to be financed by somebody with capital to burn."

Kengle hesitated. "It could have been the Sudanese," he said. "They've been asking for the diamonds back for years. It's possible, isn't it?"

"Hardly. If they had the diamonds they'd want to put them on public display, and that would be an admission of guilt. No, I think they were taken by someone who didn't give a damn about their monetary value. I think our culprit had some other motive. Revenge maybe. Some kind of personal grudge. Maybe whoever it was hated Sir Stephen Coffey himself."

"Commander, Sir Stephen has been dead for more than thirty years."

"I realize that. But is it possible there's somebody still alive who considers they have a better claim to those diamonds than he did?"

"I don't see how," Kengle said firmly. "The diamonds were discovered back in eighteen ninety-eight. So everyone involved would be long dead by now."

"What about their descendants? Sometimes these things get passed from generation to generation."

Kengle appeared unconvinced, but settling back in his chair he looked round at the assembled executives. "Very well," he said, "what *were* the circumstances of the diamonds' discovery?"

Ben Crowley said, "Nobody knows, Tom."

Kengle blinked. "That's impossible."

"It's the truth. I ran an investigation into the story myself. Thought we might get a little press coverage. I came up with a big fat zero."

"A diamond discovery that size? Somebody must have written something, for God's sake. Did you check Sir Stephen's memoirs?"

"He skims over the whole event."

"What about Winston Churchill?"

"He wrote a letter to his mother after the fall of Khartoum, but all he mentioned was finding a wounded soldier in the Sudan who spoke of some diamonds. The man later died in a British field hospital."

"And the military authorities?"

"Another blank. Their records were either lost or destroyed."

Kengle shook his head in disbelief. In all his years with the corporation he had never bothered to investigate the precise details of the diamonds' discovery.

"Did you try the newspapers?"

"Plenty of stories about the diamonds, but nothing concrete."

"This is incredible."

Commander Webber interrupted. "What was Sir Stephen Coffey doing in the Sudan in the first place?"

"He was serving in the British army," Crowley explained.

"I see." The commander toyed with the glass at his fingertips. "And while he was there he came across a diamond hoard that turned him into one of the richest men in the world. Yet for some reason, no record exists of how that hoard was found. Does that not strike you as strange?"

Kengle took out a small notebook and opened it on the table. He unclipped a pen from his inside pocket and unscrewed the top. "The commander is right," he said crisply. "I think we'd better start at the beginning, don't you?"

THE RAIN POUNDING on the windowpanes had slackened to a thin drizzle by the time the executives finally departed, leaving Kengle and Ben Crowley alone in the boardroom. "What do you think, Ben?" Kengle asked. "Was the commander fantasizing?"

"Who knows, Tom?"

"Eighteen ninety-eight! That was practically the Dark Ages." He pursed his lips speculatively. "It *is* strange, though, that there's no information to be found. Almost as if somebody's tried a cover-up."

"I was thinking the same thing myself."

"I'm worried, Ben. What if Commander Webber talks out of turn? He could damage Sir Stephen's reputation, drag it through the gutter."

Crowley sighed. "Tom," he said, "Sir Stephen Coffey's been dead since nineteen fifty-four."

"Not to me he hasn't," Kengle told him bluntly. "To me he's still here. I can still feel him like a palpable presence in the corridors, in the offices."

Crowley frowned. He had worked for Kengle for a good many years, liked him, respected him, regarded him as a close personal friend. But in one area, Kengle exasperated him beyond reason—his adulation of the corporation's founder.

He said, "Tom, you always talk about that old character as if he was some kind of god."

"Coffey *was* a god," Kengle declared, smiling. "I tell you, Ben, we'll never see his like again. He went into the wilderness and came out with a fortune beyond men's dreams. He created an empire that stood the business world on its head. And not content with that, he used his billions to help the weak, the poor, the destitute."

Kengle peered up at the massive portrait hanging on the boardroom wall. The painting, commissioned in 1936, showed the organization's founder sitting with his wife in the garden of their Dorset home. Coffey was a striking man with eyes of a clear and penetrating blue and a handsome, hawklike face. Coffey's wife, Victoria, seemed beautiful and aloof. She looked like a woman who would make her own decisions, who would never be dominated.

"You know," Kengle murmured reflectively, "when they first asked me to take over the Coffey Foundation I was barely thirty-eight years old. I couldn't believe it. I used to stand for hours looking at this picture, trying to visualize the kind of man Coffey must have been. Damn it, now I feel I've let the old boy down."

"One of these days, Tom," Crowley said, "I'm going to tell you the truth about Sir Stephen Coffey. There was something odd about that man, something that never quite sat right."

"Like what, for God's sake?"

Crowley sighed. "Tom, this mystery over the diamonds, it's not the only strange thing going on around here. There've been weird things happening for years. I've never mentioned them before because . . . well, there didn't seem any point. But now . . ." Crowley shrugged.

"You'd better explain yourself," Kengle said.

"Ever hear of a group called the Driscoll Dozen?"

Kengle shook his head.

"It's a committee. It exists right here in the Foundation."

"That's ridiculous. How could it exist without me knowing?"

"It's a sort of secret society. Coffey and his wife were founder members. Their daughter was a member too, the whole time she was running the organization. The others I was never able to identify, but I do know they met on the first Monday of every month."

"To do what?"

"Your guess is as good as mine. There were no minutes kept, no written records."

Kengle felt puzzled. There was an intensity in Ben Crowley he had never seen before. He found it vaguely disquieting.

"Years ago," Crowley went on, "I discovered something I've never shown to a living soul. I'd like to show it to you now. Come down to my office."

Wonderingly, Kengle followed his bodyguard along the corridor. Inside his own room Crowley bolted the door, then moved to the window and carefully closed the shutters. Switching on the desk lamp, he knelt down and unlocked his bottom drawer. He drew out a cardboard file and placed it on the desk top. "When I first joined the Coffey Foundation," he said, "I came fresh from the CID. I'd only been with the company a month or two before Sir Stephen Coffey died. Part of my job was clearing out his personal effects. I found these among his belongings."

He opened the file, took out a letter and handed it to Kengle. "This is a copy of a cable from Sir Stephen Coffey to a certain Garry Kurtzman. Read it."

Kengle held the paper under the circle of light. His eyes scanned the typewritten sentences. "Dear G," it said, "Good luck with the Los Angeles project. If Barney brings off his end of the deal, I will attempt to join you at the beginning of next week. Sorry can't speculate on how many expected for dinner. Phone soonest. S."

Kengle read the paper through several times before handing it back. "It's meaningless," he grunted.

"It could be innocent, of course. On the other hand, it could also be in code, a cryptogram. I found nearly a dozen like it."

"So?"

"So nothing. I was never able to get them unscrambled. But I also found these."

He took out a faded photograph and pushed it into Kengle's hand. "That was taken in Miami, Florida, thirty-four. The man with Sir Stephen Coffey is Garry Kurtzman. Here's another. This one was taken in Washington, in forty-two. It shows Kurtzman with Sir Stephen and Lady Coffey. Here they are again in London, in nineteen forty-six."

Kengle frowned. "What are you getting at, Ben?"

"Kurtzman was a notorious American gangster," Crowley told him evenly. "A close friend of Lucky Luciano. After the war, when organized crime in the United States went 'legit', he acted as the mob's personal launderer, taking the money from a thousand dirty rackets and processing it through respectable business concerns."

Kengle said nothing, but he felt his throat contract.

"Look at this," Crowley continued, handing him another photograph. "Las Vegas, nineteen forty-seven. Sir Stephen and Lady Coffey were somewhat elderly then, but just cast an eye at their entourage. There's Kurtzman again. And at his side Bobby Diapoulas, Hank Manera and the *capo di tutti capi* of the Mazoni family, Aldo Barello. Quite a gathering, eh? Strange bedfellows for people of the Coffeys' reputation."

Kengle felt the colour drain from his cheeks as he studied the figures in the photograph.

"What are you trying to say, Ben?"

"Tom, even with those diamonds behind him, have you ever wondered how a man like Sir Stephen Coffey could build up such a fortune completely from scratch?"

"He was a genius, that's how."

Crowley nodded. "It's possible. But for someone with no business experience at all, I wouldn't call it genius, Tom, I'd call it a bloody miracle."

Kengle was angry and tense. "Spit it out, Ben. What are you implying?"

"Tom, is it possible—just remotely possible—that Sir Stephen Coffey built up his fortune not through personal enterprise, but through an association with the American underworld? That he used his bewildering array of front companies, the dozens of charitable ventures the Foundation set up, to cream off fat profits made by laundering money for the American mob?"

"Are you seriously trying to tell me that this empire has been built on things like narcotics, extortion, prostitution? Are you asking me to believe that this world-famous humanitarian was nothing more than a cheap, vicious crook?"

"The Foundation itself is legitimate, Tom," Crowley explained reasonably. "I'm suggesting it's the Driscoll Dozen which launders the money supplied by organized crime."

Kengle leaned against the table. He was breathing heavily. "There's a basic flaw in your argument," he said softly.

"What's that?"

"Why would a man who was already richer than Croesus turn his hand to crime? It doesn't make sense."

Crowley sighed. "Tom, Coffey wasn't as rich as you think he was. He was serving with the British army when he discovered those diamonds. Strictly speaking, they came into the category of spoils of war. When Coffey claimed them for himself he had to reach a compromise with the military authorities. The largest and most valuable stone was presented to the British nation and became part of the Crown Jewels, the others he was allowed to keep on condition that he never disposed of them separately, or outside the boundaries of the British Isles."

"I know all that," Kengle snapped.

"Then can't you see? Without splitting the collection or taking it out of the country, Coffey could never find a buyer. The Crown had been wickedly clever. They'd kept the diamonds on British soil and ensured that Coffey would be their custodian. That collection must have seemed like a millstone round his neck."

For a long moment Kengle stood in silence. "Ben," he said hoarsely, "I've got to know if what you're telling me is the truth."

Crowley nodded. "I understand. But there's only one person alive who can answer that. Coffey's daughter, Lady Catherine."

Kengle stared at him, his face stricken. He stabbed the button of the intercom. "Miriam," he said, "tell my driver to pick me up in front of the entrance lobby. If anybody wants me, I've gone to Dorset."

Chapter Three

The house stood on a broad promontory of land surrounded on three sides by deep grassy combes where the ground rippled and undulated towards the grey sheen of the distant ocean. It was a large house with granite walls and soaring watchtowers. Kengle studied it moodily as his driver turned in at the gate.

The London rain had given way to the gentle sunshine of an English summer evening, and seldom had Kengle seen the countryside looking so beautiful. He had stopped only once during the long drive south—at his local library to pick up a book on the 1898 Sudanese campaign. But though he had tried hard to read he had found concentration difficult as his brain worried at Ben Crowley's disclosures.

It just wasn't possible, he thought. He couldn't have run an organization for six whole years, six years in which he had become closely and personally involved in every facet of its operation, without being aware that something didn't sit right.

The car swung to a halt in front of the huge grey stone mansion and Kengle got out and went to knock loudly on the heavy oak door. It was opened a moment later by Evans, the butler. His eyebrows lifted as he recognized Kengle. "Why, Mr. Kengle, sir. Lady Catherine is in the rose garden. I'll tell her you're here."

"Don't bother," Kengle answered, "I'll tell her myself."

Clutching his briefcase, he followed the footpath round the side of the house.

Lady Catherine was pruning the rosebushes which bordered the stone patio. She was dressed in denim dungarees and her grey hair was covered by a bright silk scarf. Kengle's lips twisted into a wry grin when he saw her. For nearly thirty years Lady Catherine had run the Foundation single-handed after her parents had died. Only when age and ill health had begun to take its toll had she agreed to step down, allowing Kengle, at the board's invitation, to assume the presidency. But she had disapproved of him from the beginning, insisting that he was too young, too inexperienced, to take over the Coffey Foundation. Their relationship had always been a difficult one.

Lady Catherine did not look up as Kengle approached. She was crouching over a particularly extravagant bloom, snipping at superfluous stalks with a pair of secateurs, and when Kengle's shadow fell across her she said, "I named this after my mother, Victoria. It's a new variety. Like it?"

"Very pretty," Kengle murmured.

She straightened, peering directly into his face, her small eyes shrewd and hard. "I had a feeling you'd turn up sooner or later."

"How's that?"

"You always do, when trouble arises."

Kengle shifted his briefcase to his other arm. The old lady always made him feel uneasy. Partly, he supposed, because she was Sir Stephen Coffey's daughter, but there was something else, a kind of indefinable haughtiness as if Lady Catherine could never rid herself of the conviction that she was in the presence of an inferior being.

"I have to talk to you," he said.

"Do you indeed? I hope you're suitably ashamed of yourself, young man."

Kengle sighed. "Lady Catherine, it's not the diamonds I've come about. At least, not directly."

"What then?"

"I have some papers I'd like to show you. Personal things. Photographs, letters, a few legal documents. They belonged to your father."

She frowned. "My father's been dead for more than three decades. What possible significance could such articles have today?"

He hesitated, then said gently, "Lady Catherine, it's about the Driscoll Dozen."

Not a flicker of expression crossed her face, he had to admire her for that, but her features seemed to settle into a frigid mask. She stared at him in silence; then, peeling off her gloves, she said, "I think you'd better come inside."

She dropped the secateurs onto a nearby deckchair and Kengle followed her across the patio and through the rear entrance into the mansion. The corridors were panelled with oak, their walls lined with oil paintings. The butler met them in the hall and Lady Catherine said, "Evans, I don't want to be disturbed before dinner, is that understood?"

"Yes, my lady," he replied dutifully.

She led the way into the library, carefully closing the door behind them. Then she indicated an armchair. "Sit down," she ordered.

Clutching the briefcase on his knee, Kengle sat. The old lady settled herself opposite him. "Now," she said, "tell me what this is all about."

Kengle opened his briefcase and took out the cardboard folder. "This file," he said, "was compiled by my chief security officer, Ben Crowley, from personal papers he found amongst your father's things. Some of them are messages, possibly in code. They are addressed to a certain Garry Kurtzman, a notorious member of the American crime syndicates. You will admit, ma'am, he makes a rather strange associate for people of your parents' reputation unless—and I hesitate to say this—unless Ben Crowley's suspicions contain an element of truth."

"What *are* Ben Crowley's suspicions, Mr. Kengle?"

"He believes that for many years now the Foundation has been used to launder money for the American mob. He believes this operation has been conducted and controlled by a secret society within the Foundation called the Driscoll Dozen."

She held out her hand for the file. Carefully she sifted through the papers inside, studying the photographs intently. At length she said, "Ben Crowley is a damn fool. We should have retired him years ago."

"But Lady Catherine, can you explain the existence of this material?"

"There's nothing to explain. It's perfectly innocent."

"Innocent, ma'am? I would hardly call it that."

Her eyes studied him. "How much do you know about my father?" she demanded.

"Until today I thought I knew everything. Now I'm just not sure any more." Kengle shifted uncomfortably in his chair. "Lady Catherine, I have a question to ask you and it is very important that you tell me the truth. Was there something in Sir Stephen's early life which you've deliberately kept secret?"

She peered at him sharply. "Like what?"

"I don't know. Something unsavoury perhaps? Something you wouldn't want people to know?"

Reaching back, she drew a shawl from the back of the armchair, gathering it round her shoulders. The gesture was a reflective rather than a conscious one, as if she was somehow playing for time.

On impulse, Kengle said, "Something to do with the Churchill Diamonds?"

"I don't know what you're talking about," she snapped.

But it was already too late. Kengle had seen the glimmer of alarm flash across her eyes and knew he had touched a sensitive nerve. He leaned forward. "Lady Catherine, did Sir Stephen Coffey do something in the summer of eighteen ninety-eight which resulted in some way in the jewel robbery which took place this morning? You know why those jewels were stolen, don't you, ma'am? And you know who took them. It had nothing to do with monetary gain. It was something else. Am I right?"

The old lady's eyes left his face. Then she nodded.

Kengle felt triumph gathering in his chest. "Lady Catherine," he whispered, "if I'm to carry on as head of this organization, I have to know."

"That's impossible. It's too dangerous."

"Why?"

"Please don't ask. I can tell you nothing."

Kengle was silent for a moment, thinking. He knew if he pushed too hard she would close up like a clam.

He decided to try a different approach. Rummaging inside his briefcase, he took out the book he had borrowed from the library. "I did a bit of reading on my way here this evening. This is an account of the British reconquest of the Sudan in eighteen ninety-eight. Fascinating tale. Did you know the Anglo-Egyptian army assembled for the task was the finest in our history? It numbered nineteen battalions of infantry, ten squadrons of cavalry, four field batteries and a camel corps of eight companies. The officer in command of the expedition was Kitchener. Quite a character, it seems. He could have dashed downriver to engage the dervish forces at Khartoum, but instead he opted for a more cautious advance, reinforcing his supply route all the way."

Lady Catherine hesitated. She realized she was being drawn deliberately into this new field of discussion. "That's quite true," she declared in a cautious voice, "he laid a railway track from Wadi Halfa to Fort Atbara, a distance of two hundred and fifty miles across some of the most uncompromising country in the world."

"And he used it, Lady Catherine, to ferry carriageloads of men and equipment southwards. Am I right in thinking, ma'am, that among those men was your father, Sir Stephen Coffey?"

She nodded wearily in agreement.

Kengle leaned forward. "Begin there, Lady Catherine. Tell me what happened after your father arrived in the Sudan."

She looked at him, her expression calm. "Mr. Kengle, knowledge can be a dangerous thing. Forget Stephen Coffey. Continue to run the Foundation as you have done, and in a month or two this entire episode will have been forgotten."

"Supposing I refuse?"

She paused for a moment, then she said, "I know your temperament, Mr. Kengle. You have chosen to idolize my father. If I tell you the things you wish to know, it could have the most disastrous consequences, not only for the Foundation itself but for you as an individual."

"Lady Catherine," Kengle murmured, "I must have the truth."

She laughed shortly. "The truth? What makes you think you could believe the truth? You would have to know my parents as I knew them, their secret thoughts, their secret desires. Then maybe, just maybe, you might begin to understand."

Kengle settled back in the armchair. A curious feeling of dread seemed to lodge in his chest as he studied the old lady in the pale light of the early evening.

"Tell me about it," he said.

It BEGAN IN 1898, in the Sudan.

The camel tracks formed a ragged trail which meandered diagonally eastwards away from the railway line. They were flanked on one side by a series of jagged outcrops and on the other by rolling sand dunes, some nearly fifty feet high, their crests cluttered with acacia trees and clumps of twisted camel thorn.

Lieutenant Stephen Coffey of the 10th Westmorland Lancers, dark-haired, slimly built, raised his arm to bring his troop to a halt, and after glancing briefly at the ground motioned to Sergeant MacAngus to examine the tracks more closely.

Coffey's eyes were startlingly blue, forming the focal point of his entire face, and across his cheeks the sun had burned a livid weal below the shade of his pith helmet.

MacAngus, by contrast, was a rawboned, heavy-shouldered man with skin the colour of burnished copper. He strolled lazily towards the camel tracks and began to scrutinize them carefully.

Coffey sat in silence, watching his sergeant. He knew MacAngus was a thousand times better than the Arab trackers the army employed, most of whom were spies for the khalifa, the dervish ruler, anyhow. He watched the sergeant pick up one of the tiny balls of camel dung, crumbling it between his fingers. "Droppings're still warm," MacAngus said. "They canna be far in front of us, sir. Ten, twenty minutes mebbe."

"Dervishes?" Coffey asked.

"Looks like. No more'n ten, I'd say."

Coffey thought for a moment. He had twenty-one men in his own troop, counting himself and MacAngus. But his orders had been clear. Patrol the railway, report sightings of dervish movements but under no circumstances engage the enemy.

Lieutenant Coffey was bored. He had been in the Sudan for more than four months now and most of his days had been spent guarding the train installations, and combating the heat, the flies, the monotony and the discomfort. He was eager for action, eager for excitement; but he knew that if he attacked and lost, he would face an immediate court-martial.

Sergeant MacAngus rose to his feet. "There's something else, sir." He indicated a series of dark stains on the ground. "Blood," he said simply. "Somebody's hurt. Man or animal." He indicated a separate line of tracks with his foot. "This one's a wee bit older than the rest, two or three minutes mebbe. See how the rear tracks look smudged, as if the creature was dragging its hind leg. My guess is, whoever's riding it is on the run."

Suddenly, like a twig snapping in the dry thin air, they heard the crack of a rifle shot. Coffey froze in his saddle, listening hard. Another shot rang out.

Coffey glanced at Sergeant MacAngus. "Close," he whispered.

MacAngus nodded. "Aye. Just over yon ridge, I reckon."

"Remount, Sergeant," Coffey snapped.

He ordered the troop to remain where it was and, with the sergeant following, trotted up the trail to a narrow finger of rock which descended steeply into a gully on the other side. Below him the earth sloped into a steep "V" formed by a dried-up riverbed. At the very tip of this "V" a man crouched among the rocks, an Arab in soiled robes and dirty headcloth, firing spasmodically with an ancient Remington.

As Coffey watched, another man, his body blue-black in the flushed light of evening, rose from the spot where he had been hiding and scuttled across a stretch of open ground, dropping to a crouch behind a cluster of camel thorn. Coffey spotted eight more figures, all clutching shields and spears.

"Fuzzies," Coffey whispered to MacAngus, using the nickname given by British troops to the Beja hill tribesmen. The Bejas were a primitive people, poorly armed and badly led, but they fought with a ferocity and courage which had wrung a grudging respect from their British and Egyptian adversaries.

The small group of men slowly worked their way towards the solitary Arab who, trapped in his arid cul-de-sac, could only fire futilely each time he spotted a flash of naked skin.

Coffey could see the sprawled figure of the man's camel which had collapsed, wounded, leaving its rider to the mercy of his pursuers. The Beja's own mounts stood in a group on the rim of the gully.

"Now here's an interesting situation," Coffey said, chuckling under his breath. "A dervish under attack from his own people. The question is, do we sit here and watch the fun, or invite ourselves down to the party?"

More than likely the Arab was an enemy, a deserter from the Khalifa's army, or possibly a thief who had rebelled at the thought of the dervish punishment—the cutting off of the culprit's hands—and had decided to make a bolt for freedom. Risking the lives of British cavalrymen for such an unsavoury creature would hardly be justified, in the eyes of the British high command. On the other hand, the Bejas were indisputably the enemy, and those tribesmen down there offered a tempting target.

Coffey came to a decision. "Sergeant," he ordered crisply, "order the men to right wheel into combat formation."

The troopers moved into position along the gully's rim, their lances poised in the evening glow.

Coffey drew his sword. The sound of the blade sliding from its scabbard made a soft metallic rustle on the still evening air. Sergeant

MacAngus sat with his reins gripped tightly between his teeth. He had left his sword still sheathed, and instead gripped a revolver in each fist.

Slowly Coffey raised his sword high in the air, and almost in slow motion the lances lowered. Coffey took a deep breath, then, with one swift motion, he brought the blade down and the line of cavalry broke into the charge.

The ground sloped so steeply that Coffey found most of his attention taken up with steering his Arab pony down the treacherous hillside. The tribesmen had spotted them at last and were coming forward to meet the British attack, their long spears poised for action. In spite of himself Coffey felt a tremor of admiration. Savage and cruel the dervishes might be, but there was no disputing their courage.

Coffey steadied his pony as they reached the gully floor. He became icy calm as he glimpsed ahead the little cluster of sandy rocks and the blue-black bodies flitting between them. In front of him, as if from nowhere, a man rose suddenly. His arm was drawn back, his spear poised and aimed as he crouched in Coffey's path, motionless and unafraid. Coffey swung his sword blade to the left, clipping and deflecting the spear tip as its shaft left the thrower's hand and swished past his face.

Coffey barely had time to swing his sword in a backhanded curve before the tribesman blocked the blow with his shield, and, drawing a wicked-looking twelve-inch knife, dived directly under the heels of Coffey's pony.

British cavalrymen had learned to their cost the effectiveness of the dervish on foot. Agile as a monkey, he could roll under the very hooves of a cavalry charge and hamstring the horses from behind. Coffey saw the tribesman slash at his pony's legs, and by sheer physical strength hauled his mount round just in time. Leaning sideways out of the saddle he swung his sword viciously downwards, feeling a jolt run along his arm as the blade connected with the tribesman's wrist, amputating the hand. Blood spurted from the man's forearm but he stared up at Coffey, showing no sign of fear or pain, and scrambled in the dust for his fallen knife. Coffey didn't give him a chance to use it again. Leaning forward, he drove the point of his blade into the warrior's throat, pinning the man back against the desert floor.

Coffey felt sick as he wheeled away. He could see the rest of the tribesmen retreating, scrambling for their camels along the gully's rim. The attack had been short, sharp and effective. Coffey waved his sword arm in the air. "Let them go," he yelled.

He was already ashamed of his eagerness to fight. He glanced round the gully bottom. Four tribesmen lay dead in the dust, but he noted with relief that there were no British casualties. Apart from a few scratches the troop appeared unscathed. They were laughing breathlessly, surprised at the success of their assault.

430

Sergeant MacAngus looked as calm as ever. He sat reloading his revolvers. Coffey saw the Arab they had rescued coming towards them, holding his Remington loosely at his side. He was a big man with a dark bearded face and wild flashing eyes. For a moment Coffey thought he was smiling, then he saw the impression was a false one, created by a jagged scar which sliced through his left cheek and twisted the side of his mouth into a manic grin.

"Our friend doesn't look too happy to see us," Coffey murmured softly.

MacAngus grunted, and, slipping one of his pistols into its holster, rested the other across the front of his saddle. "Ye'd better stay out of my line of fire, sir. If the bastard tries to use that Remington, I'll blow the top of his head off."

Coffey spurred his mount forward and brought it to a halt, swinging the beast sideways as he studied the Arab's approach.

"That's far enough," Coffey ordered.

The Arab halted and stared at him wildly. Then he said in impeccable English, "You certainly came down that hillside like the hounds of hell. I thought it was the devil himself coming to carry me off!"

Coffey's eyes widened with surprise. "Who are you?" he demanded.

The man saluted casually. "Lieutenant Walter J. Driscoll, Military Intelligence, under the command of Major Reginald Wingate."

Coffey whistled under his breath. Wingate's reputation was legendary. Using dubious information and very little financial backing, he had set up a sophisticated network of agents which operated behind enemy lines.

"You've been living with the dervishes?"

"On and off, for the past eight weeks," Driscoll grinned.

"What are you doing here?"

"Well, I was trying to reach the railhead when those Bejas picked up my trail. They'll have a go at anybody if they think there's an ounce of profit in it. Bandits, the lot of them. How far off are we?"

"About an hour's ride, no more."

"Who's in command there?"

"Colonel Philip Guthrie."

"I have to speak to him right away."

Coffey nodded. He knew if the Beja tribesmen had reinforcements in the vicinity he would be well advised to get his men back to camp as quickly as possible. "Is your mount dead?" he asked.

The lieutenant nodded. "One of those blighters got him with a spear-thrust early this morning. It's a wonder the poor beast managed to survive so long."

"Well, we'll just have to ride double. Think you can clamber up behind me? It won't be comfortable, I'm afraid."

Chapter Four

The camp stood on a bend of the river, bordered on one side by desert scrub and on the other by the muddy Nile. It was nearly a mile across, secured by lines of thorn bushes staked down to form a *zariba* or palisade. Inside the central gate rose the grass huts and blanket shelters which marked the bivouacs of the Egyptian and Sudanese brigades. Towards the centre fluttered the white tents of the British division. At the railhead, a solitary locomotive stood on the tracks, hissing steam between its massive wheels.

Coffey rode in. No sound rose from the men behind him other than the clinking of their accoutrements. The patrol had been long and arduous. They had ridden far and tasted blood. Now they were weary and ready for bed.

Coffey could hear Lieutenant Driscoll grunting behind him in the saddle. He knew how uncomfortable the journey must have been for Driscoll, perched on the edge of the leather rim, but Driscoll had never complained. Curiosity filled Coffey as he thought of the Englishman living, sleeping, breathing in the very heart of the dervish stronghold.

"It's a miracle you've managed to survive, living with those savages for eight weeks," he said.

"That's no miracle, Lieutenant," Driscoll muttered, "just common sense. I've learned to think the way they think. Most of the time I'm a dervish myself. The dervish may be savage but he has a simplicity of nature that appeals to my basic instincts."

"How can you talk like that when he keeps seven eighths of his countrymen enslaved?"

"Well, the dervish doesn't look at things the way we do. He sees slavery as a natural part of life. And the slaves are not treated badly, by European standards."

Coffey drew to a halt at the camp commander's tent. The red flag of Egypt fluttered from its roof and two sentries in brown jerseys and blue puttees guarded its entrance flap. With a murmur of relief, Driscoll slid to the ground. "In case I haven't done so already," he said, "I'd like to thank you for saving my life."

"A pleasure, Lieutenant," Coffey told him, as he shook the officer's hand.

Coffey watched him duck beneath the tentflap, then, handing over his pony, he ordered MacAngus to dismiss the troop and made his way to his quarters. It had been a long day and he was feeling desperately tired.

His nostrils picked up the odour of engine oil, blancoed webbing, horse sweat, tobacco smoke. Coffey loved the army. From the beginning he had felt at home here. The sad thing was, the army did not love

Coffey. He was someone who did not know his place. A man of his social background clearly belonged in the ranks, and the fact that he had aspired to higher things made him something of an untouchable among his fellow officers. His father, a poor farmer who scratched out a living from the harsh hill country of the Cumbrian fells, had sent Coffey to officer school with what savings he'd managed to scrape together, in the belief that he was giving his son a reasonable start in life. But Coffey had quickly discovered that in the British army of the 1890s a subaltern's pay was simply not enough to keep a young man: mess bills, uniforms, dining-in nights, soldiers' charities, even the simple cost of providing and looking after one's horse ran far above the meagre remittance offered by the Crown, and while Coffey's associates supplemented their incomes with regular allowances from their families, he had been reduced to the dubious expedient of gambling, in an effort to make ends meet. In the snobbish establishment of the Victorian army, gambling, although a respectable pursuit for officers with money to burn, was an unthinkable social disgrace when a man did it in order to survive. Coffey was tolerated, but the fact remained that, despite his unarguable assets—intelligence, flair, ability, imagination—he was a social outcast.

And yet he was about to emark on the greatest adventure of his life, an adventure which would turn him into one of the wealthiest and most powerful men in the world.

SERGEANT MACANGUS lit a cheroot, peering contentedly at the stars. It was the time of the day he liked best, when night brought a blessed respite from the heat of the sun, and the harsh metallic earth smell which came drifting in from the desert conjured up memories of his early youth. MacAngus felt at home in the desert. He had spent many years with the British army in India, had served on the Khyber and in the desolate hill country of Afghanistan. He did not hate wild places as some of the others did, and he did not fear them either. Instead, he welcomed their harshness like an old familiar friend.

He felt tired as he strolled back to his tent, his body moving lethargically. When he reached his bivouac door, he found Sergeant Blakey of C Troop waiting outside. Blakey was not a particular friend of MacAngus's, and though they were on amicable terms, their relationship was principally a working one.

"Blakey," MacAngus said, "I thought ye were up in Cairo."

"Came in on the evening train," Blakey told him.

MacAngus picked up a tin dish, walked to the line of water guerbas, and filled it to the brim. He felt the cool droplets of moisture splashing across his wrists.

"How did your leave go?" he asked, over his shoulder.

"Vigorous, as usual," Blakey said. "But there's something else I want to talk to you about, Mac."

"Aye?"

"There was someone in Cairo, waiting for that train. Man named Lewis."

MacAngus leaned forward and splashed water over his face and neck. The name meant nothing to him, but then names seldom did.

"Said he worked for Scotland Yard."

MacAngus's great head swung upwards, and he peered at Blakey through the darkness. Water dripped from his nose and chin.

"He was looking for you, Mac. Had a photograph, warrant, the whole lot."

MacAngus stood rigid for a moment, then without a word he turned, still dripping, and plucked a towel from the guy rope.

"He said the charge was murder," Blakey added gently.

MacAngus went on towelling his face, the muscles in his arms rippling in the firelight, and, watching him, Blakey looked uncertain. "Just thought I'd let you know," he said. "I told him nothing and he'll get nothing from the army either. But it might be a good idea to make yourself scarce for a few days. Keep out of the way until the bastard quits snooping around."

MacAngus stared at Blakey calmly, no expression on his face. "Thanks, Walt," he said.

Blakey nodded and shuffled away through the darkness. For a long time MacAngus stood looking after him. Then he moved inside the tent.

"AT EASE," Colonel Guthrie ordered. "I suppose you're wondering why I sent for you, Coffey?"

"Yes, sir."

The colonel was sitting at his desk, sipping a mug of steaming tea. Beside him stood Lieutenant Driscoll, still wearing his Arab robes. Guthrie was a barrel-chested man with heavy jowls, greying hair and brown blotches on his cheeks formed by constant exposure to the wind and sun. His rare gift for handling troops of different nationalities, and his reputation for coolness under fire, had made him a celebrity in Kitchener's army. He indicated the man standing beside him. "I believe you've already met Lieutenant Driscoll?"

Coffey nodded to Driscoll, who grinned back.

"I've heard about your little escapade tonight," the colonel said.

"Yes, sir."

"Impetuous," Guthrie continued tonelessly. "As far as you were concerned, Lieutenant Driscoll was an enemy dervish who'd fallen out with his own people. You had absolutely no right to interfere."

"No, sir."

"Under normal circumstances," the colonel went on, "I'd have your hide for what you did tonight, but as it happens I'm both relieved and grateful. You did us a considerable service. Lieutenant Driscoll is not a man we'd care to lose." Colonel Guthrie examined his desk top, brushing flies from his blotting pad. "Lieutenant Driscoll has brought me a piece of disquieting information," he said. "Disquieting, because I am unable to act upon it in an official sense. At the same time, in the name of humanity I feel equally unable to ignore it."

Coffey waited for the colonel to continue. A slight breeze ruffled the tent walls.

"Come over here," Guthrie ordered. "I'd like you to look at something."

Coffey followed the colonel to the back of the tent where a large wall map was hung from one of the ridge poles. "Recognize this?" Guthrie asked.

"Looks like an outline of the Nile."

"Correct. But with one small difference. This isn't the Nile as it is today, but as it appeared thirteen years ago, before the fall of Khartoum. When the dervish armies laid siege to the city, they swept across the Nubian Desert occupying all the towns and villages along the riverbank. One of those towns was El Serir, situated just below Khegga." Guthrie's finger stabbed at the chart. "Most of the inhabitants were slaughtered in the initial holocaust," he said. "The lucky ones were sold into slavery."

"The events at El Serir were well documented at the time," Coffey said.

"Indeed they were, Lieutenant, but the full story was never told in the British press. A number of Europeans were taken prisoner, for example, but to avoid distress to their relatives, they were listed as having been killed. Happily, they are now dead. Their sufferings are over. They were taken to Hamira, to the prison fortress there. I don't know what you've heard about Hamira, Lieutenant, but it's understood to be a dervish hellhole. The captives were kept in a small communal cell with the barest sanitary arrangements. Their clothes swarmed with vermin. They seldom saw the light of day. According to reliable witnesses, someone died every night. It's hardly surprising that most of the Europeans succumbed during their first year of captivity."

"Most?" Coffey echoed softly.

"Among them was a British missionary, Charlton Routledge, and his daughter Victoria. According to Lieutenant Driscoll here, they appear to be very much alive."

"I talked to a dervish who saw them at Hamira only last month," Driscoll said. "The old man was released from the prison about eight years ago. Now he spends most of his time helping the local craftsmen at the carpentry shop."

"And the girl?"

"Slave, naturally. That's the dervish way."

"Can you imagine it?" the colonel growled softly. "The girl was little more than a child when she was taken. Today she's a grown woman. She's spent thirteen years of her life in the hands of barbaric savages. Strictly speaking, I have no right to interfere at all. Hamira lies to the west, one hundred and forty miles across the desert. The British advance must continue south down the Nile to Omdurman and Khartoum. There is no hope of the Routledges being rescued for some considerable time, unless . . ."

"Unless we send in a flying column with the specific intention of bringing them out," Coffey said.

Guthrie nodded. "It would be a mission of mercy, Lieutenant. Dangerous in the extreme. It would mean not only crossing the Baiyuda Desert, but moving through country crawling with the enemy. I've no doubt you've heard lurid stories of what happens to men who are taken prisoner by the dervishes."

Coffey felt tension rising inside him. "With respect, sir, I understand clearly your concern for both the lady and her father, but it's one thing to send a reconnaissance patrol along the area covered by our railway, and quite another to venture through hostile territory without support troops. We wouldn't survive a day."

"I agree," Colonel Guthrie admitted. "If we attempted to send a column across the desert, it would be cut to pieces. But Lieutenant Driscoll here has suggested an interesting alternative."

"Instead of taking an entire troop, we go ourselves," Driscoll explained. "Three men, four at the outside, dressed as Tuareg tribesmen. The Tuareg belong to the Kel Ahaggar, more than a thousand miles across the Sahara. They have a tradition of covering their faces, so if we run into dervish cavalry we'll be nicely disguised. Also, the Tuareg speak a language virtually unknown in the Sudan, which means that if we are questioned by dervish patrols, their suspicions won't be aroused if we fail to understand."

There was an air of madness about Driscoll. Partly it came from the wolfish grin, but there was something else, an element of wildness, of reckless irresponsibility that filled Coffey with a feeling of deep unease. He sensed the colonel's eyes upon him.

"I know what you're thinking, Lieutenant. It's a harebrained scheme, with little chance of success. Even if you did manage to run the gauntlet across the desert, you'd still be faced with the problem of springing Miss Routledge and her father from under the dervish noses and spiriting them back to safety. I couldn't blame you if you decided to refuse."

He hesitated and looked down at his hands. "I also know the problems you've been facing since your arrival here," he said softly.

"Problems, sir?"

"Your finances."

Coffey swallowed, feeling the colour mounting in his cheeks. "I've always paid my debts, sir," he answered stiffly.

"Of course you have. The point is, I've always regarded you as one of the most promising officers in the regiment. Unfortunately, because of the curious structure of the military world, it has not been possible to acknowledge that fact. The British army has existed for more than a thousand years on a foundation of privilege and inequality. I want to help you in every way I can, but you must understand that I am bound by the system.

"On the other hand, should you become involved in, shall we say, an undertaking of an audacious nature, one which might save the lives of innocent civilians and perhaps even attract the attention of the press, then any shortcomings you may suffer in the financial sense would, I am sure, appear unimportant by comparison."

Guthrie paused and studied Coffey coolly in the lamplight. "What I am saying, Lieutenant Coffey," he added softly, "is that some kind of spectacular personal success . . . would make it much easier for me to recognize your true value to this regiment."

Coffey struggled to keep his face impassive. He was being manipulated and he knew it. But he could see no way of withdrawing gracefully.

The colonel looked down at his desk. "Lieutenant Driscoll has proposed a strike force of three or four mounted men to bring the Routledges back," he announced. "He's asked for you to take command. Naturally I can't order such a thing. All I can say is, please consider the plight of this unfortunate young woman and her father."

Coffey swallowed. Almost in a dream he heard his voice say, "I . . . I'd like to give it a try, sir."

Colonel Guthrie nodded. "Thank you, Lieutenant. I never doubted it for a moment. The intention is to depart tomorrow evening on the gunboat *Zafir*. It will transport you upriver behind the enemy lines. From there you will cross the desert to Hamira and effect the rescue of the Routledges by whatever means are necessary. Lieutenant Driscoll here will ride with you as guide and interpreter. Let him do the talking. He knows the enemy and the way they think. If you're intercepted, he'll explain that you're Tuareg warriors travelling home from Mecca. In addition, I'm giving you Sergeant MacAngus and Second Lieutenant Benson."

"Benson?"

Benson was a young officer who had arrived at the railhead fresh from Sandhurst barely six weeks earlier. He represented everything Coffey hated about the military class system: snobbery, arrogance, disdain. He had been quick to sense Coffey's humble background and quicker still to take advantage of it, taunting Coffey mercilessly until at last Coffey had taken him to the back of the railhead and thrashed him to a standstill, splitting his cheek with a vicious right hook that had laid Benson cold. Since then, Benson had stopped his sneering, but there was no mistaking his hostility.

"With respect, sir," Coffey declared, "I'd prefer someone else, if it's at all possible."

Guthrie frowned. "I can't afford anyone else, Lieutenant. Benson is expendable because of his lack of experience."

"You don't understand, Colonel. Lieutenant Benson and I have certain . . . differences."

Guthrie belonged to the old school. Duty was everything. A man played his part, whatever the circumstances. "I can't adapt strategies to fit the rivalries of my junior officers, Lieutenant," he declared coldly. "It's a war we're fighting. You'll make a point of getting on together for as long as it's necessary."

"Yes, sir," Coffey muttered.

"I shall dispatch two troops of Sudanese cavalry to wait for you at the old ruined fortress of Malawa, eighty miles southwest of Atbara. They'll have fresh horses, water and supplies. If, once you're clear of Hamira, you can reach Fort Malawa, your troubles will be over. Any questions?"

Coffey shook his head and the colonel, as if he knew the madness of what he was asking, looked relieved. "Good," he said.

THEY SET OUT on the evening of 11 July, on board the gunboat *Zafir*. The gunboat crews were regarded as the swashbucklers of the British troops, for while the rest of the army made its slow tortuous advance southwards, the river craft were already venturing more than a hundred miles behind enemy lines, steaming cheekily under the noses of the dervish riflemen, to blast their flimsy *nuggar* boats out of existence.

It was nearly midnight when the *Zafir*'s captain brought his craft alongside the western bank and the sailors waded ashore, tying her forward and aft to stunted acacia trees.

Standing on the bridge with the gunboat's captain, Commander Keppel, Coffey peered down at the shattered wreck of an Arab *dahabeeyah* which had run inelegantly aground. Its wooden hull was splintered and torn and the remains of its crew lay lifeless and bloody across its battered deck. Coffey counted eight bodies on the craft itself, and a ninth floating face-down in the water.

Commander Keppel followed Coffey's gaze. "I see you've spotted our friends down there," he said. "Not a pleasant sight, are they? We had a difference of opinion early this morning. A test of wills, you might say. They insisted on trying to blow us out of the water."

Coffey studied the stricken *dahabeeyah*. In its stern he spotted an ancient cannon, so old that its metal was smoothed by centuries of handling. By its side stood a barrel caulked with tar. Gunpowder, Coffey thought wonderingly. It was like a relic from a distant age.

"Against your Maxims, those poor bastards wouldn't stand a chance," he whispered.

"Quite right, Lieutenant. You've witnessed one of the tragedies of this war. The enemy are fighting the way they fought against the Crusaders, six centuries ago. They're using the same weapons, the same antiquated cannonry. We, on the other hand, have all the aids of modern science at our disposal. Hardly an equitable conflict, is it? Still, once you leave the safety of the *Zafir*, you and the dervishes will be more or less on equal terms. I have a sneaky feeling you'll be ready to sell your soul for an efficient Maxim then."

Coffey fell silent, staring thoughtfully at the wrecked boat.

Like his three companions, he was now dressed in loose baggy trousers acquired from the local Greek merchants, a white gown, blue *jellaba* and black cotton headgear which covered almost his entire face. Only his eyes remained exposed. He felt ludicrously theatrical in such an unorthodox outfit as he stood watching the camels being unloaded, roaring in protest as the Egyptian troops dragged them down the flimsy gangplank and began to strap saddles to their unwieldy backs.

"Not exactly pretty brutes, are they?" Commander Keppel said.

Lieutenant Driscoll, overhearing the remark, paused on the gangplank, chuckling. "I had the troopers plaster them with mud," he explained. "Trouble with the Camel Corps is, they groom their mounts every day. Now a clean well-groomed camel is an immediate giveaway to a shrewd-eyed dervish. The natives like to keep their animals coated with dirt to prevent them getting colds at night."

"Camels don't get colds," Coffey echoed unbelievingly.

"Oh yes, they do. They're a lot frailer than you realize. Try ill-using your beast and he'll lie down and die on you without warning. He can stand heat, drought, flies and dust storms, but he has to be cosseted in between."

Coffey shook his head as he followed Driscoll down the gangplank to the shoreline. He was putting the finishing touches to his equipment when Lieutenant Benson, dressed similarly in Tuareg costume, moved from the paddle boat to join them. Benson was a slim young man with a cold, aristocratic face. His skin was pale, his eyes hard, and there was a livid scar on his cheek where Coffey's fist had opened up the flesh during their fight at the railhead.

Coffey studied him coolly. He felt uncomfortable having Lieutenant Benson with them, and Benson, for his part, seemed equally dismayed at the prospect of Coffey's company. He stared through the darkness with undisguised distaste. His teeth, knocked crooked by the blow from

Coffey's fist, were now parted in a V-shaped aperture at the front.

"This your idea?" he demanded softly. "This whole crazy escapade?"

"No. If you want somebody to blame, try Lieutenant Driscoll."

Driscoll grinned at them wildly, his eyes flashing in the shadows. Benson's face remained cold. "It wasn't Driscoll who asked for me."

Coffey looked at him. "No, I don't suppose it was."

"You know damn well I'm a stranger here. I've no experience of the desert."

Suddenly Coffey understood. It wasn't the thought of riding with Coffey that Benson objected to. It was the mission itself. "You'll learn," he said gently.

"Do you take me for an imbecile? I know damned well what you're doing. You're dragging me into that emptiness so I'll be helpless and alone. You're trying to kill me."

Coffey grabbed the front of Benson's robes, pulling him close.

"Listen," he said quietly, "I didn't ask for you to go on this expedition. I advised against it, but the colonel overruled me. I didn't want to go myself. But since we have to, and since our survival for the next days will depend to a large degree upon each other, I suggest you put aside your feelings towards me and get your stupid backside into that camel saddle."

Balefully, Benson glared at him, then, jerking his camel into a crouch, he carefully mounted. Great stars hung in a flawless sky as the four men set off away from the shoreline. Cicadas screamed from the grass tufts and the air felt soft against their faces. Ahead of them as they rode, hollows and fissures lay like simple patterns on a flat unending landscape.

Commander Keppel stood on the *Zafir*'s bridge, watching them fade into the darkness.

"Think they'll pull it off, sir?" his aide asked.

Keppel sighed and shook his head. "Not a chance," he said. "Once beyond the river they'll be in a land as arid as the surface of the moon. They'll be alone and beyond the reach of military assistance, surrounded by sixty thousand hostiles. It's just a bloody sad waste of four good men."

Chapter Five

The reg fell in a series of softly undulating slopes, bordered to the east by rolling foothills which looked almost blue in the afternoon haze. Coffey lay among the rocks, training his field glasses on the waterhole below. He could pick out only dimly the crude timber pulley structure that straddled the desert well, and by its side the rough outlines of two thorn zaribas—constructed, he supposed, for defensive purposes. Beyond them, he spotted the black hummocks of nomad tents, and the minuscule figures of men moving about.

He handed the field glasses to Lieutenant Driscoll, who studied the scene in silence for a moment. For three days they had moved steadily westwards, encountering occasional straggling bands of dervishes, avoiding them when they could, bluffing it out with Driscoll doing the talking when they couldn't. Now their water guerbas were running low and Coffey knew that if they didn't replenish them soon, they could run the risk of dehydration.

"Any idea who they might be?" he asked.

Driscoll shrugged as he handed the field glasses to Lieutenant Benson. "Looks like a slave caravan on its way north from Central Africa."

"Think they'll move on if we hang about long enough?"

"Hard to say. If they've come up from the bush country the men will be tired. They could decide to rest for several days."

Coffey swore. He had been afraid of that. "We must have water," he declared.

Driscoll rubbed his nose. After three days in the desert his face-veil and *gandoura* were coated with orange dust, his eyes rimmed red from the sun. "Why don't we ride in and take our chances?" he suggested.

"There must be thirty warriors round that waterhole," MacAngus warned.

"True. But they have no reason to attack us. We're a party of Tuareg travelling west to our homeland. You're forgetting desert hospitality. We'll have to bluff it out, the way we've been doing. If those tribesmen have slaves with them, they'll not run the risk of damaging valuable property by starting a shooting match. Let me do the talking."

Coffey nodded dubiously. "We'll give it a try," he agreed, "but be ready to move like hell if those bastards turn unfriendly. We won't stand a chance down there once they've got us surrounded."

They mounted and rode in slowly, making, Coffey knew, quite a sight against the skyline, their blue robes and heavy face-cowls fluttering in the wind, their saddle ornaments reflecting the desert sunlight, their rifles resting casually across their thighs. Between the cluster of nomadic tents he could see the pale columns of smoke from the cooking fires; enamel pots dangled from wooden trestles and bundles of food hung in the branches of the few spindly trees. At the well, a group of young warriors were busy drawing water, pouring it into huge earthenware jars. In front of the tents, turbaned elders sat watching the strangers approach through timeless, implacable eyes.

Drawing closer, Coffey saw for the first time the reason for the thorn zaribas. They had been constructed not for defensive purposes, but to serve as makeshift prison stockades, for, crouched inside, strapped by the neck to heavy wooden logs, were thirty or forty black men and women. Their hands and feet had been tied with leather thongs. Because of the heavy tree trunks which linked them all together, it was impossible for one to move without causing pain and discomfort to the others, and Coffey could well imagine the agonizing misery of squatting for long hours in the blistering sun.

Beyond the waterhole the ground flattened into a pebbly plain and here, tied to a wooden stake sunk deep into the ground, Coffey spotted another black man, this one clearly a troublemaker, for a tall sapling had been bent over and its tip strapped to the offender's skull. Now, his muscles and sinews were desperately straining as he strove to withstand the ferocious pressure tearing at his neck.

Coffey felt his stomach quiver. It was clear that as the victim's strength gave out, the remorseless tug of the sapling would steadily intensify, until by morning, or noon tomorrow at the latest, it would spring upright, ripping his head from his shoulders.

Lieutenant Benson nudged his camel alongside. "Look at that poor devil," he whispered. "My God, have you ever seen such barbarism?"

Coffey muttered in assent. He jerked his camel to a crouch and dismounted, struggling to quell the anger bubbling inside him.

"They'll probably offer us tea," Driscoll explained. "If they do, drink it quickly and lick your lips to show that it's appreciated. If they offer four rounds, that means it's not convenient for us to stay and we'll have to move on as soon as we've filled up the waterskins. If, on the other hand, they offer us three rounds and no more, that means they'd like us to remain a while as their guests. It would be churlish to refuse."

Coffey nodded and Driscoll, after tying his animal to a clump of camel thorn, crossed the compound towards the watching tribesmen. He reached the elders and after a short consultation called Coffey, Benson and MacAngus over.

The tea was served in tiny glasses, very sweet and minty. Coffey found it not to his taste, but, remembering Driscoll's instructions, he gulped it down appreciatively. The glasses were filled three times and no more. A good sign.

"We're in luck," Driscoll whispered. "These are people of Dawasir. They've been south, replenishing their slave complement, and they're anxious for news of the war against the infidel. They've invited us to stay the night. They say we can have the *caravanserai*—that's the stone shelter beyond the zaribas."

Coffey glanced at the caravanserai, a flat-roofed pillbox of a building, constructed as a shelter for travellers camping by the waterhole.

"You trust them?" he asked.

"Not entirely. But it would be an insult if we attempted to leave. Once inside those walls we should be reasonably secure. Get the *guerbas* filled and I'll keep them talking while you see to the defences."

The groans of the man tied beyond the waterhole rose on the air in a bizarre symphony.

"What about him?" Coffey asked. "We can't just sit here and let them torture him to death."

"Frankly, I can't see that it's any of our business. He's the Dawasirs' property."

"He's a human being, for heaven's sake. Can't we buy him?"

"With what, old boy? We need every damned thing we've got. The camels, the rifles."

"Persuade them then."

Driscoll sighed. Shifting back on his haunches, he made a great show of dusting the front of his robes. "Look here," he said reasonably, "I seem to have convinced our hosts here that we are indeed who we say we are. But if I start arguing about the way they treat their slaves, they're bound to turn suspicious. After all, we Tuareg are supposed to be noted slavers too."

"We can't leave him, Driscoll. When we go, we must take him with us."

"Are you mad?" Lieutenant Benson hissed. "It's cruel, but it has nothing to do with us. We're here for one purpose only, to rescue Miss Routledge and her father. Bring that black along and you'll endanger not only our lives, but theirs as well."

Coffey was silent. He knew Benson was right. His job was to replenish the guerbas and press on as swiftly as possible. But something inside him rebelled at the thought of leaving the black man to such a slow, hideous death.

"Benson," he said, "we keep telling ourselves that the main purpose behind this war is to try and abolish slavery. How can we help the Routledges and ignore the sufferings of this poor devil?"

Benson turned away, disgusted but, by contrast, Driscoll's wild eyes glittered with amusement. "This really is highly irregular, old fellow."

"I'm aware of that," Coffey said quietly.

"You realize, of course, that we're hopelessly outnumbered?" Driscoll chuckled. "Not to worry. We do have one thing in our favour."

"What's that?"

"Smell the air. Dust storm. I can sniff them ten miles away. It's heading in this direction. It'll be here in an hour at the latest."

Coffey felt hope surge in his chest. "We'll wait, then."

Driscoll laughed. "That's right," he said, "we'll sit tight till the storm breaks, then while the Dawasir shelter inside their tents, we'll cut loose your friend and bolt like the blazes out of here."

NIGHT CAME SWIFTLY to the desert. One minute the land was caught in the flush of the setting sun, the next the sky was dark and full of stars. Coffey sat in the caravanserai peering out through the narrow window-holes, waiting for the dust storm to strike.

The wind came gently at first, stirring the palm trees, lifting the sand in circular spirals which whirled across the ground. There was a different feel to the air. Within twenty minutes the wind was stampeding across the desert like a living force, covering the entire campsite with a thick orange cloud. The Dawasir protected their heads with the hoods of their *jibbahs* and crouched motionless on the ground.

Clutching his rifle, Coffey sat studying the men facing him. Outside, the storm whipped its dust clouds against the caravanserai wall. "Everyone clear about what they're doing?" he demanded.

They nodded silently.

"Lieutenants Benson and Driscoll will head straight for the camels. Sergeant MacAngus and I will take care of the prisoner. Avoid trouble if you can, deal with it swiftly if you can't. Above all, do *not* fire your rifles."

He felt a fleeting tremor of anxiety, but dismissed it at once. He had made his decision, he would have to see it through. "Right, let's go," he snapped.

Sergeant MacAngus moved first, ducking beneath the door frame, battling his way into the open. He staggered momentarily, knocked off balance by the incredible force of the blast. Then he recovered and stumbled headlong into the thick orange fog.

Coffey followed, his heart thumping. The power of the wind seemed almost beyond belief. The sand came from everywhere, there was simply no defence against it. Even his face-cowl gave no protection against the harsh grains which found their way inside his clothes and stung his skin.

There was no sign of movement from the Dawasir; they were still huddled within the protection of their voluminous robes, waiting with the eternal patience of all desert creatures for the storm to pass. Ahead, Coffey discerned the outline of the unfortunate black man, his head and body completely furred by dust. MacAngus was slicing with his long curved sword at the rope holding the negro's skull. Coffey saw the line snap and the sapling spring free. A low moan of relief issued from the victim's lips.

MacAngus swiftly severed the thongs which bound the prisoner, who tried to rise, but collapsed instantly onto the ground. He had been tied too long, his limbs had lost all feeling.

Coffey hooked his wrist under one armpit, MacAngus took the other, and together they half carried, half dragged, the man towards the waiting camels. Coffey saw the camels grouped together in the storm, he saw Benson and Driscoll mounted and waiting. Then, like ghostly shrouds, dark figures suddenly reared up in his path, their robes moulded against their bodies by the buffeting gale.

A man seized him by the arm, fingers digging deep into his flesh. Letting go of the negro, Coffey turned and swung the hard wooden stock

445

of his rifle butt. Even above the thunder of the storm he heard the snap of bone as his blow broke the attacker's wrist.

Wildly, through the waves of dust, he glimpsed a figure leaping towards him, robes whipping to and fro like a schooner's sail. He caught sight of the glint of a long curved sword as it swung down in a vicious arc aimed directly at his skull. He blocked the attack with his rifle barrel and then, without pausing, jerked up his knee, stabbing it hard into the tribesman's crotch. The man's cry was lost in the howling of the wind.

Coffey leaped forward, swinging the rifle, scattering his assailants by the sheer fury of his onslaught. The attackers fell back, pausing to re-compose themselves. Without hesitating for an instant, Coffey staggered across the shifting ground, seeing MacAngus strapping the helpless negro to the shaggy back of their baggage animal. Coffey mounted his own beast at the run. He turned once to check that MacAngus was ready, then they pounded frenziedly into the dustbound night.

MORNING BROUGHT a tranquillity that surprised them all. The wind had dropped and the air was still as death.

They rode in silence, their robes coated with orange dust. Behind, Coffey could see more dust churning skywards in an ominous swirling column. He knew what it was. The Dawasir, riding in close pursuit. The suddenness of their escape had gained them a momentary advantage, but not for long. The enemy mounts were rested and fresh while their own were weary and worn by the long journey from the river. It was only a matter of time before they were overtaken.

A feeling of hopelessness and despair filled Coffey; it was not so much the imminence of capture which depressed him as the knowledge that if he hadn't been so pigheaded none of this would have happened. He reined in his camel, calling a halt. He looked back at MacAngus in the pale light of the early morning.

"How is he?" Coffey demanded, nodding to the motionless figure strapped to the baggage camel trailing in MacAngus's wake.

MacAngus shook his head, his face sombre, and Coffey felt alarm spreading through his body. Dammit, the man couldn't have died after all they had gone through. Without a word, he kicked his camel forward, reaching down to seize the man's hair in his fingers. He jerked the head upwards, staring into a face caked with dust. The eyes were open, staring sightlessly at the sky. They had been too late.

Coffey took out his knife and carefully cut the bonds holding the man to the saddle. With a muffled thud, the corpse slid from its perch and collapsed to the ground.

Lieutenant Benson glared at Coffey, fury blazing in his small pale eyes. "You fool. I told you it was insane to help this man."

Coffey wheeled away without answering.

446

Lieutenant Driscoll looked at him sympathetically. "I hate to say this, old fellow," he muttered, "but unless you do something drastic, I'm afraid those beggars will overtake us before lunchtime."

Coffey's eyes narrowed as he studied the column of dust smearing the sky behind them. Driscoll was right. It would be a miracle if their camels lasted even that long, the pace they were setting. Something had to be done to slow the Dawasir down, and since he couldn't do it himself, and since Driscoll was too important to their survival, and since Benson was inept and inexperienced, there was only one candidate left. Coffey looked at Sergeant MacAngus, feeling a momentary surge of guilt at the thought of what he was about to ask. MacAngus was more than his sergeant. He was also his friend.

"Mac," Coffey said, "somebody's got to draw them off."

"Aye." MacAngus seemed unsurprised by Coffey's statement. "In Afghanistan," he said, "the natives used to play a game called Shu-shu Kairi. There's a move in Shu-shu Kairi where you think your opponent's going one way when really he's heading somewhere else. Now, a man wi' his wits about him might lead those Dawasir a merry dance."

"Can you do it, Sergeant?" Coffey demanded gruffly.

MacAngus stared back at the way they had come, his eyes slitted against the sun. He nodded. "And afterwards I'll catch ye up in my own good time, sir."

Coffey watched as the Scotsman dismounted and began to cut himself clumps of spiky camel thorn. When he was satisfied he had enough, he tied them into a bundle and fastened the bundle to his saddle, dragging the tangled vegetation behind his mount.

"Ye'd better keep them animals steady, sir," he ordered. "Watch the dust, and when ye see the Dawasir take off after me, move like the blazes out of here. I'll be along soon after nightfall."

He set off towards the east, dragging the ragged bundle behind him. Dust rose on the air, trailing in his wake in a churning twisting column.

The next few minutes were anxious ones for all of them. Coffey studied the dust clouds through his field glasses, training them first in the direction of the pursuing Dawasir, then switching to the minuscule figure of Sergeant MacAngus vanishing steadily over the skyline. His nerves tightened as the seconds stretched.

Then with a sense of triumph he watched the Dawasir dust cloud swing to the east as the riders turned their mounts towards Sergeant Mac-Angus's decoy. "They've taken the bait," he murmured.

MACANGUS RODE HARD through the long hours of morning and into the afternoon. He knew his camel was tired, and he knew too that a tired camel was a dangerous liability. He could see the mountains a long way off, sharp craggy peaks bursting out of the desert floor, and he steered

447

towards them. Twice he paused to drink from his guerba and study the dust clouds behind. His pursuers were gaining, no question, but MacAngus did not feel alarmed.

As he headed northeast, the terrain began to change in slow subtle ways. The flatness broke up, swelling into a series of dark brown humps etched against the sky. The wind blew fierce and surprisingly cool.

MacAngus did not resent Coffey sending him off alone. Their camels, weary and dispirited, could never outride the fresh mounts of the Dawasir. Only one man could give them the respite they needed, and he was that man. MacAngus liked Coffey. He saw in Coffey a man like himself, destined to struggle for his very existence.

But Coffey had one advantage MacAngus couldn't lay claim to. A clean slate. Coffey was not a wanted man.

Riding eastwards, a mile in front of the Dawasir slavers, MacAngus thought about the Scotland Yard detective searching for him, and reflected on the night, fifteen years earlier, in the little Ayrshire town of Kilbirnie, when he had taken on the Procurator fiscal's son in an alley behind the dance hall. He couldn't even remember what the quarrel had been about. The fight had started fairly enough, the two of them trading blows, and then to MacAngus's surprise the fiscal's boy had pulled out a knife. The end had been quick, brutal, sordid, and MacAngus had been running ever since. For a while the army had offered refuge, anonymity. Now it looked as if that was coming to an end.

MacAngus steered his camel eastwards through the long afternoon until at last, when nightfall came, dowsing the incredible heat of the day, he had reached the first rugged slopes of the foothills.

He rested his animal, cutting loose the trailing bundle of camel thorn, and, taking the guerba from the saddlehorn, drank copiously, saturating his body with liquid. He no longer felt any sense of danger, for he knew no man could match him in the mountains. He soaked his face-cowl with water and rubbed it over the camel's nostrils, talking soothingly as he did so. He led the camel up the steep slope until he found the spot he was looking for, a narrow ravine cluttered with spiky scrub. When he was satisfied the beast was suitably concealed, he groundhitched it to a boulder, leaving just enough line for it to reach the scattered clumps of vegetation if it needed to, without wandering into the open.

Then he began to climb, hearing the soft shuffle of the incoming riders and the almost indistinguishable murmur of their voices on the cool night air. They were close. The slope grew rougher, the outcrops more even, and he slowed his pace as he pressed on steadily upwards. Small bushes grew among the rocks, scratching his ankles. Deliberately, he showed himself in the moonlight. He heard the dull crack of a rifle somewhere to his left. The bastards had seen him. Good.

Crack—crack. More shots. MacAngus grinned behind his face-veil as he picked his way across the twisting network of rocks. The damn fools were as excitable as children. He could hear them barking at their camels to kneel so that they could dismount.

The slope ended on a small plateau, wide enough for a cavalry squadron. MacAngus paused, looking back. He could see his pursuers scrambling up towards him, wrestling their rifles and spears through the tortuous maze of boulders. At the foot of the slope, almost hidden by the darkness, their camels waited, guarded by a solitary figure cradling a long-barrelled rifle.

Grinning savagely, MacAngus turned and ran across the plateau, making for the rocks above. The gradient was steeper here, the contours blending to form a series of fractured cliffs. He found a narrow chimney and squeezed into it, knowing his dark *gandoura* would merge perfectly with the shadows. He was standing there motionless, struggling hard to control his breathing, when the first warrior came panting up the incline. MacAngus saw the man's face, the swarthy cheeks and long hooked nose. He waited, the harsh rock pressing against his spine and skull. The Dawasir peered round, then scrambled stubbornly on, picking his way towards the starlit summit.

The others followed, stopping from time to time to check the gullies, cracks, vegetation clusters. MacAngus waited until his pursuers were well above him before he left his place of concealment and crossed the plateau at a run. There were no shots, no cries of warning. His flight was unobserved. Down the slope he slithered, making good time. Then, as he approached the bottom, he slowed his pace. He could see the camels just below, and a Dawasir warrior sitting on a rock guarding them.

Stealthily, MacAngus moved closer, his sandalled feet making no sound on the sand. He drew a knife from inside his robe. It would be a clean death, swift, neat, silent. But just as MacAngus was about to strike, a sliver of starlight lit the tribesman's face, revealing not some grizzled warrior but a young boy with smooth cheeks and almond eyes. Quietly MacAngus sheathed the knife and picked up a small rock. When the boy turned away, MacAngus moved swiftly and, without pausing, brought the rock down on the herder's unprotected skull. With a muffled groan, the boy pitched senseless into the dust. MacAngus moved about the Dawasir beasts, kicking them to their feet. Roaring and protesting, they began to trot angrily across the open reg floor. Shots rang out as MacAngus mounted, and he laughed crazily as he slapped the animals into a run. There were more shots as he turned back the way he had come, driving his newfound camel herd into the desert night.

THE WADI WAS SHALLOW, protected on both sides by ridges of crumbling red rock. On its floor parched scrub grew in ragged abundance. Here, Coffey had called a halt. Through the scorching heat of the afternoon and well into the hours of darkness they had crouched in the gully's bottom, resting their camels, resting their bodies, waiting patiently for MacAngus's return.

Coffey lay with his head against his camel saddle, staring at the stars. He was taking a risk and he knew it. Too much time had elapsed already. But he was determined to give MacAngus every chance.

Hearing a sound, he looked up to see Lieutenant Driscoll approaching. "May I ask how much longer you intend to go on waiting?"

When Coffey didn't answer, Driscoll squatted down at his side. "Even if your sergeant does manage to shake those beggars off, which I doubt, how do you expect him to find us in this little lot?"

"He'll be here," Coffey insisted stubbornly.

"My dear fellow, I want him to survive as much as you do. He's an excellent man to have around. But the fact remains that he's taking on the Dawasir on their own terrain. His chances are pretty slim."

"You don't know Mac," Coffey said. "He can move like a ghost through the desert. No Arab can match him."

Driscoll was about to speak again when suddenly he froze, listening intently.

"What is it?" Coffey hissed.

"Someone's coming."

Coffey scrambled to his knees. He heard the sound of camel hooves on the soft crumbling earth. The snick of a rifle bolt echoed in the night as, fifteen feet away, Benson cocked his weapon and lay in waiting. Coffey drew his pistol. "How many do you think?" he whispered.

"Sounds like a whole bloody army," Driscoll said.

"The Dawasir?"

"Can't be anyone else. Sorry, old boy, looks like you've muffed it."

Coffey drew his breath. He saw the animals first, then a figure swung into view, tall, angular, familiar. "Mac!" he exclaimed with relief.

It was MacAngus, hurrying the camels along, shepherding them like a herd of cattle. He reined in and grinned at Coffey crookedly. "I thought ye could do wi' a few extra beasties, Lieutenant," he said.

Chapter Six

Victoria Routledge scooped up a handful of salty earth and dropped it into the muddy pit in front of her. She watched the dirt sink slowly to the bottom and thin flecks of coarse-grained salt rise like bubbles to the surface. Eventually, in the heat of the sun, they would form a crust which she could scrape off and mould into salt blocks for the storage of food and other necessities, a function she had learned well during her thirteen years of captivity.

She was a tall woman, statuesque in the classic manner, though with a strong expressive body. Her face, tanned to a dusky gold by the desert sun, carried an air of innocent purity only mildly diminished by her sensual mouth.

Beyond the salt pits lay the village, an uneven sprawl of mudbaked cubes and sand-coloured turrets. Turbaned traders crouched in the marketplace, exhibiting their wares on palm-leaf mats.

The dervish stronghold held no surprises for Victoria Routledge, for she had grown to maturity amid its arid confines; from the moment of her capture at the age of fifteen—an event she recalled with terrifying clarity—she had been condemned to the lowest order on the social scale. Her life and destiny belonged to her owner, the village emir, and she was forced to exist like a nameless ghost, dutiful and servile, demanding nothing, obeying everything.

Victoria had worked hard because it was her nature to do so, and she was respected greatly for this by the dervishes, for though slaves were plentiful, good workers were rare. Not only was Victoria allowed the freedom of the village but even the freedom of the surrounding countryside, and many times she could easily have run off, though what good it would have done she could not imagine, with more than a hundred and fifty miles of blazing desert between her and safety.

Nevertheless, she dreamed continuously of escape and for hours would stare across the empty flatlands thinking of a world she could scarcely remember—cobbled streets, gaslit cafes, hansom cabs, flouncy dresses. She held fiercely and determinedly to the memories of her former life as if only through them could her true identity be preserved.

When she had finished storing the last of the salt blocks in an earthen vat, she rose and made her way to the central marketplace. A group of women in indigo blue robes, with tattoos on their chins, sat cutting up tomatoes in the sun. Children trotted gaily through the alleyways.

As Victoria crossed the square she spotted a young man watching her from under a mud-walled archway. He wore a long white *jibbah* and a woollen skullcap. His face was narrow, his features elongated. He stared at Victoria with yearning in his moist, soulful eyes, and she felt a flash of anger stir inside her.

The young man's name was Shilluk, and for several weeks now he had followed her everywhere. Victoria knew that Shilluk, a young nobleman of the Garu caste, had already approached the emir with a view to buying her, and although the emir had so far refused (Victoria was a good worker and he had no wish to lose her), she was uncomfortably aware that if Shilluk continued to increase his offer, sooner or later the emir might relent.

Victoria had no desire to change masters. Her position was lowly, but as the emir's property she was protected by law and never molested. Her

451

body remained inviolate. With Shilluk as her owner, she knew that her inviolability would come to an end.

Leaving the marketplace, she entered an arched portico which led to an inner courtyard; it was the workshop of the village artisans where, since her father's release from the abominable prison block eight years before, he had worked as a joiner and carpenter. Victoria could scarcely believe the change which had taken place in her father since his captivity. Once he had been a fleshy, full-bodied man. Now he looked at times like a living corpse, his skin dried and cracked by the desert sun.

He was chiselling a piece of wood as Victoria entered. The rest of the courtyard was deserted, the other workmen following their customary practice of sleeping through the hottest part of the day. Victoria's father looked elated, as if filled with some secret knowledge he could barely contain. When he saw her coming, his features lit up exuberantly. Then he noticed the look on her face.

"What's wrong?" he demanded quickly.

"That Shilluk," she said, "he's following me again."

Routledge put down his chisel. "He's getting to be a menace, that one. According to Cassato, he's sent north for an albino camel so that he can increase his offer to the emir."

"Will the emir accept?"

"Hard to tell. Owning an albino would make the emir quite a celebrity. On the other hand, he's a wily old beggar. He's determined to push up your price as high as he can."

"But Father, what are we going to do if the emir agrees?"

Routledge ran his fingers over his gaunt face. "There's only one thing we can do, Victoria. We must try to escape."

Victoria looked at him with exasperation. "You know it's impossible. They'd run us to earth in no time, and the penalty for running away is death."

"We could steal a couple of camels. Travelling by night we could steer by the stars. If we head due east we're bound to hit the Nile. There, we could buy fresh mounts and make our way to the Egyptian border."

"Buy? We haven't a single possession in the world we can call our own."

Routledge peered at Victoria, smiling secretively. "I wouldn't say that at all. We have a great deal to bargain with. Two days ago, I wouldn't have contemplated escape. Now, I can think of nothing else."

"Father, what are you talking about?"

"Come over here. I have something to show you."

Mystified, Victoria followed him to the corner where the tools were kept. Routledge fumbled among the shadows for a moment, then he dragged out a heavy bag. Unlacing its top, he tipped some of its contents onto the bare earth floor. A number of large stones, light green in colour, scattered across the ground. When Victoria picked one of them up, its surface felt oily to her touch. "What are they?" she asked.

Her father grinned at her. "The biggest fortune you're ever likely to see in your entire life," he whispered. "Diamonds, brought up by caravan from Central Africa."

"Diamonds?" Victoria echoed incredulously. "This size?"

"That's right. Aren't they marvellous? The idiots are using them on their drill tips to bore holes in metal and timber. Can you imagine it?"

"Father," Victoria muttered in a wary voice, "are you sure about this?"

"Yes, I'm sure. If these ever got onto the market, they'd throw the diamond world into a turmoil."

Victoria stared down at the dull, greasy stones, mesmerized. Diamonds. Why, they were enormous!

A new thought occurred to her, something she had never dreamed of before. What if she returned to her own world as a woman of wealth and influence? Surely it would make some kind of sense of the wasted years in between?

"What you see in this sack," her father went on eagerly, "is almost impossible to evaluate. These gems are priceless, Victoria. If we can only get them out of here, we'll be free at last. On the Nile we'll find Greek merchants who will recognize their value. We'll be able to buy fresh camels to carry us into Egypt. Once back among our own people . . ."

Victoria knew the desert was more than a hundred miles across. Between them and the river lay trackless sands and bands of savage tribesmen. She hadn't the heart to tell him once again that they would never make it.

Chapter Seven

The old lady fell silent for a moment, and Kengle shook himself. He had been so enthralled that he had completely lost track of the time. Glancing through the window he saw the sky beginning to darken and he looked at his watch. Goodness, he thought. Is it that late?

The old lady was studying him with amusement. Her attitude had softened considerably since he first arrived, he noticed, and he guessed it was probably the first time in her life she had unburdened herself so completely.

"You must stay for dinner," she said, making it sound like a command rather than an invitation.

"I have to get back to London," he told her. "I have an important meeting in the morning."

"Don't be so impatient, Mr. Kengle. The things I have to tell you cannot be hurried."

Kengle felt his inquisitiveness returning. She was right, he thought. Her story had completely absorbed him. He looked at her curiously. Then a bell echoed through the corridor outside.

"That will be Evans calling me in to dinner," she said. "Will you stay?"

Kengle hesitated. He had things to do in London. And yet . . . time seemed to have lost its relevance. Suddenly he knew there could be no question of his leaving.

The meal was pleasant and informal. Lady Catherine talked incessantly as she ate, but she was careful, Kengle noticed, to keep the conversation on a mundane level. Clearly she wanted none of the servants to overhear her story.

Kengle, for his part, was seething with impatience. Only when dinner was over and the servants had finally withdrawn, was he able, with coffee and brandy at his side, to reopen the subject.

"So your mother had been a dervish slave? I had no idea."

"That's hardly surprising. The story was kept a strict secret by my family. You must understand the times, Mr. Kengle. For a respectable Englishwoman, such an experience was regarded as the worst kind of social disgrace. After the fall of Khartoum, the British had virtually withdrawn from the Sudan, and for the next thirteen years they had to live with the ignominy of defeat. That is, until the expeditionary force of eighteen ninety-eight. Ironically, the dervish leader, the Mahdi, died only five months after my mother's capture. But he was succeeded by a new ruler, the khalifa, who was just as ruthless, just as fanatical."

Kengle swirled the brandy in his glass. "And the diamonds, the ones your grandfather discovered in the carpenter's workshop, they became, of course, the Churchill Collection?"

"That's correct. If Charlton Routledge had not been a dervish prisoner, he would have known about the diamonds already. They'd been stolen from a sultan's caravan on its way to Bambari, and there wasn't a soldier in Kitchener's army who didn't dream of discovering for himself those legendary riches."

"And through all this time your grandfather and this young, innocent girl continued to exist in a world which must have seemed, to their eyes, utterly foreign and barbaric?"

The old lady smiled. "Yes, it's hard to conceive of in this day and age. My mother lived with the dervishes for thirteen years. But she hung on defiantly until at last, when she must have despaired of any hope of rescue, there came riding across the desert four men whose lives would become inextricably bound up with her own."

FROM TWO MILES OUT, the village looked like a handful of brown sugar cubes scattered across the desert floor. The buildings seemed to ripple into each other, their contours blending in the heat. Coffey reined in his

camel and waved the others back. Hamira, he thought, experiencing a momentary sense of jubilation at the thought that they had crossed mile upon mile of hostile desert using nothing more than a battered ship's sextant strapped to Driscoll's saddlehorn. He suppressed the feeling quickly. There could be watchers on the hill slopes, dervish patrols. It was time for caution.

In a little hollow choked with acacia trees they hobbled the camels and held a hasty council of war. "The difficulty, as I see it," Coffey explained, "is that there's no way of approaching the village without signalling that we're coming. Any attempt to will raise a dust cloud a mile high."

"Why don't we go in at night?" Benson suggested. "They won't see our dust in the dark."

"We can't go stampeding through the whole damned village looking for the woman and her father. We've got to locate them first."

"Lieutenant," Sergeant MacAngus said slowly, "yon village is at least two miles away. Even with field glasses we'll see precious little at this range and the longer we hang about, the greater the chances of discovery."

"You're right. Surprise is the only advantage we've got. We really ought to move at once."

"Why don't we simply ride in and ask for a night's lodging?" Driscoll said. "I suggest we choose the six stoutest Dawasir camels, four for us and one each for Miss Routledge and her father, and leave them here with Sergeant MacAngus. The rest we'll offer to the village headman."

"You mean a bribe?"

"It's very difficult to be inhospitable to people who come to your home bearing gifts."

Coffey considered for a moment. It seemed a reasonable idea. "Very well," he agreed. "Bluff has brought us this far. Maybe it'll work again. Sort out the camels and let's get started."

They made their preparations. Coffey climbed into the saddle and set off across the desert reg, Benson and Driscoll following discreetly, shepherding the spare camels. Coffey's throat was dry and he felt fear rising inside him. He recalled stories of how the dervishes treated their prisoners, of eyes prised out, skin flayed off, limbs severed. The tension within him steadily intensified.

He watched the flat-roofed houses gradually taking shape. Turrets rose in the sunlight, the parapets moulded into crude battlements etched against the sky. Soon he could see streets, narrow and winding. The buildings took on new definition, with terraces and archways and little flights of steps worn smooth by thousands of sandalled feet.

They got within four hundred yards before the alarm sounded. A small boy tending a herd of goats spotted their approach and set up a series of highpitched yodelling noises.

"There goes our anonymity," Coffey murmured.

They reached the mud-walled outdwellings and people appeared in the doorways; black-robed women, tiny children, turbaned tribesmen, all staring at them with expressions of amazement. A few emaciated donkeys stood chewing docilely at battered feeding pails.

Suddenly they were surrounded. On all sides, excited faces peered up at their own, women in heavy black veils, children with hair tufts sprouting from closely shaved crowns, dark-eyed warriors wielding spears, swords and long-barrelled flintlocks, all of them caterwauling in a highpitched way that made Coffey's senses reel.

"What the hell do we do now?" Coffey shouted at Driscoll.

"Sit tight. We can keep this up just as long as they can."

For nearly ten full minutes they sat in silence while the sea of people yelled and swayed and their camels snorted in protest. Then, just when Coffey thought he could stand it no longer, the tumult suddenly subsided and a blessed silence settled round them.

The crowds parted, and down the centre of the street came a thickset man carrying a staff carved in the shape of a snake's head. Slowly and imperiously he walked towards them, followed by a group of what Coffey assumed to be the village dignitaries.

"The emir," Driscoll whispered. "Dismount slowly and stand beside your camels. Let me do the talking."

Coffey slid to the ground. Struggling to maintain an air of dignity, he stared back at the savage features glaring into his.

Driscoll meanwhile was going through the elaborate greeting ceremony. Nobody in the world could be quite as graceful as a dervish when he had a mind to, Coffey thought, bowing and scraping, delivering grandiose flatteries. And all the time the two men were watching each other like hawks.

The people waited in silence, hoping Driscoll's explanation would prove inadequate, so that they could press on with the more interesting business of severing limbs and heads.

Driscoll indicated the Dawasir camels, conveying by expressive gestures that they were now the emir's property. When the complex greeting ritual had been exhausted, he eased sideways and said through his face-veil, "The old boy seems satisfied with our story. He thinks it's unusual to find Tuareg nobles wandering so far east, but he's delighted with the camels and he's invited us to spend the night as his personal guests."

"Thank God," Coffey breathed.

"There's just one slight difficulty. As a sign of good faith, he's asked to see our faces."

Coffey felt his insides turn icy. "Can't you talk him out of it?"

"I've tried. I've explained that according to our beliefs, displaying our features would be the worst possible kind of insult, but he's adamant. Says he doesn't care about that; says it's so rare to meet tribesmen from such a distant country, he'd like to see what we look like."

"Dissuade him," Coffey ordered. "Tell him we've sworn for religious reasons never to reveal ourselves to man or beast. One look at our white skins and he'll know we're impostors."

"Why should he? We're probably the first Tuareg he's seen in his life. Still, I'll try the religious argument and see how he responds."

He spoke again to the emir, keeping his voice carefully deferential. The man listened in silence until Driscoll had finished and then, without bothering to answer, he barked out a command in a sharp guttural voice and instantly a group of tribesmen seized Lieutenant Benson by the arms. Before Benson could protest, one of the men had reached up and whipped the black cowl from his face.

There was a moment of frozen stillness. Coffey held his breath. Benson looked startled, his eyes bright, the scar on his cheek crimson against his pale skin. His mouth hung open in an involuntary gasp and his teeth, with their V-shaped gap, gleamed in the sunlight.

Coffey felt his heart sink. Their masquerade was over. There was no disputing it, Benson looked every inch an Englishman. Instinctively, Coffey's hand crept beneath the folds of his *gandoura*, his fingers locating the handle of his Browning revolver.

Then a strange thing happened. The people fell back on all sides. The crowd receded and a weird wailing sound rose from a thousand throats, hovering mournfully on the air. Coffey frowned. Something inexplicable was happening. The expressions on the faces of the villagers had changed from malevolent glee to an air of universal awe and reverence. Before his astonished gaze, men, women, children, even the chubby figure of the emir himself, prostrated themselves on the ground. Suddenly the Englishmen were the only figures left standing in the entire street, and Coffey stared in amazement across the sea of lowered heads. He turned to Lieutenant Driscoll. "What the hell is going on?"

"It's Benson," Driscoll whispered. "They think he's the reincarnation of the Mahdi, the last dervish ruler."

"Why?"

"Look at his teeth. That opening in the front is a sign. It's laid down in the scriptures. And the birthmark on the cheek."

"But that's not a birthmark, it's a scar. I gave it to him myself, at the railhead. And his teeth are crooked because I knocked them that way with my fist."

"The dervishes don't know that. They think Benson is the saviour they've been waiting for. They think he's the Mahdi returning to lead them against the infidel."

"Benson's not even the right colour, for goodness' sake!"

"Who gives a damn about colour? He carries the signs, that's all the dervishes care about."

Benson looked dazed and uncertain. He stared down at the bowed heads pressed meekly in the dust. "You mean, they think I'm some kind of god?" he whispered.

"Well, not a god exactly. More like the son of the Prophet. Among the dervishes, that makes you a very powerful individual indeed."

"But I can't even speak their language."

"Who cares? As long as they think you're the Mahdi, you can say what the hell you like. Nobody's going to argue."

Coffey thought quickly. It was a chance in a million. But if they wanted to utilize it, they would have to act quickly. "Tell them to get up," he ordered. "Ask the emir about Miss Routledge and her father. Tell him we'd like to see them as quickly as possible."

"We'll have to give him a reason," Driscoll argued.

"Say the Mahdi has heard about the lady's beauty and wishes to view it in person."

"That's pushing it a bit, squire."

"All right. Say we want to question them about the ways of the infidel. For strategic purposes, of course."

"That's better," Driscoll agreed.

He began to speak in loud, ringing tones, and gradually the villagers clambered to their feet. The emir barked a command, and some of his henchmen elbowed their way back through the tightly packed throng while Coffey waited nervously. He had the unpleasant notion that the tribesmen might at any moment decide to hurl themselves upon Benson, in sheer adoration.

After a few minutes he spotted the emir's men returning, escorting a wizened scarecrow of a man in a ragged *jibbah*. Walking by his side, moving with a slow fluid grace, was a tall suntanned woman dressed in Arab robes. Her features were stunning in their symmetry, but it was not the woman's beauty which impressed Coffey so much as the innate strength which lay in her face.

The couple stopped when they reached the gathering, and Coffey was surprised to see no flicker of emotion in their eyes. Then he realized that in their Tuareg robes he and his companions looked little different from the hundreds of other warriors who thronged Hamira's marketplace.

To Driscoll he said, "Tell them to let go of the man."

Driscoll repeated the order in a flat voice, and at a word from the emir the two tribesmen on either side of Routledge released their grip on his arms. Routledge looked awestruck for a moment. Then, to Coffey's consternation, he began to cry.

His daughter slipped an arm round his shoulders, holding him close, and with a visible effort he regained control of himself.

"Can we take them out of here without these people trying to stop us?" Coffey asked Driscoll in a low voice.

"Not a chance. Getting out's going to be a damn sight tougher than getting in. Now that they've found the Mahdi, they'll want to hold on to him. The emir has invited us to stay at his home as his guests. They're planning a little celebration tonight, a festival to herald the imminent downfall of the infidel. It would be imprudent to refuse. Whether we like it or not, old sport, I'm afraid we're stuck here."

"Will they allow us to wander in the village at will?"

"Possibly, if Benson demands it. No one, not even the emir, would wish to oppose the son of the Prophet."

"Tell them we must have solitude to concentrate on our next campaign. Say we'd like to acquaint ourselves with Hamira's defences while we contemplate the destruction of the British. Tell them anything you like, only for heaven's sake get them out of here."

"I'll give it a try," Driscoll said.

As Driscoll repeated Coffey's instructions, Coffey noticed a subtle change in the woman's expression. She had caught the unmistakable rhythm of the English language. Now she was staring intently at Coffey.

The emir, after listening to Driscoll for a moment, began to address the throng in a high wailing monotone. Slowly, reluctantly, they began to drift away, moving into the side streets and alleyways. In a few minutes, the little thoroughfare was almost deserted. The emir was the last to leave. After repeating his offer of hospitality he turned with an obvious air of regret and began to shuffle back the way he had come, followed by the tiny cluster of village headmen.

As soon as the tribesmen were out of earshot, the girl said in a breathless voice, "Who are you? What are you doing here?"

"Miss Routledge?" Coffey asked. He tugged the cloth from across his face. "Lieutenant Coffey, ma'am," he told her, "of the 10th Westmorland Lancers. This is Lieutenant Driscoll, and Lieutenant Benson. We've come to get you out of here."

Slowly she raised one hand, pressing it hard against her lips. Her eyes widened.

"In the hills behind the reg," he went on quickly, "we have camels, water and provisions. With luck, we hope to be back behind the British lines in two to three days."

"The British are in the Sudan?" her father whispered.

"Yes, sir. Kitchener's army is marching south down the Nile to Khartoum. The days of the Khalifa are already numbered."

Suddenly, for the second time, the man began to cry. Tears were rolling helplessly down his ravaged cheeks. Coffey stood in a paroxysm of embarrassment. It was the woman, still cool, still totally controlled, who reassured him.

"You must understand, we've waited so long for your coming. In the beginning we expected you almost every week, and then, as the months spread into years, I think we came to regard the very thought of rescue as little more than a ridiculous dream."

It took her father several minutes to regain control. "Forgive me, Lieutenant," he said to Coffey, "I am not usually so emotional."

"I understand, sir. I've no doubt every one of us would react similarly in the same circumstances. For the moment, however, we need your help. By an extraordinary stroke of luck, the dervishes appear to have taken Lieutenant Benson here for a reincarnation of the Mahdi. Apparently that gap in his teeth and the scar on his cheek have been predicted in ancient writings. Which means that, for the moment at least, we're perfectly safe. The question is, if we can find a way out of here, are you ready to ride?"

"Of course," the man said. "We'll do anything you wish. But we can't leave yet."

"Why not?"

Routledge hesitated. He looked at his daughter, then back at Coffey. "There's something I must show you," he said. "Come with me, please."

Puzzled, they set off along the street, following Routledge round a palm-fringed pool where women in bright robes sat scrubbing their laundry on the rocky bank. Coffey noticed the glances cast in their direction and with a sinking heart realized the sheer impossibility of making any move undetected.

Routledge walked with a slow shuffling gait, and from time to time his daughter reached out to steady him. The townspeople followed at a discreet distance.

Routledge ducked under a heavy stone archway and they found themselves in a tiny courtyard with smaller arches round its edge.

"Better tell your friend to remain in the doorway," Routledge advised. "Those villagers are bursting with curiosity and we don't want to be disturbed for a minute or two."

Benson turned and stood beneath the arch, staring stonily into the street beyond.

Coffey peered round the courtyard. Among the shadows he could see a cluster of primitive carpentry tools.

"What is this place?" he asked.

"A workshop," Routledge said. "I help out here most days. A few years ago the dervishes moved me from the prison block so that I could help the local craftsmen. Come over here."

He shuffled under the arches to the corner where the tools were kept. After fumbling among them for a moment or two, he dragged out a heavy bag and began to unlace its top. "Hold out your hand," he instructed.

Coffey did so, mystified. Carefully, Routledge tipped up the sack and spilled some of its contents into Coffey's palm. Coffey rolled the stones about, holding them to the light. Routledge stood watching him, an expectant smile on his face. "Well?"

"Well what? Looks like bits of fractured glass to me."

"Not glass. Diamonds. Uncut diamonds. The biggest you ever saw in your life."

Startled, Coffey sucked in his breath. He looked at Driscoll and Driscoll stared back, his eyes glittering fiercely.

"Of course," Coffey whispered. "These are the diamonds which were stolen from that caravan in Central Africa. The whole British army's on the lookout for them."

"The fools here are using them for their drilling tools," Routledge said.

Coffey's senses quickened as he jiggled the stones in his palm. "Diamonds this size, and in such quantity," he breathed. "Why, their value . . ."

"It's impossible to calculate their value, Lieutenant," Routledge said. "That's why we can't under any circumstances leave them behind. If the khalifa ever learned what his people are harbouring here, he could lay hands on enough funds to keep this war going indefinitely."

Coffey nodded. The logic of Routledge's statement was irrefutable. It was their duty to carry these gems out of harm's way. But surely that was as far as their responsibility went? Lack of money had blighted Coffey's life. He had been forced to eke out a miserable existence while other officers sauntered along in comparative ease, supported by wealthy families. Was that just? Supposing they held on to the diamonds? He could pay all his debts, and remain solvent for the rest of his life. How often did a man get a chance to do that?

Keeping his voice calm and dispassionate he said, "Mr. Routledge is quite right. There's enough in this sack for the khalifa to finance a dozen wars. It's our God-given duty as officers and Englishmen to see that when we break out of here, the diamonds go too."

Chapter Eight

The feasting started at dusk. Driscoll had been right in one respect—the villagers, though they struggled to subdue their curiosity towards Lieutenant Benson, submitted in the end to their natural feelings and refused to leave his side, touching his robes, stroking his cheeks, bending to kiss his sandalled feet. At Coffey's suggestion Benson surrendered himself to their attentions. What was more alarming was that from the outlying desert, parties of tribesmen came riding in to witness the wondrous phenomenon of the Mahdi's reincarnation until, by nightfall, the village population had swollen to almost twice its original size.

On the other hand, Coffey and Victoria were allowed to wander the streets at will, and Coffey took advantage of the festivities to resaddle the camels, replenish the water *guerbas* and strap the diamonds to his animal's back.

Victoria stood beside him in the darkened courtyard. Now that the initial shock of the Englishman's arrival had passed, she had a chance to think things out. She was going home. Soon she would be free.

Strangely, the realization made her feel uneasy. She had dreamed of it so long that now the moment had come she visualized a world whose dimensions were inestimably greater than the one she lived in. Coffey, pale and handsome, belonged to that other world. In his features lay the hallmarks of civilization: an elusive grace, a touch of humour, even, she thought, a hint of arrogance. In the thirteen years of her captivity, he was the first man who had aroused in her the faintest semblance of physical awareness.

Her response filled her with strange emotions.

"That should hold it," he said, putting the last touches to the leather strap which secured the diamonds to his saddlehorn.

"What will happen to the diamonds after we get back?"

He hesitated. "Property of the Crown, I expect. Isn't that the law?"

The law? She could not countenance the thought of any law, civilized or not, taking the diamonds from her. They belonged to her and her father. They had earned them, suffered for them.

She stared at Coffey, noticing his dirt-smeared cheeks, the thin lines at the sides of his mouth, the stubbled chin where he had pulled aside his face cowl.

"You haven't told me your first name," she murmured.

He looked at her with surprise. "It's Stephen."

She repeated it. "It's a nice name," she said.

His mouth twisted into a crooked grin. "What's yours?"

"Victoria."

"Even nicer."

"Nobody's called me that for years. Apart from Father. Slaves aren't worthy of a name."

"Well, you won't be a slave much longer. Once we reach the ruined fortress at Malawa, there'll be two troops of cavalry waiting to escort us to the Nile. After that, it'll be Cairo for you, then back to England."

She breathed deeply, filling her lungs with the dry night air. She could see the stars framed in a perfect square above the courtyard's rim.

"Lieutenant Coffey, those diamonds don't belong to the Crown. If you hand them over, we'll never see them again."

Coffey's features hardened. He stared at her in silence. Panic seized her, and she went on quickly, "There are enough diamonds in that

463

saddlebag to make each of us rich for the rest of our lives. All you have to do is forget to mention them in your report. Nobody's asking you to betray your role as a British officer. You'll have done what you had to do, taken them out of the enemy's hands. But instead of turning them in . . ." She paused, her heart fluttering wildly.

Coffey studied her for a moment, his features rigid. "Who put you up to this?" he demanded. "Your father?"

"Nobody. I've spent thirteen years of my life in this hellhole. While other girls my age were going to dances and buying pretty dresses, I was living the life of an animal. Can't you see, those diamonds are compensation for everything I've gone through."

She stopped, staring at him defiantly. She was ready to fight for what was hers. This was her entire future.

Suddenly Coffey chuckled. "You've thought it all out," he whispered.

"I've had plenty of time for thinking," she said.

"Well, if it makes any difference, the thought of keeping the diamonds had entered my mind too."

"You mean . . . ?"

"I mean we split them among the six of us, equal shares."

He was laughing now, his eyes dancing in the starlight. He was on her side. It seemed a miracle. "That's wonderful," she exclaimed.

"Is it a deal?"

"It's a deal," she declared, solemnly shaking his proffered hand.

His face sobered. "First, however, we've got to escape, and that won't be easy, the way those villagers are hanging round Lieutenant Benson."

"What do you plan to do?"

"We need a diversion. Once the feasting's at its height, I intend to set fire to some of the buildings. There'll be lots of smoke, lots of confusion. When the panic starts, I want you to grab your father and the two lieutenants and bring them here as quickly as possible. Think you can do that?"

She nodded.

"Remember, it won't take the dervishes long to realize the fire's only a blind, so there'll be no time to waste. Go back to the marketplace and wait for the flames. After we're out of here, then we'll talk about riches."

The marketplace was so crammed it took Victoria some time to locate Lieutenant Benson. He was sitting beside the emir, looking dazed, as the women selected morsels from the bowls in front of him and popped them into his mouth. At his side, acting as interpreter, sat Lieutenant Driscoll. Next to Driscoll she spotted her father. He too seemed bewildered by his newfound status, unable to accept the sudden transition from slave to honoured member of society.

She stationed herself at a point where she was directly in Driscoll's line of vision. In the centre of the square women danced, clapping their hands and moving their bodies to the beat of the drum, their eyes fixed trancelike in the glow of the cooking fires. The dancers faded into the crowd and the village men took over, holding sticks and stamping their feet in the sand. In and out they moved, beating their staves frenziedly into the soft crumbling earth.

She straightened up, startled. The entire square had come to a standstill, the people frozen into a mute tableau. She caught the scent of fumes, the unmistakable odour of woodsmoke. And with it came something else—tar perhaps, or oil. Coffey had started his fire. Her pulses quickened. Craning her neck with the others, she saw the flames rising over the rooftops, the smoke billowing and thickening.

Coffey had gone to the new part of the village where the dwellings were timber-built, where the woodwork had dried like tinder in the daily heat. Within seconds the fire was leaping among the terraces and the skyline was turning into a solid red wall.

With shouts of alarm, the people stampeded towards the blaze, carrying Victoria along with the sheer force of their momentum.

Victoria spotted Driscoll clutching her father by the arm, battling his way towards her. "What's happening?" he shouted.

"It's Coffey," she yelled back. "He started the fire as a diversion."

"Where is he now?"

"At the workshop, waiting with the camels. He said to get there as quickly as possible."

"Right. Look after your father. I'll fetch Benson."

Victoria held on to her father's elbow. She could feel him trembling as he was jostled by the panic-stricken throng. Victoria guided him sideways, elbowing her way furiously against the tide. People were cursing, tripping, falling. She scampered over them without a pause. If she hesitated, she knew they would be lost.

The short scramble through the heaving streets was like a nightmare. Flames danced everywhere, transforming the night into glorious day. Victoria found the alleyway where the workshop stood. It was empty, thank God. The great mass of the populace was stampeding towards the flames. She ducked under the archway and spotted Coffey holding the camels by their bridles.

"What about Driscoll and Benson?" he asked.

"They're coming."

"They'd better be quick."

Something clattered behind her and she turned, startled, as someone ran beneath the archway towards her. Pale robes rustled in the darkness and a face appeared through the stifling smoke. It was Shilluk, the young man who had tried to buy her from the emir. For a full moment Shilluk stood staring at the scene inside the courtyard, his dark eyes taking in

Coffey, the loaded camels, her father already struggling behind the hump of the nearest beast. Then, glancing at her swiftly, he turned and scrambled back the way he had come.

"Stop him," Coffey yelled.

Benson and Driscoll heard his shout as they rounded the corner. Driscoll hesitated, taken by surprise, but Benson lunged furiously, grabbing for Shilluk's robes. He was too late. Shilluk easily evaded his clutches and stumbled on into the darkness.

Coffey swore. "Who was that?"

"His name's Shilluk," Victoria said. "He's been following me about for weeks."

"Think he's guessed what's going on here?"

"I'm sure of it."

"Then for God's sake mount up before he sounds the alarm. Benson, you carry Mr. Routledge. I'll take Victoria."

It was awkward riding double on a camel: its spinal structure was not built for comfort. Victoria crouched behind the hump, holding on to Coffey with both hands as they lurched under the archway and into the street beyond, the camel moving with a loping, ungainly rhythm. Her chest tightened in terror as she spotted, immediately ahead, a throng of warriors with drawn swords. Shilluk, she thought. He had warned them.

Coffey barely hesitated. He kicked his camel straight into the thick of the mob and Victoria, gulping, saw his hand come out, drawing something from deep inside the folds of his robe: a heavy revolver.

A man grabbed at their saddle, holding on with one hand while he swung his .sword with the other. With a fractional movement of his forearm, Coffey shot the top of the man's skull away. Victoria saw the man pitch headlong into the dust.

A spear zipped past her head. Coffey was firing furiously now, driving his camel forward as the crowd fell back before him. Victoria felt a hand grasp at her ankle and she lashed out desperately with her right leg, but the man was suddenly leaping up, his hands groping for her throat. She screamed, and Coffey swung the revolver in a wild backhanded curve. There was a sickening crunch and the warrior slid with a muffled grunt into the dust.

Coffey went on slashing with the empty revolver at the swirling throng of faces. Victoria felt sick as she struggled to keep her balance on the dipping, lunging saddle. With a stab of alarm she realized she was falling, the ground rushing up to meet her. She sprawled in the dust. At her feet, the camel thrashed out its life in a frantic tattoo of death. A spear protruded from its chest.

Terror engulfed her. They were down and completely surrounded. But the tribesmen were bewildered, stumbling round like excited children.

She saw Coffey crouching in the dust, calmly reloading his revolver, his movements sharp yet unhurried. A dervish leaped towards him, yelling insanely. Coffey snapped the chambers shut, drew back the hammer and shot the man dead through the chest.

Driscoll turned towards them, kicking his camel through the bobbing heads.

"Come on," Coffey shouted, grabbing her arm and pulling her forward. Driscoll's camel skidded to a halt, and she mounted without waiting for the creature to kneel.

Coffey grabbed the camel's tail, firing with his free hand into the buffeting mob. She heard her father's voice rising above the melee. "The diamonds, don't forget the diamonds!"

But it was already too late. With Coffey holding onto the animal's tail, Driscoll kicked its flanks with all his strength, and they thundered furiously into the desert night.

Chapter Nine

MacAngus heard them coming through the darkness. Reaching for his rifle, he scrambled down the hillside to where the trail curved beneath the starlight. He saw the shadows merging, taking on solidity, the camels strangely distorted as they reared, double-loaded, out of the night. He recognized Driscoll kicking his animal into a crouch. There was a woman clinging desperately to Driscoll's waist. Her hood had come off and her hair was tumbling crazily over her shoulders.

Lieutenant Coffey dismounted, his face scarlet as he gasped for breath.

"What happened?" MacAngus asked.

Coffey's chest rose and fell heavily, and sweat trickled down his face. "They cut us off."

"Anybody hurt?"

"Don't think so. We lost a camel though."

"What about the old man?"

"Benson's got him."

MacAngus saw a second camel looming through the greyness. Riding it, he recognized the slim outline of Lieutenant Benson and behind him a small sinewy figure in a dirty *jibbah*. MacAngus watched Benson and the old man dismount.

"Is Miss Routledge all right?" Benson asked Coffey.

"She's fine."

"What about the diamonds?" the old man demanded.

"We left them behind."

MacAngus's eyes narrowed. "Diamonds?" he echoed.

Coffey stared at him, his flushed cheeks calming as his breathing slowly steadied. In a few terse sentences he outlined the details of Routledge's discovery.

"We can't just abandon them," Routledge protested.

"I don't intend to," Coffey told him.

"You're not suggesting we return to Hamira?" Lieutenant Benson's cheeks were pale as death.

"We have no choice."

"You're crazy. Those stones don't even belong to us."

"Who do they belong to, Benson?"

"The Crown, of course."

"Why? Because they were taken in combat? Well, that's not strictly true, is it? If they belong to anyone at all, it's to Mr. Routledge here, and I have a feeling he'll be happy to share them with the rest of us if we can only get them back."

Routledge nodded.

"Our job was to rescue these people," Benson declared in a cold voice. "That's what we came for. Let's forget the diamonds and concentrate on staying alive."

"The situation's altered now, can't you see that?" Coffey said reasonably. "If those diamonds find their way into the khalifa's hands they could change the tide of this entire war. When the dervishes see them strapped to my saddlehorn, when they realize the risks we went through to carry them back to the British lines, they're bound to guess the truth. Of course it's important to rescue the Routledges. But what's more important still, for Kitchener, for the whole British army, is to get those diamonds out of Hamira."

"Why don't you tell the truth?" Benson hissed furiously. "It's not Kitchener you want those diamonds for."

"No," Coffey admitted honestly, "I want them for all of us. But that doesn't alter the fact that it's our duty to remove them from dervish hands. Mind you, I'm not risking my neck to turn them over to the Crown. When we get them back they'll stay in our possession. There'll be a simple omission in our report, nothing more. What do the rest of you think? Driscoll?"

Driscoll whistled softly. "I don't know, old boy. Strictly speaking, what you're suggesting is illegal."

"Are you with me, yes or no?"

Driscoll nodded, his lips twisting into their crooked grin. "How much do you estimate those diamonds are worth?"

"Millions," Routledge promised. "They'll have to be cut, of course. They'll be considerably smaller by the time they're ready for the market, but their quality is inestimable."

"Sergeant?"

"I'm your man, Lieutenant," MacAngus whispered.

468

"That leaves you, Benson. Make up your mind. Are you with us or against us?"

Benson looked unhappy as his eyes flickered from one to the other. They stared back at him stonily. "Very well," he whispered at last, "if you've all decided."

"Good," Coffey breathed, wiping his face with his sleeve. "We're still faced with the same basic problem though. They've got the diamonds." Glancing into the darkness, he studied the way they had come. "The dervishes will expect us to head east towards the Nile. But they can't follow our tracks in the darkness, so I suggest we double round and re-approach the village from the other side."

"We can hardly ride in again, squire. Not openly, anyway. One look at our *gandouras* and they'll cut us to ribbons," said Driscoll.

"With a bit of luck there'll be nobody in those streets but women and children. Most of the men will be out looking for us."

"But we can't spend the entire night searching the place room by room."

"You're right." Coffey looked at the old man. "What do you think? If the dervishes have something valuable in their possession, where do they put it for safety's sake?"

"There's only one place," Victoria said. "The prison block. It's the only building in Hamira you can actually lock."

"What about the inmates?"

"It's empty at the moment."

"Then that's it," Coffey muttered. "Got to be. I'll go alone." His eyes rested on Victoria's face. "Is there some place the rest of you can hide?" he asked her.

"There's the dyeworks on the opposite side of the town. It's a good hundred yards from the village outskirts."

"Sounds perfect. We'll double back in that direction."

"One moment, Lieutenant Coffey," Victoria murmured. "How do you intend to find that prison block? You've never been in Hamira in your life before tonight. Take someone with you. Someone who knows the town. Myself."

"I can't let you take that risk. It's too dangerous."

"I've lived with danger all my life. At least this time there'll be some purpose behind it."

He sensed the determination within her. He did not like the idea, but her logic was irrefutable. "Very well," he agreed, "we'll go together."

"Ssshhh," Driscoll whispered hoarsely.

Coffey held his breath and they strained their ears in the desert stillness. Dimly, like a muffled roll of thunder, they heard the pounding of camel hooves on the soft earth.

"They're coming," Benson whispered.

"Didn't take the bastards long to pull themselves together," Driscoll grunted.

"We've hung about long enough," Coffey snapped. "Transfer the water *guerbas* and let's get the hell out of here."

THE WARRIORS RODE through the desert in a ragged line. Their eyes gleamed with the savage determination of men who have seen their most cherished beliefs affronted. They carried swords, lances, old-fashioned flintlocks, and as they rode they scoured the earth for telltale signs.

At their head rode the emir, his fat belly wobbling with the loping movement of his camel. The foremost warriors carried flaming torches which they held as low as they dared, to cast a flickering glow across the desert's surface. The fire had taken them by surprise, but more bewildering still had been the realization that the man they had welcomed as the Mahdi had been an impostor of the vilest kind. It was their sacred duty to exact vengeance.

The column slowed as the leaders paused, searching the earth for fresh tramplings. There was a moment of indecision, then a man gave a guttural cry, claiming he had spotted tracks leading eastwards—towards the Nile. Spurring their mounts, the tribesmen pushed on into the darkness.

As the riders moved off, one figure remained motionless, staring thoughtfully at the desert floor. His name was Abu Ababdeh, a young noble, barely twenty-three years old, who had already gained a formidable reputation for his judgment and powers of reasoning. Now, something made Abu Ababdeh hesitate. As he sat like a statue in his camel saddle his eyes narrowed to slits.

The emir's column was thundering eastwards, lost in the fervour of pursuit, but there were no tracks to substantiate the idea that eastwards was the right direction. A man with his wits about him might double back and strike north. That was, assuming always that escape was his main objective. On the other hand, Abu Ababdeh reasoned thoughtfully, drawing out the emir's fighting force could be the first move of an inspired commander about to launch an attack upon the village itself.

As Abu Ababdeh pondered in silence, a group of about twenty men disengaged themselves from the main dervish force and turned back towards him. They were his own followers.

As Abu Ababdeh watched them gather round him, he came to a decision. Wheeling his camel, he barked out an order, and the warriors followed him back towards the village of Hamira.

COFFEY SAW THE BUILDING ahead. It was larger than he'd expected, its walls cracked and arid. The dyeworks' roof was flat, and beneath its surface the tips of timbered ceiling struts stuck out. Beyond it, the land

470

stretched in a hush of misty starlight to the first straggling outbuildings of the village perimeter.

Coffey reined in his camel and studied the scene in silence.

"Sure it isn't occupied?" he whispered to Victoria, perched behind him in the darkness. "Sentry perhaps? A caretaker?"

"Nobody."

"Just the same, I think we should approach with caution," Coffey said, kicking his camel to a crouch and dismounting. Drawing his Martini rifle from its holster, he checked to see it was loaded. Then he cocked it loudly. "The rest of you wait here. Lay down a line of covering fire if anything happens. I'll wave you in if the building looks safe."

He made his way across the open ground, zigzagging from boulder to boulder, using what cover he could. He reached a point almost thirty yards from the building's exterior and hesitated, crouching low in the dust, his eyes scanning the dyeworks' windows for any flicker of movement.

The building stood like a sepulchre, silent and remote. Gritting his teeth, Coffey rose and scuttled across the last thirty yards, slamming to a halt against the earthen wall. He glanced back to where the others waited in their saddles, the men holding their carbines in readiness.

Taking a deep breath, Coffey turned and rammed his foot against the timbered door. It swung open easily. He could see a massive room, thirty yards long, the floor pockmarked with huge pits. At a cursory glance it looked like a chessboard, but each chamber was filled with a different coloured liquid: black, green, indigo, scarlet, blue, yellow. Above the pits, great shrouds of cloth, already dyed into a multitude of hues, hung across the timbered struts to dry.

Relaxing slightly, Coffey pushed into the dyeworks' interior. The odour of the dye-pits hung in his nostrils like the smell of rancid butter. He waved the others in, watching them guide their camels through the narrow doorway.

"What happens now?" Driscoll asked, tying his camel to one of the drying-spars.

"Victoria and I go into the village," said Coffey. "The rest of you wait here. We'll get back as soon as we can. If dawn breaks and we've still not shown up, make a run for the river."

Victoria moved to her father and held him tightly. His arms slid round her waist, pulling her close, and his eyes glistened as he kissed her gently on the forehead.

Coffey peered at Victoria. "Ready?"

She nodded silently, and together they strode off towards the settlement. The shadows gathered round them, and Coffey felt the fear starting deep in his chest. He was gambling everything on the slender hope that the entire population would be drawn to the scene of the fire, that the streets would be empty and deserted. If he was wrong, there would be no hope for either of them.

They covered the first fifty yards at a decent pace, not troubling to hide their movements. From this distance the village looked like an anthill. Flames still licked from the rooftops and the pungent odour of smoke reached them across the barren landscape.

The first outbuildings reared through the darkness and instinctively they slackened their pace. There was no sign of movement. The rabbit warren of streets appeared abandoned. Only the reflection of the flames and the distant murmur of people gave any indication that human life existed.

Coffey moved on, Victoria following, and slowly the houses gathered round them, the streets twisting and turning, following no discernible pattern. Now Victoria took the lead, picking her way with easy confidence.

Coffey felt strange having a woman with him. He was acutely conscious of her closeness, of how long it had been since he had found himself in such intimate proximity to a female. He felt awkward in her presence.

"How much further?" he asked, his nerves stretched to breaking point.

"We're nearly there. I brought you the long way round for safety's sake. The other route runs by the site of the fire."

Abruptly the street opened, widening into an empty square with alleys running out of it in all directions. At the centre rose a blockhouse of sorts, its walls windowless and stout, encircled by a formidable palisade. The palisade was twelve or fifteen feet high, its top sharpened into a series of jagged points, but Coffey noted with relief that the gate hung open on its hinges. Beyond, he could see the studded metal door of the building itself, sealed with a massive bolt held firmly in place by an old-fashioned padlock.

"Is that it?" he whispered. "What about the guard?"

"There isn't one. Nothing to keep an eye on."

"Except the diamonds."

She smiled. "If they're really in there, it would take an army to break through that metal door. The dervishes know that."

"Come on," he hissed, seizing her wrist.

They scrambled across the open ground, darting through the massive gateway. On the doorstep, Coffey studied the bolt and padlock with dismay. The place looked as solid as the Bank of England. Victoria was right. They would need a squadron of cavalry armed with battering rams to pound through that little lot.

Examining the lock, he ran his fingers over its uneven surface. It was rusty with age, probably nearly a century old. He peered back across the square. Dare he run the risk of a shot? In this stillness, the sound

472

would be alien, unmistakable, hard to ignore. Yet there was no other way.

He reached inside his *gandoura* and drew out his Browning. "Ease back," he ordered.

Victoria moved aside without a word, edging against the wall. Coffey took two paces backwards and held the Browning at arm's length, gripping his wrist with his free hand. He aimed the gun at the keyhole and squeezed the trigger. His hand jumped as the revolver cracked. The shot was like a cannon going off in the stillness, its echo reverberating through the empty streets. The padlock jumped like a firecracker, smacking wildly against the iron door. He could see the hole where the bullet had gone in, but the lock remained firm.

Coffey swallowed and looked at Victoria. He noticed her fists were clenched tight. He hesitated, then fired again. This time there was a metallic clanging sound and the padlock flew from its moorings, slithering across the ground.

"We're in," he said excitedly. And slipping the revolver inside his *gandoura*, he drew back the bolt and slid open the heavy door.

RIDING THROUGH THE MARKETPLACE, Abu Ababdeh heard the first shot echoing above his head. He reined in his mount, raising his arm to draw his followers to a halt. He remained motionless, trying to assess the direction from which the shot had come. Then his camel grunted nervously as a second shot rang out.

The sound ricocheted through the empty streets, hurled from building to building. Abu Ababdeh made his decision quickly. Barking out a guttural command, he galloped briskly in the direction of the village jail.

COFFEY AND VICTORIA found that the prison interior looked as desolate as an empty grave. The ceiling was high, the floor was covered with straw. Rats darted across the filthy surface. The stench of decay filled Coffey's nostrils. Along one wall, small ovenlike compartments had been shut off from the rest of the interior: special quarters, Coffey guessed, for high security prisoners.

Coffey checked each of the cubicles in turn. They were all empty. He moved round the main cell. Heavy chains hung from the walls, iron rings where prisoners would be manacled. There was no sign of the diamonds, nothing but straw and rat droppings.

Coffey spotted a ladder leading to a loft above. "What's up there?" he asked Victoria.

"The overflow," she told him. "When the prison got crowded, they pushed the more unfortunate occupants upstairs. It's so close to the ceiling, it gets like an oven in the heat of the day. Nobody lasted more than a day or two."

"Let's take a look," Coffey said, climbing the ladder.

The upper storey was marginally cleaner than the one below, but just as empty. The ceiling at this point was barely three feet high, and Coffey had to crawl on his hands and knees to check the furthermost corners. A few bales of dark cloth lay stacked against the wall, covered with sand and dust. Coffey pulled them out and examined the space behind them. Empty.

"Anything there?" Victoria called from the top of the ladder.

He shook his head. "We're wasting our time. There's been nobody inside this building for years."

A feeling of dismay rose in him, a fury directed more at himself than at the circumstances. That they had taken such a risk for no reason was almost more than he could bear. He slithered back towards her.

"Think," he said. "Where else might they have put those diamonds?"

"There's nowhere else," she insisted. "This is the only safe place in the whole of Hamira."

Coffey was conscious of panic threatening to engulf him. They had been crazy, coming back to the village like this. At any moment their presence might be discovered.

"Ssshhh," Victoria exclaimed. "Someone's coming."

Coffey took her arm, pulling her off the ladder onto the creaking timbered floor. Easing forward he peered down through the open doorway and into the street beyond. Dust rose on the air, and in its swirl a body of mounted men wheeled into view, the ugly grey snouts of their flintlock rifles outlined against the stars. Dervishes.

At his side Coffey felt Victoria trembling. "What will we do?" she whispered.

He glanced back at the far wall where the bales of cloth were stacked. "Come on," he murmured, and holding on to her hand, he wriggled backwards, pulling the bales aside. "In there," he ordered.

They squeezed into the narrow space betweeen the bales and the wall, their bodies locked tightly together. Coffey used his free hand to ease the bales back into place. There was barely room enough to breathe, and he could feel Victoria's heart thumping against his chest.

Feet scraped on the floor below. Voices rose in an indistinct murmur. The light from blazing torches filled the cavernous room.

Coffey found Victoria's hand and squeezed it gently. She was shaking. More voices. Then a sharper, more commanding tone, barking out an order.

Coffey heard the ladder creak as someone slowly climbed it. He held his breath, training his eyes on the point where the ladder ended. A figure rose through the gloom, robed and bearded, clutching a blazing torch. For a moment the Arab remained motionless, perched on the ladder's topmost rung, his torch lifted aloft. His eyes settled on the bales of cloth. Grunting, the warrior eased himself over the ladder's top and began to edge slowly towards them. Coffey's fingers left Victoria's hand and crept down his stomach to the folds of his *gandoura*. Reaching inside, he gripped the handle of the Browning.

The man crawled nearer, so close now that Coffey could see the sweat glistening on his forehead. Gently, and as softly as he could, Coffey drew back the hammer. The movement made a muffled clicking sound in the heavy darkness. Coffey waited, watching the tribesman warily. The man gave no sign that he had heard. He was still moving towards the cloth bales with dogged determination.

At that moment someone shouted from below. It was the same commanding voice Coffey had heard when the dervishes first entered. The man hesitated, glanced briefly at the cloth bales, then turned back the way he had come and slowly descended the ladder.

Coffey breathed deeply. He heard a muffled sob of relief choke in Victoria's throat. Slipping the Browning back inside his *gandoura*, he again reached down, gripping her hand.

They were safe for the moment, but for how long? The dervishes were checking the buildings round the square one by one. They would have to remain where they were until daybreak. Their chances of escape were terrifyingly slim.

MACANGUS STOOD at the dyeworks door, staring out into the darkness. Some of the tribesmen had returned, he could tell. Coffey and Victoria were trapped, their escape route blocked. MacAngus swore under his breath. He turned back to the others, sprawled on the ground, resting. In the darkness the camels stood like blocks of stone.

"What's happening out there?" Driscoll asked.

"They're back," MacAngus said.

"Dervishes?"

MacAngus nodded. "Not the whole force, but enough to make things tricky."

Driscoll scrambled to his feet and moved to the door, looking out through the narrow opening. He whistled softly under his breath. "They're searching the village house by house," he whispered.

"How can you tell, at this range?" Benson snapped.

"I'm like a cat. I see in the dark," Driscoll told him, flashing his lop-sided grin.

"What are we going to do?" Routledge asked, his hands fluttering nervously.

MacAngus guessed he was thinking about his daughter. He didn't blame Routledge for feeling worried.

"They're coming this way," Driscoll murmured.

MacAngus joined Driscoll in the doorway, gazing out at a cluster of riders facing in the dyeworks' direction. One rider moved towards them, the others turned back into the rabbit warren of streets. MacAngus watched the man guiding his mount across the barren ground, his ancient flintlock rifle resting casually over his thighs.

"Move back into the shadows, sir," he whispered.

Driscoll edged away from the door.

MacAngus drew the long curved sword from his belt. Outside, the hoofbeats came steadily closer. The man was clearly in no hurry, MacAngus thought, and his hand tightened on the sword hilt as he pressed himself hard against the wall.

The hoofbeats stopped. MacAngus heard a soft scuffling noise as the rider dismounted. Clop, clop, the padding of his sandals reached them through the heavy timbered door. Then, with a little squeaking sound, the door swung gently open. MacAngus glimpsed the warrior framed against the starlight. The man's robes fluttered in the wind. He peered into the darkness, his eyes widening instantly as he detected the huddle of figures frozen in the breathless hush of discovery.

MacAngus drove his sword arm forward, feeling the blade slide smoothly in, almost to the hilt. He twisted the sword expertly before drawing it free.

The warrior was still standing in the same position, his mouth gaping open, his eyes already clouding into the blue-marbled milkiness of death. MacAngus seized the front of his robes and jerked him inside, letting him fall to the floor.

The man's chest was rising and falling rapidly as he battled for breath.

"Ask him about the diamonds," MacAngus snapped.

Driscoll dropped to his knees and spoke rapidly into the warrior's ear. The man's hand lifted in silent entreaty and he muttered a few hoarse words. They watched the life draining out of him like a visible force.

"What did he say?" MacAngus demanded.

Driscoll glanced up at him. "The diamonds aren't in the prison block at all. They're not even in Hamira. The bloody emir's taken them with him!"

MacAngus swore. "Ask him how many men have followed the emir."

Driscoll looked down at the warrior again, but the man's eyes had glazed and his arms were stretched motionless at his side.

"He's dead, I'm afraid."

"Help me pick him up, sir," MacAngus said fiercely.

Driscoll's face looked blank. "What for, squire? I tell you the man is dead. Like a piece of mutton."

"Aye, but we've got to get Lieutenant Coffey and the girl back. I have a plan. Pick him up for God's sake. And somebody duck out there and grab his camel. We'll need that animal to take the place of the one we lost."

Driscoll studied him in silence for a moment, then, impressed by the intensity of the sergeant's tone, reached down without a word and took hold of the warrior's head. Together, they lifted the dead man from where he was lying and carried him carefully over to the dye pits.

COFFEY LAY IN THE STILLNESS and listened to the dervishes scouring the street outside. He was still holding the girl, his body pressed hard against hers in the confines of their narrow hiding place. Now that the first flush of danger had passed he was becoming increasingly aware of their physical contact. Despite their perilous position, his body started to respond. He shifted, trying to ease himself back.

"What are you doing?" she whispered.

"Getting more comfortable," he said.

Victoria had stopped trembling, he was happy to note.

"How long must we remain here?" she asked.

"We can't leave now. The streets are alive with dervishes."

"But in another few hours it'll be morning. We're trapped, aren't we? When dawn breaks, we won't be able to move."

He edged back still further so that his arm no longer pressed quite so disturbingly against the softness of her breast. "We'll get out, that's a promise," he whispered.

She was silent for a moment. "We should never have come back like this," she breathed. "We were lucky enough to escape the first time."

"We'll make it, I tell you."

His voice was fierce and insistent but behind its intensity he felt the emptiness of his words and knew she sensed it too. He tried to turn his mind from the danger outside, concentrating instead on the pleasant, comforting touch of warm flesh beneath his fingers. Softly, he chuckled.

"Why are you laughing?" she asked.

"I was just thinking. Here we are wrapped together like a couple of silkworms, yet before today we'd never even spoken to each other."

She looked up at him through the shadows, her eyes glittering. "Are you married?" she asked.

The directness of the question surprised him. "No," he answered stiffly.

"Why not?"

He hesitated. Then he smiled. "Can't afford it. That's what everything comes down to in the end: money. It takes me all my time to pay my mess bills. If I had a wife to support as well . . ." He shrugged, leaving the sentence unfinished.

She was silent for a moment, then she said, "Is that why you want the diamonds so much?"

"That's why."

"Money isn't everything, you know."

He laughed bitterly. "Not when you've got it."

"There are more important things. Being free, for one."

"Without money? Call that freedom?"

"It's better than slavery. Anything is. Why are you so bitter?" she whispered.

"I'm not bitter. What makes you say that?"

"You're like a volcano threatening to erupt."

All at once the tension seemed to flow out of him. "You're right," he admitted, "I *am* bitter. And I've no reason to be, God knows. I've been luckier than most. But luck by itself isn't enough. Not when you're up against a system like ours."

"Then why are you in the army?" she asked.

"It's a good enough career for a young man with limited assets and dubious prospects."

"But you're not the soldiering type."

"Why not?"

"You're too . . . gentle," she said.

Her answer surprised him. To his knowledge, gentleness had never been one of his virtues. Anger certainly, the bitterness she had so accurately discerned, occasional bursts of murderous rage when the iniquity of his position became too much to handle, but gentleness—never.

"Nobody's called me that before."

"When you live with the dervishes, gentleness becomes very important. There's something about being a slave that destroys your very soul, if you let it."

"I can't imagine that happening to you. You're too controlled."

"I'm not as controlled as you think. If you want to know the truth, I'm scared. I don't mean scared of the dervishes. I mean of people. Of going back to a world I no longer belong in. Will people accept me out there? Civilized people, I mean?"

The question carried an artlessness, an almost plaintive innocence he found curiously endearing. "A woman who looks like you," he said, "will be accepted anywhere."

"Am I attractive, physically attractive, in a civilized sense?"

Her directness startled him. "I find you . . . extremely attractive," he admitted softly.

She seemed to consider this, and he wondered what complexities were drifting through her mind. A man could be forgiven for losing his head in such circumstances, he thought.

She peered at him. "The dervishes regard the pleasures of the flesh as one of the great essentials of life. They seldom drink or smoke, but making love is as natural to them as saddling a camel or milking a goat. They look upon our so-called European standards as puritanical and absurd."

Something in her voice made his pulses quicken. He lay motionless, his face barely an inch from her own, trying to quell the impulses rising inside him.

"I have never known a man in the true sense, not in the real sense."

His breathing seemed to stop. He struggled to keep his face impassive, scarcely daring to believe what she was saying.

"I want to now," she whispered, "I want you . . . I want you to make love to me."

He was filled with a frantic, impossible-to-ignore excitement. His throat tightened and the blood throbbed in his temples. Leaning forward, he kissed her on the lips. It was a tentative kiss, gentle and exploratory, but within a second his emotions seemed to career out of control.

And then, as the pounding in his skull intensified beyond endurance, a new sound intruded upon his consciousness, a scream too high and shrill to be construed as human, yet human it was. He felt the hairs prickle on his neck as the sound rose, growing louder, harsher, filling his brain.

ABU ABABDEH HEARD the scream at the same moment. He jerked back his camel, listening intently. Around him, his men froze.

The wail echoed across the rooftops, fading as suddenly as it had started, leaving only the shuffling of the camels and the distant crackle of burning buildings.

Abu Ababdeh knew where the shriek had come from. The dyeworks. He kicked his camel into a trot, and with murmurs of excitement his men followed.

A feeling of unease filled Abu Ababdeh as he rode through the night. Screwing up his eyes, he detected in the distance a crimson glow flickering eerily in the surrounding gloom.

Drawing closer, he heard murmurs of consternation rising from his men and he slowed his camel to a walk. The glow was taking shape now, clearly discernible at close quarters. A fire. Not a raging inferno like the one behind them, but a small dancing flame just large enough to illuminate the figure of a tribesman strapped to a wooden frame.

The man's arms were outstretched in the manner of a priest reciting the Koran, and his head was drawn back, fastened to the upright post by a leather thong, the eyes gazing sightlessly into the night. His head and body had been dyed a variety of brilliant colours, purple, blue, indigo, orange, green, all flickering luminously in the pink glow of firelight.

Abu Ababdeh was not an educated man. He had grown to manhood among primitive people and his instincts were primitive also. The sight of the lifeless warrior, his arms outflung in wordless embrace, his robes and features stained into a grotesque complexity of hues by Driscoll and MacAngus, filled Abu Ababdeh with superstitious dread. His eyes

479

bulged fearfully, and behind him he heard the whispers of his men as they drew up their camels, staring with trepidation at the macabre figure poised before them. Without waiting for their leader to give the word, they wheeled crazily and pounded back the way they had come.

Abu Ababdeh cast one last look at the purple skull, then he too turned his camel and followed swiftly in his warriors' wake.

COFFEY LISTENED to the sound of the tribesmen leaving, scarcely able to contain himself. They were riding off to investigate the source of the scream, he realized. For a minute or two at least, the square outside would be empty. It was their one chance of escape.

"Come on!" He clutched Victoria's hand, and they rose together and scurried across the timber floor, and scrambled down the ladder and through the open doorway. They sprinted through the network of streets, aiming for the open desert.

Coffey heard someone moving towards them and slithered to a halt, pulling Victoria back. Instinctively, his hand groped through his robes, fumbling for the ribbed grip of his Browning.

A rider broke into view, dragging a pair of riderless camels behind him. His headcloth fluttered in the wind as he skidded to a halt, swinging his mount sideways between the silent buildings. Coffey recognized the tilt of the head, the heavy set of the shoulders.

MacAngus, he thought jubilantly. The sergeant's face looked flushed in the stillness as he waved them impatiently forward.

Coffey ran to the first of the camels and jerked it into a crouch. He helped Victoria into the saddle, then mounted the second, and with a click of his tongue followed furiously in MacAngus's wake.

Chapter Ten

The plain shimmered in the heat. Flat as a pancake, it merged into the blinding glare of the sun, losing its density, paling in slow subtle nuances of colour until it was impossible to tell where the earth ended and the sky began. To Coffey's right the outlines of the adjacent mountains looked strangely blue in the early morning.

He lay flat on his belly in the camel scrub, training his field glasses on the vast wave of warriors advancing steadily across the desolate reg. They moved slowly, studying the ground, puzzled that the runaways had left no tracks to follow.

Coffey had ridden through the night in a desperate effort to outdistance them, but now, with the first heat of the day gathering on the gridiron of the desert floor, he felt his spirits sink as he counted two or three hundred men. He could pick out the emir clearly, his fat form

swaying with the uncomfortable rhythm of his camel's gait. A pale blur adorned his saddlehorn. The bag of diamonds.

Pushing the field glasses into their leather case, Coffey edged back to where the others were waiting. They studied him expectantly.

"He's got them all right," Coffey confirmed. "However, there are roughly three hundred men out there, and only six of us."

"Got anything in mind, squire?" Driscoll inquired casually.

"Not a thing. But I'm open to suggestions."

Sergeant MacAngus spat on the ground. "Och, it's not as hopeless as it looks, Lieutenant."

"How's that?"

"When I was serving in Afghanistan, there was an old Pathan warrior called Khaima Rakhri. With less than thirty men he held off the whole British army for damn near seven years. It seems to me if Khaima Rakhri could do it, we can too."

"How?" Coffey asked.

"Well, what we need for starters is a new chain of command. Let's forget the army for a wee bit. When it comes to something like this, we need somebody who thinks like a Pathan."

Coffey frowned. He had noticed a new confidence in MacAngus since the discovery of the diamonds.

"I'm suggesting that until we get them diamonds back, I take over," MacAngus added simply.

Coffey stared at him, thunderstruck. He hadn't been mistaken. MacAngus *had* changed.

"Think it over, Lieutenant," MacAngus argued reasonably. "What difference does it make who gives the orders and who obeys them? The only thing that matters is who gets rich in the end."

Coffey knew that what MacAngus said made sense. In a situation like this, the sergeant had more experience, more natural cunning. "Very well," he said, "until we have the diamonds back, you may assume temporary command."

Driscoll smiled. "Congratulations on your promotion, Sergeant."

MacAngus ignored the remark. He was already concentrating on the problem in hand. "The first thing we must do," he said, "is choose our ground to fight on. Them dervishes are heading across the open reg. Now, no Pathan in his right mind would fight in the open. We need to lure them into the mountains so we can use the land as an ally. Also, after we've got what we came for, we have to make sure they don't overtake us when we run for Fort Malawa."

"How do you intend to accomplish that?" Coffey asked.

MacAngus squatted on his haunches, drawing a line in the dust with his finger. "The dervishes have been riding all through the night, fully loaded. They're moving slow, looking for our tracks, but by sundown

482

their camels will be weary. Now, a shrewd Pathan would give his mounts a rest, then send them out empty-saddled to cut across the dervishes' path."

"Why?"

"They would move faster than ones with riders on their backs. And they'd be a damn sight fresher at the end of the day. Now, we choose the lightest man we've got. He takes the animals in a wide arc, switching from beast to beast so they don't get overtired. He cuts in front of the dervishes, and when they spot his tracks they take off after him. He keeps on wearing them down, bit by bit. Then he leads them into the foothills. We'll be waiting, by the time they get there."

"How?" Coffey asked.

"We walk," MacAngus said. "I estimate them foothills to be no more'n five miles off, maybe even four. We cut across the desert on foot."

Coffey considered for a moment. "Makes sense so far," he said. "The question is, who goes with our camels? Strictly speaking, Mr. Routledge is the lightest, but these beasts, even roped together, will take quite a bit of handling, and Mr. Routledge's hardly in the best of health."

"I'm every bit as light as my father," Victoria said pointedly. "What's more, I'm perfectly capable of leading those beasts all the way to Khartoum and back if necessary. I did it often enough at Hamira."

"No." Coffey's voice was sharp. "It's too dangerous."

"The lady makes sense," MacAngus told Coffey. "I reckon she'll be safe enough as long as she doesn't dawdle."

Victoria smiled as she rose to her feet. Her manner seemed light, almost jaunty. Unhappy, and struggling not to show it, Coffey rose with her. There was a strange inexpressible yearning in him that he had not experienced for many years. Now a sour pall of dread had gathered in his belly. It wasn't right, letting her go like this, but he could think of no way of changing the others' minds. "Be careful," he warned.

Fifteen minutes later, Victoria was riding eastwards across the reg, trailing the camels behind her. Coffey watched her go, the muscles tightening in his throat. Something was happening to him which he couldn't quite fathom. Always in the past he had understood his feelings. Now, for the first time, he was experiencing an elusive melancholy. Watching Victoria ride off, he swallowed uncertainly. Then he flung his water *guerba* over his shoulder and set off after the others.

If that breathless encounter in the prison block at Hamira had been just an instinctive reaction to the urgency of the moment, he thought, why then did it bother him so much? He shook his head as he strode resolutely on.

Victoria, for her part, riding eastwards with the camels, was going through the same emotional crisis. What had possessed her? she wondered. To demand that Coffey, a perfect stranger, should make love to her? That moment in Hamira had been little short of madness. And yet, she could still recall the tautness of his body, the hard resilience of muscle and sinew. The memory caused a gnawing longing that threatened to consume her completely.

Victoria jerked hard on the rope, forcing the camels to quicken their pace. She could see the dervish dust cloud far to her left. It would take her several hours to circle round in front of them. She would put the thought of Coffey from her mind for the present. With the diamonds in their possession, she would have all the time in the world to think of him.

IT TOOK COFFEY and his party four hours to reach the first rambling ramparts of the foothills. Here, high cliffs rose to a central plateau, the cliffs forming a natural amphitheatre ten or fifteen miles across, broken in places by a series of narrow gullies which split the walls into a honeycombed network of twisting passageways barely wide enough for a man to ride through.

Sergeant MacAngus surveyed the labyrinth with an appraising eye. He eased himself into the first of the openings, clambering upwards over the loose scree to peer at the rocky cliffs above. "We'll cut down camel scrub," he declared. "Build cradles at the top of the gully. Then we'll fill them up with rocks and shale."

"Only a maniac would enter this gully unprotected," Coffey told him flatly. "Those dervishes will smell an ambush a mile off."

MacAngus grinned. "That's just what I'm counting on, sir," he said.

Coffey was baffled, but shrugged resignedly and, under the sergeant's directions, they set to work cutting down the thick clumps of thorny scrub, using pliant saplings to build rough-hewn cradles at the ditch's rim. The work was arduous and time-consuming. MacAngus strapped the saplings together with the leather thongs from their *gandouras* and, when at last he had finished, he looked at the cradles approvingly.

"Now we fill them up," MacAngus ordered, scooping up a heavy rock and dropping it into the first cradle.

They followed MacAngus's example, gradually packing the flimsy frameworks until they were piled high with jagged stones. Then they stood round gasping, their bodies drenched with sweat.

"Even if we manage to lure the dervishes in here, which I doubt," Coffey murmured, "there's no guarantee the rocks will fall in the right direction when we cut these cradles loose."

"Who said they were meant to fall anywhere at all?" MacAngus asked him cryptically.

Coffey was about to speak again when suddenly Driscoll whistled from the top of the gully. "Somebody's coming," he shouted. "Looks like Victoria."

Thank God she's safe, Coffey thought.

484

"Get down where she can see you," MacAngus ordered. "Signal her to steer the camels over here."

Coffey scrambled down the rocks, his heart fluttering rapidly. He reached the reg and saw the cluster of riderless camels moving towards them, Victoria mounted on the foremost beast.

He waited until she was almost within hailing distance, then waved his arms frenziedly until she turned the camels in his direction. Coffey watched them drawing closer, and pointed towards the mouth of the gully. She nodded to show she understood.

The long ride had covered Victoria with a thin layer of dust. Her hair was scattered in the wind, and now hung in loose tresses round her face.

Coffey grinned at her as she entered the ditch below him. He scrambled down the rocks to meet her, helping her to dismount. "How'd it go?" he asked.

"Like clockwork," she told him, but he knew she was lying. He could see the strain in her face.

"Are they coming?"

"I think so. They switched direction as soon as they crossed my trail. I watched their dust cloud."

"Good," Coffey declared. "At the very least we've now got fresh camels to take us to Fort Malawa."

They heard a rattle of stones as Sergeant MacAngus came sliding down towards them. "Everything all right?" he asked.

Victoria nodded silently and MacAngus turned, studying the rocky cliffs above. "If we can move our animals up to the plateau," he said, "those dervishes will have to find a way round the cliff bottom before they can follow us. When we've got the diamonds, it could give us a two-maybe three-hour lead."

"You'll never get camels up there."

"What about the scree slope?"

Coffey peered at the giant bridal veil of loose stones falling in an almost perpendicular wave from the plateau to the valley below. "A man might do it, or a dog maybe, but a camel, never."

There was a look of determination on MacAngus's face such as Coffey had never seen before. Without a word, MacAngus took the rope from Victoria's hand and untied the animals one by one. He removed their ropes and knotted their ends firmly together. Then he moved to the scree slope and began to climb, paying out the line behind him. The loose stones rolled beneath his feet as he scrambled steadily upwards, his sandals slipping on the unstable surface.

When he reached the top he leaned forward and peered round. The plateau meandered steadily eastwards, vanishing into the distant heat haze. A good escape route, he thought approvingly. The ground looked solid underfoot.

Just behind the cliff edge, there was a large smooth boulder. Sergeant MacAngus wound the rope round it and began to descend the scree slope. When he reached the bottom he had two separate rope-lengths with the centre looped round the boulder above.

The others watched, mystified, as MacAngus tied one end to the first of the camels, the other to three of the remaining beasts bunched tightly together.

"Think ye can drive these beggars in the opposite direction?" he asked Driscoll.

Driscoll grinned, realizing for the first time what the sergeant was up to. He seized the three beasts by their halters and began to lead them away from the cliff. Roaring in protest, they strained against the rope. The line rose in the air, tightened, became taut as a bowstring round the boulder above. Breathlessly they waited to see if it would take the strain. Driscoll hauled on the halters, pulling the camels forward, and slowly, relentlessly, the rope began to move.

As the first camel was dragged unwillingly towards the scree slope by the insistent pressure of its three companions, MacAngus gripped the animal's bridle, adding his own strength to the force pulling from above. The camel reached the slope and began to scramble upwards. When it felt its feet sliding on the loose shifting rubble, it shrieked loudly and tried to jerk back but MacAngus held on to its halter, and, spitting and protesting, the camel was dragged up the steep rugged incline by traction from below. The second camel followed in a similar manner, and when MacAngus had two animals on the cliff top, he switched tactics. Instead of using the boulder, he fastened the free end of the rope to the camels on the plateau, and used the direct upward pull from above to bring up the other beasts one by one. In the space of barely three hours, the entire party, camels and humans alike, stood safely on the cliff top, the plateau reaching away before them.

Coffey shook his head in wonder. "Sergeant, you're a marvel," he breathed. MacAngus shrugged. He was in no mood for compliments. Only one thing mattered, to his mind. The diamonds. He turned to examine Lieutenant Benson's camel. Dangling from the saddle was a bulky skin carrier.

"What have you got in there, Lieutenant?" MacAngus demanded.

"Just a few odds and ends," Benson said.

"Empty it," MacAngus ordered curtly. "Bring it, and come with me."

Benson hesitated, clearly resentful of the sergeant's tone. He glanced at Coffey and Driscoll for support, but they stared stonily back. In the end, Benson conceded defeat.

"Where are we going?" he asked sullenly.

MacAngus's sunbaked features creased into a network of wrinkles caked with dust. "On an old-fashioned Pathan snake hunt," he grinned.

IT WAS ALMOST DUSK when the dervishes reached the foot of the great cliffs. The rock cast shadows across the orange sand. The emir reined in his mount, looking suspiciously at the point where the camel tracks meandered into the mouth of the narrow gully. He stared balefully from left to right and his warriors waited in silence, the same thought in each of their minds. The gully was narrow and precipitous. There was one way in and one way out. There could be no logical reason for the escapees to enter it at all except for the purpose of an ambush.

The emir barked out a command and two of the tribesmen dismounted, scrambling up the incline towards the gully's mouth, and gingerly edged their way over the ragged jumble of rocks. When they reached the end of the gully, they spotted the wooden cradles MacAngus had built so meticulously, high on the upper edge. Drawing back the way they had come, they related their findings to the waiting emir, who nodded grimly. His assumption had been correct. The runaways were waiting to attack them inside the gully walls.

He studied the cliff face intently, shading his eyes against the setting sun. A second gully, even narrower than the first, cut into the rock at an angle, climbing steadily to a point overlooking the rim of its companion. A small party of men might be able to scale it and surprise the ambushers.

The emir grunted an order and the nearest warriors fell into line beside him as he rode towards the mouth of the second gully. Inside its opening, MacAngus crouched among the rocks chuckling under his breath. His strategy had worked. The dervishes, glimpsing the cradles, had decided to use the parallel gully to launch an ambush of their own.

The spot in which MacAngus was lying was a far from enviable one, however. The cliff rose perpendicularly above it, and his little cluster of rocks offered only a fractional amount of concealment. But he had instructed the others to leave the rope dangling on the scree slope so that when the moment came he could use it to escape to the summit above.

Everything now depended upon Coffey and the others on the cliff top. It was all a question of timing, he had impressed that upon them again and again.

He watched the riders drawing closer. Behind them, on the broad expanse of the desert floor, the great army of men waited silently.

MacAngus eased back the hammer of his Colt with his thumb. The riders drew nearer, until MacAngus could see the emir plainly, his saddlebag with its precious cargo slapping against his animal's flank.

Something whistled through the air. Framed against the sky a coiled shape twisted, falling in an almost perfect arc to land among the riders grouped below.

MacAngus saw the emir's mount start in panic as it glimpsed the snake wriggling viciously beneath its feet. Another shape fell, then another.

487

Then the air was alive with twisting, wriggling snakes streaming like raindrops from the rocky heights above.

The dervishes were caught in a welter of panic and confusion. Their mounts, half crazed with fear, plunged frenziedly in the narrow twisting defile. The riders struggled to retain their balance. A snake fell on a man's neck, wrapping itself instinctively round his throat, and MacAngus heard him cry out as its fangs sank deep into his jugular.

MacAngus came out from his hiding place and ran unevenly towards the emir, his feet dancing across the rocks, dodging the twisting tendrils of snakes wriggling and darting between the camel thorn. He drew his long curved sword, ducking and weaving through the milling camels. He drew level with the emir and, thrusting the Colt inside his robe, snatched at the flesh on the man's mountainous thigh. The emir lashed down at MacAngus with his riding whip, and MacAngus pushed upwards with all his strength, tipping the man inelegantly from his perch. The emir hit the ground in a cloud of dust and lay there gasping. A snake darted over his ankle, vanishing under his robes, and with a shriek of panic he scrambled to his feet, twisting and dancing insanely in a vain attempt to dislodge the intruder. He yelled as the snake bit deep into his ample flesh, then he fell to the ground again.

MacAngus cut the saddlebag strap with his sword. Clutching it firmly in his free hand, he turned and ducked back the way he had come. He reached the foot of the precipitous scree and grabbed at the dangling rope. Frantically, he drew the knotted loop over his shoulders and under his arms, and jerked hard on the line. At once he felt the pressure from above as the others began to pull him upwards. He scrambled up the steep sliding surface, gripping the rope with his free hand. A wild elation filled him. He had the diamonds firmly in his grasp.

A shot rang out and a bullet ricocheted against the rock beside him. The dervishes had seen him running. Even amidst the confusion below, there were cool heads intent on bringing him down.

MacAngus stumbled. His ankle caught against a boulder and he felt himself pitch forward; the saddlebag fell from his fingers, tipping open among the shale. He tried to snatch it back but the rope dragged at his waist, hauling him on.

In a fury, MacAngus tore off the loop of rope and scurried back the way he had come. Dimly he heard Coffey's voice calling a warning. Two tribesmen had dismounted and were working their way up the incline towards him.

MacAngus reached the saddlebag and began to rake through the rubble, scooping up the spilt diamonds and stuffing them frantically into their leather container. He heard Coffey's voice again—"Mac!"—and peering up, saw the nearest tribesman almost upon him. He snatched out his gun. The weapon jerked as he fired, and the man's left eye

488

vanished in a spurt of blood. He fired again, and saw the second man fall back. Then a fusillade of shots rang out from below and MacAngus saw men swarming up the scree slope towards him, their features twisted in fury.

Clutching the saddlebag against his chest, he scrambled furiously up the precipitous incline. At the top he found the others mounted and waiting, Lieutenant Benson holding the spare camel by its bridle. MacAngus mounted at the run, waving the saddlebag triumphantly at his companions, and before the first of the dervishes could breast the rocky rim, they had turned their animals eastwards and were galloping out of the setting sun.

Chapter Eleven

Fort Malawa stood in a flat saucer of land, flanked on one side by a few palm trees. Its walls were largely intact, though in places Coffey noticed that the outer palisades had crumbled away. He shifted wearily in his saddle and tugged the field glasses from their leather case.

All through the night they had ridden hard, Coffey plotting the route from the battered ship's sextant strapped to his saddlehorn, and when morning came, they had struck diagonally across the flatness of the open reg.

Now, staring down at their first glimpse of Fort Malawa, Coffey felt a spasm of uneasiness as he spotted a handful of birds fluttering above the edge of the parapet. There was no other sign of life.

"Vultures," Coffey whispered.

Driscoll whistled softly. "Place looks deserted, squire."

Coffey pushed the binoculars into their case. "Mac, give the diamonds to Lieutenant Driscoll. You and I will ride down and investigate."

MacAngus unstrapped the leather bag from his saddlehorn, and kicking his camel obediently forward he followed Coffey down the steep crumbling hillside.

Coffey's first intimation of what was to come was the sight of a severed head impaled on the crumbling gatepost. He braced himself as he rode into the fort compound, but nothing prepared him for the horror of what they found there. Bodies sprawled on the ground, hung staked to the walls, dangled from the parapets. Most of them had been dismembered, the various parts spread round the compound in macabre disarray. Coffey reined in his camel and sat in silence, his stomach lurching as he peered at the desecrated corpses of Guthrie's Sudanese cavalry.

"What kind of animals would do a thing like this?" he breathed.

"Dervishes would," MacAngus said. "It's the dervish way."

Above Coffey's horror rose the realization that the reinforcements they had been counting on were no longer here. Desperately, he tried to force himself to think. They were worn out, animals and men alike. They were still eighty miles from the railhead, a distance which, in their present exhausted state, might as well be eighty thousand. They had no hidden resources of energy or strength, no last vestiges of endurance.

"We'd better scout around," he sighed. "See if the dervishes left anything worth salvaging."

For the next fifteen minutes he and MacAngus moved around the compound looking for water *guerbas*, ammunition, anything at all which might alleviate their desperate situation.

When he had finished his unsuccessful search, Coffey met MacAngus at the compound's centre. "We'd better get back to the others."

The little group of riders sat watching their approach from the hilltop. Driscoll waited until Coffey had reined in his mount, then lifted his eyebrows inquiringly.

"Dervishes beat us to it," Coffey told him. "Every damn soul massacred."

Driscoll was silent for a moment, staring at the fort. Coffey glanced at Victoria. Her cheeks were pale as buttermilk and he could see the faint gleam of fear in her eyes.

"Water?" Driscoll asked.

"Not a drop."

"That puts us in rather a difficult position. There are no waterholes between here and the railhead, and what's left will barely last the night."

"We're not making for the railhead," Coffey told him curtly. "We're heading for the Nile."

Driscoll frowned. "We're too far south. There'll be dervish patrols all along those riverbanks."

"We've got to have water, Driscoll. I'd rather take my chances with the river than the desert. Who knows, maybe we'll run into one of Kitchener's gunboats."

Driscoll nodded. "Whatever you say, old boy. However, we ought to rest awhile."

"Rest is exactly what I had in mind. How much of a lead do you think we've got?"

"Quite a bit, I should say. It would take those dervishes hours to find a way round that mesa and pick up our tracks again. We can thank the sergeant for that."

"Then we'll remain here until morning. We'll take turns at sentry duty, four hours per man, Benson first. When dawn breaks, we'll saddle up and head for the river."

It was a poor camping place, Coffey realized, the ground littered with stones, the air filled with the smell of rotting flesh, but they were too spent to move any further.

Coffey watched Victoria remove the blanket from under her camel's saddle and spread it over the sharp stones. He moved towards her, helping to arrange her bedding. "You mustn't be frightened," he told her. "We're not finished yet."

She sighed softly, stretching out on her side. "You're such an optimist," she whispered.

He squatted down beside her. He felt glad of a woman's presence, as if in some strange way it alleviated the burden of his own position. Around them, the others were making themselves comfortable for the night.

"I've been hoping for a chance to talk to you," Victoria said gently.

"Why's that?"

"What happened back there in the prison block . . . I don't know what you must think of me. It was madness, of course. I'd gone a little crazy, that's all." She hesitated. "As far as you were concerned, it might have been anyone—any girl."

Coffey shook his head. "You're wrong."

Victoria smiled, settling back her head. "I just wanted it understood between us, that's all."

Coffey took the blanket from his own camel and spread it on the ground. Who could understand the ways of women? he thought. The memory of their encounter unsettled all his senses, but Victoria could only think about whether or not he held her cheaply. As if he could. She was the best thing that had ever happened to him.

He lay down exhausted, shutting his eyes, and within a minute he was fast asleep.

COFFEY WOKE TO FIND Driscoll shaking him. The sky was dark, and Benson was crouching at Driscoll's side. Something in their eyes made Coffey's senses quicken. "What is it?" he hissed. "Dervishes?" He groped for his pistol.

"Nothing so mundane, I'm afraid. It's MacAngus. He's run off."

Coffey rubbed his face with his fingertips. "What are you talking about?"

"The diamonds," Benson hissed. "He's taken the diamonds."

Coffey felt his stomach contract. MacAngus? he thought. Impossible!

"Who was on sentry duty?"

"I was," Driscoll said.

"Didn't you see him leave?"

"*See* MacAngus? That man moves like a cat."

Coffey was conscious of a bitter sense of betrayal. It couldn't be true, surely? MacAngus was more than his sergeant, he was his friend. Coffey could recall a thousand times when he had gambled everything on the sergeant's shrewdness and judgment. How could a man be capable of such treachery? Coffey felt the fury inside him transmute suddenly into cold and resolute hatred. No enemy is despised so much as the friend who turns against you. "Which direction did he take?" he asked.

"Northeast. He's heading for the Nile all right, but he clearly intends to cross it higher up, where the dervish patrols will be less concentrated."

Coffey nodded. That was MacAngus all right. With damn near all his water gone, he was striking out for the furthest point. An audacious move, but if he pulled it off he would be clear of the dervishes by sunrise. Then he'd have only the British to worry about.

"We've got to go after him."

Driscoll looked doubtful. "We're one camel short, squire."

"If Miss Routledge and her father rode double, do you think you could get them to the river? I'll take Lieutenant Benson and see if we can run the sergeant down. Once we've recovered the diamonds we'll move south to join you."

"And then?"

Coffey sighed. "God knows," he admitted honestly. "We can only pray, I suppose."

VICTORIA RODE THROUGH the cool of the predawn morning, adjusting her body to the monotonous rhythm of her camel. Behind her in the saddle she could feel her father holding gently onto her waist. Driscoll trotted ahead, his soiled robes fluttering in the wind. Victoria's body felt stunned. The few hours' rest had scarcely revived her.

It mattered little to Victoria if MacAngus had stolen the diamonds or not. Twelve hours ago they had seemed the most important thing in the world. Her few blessed hours of freedom had made her realize one overpowering truth—she wanted to live, she wanted it more than anything.

But she wanted Coffey too, she realized with a small tremor of shock, recalling the way his eyes crinkled each time he smiled, the way the dust coated the hollows beneath his cheekbones. He was a fine man, she thought, hard and decisive when he had to be, gentle and kind when he didn't. Pray God they would come out of this all right. It would be a dreadful irony if she lost him now, after the empty years of loneliness.

Dawn came slowly, starting in the east, a pale sheen spreading rapidly across the faultless sky. Soon the land took on new dimensions and she felt the warmth of the rising sun striking down on her face and chest. The countryside changed subtly, the stony reg giving way to lusher scrub and sporadic clusters of stunted palms. The vegetation thickened. "How much further?" she asked Driscoll.

"Can't be far. See how the animals are hurrying. They smell water already."

"Shouldn't we slow down a bit? If we're approaching the Nile, there could be dervish patrols about."

492

"Better to get there before the sun climbs high," Driscoll said reasonably. "Then we can hide ourselves in the scrub along the bank. Here we stick out like cherries on a Dundee cake."

His voice broke off and she saw him lean back in the saddle, hauling on his reins. Peering ahead, Victoria froze. They had ridden unsuspecting into a little hollow in the desert reg. It was scarcely deep enough to be termed a wadi, but so gentle were its contours it had been impossible to discern on the flat shimmering floor. In the bed of this shallow depression, a group of dervish tribesmen were busy saddling their camels. The early morning sunlight fell in slanting rays across the carved ivory stocks of their ancient rifles.

The tribesmen themselves were just as startled as Victoria and Driscoll and for a moment they also froze into a silent tableau. Then Driscoll pulled himself together. "Back," he shouted, "get back to the scrub."

Victoria jerked hard on the camel's reins. She heard her father give a startled exclamation of surprise, then they turned in one fluid motion, and with Driscoll flanking her she whipped her mount furiously into a desperate stumbling sprint. She could see the thicket ahead, green and prickly on the arid reg. It would offer them cover of sorts, though for how long she scarcely knew.

Shots rang out as the dervishes recomposed themselves. She felt her father jerk, and knew at once that he had been hit. She felt his fingers slacken on her waist.

"Father," she gasped.

The saddle creaked, and the weight behind her suddenly lightened as he tumbled helplessly into the dust. She dragged the camel to a halt, skidding wildly.

Her father was sprawled among the rocks, his face pressed against the ground, the upper part of his skull blown away. Horror engulfed her. Waves of nausea came rippling upwards through her.

"For God's sake, don't stop," Driscoll bellowed. "Can't you see he's dead?"

He turned back towards her, seizing the bridle, and with Victoria clinging sobbing to the saddlehorn, he pounded furiously on towards the cluster of prickly scrub.

More shots. Dimly she heard the bullets streaking through the air above her head. She felt no sense of danger. She was caught in a paroxysm of shock and disbelief.

Suddenly Driscoll jerked upright, blood spurting between his lips. His hand left her bridle, clawing futilely in the area of his lower spine. He rolled sideways, hitting the ground shoulder first, scattering the sand in a shower which sprayed across her legs.

Victoria slid off her camel. Driscoll was lying on his side, blood spreading across the front of his *gandoura*.

Sobbing helplessly, she seized him by the armpits and began to drag him backwards across the sand. She was only dimly conscious of the dervishes mounting and turning in her direction. She reached the thicket and let Driscoll drop, tears streaming down her cheeks.

"The rifle," Driscoll croaked. "Fetch the rifle, *hurry.*"

Victoria stared across the desert flat. She could see Driscoll's camel chewing contentedly at a clump of thorn. The stock of Driscoll's Martini protruded from the saddle holster. Victoria sprinted back as hard as she could run. She could see the dervishes drawing closer. She managed to reach the camel and fumbled desperately with the leather buckles,

drawing the Martini free. It seemed incredibly heavy in her grasp.

"Bring it over here," Driscoll croaked, grimacing with pain. "The ammunition pouch too."

Still weeping, Victoria scurried back clutching the rifle and saddle-pouch in her trembling fingers. Driscoll propped himself against a boulder. He took the Martini from her hands and levered a cartridge into the chamber. He released the safety catch and snapped off a shot which brought the leading dervish down in a flurry of whirling arms and legs. Driscoll fired again, and a second rider tumbled from his saddle. The others turned back, sliding from their mounts and running for cover.

495

Driscoll lowered the rifle and propped his head against the rock. Sweat streamed down his face. "That'll hold them for a bit," he murmured weakly. "They'll probably get us next time, when they get their nerve back. That's if the sun and thirst haven't finished us off first."

MACANGUS SAW THE RIVER through the thin haze of the early morning. He'd known he was close, he could smell it.

The long ride across the empty sands had drained his strength. But it wasn't the tiredness which worried him so much as the other feeling that had settled stubbornly in his gut. His brain returned with nagging persistence to the bag of stones joggling at his thigh. He was ashamed, ashamed of what he had done to Coffey. He had never turned his back on a friend before.

But the diamonds had been too important to ignore. They could buy him a new identity, a new life out of reach of the law. They offered more than a future. They offered survival.

He found a little spot where water seeped through sand and pebbles into a natural crystal-clear pool, and, lying down, he lowered his face and gulped the precious life-giving liquid into his body. His mount also drank.

The banks looked empty, cluttered with thick patches of scrub and mimosa, but he knew there would be villages higher up, and dervish patrols riding between them. Following the river would be dangerous and foolhardy unless he moved inland. A mile or two should do it. MacAngus replenished his water *guerba*, then remounted and set off along the riverbank. The river bent like the sweep of a longbow, and MacAngus frowned suddenly as he spotted, above the crumbling red bank, vultures dipping and wheeling in clumsy confusion. There was something dead up ahead. He could smell it already, the same chilling odour that had settled in his nostrils at Fort Malawa. He unslung his Martini rifle as he nudged his animal forward.

At a point where the river bent, with the water running dark over cold flat stones, the shattered wreckage of an Arab *dahabeeyah* lay keeled over on its side. MacAngus could see its crew's remains, sprawled about the deck. Then he remembered. This was the wreck they had seen the night the gunboat put them ashore. Unwittingly he had come upon the very spot from which they had started.

MacAngus dismounted and led his camel down to the water's edge, leaving it to drink there while he moved towards the battered shell of the boat. He counted eight bodies in all, and a ninth still bobbing in the shallows. In the stern lay the ancient metal cannon and the tiny gunpowder barrel caulked with tar. MacAngus shook his head in wonder. The dervish crew, using a weapon centuries old, had taken on a British patrol boat armed to the teeth with modern artillery. It was an unequal struggle. Even the khalifa must realize the inevitable outcome of the war he was fighting.

MacAngus was thinking this when he heard, quite distinctly, the rasping snort of a camel. Scrambling up the riverbank he threw himself flat between two clumps of mimosa. He was able to discern, through the shimmering waves of morning heat, two riders coming hard towards him, clad in the dark blue robes and black headdress of the Kel Ahaggar Tuareg. The man leading he recognized instantly: Coffey. The way he sat in the saddle was unmistakable. The other one would be either Lieutenant Benson or Driscoll.

Damn fools. Instead of running for the river to the south, they had followed his tracks, the tracks he hadn't even bothered to conceal, calculating that no one would be crazy enough to come after him.

Coffey was after the diamonds, MacAngus's diamonds, his future. There was only one answer MacAngus could see.

He slipped a bullet into the Martini's chamber and licking one finger he carefully moistened the front sight to give him aim. He settled his cheek to the stock and levelled the barrel at Coffey's chest. He did not want to kill Coffey. He liked him better than any other officer he had served under. But he did not want to lose the diamonds either. MacAngus was prepared to kill anyone for them.

Coffey had slowed his pace, seeing the river ahead, and now his outline offered a target MacAngus just could not miss. One light squeeze, gentle as a desert wind, and Coffey would go tumbling lifeless out of the saddle. MacAngus's finger tightened on the trigger.

Nothing happened. He waited like a man caught in a seizure, unable to move. Swearing softly, he lowered the weapon. He couldn't kill Coffey, no matter what, he should have realized that from the beginning. If he wanted to hold on to those diamonds, his only hope was to find some way of staying ahead, of crossing the river maybe, and heading up north on the opposite side.

A sudden commotion caught MacAngus's ear, and craning his head he glimpsed eight mounted horsemen riding across the skyline. MacAngus's mouth gaped open in astonishment. Clad in chain mail and heavy armour, the horsemen looked like medieval crusaders, the sunlight glinting fiercely on their metal shields and helmets. Worse, they were riding swiftly towards Coffey and his companion.

VICTORIA CROUCHED among the camel scrub and listened to the monotonous rhythm of the dervish rifle fire. For more than an hour the tribesmen had kept up a steady barrage of shots, most of them falling far wide of their target, for their weapons were ancient and notoriously unstable.

Driscoll was dying. Victoria had struggled desperately to staunch the blood pouring from his wound, but death was inevitable. Driscoll's strength was fading with each passing minute, and soon he would be too weak to raise the Martini to his shoulder. Poor Driscoll. Though she scarcely knew the man, she liked him, trusted him, felt secure in his company. He had risked his life to rescue her, and by that act of deliverance had lost his own.

Victoria had already made up her mind what she would do. When Driscoll had gone, she would take the rifle and blow out her brains. She had watched him operate it, knew now how to load and fire.

Driscoll coughed painfully as blood choked in his throat. His eyes looked glazed as they focused with difficulty on her face. "Listen to me. You've got to make a run for the river," he croaked.

"And leave you behind? What do you take me for?"

"Take my camel," he choked. "It's still grazing at the back of the thicket. Steer due east into the sun. The Nile can't be far. Another few miles, possibly less. At least you'll have water."

"Lieutenant Driscoll, I am not going anywhere without you."

"You must go now. I can't keep this up much longer."

Unable to help herself any longer, Victoria felt the tears springing to her eyes. Her shoulders shook as sobs racked her body.

"I hope you're not crying for me," Driscoll said. "I never could stand to see a woman's tears. Take what's left of the water," he muttered, "I won't need it. Leave the rifle and ammunition and I'll do what I can to hold the dervishes off until you get clear. But for God's sake, hurry."

Victoria controlled herself with an effort. Driscoll was right. There was no sense in both of them dying. Her chances were slim, but it was worth a try. Leaning forward, she kissed him lightly on the forehead.

"Go now," he whispered. "You've wasted too much time already."

Gently Victoria eased backwards through the thicket.

"Miss Routledge?" Driscoll croaked. She glanced back. "Make sure everyone knows what a hero I've been, won't you? I'd hate to think I'm doing this for nothing."

Victoria nodded, unable to speak, then turned quickly away and wriggled forward to where Driscoll's camel squatted in the scrub, its rubbery lips chewing contentedly at the vegetation. She slid into the saddle and slapped the animal to its feet. With the tears still streaming down her cheeks, she kicked the camel's flanks and rode into the sun.

Chapter Twelve

Coffey stared in amazement at the line of ironclad riders galloping towards him, their polished helmets and breastplates glittering. "My God," he whispered, "will you look at that."

"They're . . . they're knights in armour," Lieutenant Benson breathed.

"Dervishes. Can't be anything else." Coffey glanced swiftly round. Scrub cluttered the land in all directions. Ahead, the Nile gleamed in the morning sunlight.

"The river's our best chance," he said. "If they follow us into the water wearing that lot, they'll sink like stones."

He kicked his camel into a run, conscious of Lieutenant Benson following, conscious of the river shimmering ahead, deep and green and cool. He galloped across the last few yards, dismounted at the run and stumbled headlong into the swirling current, feeling the water soothe his fevered skin. The riverbed seemed treacly, tugging at his sandals as he waded forward as fast as he could, pushing against the current until his toes had left the bottom. His robes bunched up, lifted high by the bobbing tide. The heavy fabric clung to his thrashing limbs, dragging him back.

Benson overtook him, swimming hard, his pale face glistening through the spray. At eye level, Coffey could see flies dancing across the rippling surface. Ahead, so far away it seemed little more than a hazy ghostline, lay the opposite shore.

To the north, the river narrowed, the water tumbling into the frothy tumult of a raging cataract. Coffey glimpsed the dark hummocks of rocky islands rearing out of the white-capped spray.

Behind them, the armoured warriors had come to a halt along the riverbank, making no attempt to follow. Instead, they were watching and—Coffey froze as he realized this—laughing, actually laughing.

He felt a chill sweep through his body as he spotted a boat, just ahead, swaying towards them out of a narrow inlet, its brown triangular sail billowing in the wind. A *nuggar*. Gathered along the vessel's hull dark-skinned dervishes grinned savagely as they waited with poised spears for Benson and Coffey to come within range.

"We're trapped," Benson choked, kicking wildly as he struggled to change direction.

The boat drew nearer, and instinctively they struck out for the shore, though Coffey knew that no sanctuary lay in that direction, for already the mounted warriors were clustering at the water's edge.

Coffey saw spears curving through the air above them. Something clipped his skull and pain shot through his brain as blood trickled over his hair into his eyes.

Then something echoed in his ears, a distant vibrating thunder. Coffey glanced back as the prow of the *nuggar* suddenly erupted in a great shower of splintered timber. The men who a second before had been laughing and dancing along its hull were scattered across the river's surface.

Coffey struggled to discern the meaning of this new development.

Dazed, he trod water as the explosion's echoes reverberated in his ears. The *nuggar* was listing now, the remnants of its crew running up and down the deck, shouting in panic.

Coffey squinted along the riverbank. He could see something at the water's edge, a boat of sorts, or what was left of one. Crouched in its stern he spotted a tall, rawboned man with craggy cheekbones, leaning back against the vessel's mast, fumbling with an ancient metal cannon. MacAngus!

The roar came again, accompanied by a vivid flash. And this time Coffey could hear the rush of grapeshot as it swept across the river's surface.

He saw squirming bodies splashing in the water.

Benson stared at the scene in bewilderment. "What the hell is happening?"

"It's MacAngus," Coffey shouted jubilantly. "He's blown them out of the water with their own cannon! Come on," he urged, "let's swim for the opposite bank."

MacAngus watched the remains of the *nuggar* slowly sinking. He could see Coffey and Lieutenant Benson swimming determinedly away. It had been a chance in a million, he realized. He'd half expected the old cannon to blow up in his face. But the gunpowder had done the trick. And the second time he fired, that grapeshot had cut down everything in its path. He was glad Coffey and Benson hadn't been a few yards closer or it would have torn them both to bits.

MacAngus let his gaze sweep along the shoreline. The armoured warriors were staring at him dumbfounded. For several seconds they sat frozen in their saddles in amazement. Then, gripping their lances, they turned in his direction, kicking their horses into a gallop.

MacAngus clambered ashore and raced for his camel. He knew the animal was on the brink of exhaustion, but the dervish mounts were weighed down with the chain mail they were carrying. He still had a chance. He kicked his camel into a run, steering it furiously through the thorny mimosa to the brightness of the empty reg.

Yelling insanely, the dervishes thundered relentlessly in his wake.

VICTORIA SCARCELY KNEW how long she had been riding. Her camel was on the verge of collapse and in every direction the desert stretched away interminably. Her spirits drooped as she considered the hopelessness of her position. Never in her life had she felt so terribly alone. Her father was gone, Driscoll was probably dead by now, and Coffey was off on a wild-goose chase of his own.

She rode almost without thinking, following a spine of rock, crossed a narrow *wadi* and entered a twisting tangle of vegetation. The river couldn't be far, she reasoned.

Suddenly, a fusillade of shots broke on the bright morning air, and Victoria straightened in the saddle, sucking in her breath. The shots came again, rattling in her eardrums, and behind them she heard the sonorous boom-boom of deeper explosions. Artillery. Victoria's heart began to pound.

She left her camel grazing in the scrub and scrambled up a sandy incline. The broad sweep of the river swung into view, its water sleek and slow-running as it looped beneath her in a massive arc. The Nile!

On the opposite bank dervish warriors in white robes crouched among the mimosa firing their rifles at a white-painted sternwheeler chugging sedately through the central channel. Victoria stared incredulously at the gunboat. The vessel was three-tiered, with metal palisades built along its decks, and from its mast the Union Jack fluttered merrily alongside the Egyptian white star and crescent.

She could see men moving to and fro like tiny ants, and a flash of flame emerged from the gunboat's stern. Almost simultaneously, the deep satisfying boom of artillery came resounding towards her, and on the opposite bank a column of earth mushroomed into the sky, tossing men and animals contemptuously aside like confetti.

Keeeeruuuumph! Another shell exploded. Screams of pain and terror rang in Victoria's ears, and this time the dervish warriors left their positions and began to scramble panic-stricken away through the thick thorny scrub.

Victoria was within a hair's breadth of safety, except for one thing. In her dervish robes, she looked identical to the savage tribesmen engaging the gunboat from the other side of the river. If she rose from her position, the artillerymen would simply swing the lethal Maxim in her direction. She felt a surge of panic as she watched the great craft drift majestically round, heading back the way it had come. An idea came to her. The men on board must realize beyond any question that she was a woman—and a white woman at that. She began to fumble with her robes, drawing them feverishly over her head. Her face and arms had been tanned by the sun, but the rest of her was pale as alabaster as, naked, she rose and stepped up to the riverbank, standing outlined against the sky.

Staring across the water, she willed the gunboat to stop, willed the crew to look in her direction. A startled, inarticulate cry echoed across the current and Victoria felt triumph in her breast. They had seen her.

She walked slowly down to the river's edge and entered the water. It was many years since she had tried to swim, but she moved her arms and legs persistently and she was gratified to see, when she paused for breath, that the gunboat was some distance nearer.

A knotted rope was lowered from its gunwale, and, with her hair hanging in sodden strands around her shoulders, Victoria was hauled up

501

to the vessel's deck. A young officer helped her over the rail, his eyes bulging at the sight of a naked white woman clambering out of the river fifty miles behind the dervish positions.

Minutes later, wearing a naval tunic, Victoria stood on the bridge and gabbled out her story to the astonished gunboat commander.

THE MOVEMENT OF THE RIVER distorted Coffey's senses. His brain was spinning as blood from his head wound trickled relentlessly into the tumbling stream. I can't keep this up much longer, he thought.

Suddenly he realized why the current was moving faster. They were being sucked downstream into the boiling waters of the cataract.

Benson spotted the maelstrom ahead and his glistening face turned visibly paler. "Kick," he bellowed. "Kick, for God's sake."

But Coffey was spinning along at a dizzy rate, his body cold and numb, the pain in his head accentuated by each beat of his heart. His sight blurred as he went under. Then his head broke the surface and he spotted Benson splashing towards him. A hand gripped Coffey's shoulder, dragging his head higher. He heard Benson bellowing, "Kick, damn you! Do you want to get us both killed?"

Coffey lashed out with his feet, thinking in that fractional moment how strange it was that Benson of all people, his old enemy, should be helping him now.

And then the torrent was all round them, seething and boiling, battering their bodies from every direction. Above the ferment Coffey glimpsed jagged columns of rock rearing in their path. Once again he felt Benson's hand gripping his shoulder, Benson's voice yelling into his ear, "Harder! Harder! We've got to get to that rock."

Coffey struggled. Dimly, at one point, he caught a glimpse of the opposite bank, but before he could get a grip on his senses, the river came leaping in again and he spotted the nearest rock almost upon them. It reared above the spray, sharp and angular. Benson had one hand gripping the outcrop, the other holding onto Coffey's robe. Coffey heard the robe tearing, heard Benson shouting, heard the river roaring, and clenched his teeth as the torrent thundered against his skull.

MACANGUS HAD FELT his camel staggering for more than a mile now. He drew to a halt. It was cruel to punish the poor beast further. Better to choose a place for them both to die.

Behind him, the horsemen pounded triumphantly in for the kill.

MacAngus didn't bother to take cover. He spat on the ground, stuck a cheroot in his mouth and lit it carefully. Then he loaded his Martini, laying the rest of the cartridges in the sand where he could get at them if he needed to. All the while, he watched the horsemen's approach with steely absorption.

He let them get within thirty yards, then he brought the Martini to his shoulder, took aim and squeezed the trigger. Metal hit metal, and MacAngus saw the leading rider throw up his arms and tumble from the saddle.

Biting hard on his cheroot, MacAngus cleared the chamber and slipped in a fresh round. He watched his next target swing into frame then—crack—a man's helmet buckled inwards as he went into a backward somersault.

MacAngus was ejecting the cartridge case when suddenly he was lying flat on his back, staring at the sky. He frowned, then the echo of a rifle crack reverberated in his ears and he realized he had been shot. He had been unaware that the dervishes were carrying rifles.

He felt no pain, that was the strangest part, only a curious numbness which crept through his abdomen to his lower chest. His Martini was lying several feet away. He groped beneath his robe, his fingers locating the ribbed handle of his Navy Colt. He dragged it out, and drew back the hammer. The foremost warrior was almost upon him and MacAngus saw the man's face quite clearly beneath his shiny steel visor. MacAngus fired, holding the pistol at arm's length.

The bullet caught the front of the dervish's breastplate and ricocheted upwards, entering the man's skull beneath his chin.

The warrior almost landed on MacAngus's chest as he hit the ground and rolled over in the swirling dust. MacAngus switched his aim, firing twice at the next rider, seeing only his outline framed against the sun as he reared up in the saddle and wheeled away, clutching his side.

MacAngus waited. Three shots left, he thought. Only three. There would be no freedom now. No fresh start, no new identity. He had betrayed his friends, turned his back on everything he believed in, and for what?

So MacAngus waited for the warriors to come. The minutes stretched out and nothing happened. Cautiously he lifted his head, squinting through the glare. There was not a soul in sight. Puzzled, he let his head drop back, feeling dizzy and nauseous.

He did not hear the soft rattle of accoutrements, nor did he see the brown jerseys and sand-coloured trousers of an Egyptian patrol led by a young British subaltern riding slowly towards him through the blistering sunlight . . .

FOR MORE THAN AN HOUR, Coffey and Benson lay sprawled on the rock, with the river roaring around them.

"How's the head?" Benson croaked, his voice strained and distorted.

"Throbbing."

"Bound to. Nasty cut you've got."

"I was finished, back there." Coffey whispered. "If you hadn't hauled me out I'd have gone straight to the bottom. You saved my life. Why didn't you let me drown?"

"I don't know," Benson admitted frankly. "Just couldn't resist the temptation to play the hero, I suppose."

Coffey's lips twitched painfully into a smile. "I'm beginning to suspect that underneath that cold exterior you're really a decent human being."

He closed his eyes. He wondered about Victoria. Was she still alive? Would she make it through to the British lines? He wished sadly that he had known her better.

Benson interrupted his thoughts. "We can't stay here. We'll burn to a cinder on this rock."

"We could take our chances in the water."

"We'd never make it." He was right.

"Think Driscoll got through?" Benson asked, after a while.

"Maybe."

"It's MacAngus I'm envious of. He's still got the diamonds."

"Bastard."

"He saved our lives, remember?"

"Doesn't alter the fact he's a bastard."

Soon it grew too hot to talk and they passed into silence, their bodies stretched across the rock. The morning lengthened and Coffey closed his eyes, listening to the roaring of the current. Soon he lapsed into long stretches of mindless torpor.

It was Benson's voice which brought him back to consciousness. "Coffey," Benson hissed, "look up the river."

Coffey blinked, screwing up his eyes against the glare of the sun. Something danced in his vision, blurring weirdly. As he watched, it gradually came into focus. He spotted a Union Jack fluttering in the wind. White-painted decks gleaming in the sunlight. Smoke curling from a blackened funnel. A British gunboat.

"Is it a mirage?" Benson choked.

A wave of elation swept through Coffey's battered body. "It's no mirage," he croaked excitedly. "That's Victoria on the deck. Wave your arms, Benson. Wave them hard, for God's sake. I think we are going to be rescued!"

LATER THAT DAY, when Victoria picked up the teapot and refilled Coffey's cup, she was dressed in the uniform of a Seaforth Highlander, complete with kilt. The jacket was at least two sizes too big for her.

They were sitting in the empty mess tent, the sounds of life and movement drifting in from the camp and the railhead outside. Several hours had passed since Coffey and Benson had been rescued from the cataract, and Coffey was beginning at last to absorb the realization that he was not after all on the threshold of death, but safely back amongst his own people. His wound had been dressed, he had delivered his report to Colonel Guthrie and, apart from a desperate weariness which seemed to pervade every limb, he felt, in the circumstances, surprisingly fit.

"I'm sorry about your father," he said.

"My father died a free man," Victoria answered gently, "and he felt no pain. That's something to be thankful for."

"I wish things could have been different, that's all. A man who's suffered so much ought to have been able to live out his life in comfort and peace."

"Well, he's at peace now. Lieutenant Driscoll too."

Coffey was silent as he stirred his tea. He felt a flash of anguish as he thought of Driscoll, recalling his wild eyes, the jagged scar, the twisted grin. The news of his death had saddened Coffey greatly. "There'll be a decoration," he murmured.

"He was a very brave man."

Coffey nodded. Leaning back in his chair, he ran his fingertips over the padded dressing on the back of his skull. His head was still tender, but it would soon heal. "What about you?" he asked. "Feeling better?"

"I'm recovering," she smiled. "A cup of tea does wonders."

They were strangely uneasy in each other's company, as if the knowledge that the past was over, and there would, in spite of everything, be a future after all, unnerved them.

Victoria glanced down at her cup. "You know, I never really thanked you for what you did for us, my father and me."

"That was our duty," Coffey said. He looked at Victoria. "What will happen to you now?"

"That's up to the mission people, I suppose. They'll have to accept some responsibility for me, with my father dead. They'll send me to Cairo, I imagine, then back to England as soon as arrangements can be made. I've been away so long it'll seem like another world. What about you?" she asked.

He felt strangely morose at the thought of her leaving. He shrugged. "I go where the army sends me."

She stared at the ground. "I'd hate to think I'd never see you again."

Something caught in Coffey's throat. He studied her face, her eyes, her mouth, aware of a sensation that was startling in its intensity. He heard himself mutter, "Let me know where you are in England. I'll visit you when I'm home on leave."

"Promise?"

"I promise."

His voice seemed to falter as he recognized the emptiness of his words. What if he lost her completely? The realization jolted him.

"For God's sake," he said suddenly, "why are we talking like this? You know damned well I can't bear the thought of you going away."

A faint smile touched the corners of her mouth. "But we scarcely know each other."

"Does it matter?"

"I'm a savage, remember? A slave."

"Stop talking rubbish. I want you to stay here. With me."

She was smiling openly now. "Wouldn't that be rather irregular?"

"You can tell the mission people you've changed your mind. You're not going back to England after all."

"You're a very persuasive man, Lieutenant."

"Give me your answer. Yes or no?"

Without a word, she rose from her chair, moved towards him and bending over, kissed him on the mouth. He felt her body soft against his chest. She leaned back, looking at him. "Satisfied?" she whispered.

Never in his life had he experienced such happiness. He was about to answer when the tentflap was thrust rudely aside and Lieutenant Benson entered. Benson was dressed in his khaki uniform, his sprucely scrubbed face still displaying the rigours of his desert ordeal, his cheeks and throat scorched red by the blazing sun. He hesitated, taken aback at the sight of Victoria caught in Coffey's embrace, and Coffey could tell by the look in his eyes that something was wrong.

"What's up?" he demanded.

"They've just brought MacAngus in," Benson said.

Coffey's body stiffened. He had forgotten MacAngus in the excitement of being rescued. Now a savage resentment settled in his breast. It mattered little to Coffey that MacAngus had saved their lives at the river. All he could think of was the overwhelming bitterness of betrayal.

He rose to his feet, kissing Victoria lightly on the forehead. "Wait here," he ordered. "I'm going to have a little chat with that sergeant of ours."

"It's over now," she said earnestly, "can't you see that?"

"No," he answered in a clipped voice, "it's only just the beginning."

There was no question of forgiveness in Coffey's mind. Only a burning desire to bring things into the open. With Benson at his heels he strode swiftly through the crowded campsite to the hospital tent.

Sergeant MacAngus lay on the furthest bunk. When he heard them coming his eyes opened and he looked at them. No expression crossed his face but he closed his eyes.

"Well," Coffey said, drawing to a halt at the foot of the bed, "I'm glad to see that you at least have the grace to look ashamed."

MacAngus didn't answer.

"I suppose you think you're a bloody hero, blowing that boat out of the water the way you did?"

MacAngus considered this for a moment, then he nodded modestly.

"I want those diamonds, Sergeant," Coffey said quietly.

Silence.

"Hand them over, damn you."

Lieutenant Benson coughed uncomfortably. "Be reasonable, Sergeant," he said in a soothing tone. "Those diamonds belong to all of us. I know what you did for us, and we're grateful, believe me. If you hadn't fired that grapeshot we'd have been cut to pieces at the river back there. But that doesn't alter the fact that the diamonds are our communal property."

"I didn't fire any grapeshot," MacAngus snapped.

"What's that?"

"I didna have any grapeshot. I used the only damn thing I had."

Watching, Coffey saw a shock run through Benson's body. Benson turned to look at him, his cheeks pale, and a cold chill gathered in Coffey's stomach as the terrible truth settled in his mind. "You fired the *diamonds?*" he whispered.

MacAngus nodded.

Coffey felt his legs turn rubbery. Stunned, he struggled to recall the moment at the river when he had heard the grapeshot on the hot morning air. It couldn't be true, not after all they had gone through. He had thought his life was beginning afresh. Now his dream was being shattered in a manner so ludicrous, so unutterably grotesque, he could barely believe it.

To Coffey's astonishment, Benson started to laugh. He doubled over, choking helplessly.

Coffey turned to MacAngus with an expression of bewilderment. Even MacAngus was laughing, cackling drily from his bandaged chest. Unable to help himself, Coffey felt his own laughter begin, bubbling up in his stomach, bursting from his throat. Caught in a spasm of hysteria the three men roared in unison.

Chapter Thirteen

Kengle looked at the old lady, thunderstruck. "I . . . I don't understand," he whispered weakly.

She chuckled. "It's perfectly simple. The diamonds are lying in the mud and silt on the riverbed."

"Then what on earth . . . ?"

"The Churchill Collection? Strontium titanate. Superb imitations, but strictly synthetic. Crystals cut and polished to look like diamonds, but lacking the hardness and lustre of the real thing."

Kengle took a deep breath. "Are you telling me the stones stolen this morning were nothing but fakes?" He felt suddenly weak and shivery. "It's insane," he breathed.

The old lady smiled, her eyes glittering as she savoured the effect her words had created. "Only a single stone survived from the original hoard," she explained. "The one Churchill found lodged in MacAngus's belt. He turned it in to the military authorities and it now forms part of the Crown Jewels. The army, of course, had been well aware of the diamonds' existence, and it wasn't difficult for my father to convince them he had the others still in his possession. When they ordered him to hand them over, he refused adamantly. In the end, a compromise was reached. MacAngus's stone would remain the property of the Crown, and Coffey could hold on to the rest, providing he undertook never to sell them outside the British Isles."

"And then he had fakes made?" Kengle muttered.

"Excellent fakes, Mr. Kengle. Perfect in every detail. Only a professional would have been able to detect the difference. Happily, the only *diamantaires* ever to examine them closely were men in my father's employ, members of the Driscoll Dozen."

"The committee set up within the Foundation?"

"Precisely. Their job was to administer all details concerning the diamonds' safety and welfare. They included lawyers, insurance brokers, diamond experts, businessmen, all carefully screened and vetted. Only the most trusted associates were invited to join that elite little assembly. They were paid handsomely to ensure that my father's secret would never be disclosed. You see, Mr. Kengle, when Lieutenant Coffey returned from the Sudan, he found he was a national celebrity. Stories about his newly acquired wealth appeared in every newspaper in the country. On the strength of those fabulous diamonds he was able to borrow vast sums of money and use that money to lay the foundations for his future business empire."

"But surely, I'd have thought the financiers would have wanted to examine his collateral?"

The old lady smiled. "My father was fast on his feet," she explained. "The experts who did the examining were invariably members of his own committee. Because of the privations of his youth, Mr. Kengle, my father was filled with a burning need to succeed. He took risks, extraordinary risks, and he took them with other people's money. But the fact remains it was his own extraordinary talent that allowed his business ventures to grow and flourish. Of course, he never had to worry about financial backing. Whatever he wanted to borrow, people were only too happy to give. After all, was he not the owner of the most extravagant diamond collection in the world?"

Kengle shook his head. "It's unbelievable."

"Yes, my father was always conscious of the delicate game he was playing. Even the people who insured the diamonds were part of the bewildering array of front companies set up by the Driscoll Dozen."

508

"And it was the Driscoll Dozen which ordered this morning's robbery?"

"They had no choice. The British government was about to put pressure on the Foundation to return the collection to the Sudanese. You can imagine the effect that would have had. However, no one will be the loser. The insurance companies belong to the Foundation anyhow. And as time goes by, the Churchill Diamonds will simply become one of the world's great unsolved mysteries."

Kengle was stunned. It was too much to assimilate. "What about Ben Crowley's file? The links with organized crime?"

The old lady laughed drily. "There never were any links. My father simply used his money to help his two fellow conspirators. He backed Lieutenant Benson's political career, and Benson eventually became part of Churchill's wartime cabinet in 1941."

"And Sergeant MacAngus?"

"MacAngus was wanted by the British police. My father bought him a new identity."

"So the sergeant didn't die in the desert after all?"

"Of course not. The man was as strong as an ox. He went off to the United States as Garry Ulterfeld Kurtzman. Unfortunately, he got himself into bad company and became a notorious figure in the American underworld. But that didn't stop him and my father remaining firm friends. Those letters and cablegrams Ben Crowley discovered were perfectly innocent. Both my parents visited MacAngus frequently throughout his lifetime, but there were never any business dealings between them."

The clock striking three made Kengle jump. He was suddenly aware of the darkened room, and struggled to assemble his senses. "I have to go," he said. "I must . . . leave. Immediately. I have an important meeting in the morning."

"What will you say there?" she whispered.

"Say?" He blinked at her. "I'm not sure," he admitted.

He pushed back his chair and rose unsteadily to his feet. "It's too early to take all this in," he said. "I'll ring you from the office when I've sorted things out in my mind."

The old lady was silent for a moment, then she said, "Mr. Kengle, my father lied in order to borrow money. He was wrong to do that, and I can't deny it. But the things he achieved were achieved by his own ability. He created a fortune, and rather than keep that fortune to himself, he used it to help others. He started with the unfortunates in his own society, the poor, the helpless, the underprivileged, then he extended his activities to Africa and the Far East. He was a good man, humane and compassionate. You have in your possession enough knowledge to destroy his reputation for ever."

Kengle frowned at her. "You misjudge me, ma'am," he said. "It is my own future I need to consider. If you knew me better you would understand I could never do anything to harm the Foundation. Ben Crowley's file will be destroyed at once. Your father's reputation will be safe with me."

For the first time that evening the old lady's expression visibly softened. "I was wrong," she admitted softly.

"Wrong?" he echoed.

"When they wanted to make you Foundation president, I voted against the proposal. I thought you were too young, too green, too headstrong. Now I realize I made a mistake. You *are* the Foundation, Mr. Kengle. I hope you will continue to run it as brilliantly as you have for the past six years. We need you."

Kengle nodded silently. For the past few hours he had been transported to a world beyond his wildest imagination. It was a world that had gone now, for ever. The people in it—Coffey, Driscoll, Victoria Routledge—had become as real as his most intimate acquaintances.

He walked to the door, pausing with his hand on the knob and glancing back. "You know, one way or another," he said, "your parents played a damned good joke on us all. The funny thing is, I can't help feeling that I can hear them laughing still."

She smiled, tears rolling down her cheeks. Kengle smiled back. Then he went out, closing the door gently behind him.

A light rain was falling as he was driven back to London in the cool softness of the early morning.

BOB LANGLEY

Bob Langley is probably best known as one of the presenters of "Pebble Mill at One" and "Saturday Night at the Mill". His television career, which has since broadened into a wide range of reporting and presenting assignments, takes him to all sorts of places, giving him plenty of material for his novels.

Langley, who grew up in Newcastle, left his first job as an insurance clerk in order to take off for America, where he spent three years doing any sort of work he could find, from fruit picking in California to working in the tobacco fields of the South. On his return home, Tyne Tees television invited him to appear on a local programme to talk about his experiences. They were so impressed with his performance that they asked him to join them as a scriptwriter and, later, a presenter. In 1969 he went to the BBC, and worked for two years as a newsreader, in London—and subsequently as a reporter on the news programme "24 Hours". It is still highly topical reporting that he likes best.

He visited the Sahara some six years ago, before he began writing *The Churchill Diamonds*, which is his eleventh novel. "The landscape was quite spectacular," he recalls. "Just like *Beau Geste*, with oases surrounded by palm trees and mirages shimmering in the distance." His aim was to write an adventure story which spanned the past and the present. "I used Churchill as a link, because he's a figure from a past era, but also someone from our own age."

During pauses in his busy schedule, Langley likes to retreat to the Lake District, where he and his wife Pat live in a house with magnificent views over Derwent Water. "When I'm coming home and see the rolling hills in the distance, the tension falls away."

His next book will tell of an Argentinian plot to destroy the *Conqueror*, the submarine which sank the *Belgrano* during the Falklands War. It will undoubtedly be full of true Argentine flavour, because that's another place Bob Langley has visited in the course of his constant travels.

PICTURE CREDIT. Page 403: Roger Barrett.

M145